KARL AND ROSA

Karl and Rosa

November 1918
A German Revolution

A Novel by

Alfred Döblin

Translated from the German by
John E. Woods

FROMM INTERNATIONAL PUBLISHING CORPORATION
NEW YORK, NEW YORK

Printed in the United States of America

First U.S. Edition

Library of Congress Cataloging in Publication Data

Döblin, Alfred, 1878-1957
Karl and Rosa.
(November 1918)

Translation: Karl und Rosa,
the third part of the author's trilogy, November 1918.
1. Liebknecht, Karl Paul August Friedrich, 1871-1919—Fiction.
2. Luxemburg, Rosa, 1871-1919—Fiction.   I. Title.   II. Series:
Döblin, Alfred, 1878-1957. November 1918. English.

PT2607.035K313   1983   833'.912   83-16461

ISBN 0-88064-010-3
ISBN 0-88064-011-1 (pbk.)

CONTENTS

BOOK THREE
Antigone and Ancestral Guilt

BOOK FOUR
The Challenge Is Made and Accepted

BOOK FIVE
The Revolution Is Lost
Even Before the Battle Begins

BOOK SIX
The Hour When the Dead Hear
the Voice of God

BOOK SEVEN
Police Headquarters;
or, The Black Swan Takes Flight

BOOK EIGHT
The Murder of Karl and Rosa

BOOK NINE
The End of a German Revolution

I*n the midst of life*

death surrounds us;

Whom shall we seek

That we may find grace?

(Traditional hymn)

BOOK ONE

In Prison

She Had Imagined Things Different

She had imagined things different.

It was February, 1915. She meant to go to Holland, to a women's conference. The evening before her departure, the Berlin police picked her up at her apartment and drove her in a green car to the women's prison on Barnimstrasse. It made no difference to them that she was a "political" prisoner. She had to strip down to her chemise and let them run their hands over her, twice in succession; the tears welled up. She was angry at herself afterward for being so weak.

She served a one-year sentence—in the middle of the war, when her work was needed—because in Frankfurt two years previously she had declared: "If they expect us to take up their murderous arms against our brothers in other nations, then I say: No, we will not do it." (But sad to say they had done just that.)

She sat in prison. Reports of victory came thick and fast. At the beginning she had been able to smuggle out a brochure about resistance, but then all contact with the outside stopped. Karl, her comrade-in-arms, was drafted and was digging ditches along the Dvina on the Russian front.

And what had happened to dear Hannes, sweet Hannes, her friend of recent years? He was sent into the field as a doctor and soon proudly reported back wearing the Iron Cross. She wrote to him. "Six months ago I looked forward to prison as if it were a holiday, but now . . ."

Oh, she had such an intense longing to get out of there, was so painfully anxious. She lay there in the long nights, consumed with it. Life was trickling away, now was the time to be out there working for the revolution against Prussian militarism. The masses were waiting for a sign, someone should now be calling them to battle.

And she should be out there now too—for her own sake and for Hannes, just as Heine had put it: "No longer young, nor hale and hearty, I sit here in my old man's jacket. I'd love to love again, go to a party, be happy, gay—but sans the racket."

Free at last. 1916. And now she is out surrounded by people. They sing her praises. But she—she seems unable to do things right anymore. The brochure she had had smuggled out is published, signed: Junius. It rumbles to a theatrical conclusion:

"The insanity of war will only stop, the bloody demon of hell disappear, when the workers of Germany, France, England and Russia finally awaken from their drunken stupor, extend the hand of brotherhood to one another and drown out the bestial hymns of imperialism with the thundering ancient battle song of the working class: Proletarians of All Nations, Unite."

There were still some happy moments. They thought of founding a revolutionary party. And then came May 1st, when Spartacus brazenly summoned the masses of workers in Berlin to a demonstration against the war.

What a magnificent time there on Potsdamer Platz in Berlin! The police have occupied the area early that morning, but the workers come nevertheless. Their numbers grow. Thousands of them. And then Karl appears, Karl Liebknecht in the uniform of a common private. She stands next to him. Someone shouts: "Karl, Karl — Rosa!" She waves and laughs. She speaks. But Karl's voice roars over everything else: "Down with war! Down with war! Down with the government!"

Then the police move to arrest him with sabres drawn. Rosa and others throw themselves between them. He goes on shouting. She watches him waving his right arm. The cavalry gallops up, Karl is arrested. The tumult is overwhelming. He is led away. People mill about angrily on the square and in the streets leading to it for hours.

Meanwhile Rosa is sitting with little Sonya, Karl's wife, in the Café Fürstenhof, and they are happy, rapturous. They drink their coffee and eat pastries. They gossip and exchange tales of the struggle. Their volleys of laughter cause a sensation.

What a volcanic May 1st!

But in June Karl is sentenced to two and a half years imprisonment, and the sentence is later increased to four years.

And shortly thereafter they arrest her as well.

And this time they do not use some past offense as a pretense. This time they are as serious about it all as she had meant to be herself. They sentence her to indefinite preventive detention.

And now prison has swallowed her up.

The time to be merry, to burst into volleys of laughter, is long past.

She is transferred from the louse-infested cells of Berlin police headquarters to Wronke, and from there to the gloomy brick confines of the women's prison in Breslau. To all appearances she bears up well. She tells herself she does, writes the same to others, she has been imprisoned in Russia and Poland before this, after all.

But she is forty-six years old now, forty-seven. Her hair is losing its color. The war rages on out there, with murder, famine, and pestilence. The storm of revolution sweeps across Russia, and an unbelievable rumor finds its way into the prison: Lenin, the most radical revolutionary of all, has sold himself to the German General Staff and has been allowed to travel through Germany to Russia. Lenin is already in St. Petersburg.

Inside, Rosa begins to tremble. She knows nothing, comprehends nothing. She is afraid of everything and anything. She becomes upset at the sight of titmice seeking food at her window. To calm herself she begins to translate: Korolenko. You have to protect yourself from the stress of prison.

Then, in November, two pieces of news arrive simultaneously: this incomprehensible man named Lenin and his Bolsheviks have toppled Kerenski in St. Petersburg—and Hannes is dead. Hannes has fallen, Hannes Düsterberg, her darling, her only love.

They were waiting for the war to end. They had wanted to travel when it was all over, somewhere in the south, to enjoy life, no more politics, no meetings, no newspapers.

She stammers. "I can't get over it. Can it be possible?" It's like a voice gone mute in the middle of a sentence. I don't comprehend it. Is it possible?"

But her life has not ended yet. Many more things will still be possible.

January 1918. Women's prison in Breslau. A small, white-haired woman stands at the portal of the courtyard of the supply wing with its high walls and weeps. The soldier has finally stopped cursing and beating the oxen. The heavy cart has made it over the threshold. The women prisoners run up and grab things from the piles, torn military jackets, and take them back to their cells to be mended. The young soldier tosses his cap up under the seat, wipes the sweat from his brow and mouth, and asks where the canteen is.

The female guard who has been helping unload from the rear of the cart calls out over the heads of the women, "What do you mean, canteen? That too? Ain't any, slavedriver."

He hitches up his trousers. "Slavedriver, hah! Nobody sheds tears over us neither." And he leans against the wall, thrusts his hands into his pockets and starts whistling to himself. One of the oxen is bleeding. Its thick hide has cracked open.

The small, white-haired woman approaches the soldier and examines his young, red face. He is a squat fellow, has closely cropped flaxen hair and a little moustache. On his right cheek, just above the cheekbone, is a bright red, star-shaped scar. When the woman just stands there in front of him, saying nothing, he stops whistling, bends forward suddenly and blows a puff of air at her nose. When she flinches and turns away, he laughs at her as she moves off and bellows, "Hey, hey, look how she waddles! She waddles like a duck."

In her cell Rosa writes a letter to Karl's wife:

"Sonya, they were beautiful, Rumanian oxen, used to their freedom. One of the beasts was bleeding, looking straight ahead like a child in tears that doesn't know how to escape its torment. But that is how life is, Sonya. Despite everything, we have to accept it, brave and undaunted."

The pen slips from her hand. She realizes she is talking to herself again.

The young soldier drives the oxen out of the prison yard. Whip in hand, he trots beside the open cart through the narrow streets to the depot, unharnesses the beasts, leads them to a pump and pours a bucketful of water over each of them. Then he drives them into their stalls and pours out fodder for them. He bangs each of them between the horns with his fist, saying, "Lazy bum, greedy-guts!"

Then he washes at the pump and takes a seat on a bench in the warm, smoky canteen next to other men who are already eating. He slurps away at some hot cabbage soup. But when he takes a bite of the pasty wartime bread, he spits it out and tosses half a crusty loaf under the table. The others, home guards, ask, "What are you doing, plow jockey? Are you going to pick that bread up right now, or not?" He has to pick it up and place it neatly next to him. And they prophesy that he'll eat it soon enough, since he won't get any more until he does. They've already given him one sound thrashing recently. At that he lets out a cowardly "bah" and wolfs down his potatoes. Once he is done, he stands at the door, turns around to them and spits over the threshold. Before they can grab him he is in the sergeant's office and they can hear him reporting back safe and sound. They're satisfied. They've gotten rid of him. He's now up for two weeks home-leave.

And next morning he is standing with a few others at the main station, equipped as if for a march out into the field. They all climb into a third-class car. The Red Cross provides them with coffee and dry buns through the window. They are already asleep before the train pulls out.

He is a rifleman by the name of Runge, who has never been able to please anyone in life. He knows that they don't want him at home either. But that doesn't matter. Doesn't matter at all.

Night has fallen over the prison. The crows have flown away, off to sleep, high over the courtyard in a broad, easy curve. Heaven's darkness lies on the prison walls and hides their ugliness. (Judge not, lest ye be judged!)

Rosa lies there and listens to the strange, staccato call of the birds.

The hour of despair has come. She throws herself onto her stone-hard bed.

I murdered him. I allowed him to go out there. And didn't think for even one moment that he could be killed. I thought of everyone else, of the hundreds of thousands of anonymous faces. It was for their sake, for men I didn't know, that I wrote against this shameful war. But I did not think about him. Oh, I was a great altruist.

She trembled and bit her lips. A terrible cold flowed through her.

I always knew what others needed. Poor Hannes found his way to me. I loved him. He was my Hannes, and in that moment I no longer worried about him.

She sat up on the edge of the bed, sat there for hours in the darkness, a heavy torpor pressing upon her.

Just look at how the Prussians, militarism, everything that I wrote and preached against, have got hold of me now too.

She scratched and clawed at her temples.

They have taken him from me. They have revenged themselves on me. I wasn't dead enough for them in prison. They murdered him out there to get at me and then sent my letters back.

Her tears streamed down in the darkness. She sobbed, her eyes closed, sometimes so loud that someone next to her banged on the wall. The following morning she drank her coffe-soup later than usual.

But that's how it is. I'm a war widow. I didn't know what it was like to lose someone. Yes, it's a thousand times worse than I thought. I should have dealt differently with those murderers. And now I'll have to die right along with him from morning till evening, and on through the long nights. And when night is over, the sun will return and will lead me forth to the next piece of dying. I'm locked in like Antigone in her bridal chamber, buried alive within these walls. Who will save me?

Hannes, come, help me! Come, my darling, my love, come to me. You have no body now to stop you, the doors and walls cannot hold you back. Forgive me for what I did to you. Look how they're punishing me. They have let me go on living and have taken you.

Simply close the books on them, Hannes. You can't have vanished, your body is lying somewhere in the earth, so your soul must be there too. There are laws about the preservation of energy and matter. You can't simply have vanished. Then don't hold yourself back from me. Come, Hannes, whom they've listed as dead because you give no sign of life. And why should you give a sign to them, for whom you were always just a number. You have settled accounts with them, finally, even more thoroughly than I have. But with me—you haven't even begun with me. You know that, Hannes.

So be here. Don't hide from me. I'm no sorceress. I can't conjure you up. Come then!

She whispered incessantly, "Hannes, Hannes."

She kept herself awake with that cry until the first birdcalls.

The crows fly in a broad, easy curve above the prison yard out into the fields.

Rosa lies there and listens to the birdcalls. They gurgle: caw, caw. It sounds as if they were tossing small metallic balls to one another.

The bed is hard as stone, but Rosa no longer knows that she is in prison. She is no longer young, has all kinds of ailments (you old hysterical female, you, she curses to herself), she lies on the hard bed, sleepless, stares at the light of the lanterns on the ceiling, hears the heavy, slow steps of the sentry—and is intoxicated. Enveloped in bliss.

On her table is the picture of Hannes that Luise sent her. He looks so worried. She comforts him, he shouldn't be unhappy, there is really so much happiness in the world.

Death. What an empty word. I have you. Who can take you from me. What does the word "death" have to do with us. As long as I have arms and legs you are not lost to me, and when I no longer have them, then we'll be together. Hannes, I have so much happiness to give. Open your mouth, my boy, open it wide, come take! Ah, what ecstasy! Take something of my happiness from me.

"Why are you so happy, Rosa?"

"Do I know that? Do I know everything?"

"I had to die out on the front, and we can't travel together anymore."

"We'll have all that, Hannes. Have patience. I'll travel with you, I'll take you along as my traveling companion without a ticket. I'll smuggle you in everywhere."

"But how? And where? How will you carry me, Rosa?"

"I'll carry you in my hair. My hair is still heavy and full. It's almost white now, which makes people think I'm old. Am I old, Hannes?"

"How are you going to carry me in your hair?"

"I'll not wear a hat. I'll balance you the way a peasant woman carries her pitcher, on my head, or I'll pull you down to my heart. Oh, it will be beautiful Hannes. There was always something that bothered us, first I would bother you, then you—forgive me—would bother me. Now I'm lying here in this cell, while the sentry watches our rendezvous. Isn't that magnificent? We'll laugh in their faces. And you'll say heavenly things to me, and I'll be completely yours."

"And what happens to the revolution, to your party?"

"I'll just be Rosa without a revolution and without a party. Rosa just for you."

"And the birds and the flowers, and your cat, Mimi?"

"We'll take them along. Oh, we'll take a lot more things along, Hannes, the vast sky, the stars, spring, the sunset, twilight. We can take them all with us, no one will notice, people are much too busy with their war."

"And music, Rosa? The songs by Hugo Wolf?"

"Yes, and your Romain Rolland, your Jean Christophe, oh how I look forward to our journey!"

It is bath day. The snow that fell the night before is being swept from the supply-wing courtyard. And the gray cobblestones on which the prisoners trudge the whole year long are visible again.

Look, the women over there like the snow too! One of them has her window open and is reaching out through the bars to grab a handful of it. Who might that be? A human being like myself, locked up, powerless, condemned to wither away here. Behind each set of iron bars across the way is someone like me, who gazes out at the snow and takes heart a little at the sight. We are the ones society can't deal with, and builds walls around because it can't.

The door to her cell is unlocked. The trustee enters, a prisoner herself, a young, slender woman who has her head bound up in a bright linen scarf. Her face is drawn, the skin pulled tight and white as chalk. Rosa examines her today for the first time. She had some bad

9

experiences in the Barnimstrasse prison in Berlin once with just such a lovely, masklike face. Today she feels the urge to make small talk. The snow has softened her—and she is secretly afraid of herself.

The sullen prisoner leads Rosa into the steam-filled bathing room and leaves her there alone. Light falls into the room from a high, narrow window. Rosa remembers the bathroom in Wronke and a butterfly that she breathed back to life. Now she is in Breslau, it is winter. She is sitting in a bathtub of warm water on a bright morning and thinking about the young men who even now, at this very hour, this minute, are dying out there.

Here I sit in my tub like some fat burgher's wife, warming my body. And what should I do? We tried hard. I could shout, Karl could shout, and a couple dozen others with us. And we let them lock us up and that was all we could do. Because you can't do anything against the will of the masses. Their lethargy is stronger than we are. When the time comes, they obey again, take up their rifles and shoot for kaiser and king. They don't want it any other way. Young Friedrich Adler shot Prime Minister Stürgkh in Vienna. It made no difference. They've got cowardice in their bones. And that's what the crooks depend on. And here I sit in the tub and warm my body.

People don't want us. People want to be left in peace.

(She slapped at the water with her hand.) There's something damnable about politics. All that work for nothing. That's how things started with me, very young; that's how it stole my life from me. I was supposed to stay in bed because of my hip, in Warsaw. And mother said, "Why would you want to get up?" But I couldn't take it, and early in the morning, when all the others were asleep, I would go to the window in my chemise and look down into the courtyard, where long, lanky Antony was standing with his wagon, and then I'd search out across the roofs, way out over the roofs, for life, for true, full life. Out there, beyond the roofs, that's where life must be, far away. I ran after it. I always thought it lay just beyond those roofs. I never reached it. That's what has turned my hair snow white. That's what killed my Hannes.

(She closed her eyes.) A lot of help all your cleverness was, Rosa Luxemburg. You were dreadfully clever, but not clever enough. The Moloch has devoured you.

Don't gnash your teeth, Rosa, don't tremble. You have lost your way. At least you're sitting in a warm bath. Be content with your bath.

As she hurried back along the icy corridor to her cell, the woman with the white, masklike face stood at her door and opened it, her eyes lowered. Rosa pulled her into the cell with her and asked her her name.

She was called Tanya.

Polish or Russian?

Polish.

She whispered in Polish. She asked if Tanya would be in the courtyard that afternoon? The prisoner threw Rosa a look of suspicion. Yes, she would be in the courtyard.

I don't know what I want from her, Rosa thinks as she throws herself on her bed, but if someone doesn't come along soon and give me a kick, I'll go crazy.

Lenin Has His Revolution

At this point the Russians are out in front of the Germans by several lengths. They already have their defeat behind them.

And they have what a handful of people locked in German prisons can only dream about: revolution. They have put their czar to flight and toppled a compromise government. There is no longer a military dictatorship. The prisoners have been set free from their dungeons, the exiles have returned home. It is freedom's turn, the freedom for which over the past decades the avant-garde of fighters has been hanged, shot or sent off to Siberia.

And in Petrograd Lenin is hard at work trying to show the others what a revolution looks like, something about which there is a difference of opinion.

And to resolve the matter quickly his way, the first thing he wants is to be rid of the Germans still occupying his country.

But General Ludendorff is more interested in beating a dead horse than in making peace. When Trotsky realizes this at the conference in Brest-Litovsk, he returns to Petrograd to ask Lenin's advice. You can in fact ask the man for advice.

Lenin is busy sniffing out a rather large collection of men and women that has arrived in Petrograd with the intention of instituting a constituent assembly. They can prove that they have been legally elected, and in fact have received considerably more votes than the Bolsheviks. That does indeed impress Lenin.

He has the commissioner of elections arrested, and then he names a new election committee, and since the matter cannot be drawn out any longer, he fixes January 18th—it is now 1918—for the opening of the assembly that these men and women are so intent on. As far as he is concerned, the battle royal can begin.

Given the curious course that the revolution has taken thus far, several people already know what they can expect from Lenin, from this man with whom they fought shoulder to shoulder to bring down capitalism and imperialism. (He, of course had always kept his own counsel.) They attempt to assassinate him. This misfires. They want to kidnap the Bolshevik people's commisars. That misfires as well. They come to the conclusion that their theories about socialism are correct, but that prospects for realizing them don't look good at the moment. (Could it be they have made some errors in their calculations?)

With anxious hearts, full of forebodings—completely convinced of their ideas, but worried about those errors in calculation—they approach the Tauride Palace on the assigned date. They deeply resent the treachery and the methods of the Bolsheviks. Their rage burns within them.

In the meantime Lenin has ordered up a Latvian rifle regiment, men who are indifferent to these Russian domestic quarrels.

And when on January 18th the elected representatives of the people, men and women alike, approach the Tauride Palace, they sense something, but are not sure what. They feel as if they've been set back into days long past. Everywhere rifles and bayonets bristle. Their credentials are taken from them, checked. Latvian riflemen and Red Guards occupy the entrances to the building. Inside the building, machine-gun emplacements have been set up. Why had there even been a revolution? Weren't they supposed to meet here and proclaim the will of the people?

At four that afternoon they are finally ready and the meeting is opened. Following established parliamentary usage, the strongest party nominates its senior member as provisional president—in this case the Social Revolutionaries.

At this point, Sverdlov, chairman of the Petrograd Soviet—who most certainly is quite out of order—pushes his way up to the president's chair, takes a seat amidst a general cry from the indignant and dumbfounded assembly and, without even asking for the floor, let alone having received permission to take it, reads aloud a statement from the Soviet of People's Commissars, which declares this worthy Constituent Assembly to be dissolved forthwith should it not recognize the reality upon which it is based—by which he means the events leading up to the establishment of Soviet power.

The reaction of the worthy constituent representatives is expressed in various cries, the tamest of which is: "Go wash your bloody hands, you murderers."

There had indeed been all sorts of executions by firing squad. But the Bolsheviks found themselves in a strong strategic position: they had the whole city of Petrograd, the site of the Assembly, and they controlled the Latvian regiment. They could therefore take such curses lightheartedly.

Whereupon they elected as president of the Constituent Assembly a certain Chernov, who had served as minister of agriculture under Kerensky, that man of compromises who had since fled. Amid surging applause, the man now took the chair that Sverdlov had warmed up for him and then vacated and, without pausing to consider what he was doing, he proceeded to attack the Bolsheviks for the many difficulties they had put in the way of the true revolution. In passionate phrases he celebrated the democratic constitution of the nation, so long and earnestly desired; to the writing of which they would now proceed posthaste.

The Bolsheviks had seen to it that the galleries were packed with their people. When the Assembly applauded, those up above booed; when the Assembly booed, those up above applauded enthusiastically. There were differences of opinion, so to speak. But they were not dangerous, since the one faction was up above and the other down below.

And if some scholar, having shown the appropriate documents at the door, had appeared between 6:00 and 8:00 P.M. on January 18, 1918, at the Tauride Palace in Petrograd for the purpose of studying certain social phenomena, he would not only have found the whole affair perfectly natural, but would have praised the arrangements that separated those above from those below. The Homeric gods, to be sure, would have seen to it that there was a greater interchange. They would have determined soon enough that there were stairways connecting those above with those below, and would have used these stairways to establish contact between the two masses. As a result, there would have been dreadful scuffles and shoot-outs between the Mensheviks and Social Revolutionaries from below and the Bolsheviks from above, with Pallas Athena and Mars and Apollo in the thick of things shouting directions like: "Give it to him. Right on the nose. Ivan, sock him one. Nikolas Nikolayevitch, pull your knife, draw blood. Konstantinovitch, grab your axe and part his hair for him."

Lenin, sitting there in Petrograd—later Leningrad—did not get involved. He waited. At one the following morning the incident he had been waiting for occurred.

The majority made a motion, the Bolsheviks made a motion. The Bolsheviks claimed priority, lost the battle, and that was the end—they left these inhospitable quarters and returned to Lenin, to their

Latvian riflemen and Red Guards, in order to lodge a protest.

Lenin was at the Smolny Institute and lent a sympathetic ear to their lament. He praised their great steadfastness, their heroic patience, and opened his heart to them. He told them not to get upset at this incident. And he discussed the matter with his friends on the executive council and wrote a penciled note:

"The members of the Constituent Assembly, elected on the basis of lists drawn up before the November Revolution, represent the Old Order dominated by men of compromise and military cadets. It is clear that a constituent assembly made up of such people can only be a prop for the bourgeois counterrevolution. Wherefore the Central Executive Committee declares the Constituent Assembly disbanded."

He stuck this paper in his pocket and walked over to the brightly illuminated Tauride Palace. It was a refreshing stroll, partly because of the pure night air after the stuffiness of the Smolny Institute, partly because of the paper he had in his pocket. At the ground-floor entrance to the palace he gave the paper to the commander of the guard and told him that everything he needed to know was written there, but that there was no hurry. They could go ahead and wait for the meeting inside to adjourn.

The commander said that the guards were already quite tired. Could they not perhaps, even though it was early . . . ?

Lenin gave him a sympathetic pat on the shoulder, smiled, said "adieu" and left.

Around four that morning, the commander was still waiting with his guards. They were not yet finished in the main hall. They were debating the central article, the one concerning ownership of land. Finally there came the rumble of applause, they had done it, the land had been apportioned. The gallery had long since ceased to respond, firstly, they were tired too, and secondly, they already knew how things would develop from here on.

And behold! the doors to the hall open and the commander of the guard pushes his way in. He looks about. He shoves his way between the deputies who have taken to their feet, cheering and applauding as they stand in the aisles. He makes his way to the front without anyone noticing. They all are thinking what a historic moment this is. It is indeed, but in another sense than they think it to be.

The commander elbows his way up onto the podium and stands next to President Chernov, who is enjoying the sight of the ovation in the hall. The commander tenderly lays a hand on his shoulder (it's how fate raps at the door).

"Don't you think it's time to adjourn, Mr. President?" the soldier whispers, pointing to the clock up on the balcony railing. He also takes Lenin's note from his pocket and gives it to Chernov. "Here, read this. The Assembly is hereby dissolved anyway. And besides, the guards are so tired."

The soldier turns around as people down on the floor begin to notice him. And suddenly stillness reigns—all eyes focused on him; he turns around in embarrassment to face the Assembly and asks them to go home as well, the guards are really very tired and the hour very late, four in the morning.

Chernov hurled back the answer that his delegates expected from him. "We understand that, Commander. The members of the Assembly are just as tired as your soldiers. But we are concerned here with preparing the legislation that all of Russia is waiting for."

The soldier is not expecting this, he scratches his head and stands there silent and humiliated. Chernov meanwhile scornfully moves on to the day's agenda, ignoring the stupid, impudent fellow simply by beginning to speak. His topic now is the peace treaty being prepared in Brest-Litovsk, though there has been in fact no authority granted to the Bolsheviks to negotiate it. And suddenly he is overwhelmed by the spirit of his former boss, Kerensky, and he pleads with the Allies so far away to side with Russia and democracy.

In the meantime the commander slinks out of the hall, meek and unnoticed, Chernov having thrust the note back into his hand. Outside he reads the note aloud to his comrades, who thought that he was finally getting the assembly to adjourn. Instead he waves the note and admits sadly, "I couldn't carry it off, they won't face facts. What'll we do?"

They think that things are crystal clear—they have to put a stop to this. And so one of them goes to a technician in the cellar, and he understands the whole thing too—and simply shuts off the electricity.

At that moment the people in the gallery, who have already fallen asleep, wake up and begin to crow as happily as roosters at sun-up. A tumult ensues in the dark hall, people shout, threaten, step on each others' toes. But they really have no choice, they must leave. In the crush they complain bitterly what a shame this is for Russia; other nations will once again get an impression of the new democratic Russia of which one can only be ashamed, and the monarchists will laugh in mockery at this version of self-government by the people.

While they complain and crowd their way out, while the gallery meows, Chernov speaks his final word from the podium; he is barely audible but he speaks out nevertheless: "I hereby declare the Russian state to be the Russian Democratic Federal Republic."

"Hereby," he says. In all the uproar it is impossible to determine what he means by here, here in the darkness of the hall, here in the uproar or here amid this concert of meows.

The following noon, a number of deputies who still had not noticed anything walked over to the Tauride Palace to see how things were going with the Russian republic proclaimed only yesterday. But this time the Latvian riflemen and the Red Guard had been positioned in such a wide circle around the palace that no one could even get close. And they were not at all interested in credentials. The deputies took fright at this and stared at each other. Was this supposed to be the new republic? Is this what they called a revolution? This was treason, counterrevolution.

But it was Lenin.

Trotsky had just given him a detailed account of how things were going with Brest-Litovsk, and Lenin replied, "What a mess. These Germans are brutal, but they're candid, which is more than you can say for the Western democracies. We dare not have any illusions about them, these former allies of ours. At least as far as our Constituent Assembly goes, disbanding it was the best thing to do under the present circumstances. A total and open liquidation of formal democracy in the name of a revolutionary dictatorship."

Trotsky looked out at the street below where they were busy putting up a barbed-wire barrier across the snow. "And how did they behave?"

"Who?"

"The delegates, last night."

Trotsky took cigars from the breast pocket of his leather jacket. "Havana, got them in Brest-Litovsk, a bribe."

Lenin sniffed one. "Are you sure they won't explode when you light them?"

Trotsky lit his, it smelled good.

"Last night," Lenin laughed gleefully, "I sure would like to have seen them last night. They had composed long orations, every one of them with a stack of reforms in his pocket. And then my little commander comes in, yawns and grouses, 'I'm tired, I really am so tired' and turns the lights out on them."

The metalworkers in Berlin want peace. They strike in protest against the outrageous demands made by the Germans at Brest-Litovsk.

They prepare a flyer that reads:

16

"Fellow workers, men and women! Work has stopped in all the factories in Vienna and Budapest for five days now. We must finish what our Austro-Hungarian brothers have begun.

"The resolution of the question of peace lies with the German proletariat. We will fight for as long as it takes for our basic demands to be truly met with no amendments. Lifting of martial law, of censorship, of all limitations on the right of assembly, and freeing of all political prisoners. Those are our conditions; they are necessary for the continuation of our struggle to erect a people's republic in Germany and for an immediate and general peace.

"Workers! Before we leave our factories, we must follow the Austrian and Russian models and vote in free elections for deputies who will be given the task of leading this battle and the ones to come.

"On to battle! One for all, all for one!

"Awaken, workers, recognize your strength! All the wheels will stop if your strong arms wish it!

"Down with war! Down with the government!"

Four hundred thousand workers struck in Berlin on January 28th for peace without annexations or reparations, for the right of self-determination for all peoples, for the participation of workers' representatives at the peace negotiations.

A genuine ad hoc committee had formed, with Haase, Ledebour and Dittmann, plus Richard Müller from the Revolutionary Shop Stewards. But the worms were in the apple already, namely Ebert and Scheidemann from the old Social Democratic party.

The committee met, the number of those on strike increased to half a million. The wheels of the war industry literally stood still. The government proclaimed still more stringent martial law, set up special courts-martial. The strike lasted until January 31st. Then the parts the worms had eaten away became visible. The socialists negotiated with the government, even the Independents softened, causing the commandants in the several provinces to decide that the moment had come to place seven major factories under military control and to proclaim that if work were not resumed by Monday, February 4th, workers would be inducted into the army or else be subject to punishment.

The Spartacus League roared: "Meet force with force, we'll hold our ground. The issue will be decided nowhere but in the streets. Down with war, down with the government!" Work was resumed.

General Ludendorff was not to be stopped, either from within Russia or from without. He told the Russians, who were unwilling to swallow his conditions, that the armistice was terminated and began to advance. The German army took Pskov, where the Czar had been forced to abdicate the preceding year, and Mohilev, where last December the Bolsheviks had taken from his railway carriage the last commander of the czarist forces, Duchonin, and executed him.

For Wilhelm II's Germans this was an amusing war. General Hoffman declared, "This war has the charm of novelty. You simply load a squad of men onto a railroad car, give them a couple of machine guns, have them ride to the next station, take prisoners, travel on ahead, and that's how they conquer Russia."

The German terms for peace were therefore frightening. Neither Trotsky nor Stalin was for signing them. Lenin, however, wanted his revolution. His sly little eyes sparkled. "You can't make a joke of war. That's what you still don't understand. The revolution is in danger. When Napoleon had conquered these same Prussians that we have now in front of us, they concluded the Peace of Tilsit with him. Napoleon was not looking well. So they signed his treaty. After a few years there wasn't any more Napoleon. I shall sign my Peace of Tilsit."

They were of the opinion it would be difficult to have people accept it, that it would hurt the cause of the revolution. He scoffed, "Do you think so? We'll see!"

The little bald-headed man kept right on smiling his gentle, ironic smile when the Petrograd Soviet and the Central Committee greeted him with cries of "Down with him, down with the traitor!" He mocked them. "I understand why you're so upset. But what do you suggest instead? Can you hold back the German army? Can you muster an army? Our trenches are empty. You can comprehend that much. Our soldiers have had enough of this war. They want to rest, and are more interested in what peace and our revolution will bring them. Your enthusiasm is fine and dandy, but where are your weapons? You can't make war with protestations. Where are the weapons? Let me in on the secret. If you can't, then I say, one shouldn't make oneself a slave to one's own phrases."

They answered by saying he should simply let the Germans march on ahead. But he would not consent to that. "If we pull back to the Urals, within a month we'll have to sign a treaty with terms a hundred times worse."

The Petrograd Soviet voted "yes" with him, while in the Central Committee they bellowed, "German spy! Judas! That's what we get for calling you back to Russia." But he found his majority.

A great cheer arose in the German Reichstag in Berlin when the government proclaimed the "Peace of Brest-Litovsk," under the terms of which Russia lost forty-four percent of its population, in addition to half of its industrial enterprises and nine-tenths of its coal mines. It was clearly a modern peace treaty.

Representative Stresemann declared, "It was not the negotiations with Trotsky, nor the peace resolution of the Reichstag, nor the Pope that brought us peace in the East, but the advance of the invading German army." Another socialist blustered, "We Social Democrats would never have signed such a treaty."

Lenin could not allow himself to be seen on the streets of Petrograd. People whom he had damned as compromisers and fence-sitters in the past founded a newspaper directed against him, *The Communist,* for which Radek and Bucharin, Kollontai and Dybenko all wrote. He pushed his abominable treaty through the last hurdle, the All-Russian Soviet Congress.

But he no longer felt at home in Petrograd. It lay directly in the German line of fire. He wanted to go to Moscow. The revolutionaries from October 1917 raised a cry of lament. "We won't surrender Petrograd, the cradle of the revolution. Petrograd and Smolny."

"Stupid sentimentalists," Lenin swore while he packed his bags. "Once we are sitting in Moscow, we'll make the Kremlin our symbol. What idiots."

He felt surrounded by nothing but romantics and morons. He treated Bucharin and his hangers-on as if they were schoolboys.

And he won the day by transferring the capital to Moscow. Ludendorff now had his eastern border secured and could plunge back to the west, right into Foch's dagger.

A Wedding in the Cell

The woman with the mask of tragedy walked with Rosa in the supply-wing yard. Rosa thought, what shall I talk to her about, they're watching us, we'll get into hot water.

She asked Tanya, "Why are you here?"

Tanya smiled. "I stole things."

"You didn't have a job, is that it?"

"Oh no, sure I did."

"And? You had a boyfriend, right?"

"Yes." The white mask cast a glance toward the men's penitentiary. "He's over there."

Rosa: "Do you see him sometimes?"

The pale woman nodded. "They gave him three years. Burglary. He only has one eye. They shot the other one out."

"Which means he did some shooting too."

Tanya's face registered nothing. "The bullet is just above the nose and can't be removed."

She cast a hurried look at Rosa. "Do you have someone over there too?"

"No."

"Must be nice to always read like that. What's in them books?"

"How to make things better for people, Tanya. How to educate them better, so they'll know what they need."

The white mask winked, there was no telling what the wink meant. "And how do the people who write these books find out what we need?"

Rosa: "What you need, for instance?"

Tanya giggled. No, of course not her, they didn't have to write on her account.

"And why not for you, Tanya?"

And that amused Tanya so much that she laid an arm on Rosa's shoulder and laughed loud and heartily. Rosa was downright embarrassed. Two women walking in front of them, moreover, laughed at the same time and turned around to look. They seemed to understand why Tanya was laughing. Rosa was just plain stupid.

Rosa walked around alone for a while longer, angry at herself. Then it grew too cold for her, and she thought of her cell, and—at once she was like an alcoholic who walks by a bar.

She had to go in. The impulse was so strong there was no resisting it. She scolded herself as she went: I'm going back to my den of iniquity. She knew in her bones that she was going to get involved with "him" again.

And she had already done just that before she reached the cell. She kept on castigating, mocking, damning herself for it, "You're going crazy, Rosa; you're wrecking yourself." But that was all on the surface. Down below she was already arguing with "him," was up to her ears in a heated debate with him. "Prison psychosis," she cursed, but her eyes stared straight ahead.

He maintained, "You were always telling me that I didn't understand this and I didn't understand anything about that. That of course I might know something about medicine, or about literature, but that when it came to people, the world, the state—ha! We were all sheep, even Luise. And who was it that knew something? Just you politi-

20

cians, just the Marxists, the theoreticians. They're stuffed full of wisdom. You listen to Tanya. You don't think she's so dumb, do you, even if she hasn't read anything? And what's become of all your book-learning? Just look what they're doing in Russia, how they're hacking away at each other. What erudition! Which of them has got a corner on truth?"

"That's how it always is with science, Hannes. Even in physics and astronomy there are different theories."

"Ah, Rosa, don't try to defend yourself, don't say something you don't believe. How far did all that get you? What do you have to say about me? Tell me, what about me? I'm a—hallucination, is that it? Hal-lu-cin-a-tion. Hal-hal-lu . . ."

The voice muttered, cursed, laughed and was lost. Rosa listened in alarm. "I can't understand, Hannes. Don't be angry with me. Don't you be angry, too. I really have no one."

"No one," he mocked. "Grab hold of your nose, tug your ear, slap your thigh, there's someone, a hundred pounds and more of someone. And what do I have?"

"What do you want," she begged. "Don't start in with that again."

"I know, we're going to go on a trip together. A beautiful trip, in your hair. If only I don't come tumbling down. I want to do some real traveling, in the flesh, in an express train, first class, with cushions, with luggage, to Switzerland, to Italy."

"Did you love me that much, Hannes? Would you like to do that? You were always so quiet."

"Sure," the voice lied (Rosa sensed that Hannes was lying, but the lies made her happy), "I always held back somehow."

"What shall I do, Hannes? What do you command me to do?"

He: "Finally you understand that you have duties to fulfill. Every morning when you wake up and they bring you coffee, go to the window, look out and call me. You are to call me often, do you understand? And if I don't answer at once, that's not important. You have to call loudly for me, keep on calling for a long time, with your whole heart. Passionately, Rosa, otherwise I can't come; passionately, as you did those first days. Without that I can't come."

"I can't imagine where you are, my love. Stay close to me. Don't get lost again now."

"You can call me in whatever way you want, but you have to do it. It must come from deep inside you. What will you say? You will say, 'Hannes, sweet Hannes, my dear Hannes, the coffee is so bad, it's war coffee, and prison coffee besides, chicory, but it's all I have, and all I can offer you, and I'll share it with you. Sip it with me. Sip slowly, Rosa, so that I don't choke on it. And now give me your bread to gnaw on."

"This ghastly bread, Hannes!"

"I'll eat it with you. You owe me that much. On Wednesday, when you take the spoon in your hand . . ."

"Hannes, I'll feed you then. I'll feed my little, invisible child. I look forward to it. I'm so glad that I have you all to myself alone and that no one knows about us. A new prisoner is here, one boarder more."

"You'll make room for me with you?"

"You are to come join me, my poor Hannes. I'll not leave you out there in the cold."

"And where shall I bed down?"

"Wherever you want."

"I'm not a shy person, Rosa, be careful. If you're sitting down to a meal, I'll take your soup away from you, I'll eat the tin spoon itself."

"Are you that hungry?"

He sobs. "We don't have anything, really. What are we? We're nothing if someone like you doesn't help. We're worse off than beggars, we're casualties. We never really had a life, and how long will death like this last for us?"

And all reluctance was gone. She went on translating, writing her letters, speaking to Tanya, reading her newspapers, but—he raged about her cell.

Whenever he meddled too much, she had to push him back. "Now Hannes, I beg you, there's a limit to everything." But apparently he did not recognize such limits, he behaved like some obstreperous child. Out of the blue he would surprise her with a reproach for some banal occurrence in the past. He was arrogant toward her, took on a tyrannical personality. She always had to yield to him, one hundred percent, and after his tantrums she had to beat her breast and beg for forgiveness. At the end of such debates he would soften; she recognized the symptoms, he would grow weary, his rage had exhausted itself, and she would fall asleep with him.

The joy she felt having Hannes living in her cell was sometimes so overwhelming that she would cover up his picture to keep from going mad.

After the unrest in January, things were quiet in Germany.

Rosa felt the need to get out of her cell. If only they would grant her a few days' parole. She petitioned for it. They knew that she was often confined to her bed and was not well. The petition was denied. It was clear that she was to remain in her cell until Germany had defeated the whole world. She collapsed again.

Her birthday was March 5th, she turned forty-eight.

On the eve of her birthday, before they turned out the lights, she asked that books and paper be put on her table—here in this little cell that would probably be her grave. Then she pulled her chair up to the table and tenderly, devoutly—a veritable ceremony—she took from the cupboard a carefully folded towel, her own personal property. It had grown totally quiet in the building, it would soon be eight o'clock, and the sentry downstairs was being relieved. Rosa spread the beautiful white towel over her arm and laid it carefully over the back of the chair. It fell gently down over the seat; she smoothed it out. Then she got a second cloth from the cupboard as well, a small, blue embroidered scarf that had been given to her once as a present, and she laid it at the head of the towel. And now everything was correct. She tenderly pressed her face to the little blue scarf. The signal for the hour of the spirits had been given. He could come now. The lights went out. He would come tonight perhaps.

She no longer resisted. She no longer worried about "crazy notions," "obsessions," "hallucinations," etc.; she no longer gave herself scientific lectures complete with warnings, threats, and "firm decisions." It was all in vain and stupid as well. Rosa came to the conclusion that her mind was clear and logical, she was still working in the same old way with her books, was translating—and the scientists who wanted to convince her that she was suffering from fantasies knew nothing about it. Not any ordinary professor or pater familias could have experiences of this sort. They were her experiences, her discovery.

On the eve of her birthday she sat there in the dark on the edge of her bed next to her chair. There she sat, deserted and alone.

A résumé of the year past, a view to the future: no party, no revolution, no life, just this cell, this grave and this desolation.

The pain of it broke through. Despair raged inside her. Look about you, Rosa; that's everything we have. She fingered the towel. That is what we have left.

Early the next morning, Tanya came in with coffee and bread, and at once handed Rosa a little bouquet that she had tucked away under her apron, and smothered Rosa with kisses. After she had gone, Rosa lay there quietly for a long time, then reached over to grasp the scarf, to touch his picture, her fellow sufferer.

She gazed at him, greeted him tenderly. She begged him to forgive her on this day for all the things she had done wrong, for all her rudeness in the past.

"It's your birthday, Rosa, I know. Congratulations. But why so solemn?"

"You've noticed that?"

"But of course."

I have a surprise for you, Hannes. I don't know whether I will ever leave this cell. I'll be buried here in Breslau. And what I would like— you can say no if you want . . ."

"Go ahead and say it, my Rosebud."

"Rosebud, you say. And the rough-and-tumble lad plucked a rose-bud from the heath. I'll not scratch you I guarantee. I have decided, Hannes, that we should marry. We shall be wed today."

"Wed?"

"That is what I want from you as my birthday present."

"Are you serious?"

"Yes. It's my birthday, and I want to marry you. I don't need anyone's permission, anyone's consent—except yours."

He didn't seem to believe her.

"What surprises you about that, Hannes? You must see that things can't go on like this with us. You come to me, I invite you here, you live here with me. It's time we made things legal."

"Of course, of course," he muttered, apparently preoccupied with something.

"Well, Hannes?"

He seemed embarrassed. He muttered several "hmms" and said, "well, well." Finally he managed an answer. "Rosa, it won't work. You can't marry me, not in the state that I find myself in."

She was annoyed, realizing what he was driving at. "What state do you find yourself in then, my silly Hannes? What state do I find myself in here in this cell, for life? Forty-eight years old, a miserable old woman, looking like a witch."

"But you're alive."

"I expected you to say that. I'm alive. It would take someone like you to say that I'm alive. Because I weigh a hundred pounds and give those hundred pounds coffee, soup and bread to eat every day, that means I'm alive. Hannes, that sort of nonsense does not improve just by repeating it. Sure, I weigh a hundred pounds. But they only cause me trouble. They give me a headache, a tummy ache and ghastly gut aches."

He said nothing.

"Why are you trembling, Hannes?"

Apparently he was terribly upset about something.

"I can't believe you're serious about this, and that you have invited me to join you, Rosa. Rosa, you don't realize what it means to live without a body. When you're alive, it grieves you to lose one single organ, just one eye, just one hand. But when you have lost your whole body, suddenly, in battle, unexpectedly—you've already made arrangements for this and that, you've got little things to take care of that afternoon, you've just received a package from home and haven't even opened it yet, all that sort of thing—and suddenly it's all gone, and there you are, you try, you struggle, you wrestle, you can't do it, you're cut off, the entrance has been buried under an avalanche—ah, Rosa, do you know what it's like to hear the pickax that's digging you out, the voice that calls to you, keeps on calling without growing weary until they reach you. You yearn for nothing so much as for a body."

"But why is that? Why yearn for this wretched body? You're trembling Hannes."

"I can't give you an answer, Rosa."

"But you only have to come to me whenever you want. I'm inviting you. I don't know—whether you find me enticing, the way I am now."

"Oh, you're enticing enough, Rosebud."

"Come."

And at once he whispers from very close, "Close your eyes, Rosa. Your mouth, give me your mouth."

Something icy touched her lips and breathed against her teeth and stroked her tongue. It trickled down her throat, down her gullet. It dipped into her breast, into her body. She felt how it spread through her limbs down to the tips of her fingers and toes.

Her teeth chattered. Her body shivered and convulsed. But she stood her ground. She pulled the blanket over her, to warm herself. But it had taken hold deep within her, this icy cold, down into her bowels. She moaned, "Hannes, oh, you are cold."

She whimpered, she turned around. It flowed through her body. A wedge of ice was driven into her breast.

He moaned. Slowly he spoke, he seemed to be feeling better. "You see, Rosa, it's good."

Rosa: "Is that death, Hannes? Is it so ice-cold?"

"That is the steppe, Rosa, where I fell, the Russian snowfields. There I lay face down from a single shot until I froze to death."

"I can't bear it, Hannes."

"We're celebrating our marriage, Rosa. You invited me. It is good here with you. Ah, how good it is. I'll never let you go. Oh what bliss! Oh this human warmth! How grateful I am to you, Rosa. Human skin, human flesh, hair."

The cold subsided within her. She felt the pulsing of her blood. She had not frozen stiff. She still kept her eyes closed under the blanket. She forced herself, pressed out the words. "Are you there, Hannes? Is it still good now?"

"It's so good, Rosa, you wouldn't believe it."

"I'm glad. That—bit of warmth, even if I can give you nothing else."

She struggled with herself, it was still unbearable. "Don't worry about me, about what I'm doing, Hannes. I'll give you everything I have, go right ahead and warm yourself on me."

And she felt herself embraced, kissed on the eyes and mouth, and she did not feel so cold anymore.

Her arms, which till now she had held crossed on her breast, loosened and fell down to her sides.

He said, "Oh, it's good. You've taken me in, poor Hannes, in."

"Yes, stay here in my house. Stay under my roof. I'll keep you forever."

She could finally breathe easily. The block of ice in her breast had melted, but frost still lay upon her skin.

She opened her eyes. There stood the chair with its spread and the little blue embroidered scarf. Flowers on the table, his photograph there on the bedspread in front of her. It was broad daylight, the 5th of March, her birthday. She lay in her cell, in Breslau. Outside, prisoners were shouting as they walked by.

And she—bore him within herself. She was with him, just think of it: with him.

She spoke to him, "Hannes, you are with me. I am a remarkable specimen of humankind. I have two souls."

"Yes, Rosa."

She heard him beside her, outside of her, it was magical, but where was he hiding?

"Are you hiding in the pillow, Hannes?"

"You know where: in your body."

"I'm embarrassed, Hannes. That's really awful. A great big strong, handsome man like you inside a sick woman?"

He hummed a tune, and to her surprise she heard him sing, "Ah, if you only knew how the fishies love it in the stream."

They giggled together.

26

Rosa: "We are living closer together than Siamese twins. You breathe my breath, you see out of my eyes. You eat when I feed myself. I taste all the food for you. But you'll have to put up with my stomachaches right along with it."

He uttered some unintelligible sounds.

Rosa: "You're grumbling like a mole."

He: "I'm on leave. Soon I'll go to sleep and sleep for hours on end."

"Go right ahead, Hannes. I'm happy that you've finally arrived. My warmest greetings."

He wheezed, "Warmest greetings, Rosebud."

"My name is now Rosa Düsterberg. That sounds lovely."

"And I'm Hannes Luxemburg."

"But my name isn't even Luxemburg. I'm Frau Lübeck. Years ago I married a man named Lübeck, just for reasons of citizenship."

"That doesn't matter to me."

"I only wanted to confess it to you, Hannes. I have all sorts of other things to tell you as well."

"What? Let's have a general confession, please."

"For example, for example . . ."

"Well, come on."

"For example—it's too hard for me."

"Rosebud, I can't relieve you of what you feel is your duty."

"For example: that I really have nothing to confess. Oh, I'm so ashamed of myself."

"What is that supposed to mean?"

"I'm behaving like some teenager. Because you're my first real love. I had an affair with Jogiches, when I was in Zurich, twenty years ago. We lived together, he was my teacher, my lord and master; a school-girl's crush, I used the word 'love' and believed it, but it was only politics. I never was guilty of that confusion later. I saw you in a quite different light. Not even for a moment was there any politics mixed up with you."

He muttered, "I know. I was dumb Hannes. You were one of my first patients, bellyache and colic."

"And I still have them. You didn't cure me. Pure hysteria. I'm an easy case to diagnose. Do you know, if a doctor would come in now, a specialist like yourself, he would claim you are only some obsession of mine."

"Just let him," Hannes growled, "just let him."

"He would say: we'll cure you of this Hannes. Since when is there such a thing as a soul? Theology, mysticism? Old wives' tales from the Dark Ages, nothing more."

Hans sighed, "That's what I thought too, until I became one my-self."

She laughed. "Oh, Hannes, it's so lovely to be hysterical. Life would be hard to live without hysteria."

"Why did you go running to a doctor then in the first place?"

"Because you were so splendidly dumb. And when you still didn't catch on, I came back again and again, and fell more and more in love with you. I always had some story or other to tell. One time I was doing better, another time I was doing even better, and then I would weave in some little set-back, so that things wouldn't proceed too swiftly."

"So that's how you robbed me of my precious time, is it?"

"And then came the last, really serious set-back, when for the twentieth time you listened to my heart, and I took the stethoscope from you—I can still see the face you made—used it to blow directly into your face, laid it on the table beside you—and laid my hands on your shoulders."

"I can still recall that moment too."

Rosa had grown very warm. She had her Hannes beside her, it was incredibly lovely. "If the women out in the courtyard knew that I am lying here with you. — Don't look outside, Rosa. Keep your face under the blanket."

"I can hear the women easily enough. I've gotten used to them. I'm quite at home here, you see, together with my dear husband. Did I annoy you all that much that time, when I put my hands on your shoulders?"

"You stood up and looked me in the eye."

"And then I laid my head on your shoulder."

"What was there about that young doctor in Stuttgart?"

"Nothing."

"Tell me, Rosa."

"Nothing. What can you say about the person you love?"

She lay there, her expression one of happiness.

He listened. "What's the matter, Rosa?"

She hummed an old song. "Two souls and yet one thought, two hearts and yet one mind. We have one heart and two minds, but no thoughts at all. Listen to my heart, it's going tick-tock. The 'tick' is you, the 'tock' is me."

She thrust her arm across her face. "It's wonderful, Hannes. I feel like a mother with a child."

And suddenly she began to complain, "And why did you wait until now, Hannes? I had nothing. You're here with me now, Hannes, there are no secrets between us. You knew so many girls. Why didn't you just take me as one of them? Why did you always have to worship me from afar, write poems in my honor—but not follow through to the conclusion? Why did you always deny me that? I was human after all, you know."

"Did you miss that, Rosebud?"

"Oh, how ashamed I feel. Did you miss that? You wouldn't have asked some other girl if she missed that."

"Oh, forgive me, Rosa. Please, don't hold it against me. I looked up to you too much. I thought that physical things . . ."

"And now you think differently about physical things, right?"

"Rosa, forgive me. Forget all that. I adored you. You were the true, the sublime female for me, the woman of my dreams, you were so clever."

Tears stood in her eyes. "Don't you say that I was clever, too."

He: "Whenever I thought of you, Rosa, I felt myself exalted—and at the same time I yearned for you, yet did not dare to act. Out in the field, before I would fall asleep, I always saw your sweet brown eyes, your lofty brow."

"That's better. That's the kind of man you were, and because you were that way, I didn't lose you."

"You have such energy, Rosa."

"Nothing but yearning and love. Love that has never been expressed as love. May this day never end."

The Tragic Mask

Spring came. Rosa wrote to Sonya, Karl's wife:

"In your card to me you ask why everything turned out like this. What a child you are. That's how life has always been. It's all a part of it, suffering and separation and yearning. You must always take it as a whole—and find it beautiful. I would not want to miss any part of my life and would not want anything to be other than it is."

(That is indeed what she wrote. Why not console the others, why not pretend as if—. If Sonya only knew how things stood with me.)

"Don't you remember, Sonya, the time we were in the Botanical Gardens with Karl? It was early morning and we heard the nightingales, and saw a tall tree that was still completely bare of leaves but covered with masses of shining white blossoms. We racked our brains trying to figure out what kind of tree it was. For it was clear that it wasn't a fruit tree. Now I know that it was a white poplar, and its 'blossoms' were young leaves. I can see just such a poplar here, and songbirds are sitting in it.

"At that time, on that same day in Berlin, you were both with me. Do you still remember? It was so beautiful. Around midnight, as we were saying good-bye, a delightful breeze heavy with the odor of jasmine entered the room through the window open to the balcony, and a Spanish song that's a favorite of mine occurred to me, and I recited it for you:

> Praise him at whose command the world was knit.
> How glorious in every hill and vale.
> He made the sea, both deep and infinite,
> He made the ships that on the sea do sail.
> He made man's Eden, light eternal once,
> He made this earth—and your countenance.

"A great big bumblebee has just flown into my cell, Sonya, filling it with its droning. What *joie de vivre* there is in that sated sound! He bears the fields with him into my cell, hard work, warmth, the perfume of flowers."

Spring had truly come, despite the history the world was busy making. It was even a month to six weeks too early, which bothered Rosa, and she asked Sonya to go to the Botanical Gardens on some sunny day to see whether the orioles and wrynecks had really begun to sing. It was the most important thing to her in all the world (please don't laugh, Sonya!), except for the outcome of the battle of Cambrai.

That battle, by the way, proved inconclusive. The slaughter continued. And at home the political repression grew. People were arrested, and among the new prisoners was Rosa's old friend, the so skillful Leo Jogiches. They brought the news to her, she caught fire, she threw her Korolenko translation to one side and wrote a Spartacus letter:

"So that is how things stand now: the German proletariat missed its chance to jam the spokes of the wheels of the imperialist chariot, and as a result it is now being dragged all around Europe by that same imperialism, overpowering both socialism and democracy.

"Yes indeed, the German worker is tramping on the bones of the revolutionary proletariat of Russia, the Ukraine, the Baltic nations and Finland, across Belgium, Poland, Lithuania, Rumania, and on across France. He wades onward up to his knees in blood in hopes of planting the flag of victory for German imperialism.

"But every military victory that the German cannon-fodder help achieve out there means a new triumph for the reactionaries inside the

Reich. With every attack on the Red Guard in southern Russia and in Finland, the power of the junkers to the east of the Elbe grows and with it pan-German capitalism. With every battered city in Flanders, a bastion of German democracy is lost."

"Well roared, Lioness!" a voice said. Of course he would have to stick his nose in. She got on well enough with him, at least it seemed so to her; she had a good life with him, and having him made her gentler, more patient. But she treated him a bit like some bagatelle. She had him, and that seemed to take care of things as far as she was concerned. But he was like a child: restless, a cry-baby, insistent.

"What's that supposed to mean?" she laughed, responding to his jibe of "Well roared!" "First, you understand nothing of these things. And secondly, Hannes, my darling Hannes, don't exaggerate. I still don't have to take you seriously; no, absolutely not, not even now. I'm still holding the last card in the trick. You're a delusion, a hallucination, a white lie, whatever you want to call it."

"Is that what you think? What you'd like to believe? I'm a delusion, an illusion? You hear me, feel me. And I will provide you with other proofs as well."

"Well now you've got me curious, doctor. You're funny. I'll simply think you away, erase you. Think about that. Especially if you don't stop looking over my shoulder."

These were the little jabs by which she defended her position as "lord of the manor." She really didn't mean it so seriously.

One afternoon, Tanya was sitting next to her as she sat bent over on the bed; Tanya shook her and laughed out loud. Rosa sat up straight. "What's the matter?"

Tanya: "You're sleeping in broad daylight. You're dreaming."

"So what. I dropped off. Why are you looking at me like that? What's the matter? What is there to laugh about, Tanya?"

"You dream the way a rabbit does, with your eyes open. When I came in I heard you talking. You sit there and give orders."

"What—did I say?"

"Hurry up. Get a move on. Bring me the first-aid kit. You were dreaming about a doctor. Then you did the bandaging and all of a sudden you were silent."

"And then?"

"Then you lay down on your bed."

Tanya patted Rosa's hand; she whispered, "You had a boyfriend, a doctor, right?"

"Nonsense," Rosa said, "just dreams. I don't know anything about it."

Rosa was frightened. So that's it. I dreamed about him. But—I wasn't dreaming at all. I don't remember anything about it. But I have a hunch. That's just like him. He's making things cozy for himself here with me. He's abusing his guest privileges. He's feeling right at home already. In my sleep, of course in my sleep. Where can he be hiding? I'd like to nab him by the ear.

Of course he did not respond. There arose a certain tension between them. Rosa was alarmed.

Then came an annoying affair with Tanya. Tanya had learned the rudiments of reading and writing from Rosa, but she pilfered a little, too. As a trustee she found her way into a lot of cells, which made it possible for her to do her spying. They once found money and chocolate on her. Rosa was asked about the chocolate. It was true, it was her chocolate; she told them she had given it to Tanya as a present. They used the occasion to search her cell as well, searching for suspicious papers. Rosa had indeed made some rough drafts, but had destroyed them in the nick of time.

Tanya did not come by for eight days. When she did appear, at the first moment when the coast was clear she fell on her knees before Rosa, kissing her hands, thanking her "for your help with the chocolate" and asking Rosa to forgive her, she only took the chocolate for Michel, her sick friend in the men's prison. Rosa was outraged that Tanya would kneel in front of her and pulled her up. She used this opportunity to interrogate Tanya about the spying she did for the prison administration.

"But I have to do it," Tanya sobbed, "otherwise I'll lose my job as trustee, and then I won't be able to do anything for Michel."

It turned out that she had found a way to smuggle things into the men's wing on a regular basis. Over and over again she begged Rosa to forgive her and blamed herself for her wickedness. Then she quieted down, swore to change for the better, and promised that in the future she would do everything for Rosa that she could. From then on, Tanya regularly told her what was happening both in their own building and in the men's wing. This irritating episode resulted in Rosa's being watched more closely, in her books, letters, and writings being checked, but Tanya's devotion to her made up for much of that.

Their principle topic of conversation was Michel's illness. Apparently a fragment of bone in the wound where Michel had been shot had become infected, and they were afraid that the inflammation would spread to his brain. Rosa and Tanya were frightfully worried. Tanya received daily messages from the infirmary across the way via a carefully organized grapevine. Rosa's opinion was that with such a serious illness as Michel's, he ought to be taken out of the prison infirmary and transferred to a municipal hospital. That put a bug in Tanya's ear. She succeeded in getting a nurse to suggest this to the prison doctor so that apparently the doctor and the warden did discuss the issue—with the result that one day the doctor informed the nurse with a shrug that they were adequately equipped for a case such as this and that a surgeon would be brought in. The municipal hospitals had to be kept available for the military.

Tanya wept. "They'll let Michel die like a dog." Rosa had her hands full calming her down.

And so spring passed in the prison, and the momentous summer of 1918 began.

And with the advent of summer's heat, Rosa felt the urge to go on a honeymoon, with him. She had promised it to him, and it was high time arrangements were made. Because the war could go on for a long time yet.

At this point, Tanya brought her a book out of the prison library that Tanya liked because of its pictures. It was about Breslau, with its historical monuments and other tourist attractions. Tanya explained the pictures to Rosa, and Rosa had to read the text to her.

They learned about a great exposition hall that had been built just a few years before, in 1913, and could easily hold more than a hundred thousand people.

Tanya asked naively, "What for?"

Rosa answered, "I don't know, Tanya. Maybe so they can fight their war."

Tanya, however, knew what for, for the Midsummer Festival, for beer tents and hot-dog stands.

Rosa said, "Here's something about someone named Konrad Kissling."

"Kissling," Tanya replied, "don't know him."

Rosa: "He lived eighty years ago. He came from Middle Franconia and opened up the first beer cellar in Breslau, on the boulevard, for Bavarian beer."

Tanya said very seriously, "They're probably right."

Rosa: "Sure they are. The Schweidnitz Cellar."

Tanya crowed, "Is that in there? I know the place."

She looked at the book. Rosa showed her the place, but Tanya considered it impossible that something like that was in the book.

"What happened there," she asked excitedly, "to make someone write about it?"

"Oh, nothing unusual. Someone wrote about it because," she hesitated, it was difficult to explain really, "because people write down things that happen in the world. For instance they mention here, 'Once the Kaiser sat at a table in the Schweidnitz Cellar and drank his beer, without letting anyone know who he was, just like anyone else. But before he left, he wrote something on the table in chalk.'"

Tanya nodded happily. "In chalk, that's true. He had the waiter give him the chalk. After every mug you drink, the waiter makes a mark on the table."

Rosa: "The Kaiser wrote: 'If some people knew who some people were, some people would show them sometimes more respect.'"

Tanya's face was serious. "He was offended. Sometimes they don't have good manners. It depends on the time of day. — But why did the Kaiser go in there in disguise?"

Rosa: "It's hard to put yourself in a kaiser's shoes." (She wanted to laugh out loud, but she contained herself.) But Tanya, the prisoner, first paused to consider why the Kaiser would go in there "in disguise" and drink his beer, and she felt ashamed for her hometown of Breslau that people had once again shown such bad manners in the Schweidnitz Cellar.

"A kaiser," Tanya declared to her older friend, "doesn't have things so easy all the time. He sits on the throne and he's got to run things. He doesn't have any time for his family or for himself. Just think of all the petitions from people who want a pardon or feel they're innocent or want their case opened again. Even if his prime minister reads it all, he's still got to give his opinion too. And then—if there's a war. His sons are sent to the battlefield, he's left alone with his wife. And all those battles."

Rosa: "Who is responsible for war in the end, Tanya?"

Tanya's face registered her surprise. "That's part of it all. If you're a kaiser and running things and you've got a nation with generals and soldiers, then war's a part of it all."

Rosa: "Hm, hm." Not bad. It's a part of it all. She looked at the book again. "At one time in Breslau there was a House of Silent Music."

"I don't know nothing about that."

"On Altbüssergasse. In the thirties, in the last century, during Advent one year, mysterious music was heard, as if singing nuns were going by in a procession."

If Rosa had been reading the book for herself, she would have skimmed that part. But now she had to stop at this point, responding to the attentive look on Tanya's face. Tanya whispered that something like that had happened in her own village in Poland, at a spot that had once been a cemetary. Ghosts had come out at night, also during Advent, and started singing.

Rosa: "Did people see the ghosts?"

"Lots of times. They'd disappear then after Advent. They're the ones who can't find any rest."

Rosa laid the book down and stared straight ahead. Without glancing at Tanya, she asked, "Why can't they find any rest?"

"They're poor sinners. They died without finding rest. And now they come back to where they've lived and where their graves are and want to make up for it all. That's why they come during Advent, when the Lord is about to be born."

Rosa passed her hand across the book. Hannes and I, poor sinners, absurd, ridiculous. I love him, I have the power to draw him to me here, and he cannot die without me. He wants to live, we want to live, both of us, we can't tear ourselves away from this life.

She read on. "This occurred on through the thirties of the last century and was repeated every year during advent. Then the cellar was walled up, and since then the mysterious nuns have been heard no more."

Rosa smiled archly. "Those were nuns, Tanya, not poor sinners. What would make an innocent nun wander about after death?"

Tanya: "More than likely there's something special about them. Maybe," she became very mysterious herself, "they were allowed to return during Advent to their cloister because they wanted to celebrate the Lord's birthday. But—why did they do that, wall it up I mean?"

"You think they shouldn't have done it?"

Tanya shook her head. She sat there, shuddering with horror.

And Rosa—said nothing. She said nothing.

A Ghost Gets His Way

When Tanya had left, she left the little book lying open at the illustration of the "House of Silent Music." She closed her eyes. She tried to initiate a conversation with him.

He was almost always around. She sensed his presence in a lighter air that surrounded her. Sometimes it seemed to her as if she carried this lighter, cooler air around with her like an aura. On occasion he would pat her shoulder or give her hand a little tap. Sometimes it was as if he were a fur collar laid about her neck. On her head, however, in her hair, where she had imagined him, he never came to rest. He

35

avoided her eyes as well. He seldom spoke. Often he would not even respond when she called out to him, so lost in himself after what he had had to go through out there. His presence hardly bothered her. She moved about quietly, like a mother in the presence of her sleeping child, always alert, her thoughts trained on him. That was how she lived together with her invisible bridegroom, her husband, of whom it was said he had fallen in the war and lay buried in the snows of Russia. She had heard at one point that friends had looked for his grave on those Russian battlefields. That amused her. I could tell them a thing or two; I could ask him about that myself. But why bother to talk about unimportant matters. He is here. He's been acting strangely for several days now. (She also knew, without making much of it, that he played a role in some way in her fainting spells.)

Now that Tanya had left, she turned to him.

"Hannes, did you hear that? Hannes, my darling guest, my other self, what do you have to say about the 'House of Silent Music'?"

"Who is she?" Hannes asked.

"A prisoner like me. She does work in the cells. She—believes in ghosts, in spooks. She says some peculiar things about them."

"Why does that upset you? Do you believe in ghosts?"

She, tenderly: "Me? — no. You're not a ghost."

"A while ago you wanted to turn me into a hallucination. And now I'm supposed to be a ghost, is that it? But I'm not one, Rosa. But—you are one."

Rosa went rigid. They had not had a conversation for a long time now. What had he been thinking about in the meantime.

He repeated it. "You're one."

She became angry. "Stop talking nonsense, Hannes. I'm not in the mood."

"Don't you feel that you're a ghost, Rosebud? Just because you still have arms and legs, you're not one, is that it? What sort of life can even be called life that's lived out behind bars, locked up in a little cell, with a high wall outside? This whole moldy world."

"What's all this, Hannes? What are you driving at?"

He was so impatient, grim, irritable; the tone of his voice was anything but endearing.

He kept on pushing. "You're a woman, Rosa, and so you're moody. Maybe you called for me that first time only because you wanted your stay here to be a bit more comfortable. Well here I am. It's not right to be so egotistical. A person ought to think of others."

"Which means, which means? What am I supposed to think of?"

It seemed to be getting out of hand. She was trying to parry his attack by making a literary joke. "Aha, I understand now: 'Our thoughts rest easily, lie side by side, whereas realities must needs collide.'"

"Correct. That's it. We have one body. These are confining quarters, where each must be considerate of the other. Which I most certainly am. But you talk, you think, as if I weren't here at all."

"Oh but Hannes my dear, quite the contrary."

"What, for instance, is the point of this conversation with Tanya? You know full well that I'm listening. I have to listen because of our confined quarters. The walls are thin."

"And what is your point?"

"You snoop around after me. What was the purpose of that silly talk about nuns in cellars who sing while they haunt? Why that annoying digging around investigating their past, looking for their sins, for their intentions and so on?"

"Hannes, it simply happened that way. No offense intended. Really, I do everything I can to be considerate of you."

"If only I could see some of that. Not that I want to boast about myself, my dear Rosa, but I don't meddle when you're speaking to some prison official or other, for instance, when you're complaining about your mail or visiting hours—although I most certainly would adopt another tone if it were me."

"And what kind of tone would that be?"

"The tone appropriate to dealing with civil servants. A courteous one. You shouldn't always play the prima donna, the political prisoner, the *enfant terrible*."

"I beg your pardon, Hannes, but that's my own concern."

"Just what I said—that's what one calls being considerate."

"But it's not something we need to argue about now, is it."

"I wanted to show you—my good manners, the way I try to oblige you. You won't dispute the fact that I allow you total freedom. But I have the feeling I'm no better than a criminal who's being hidden away in the house."

"Hannes."

"And that is definitely not who I am. I have proven who I am. I am being ignored, slighted, I'm used and abused."

She whines, "But I've pampered you, Hannes. You're my sweetheart, my lover. What are you thinking of doing? Do you want to leave me?"

He, roughly: "Leave you—just how do you figure I can do that?" He gives a short, cynical laugh, wouldn't that suit you just fine. "Rosa, there have to be some changes made. We've been brought together by dreadful circumstances. We have to make shift somehow; we live, as you've put it, under one roof together. But that doesn't mean that I'm your boarder."

"Certainly not." (Good heavens, what is all this?)

"Now that you have invited me in, and now that I've accepted with sincere gratitude, certain consequences must follow. It's out of the question for one of us to play master of the house."

Anxiety swelled within her. She did not know what it was she felt. She was dizzy, but she managed to stay sitting up.

"Hannes, you have the same right—you have even more rights than I. It's only through you that I'm alive; I have you to thank for any joy in this life. I was desperate—everything, everything I have is yours." (What will he demand now? What is wrong with him?)

"Fine, fine," he said, "that's a fine turn of phrase. But if it's not just a fancy phrase of yours, then you'll have to follow through with it."

"But what can I do for you? I'm only Rosa Luxemburg, locked up in the Breslau women's prison, a political prisoner."

"Oh go on, locked up as a political prisoner. You can just cut that sort of talk. I heard enough of that long ago. I don't want to be locked up here forever myself just because of that. It's unjust of you to demand that of me. You can't treat me like that. I want out. I have to get out. I have to get out. I'll break out."

"Hannes, my dearest Hannes."

"That doesn't help me much."

"For heaven's sake, what do you want me to do? I'm a sick, weak, old woman. How am I supposed to break out of here, with my bare hands?"

"It can't be done with those hands of yours, that's for sure. But what if we use my fists?"

She couldn't believe it. "You want to take my own hands away from me?"

He whispered vehemently, wildly to her. "Don't betray me. Keep ever so quiet. You'll see who I am."

"Oh please, not that, Hannes, we wanted to stay together, we wanted to love one another."

"Rosa, something has to happen."

And something happened, sooner than she expected (or feared). It happened the very next morning as she awoke.

She found herself lying in bed, her limbs heavy, a strange, dull pain in her lower back, and her left arm (she was terrified as she went to lift it) was bandaged up to the shoulder. She had been lying with her face

38

to the wall. Now she turned her head to the window. There sat Tanya, watching her, attentive to her every move.

Tanya bent down to her, smiling. "How are you feeling, Rosa?"

Rosa looked at her questioningly.

Tanya: "You had a hard night, Rosa."

"Why? What happened?"

"What did happen, Rosa? You tell me."

"I don't remember anything."

"Nothing at all?"

"No."

Tanya: "You woke up the whole place. You were a one-woman revolution. It was terrible. It took us a whole hour to calm you down."

Rosa stretched out the bandaged arm and then reached up to her head.

"We had to call a guard. We couldn't manage you. You wanted to break down the doors. You even attacked the guard. You gave us all bruises. He had to haul off and slug you a couple of times. It was awful. But then you finally gave up."

"I—I don't remember anything."

"We saw how things were right off. You didn't even recognize me. You were so strong. There were three of us, and we couldn't handle you. That's why we called the guard, and he was amazed, too, at how strong you were."

"Me, strong?"

"I'm glad you've gotten hold of your senses again, Rosa. The director was here a while ago. He said that if you have more fits like that you'll have to be put in the infirmary."

"Me, having fits, Tanya? Why that's nonsense, what are you talking about?"

She buried her face in her pillow and began to cry miserably while Tanya stroked her hand.

It was his fault. She had had such pains. That's how he treated her. He had wanted to escape. He had taken control of her in her sleep.

What crime have I committed. I was alone, I was desperate, I clung fast to him. He wanted to escape, and so I called him, I gave him all the love I am capable of—and that he was capable of, too. My life, this life I've thrown away, I wanted to live it again. I brought him here, I had him, he had nothing else after all, they had destroyed him out there on the battlefield. I said, come to me, Hannes, it won't be like before, but we'll be together, forget all those awful things, forget the misery of your life, today is today, and now . . .

Tanya had to report to the kitchen. When she came back, Rosa was lying peacefully looking up at her. "Can you stay with me, just for a little while Tanya?"

"I've been told to do just that, Rosa. I only had to look after something else."

Rosa was struggling with herself. "Tanya, I'm not ill. Believe me. I won't go to the infirmary. I'm fine here in my cell."

"That's where you'll stay, too, Rosa."

"Tanya, it wasn't me last night. Believe me. How would I ever come up with the crazy idea of trying to escape from here. I've been here for a long time now. I would have let you in on it. It—was someone else, a friend of mine."

"Rosa, it's all right. We're glad you're with us again."

"No, it wasn't me, Tanya, he ravished me."

"But it was you, Rosa. Don't get upset now. I saw you with my own eyes. Just look at your arm. I put you in bed afterward myself."

"It wasn't me. You know I don't have strength like that."

"Of course you had it. I wouldn't have believed it, but you did."

Rosa: "It was someone else. A friend of mine. He did it."

Tanya opened her eyes wide. "A friend of yours?"

Rosa pointed to the photograph on the windowsill. "It's him. My friend. — He was killed in the war."

Tanya sprang back.

Rosa: "You won't tell on me, will you? He's dead, he comes to see me. And he does that to me."

Rosa thought while she was saying this: let him go ahead and hear. He's got to know that it can't go on like this.

Tanya gave the picture a horrified look. "What does he want?"

Rosa: "I don't know. He is seeking refuge here with me. He was still so young. I love him so. His name is Hannes. Even if he does treat me like this, I still care for him."

Tanya: "You've been bewitched, Rosa."

"No. He comes to me. He was killed. He didn't want to die. We wanted to have and do so many things together after the war."

"You weren't able to get married, Rosa?"

"No, no, we weren't."

Tanya put her hands to her face. She stood up and stood with her back to the wall where the picture was. "I'm afraid."

"He won't hurt you. He's so gentle. It just comes over him sometimes. You've got to help me. I don't know what else he may try to do to me."

"He will murder you, Rosa."

"Don't go believing things like that, Tanya. He's my sweetheart; I called for him myself."

Tanya threw up her hands in terror. "You should never have done that. How could you do that, Rosa. Now he's here. We'll ask for you to be given a different cell. Maybe he won't find his way there."

"Tanya, I don't want to do that. You won't tell another soul about this. Give me your hand on it. He wants out, he suffers so here in the cell. That's what made him so violent. What can I do?"

Tanya sat down next to Rosa on the bed. "Is it really the same man as the one in the picture? Does he really come to you?"

"I told you he does."

"Then you will have to pray, Rosa, for him to find peace."

"But I want to have him. He is my one real happiness."

"You've treated him unfairly. You don't understand. You don't dare do this."

"Without him, in this cell, with no end in sight, never. I can't do it. We were able to enjoy one another while he was alive, and now you want me to drive him off."

"Rosa, he can't stay here with you. He'll drag you to your ruin with him. We have to pray for him."

Rosa closed her eyes. "I want to keep him here. He's mine. And I'm his. I want to keep him for ever and ever."

Tanya first stood up and then knelt beside the bed. She sobbed, "I love someone in just the same way. If only he stays alive."

They gave Rosa sleeping pills and sedatives. She dozed away a few days. The pain in her back subsided, they unbandaged her arm, revealing green and yellow bruises; it hurt her to move it. At one point Tanya asked her, "Aren't you afraid of him, afraid he'll come back?"

Rosa: "I'm never afraid of him. Are you afraid of Michel?"

Tanya stood there amazed. "Is it really like that?"

She brought her a few wild flowers and put them in a waterglass on the table, shyly. There was no way of telling for whom the flowers were meant.

Rosa, however, went about things shrewdly. She gave him no cause for offense. She wanted to prevent him from doing any more stupid things.

He was nowhere to be seen. She thought: it's his bad conscience— or is it something else again? She would have to get hold of him. There was no way of knowing what plans he was hatching behind her back.

41

She thought it over: what is wrong with my quiet, well-behaved boy that he's become so cunning and violent, downright cruel? Did the war do that? I haven't seen him for a long time now. He's really dangerous. He'd just love to toss me out of my home here.

She had never actually been able to see him with her eyes. But then, one day after the sun had set, as the cell lay in twilight and no light had been turned on, she became aware of him because of his soft sighing. He was sitting under the table, all in black, hunched over, his head in his hands. He took no notice of her. She called to him, "Hannes. It's you. What are you doing there?"

And he was gone.

Another time, after she had spread out the towel and the scarf, he sat silent and dejected on the chair, his head resting on the tabletop, lost in gazing at his own picture.

He sadly turned about after a little while and offered her his hand. "Forgive me, Rosa."

Those were his first words since that awful night. She could not answer him for happiness.

She looked at him and understood everything: he wanted out, he could not bear it in this cell. But what could she do?

"Rosa, I want out. I ask nothing else."

And he stared into her eyes and raised his strong right hand. She realized how dreadfully serious he was. This man, her Hannes, was capable of anything. There was no talk of the love they shared; he was driven unmercifully and he held fast to her.

And she received proof of how serious this was the next morning. In one corner of her cell lay a small cardboard box in which Rosa kept her underclothes and blouses, since her cupboard was stuffed full of books and papers. When she got up she found the lid to the box out in the middle of the room and all her things scattered on the floor. Rosa was beside herself (someone had been in her room), and she buttonholed Tanya. Who had dared do such a thing?

Tanya looked at the mess in surprise. It wasn't her, it really wasn't. But then who was it? It certainly was outrageous, Tanya said, she would make inquiries with the matron. But she didn't know anything about it either and was angry. Rosa had best be careful about making accusations; could it be that someone was trying to steal her blouses.

Tanya returned.

Rosa was waiting expectantly for her, spoiling for a fight.

Tanya sat down silently next to her.

Rosa: "Well then, who was it?"

Tanya looked firmly at her and laid an index finger to her mouth.

Rosa did not understand. Then Tanya turned her head in the direction of the photograph.

Now Rosa understood. She opened her mouth in horror. Then she let her arms fall to her sides and slowly shook her head. Tanya patted her hand. They did not speak.

Then Tanya said, "What does he want?"

Rosa: "With my clothes? I don't know."

And suddenly it dawned on her. She held one hand to her mouth and laughed aloud. She laughed and laughed.

"That's just like Hannes, Tanya, just like him. It's him all over. He's looking for men's clothes."

"Men's clothes?"

"Yes, in among my blouses and camisoles. He wants to get out of here. He won't give up. He thinks that if he's wearing trousers he can do it."

Rosa pulled Tanya down to her, she infected Tanya with her laugh, they giggled together. "He thinks he'll find men's clothes and a coat among my things, and then he'll break out, with me, if you can imagine, with my woman's legs and fat as I am. He's annoyed that I'm a woman. Oh, what an idiot he is."

Rosa let go of Tanya. She had an idea. "Tanya, he wants to play a trick on me. That's apparent. He's up to something. What I may think of it makes no difference to him at all. For all he cares I can break every bone in my body. We'll beat him to it. You'll have to help me."

Tanya protested vehemently.

Rosa: "I need men's clothes. We'll make a fool of him. He'll soon see that I am still very much here."

Tanya wanted to run away. Rosa held her tight. "Tanya, you're going to help me. You have to. You have the clothes that need mending, the uniforms. It would be no problem for you. You just come in here and sit down beside me and mend. I'll—stay lying on the bed. I'll pretend I'm sick. You won't say anything to anybody."

"I'm not staying here if *he* comes."

"You won't have to. He won't bite you, Tanya. You only have to look at him to see what a good man he is."

"He's a ghost."

"You and your crazy ghosts. He's harmless and stupid. You'll—let me think this out—you'll sit here and sew and then get up and leave all of a sudden with everything lying here."

"I won't do it, Rosa. I won't do it."

"Then, when he's standing there in his men's clothes, in a uniform, you'll come back in. Oh, Tanya, will I ever give it to him. Just imagine what I'll look like in a man's uniform. I'll die laughing."

"I'm afraid, Rosa."

"As soon as he starts rattling at the door or at the window, you'll come in. It will be incredibly funny. Me in a man's clothes. Good heavens if only I could see it myself."

"That's enough, Rosa."

"Tanya! Dear, sweet Tanya, get some men's clothes for me. I have to teach him a lesson. He must learn not to do such stupid things."

"Won't you be embarrassed, Rosa, wearing a man's clothes?"

"He's the one who should be embarrassed. You'll die laughing."

Tanya had no choice but to sit down the next morning in Rosa's cell with a bundle of mending and to work at it. To get a foretaste of her joke, Rosa tried the clothes on. Naturally nothing fit, the trousers were too tight and too long, they wouldn't fasten at the front and at the rear they were beastly tight. Tanya was grandly amused by this masquerade; since she didn't have any suspenders, she tried to tie the trousers with the broad string of an apron, but the effect was all too improvised. They gave up in delight and threw the playthings to one side. Tanya had other things to do and departed.

That afternoon she sat back down again with Rosa and began once more to do her mending, and in the evening she left it all lying there. Rosa was pleased as Punch. She gazed at the clothes, waiting for him to announce himself. She stayed awake all night long, sitting up, walking about. She didn't want to let him catch her napping. She tried to entice him, but without the necessary fervor without any real warmth. And he did not come. He pretended not to hear her.

When Tanya looked in the next morning, Rosa was very tired and lying fully clothed on her bed. She shook her head. "Nothing new from the war zone, Tanya."

Tanya was glad. She brought some coffee and said she would return in an hour. But it wasn't until two hours later she came. Rosa had drunk her coffee in the meantime and had fallen asleep, exhausted from the long night of waiting.

The morning wore on, bringing the busiest hours out in the court-yard. The prisoners were let out, some for work, some to walk in the yard. Wagons drove in and out, crates were being knocked down to kindling over near the kitchen, tubs and basins were being carried about.

Suddenly two women who were working near one wing of the building, dragging an empty tin tub back to the kitchen, noticed a strange person come out of the building and awkwardly march down the low steps leading to the courtyard.

It was apparently a man (or was it?). At any rate a queer fish. He had a full, ashen face and fixed goggle eyes. He had pulled a soldier's cap over his thick white hair, pushing it so far down over his face because it was apparently much too small for him. He wore an old grayish green soldier's jacket from which pieces of white thread hung everywhere as if the jacket had just come from the tailor. The jacket was too tight for him, moreover, it could not be buttoned at the neck, and so the man had left the collar open. The jacket couldn't be closed across the chest either, and incredible though it seemed, some white linen, a shirt perhaps, bulged out from it. The trouser legs were much too long and wound like the threads of a screw down to his small feet, which were stuck in brown slippers.

The two women carrying the basin could not believe their eyes. Other women behind them began to take notice and stopped in their tracks, just as dumbfounded. What was it? A man? A woman? It was a woman of course, but what was it all about, who was it? Some laughed, but that only lasted for a moment. For a while the rest of the yard was as noisy as ever, here just the opposite happened—total silence reigned in the vicinity of this strange creature, like the calm air surrounding a storm. The creature waddled slowly across the yard, moving in a straight line on past them toward the open courtyard door. One woman who had approached it fully unsuspecting, suddenly let out a scream and ran away. The whole courtyard was on the alert now, and people came from all sides to see what was happening. Two matrons recognized, as did several other women, that the creature was Rosa, and they remembered what had happened to her several days ago.

The matrons bravely walked up to the creature and patted it on the shoulder, admonishing her. "Rosa, be reasonable now, Rosa. Wake up."

But when one of them tried to take the creature's cap away as it waddled on ahead, she was countered with a hefty blow and shoved to one side. The cap sailed to the ground, and the creature waddled on bareheaded, not bothering to bend down and pick it up, its long white disheveled hair now falling down its back.

"She's gone loony," the prisoners shouted to one another. The matron called for the guards, her cry of "Guards!" sailing across the yard to the main gate. Both sentries, their rifles in hand, ran over. People made way for them.

Everyone knew that it was Rosa.

And now the battle between the creature and the soldiers began. In order to have their hands free, they leaned their rifles against a delivery wagon and approached the ungainly creature as it strode on, skirting a clutch of women who fell back before her.

One of the guards planted himself in front of the creature. "Halt, where are you going?"

The man was not unafraid. It was a woman, that was true, but she looked terrifying. And now, since he stood there with legs spread and arms outstretched, the creature had to halt. It stammered in a hollow voice, "Let me by."

The other sentry came up behind the ogre's back while it continued to plead, "Let me by, get out of my way." The man grabbed the creature's left shoulder from the rear, but it wheeled around at the same moment, snatching hold of the hand on its shoulder and flinging it away, along with the man attached to it, with such force that the man stumbled and fell. The creature stood there in the open now, like a boxer with fists held up before his chest, and emitted a ghastly rough, gutteral sound like the howl of an orangutan. "Dear friends, step aside! Let me by, dear friends. I'm doing you no harm."

But that had no effect at all on the sentry who had taken offense at the sad fate of his friend. He threw himself at the creature, who in turn began beating him with unbelievable rage. But he hit right back, and growling and spitting the creature had to retreat to the yard wall, its uniform gaping wide at its chest now, where it hid behind an empty wagon. There it barricaded itself in.

The second sentry, scrambling to his feet again, ran up now, hoping to set things aright. The monster was boxed in behind the wagon, waddling back and forth from one side to the other, sticking out its head, baring its teeth, threatening and babbling at them. Its trousers had fallen down around its knees by now, and a woman's white underskirt was visible. It had trouble walking with the trousers down around its knees, and when it tried to free itself of them it stumbled and fell under the wagon. And with that, the two sentries dragged it out. It ranted and flung its arms about, it howled and begged, "Let me by, dear friends, let me by. Have pity, have pity on me."

It was ghastly to have to listen to it. Then she was dragged out, like some fish flopping around in a net, like some horrible octopus, a sea monster caught in a net but spreading terror even when beached. Many of the women ran away in fright. Once the soldiers had the beast out from under the wheels, they held its knees to its chest and bound it with their own leather belts. Then they dragged the body, immobilized in its bonds, by the feet and shoulders across the courtyard and into the building that housed the infirmary. In the corridor now—as they moved carefully along it with the creature gurgling and gnashing its teeth—a nurse from the ward, where the alarm had already been sounded, came running toward them and gave it a short of morphine.

The monster lay bound to the bed, its face bluish red and bloated. Slowly it calmed down. The wildly bulging eyes retreated and closed. The shot had its effect. The face changed and took on the features of a sleeping woman. They loosened the straps.

It was mealtime.

When Rosa awoke at around five that afternoon, she experienced a pleasant sensation, and it took a long time for her to orient herself, for she kept sinking back into that pleasant world and falling asleep.

Finally—it was six and the lights had been turned on—she was able to keep her eyes open, and she fixed them on the nurse. What was happening? — Where was she?

She was given a cordial answer: in the infirmary. The medical health officer on duty at the prison was just making his rounds at the moment, and he was called in. He and the prison doctor had together already interrogated the trustee named Tanya. They had not been able to get much out of the uneducated woman. She said, as did several others who had been present at the scene in the courtyard, that Rosa was "possessed."

Rosa recognized the pudgy little doctor with the full-moon face. He was a man who liked to make jokes, make light of people's ailments with his jokes—what else could he do? He could not, given the nature of things, help much in the first place, still less in a war, and not at all in this prison. So at least he had his good spirits to offer, and the patients had to be content with that: eat up, kid, that's all there is. And so this wag came slowly over to her with cautious steps (less for the purposes of a joke than because of his asthma) and caught his breath again at Rosa's bedside. He took a chair, sat down, set his pince-nez on his nose, the old-fashioned kind that dangled from his vest on a broad ribbon, and gazed at Rosa. The old nurse, a large, angular woman who knew the doctor well, stood at the head of the bed and waited for the expected joke.

"Didn't recognize you at all, Frau Luxemburg," he began in his high voice, a laugh always just in the wings. "Quite amazing, my highest respects. Major attack of hysteria, a truly major one. Rosa

Luxemburg. I had assumed a few valerian drops were the answer. Or some pastry. A major"—he opened his arms to embrace his surprise—"a truly major attack of hysteria."

He waited. She listened. She had nothing to say. He couldn't find an opening then. He would have to do it all on his own. "Didn't you notice anything before this? Small attacks or whatever? What? Nothing? Well then, that's all right too. The people out in the courtyard got an eyeful you can bet. That was quite an audience you had. Rosa in uniform. Haha. But the uniform didn't fit, did it?"

The nurse laughed. The five other women lying in the ward's beds looked sullen, they wanted to be treated and all they ever got was jokes.

"But now tell me," he sniffed and rapped his jawbone with his pince-nez, "you really don't remember anything? Or a little bit perhaps? Complete amnesia? Were you trying to mock the uniform? A bit of that don't you think, hm? You're an educated woman after all, and you're probably aware that in a state like that, a lot of things emerge that were better left undone, in bad taste. Just like when a person's drunk: *in vino veritas*. Cross your heart: only a little satirical farce with the uniform? Right? Propaganda, right?"

At this political teasing, Rosa collected herself. "Why am I lying here? What do you mean "a major attack of hysteria'?"

"Reasonable question. You were in a semiconscious state and in that condition you put on soldier's clothes, a uniform, and went walking like that out into the yard in broad daylight and said you wanted out of here. A crazy notion, I'd say." The nurses giggled along with him.

"I wanted to get out?"

"Which resulted in a minor scuffle, though not as bad as the one in your cell recently. But you won't give up. Resistance to civil authority, just what we've grown accustomed to expect from our good Frau Luxemburg."

He touched her hand with the pince-nez.

The hand jerked back. Rosa bit her upper lip. She said resolutely, "I would prefer to go back to my room."

"Prefer, prefer, you really don't seem to realize what a 'semiconscious state' is. Where would that get us, do you suppose? Hm. I don't even really know whether we can keep you here."

"What is that supposed to mean?"

He shook his head, he chuckled, he sought again to touch her hand familiarly, which she avoided once more. He stood up and got his wind. Then he looked down at her, sniffed and departed. The nurse followed him to the door, where they whispered.

48

When the nurse came back to Rosa's bed, Rosa learned that she would remain here for the time being.

"But what does that mean, for the time being?"

The nurse sniffed just like the doctor, and gave no answer. She was about to move on when Rosa repeated her question.

Already beside the next bed, the nurse answered, "I can't always be standing there next to you, waiting until something else happens. We're not set up for that sort of thing. There are other institutions available for that."

"What sort of other institutions?"

"An insane asylum, if you must know. We don't have the necessary personnel. —But then, what's so bad about that? If it were me, I'd rather be in an asylum than here. —Besides, it's not so far from here either."

Rosa lay there with her eyes closed, still pleasantly tired. She knew now how things stood with her. She was lying in an infirmary with every chance of being transferred to the insane asylum.

She was in "his" hands.

(I've got to tell someone all this, the cry rose up in her. I'm lost. I need help. Who is going to save me? He's a demon. I let him get far too intimate with me.)

She looked about the room. The poor, malcontent faces. No one would believe me. They would send me to the asylum the minute I opened my mouth.

She cried softly.

They gave her sedatives and sleeping pills. She dozed away one week and then another.

*

A New Man Must Be Created

"We have to create a new man," Lenin shouted, raising his fist. "This one is worthless."

He had succeeded in transferring the government from Petrograd to Moscow. He wanted peace, so that, undisturbed by enemies, he could set his revolution in motion.

The peace treaty with its outrageous conditions demanded by the Germans had been accepted. Bucharin ranted, and in his new magazine, *The Communist,* he called Lenin a "Russian Kautsky," an "opportunistic lying windbag." The idealistic socialist revolutionaries, the old conspirators, left the government in order not to compromise themselves by cooperating with Lenin. They indeed had intended a different revolution from his, they wanted "socialism."

"We have to create a new man," jeered Lenin, who had retreated to Moscow in order to carry out his revolution.

Man, in his present state, is worthless. People are dumb and soft, sentimental idiots with a bourgeois love of comfort; mystics, pious and lazy, and, as a result, criminals. We must declare war against them, destroy them root and branch. The remnants of the old tyranny must be smashed. Not just its army, its administration, its legal system, but also, and above all, its hidden bastions in people's minds, in their ideas, ideals, faiths, religions, metaphysics, emotions.

They reproached Lenin for signing the Treaty of Brest-Litovsk, by which millions of Russian workers were placed beneath the heel of German militarism. He had surrendered them to pan-Germanism, the goal of which was to conquer and enslave the whole world.

He answered with his sly smile. "The treaty has been made, that's true. But the Germans have already broken it a dozen times. And I have broken it thirty or forty times. A treaty means nothing. There is no justice that can exist between two classes."

Petrograd was on the verge of famine. The prosperous farmers held back delivery of their grain, they had not even brought the back harvests of 1916 and 1917 to the mills. The land was entirely in the hands of kulaks, city people, and the rich.

Lenin founded a Committee of the Poor. They took this grain away from the farmers and the wealthy who had hoarded it; they left them only as much as they needed for themselves.

In retaliation, the farmers and the rich took up arms against the Bolsheviks. It was a bloody summer. The starving and the desperate fought mercilessly against the starving and the desperate.

A new man had to be created.

There were Czechoslovak prisoners of war in Russia. They had taken up positions beside the Bolsheviks and fought with them against the Germans in the Ukraine. They now wanted to cut a path through the vast nation, to cross Siberia to America and then defeat the Germans in France, since they could not defeat them in the Ukraine. They had weapons. The Bolsheviks wanted to take their weapons from them, but they would not permit it.

And when the Bolsheviks under Trotsky tried to halt their train in the Urals, a battle ensued and the Czechoslovaks ran right over the Bolsheviks, fighting their way to Siberia. There they occupied Samara.

Already gathered in Samara were social revolutionaries, sentimentalists and idiots, as Lenin called them, who still wanted socialism in the old style—that is, freedom and democracy—and wanted it now. They did not concern themselves with what the country needed; for them, freedom and democracy came before everything else, and Russia could perish in the attempt to have them. They did not see that one first had to exterminate the old nobility and the bureaucracy and the rich bourgeoisie, along with their intellectual flunkies, and that one would first have to build factories and provide electrification for the whole country in order to exterminate poverty. And only then could one begin to talk about freedom and democracy.

Lenin had not let the sentimentalists and idiots convene at the Tauride Palace. He chased them clear across Russia. They fled to Siberia. And there they sat now in Samara, trying to pick up where they had had to leave off on that historic night in the Tauride Palace when the commandant of the Latvian regiment had turned the lights out on them. There was now no shortage of light, but of power. Which was why they were glad to see the Czechoslovaks march into town; they too were fleeing from Lenin, but they had weapons. And without hesitating, they placed themselves under the protection of these Czechoslovak prisoners of war; and they could redistribute Russian farmland to their hearts' content, could convene and deliberate. It was a problematical pleasure. It was also their sad fate that they had to place the government of the first constitutional Russian republic under the protection of prisoners of war.

But they had been chased off into the wilderness of Siberia, and if need be they would travel to the beaches of the Pacific and plant their banner there to preach the brotherhood of mankind under socialism— seeing that mankind would not accept it—to the fishes.

During this dreadful year of 1918 there was however one man in Russia whom no one attacked, and who received applause from all sides. This was a Ukrainian named Machno.

He had a fabulous slogan. It was short and sweet: "Kill all civil servants, kill them without prejudice, no matter what party they belong to or what government gave them their posts." This was the sort of universal freedom that Machno wanted to establish. As far as poverty was concerned, he printed up paper bills that read: "The counterfeiting and forging of this money is absolutely not punishable by law under any circumstances."

Whereupon supporters streamed to Machno from all sides and parties. Neither the democratic constituent assemblymen in Samara nor the Bolshevist Lenin in Moscow could compete with him. He was the real liberator of Russia. In hordes they swore their allegiance to him—

their oath reading that they were prepared to carry out every order of their commander so long as he didn't happen to be drunk at the moment.

And while the tide ran high for Machno, the hundred-percent hero of liberty, Lenin, back in Moscow, had to be careful that no one assassinated him. He sat inconspicuously with his wife and sister in the Kremlin in Moscow, drank his tea, ate black bread with butter and cheese, and when he had polished that off, his sister would wander about the palace in search of marmalade.

But Maria Spiridovna was a wild-eyed revolutionary who had once murdered a high czarist official and been banished to Siberia for her crime. That they hadn't executed her at once, for that remarkable act of mercy on the part of the old judicial system, Lenin could find no excuse, especially since she openly attacked him in the Congress of Soviets with the authority of an experienced revolutionary.

She called Lenin a traitor and a liar. He was lying to the farmers who wanted land. He had something entirely different in mind than the welfare of the Russian farmers.

She screamed (Lenin thought it was hysteria), "As far as Lenin is concerned, you all belong on the dungheap. People aren't people to him, they're manure for his plans. There is no difference between the mass-murderer and butcher of mankind Ludendorff and Lenin; people mean nothing to either of them. To them they're only pawns in the game. But I'm telling him and I'm telling you, comrades of the Congress of Soviets: if the peasants of Russia are now to be enslaved, regardless of whether they are Bolsheviks, social revolutionaries or independents, if they are degraded and oppressed, if they are enslaved as peasants, as human beings—then you will again find in my hand the same pistol that I was forced to use to defend them once before."

While the storm of applause was still raging, Trotsky, Lenin's faithful helpmate, stood up. He was greeted with a yowling scream of rage and protest. The chairman was the same Sverdlov who had had the job of intimidating the Constituent Assembly. He now rang his bell and tried to yield the floor to clever Trotsky with his pointed beard. He did not succeed.

At which point bald little Lenin stepped up to the podium, still wearing the same old trousers he had worn on Spiegelgasse in Zurich. Sverdlov turned around to him. With a gentle smile, Lenin took him by the lapel and whispered something to him. At that, Sverdlov put down his bell, inaudible in any case and sat down. Lenin stayed on his feet beside him and smiled out at the seething assembly. Curses were hurled at that bald head. He turned it to the right and left as if to catch them. Gradually they gave up.

They had said everything there was to say, after all, and he had heard it. Now let him try to answer them.

And indeed, he raised his hand and began to speak. And resentment, rage, and hate began to oppress the hearts of those who had just given such full vent to their emotions.

Lenin explained to them how things stood. He acted as if they had no notion of the facts. They had indeed had all sorts of good and reasonable things to say (he spoke conciliatorily), but, when seen from up close, matters were not as simple as they appeared from a distance. In a revolution one must constantly learn anew, even unlearn some things. That was wearisome and often unpleasant, especially when one had one's principles, but one must keep pace with the revolution. He explained to them how he himself had come around to making a peace such as the one of Brest-Litovsk. It was a matter of necessity. He demonstrated to them the difficult situation the nation faced as the result of war. He pointed out that they had a famine to deal with and that they must use every means available to deal with it. One could not make allowances for people who in such a situation considered their ideals more important than millions of starving people. Then he went on to attack the very same Treaty of Brest-Litovsk, but only in order to ask his opponents what other treaty they might have been able to conclude themselves, one that would provide for peace with the Germans so that the revolution might be advanced.

When he finished, the assembly stood to a man—with the exception of a small group—and applauded. Lenin accepted this approval with gravity, shifting his blazing eyes coldly to the mute row of his opponents. This was then followed by an outburst of rage on the part of the Congress against Count Mirbach, the German envoy who had been watching the proceedings from a private box—and who was found murdered in the embassy the next day.

Lenin considered the murder stupid, "the work of monarchists and people who want to get us into war with Germany for the benefit of French and English capitalists." To the disgust of his friends, he expressed his sympathy to the German government (on which occasion, by the way, the German word for "sympathy" could not be ferreted out—someone had found the word for "pity" and they had to send for Radek, who rescued them).

Lenin's opponents then murdered General Eichhorn in Kiev. A whole troop of social revolutionaries mowed down Uritsky, the chief of the secret police in Petrograd. And ultimately they decided to go for Lenin himself. He had spoken to the workers at the Michelson Factory in Moscow, and was already standing on the running board of his car when two women approached him to ask a question. But it was less a question than an answer. He was struck by three bullets, the first in the spine, the second in the shoulder, the third in the hip.

It was a matter of life and death, and he suffered terribly. He mumbled, "Why didn't they finish me off?" But after three weeks he once again took up his work, his revolution, his battle against the sentimentalists, the idiots, the ideologues.

Within three days after the attempted assassination of August 30th, five hundred people had been executed. Fourteen days later, Petrovski, the People's Commissar for Interior Affairs, issued an order: "An ample number of hostages are to be taken from bourgeois and military circles. All right-wing social revolutionaries are to be arrested. The least resistance is to be countered with mass executions."

And Lenin himself, in the last weeks of his recuperation and back up to snuff, telegraphed the commanding officer of the Fifth Army, who was in the thick of battle against the Whites and non-Bolsheviks: "I expect the suppression of the Kasan-Whites, Czechs and Kulaks to be exemplary in its ruthlessness."

He later sent the following explanatory remarks to the workers of America:

"The bourgeoisie of international imperialism murdered ten million people and maimed and wounded thirty million more. When our war here claims a half million or even a million victims, the bourgeoisie declares: the earlier sacrifices were justified, these are not. The workers will judge otherwise."

Lenin had a friend, Maxim Gorki, the writer. They had been together in Capri for a long time, during the long-ago days of exile and expectation. Lenin even permitted Gorki his idealism.

And when, following the attempted assassination, Lenin took up the chase with special rigor, Gorki confronted his friend and said, "When I see you and your people at work, I am often reminded of the Dominicans from the medieval Inquisition. You try people's hearts and souls. You play the exorcist—I saw that done once in my home-town. The sorcerer cast out the devil. Just as you," Gorki laughed easily, "just as you would like to drive the devil out of Russia. But you've gone too far. You're driving the people out with him."

Lenin shrugged.

Gorki: "What is really happening here? Is all this only an idea of yours, something you've thought up, a fancy, or do you really feel for the people?"

Lenin then gazed attentively at his friend, and that gentle mocking smile of his played once again about his mouth. "I feel sorry for you intellectuals."

54

A Mysterious Journey Around the World

Discharged from the infirmary, Rosa was once again sitting in her cell one rainy day with Tanya, who was mending gunny sacks, reading to her from the book about Breslau that Tanya found so interesting. This time a small atlas lay next to the book, and Rosa was using it to show Tanya where Breslau was located and what all else there was in this world.

Tanya was fascinated. This here, the blue part, was water, the sea, the ocean. It flowed all around the earth, like a clear glaze poured over brown cake. The black lines in different countries were meant to be rivers. Rosa showed her Warsaw, where she had grown up, and Vilna. That was Poland, she said, and this whole country belonged to Russia, and Russia was incredibly big, and there was a revolution going on there now, and leading it were Lenin and Trotsky and other people she knew. Russia reached as far as the sea, and this here was called Siberia, the place where the Russian czar always sent people he was afraid of, and ordinary criminals too, prisoners just like in Breslau, men and women, and they had to work in mines there and build roads. "At one time I came very close to being sent there too. But then I got sick. If I hadn't come down with that illness, maybe I'd already be dead now."

They laughed. Tanya: "Was it the same sickness you have now?"

Rosa laughed loudly. "It's always the same. It keeps right on. It'll keep on going longer than I do."

Rosa: "And then comes China. And down here, more to the south, it gets warmer and warmer. India, Africa."

"Where the Negroes live," Tanya added, her chin propped in her hand, following it all eagerly, her eyes glued to the map. It was exciting. If you followed the map still further it got even warmer, but only for a while, then it got cold, much colder again. The people on the earth in the many different countries were white or yellow or red or black. There weren't any blue people, Rosa had no explanation for why not. They both laughed heartily and decided that mankind had only tried white, yellow, red and black up till now; maybe someday they would be blue as well, and that that would be the race of the future. Up at the North Pole was where Eskimos lived; they wore polar-bear hides and lived in ice houses, and in Africa the Negroes ran around practically naked.

An astonished Tanya repeated the names she heard and traced her finger across the map, from the middle up to the top where it got cold and then back down again as if she could feel the change. She was perplexed, played the game once more and shook her head. Finally she stood up. She had to get back to work. Still uncertain about it all, but pleased, she kissed Rosa's hand (something she persisted in doing) and turning to the door she made their customary sign of farewell, an index finger to the lips—"mum's the word."

Rosa sat there alone. It seemed to her that while she was talking with Tanya, "he" had been looking over her shoulder.

He had not appeared to her for a long time now; an estrangement, but one that was mutual. She had wanted to break off with him while she was in the infirmary, because of his underhanded tactics and brutality, because of his almost incomprehensible egoism. She remembered how she had indulged him, and she shuddered. She wept a great deal; he was not a friend, not a lover, but a liar, a swindler, a brute. She wanted to accept the so-called "diagnosis" of the little health officer, that she suffered from "hysterical lapses into a semiconscious state" and that Hannes was only an obsession. She wanted to rub Hannes's nose in the idea and degrade him to an illusion.

But that was not so easily done. Besides which it was probably— pure nonsense.

When she had returned to her cell (my "den of iniquity"), Tanya reported to her at last the full details of what had transpired that morning. How she, Tanya, had first been made to leave, leaving the clothes in the cell. How Rosa had then dropped off to sleep, and then how the masquerade they had planned had come off—but in a way totally unlike what she had expected.

Rosa: "How do you mean?"

Tanya put her hand to her eyes. "It was terrible, Rosa. You shouldn't do such things. I went to see the chaplain afterward and made a confession. He said it was horrible and sinful and that I should warn you. That you were a bad person."

Rosa was impatient. "But what happened then?"

Tanya: "We were going to have a laugh, remember, when he put on the pants. But nobody laughed. They all saw how things stand with him. Rosa, he's a poor sinner, a poor lost soul burning in purgatory. Leave him alone, you're committing a sin."

Rosa knew this old song. But the description did make an impression on her. She saw her Hannes again, the young man, how he had been left there on the battlefield, how he could neither live nor die, how he tried to force his way back to life, to his life, into her life.

What nonsense to call him a poor sinner, my Hannes. I would like to know what sin he ever committed. They did not let him live. And even if I wasn't able to prevent this godawful war, I will at least accomplish one thing: I'll stand by my Hannes when he needs me.

Once Tanya had gone, she sat there in her cell and waited.

She joked with him.

You're holding something against me? Why? I only wanted to have some fun with you. Really, it was a stupid thing to do, but you shouldn't take it so seriously.

Hannes, what are you up to? Tanya thinks you're in purgatory. My guess is you're inside the pyramids, walling yourself in, hiding from me.

Come on, come on, climb out of your sarcophagus.

She closed her eyes tight and tapped his photograph.

She looked at the end of her finger. Maybe it's magnetic and I can pull him out of his picture.

I'll move over to the edge of the bed. You can sit on the chair.

She got up and began the old ritual, laid out the white towel and the scarf on the chair.

The gentleman is very fussy. He requires a long and carefully thought out invitation. Here, a flower for you. My good husband has up and left me. Come back, Hannes, all is forgiven—and please forgive me, too, please! Your obedient servant, Caroline, Rosa, née Luxemburg.

She laid her right arm tenderly on the arm of the chair.

As in those first days of our love. She listened in his direction.

He didn't say anything, he didn't come.

She gave up. I want to forget him. She translated some Korolenko. But the thought of him wormed its way in everywhere. It was as if Hannes's shadow were being cast ahead of him, but only to vex her, to punish her.

She begged. She insisted. She pushed the books to one side. She felt it all thrust down upon her, enveloping her.

He would not come, he would not come. Her yearning for him, her sense of abandonment. And again the horror, the hatred she felt for this existence, for this cell, for Tanya, for herself.

I don't want to live. I don't want to live anymore. I don't want to exist. To see light anymore. No newspapers, no battles, no revolution, no peoples and nations. That I ever got involved was a curse. It only meant that I was beaten, hounded, tormented, until I finally landed here, flung alive into my grave.

I should forget about me, and forget about you, the man they killed. I accuse myself, Hannes, I am guilty of your death. I took such delight in how handsome and smart you looked. I loved you so tenderly, and still I did not hold you back with both hands when you said you had to do your duty, even though you loved peace, even though you loved France, but it was your fatherland that was calling you and you would do your share. You said it with such assurance then, and I could have kissed you for it.

Not to see the sun anymore, not to see light. I let you go. And you fell on the battlefield.

Look, Hannes, I've gambled my life away, too. So come to me, don't deny me that. Show me your sweet face. Let me hear your voice, if only in the tiniest whisper.

And you, you, only you, no one else but you, nothing but you.

"Where he is not, there is my grave, the world then all, all turns to gall."

Oh, to possess you, to leave the world far behind with you.

Oh, you out there, you people, let me alone. Let me be, you sunrises and sunsets.

Oh, let me alone, birds.

Leave me in peace, bees.

And all you plants, I can't go on.

Sonya, Luise, Leo—all of you, I don't want you anymore. You've pursued me so long. I've given you all so much of myself. Grant me peace.

Ah, Hannes, protect me. Help me, my Hannes, so that they will let me reach you. Believe me, I want nothing but that. Hannes, my darling, I'll deny you nothing now; look how I'm weeping and no one is here to stand by me. Keep your hands off of me. See what's become of me, an ugly old dishrag, that's what I've become after all those long squabbles, the noise, the meetings, the congresses—and when the going got rough, they all turned coward and it was as if I had never existed.

What's the point of it all?

And for the sake of that to forget you and let you die, and never, ever to see you again.

(She bit her finger, hard.)

A dogmatist, a know-it-all, a loud-mouth, that's what I was. I called upon everyone to become aware of things—what I called aware; for them it was just a bauble that they traded off for their patriotism. But I did not call myself to awareness. And I did not become aware. I rotted away. Too late now? Tell me it's not too late, Hannes. Be merciful, Hannes.

Come.

And he came.

As she once again waited for him, doggedly, tensely, desperately, cursing herself—he came, without any advance warning.

He could not be seen, of course. He never managed to be truly visible. But now, after his long absence, something had happened to him.

When Rosa closed her eyes till they were just open a crack, so that only a trace of light could filter in—there he sat. Her heart beat high.

He sat there, blurred, misty, but with the clear outlines of a man in a chair bent over a table. Was he holding his head with one hand? Didn't he heave a sigh?

He seemed to be exhausted. He pushed his hand away from his brow. What a peculiar hat he was wearing! Hannes had never worn a hat like that—broad-rimmed and with a long feather that lay flat against it and then billowed down and away. What ever had possessed Hannes to wear that?

He said nothing, he tried to catch his breath, he must have had a long journey behind him, and she did not disturb him. Sitting on the edge of the bed, she was too deeply absorbed in watching him. The longer she gazed, the more definite the image that emerged. He was indeed wearing a huge, grayish black hat that she first mistook for a cowboy hat, but the immense feather bothered her. His left hand, which he held to his brow, was thrust into a yellow leather glove with a broad cavalier cuff that lay along his forearm. He wore a heavy, broad leather jacket that covered his chest, but it was not the normal leather vest of a rifleman either. And there was even a wide white lace collar, what finery, what elegance. All the while enveloped in a haze.

"Hannes," she said, since he did not speak, "Whatever has happened to you? Where have you been gadding about?"

He sighed, "I'm tired."

She had to strain to hear his voice. It was definitely his voice, but he sat there so downcast, despite the elegance. His new life seemed to overtax him.

She had to cough, her eyes and nose stung from the smoky haze that Hannes brought with him.

"What has happened, Hannes? What is that mist that you have around you?"

"It's gunpowder. We've been fighting the Swedes."

"Who?"

"The Swedes. We had our hands full."

"But the Swedes aren't even in this war."

"We challenged them near Lützen as they were about to advance. What a dreadful butchery it was. There King Gustavus Adolphus met his maker. They can't find his corpse."

Rosa jerked back. "You're crazy, Hannes. What are you talking about?"

Then he turned his face to her and she had to suppress her scream. He looked ghastly. His left temple and cheek had been split open by a horrible blow, his left eye was losing fluid. (Her sense of guilt: I did that to him.)

"It was wild, Rosa. We held up our end."

She let her hands fall into her lap, speechless.

"That's how it goes, Rosa. You fight it out, now here, now there. Not a moment's peace. I'm glad you called me."

"If only you had stayed here with me."

"That couldn't be, Rosa. I apologize for that upset a few days ago. I was an idiot. You were only too right about me. I—had to try things another way."

That ghastly look of his. But what was odd was that his image did not stay the same, the wounds from the saber blow didn't seem so deep anymore, the rim of the hat faded, the long feather dissolved.

"What are you up to Hannes? If only I could understand you. Why don't you want to be here with me?"

"Things are different with us. We can move about even without our bodies. Can we ever! It's completely different from when you have a body. Everything is possible for us. We can go to every country, every continent. We can travel in every time period, anywhere in the past. Nothing is closed to us."

"In the past?"

"Like lightning, here or there."

"What are you looking for in the past, Hannes?"

"We have no present. We have to go back into the past."

"You have to?"

A shudder ran through her, she controlled herself.

He: "What are you supposed to do with the present? What does it offer? Look at me. I don't have to explain that to you."

She: "Take me along, Hannes. For a long time now I've wanted to see things up close, things in the fourteenth century, so much is unclear to me."

He sat there now without a hat, his hair had returned to its usual length, the left side of his face was still slightly darkened.

"We don't go into the past to learn anything. We follow all paths that lead back. We're searching. At every turn something rises up against us."

He groaned. He had braced his right arm firmly on the table, he held his head up rigidly, his brow furrowed.

60

"We search and burrow and dig. We hurtle down through the centuries. You could almost say we are wolves in flight. Rosa, once we have been torn from this world, we are damned to begin life anew at some point, to pick up all the old threads, to attempt to make good all our mistakes, to fight all our battles once again, to topple all the empires once more and make republics of them, set up dictatorships, topple the dictators."

"And why must you do all that, Hannes?"

He sat there rigid, an unaccustomed, proud, defiant look on his face. Then he replied coldly, without any change of expression, "We are sitting in a trap."

She searched and searched his face. Yes, that was Hannes's kind face, but why was it so grave, so fierce? She did not understand. She coaxed him, "Oh come on now, my dear little Hannes. Stay with me a while. What good are all those battles? You know that yourself. Sit here next to me. Keep me company, like in the old days. Do what you like with me. But don't leave me alone. Weren't you looking over my shoulder just now when I was with Tanya?"

"Yes. Why?"

"Did you see the map? If you can go everywhere, it must be wonderful to travel with you. Go on a journey with me, Hannes. You chase around the world like some criminal, like a man fleeing on a horse. What have you done? Who is it that drives you away? Stay with me. Come on a trip with me, our honeymoon. You still owe me a honeymoon."

He looked at the opened atlas. She slid along the edge of the bed closer to him.

"Our honeymoon, Hannes." (The tears poured from her eyes, to be so close to the man she loved, a hounded shadow of a lover, and they had to take their honeymoon here in a cell, on paper.) "There are all the countries in the world. We can pick out the loveliest one for ourselves."

There was still something of his military bearing about him. He appeared to be still wearing the leather vest and to have a leather strap over his left shoulder, a belt for his sword, but otherwise he looked quite normal. She feasted on the sight—except that he was transparent, you could see the wall and the window frame through his torso, his whole body. Rosa's suggestion seemed to appeal to him. He studied the map, thought a bit, looked up at Rosa, stared again at the map.

"You want to go on a trip with me, Rosa?"

"Yes." She smiled and pointed at the atlas. "There's our railroad and everything that we need. I can't offer you more than that."

"I know. You'll go with me?"

"I'm inviting you."

His eyes sparkled.

She gave him both her hands. He wasn't cold.

She felt a swift, gentle pressure that caused her to lose consciousness for several minutes.

A Fabulous Arctic Journey

She had no illusions about what he wanted from her. But neither was she afraid.

He was the man she loved—she was ashamed of herself for having treated him so disrespectfully; she could see how he suffered. She was full of pity for him and she did not want to hold back anything from him, not anything at all.

He arrived very early in the morning now. The mere thought of him was sufficient to call him. She did not even need to prepare the chair.

She was beside herself. "I have you, I will hold onto you, I'll not let you go. At last I can make up for what I've missed, my whole rotten life without you."

"So it's a wild chase into the past for you too. But, my dear Rosa, what rotten, failed life do you mean? — You have burned your candle at both ends."

"I don't call it burning, without you, without serving you."

"Rosebud, I don't believe my ears—Rosebud wants to serve?"

"To be your subject, Hannes, darling, my husband. To throw myself before you, so that you may walk over me."

He laughed. "Russian fantasies."

"Hannes, I've laid these flowers here for you."

"Your hands flutter. Your lips are trembling."

"For you. My dear husband is sitting here beside me and I beside him. I love him, I love him and will not let him go."

When he kissed her she did not lose consciousness, she only felt weak and slightly lamed, but a filled with bliss. He beamed and blossomed. He seemed more solid. She laid a weary hand on the table, ready, if it must be, to dissolve completely.

"I've laid these flowers here for you. I could not find any better ones. There were lovelier ones in Wronki."

"O sweet flowers of this earth, meant for me, how gladly I accept you. I've missed you for so long now."

62

"And these two here as well. I picked them . . .

> With endless yearning sore,
> I've pressed them to my heart
> A thousand times and more."

"Our old song by Hugo Wolf. Do you still sing it, Rosa?"

"Only just now, with you. And do you really want to go on that journey with me, Hannes? Shall I show you the earth, all the kingdoms of the world and the glory of them?"

"Those are satanic words, Rosa. Are you Satan?"

"Anything you wish."

He looked at her in wonder with startled eyes. He said nothing. Finally he said, his expression strangely guarded, "I thought it was like that."

"What?"

He: "That—things are as you just said."

She: "That I would like to show you anything you want?"

He: "The earth, all the kingdoms of the world and the glory of them."

Rosa: "Does that frighten you? Why do you look at me like that, Hannes? Is something wrong with me?"

"No, Rosa. I was only thinking—how long I've known you. And slowly it dawns on me, what I know of you."

"I hope it's something good."

He: "You were always strong and fierce."

She laughed: "That's what you have to be when you have such a quiet boyfriend. Come on, Hannes, you needn't be so surprised— what are you staring at, what did I say? Don't ruin our trip. We'll travel in the latest, most modern fashion, as only you and I can. Faster than lightning. And now, dear Hannes, my fine man, it won't be like in your old battles. I'll see to it that you don't grow a pigtail and that you won't even so much as wear a broad-brimmed hat with a plume. We'll take off just as we are, across the world, there, across the whole immense globe. We haven't a suitcase, won't show our passports at borders."

"Hurrah, hurrah, away we go, Rosa. I'll not stand in the way."

"Do you see this black dot, that's Breslau, 51.7° north latitude, 17.2° east longitude, 400 feet above sea level. From here we can travel along the meridians or parallels, and just let anybody try to stop us."

"Let's go, Rosa. No preliminaries."

"We're heading north, along the meridian. We'll not let go of it, that way we can find our way back afterward. Because just think, Hannes, what a joke it would be if we lost our way and suddenly found ourselves sitting with the Eskimos at the North Pole. I have to be back by noon when Tanya comes with lunch."

"We'll eat together."

"Northward. I've marked our route with a pencil. It moves across rivers, mountains, forests and clouds, always holding to 17.2 east longitude."

And already he began to sigh, "Oh, my love, I can't bear being up so high. Oh, not so fast. Slow down. Let me look. Oh, the forests, the meadows, our mountains."

"Does it make you happy, Hannes, what I'm showing you? Am I a good guide? Here we are coming into Posen. Over there, more to the right lies Gnesen, but what do we care about Gnesen? Schneidemühl and Flatow hold no charms for us either; and now Schlochau, Bublitz, Schlaren, all mysterious towns. If you like we'll stop, but we still have so much ahead of us. I'm already gazing on ahead toward Scandinavia. Are you really equipped for a journey to the lands of the north, Hannes?"

"We'll see. I hope so."

"Haha, such a serious reply. We need neither woolens nor police. We hurtle across fields of snow and ice. We manage it without sleds or dogs."

"I'm afraid. We're going to fall, Rosa."

She laughed. "Then I'll hold onto you tight, by the tip of your ear. We're traveling like two vagabonds, without a penny in our pocket, armed only with impudence. On the wings of song, my darling, I bear you away."

"Oh yes, sing, Rosebud."

"And here we are at the Baltic Sea. How can I sing with a wind like this blowing in my face? There, off to the left, at 15° lies Kolberg, a place that I cannot really recommend, not for such a grand trip, not at the beginning, a children's resort, a beach for mosquitoes. I lived there once."

"Shall we take a sailboat? That one there, Rosa, with the broad sails?"

She lifted her gaze from the map. "What are you talking about? What sailboat?"

"The big one there, moving so slowly along between the two smaller ones. It must be a fishing boat that's putting out its nets."

Rosa stared at Hannes in amazement.

He: "They have room for us. The old man with the pipe at the wheel would take us on board."

It confused her that he could not be argued out of this. She sensed that she was slightly afraid of her traveling companion. Only now did she remember with whom it was she was traveling. "Hannes, forget that. We're not using a boat, we don't need a boat. We have to go on now. I want to show you the North Pole today at least."

She wanted to make a joke of it and get him to laugh.

But he said, "Rosebud, fly lower, come down closer to the water, do. I want to see the fish. Look, how they race. How they flash through the water. Whole schools. They must be herring."

She laid her arm on the arm of the chair, saying nothing. He bent down low over the map. He held his eyes close to the paper.

"Why are you bending down so close to the map? There's nothing underneath it."

What did he intend to do? What was that supposed to mean? He was hallucinating. What was he looking for underneath the map? You couldn't do anything with him, make some simple joke, have a lovely time, without his making something extraordinary out of it.

He muttered something about fish. Then finally he pulled himself away from it. And they were on their way north, full steam ahead.

She wanted to play a game with him, she wanted to go on a giddy fantasy journey, just as she had often done with other fellow sufferers in one prison or another; each of them had come up with some memories of journeys past, and if someone had nothing to remember, why then she would make something up, and the most improbable stories were always the best and funniest.

They came to Scandinavia. She spelled out the names, the heavy, clumsy words. She waded in, making up something about the lumberjacks in the mountains. (Is this Sweden? It's possible it's Finland, *mais qu'importe?*). There in the villages were little brightly painted churches (I saw ones like that in the Tatra Mountains). Brooks flowing everywhere. Water purling from the mountains everywhere.

Rosa was enthusiastic. "The land rose up out of the sea, but it's just as if the water were rushing back in from underneath."

Hannes: "The water does come from below, Rosa, and it comes from above. The earth cannot live without water. The earth would lie there dying without water. The earth is an old man. If it doesn't bathe and drink, it turns into a stick. That's why there are always clouds on the move and why snow falls, and rain, and the fog rises."

"Where did you learn all this, Hannes."

"You just have to observe, Rosa."

Rosa spelled the names, shaking her head. "Norrköping, Dannemoor, how marvelous that sounds. There are girls with wide, red skirts and high-top boots. The young men wear knee socks and look so healthy. They do quaint traditional dances. I've seen them dance them in the theater, peasant dances. But onward, onward, to use your word, Hannes. Hey, it's getting cold, and nothing but mountains and rivers. How odd, look, all the rivers flow off to the right into the Gulf of Bothnia where the land drops off, one river after the other, there's the Skellefte, then the Pite, the Lule, the Lina, the Torne; mighty rivers, torrents tearing great swaths of gravel from the mountains with them. And here we must speed now across the border, over the mountains, we cannot tarry any longer. Come, we'll make a dash for it. There must be a pass here."

"What a magnificent landscape, Rosa. The cold. Ah, the snow. What a wind!"

"Do you like it, Hannes? I'm glad. There's still a lot for you to see, we've only just started. The mountain range is narrow. We're coming now to another country, Norway, here, this narrow band here, to the coast. Narvik, that's this big town here with mines, they have iron ore, they bring the iron ore up out of the earth. We make cannons out of it."

He hummed, "The Lord who gave the earth its iron, wishes no man to be another's slave."

She gave the chair a slap. "You're still the idiot you always were, Hannes, It's just the other way around. They use iron to make slaves of men."

"It all depends on who has the iron."

She: "You can laugh about that? That's a joke? Not to me."

"Forgive me, Rosa, I'm just a poor soldier, that's all."

"Fjords, ravines, these cliffs here. Now we have to hold tight to our 17.2°, otherwise we're lost. Just think, Hannes, we're in Norway, on Ringvassöy Island, today on August 4, 1918. It is cold on the island and thrillingly dark, dusky dark. We have broken completely through the English blockade by now and have escaped them, slipped through to Ringvassöy Island. And down below, so far behind us, on the same longitude, lies Breslau, with its woman's prison, where they thought they could lock us in because we were getting on their nerves.

"There they sit down below, shooting and killing. But we are free, we're free, free."

"Come on, my Rosebud, let's move on."

"You're fascinated by the sea, Hannes. You'll get enough of the sea. I promise you more water than land."

"Let's go."

"We're already over the open sea. All of this pale blue to the north, east, west, it's all sea."

66

Hannes was delighted. If only he didn't slip away from her.

She laid her arm firmly on the arm of the chair. It was clear that he saw, heard and felt things she could not see. This frightened and gladdened her. Let him have whatever he wanted. He began to talk about dolphins and whales. Was he just going on about them, did he know these things, had he read about them—or did he really see them?

He bore her into the Arctic Ocean, across the floating icebergs.

He said, "We have to get closer. Don't be afraid, Rosa, I'll hold on to you."

Now wasn't that funny. What was he thinking of? Did he love her?

A whale hunt was in progress below. He took an avid interest in it. He talked about harpoons; she wanted to pull him away from it, but he stayed with it for a long time. Finally they put it behind them.

My God, what am I doing, what if someone were to come into the cell right now. I couldn't get rid of him, I can't just send him away, and after all, I'm the one who invited him along.

Finally he followed after her again. They had to stay close to the surface of the water. It was hard to say just how they moved. They certainly weren't flying, they simply moved—without any sound whatever, without a propeller, and moved from place to place.

He was still carrying on about his whale hunt. He told her about whales in a way she had never heard him talk before, as if he had lived among them or belonged to the species.

"We know about whales. They aren't fish at all. They only live in the sea. They could not endure life on land. They wanted to go back to the water. It was more comfortable for them in water. They could move more easily there. The ground under your feet stays still, but water lifts and supports you; there are currents that you follow or avoid. But how wretched it is on land. To live on land is to live the life of a vegetable. It's true you don't put down roots, but you can use your legs merely to drag yourself forward a bit. But whales, look at them. Whales once lived on land. They walked on four feet. They understood, they noticed something and went back to the water and learned to swim. They chose the better part. There's a whale swimming now, in a school, his family beside him, they're all strong and happy, life is good for them. He blows his steam into the air. He has lungs, really; his race has separated itself from us landlubbers, he can live in water despite his lungs."

What was it that interested him about whales, really? He was like a little boy.

"They have arms and legs, only they've fused together into fins. Some of them even have fur."

"Come, let's go on, Hannes. I'd at least like to take you as far as Spitzbergen."

It was rather eerie being with him out over the water. She thought to herself: he could drown himself and me with him.

Finally, icebergs, and they whooped for joy, and the silhouette of Spitzbergen. She showed him the coast. But it wasn't necessary to point anything out to him. He saw and heard much more than she— and quite different things. Where she would think, dream, and imagine, he was there with his eyes and ears and emotions.

He was occupied now with the herds of sea lions and elephant seals that lay on the beach.

She could get nothing out of him now. He did not answer. He saw something. He was busy and there was an aura of fear about him. Finally she heard him give a deep sigh.

As they thrust on to the north over the ice-covered interior of Spitzbergen, he once again uttered a sound. "What's wrong with us humans, Rosa? Did you see those little huts on the beach. They're stalls. They drive the seals into them, those that can't escape by plunging into the water. They surround them and the seals waddle packed together by the hundreds into the pens. And men stand there with clubs, the butchers, and beat them over the head. How hideous, how atrocious. They club them to death, one after the other."

Rosa whispered, "That's what they do with swine in the slaughter-houses."

He repeated it, mournfully, "Yes, and what we do to one another."

She wanted to get to the North Pole at least, it wasn't much further now. But he had grown so quiet.

Again he sighed and groaned. She became frightened. He turned away from her. She whispered tender words to him.

But—he was no longer recognizable.

He melted away and vanished.

But he came back, without her even calling him, and with what violence. He seemed to want to cling to her totally. This made her happy and excited her. She felt—what a strange feeling—simultaneously a restless urge, a tension that would not let her sleep and a cumbrous bodily weakness that grew and grew.

She thought: it's the excitement that's consuming me. But when she saw Hannes again she knew better. She was exchanging her life, her corporality with him.

For he became ever more visible—how it delighted her.

"My leech, my spider, my growing child," she thought. "And since I must perish, what lovelier way to perish than to give your existence to another creature, to die that new life may grow."

He walked about with her and his joy grew and grew. His tempestuous spirit experienced everything—and not just in his mind—and would not let go of her as he did so. He was able, after all, to wander freely across the fields and mountains. But he needed her. He followed the point of her blue pencil faithfully, northward along the line of 17.2°.

How reckless was his desire to enjoy the world. Yes, he enjoyed it. She felt he had never before experienced it like this, not like this. He was savage in his yearning for what had been lost.

Earth could not hold him. He shot into the clouds like a bird and plummeted head over heels into the flood of the sea and swam like a fish. And still other things happened.

She was sitting—to all appearances—in her cell in the women's prison in Breslau, at her table, her face to the courtyard where people were moving about and making noise. She was sitting in front of the harmless open atlas, a pencil in her hand, pointing to some spot or other to the north of Scandinavia. But her body trembled softly. Her eyes stared at the spot. A sweet smile played across her tightly-pressed lips.

For he was telling her (or singing): "Oh, the blue of night." (But outside it was morning and the summer sunshine was sharp and bright.)

He clung to her pencil point. She held him tightly with it. How much longer before I can't hold onto him; then he'll tug at the pencil and I'll fly away with him wherever he wants.

"The white icebergs," he sang, "stand about like ghosts in the blue night, as if someone had called to them and they could not move anymore. Look at those brown cliffs, one after the other—like children in white shirts. It's a school class out in the open country. How the snow splashes with the wind across the plain of ice. And up above, Rosa, what is that? In the ebony blue that must be the sky, that round object shedding soft light but without providing warmth and scarcely shining? Perhaps it is warm, but it doesn't warm us. Perhaps it shines, but not on us. It is brighter than the moon, but not much brighter. It is round like a circle and pale yellow like glossy straw, and there it flickers at the ends of the bluish blackness.

"The sun.

"Rosa, can you see it?

"What a miracle. What unutterable glory.

"And now here. A tumbling. Coming at us. Watch out—an avalanche."

Incredible, Rosa thought, that he is sitting next to me here, my

Hannes—and avalanches roll; they could bury us alive. We could be sitting here and get buried alive by an avalanche, here at this table. And then I'd be lying there, and whoever saw me under the table would say, she's suffocated, a heart attack or whatever, nothing more. It can happen any moment.

"Leave me behind, Hannes," she begged, weakening suddenly. "Can't you go without me?"

"Rosa, look around you."

"You frighten me, Hannes."

He was triumphant. "Take heart. We'll risk it. It all belongs to us, all the kingdoms of the world and the glory of them. The sky is turning violet. The great ball grows red, blood red; how quickly it is setting behind us. And now snow is falling. Where is the sky now? The violet turns to black, the clouds ball up together, making a single black wall that inches slowly toward us.

"Rosa, just to experience this.

"The fantastic blackness. And how the ice flashes. Where does that stream of light come from. Listen, how the sea roars. The ice cracks."

He was no longer sitting on the chair.

The chair with its magic cloths stood empty.

The whole cell was illumined with an extravagant brightness, a whiteness tinged a soft green.

The shimmer and iridescence emanated from a cherub in long flowing robes. Its arms were held in wide sleeves against its chest, its head held low, dark blond curls framing a face that seemed lost in dreams.

He swayed back and forth.

He moved about the room in a slow dance-step.

He whispered and hummed.

And when she looked up at him, her right hand still on the atlas, she saw more than she had seen till now. Inside him, amid the long flowing lines of his shirt, between his outstretched arms, what he saw became visible to her and it moved.

The icebergs plied their way through the contours of his figure, the gray ocean rolled beneath the soles of his feet. And look, the black wall of clouds pitching about behind his head and moving toward her along the part in his blond hair.

An unearthly boom and roar was heard; a cracking and breaking. Those were the ice-floes crashing into each other and breaking up. The squawling of birds. And the billowing chill.

She stared at him, the man she loved, missing in action, fallen in battle, the cherub. They were honeymooning not at all as they had planned to, going to Switzerland and Italy in the pullman car of an express train.

What was this mortal life? Why should one remain here. Why not follow him? If only he would come and take her soon.

The room grew darker and darker.

She was seized with a burning weakness (twilight, twilight, twilight) that she could not resist. It was as if he were flowing into her. Then she could no longer see him.

Ah, this sucking within her. How young he was and strong and insatiable.

My friend, my lover, my husband, my child. And this is death? This is what death is like? Take me.

Her shoulders fell, her head fell to the table. She knew as she slid toward it that she was entering a state of limitless unconsciousness, following his footsteps.

It was noon as she sat up straight. The sounds from the kitchen, the running back and forth of people bringing the meals had awakened her.

She sat in her chair. Tenderly, and ever so gravely she removed the divine cloths and put them away again. She ate her lunch, devoid of all thought.

The Spirit's Attempted Assassination

For days thereafter she did not lay the atlas out on the table. Was it fear? She did not know why herself. She thought about him a great deal. She said to herself: let me first regain my strength.

She knew she would call him again soon enough. For this was no vice, and no mere longing. It was her will. She was addicted to him. She could not shake one thought: what kind of life do the dead lead? There is no life in these narrow, heavy, rotting bodies of ours.

Was Tanya spying on her? Didn't Tanya tiptoe by sometimes, trying to eavesdrop?

Rosa did not let herself be eavesdropped upon. She no longer allowed Tanya into her confidence. What she and Hannes had between them was beyond Tanya's comprehension. And Tanya mistrusted her, too. Once Rosa even gave herself away. It happened one day when Tanya sat down with her in her cell once again to do some sewing, and during a pause reached for the atlas. Rosa sprang up from the bed and grabbed the atlas from her. Rosa forbade her to touch her books. Rosa had never spoken to her like that before.

Tanya apologized and went on working.

When Rosa looked over at her, however, and they exchanged glances, Rosa saw that the white mask knew everything.

She could not wait to be with him again the following morning; it was the climax, the goal, the apex of her life, what she had always sought out beyond the roofs of the houses. That this had been granted to her! That she had achieved this summit, after such a detour!

Trembling with excitement, she prepared his chair for him, his throne. It was the secret door through which he would enter. Then she closed her eyes and called to him, "Come now, Hannes."

He gave no sign. What was this? She opened the atlas, picked up the pencil, the magic wand in her hand. "Come, Hannes."

She felt that he was far away, very far. Why should he come to her after all? What did she have to offer him? He was a spirit, wandering about out there in the world, through all glory of the world.

And then he rushed in upon her. Good heavens, what a tempest. Would he burst open the cell? Would he whisk it all away?

She had never realized what a spirit is. An animal is an animal, a plant a plant. But a spirit changes its form and shape depending on what it is engaged in, making no distinction between inside and out.

But she saw that even more was happening. The journeys, his travels had changed him. He looked different from when he had left her. Hannes had flung himself out into the world, ecstatic, reckless, hungry and insatiable, and when he returned to her now all of that clung to him, he dragged all that earthly debris with him each time. It had followed in his train, he had plundered it all and would not let it go.

That was one achievement of his travels. Earth literally clung to Hannes. That was the cause of his cravings.

He burst in upon her like a storm cloud. She wanted to bind him under the spell of her atlas and magic chair. But he could not be held. He tugged the pencil in her hand like a dog on its leash. She was forced to dodge back and forth. What did he want? Then he was off and away again, and she did not know what that meant.

Later he reappeared as a diver, wet and gasping. He had been romping at the bottom of the sea.

Then he sailed into her cell as a crane, screaming loudly, frightening her, for she thought people would come now and everything would be revealed. But only she had heard him. No single shape was sufficient for him. The earth's surface was not sufficient for him. He no longer sang. He no longer spoke, enraptured by the world and its glories.

And when from time to time he would assume the shape of a man

72

and sit down with her as in the past, he pushed the pencil away, did not want to hear anything about journeys and brooded gloomily.

There was something painfully violent within him. She could not loose his tongue for a long time.

She knew he had a secret. His whole existence was based upon some secret. At some point he would have to reveal it. It seemed that that hour was near.

Tanya's presence was good for Rosa.

Tanya was suffering too. Rosa had often asked her what caused her extraordinary complexion? She assumed it was anemia. But now she was told the answer.

Tanya sank down onto Rosa's bed, spoke not a word, only lay there for half an hour. She only gave mute signs with her head. She coughed very softly, cautiously.

Afterward, when she sat back up again, she took the handkerchief clutched in her hand from her mouth and stared at the palms of her hands and at the handkerchief. Then she smiled. "No blood."

She was feverish, but told no one. Otherwise she would lose her position as a trustee and she held onto that for Michel's sake. Rosa understood, what would Tanya have in life if she could not help him? What are any of us without love? How sweet it is to sacrifice ourselves. (Do I even think anymore of living my life for myself? Those days are far behind me. I have learned that; Tanya knew it before I did.)

Rosa slipped Tanya everything she herself could get along without. We are real comrades, we ply the same trade, we have concluded a secret covenant behind the world's back.

It alarmed Rosa to see how Tanya scrubbed and hauled things from morning till evening. There were days when they could only exchange a single glance between them. The tragic mask greeted her from afar with moist, shimmering eyes, and teeth revealed in a delicate smile.

She once whispered to Rosa, "I've had it twice before this. I'll pull through."

Pulling through. Strangely Rosa was aroused by that idea as well, despite all her withdrawal.

And she now began to find a new interest in the world. It was an acute curiosity to understand what all this was that had driven her up till now. She felt that she had won some new relationship to the things about her.

She wrote to a girlfriend:

"Just now as I was arranging some flowers it struck me that in reality I am deceiving myself. How can I ever dare to think that I am living, still living, leading a normal human life—while out there the threat of doom hangs over the world?"

She added by way of explanation: "Perhaps it is the 'scapegoat hangings' in Moscow that have especially affected me."

Yes, the events in Moscow had attracted her attention. This was what engaged her most intensively, excited and challenged her.

For Lenin was out there working like a battering ram, hammering against the turrets of the old society, toppling one wall after the other. The edifice trembled. It could not be long now until the whole thing crashed to the ground with a thundering collapse that would awaken the whole world.

How the drama intrigued Rosa. She read how they were attacking Lenin. She defended him. What were these Mensheviks thinking, tainted with their bourgeois ideas? How was Lenin supposed to act? These foolish utopians and weaklings. They thought he would just sit back and wait while the Whites prepared a military dictatorship with all its terrors for the proletariat.

She began to take down notes again, alert and aggressive.

"In this situation the Bolshevik wing has proven its historical worth by proclaiming from the very beginning those tactics that alone could save the revolution and by acting upon them systematically. All power in the hands of the masses of workers and peasants, that was the sword stroke that slashed the Gordian knot, leading the revolution out of its constricted passage and opening for it the free plain of uninhibited development."

But then Lenin's face was revealed to her, his cynical smile. He was betraying democracy. He was setting it aside. For what purpose? To create without disruption what he called revolution.

But we are not generals commanding armies. We do not command, we battle side by side on toward the same goal.

Lenin versus bourgeois society, what is he then? A general, a dictator, a man of the past, whose methods are those of the past, he is no socialist but a bourgeois.

Rosa became empassioned by the ups and downs of the conflict with the man. What? To have thousands shot in retaliation for an attempted assassination? To shoot them down summarily, cold-bloodedly, all the while pretending to be inaugurating a socialist society? It was enough to make you long for the days of the czars, may they rest in peace, when every case was investigated and each guilty party hanged or exiled on his or her own.

She sat with paper before her and thought. We have had a great many discussions about the dictatorship of the proletariat and its relationship to democracy. Just look at him, how simply he solves the problem. The solution is: Lenin. Goethe, a German, said, "Mortal man's greatest treasure remains the individual personality." Not the man who smashes it, the dictator.

I am the dictatorship of the proletariat, Nikolai Lenin has decreed. But why? Just ask my Latvian Rifles and the Red Guard. You will receive a bang of an answer. But what do you need all that grand rhetoric for then? Let's simply call it war and victory and defeat.

In what way is his war different from that of the Germans against the French and the English? His is fought out between civilians, the other between uniformed soldiers. The brawl has moved to the home front. The illness has spread to the homeland. What magnificent progress.

Rosa jotted it down angrily:

"With the suppression of political life throughout the country, the political life of the Soviets must likewise languish. Without general elections, without unhampered freedom of the press and assembly, without free debate of opinions, life will die out in every public institution. It will only seem to live, while only one single effective pulse of life will remain—the bureaucracy.

"It is at its base an oligarchy. Most certainly a dictatorship—but by a handful of politicians. In effect, a bourgeois dictatorship."

She brooded for a while before she dashed it off:

"Real dictatorship, our dictatorship, consists in the application of democracy, not in its abolition."

And that was a sentence that gave her comfort.

She saw "him." She felt "him" in her presence. He had given up his rovings, at least for the moment. He did not budge from her side— her husband, her cellmate.

He had grown strangely more solid, one could no longer call him a "shade." Rosa feared that others would see him too. But that did not happen. Whenever he came—he appeared mostly in human form— each time he grew more solid, more opaque. She made him happy by telling him that.

"It's the reward for all my labor. I am taking the earth into myself. I attract it more and more. Among human beings a birth is an easy matter. You get a body delivered ready-made. We spirits don't have things so easy. We have to travel through heaven and earth, wade through mud and sand and slowly gather ourselves together, piece by piece. And things are made difficult for us. Oh, people don't want it to happen. They want to prevent us from traveling that path. We are supposed to take another route. To which I say: thanks, but no thanks."

Then he spoke of his ridiculous stupidity in the past in trying to steal her body straightaway while she slept—which naturally was pure nonsense.

"Because, of course, it cannot be done that way. And even if it could be, one would have it only as an emergency refuge for a few hours, and what a refuge at that."

Rosa listened enthralled. "Hannes, is that true? Really true? You wander about and have the ability to return to existence?"

"Some do it that way, try it that way, others take another tack. They plunge into some animal or other; that's the easiest way. Because there isn't anyone who can throw you out again. But what good is it to be a snake or a salamander? Or if you have whimsically cast yourself into a cat and can slink about hunting mice?"

"Do you want to become a human being again?"

"That's what we all try to do, Rosa. You must understand how it is: we were busy knitting away and then dropped a stitch, and now we try to find it again."

"In order to continue knitting?"

"Yes. But they won't let us. Won't even let us search. Won't even let us try. They don't want us to do it. They want us dead, and humbled to boot."

"Who does, for heaven's sake? Won't you finally say straight out what is bothering you?"

He groaned, "Why talk about it? What does that help? I've been through enough already. I've experienced enough shame already. I'd rather you helped me."

And he faded away, vanished, melted with a sigh.

And now he was evasively circling about her a lot. She did not understand why, actually, nor what he still wanted from her.

He would come down the corridor like anyone else, sit down in one corner of the cell and wait for her to call him. At night he often occupied the sentrybox outside and watched the guard on patrol there. This was, by the way, one of the fellows he had had a row with that day. Perhaps he wanted to give him the creeps.

Everything in the cell was drenched with him.

The song had begun with cruel pain, with desperation and longing. Then the fantasies had become part of it, conversations had developed, the courting, the bliss, a wedding grew from it—and now?

She was so anxious. The others said she was growing paler and paler. And it was true that even the smallest walks in the courtyard taxed her. She laughed: that comes from my intense love life, that's what you get from living permanently in a den of iniquity. And why not? Some do this, some do that in their cells. Some do calisthenics, others learn languages. I speak with Hannes in the tongues of angels, or devils.

"You're so hale and hearty," he said to her one morning when she called him in for a discussion (maybe he lurks nearby while I sleep, waiting to attack me). "I'm glad of that, Rosa."

She laughed. "I can well understand that, you thief. The more I have, the more you think you can get from me."

He sat there comfortably in his chair, she lay on the bed. He turned around to her.

"And because you're so healthy, I'll tell you a secret."

"At last," she said.

"Just recently, when you were talking about the glories of the world that you were going to spread before me, I intended to do it."

"Well then, what is it, Hannes?"

"I have much, very much to thank you for—whether I'm sitting here or whether I'm out wandering. I was about to perish. You called me back and held onto me. It was all your work. And with every day you give me more."

"Because you're my child, Hannes."

"Yes. I came from your breast, from your blood. But I am also the Hannes who was hit last November and left lying in the snows of Russia. My own powers alone would not have been sufficient to hold me on this earth and accomplish what I am now accomplishing. That is your work. Therefore, Rosa, I must let you in on my secret. Because you have become a part of the game now. I can't keep it to myself."

"No, you mustn't do that."

"Rosa, they—want to destroy me. I lay there in the snow, shot down, and I was not supposed to exist anymore. I was supposed to lose everything, leave it all. Not just leave everything behind that I had had up till now. I was supposed," he gnashed his teeth, "to repudiate all that I felt, desired, and cherished. I was supposed to plant something inside myself, and I could not justify doing that."

"But who wanted that of you? Who was forcing you to do it, Hannes?"

"I couldn't put up with that, isn't that right? They have pursued me since then, unceasingly. Where I fled, they followed. They won't give up. They know no mercy. They set snares wherever I go. They surround me. They press in upon me. They make my every path a cul de sac. Where I go, wherever I show myself, I am beaten back once again."

"Who does this? For heaven's sake, Hannes, who do you mean? What do they want from you? You have committed no crime. I would lay my hand in fire for you. You are my sweetheart, my very soul. I cannot bear it."

"Fine, fine. That is fine. I expected no less of you."

"Speak more clearly, Hannes. I don't understand."

"What else is it that you must understand, my Rosebud, about us? What did I understand about it before? You must renounce all that you have been. Renounce everything dear to you, damn yourself. I cannot do it, I won't do it."

"And you're right, Hannes, my darling."

"I do not recognize their kangaroo court."

"And you're right, Hannes. I would be ashamed of you if you didn't feel that way. I cannot understand it all, Hannes. But I am with you with all my heart. I am yours to do with as you will, just so you don't capitulate."

She closed her eyes. Her face glowed. She balled her fists.

She felt his kiss. "Thank you, Rosa, my darling—Satan. I'll pull through. Your strength is inside me. You are fighting inside me. They won't make me bend the knee. If you don't leave me in the lurch."

She flared up. "You call me Satan. Go ahead, call me that. If only you hold fast. Swear to me, swear, Hannes, not to give in."

He swore it.

What has happened to the people who, as they say, have "died"? Why do they wander about? What is wrong with them—he is one of them—and with those who are harassing him?

She had never heard anything but superstitious nonsense about them. Tanya could believe that sort of thing. But could she?

She was deeply shaken.

I'm crazy, she said to herself. Now I've really gone crazy. The little medical officer was right after all. He warned me not to brood too much. And of course all of these dreams I have are nonsense. I must push it away from me. I must reduce it to what it is, a hallucination and a delusion.

We live in an objective world. Everything takes its natural course. No "spirits" wander about. To be sure it does you good to meet a person you've been close to, even after his death, and when it happens so suddenly and unexpectedly as with my Hannes, then it's understandable that you can imagine things and even see and hear things that aren't there.

That is what she said to herself, while the subterranean laughter echoed and loudly proclaimed "no," rhythmically, in chorus: "No, no."

She tried to give herself orders. From now on there would be no more "hearing" and "seeing." Delusions are delusions. An obsession has no form, no arms, no legs, no mouth and cannot speak. I'll put a big sign on my door that reads, "Spirits not permitted to enter."

And this idea pleased her so much that the first thing she did was— tell Hannes, who laughed along with her about it. But he urged her to show him the map again.

"What is with the map all of a sudden, Hannes? What do you want with it again? You can find your way wherever you want to go."

"Rosa, don't make me ask again. We'll make it. We can't miss."

She sat down at the table. She opened the atlas.

"But what do you mean, Hannes? What can't we miss? I'm afraid. Someday you'll drown me."

"Show me Russia."

"Why Russia?"

He tugged at her pencil. There where the point of it touched the map was where he was. He looked and looked.

She laughed, "Hannes, I know that area. You'll find nothing but swamps and bogs there. All you'll catch is the fever, and I'll die along with you."

He pressed her. "That's the place. We're standing right there. Now they've stopped fighting. They've advanced. Hold still. Don't trem- ble. I'm looking, I'm looking."

He bent down over the table.

He looked exhausted. His eyes were set deep. He was wearing his officer's cap. In his buttonhole were the black and white ribbons of the Iron Cross. He was an army surgeon. While he searched he took off his cap and wiped his brow. Ah, at last she saw him in uniform too. Back when he had gone off to war she was already in prison. He looked handsome.

She realized that he was looking for the place where he had fallen.

He whispered, "We can risk it. Be brave, Rosa. We'll just snap our fingers at them."

"Are they still following you? Who are they?"

"Give me strength, Rosa."

"All that I have."

"I've found the spot now."

"Hold fast, my darling. You swore to me you would. Don't dis- grace me."

She did not know how it happened, but she found herself lying in front of her bed. She had slipped and fallen.

Something had attacked her. Something had grabbed her and dumped her out of her bed.

He must have used a great deal of force. Because she felt her very bones sapped of energy, and she was dreadfully thirsty the whole day. She drank down half a pot of herbal tea that Tanya brought her. (Before warriors march off to battle, they drink their courage.)

That evening, after a sultry day, a thunderstorm approached. Lightning struck the men's wing. There was a dreadful crash. And the next bolt struck the women's prison and slid down the lightning rod near her window and into the ground.

For a fraction of a second the lightning traveled in a zigzag. It flashed in her face like a flaming sword. And as she sat up in bed, turning her face to the wall, the thunder filled her ears with its scream: "Let go, let go, Rosa."

And with that she was seized with unimaginable pain, and the torment was so great that she whimpered and slid down under the covers. She was still groaning when Tanya arrived to see if she had been frightened. She herself was very much afraid. Rosa managed to utter a few words, she was suffering those same strange, hot torments. Tanya brought her something to drink.

"Why should anyone be afraid of a thunderstorm, Tanya?"

It was a downpour. After midnight the rain began again. It fell all night long, now heavier now lighter. It was pitch dark.

It might have been two o'clock when Rosa heard someone knocking. "Open up, Rosa."

It was his voice.

"I can't open it, Hannes. The door's been locked."

She must have fallen asleep then. Again the knock at the door. "Open up, Rosa."

"I can't, Hannes. The door is locked. I don't have a key."

It was still dark when Tanya set her coffee down on the table. Right afterward there was again a knock. She called out, "Come in."

The rain was pouring down, it was so dark that she could not recognize him. His voice approached.

"Clear the chair for me."

She had laid a book on it; she groped for it and laid it on the floor.

"Where are you, Hannes? I can't see you."

He pulled out the chair. She heard him sit down. Terror filled her. He had a body.

She heard him grope along the table.

"What are you looking for, Hannes?"

He had his picture, he tore it into shreds. He pushed back his chair. He turned to her. She felt an icy cold. He came toward her.

"Did you leave the door open, Hannes?"

"No."

80

"Because there's such an icy draft."

She trembled. "It's so cold. You were like that once before."

"Come closer, Rosa. Why are you hiding under the covers?"

"Hannes, I'm afraid."

It had grown lighter now. He tore the blanket back. She gave a cry.

He stood by her bed, his head hung down, his forehead ripped by a shot, his mouth hanging wide open, his eyes burst. Blood flowed down over his moustache and dripped down onto her pillow. The corpse reached for her.

He howled, "Here I am again. Now I have everything. Only one thing is missing now."

She gnashed her teeth.

"Rosa, you promised it to me."

"What?"

"Your warm blood."

He had already torn open her blouse.

She recoiled.

He bent down over her.

Tanya came in response to Rosa's shrill cry.

Rosa lay there on her bed with eyes wide open, her arms flailing about her. She came to as Tanya rubbed her hands and face, which were ice-cold and bluish white. The pillow under Rosa's head and the blanket at her cheek were bloody. Tanya showed Rosa the bloodstains when she sat back up again, clinging to Tanya. Rosa was still trembling.

"Were you having a dream, Rosa? Did you bite your lips? Or are you coughing blood, too?"

Rosa: "Help me get dressed. Take these bloodstained things away."

Tanya held her in her arms. There she sat with Rosa on the edge of the bed.

Tanya: "And you've torn up his picture? Why did you do that?"

Release, and Back into the Fray

After that it was all over.

Everyone could see that Rosa was feeling better. She left her cell more frequently, walked with the others in the courtyard, sought out conversation. It was as if she were starved and could not hear enough news and details about day-to-day affairs. The prison warden understood what had brought on Rosa's sudden renewal of interest: major battles were being lost in France; the nation was filled with deserters;

defeatists, and rabble-rousers were everywhere. Apparently Rosa was being kept informed about the latest events through some unknown source.

There was no more talk about her curious "hysterical" condition. The prison warden had at once sized up what that was about, namely an attempt to get out of her cell and into some institution less well guarded, from which she could then escape with the help of her countless accomplices. They put a closer watch on her.

Revolution was stirring in the Reich, revolution in Germany. The Kaiser, kings, grand dukes and petty dukes, generals and junkers had considered a revolution in Germany to be such an impossibility that with perfect peace of mind they had let Lenin, Russia's arch-conspirator, and his hangers-on travel from Zurich to Russia so that he could do his best for the German cause. Russia was Russia and Germany was Germany. And now suddenly Germany was no longer Germany. People dared to speak of democracy, of a parliamentary constitution, all those well-known "foreign falsehoods" smuggled into the country by the enemy to subvert the German armed forces; and now their own Reichstag committees were working at the urging of the government on a draft for a new constitution. They wanted to protect themselves from the fate that had overtaken Russia. Why not a "foreign" constitution, as long as one held the reins in one's own hands?

But holding the reins in one's own hands was as far as it got. There was talk of the Kaiser's abdicating. If only the army would hold fast.

But on October 1st, Ludendorff began to insist on an immediate armistice. Talk of the Kaiser's abdication gathered force, though the Kaiser himself turned a deaf ear to it. The government sent out more and more feelers toward the opposition. Political prisoners were freed, among them Kurt Eisner, a member of the Reichstag, and Dittmann. Rosa heard of this.

She wrote to Sonya, Liebknecht's wife. "I bore it all patiently over the years, and would have remained patient for years to come under other circumstances. But now that these dramatic reversals have taken place in the outside world, I've been psychologically bruised. If they have let Dittmann and Eisner free, then they cannot keep me in prison any longer. And Karl will be free, too, in a short time."

And the reversals, no longer merely hoped for, had come. The days of despair were over.

Karl Liebknecht was released on October 23rd.

Rosa telegraphed the Reichs Chancellor, vigorously demanding her own release. She had to wait another three endless weeks.

*   *   *

On October 26th, former Quartermaster General Ludendorff fled to Sweden under the name of Lindström.

The front held, but was falling back bit by bit.

The dams built to prevent revolution were breaking. In Kiel the stokers and sailors aboard the warships refused to obey orders. They were supposed to risk a last desperate battle with the English. They asked themselves: "And who will be the winner? It most certainly won't be us!" and they forced a return to port. Whereupon they set up a workers' and soldiers' council to govern the city, sounding the first trumpet blast of the revolution:

"Comrades and friends, the crucial moment has come. Power is in our hands. Listen to us. Rally around your elected leaders.

"No imprudent measures.

"The watchword at present is keep calm and display an iron will. Do not plunder or steal. We are close to our goal. The troops sent here to suppress our uprising have joined us."

The police were once more hunting Karl Liebknecht. He could no longer enter his own apartment. He spent the nights in a furniture van, in a workers' bar, in Treptow Park. He agitated among factory workers and had long arguments with other groups, especially with the "Revolutionary Shop Stewards," about the most effective tactics. They had notions of a conspiracy; he was for fighting it out in the streets.

A new call to arms was issued on November 7th from the "International Group of the Spartacus League."

"The hour of deeds has come. Workers and Soldiers, what your comrades and friends have accomplished in Kiel, Hamburg, Bremen, Hannover, Munich and Stuttgart you can accomplish as well.

"The immediate goals of the struggle are: release of all civilian and military prisoners.

"Abolition of all dynastic houses and dissolution of individual states.

"Election of workers' and soldiers' councils.

"Takeover of the government by deputies of the workers' and soldiers' councils.

"Immediate establishment of relations with the international proletariat, especially with the Russian Workers' Republic.

"Long live the socialist republic.

"Long live the International."

Karl Liebknecht, Ledebour, Adolf Hoffmann and the "Revolutionary Shop Stewards" had spent the night in the home of an "Independent" comrade in Schöneberg, and had risen early on the morning of November 9th to watch from the window of their corner house to see whether the factory workers of Steglitz would come. Would they come? And look, there they were.

They marched ever closer.

They sang.

The red flag flew before them.

And there were soldiers among them. This marked the end of the hiding out. What a morning—could there ever be one more beautiful?

Greetings, jubilation, speeches out in the streets. Karl and the others joined the parade. They were moving toward the imperial palace, the erstwhile imperial palace.

On Wilhelmstrasse, in the palace of the Reichs Chancellor sat the last imperial Reichs Chancellor, Friedrich Ebert, an old Social Democratic hand, a crafty fellow. He trembled even more than the generals at the idea of revolution. Because if it succeeded it would also settle accounts with him for his policy of seeing the war through to its end. He was for the monarchy. It was not hard to believe that of him. There he had been sitting in the Reichs Chancellery for one day now, and here came the revolution.

And then his own friend, Philipp Scheidemann, a Social Democrat like himself, upset the apple-cart—unintentionally; he thought he was doing the best thing that could be done. While Liebknecht marched with his workers up to the palace and proclaimed a republic from one of its windows, Scheidemann climbed into the window of the Reichstag and proclaimed the same republic from there.

The republic was proclaimed twice over; it could lack for nothing.

When Ebert, who was in the same building, heard what Scheidemann had perpetrated, he screamed in rage, "You have made a perjuror of me." But there was no repairing the damage.

Several days before, in Moscow, Lenin had declared:

"The international revolution is building. We must be vigilant. If imperial Germany falls and the new government is not an effective one, then we are in greater danger than before. Then France and England will have their hands free to deal with the Soviet Republic."

And now he sent a telegram to Vorovsky in Stockholm (the battering ram who had slammed up against the doors of the old social order, against its armies, its economy, its politics, its classes, and ever more furiously against its foundations, against religion, mysticism, humanism):

"German soldiers have arrested the emissaries of the German

generals who hoped to arrange an armistice with the Allies. German soldiers have entered into direct negotiations with French soldiers. The Kaiser has abdicated. All the ports on the North and Baltic Seas are in the hands of revolutionaries. The red flag flies above the German fleet. Tomorrow the heroes who have fallen for freedom will be buried in solemn ceremonies."

(A new man must be created.)

And now the prisons were opened—who was there to prevent it?—and the political prisoners streamed out.

Rosa stood on Cathedral Square in Breslau and spoke to a crowd of ten thousand.

On November 10th she was in Berlin. They met her at the station. Her friends looked at her with a sense of sadness. Yes, it was Rosa—Rosa Luxemburg, the fragile little woman. She had gray, snow-white hair. Did she still have the old energy? It appeared so. If anything, her eyes radiated more strength, more urgency than before.

For the moment she stood in the midst of the fray.

BOOK TWO

The People's Naval Division;
or,
The Revolution Looks for a Permanent Job

Friedrich Ebert, the Obstructionist

They had already lost the battle before they began.

For the exiled dynasties had taken precautions.

They had prepared for their downfall, but not as a private citizen would, who hastily sends his money out of the country before things go awry, but like a tree that scatters masses of seed before it withers.

Wilhelm II was able to travel to Holland, the other princes were able to hide inside the country. That left the generals and the bureaucrats. They went right on thriving happily as offshoots of the old tree. And the soil remained as well: an industrious citizenry that willingly obeyed.

And then there was Friedrich Ebert.

Friedrich Ebert let his countenance shine upon the masterless nation. He was anxious not to disturb anything here. He was anxious to prevent anything from happening and to undo what had been done.

Who Was This Man?

By strange coincidence he was born in 1871—the same year as Lenin and Rosa Luxemburg—as the son of a Heidelberg tailor. Raised in a Catholic home, he exchanged the deeply-felt religion of his parents, with its melancholy and its yearnings, for the shallow optimism of a socialist who swears by progress and organization. He was not out to accomplish grand things, nor was he comfortable with the visions of Karl Marx, with world revolution and dictatorship; he only wanted to better the living conditions of his countrymen, and did what he could to accomplish that. He joined the Party. He was a saddler, an inn-keeper, an upright citizen, a common man, without ambitions thus far—one would never have thought of comparing him to Lenin or Rosa.

He was squat and portly. His massive head had never really grown up beyond his shoulders. He preferred to conceal his eyes beneath their heavy lids, for they bugged out and had no pleasant gleam in them. A small black imperial sprouted from his chin. His most important, most conspicuous feature, however, was his legs—short, stout props, solid instruments that their owner could trust with his weight. And with legs like that he could stand firmly on a foundation of facts. If some people might stretch their necks to get a glimpse of life lost somewhere beyond the roofs of houses, if others might use a battering ram to make room for themselves, he was content. He was interested only in touching up the details.

Prior to this, hardly anything had been heard about the man. He first became a Reichstag deputy in 1912. He had somehow gained people's trust. He did not write; writing was not his strong point, there were scribblers enough in the Party. Nor did he make speeches, even though everyone gave speeches, and it caused a sensation in the Reichstag whenever a new deputy took his seat and kept his mouth shut. They assumed there was something wrong with his mouth. But when in Party caucuses he did open his mouth, it turned out there was nothing inside it except for a few small, correct remarks. They were the remarks anyone might make—but didn't. He himself was used to standing behind his bar and pulling the tap for them. And so he became a political miracle. He could let the others talk and himself say nothing.

His fame was made. He chaired committee meetings, was elected to the executive committee of the Party. He still looked like an innkeeper as before, one who knew how to quell the noise in his place; and he remained, as his friend Scheidemann attested, "a splendid fellow in the company of happy tipplers."

When the war came to an end in 1918, and all the countries involved had had enough, the need for peace and quiet surfaced among the Germans as well, and they demanded their trusty old sleeping-caps. This was warmly greeted by all the generals, junkers, and saber-rattlers who had begun to think their lives were on the line because their apple-cart had been upended and they were lying deep in the mud. They heard the average Fritz moaning and they said: we can help that man.

They yoked him to their apple-cart. And as driver they named a very trustworthy fellow: the saddler, innkeeper, Reichstag deputy and imperial Reichs Chancellor (for one day) Friedrich Ebert. He became First People's Deputy of the young republic.

He was supposed to get the old, badly battered cart rolling again. And as the imperial army marched back home under the leadership of its officers, Hindenburg and Groener thought: Now's our chance to mix business with pleasure. Let us break this young republic's neck. And so they marched three divisions into Berlin, led by General Lequis, under the motto: the Frontline Troops Return Home. But the return home and the broken neck planned for the republic were a failure. It was counter to the desire for peace and quiet. These troops were Germans after all, and they literally marched home. This came as a complete surprise to the organizers, occurring between the 10th and 12th of December 1918.

After which a great Congress of Councils took place in Berlin, where the revolutionaries wanted to turn things around and put Ebert's life on the line, inasmuch as he had been in league with the generals and saber-rattlers. And an old man, a rough-and-ready rebel in gray hair named Georg Ledebour, ascended the festively decorated podium in the Chamber of Deputies and gave vent to his indignation, to the grievance in his heart and in the hearts of many others. He shouted:

"Herr Ebert, you are a disgrace to the revolution."

And someone shouted down from the gallery, "It is a general disgrace that people here keep talking about a revolution. We are in the midst of a revolution."

The galleries, by the way, strongly resembled those of the Petrograd Constituent Assembly of 1917, and in the hall itself things looked as they had in the Tauride Palace. Only Lenin was missing. And then, too, there were no dependable Latvian regiments marching around outside. Instead, unarmed workers milled helplessly about on the street in front of the locked doors, singing the International in dead earnest. And their delegations carrying placards were allowed into the hall and permitted to pray a litany of their slogans. And why not, they were the people, they were harmless, it was touching.

And finally the driver of the upended apple-cart rose to his feet, the saddler, the innkeeper, the Reichstag deputy and imperial Reichs Chancellor, Friedrich Ebert himself, and he knew, as had Lenin in the Tauride Palace, that everything was cut and dried—only quite unlike the way it had been in Petrograd. Because Ebert had the German need for peace and quiet, and he had the generals and the junkers on his side; his accusers, however, had nothing except indignation and pretty songs. And so Ebert became enraged himself, and latched onto the great many untruths and exaggerations of his accusers. Whereupon the hall promptly shared his rage, and he could then put through his demands easy as pie: a new election for the Executive Council, the body set up as a control over the government, and the fixing of January 19th as the date for elections to a constituent assembly. And so elections were set for January 19th, and the revolutionary Executive Council was made up of none but peaceable folks, so that one could indeed say that the day had not been allowed to pass to no purpose.

"You need luck," Friedrich Ebert admitted with a sigh of relief when they congratulated him for his victory in the Congress.

"You need to have the German people behind you," said others.

"That's what I meant," said Ebert. "And you need," and here Ebert spoke only for himself, "to have the generals behind you, for all eventualities. But only at the beginning. Because later on I would like to get rid of them in order to prevent them from getting rid of me."

And then came the affair of the People's Naval Division.

The Stolen Linens

They sought out the quiet and darkness of night to do their work. There were many such nights in December.

On the other side of the Spree, in front of the Stock Exchange, there were few passers-by, nor was there any activity on the Kaiser-Friedrich Bridge, traffic moving more in the direction of Busch Circus and the Exchange Station.

And so between one and two in the morning—and if there was a lot of business, even before midnight—they would be underway, transporting things down to the water past the dispensary. Bold as brass they would pass through the inner courts of the palace. Because first of all it was badly lit, if at all, and secondly, if they were spotted, what sort of people would see them? Some sailor on patrol or the men at the fire station. But they were usually playing cards or telling stories. And if they should spot you they were not about to blow the whistle, not by a long shot. As far as they were concerned, you could go right ahead and clean out the palace and all the junk the Kaiser ever owned.

The cumbersome boats lay black on the water below. The boatsman and his wife helped stash things. Everything went smoothly.

And now they stand in front of the palace dispensary on the Spree and smoke their pipes and gaze at the silent boats. On one alongside theirs a small dog barks, still unable to calm down, the only creature upset by these events. The boatsman and his wife are already asleep again in their cook's cabin.

Gerstel, from Kiel, a former stoker in the navy, in his early thirties, frowns, scratches his beard, and says dejectedly, "Lidinski, we'll always be a pair of rascals. We deserve a good thrashing."

"More than that."

"Prison maybe. Because we're acting like thieves, stealing outright."

"That's it, Gerstel."

Lidinski, from Berlin, is younger, and a head taller than Gerstel. He stretches his long, thin neck out of the baggy military jacket. He was once an artillerist, but the French have got the cannons now.

"It's a matter of helping yourself, Gerstel," Lidinski suggests. "Nothing else. Out in the field a soldier has to use his wits."

"What do you mean help yourself?"

"If you've got no other choice and nobody's helping nobody else."

"That won't get you very far, Lidinski. What's wrong is wrong."

"But it's not your fault if one fellow won't help another. Let them mind their own business."

"You Berliners always were great at talking big. But for all that I'm standing here red-faced, and I'm telling you this is dirty business and we're thieves."

"What you're asking me then, Gerstel, is if we aren't sort of acting like common thieves. And what I'm asking you is if you're not a dumb ox?"

"What do you mean?"

"I'll clue you in right now. You're part of the guard here at the palace, keeping watch on it, right?"

"Sure, so what?"

"Then you must be a dumb ox. 'Cause, let's say you've got a grandmother or an aunt in Rahnsdorf, and she dies and leaves you a bit of land with a field of potatoes and vegetables. And you hire a couple of private guards to keep an eye out so that you don't steal the potatoes."

"Who me? But you just said that I had inherited them. Those are my potatoes."

"That's what I'm saying. There's your proof that you're a dumb ox. Because there's no need for you to hire private guards to keep an eye out to make sure you don't come and get your own potatoes."

"Lidinski, I still don't get what you're trying to say. You boys from Berlin are just too sharp for me."

"Well then, let's turn the whole thing around. For example, let's put the question this way: Who took off for Holland, you or the Kaiser?"

"Sure wasn't me. Otherwise I wouldn't be here."

"Right: him and Lehmann. So then you also know who ain't giving orders around here anymore and who is."

"We had that much all figured out in Kiel long before you guys here in Berlin got around to it."

"Right, Gerstel. Now look at Lehmann, who took a powder and left a pile of debts behind. And now if you, Karl Gerstel, go into his palace as his creditor and take some things out, seeing as he cheated and duped you—does that make you a thief? The whole damn palace belongs to you, Gerstel, don't let them kid you, and there's no need whatever for you to go fetch those duds today and pawn them the next. It all belongs to you."

"Lidinski, you Berliners are great talkers. But I just don't see where all this gets you."

They knocked the ashes out of their pipes. They were freezing. And as they walked on through the dispensary wing, they halted and stepped back into one corner. They had heard a funny noise. But it was only someone snoring in an open room. Sailors were asleep inside.

Lidinski, the tall young fellow from Berlin with his soldier's cap cocked over one ear, giggled as they groped along and held their hands to their mouths to keep from bursting out laughing.

"Hell, Gerstel, there you see what I mean. That's some notion of war they've got there. Just lie down and sleep, and tomorrow they'll land in the street so fast it'll make your head spin—or be stood up against a wall."

"I don't see things as being so dark, Lidinski, I really don't."

"Gerstel, don't you realize we've been taken in?"

They were trotting on across the palace courtyard.

This angered Gerstel the sailor, and he said, "You're always saying we're the fools. But that's as much as you know. We're waiting now for our pay as it is."

"And not getting it, right?"

"They're taking their time about it."

Lidinski laughed. "You're not going to get it either, Gerstel. You'll be tossed out. They'll make short work of you guys."

"With our division you mean? Hell, I'd like to see somebody try anything with us!"

Lidinski: "Poor bastard! Didn't you hoist your red flag in Kiel a good six weeks ago already, and elect yourself a sailors' council, and now," he giggled this into Gerstel's ear, "and now, you poor bastard, you're pilfering."

Gerstel nodded mournfully, an old sailor. "And what do they pay you for a couple of chairs."

"Yes, sir," laughed Lidinski. "Write a letter to Wilhelm in Holland, tell him to come back, 'cause the whole affair hasn't paid off."

Their firm steps echoed over the courtyard. The sailor opened a side door for the man from Berlin. When he was alone again, he sighed, yawned and trotted back to his guardroom.

Yes, they had taken a great fall, the Naval Division, the avant-garde of the revolution. They were left to dangle, waiting for their reward. They had had "their water turned off" as they say in Berlin.

What caused this? Apart from affairs in general, apart from December 6th?

December 6th had been "bloody Friday," in which the sailors had not even played any part. And that was what was so bad about it. For on December 6th a group of people had attempted a mysterious putsch in Berlin, during which a dozen people were killed (on Chaus-seestrasse), and in the course of which several people had prematurely declared Friedrich Ebert President of the Reich (on Wilhelmstrasse) and arrested the all-too-revolutionary Executive Council (on Prinz-Albrecht-Strasse). The sailors, as we said, were not even involved in this fishy affair, but their commander was, who curiously enough was a count, Count Wolff-Metternich.

The sailors did not know that in the history of revolutions the name Metternich was of no great repute, nor were they offended by the title of count. For them what mattered was that when they had arrived in Berlin from Kiel he had taken them in and provided them with funds. It was no surprise, then, that they elected him their commandant. And he took up residence with his friend, a certain Count Schüssberg in the palace, not in some ground-floor rooms, but in the grand salons. And when it came to the aforesaid putsch of December 6th it turned out, to the boundless amazement of the sailors, that their own commander had taken part in the counterrevolutionary action, procuring the trucks that were to carry off the all-too-revolutionary members of the Executive Council, but didn't.

Then and there they ripped their count from their hearts and elected a simple man named Radtke to be their commandant.

And since then their pay had not been coming through. In terms of

95

pay at least, Radtke proved to be no improvement. Their pay came through the City Commandant, where a Social Democrat named Wels was in charge, a man who couldn't stand the smell of them. Count Metternich had been able to get along better with this Social Democrat.

Worse still, there was a campaign against the sailors who had been the avant-garde of the revolution—and perhaps for precisely that reason. For example, the Guard Cavalry Rifles, who had marched with General Lequis into Berlin to no useful end on December 12th, could not refrain from proclaiming that they found the presence of the People's Naval Division in Berlin to be a personal affront to their honor. They protested, saying that the very presence of these troops in Berlin necessarily belittled them in the eyes of the rest of the world. And indeed, in saying this, the sensitive Guard Rifles had hit the nail, if not the sailors, on the head. For if in fact you are about to mug someone, and you discover a police officer right there on the spot, you naturally find his presence quite superfluous, indeed a vexation and an offense.

This was the state of things for the People's Naval Division in the latter half of December, when one fine day an unexpected personage appeared, as if summoned (or perhaps ordered up) for the occasion, in the Prussian Ministry of Finance.

Into the office there came, supported by his baton and bent over with age, dignity and care, a genuine lord chamberlain from the Wilhelmine epoch. He appeared in the company of an equally aged majordomo of the palace, and both had something on their hearts.

He, the lord chamberlain, whose grief at the decampment of the court was visible, made a deposition declaring that objects were continually disappearing from the palace, and that an end must be put to this. He had come, he said, to inform them that large inventories had been removed from the linen supply room. To give the thing a proper name, they had been removed by the People's Naval Division, which, as was well known, had made itself at home in the palace. Ostensibly such linens were being used as towels for the sailors in the royal stables and so on.

The lord chamberlain, according to whose account the court linen was drifting away, muttered truculently, "Those fellows can wipe their dirty noses with something else." He found the treasury official in complete agreement, even when he added, "They're an organized band of thieves."

All this was promptly taken down for the record.

When called to the witness stand, the majordomo could do no less than concur point for point with the testimony already given.

On a high stool behind a lectern sat the public auditor, who recorded the amazing things he was hearing. His chair spun about beneath him at the joy of it all. The chair, fused for decades now with its owner, could not get enough of spinning, so that the accountant had to use force to arrest it—all the more since the witness was getting dizzy watching, and he himself was having trouble taking down the minutes.

In a distant room sat the minister himself. The German November Revolution, determined as it was to accomplish nothing and to reverse everything that had been done until now, had come up with the idea of leaving a calling card in the various ministries as a reminder of its presence, a visiting card in human form, a man who was in fact discovered later in the rooms provided for him.

It was agreed that this man should be called a "minister," each according to the building in which he found himself, and the bureaucrats used that name when they talked about him. Because the visit the revolution had paid did interest these people, and people spoke openly about it in the ministries.

And when, following the visit of the lord chamberlain and the majordomo, the bureaucrats trooped together in the office of the public auditor, their first task was to rescue the auditor from his chair. The chair spun about in a mad whirligig and finally leaped down into the room. The auditor, having been fetched down with a pair of tongs and set back on his feet, carried the excitable chair through the room and opened a window, smiling in his embarrassment and decidedly dizzy. A cool breeze soothed the chair. Quieted, the creature sank back into its customary self-contemplation without further ado.

When the bureaucrats were assured that this was the case and the accountant had read his minutes, they agreed, in light of the importance, urgency, and stupendous character of this matter, immediately to place it before the minister. They considered the minister part of their bureaucratic household.

The minister was sitting in the office he had taken over, grateful that as yet no one had contested him for it. He was an earnest man who frequently turned his thoughts to the question of why it was he was sitting here, had to sit here, since he did have living quarters of his own. But so great was his respect for the revolution that he did not pursue the question.

The bureaucrats pressed their way in, bringing the public auditor with them. A somber choir sang in unison its grievance against the People's Naval Division, a fugue on the theme of: "Thou shalt not steal."

He listened attentively, he propped his head on his fist, he pondered. It was a biblical commandment. They plied him with theology. He was a banker, a patron of the arts, and an Independent Socialist. He found himself in great difficulty: in what capacity should he speak? In matters of theology?

As an Independent he thought: these fellows here before him, these bureaucrats, were hoping to cut the sailors down to size; a blind man could see that the sailors had in fact used the linens, and why shouldn't they take them out of the palace? In wartime that sort of thing was called requisitioning.

The patron of the arts had his say as well. What could one reply concerning the biblical passage to which they had referred? Even artists steal. One artist steals another's ideas and melodies. That is called influence. Can you call stealing towels a form of influence? Hardly. They wouldn't understand that.

And now the banker. As a banker I have my opinions about theft, but I'm not sure which ones. At any rate I would not want to initiate any discussion at this point on the topic "Banking and Theft." There's already been enough said about that.

And the upshot is, I can't arrive at any decision.

He was determined not to come to a decision.

And then it occurred to him that they persistently addressed him as "Herr Minister." Right, he was a minister. The minister of finance. And for the moment his outrage knew no limits. He requested exact information.

"What was stolen?"

"Linens," came the answer.

"What do sailors need linens for?" the Independent Socialist inquired.

"That's not the issue," came the enraged answer, "but rather that those are supplies which are under our administration."

"Were there a great many linens?" the banker grumbled.

"An enormous amount."

"Lovely, new, white linens? And did they perhaps steal paintings as well?" inquired the patron of the arts (who as a banker, moreover, would have liked to purchase these paintings.)

"Yes indeed. Lovely, new white linens. We will make inquiries concerning the paintings."

It was all clear now. That settled it. He was the minister, and people had stolen linens. That called for revenge. There could be no more doubt of it. What was required here were pure, fixed, documentary formulae, such as: "In case of involuntary manslaughter, the interment costs shall be borne by the party upon whom such responsibilities are incumbent."

He gave the bureaucrats authorization to scrape together all such formulae, phrases and cliches that they could lay their hands on for the resolution and subjugation of such a case.

And they didn't need to be told twice, not even once for that matter. They had already prepared it all and had brought it with them in written form, and he only had to initial it.

After a multitude of "insofar as's" and "inasmuch as's," after dreamily musing over clauses like: "The proprietor may defend himself with force in cases of unauthorized appropriation," their decision read:

"The sailors attached to the Ministry of Finance are to be removed from the palace and the royal stables, and an appropriation of all keys in their possession is to be carried out without prior notice."

Which action was then submitted as an official proposal of the Ministry of Finance to the People's Deputies on Wilhelmstrasse.

Sailors are Interrogated at the Ministry of Finance

In the grip of pain (and of greatest glee) Friedrich Ebert read this petition, folded it up, and rubbed his colleagues' noses in it.

He promptly passed the information on to the newspapers, and thus the public learned that the palace was literally being plundered of the shirt on its back, or as the case might be, of its towel. And by whom else but the all-too-notorious People's Naval Division.

The public demanded action.

And the government, gentle (and nervous) as it was, came to the decision, nudged by public opinion, to remove the sailors from the palace at once.

When the sailors learned of this, they became restless, and that restlessness spread to the soldier's councils of the regiments stationed in Berlin, who issued a declaration:

"Our comrades in the Navy, whom people now want to oust, were the first bearers and defenders of the revolution. Their continued presence in Berlin is therefore absolutely indispensable."

The government, however, remained unruffled, and ordered City Commandant Wels—who, poor unfortunate, had brought these sailors in from Kiel on November 12th—to get rid of them now. Wels invited their leaders to join him at his headquarters.

Now these sailors, being sailors from Kiel, were by definition revolutionaries. But because they were also Germans, and since a lot of water had flowed down the Spree since November 12th, they were likewise not revolutionaries. And in order to do justice to both realities, they had arrived at the following decisions beforehand: first, to demand their pay; second, to demand that their numbers be strengthened; third, that they be removed from the ranks of the navy and be allowed to join the Republican Defense Forces under Wels—this latter in order to be better paid.

Which meant that the counterproposal made by Wels as City Commandant struck them rather hard. They were to be reduced to six hundred men and turned out of the palace. There was to be no agreement incorporating their wishes.

Exasperated, they returned to the royal stables and spread their sulky mood among the rest of the sailors. Debates and arguments arose. And since they numbered some two thousand men and were commanded by several different officers, both senior and junior ones, the argument took on major proportions. Several differing opinions were registered, and the result of the argument was that at least two hundred men were dismissed. But these were merely men who had wanted to leave anyway and had found work elsewhere, and so this made no impression on the powers that be.

And so they muddled on, bad tempered, sulky, and irresolute; meanwhile Christmas drew nearer and still they had no money. Having to sit around there staring at the bare walls over Christmas and not being able to buy Christmas pastries or anything else after four lousy years of war—that's what they called peace? That didn't make sense to them.

But because in their distress they could not agree among themselves and because some men were just about ready to undertake ill-advised action while Spartacus was busy agitating among them, they pulled themselves together and decided to try the bureaucracy once more and knock at the door of the Ministry of Finance. We know our way around the Ministry of Finance by now. There's a mouse-gray public auditor sitting on a swivel-chair who is very anxious to know what will become of the affair recently reported to him by the lord chamberlain and the majordomo. In other offices other bureaucrats bustle about, all placed there by Wilhelm II and pained by the fact that they must receive their salary from the hands of such a dirty republic. Only because the salaries are high do they deign to accept them.

And finally, there in the ministry sits the man with the brown beard who day in and day out asks himself the puzzling question why it is that he has to be sitting here, seeing that he already has living quarters of his own. But the revolution is strict, and one may not ask questions of it. He is a minister of the revolution.

When the sailors arrive, he is not in. He is also a farmer and owns an estate, and he must be fetched back from it.

In the meantime the sailors attempt to make a deal.

They first declare to the public auditor, who listens not without some goodwill—for who does not love the pigeon he is about to roast, even when it is still in its raw state—that according to their roster from December 12th they are 3,250 men strong.

Of these, 1,450 men had been reduced to half-pay. ("What did that mean, half-pay?"—"Half-pay? Well that was half-pay."—"Fine.")

"Because of a shortage of uniforms, underwear, board, and basic pay."

"Go on, please."

"Which means eighteen hundred men still are left. Of these, eleven hundred reside in the stables."

"What do you mean reside? They're quartered there. That is not their residence."

"Certainly not, of course not. Three hundred are staying in the Chamber of Deputies, four hundred in Moabit prison, seven hundred are on guard duty."

The public auditor, a chancery counselor, wrote all this down. The chair beneath him began to rotate. The chancery counselor hovered and swung back and forth, invisible, of course, to the rude eyes of those sailors merely "quartered" in the royal stables. What heavenly joy! He floated near the ceiling, he sank back down, rotated, and took down notes.

"What else? Is there anything else, please?"

"Upon the departure of Count Wolff-Metternich, Comrade Radtke took over command of our division."

"Radtke with a 'd' or a 't' or with both?"

"With both. As he himself has publicly declared, Radtke provides, together with his staff of four aides, a leadership based on mutual trust and dedicated to the interests of the Socialist Republic."

The chancery counselor opened eyes and ears wide. The chair started to rotate. Everything stood still, including the chancery counselor's brain. He said in bewilderment, "Say that again, please."

The sailors' representative: "Radtke with both, with a 'd' and a 't'. As he himself has publicly declared, Radtke provides, together with his staff of four aides, a leadership based on mutual trust and dedicated to the interests of the Socialist Republic."

The chancery counselor looked from one man to the next, his pen in his mouth; he sucked on it, marveling, sucked some more. "And how do you know all this?"

His chair stood still, his mind was still not in gear. He leaped up and ran off to the bureaucrats.

He knocked at every door. They saw at once what had happened. The man's mind was no longer in gear. They followed him cautiously to his office. There stood seven sailors side by side. Aha, they had stolen his mind. After having stolen the linens from the lord chamberlain's palace. They had stolen sheets and handkerchiefs, and now they had pushed their way in here and robbed a poorly paid chancery counselor of his little bit of a mind.

They wanted to alert the police in the building. These twelve fat, bald, runny-nosed men roared at the seven sailors, demanding to know what they wanted here. They were outraged. They insisted they be given a candid, expanded confession.

The sailors began: According to the roster of December 12th, they numbered 3,250 men.

"3,250? That's way too many."

Of these, they had now put more than 1,450 on half-pay.

"Half-pay? What does that mean, half-pay? Are you an army, a regiment, empowered to put someone on half . . ." (In their excitement they left off the word "pay.")

"It's just an expression."

"What?"

"To say that we've put them on half-pay."

"Aha, we see. Go on, please."

"We've placed them on half-pay due to a lack of clothing, underwear, money and rations."

"Fine," said the bureaucrats.

"What do you mean fine?" the sailors now asked.

"It's just an expression. Please go on."

"That leaves eighteen hundred men. Of these, eleven hundred . . . ," the sailors stammered, hesitated—they remembered that the word "reside" was incorrect. They turned to the bureaucrats. "What should be say instead of 'reside'?"

The bureaucrats at once: "Are quartered."

The sailors: "Of these, eleven hundred are quartered in the royal stables, three hundred are staying in the Chamber of Deputies, seven hundred are on guard duty."

The bureaucrats were amazed. How could the chancery counselor lose his mind over this? Had he perhaps had none before? They had never noticed in the press of business.

They gave them a sign to continue their questioning, the main point was yet to come. And so they asked, "And further? What else, please?"

The sailors: "Upon the departure of Count Wolff-Metternich, Comrade Radtke took over command of our division."

"Radtke with a 'd' or a 't' or with both?"

"With both." And they rattled it off like clockwork. "And as he himself has public declared, Radtke provides, together with his staff of four aides, a leadership based on mutual trust and dedicated to the interests of the Socialist Republic."

The bureaucrats were so flabbergasted their mouths turned to cotton.

They could not speak. They looked about the room for a drink or water. There was no water; the chancery counselor only drank schnapps and he had hidden that. They ran out into the corridor shouting "Water!"

What happened now took place so fast that even those involved did not know what was going on, and they would definitely have denied everything had someone accused them of it later. But nonetheless it happened.

As the bureaucrats yelled for water, a gang of building personnel appeared and went to work—wild-eyed, unshaven fellows, who had just returned from the war. Wearing battle helmets, they threw themselves to the floor and took cover, shooting as they advanced. This resulted in the death of three bureaucrats and in two more being seriously wounded. The rest, still with cotton in their mouths, went on yelling for water.

And so the fellows thought they were dealing with a broken water main and dragged in life vests, which, as is well known, are kept in reserve at all ministries of finance for officials in constant danger of drowning in figures. They forced the bureaucrats, both living and dead, to put them on, then drove them out onto the fire escape, where they yelled up to them to find out if the water was still on its way or not. And when, to their amazement, the bureaucrats wrung their hands and lamented, "On the contrary, there isn't any," they resolutely upended the fire ladder, which broke into pieces as it fell, burying everyone beneath it. Things happened, as we've said, with such rapidity that those involved could not even take down the information and file it.

The collapse of the fire ladder resulted in several broken necks, three to be exact, two broken arms and legs, and in a mere two cases the victims escaped with simple death. The whole lot were immediately swept up by the house personnel without interrogation, stuffed into the nearest coal scuttles and wastebaskets, and promptly dispatched to the University Surgical Clinic on Ziegelstrasse, where the latest super-fast soldering technique for broken necks was being tested. This was used at once on those admitted—successfully. Whereupon those with broken arms and legs were dealt with homeopathically, the slogan of which treatment is: "Pain is cured by what causes it." Which meant that the wounded were placed in life jackets on fire ladders and up-ended once again, which naturally permitted healing to take its course without further difficulty. As souvenirs of this miraculous healing, the patients were awarded old-fashioned plaster casts, and afterward they were allowed to return to the Finance Ministry, where they underwent a thorough watering. At this, the plaster casts dissolved in delight, the delight spread among all those present, even among the bureaucrats themselves, who rejoiced and laughed and laughed and laughed.

And so, jovial and dripping, they all waded in to join the sailors, who were still standing there waiting for their pay (from the moment of the bureaucrats' flight into the corridor, on through their transport to Ziegelstrasse, the soldering of their necks, mending of broken arms and legs, awarding of plaster casts, and their return to the ministry, not to mention the final watering, twelve seconds had elapsed all told—which, it must be admitted, is a record time for such a procedure).

The sailors had not wasted the elapsed time themselves. They had gotten married, and stood there now with their children, grandchildren, parents, grandparents and parents-in-law, displaying, as is understandable after such a long absence from home, a great feeling for family life. Except that they had not borne up well from their long incarceration in an office; they had become a sort of parasite, termites that had forced their way through the ceilings and walls into the rooms above and adjoining. And once there, so as to have some sort of exercise, they had had to play soccer and ping-pong (many of them were already getting fat and had callouses on their rears); and they filled the Finance Ministry from top to bottom with their merry howls, mixed in, however, with other noises as well (besides the monotone clattering of typewriters): the scream of babies that had just come into the world, whom their mothers had to cradle in the ashtrays for lack of space, where they were singed by the cigars of the sailors, who in the heat of their games had not noticed their arrival.

Into this gala festival of life, the bureaucrats came storming, as banal as some utterance of People's Deputy Ebert—who was not present—and in a rage at the thought of what all had happened in the last twelve seconds, at what they had suffered, both they themselves and the public auditor, they cursed the sailors with a mighty curse. Now no one can accurately predict the range of a curse, for which reason it is wise to be careful with curses. At any rate the curse of the bureaucrats not only destroyed the sailors, but the entire Finance Ministry as well, themselves included, and an even greater misfortune might have occurred; since as the Finance Ministry fell, the buildings adjoining it on the right and left were threatened with collapse as well. Because this would have blocked traffic in the entire area, however, and because it was a case of negligent and unauthorized cursing, the curse was allowed to function only for one moment, whereupon the Finance Ministry and all its contents were restored—though with the eradication of the children born in the meantime and the whole attendant familial life—so that now there stood, just as before, only the naked sailors, clad to be sure, but naked as individuals standing there trying to find their way in these new times.

But now the strange occurrences that had overwhelmed the Finance Ministry began to infect them as well, and what happened to them was no less wonderful than the experiences of the bureaucrats. Having barely escaped both the curse and married life, the sailors now saw water before them, the very water that had flowed away from the bureaucrats. They saw it boil and seethe and surge and fizz and gush like a stream from many wells. And they believed they had been blinded by madness and spirited away upon the open sea by the sorcery of this tale. Their minds were confounded. They spoke to one another in Greek and Latin, but translated this at once into German and so exhorted one another to travel upon the sea, upon the ocean, on through the Pillars of Hercules. To this end they crept among the legs of the chairs, which proved an only partially successful maneuver given their girth. This explains why they did not move from the spot and were unable to pass those difficult straits—whereupon others sat down on the chairs in order to determine if this problem was caused by the wind or something else. They fell, into the water, into the sea, and found themselves among other men who had already climbed aboard lifeboats. There they joined them, vigorously manning the oars in hexameters, hoping to force the passage.

They forged ahead with rapid strokes across the floor of the office, and because their progress was still not rapid enough, they hoisted sails that they had pulled out of the filing cabinets and cut invisible riggings. They overturned the tables and gazed through inkwells, probing the horizon. They saw a black future ahead of them.

At this point, the bureaucrats could no longer endure it all. They took to their heels. For the difficulties of the case exceeded anything they had ever before been confronted with.

They ran to the minister. The farmer was there. As a man who had traveled much in the open air, he immediately recognized that something unusual had happened here. The gentlemen were soaking wet and very excited. The chancery officials and bureaucrats took their seats. The farmer had the heat turned up. He dried out his visitors. He asked whether he should hang them out to dry. They graciously declined.

The minister inquired what had happened. They stammered as they repeated that ominous sentence about the Socialist Republic and about Radtke with a 'd' and a 't.' They were afraid of the terrible effect this would have on the minister. But the Independent Socialist had already heard this sentence, it bounced off him as if it were nothing, some child's ball, falling impotently to the floor and rolling about the room causing no damage—much to the amazement of the chancery officials and bureaucrats, who then broke into a hymn of jubilation, praising the minister and proclaiming to the other floors of the building: "Behold the hero, flaming bright, clad in glittering armor. Terrible words bounce off from him like a child's rubber ball and roll about the room causing no damage."

Thereupon they lay down in the shade of the minister, an over-towering personality, a true date palm, a fig tree, and at once they heard pleasant music, and a soft ticking became audible: the auditors brains were purring and making their first movements. For others, saliva began to flow again. The minister passed a spittoon to each of them, he had two dozen of them in his office, since he himself spat a great deal—just in general and at his servants in particular. And when they had all let their spittle flow in concert, they entered into excited conversation and bared their souls; and the officials and bureaucrats began to laugh. They could not stop laughing.

The auditor could no longer contain himself. He had to get out, to get to his chair, to his chair, to the high chair in his office that stood immobile before the expectant sailors. As it heard the tread of its master, the chair began to sway. And as he entered and sat down upon it, it took off in wild spirals, rotating upward, and only the ceiling prevented it from screwing its way right up through the roof and into the clouds. And so it descended again, sinking down to storm its way across the room with a triple hurrah. It was purest joy. And the sailors, who had happily come to the end of their ocean voyage and passed through the Pillars of Hercules, rejoiced as well.

For they realized: the matter was going well.

And they were doing well.

The Independent Socialist bade them come to him. In the presence of the merry bureaucrats he gave them a good talking to. But he treated them with caution in light of what all had happened here.

As they entered, he was wearing a simple dark gray suit with a light tie and brown Oxfords on his feet. But as minister he immediately donned a fitting costume, a long black formal coat, a small black tie, cast off the Oxfords and chose instead a pair of black laced boots. He said (after also taking invisible scissors to the totally inappropriate beard, quickly shampooing and shaving it away—the lathering, rinsing, and powdering presented no difficulties), that he had to insist that the palace in which they were residing be vacated, by twelve noon on a day yet to be determined, but very near. By that date they must also deliver all their keys to his certified representatives.

They agreed on the fact that the sailors wanted their pay. They agreed to call this point six. That left points one through five.

And now the farmer, clad (all this of course invisible to human eyes) in a heavy jacket and mud-caked top boots and armed with a shovel, paced about the room that he held in trust for the revolution, and conversed in friendly fashion with the sailors about food, about bread, butter, eggs. They readily entered into this conversation, but then unexpectedly turned to the theme of inflation, whereupon a revolt, a transformation occurred within him. Spinning about (of course, invisibly) he cast aside his manure shovel, his muddy boots, and the whole agricultural caboodle and flung his leg with an elegant and charming motion over his chair: the representative of banking interests. He pulled his gold-rimmed spectacles from his upper left vest pocket and was a trustworthy banker, who relieved them of their fears of inflation easy as pie, which is to say kept it within certain lucrative limits. He dreamily stroked his brown, newly-grown beard. He was intrigued by the adventure of inflation. As banker he could be ruined by it or, contrariwise, thrive upon it.

The sailors, now swinging into action, bore to the minister their cares concerning the quartering of their divisions following the evacuation of the palace. As a result, they arrived at a formula for point four, according to which the People's Naval Division called upon the Finance Ministry "to provide for their disposal, by Friday, the 20th of the month, at twelve noon, eight fully furnished rooms in the royal stable, one of which must contain a safe, to serve as the division office."

The bureaucrats finally found the transition between points four and six, to wit: "twenty-four hours after these rooms are placed at their disposal the palace is to be evacuated." And they called this point between points four and six, point five.

Points one to three were filled in with official phrases that were lying all about, cut into cardboard stencils.

Thereupon the sailors marched back to the stables and proclaimed the results of their raid in the form of all the points they had won. Everything was now fair and square, and all they had to do was wait. Further instructions would come from the top.

They were accustomed to waiting (as they had proven during those ominous twelve seconds), and further instructions did come from the top.

The Sailors Have Enough and Lock Up Ebert

At the top, however, sat Ebert and Wels. On December 21st, the following memo landed on the desk of the city commandant:

"December 21, 1918
Government Payment Orders

The Council of People's Deputies directs the city commandant to pay the People's Naval Division the sum of 80,000 (eighty thousand) marks, but only upon the evacuation of the palace and the delivery of all keys to the city commandant.

From January 1, 1919, payment will be made for no more than six hundred men, in accordance with the agreement made between the city commandant and the chairman of the Committee of Fifty-Three of the Navy on December 13th.

Ebert, Haase, Landsberg, Barth, Dittmann, Scheidemann."

Wels's adjutant, a Lieutenant Anton Fischer, examined this memo, turning it back and forth in his hand (which, however did not change its content and how could it—who is Lieutenant Anton Fischer that he could effect such a thing?) Whereupon Fischer informed the chief of the People's Naval Division that he should appear at headquarters at 11:00 A.M. on Sunday, the 21st, for the proclamation of this decision.

But the sailors did not come. What? Why not? These were after all the further instructions that had come from the top. But they had come from Wels. And they would not go to Wels. They had no confidence in him. They couldn't stomach him. What did they take them for? Why were they making things difficult? Were they making fun of them? After all, they had started the very revolution that had put all these high and mighty fellows, including Ebert and Wels, in their palaces. They were the backbone of the republic, and damn it all they wanted their pay, their pay, their pay!

They had had enough. That's understandable. They were gentle and affable. But it was enough to make a revolutionary of any man.

It is Monday, December 23rd, the day before Christmas Eve. The sailors, filled with mistrust and feeling helpless (and how shabby and down at the heel they were, the erstwhile avant-garde of the revolution), made their way to the Reichs Chancellery. Along with them came two gentlemen from the Naval Committee and Tost of the Executive Council. Otto Tost, a metalworker from Berlin, had commanded the sailors at the very beginning, though only after another commandant, named Wilschorek, had been shot dead in a quarrel by a Commander Brettschneider, whom the sailors then summarily lynched while naming Tost their commandant. Soon, however, this position no longer satisfied him; he wanted to move higher still, got himself elected to the Executive Council, and there he sat now and was a big shot. And so with him and with two others from the Naval Committee, the unhappy sailors marched toward Wilhelmstrasse in search of their pay.

They were led in to see Ebert at once, and he put on his friendliest face and displayed great sympathy for their situation. But then, like a magician, he pulled a sheet of paper from a drawer and laid it before them. This was supposed to be the minutes of the negotiations between Wels, the city commandant, and the representatives of the Naval Committee of Fifty-Three. According to those minutes their forces were to be reduced to six hundred men, and there were some other nice items besides.

They were greatly astonished. (But they did not let themselves be charmed; those previous twelve seconds had hardened them.) None of them knew anything about these minutes.

And from the reports given them about these negotiations, things had proceeded quite differently. No, as far as they were concerned these minutes were invalid, they would not accept them, they were wrong.

Ebert looked at the minutes and took it all in peaceably enough. He said that he at any rate was bound by the documents. He would have to adhere to them. But the matter was not so alarming at all events, since he had it in hand, you know, and they could be certain of that. And as far as the affairs of the sailors went, exclusive of the matter of the six hundred, that too was not so alarming, for he had the matter in hand, and he would—they would be certain of it—he would see to it that the discharged sailors would be placed in the militia wherever possible. And that was what they all wanted, to join the Republican Militia at higher pay, wherever possible.

That calmed the three men, and they said they were content and promised to carry out the division's evacuation of the palace. And their pay, Ebert added at the door, would be theirs when they handed over the keys.

So was not everything arranged? It seemed so to the three negotiators, and in the royal stables people thought so too, for they were already very docile there by now. And so to bring the matter to a close at last, and to get their pay, they ordered Lieutenant Dorrenbach to take charge of the strongbox with the keys and deliver it for chrissakes to the Reichs Chancellery.

Lieutenant Dorrenbach, who was he? An enterprising fellow, just the sort the sailors loved: squat, gnarled, with dark bristly hair, sharp piercing eyes, and whatever he undertook to do he saw through to the end. He gathered a dozen heavily armed men and had them march into the guard house. There he joined them, grabbed up the steel strongbox containing the keys, rode down Wilhelmstrasse in a truck, strongbox in hand and his sailors with their rifles beside him.

Emil Barth, the little people's deputy, an Independent, was sitting in his office in the Reichs Chancellery, reading his newspaper. He sat there on exactly the same sort of chair as the auditor in the Finance Ministry. But since he, Barth, was a newcomer and a revolutionary, the chair had of course not grown to be a part of him, nor he a part of it. As a result of which, the chair beneath him stood still, that's true, but it also took no part in Barth's emotions and was ready at any moment to emancipate itself from him and to give him a kick. It therefore twitched joyfully the moment a dozen heavily armed sailors entered the room, at their head a gnarled lieutenant with a massive strongbox. The sailors formed themselves in two rows along the wall.

110

Emil Barth received a violent kick in the rear, from below, from the chair, and he stood up.

It seemed to both him and the chair that he was to be executed.

Lieutenant Dorrenbach strode over to his desk, gave his name and put the strongbox on the desk. "So, now this here is the strongbox in question. And now we've delivered it."

Barth, familiar with the whole affair, regarded the much-talked-of item with astonishment as it lay there before him on top of his paper. "Yes, fine, good. But what am I to do with it? Why didn't you go directly to headquarters with it, to Wels, who has the money?"

Dorrenbach: "That is out of the question for us. We will not go to Wels."

An elderly sailor stepped forward from the row. "We don't want to have nothing to do with Wels. You're a people's deputy. You can take care of the matter."

Barth scratched his head, gazed at the strongbox, gazed at the sailors and felt his rear end. It hurt. He exchanged fruitless glances with the chair. It had veiled itself in silence, naturally. Now Barth picked up the telephone and demanded to speak with the city commandant, with Commander Wels.

"This is Emil Barth. The sailors are here in my office with the keys, yes here with me in the Reichs Chancellery—I told you, with the keys you wanted."

"Well then, tell them to bring them over here."

"No. That's what they don't want to do. That's why they've come to me. They say that things would only end up in a confrontation if they were to go to headquarters. You know well enough what sort of popularity you enjoy among them."

"That makes no difference to me."

"So then pay. The keys are here with me, in front of me on my desk. It really would be a shame if things were to blow up just twenty-four hours before Christmas on account of a minor detail. You've got to realize these people need to be paid."

Wels: "Well then you have to realize that I insist that they bring the strongbox to me, first of all so that I can be certain that all the keys are in it, and second because it's my responsibility. As I said, whether I'm to their taste or not doesn't make a damn bit of difference."

Barth: "But look here, it must be sufficient if I assume the responsibility."

"No. It's not sufficient for you to be responsible. In that case Ebert should be the one."

Barth: "Hell and damnation, now that's just fine. We're all six people's deputies with the same rights. Ebert is not worth a cent more than I. You're saying you don't trust me. Well, all I can say then is that I understand why these people say that there's no dealing with you."

Wels: "That's all the same to me. I don't want to offend you. But Ebert's in charge of military matters. If he says yes, I'll pay up."

Barth: "Okay, fine. Let him handle the matter, since you deny me the right to do it."

The sailors, along with Dorrenbach, were listening to the conversation. Once Barth had put down the receiver and told them, "Well, you heard how things stand; so go see Ebert," they formed a circle, including Dorrenbach, and cursed softly for a few minutes. Then Dorrenbach broke it off, picked up the strongbox, and off they went to Ebert.

He is not there.

Now they've had enough. Now they've had more than enough. They've been wandering about Berlin for days on end because of their pay. They are being treated like foolish children. But they are sailors, that they are, heavily armed sailors. They'll show this pack sitting around in their offices and trying to lead them around by the nose what a People's Naval Division is.

So they march back down to the men guarding the building below. These are their own people, sailors, unpaid ones as well. They show them their strongbox, and explain how things stand and how they're being cheated and led around by the nose. And now something has to be done. That's clear to them all. Which results in Dorrenbach giving the order: "Occupy the Reich's Chancellery, no one is to be allowed in or out. There are to be no telephone calls. We're not leaving until we have our money."

Whereupon the guards on Wilhemstrasse close the heavy iron gates, place sentries at the entrance, and sailors take up position at the switchboard. Two men are given orders to run through the entire building flinging doors open and shouting to those inside: "This building is occupied, no one is allowed in or out."

This is done, and in the course of the action these fellows happen upon a large room that looks much like a cozy living room, and there sit two men at a table chowing down. The two sailors shout, "This building is occupied. No one is allowed in or out," and slam the door. They've got it good, those guys do, chowing down.

"What's this?" asks one of the two at the table, wiping his mouth in amazement. This, of course, is Friedrich Ebert, who has not yet finished his meal. Landsberg, the other fellow, is amazed as well. "No one is allowed in or out. What's that supposed to mean?" They listen to the shouts continuing at the doors of adjoining rooms. Something is wrong here. They fold their napkins, lay them in consternation on the table, and head off for their own offices.

First of all Ebert wants to find out what is happening here. His secretary, Krüger, reports that sailors have occupied the building and the switchboard. He knows no other details. So Ebert sends him around the building to determine which of the other people's deputies are there.

In Barth's office, from the opening salvos on, the chair has broken into open rebellion. As is only fitting for a chair that has finally come to its senses, it planted kick after kick. The people's deputy understands none of this, and in his amazement tries to sit down again. He still has not realized for whom the bell tolls (or in this case, the chair kicks). He has to carry on his conversation with Undersecretary von Möllendorf from a standing position, a debate about the economy, and this is how he is discovered by Krüger, whom Ebert has sent around to see who is still in the building. Barth dismisses Möllendorf at once and joins Ebert, full of dire foreboding.

"You sent for me, Herr Ebert." (No first-name basis with Ebert for him.)

With Ebert sit Scheidemann and the head of the Reichs Chancellery. (What is going on here?)

Ebert: "Did I? I know nothing about that." (Cool as a cucumber.)

Barth: "All right then, Krüger sent for me."

Landsberg: "He was only supposed to check to see if you were still here and might want to keep us company." (Mocking laughter, though inaudible.)

"What do you mean 'company'?"

"Well, you know all about it. Perhaps even better than we. We're under arrest."

"Don't make jokes. What's that supposed to mean?"

"I see. Then I'll give you the news. The sailors have locked us up in the Reichs Chancellery. We can't even make telephone calls."

Barth: "But that's pure nonsense. Can't make calls? Well, I'll see about that."

He storms out, runs to his office, to the telephone. He receives the answer that the lines are blocked. He rages, he forbids such a thing, he is People's Deputy Emil Barth, and he demands to be connected. That unsettles the men at the switchboard, and after some hesitation he gets his connection.

Ebert does not like this affair at all. But he makes the best of a bad bargain and sends Krüger down to the sailors guarding the building. Would they please send yet another delegation from the royal stables for negotiations.

When sailors emerge from the Reichs Chancellery to inform Lieutenant Dorrenbach of this, he is convinced that those fellows in there have weakened, and that he can now press forward to harvest the fruits of his decisive action. When he is once in the Reichs Chancellery, where he enters Ebert's office with several of his men, he is not a little surprised to hear that Ebert's intentions go no further than to try to convince him to give up the occupation of the Reichs Chancellery. It was a foolish act, but they'll let the matter rest at that. Now wasn't that the limit.

Dorrenbach, the rough, monosyllabic lieutenant, listens with great self-control to the little, fat, genial and pompous Social Democrat. He realizes that he is trying to pull the trumps from his hand, but he has got the wrong man. There is no mention at all of being paid, which apparently implies that everything remains as it was—they are supposed to kiss Wels's feet.

He answers icily: "No." And his companions, too, shake their heads.

The crafty man across from him now drops his smile and attempts to drape himself in dignity. He notices the mocking twitch of Dorrenbach's moustache. He thinks he has him, Ebert, in a trap. The conversation is at an end.

When the head of the Reich's Chancellery enters, Ebert does not look up from his desk so as not to betray that he's mad as hell and that the old terror has swept over him: he has seen revolution eyeball to eyeball. He quietly informs the official that the conversation proved fruitless.

Then he locks himself in, plays upon his solo instrument, secret line 998 to Wilhelmshöhe. Those clever sailors have occupied the switchboard, true, but they knew as little about the secret line to General Army Headquarters as does anyone else in the building.

Groener, quartermaster general in Kassel, rejoices greatly to hear from Berlin at such an unaccustomed hour. The calls are normally made in the evening. He carefully inquires after Ebert's health. Well, replies Ebert, he is only feeling so-so. The Spartacists, to be more precise a couple of fellows from the People's Naval Division, have locked him into the Reichs Chancellery.

"Well, well. You don't say! —"

"Yes. Has to do with matters of pay, purest formalities, it's all been arranged, these people have been incited by others."

114

Groener rejoices greatly all the more. The fellow in Berlin is in a jam, and if he is calling now he naturally wants help.

Aloud, he expresses his sympathies with this deputy of the revolution now begging for help. He cheers him up: "So you see, what a good thing it is that we have this connection." He means the telephone line. "Those fellows have blocked the switchboard of course."

"Yes, they have."

"That's what I figured. Well, we'll put everything back in order simple as pie, Your Excellency. One telephone call to Lequis and the damage is repaired."

Ebert thanks him. Groener laughs (and so now you've learned a lesson, my boy, that I hope you'll take note of).

A short while after this secret conversation, the telephone in Emil Barth's office buzzes. Klawunde, chairman of the Potsdam Soldiers' Council, is on the line, very excited. In Potsdam at that very moment, several regiments of infantry and cavalry were being shipped off to Berlin. What was the meaning of that? —

Barth is no soothsayer. He knows nothing either. They exchange their ignorance about this course of events. Whereupon Barth declares that he will go to Ebert and ask him.

Ebert, however, knew nothing about it. He sat there in his office, apparently hard at work, the epitome of calm. What nerves of steel the man must have.

He inquired about the details of this report, particularly who it was that had called it in—and appeared not to believe any of it. Then, however, since matters "military" were his concern, he said he would do Barth a favor and look into the rumor—just as soon as he was permitted to make telephone calls. Barth replied he would see to it that that was possible; Ebert simply must forbid this troop transport. "Of course," Ebert said, "just as soon as it is possible for me to do so."

Of what all it was possible for Ebert to do, however, Barth had only a vague notion. Ebert could, for example, send a personal messenger over to Wels at headquarters. Because everyone familiar with the terrain of the Reichs Chancellery—of course our good Barth was not one of these—knew that you could walk over to the Foreign Office via several interior courtyards. And it was via this route that City Commandant Wels now learned what these sailors had pulled off behind his back in their lust for pay, the very sailors who were pacing up and down Unter den Linden before his very eyes. They had occupied the Reichs Chancellery, locked up the government, and were now holding them as pawns in the game. Well then, swore Wels, the military lord of Berlin, I'll see to it that it gives them indigestion.

And immediately he set out to alert his Republican Militia in their barracks, and had come back again at once to organize in person the storming of the Reichs Chancellery and free the government, when— he himself was arrested. In front of headquarters, you see, he ran right into the rifles of the sailors.

There stood little Lieutenant Dorrenbach with his men, who had had enough and more than enough and for whom there was only one possibility: arrest them, lock them up—in short, make a clean sweep.

They led Wels to his office, where at first he still assumed that he could talk some sense into them. He threatened them; he wanted to know just where the keys to the palace were, whether Ebert had them or someone else.

The keys, little Dorrenbach answered, had long since been returned to the palace.

Well then—and Wels acted as if nothing at all had happened—he could not pay them their eighty thousand marks.

But it was certainly no longer a matter of eighty thousand marks.

It was late afternoon, almost six o'clock, and it had grown dark. Sailors were stationed in Wels's office, and now they had this fellow, the one who had given them all this trouble, the one whose fault it was that the channels by which they were paid no longer functioned—ever since they had brought down that traitor, Count Wolff-Metternich. And they had even carried the strongbox to the Reichs Chancellery. And even Barth's word hadn't been good enough for him.

And while they argued with him, a detachment of sailors moved up from the south along Charlottenstrasse and then down Unter den Linden. Another detachment of sailors, several hundred men strong, marched down Oberwallstrasse to Opernplatz. And others as well marched across the Palace Bridge. Municipal headquarters was surrounded.

But then from below there also came the rumble of headquarters' own armored cars, driving up Oberwallstrasse to counter the sailors. And from an adjoining building, once the palace of the crown prince and now the barracks of the Republican Militia, machine guns were rolled out. And the government's armored cars rattled up Unter den Linden toward headquarters, broke through the line of sailors attempting to halt them; and as they drove by they opened fire on the sailors stationed in front of headquarters, killing one of them and seriously wounding three others.

At the sound of shots and the general uproar, Wels rushed out onto the balcony and called down, "Cease fire. Don't shoot."

116

But the calamity had already occurred.

Within moments, Wels was encircled in his office by enraged sailors. They forced their way through doors and windows into headquarters. They threatened to lynch him.

From below came a shout of command. The sailors closed ranks and started to move down Wilhelmstrasse. At first they wanted to bear their fallen comrade at the head of the column, so that they could show him to Ebert. But then they dropped the idea. This was not a moment for demonstrations. They moved toward Wilhelmstrasse in double time. The iron gates that had been opened in the meantime now banged shut again.

But the sailors were not the only ones standing there on Wilhelmstrasse now. Wels's call to arms had had its effect. Columns of Republican Militia had marched up and still others were streaming in. Slowly they advanced, so that gradually a formation of troops stood between the two hostile groups: the sailors standing in front of the Reichs Chancellery, and on the opposite side of the street the militia. They eyed one another across the pavement, but did nothing. There remained in fact enough space between them for private cars to pass along the street. (For its part the city lay meanwhile in perfect peace; traffic was normal. The police had already taken matters in hand, and Wilhelmstrasse was completely cut off from Wilhelmplatz and Unter den Linden. For the police, this tumult had the earmarks of a civil brawl that needed to be isolated.)

The lynching of Wels proceeded in the same mild manner. While they were threatening him with death, their pistols aimed at him, the telephone rang. His lynchers made way for him to answer. Who was it? Why what do you know, General Lequis, of all people Lequis, who replied by asking how he was doing.

Wels answered frostily, "Not so well," and if Lequis would come by he would consider it a real favor. With that he hung up, and the lynching could proceed.

The sailors declared that they most certainly could not release him now, not after the shooting incident, not before he paid the eighty thousand marks and recognized them as troops to be stationed permanently in Berlin. It was obvious they were upping their demands. Wels was in fact willing to bite the bullet as far as the money went. But to recognize these barbarians as permanent troops was not at all to his taste, he would rather bite off his own tongue. Furthermore, he could not do so anyway. So there was nothing for it but to lynch him. But the hour was apparently a bit advanced for that. So they announced to Wels that for the time being he was under arrest, along with his lieutenant, Anton Fischer, and his secretary, Bongartz. And they transported the whole lot of them off to the royal stables.

Once again the police took matters in hand, just to keep things within civil limits and to make certain that the public was not inconvenienced while the revolution was being obstructed. Officers preceded the transport. Breite Strasse, down which the procession moved, was therefore, cleared in advance.

In the meantime, as before, the two warring parties eyed each other on Wilhelmstrasse. Many of the men on one side knew some of the others personally. Moreover, as we are already aware, it was in point of fact the ambition of the sailors to join the other side, that is to become members of the Republican Militia at better pay, something their opponents knew. It would definitely be difficult to speak of bellicosity on the part of these soldiers, since they now occupied the positions for which the sailors yearned; and they were not about to die for them on the spot.

Which resulted in conversations across the street, more or less salty and tense ones, when suddenly a shout sounded from the ranks of the soldiers to the effect that they wanted to send negotiators to the Reichs Chancellery. Well, let them have their negotiators. Evening fell, the cold intensified. The whole affair was becoming boring as time dragged on.

And so across the no-man's-land of the pavement, heading for the Reichs Chancellery, there marched a delegation of the militia—and if they did not greet one another with joy, at least they felt good about it—with Brutus Molkenbuhr in the lead and at full speed. On the far side their inimical brothers made way for them, the iron gate creaked open, and in they went.

Once inside, they expressed their trust in and sympathy for the reincarcerated martyr, Friedrich Ebert, and could not help but disapprove of the sailors' action. Now that was music to Ebert's ears. He praised them, but he warned them not to shed blood. There must be negotiations. They understood that, too, and it was what they wanted as well. They both assured each other that enough blood had been shed in the war. Whereupon they took leave of Ebert and crossed back through enemy lines in front of the Reichs Chancellery. They drove off to the royal stables.

There was a long exchange back and forth between Wilhelmstrasse and the stables until the following suggestion was accepted:

"The occupation of the Reichs Chancellery is to be ended. The hostile parties will pull back from Wilhelmstrasse, with the sailors retreating to Unter den Linden, the Militia to Leipziger Strasse."

This was immediately put into action. With heads held high, the sailors marched toward Unter den Linden. Before the militia had retreated with heads held equally high, Ebert appeared before them on the street and said:

"We have determined that the sailors have left the building. Now you must depart as well. I beg you to do everything in your power to avoid bloodshed. Return to your quarters."

There was nothing they would rather have done.

It was 10 P.M. Quick as a wink, Wilhelmstrasse lay peaceful, quiet, and dark.

One question: what had been accomplished?

The sailors had put Wels in a dark hole inside the royal stables. Commander Radtke visited him there and was of the opinion that if they were going to lynch him, they could at least provide him with a clean room. Which was then done.

What had Ebert accomplished? He was no longer a prisoner; Wels, on the other hand, was.

And what the status of the sailors' eighty thousand marks was now, nobody knew.

Bloody Christmas

At eleven o'clock a call was placed to the stables from Wilhelmstrasse: Had Wels been set free?

Answer: No.

At twelve, the same call. Answer: No.

Again at one. Answer: No.

Ebert did not go home. Lieutenant Dorrenbach had pricked him. He had stood across from him, and at that moment he knew: this was no joke. Ebert's rage, invisible to others, grew with each telephone call. Scheidemann and Landsberg stayed with him. When Radtke reported from the palace at one in the morning that Wels was still being held, Ebert had made his decision.

He said: "You cannot guarantee us that Wels will come out alive. We'll have to go in and get him, if need be by force."

He hung up the receiver and was about to call the War Ministry. The other two got involved at that point.

"The War Ministry, call in the War Ministry on that account? Everything has gone smoothly enough up till now, except for the gunfire in front of headquarters. Once you call in the War Ministry, the matter takes on an entirely different color."

"And how do you suggest we free Wels? Radtke will not guarantee us he'll come out alive."

"But to call in the War Ministry? You're against bloodshed after all." No, the other two could not see it. And in any case, to do that they would have to call an official cabinet meeting and the three Independents were missing for that.

Ebert pulled his bullneck in even more. "I'm in charge of military matters. I don't need a cabinet for this. I'll not be led around by the nose. The occupation of the Chancellery this afternoon was scandal enough all by itself. We're letting them make us the laughing-stock of the world. I insist that something be done for Wels, and I mean at once, right now."

Dorrenbach had done this to him. The other two, Scheidemann and Landsberg, did not know what to say. They sat there doing nothing, humble and unsure, while Ebert picked up the receiver and demanded to speak with the War Ministry, with Minister Scheuch. He informed him that sailors were holding City Commandant Wels prisoner at the royal stables and that his life was in danger. He had to be freed and the sailors brought to reason.

Scheuch replied, "Agreed," and passed the order on to General Lequis of the Guard Cavalry Rifles.

Ebert began at once to pace about his office in the Reichs Chancellery while his two friends sat there anxious and cringing. No discussion was ventured. They coughed—as if they had all choked on something.

When the troops had marched into the city on December 12th, General Lequis had not been able to use his cannons. Now they were to have their turn. They could speak their mind.

The participants were almost robbed of the joy of this happy occasion at the last moment, when Radtke called from the stables to report that his comrades had calmed down to the extent that they were ready to negotiate. He, Radtke, had already invited old man Ledebour to take part in these discussions, who would be arriving before the night was out.

But it is the nature of cannons that once in place they can but speak. They cannot be made to listen. Apparently the noise of their own boom destroys their sense of hearing. Radtke and Ledebour at least could not prevail. Once issued, a command from the War Ministry in

Berlin to the staff of a division in the same city travels fast, and can be executed even faster, since preparations for such an order have long since been made.

The masters of the cannon, moreover, felt very sure of their cause.

Having installed their staff headquarters in the Princesses' Palace on Unter den Linden, they sent a delegation of five men with a white flag over to the royal stables as morning dawned around seven-thirty—it is Christmas Eve Day. There are no civilian militiamen to interfere now.

At seven-fifty these envoys arrive at the stables and are led into the sailors at once. In a strident voice of command, a young lieutenant reads the following ultimatum to the men from Kiel:

"The sailors are to surrender, while all just demands they may have are to be met. All sailors in the palace and the royal stables are to assemble unarmed in the palace square.

"Ten minutes are permitted for consideration."

Without considering a thing, the sailors' council said no. The beardless lieutenant had made their answer an easy one.

At precisely eight o'clock the first cannons let loose. They were large, 10.5-cm flat trajectory guns. The attack was led by Colonel von Tschirschky.

The cannons were placeed on the Schloss Bridge and out on Werder Market. The Guard Cuirassier Regiment fired with light rifles from Französische Strasse.

The palace took a heavy beating. The bullets seemed to have a special preference for the historic balcony from which Wilhelm II had declared in August, 1914, that he no longer recognized political parties, only Germans; this was now a palpable, though actually superfluous disavowal of that remark.

At this stage, the sailors could not take any real part in any military discussion. They had only one heavy piece of artillery and some machine guns.

The shooting lasted from eight to ten o'clock. Then there was a pause while women and children were evacuated from the stables. At ten-thirty, firing was resumed.

Despite the doggedness of the sailors, this would have been a lost battle, since they had no weapons to boast of—if the battle had taken place anywhere else. But it took place in the middle of Berlin. As is well-known, rivers, hills, difficulties of terrain play a decisive role. In Berlin the difficulties of terrain were people.

At the proud and boastful boom of the cannons, civilians awoke from their sleep, understanding at once the cannons' message. They

121

came running to express their own opinions. And that they came running, rather than running away, was a sign that they understood the cannons' message.

At the Stock Exchange, proletarian hordes assembled, and this time not with placards on poles or with songs and hurrahs and boos, but with rifles held against their cheeks. Civilians came running across the Lustgarten from the direction of the museum. They grabbed two machine guns from the third column of the Potsdam Lancers and rushed forward with them. The line of sentries posted by the Whites in front of the palace was breached.

The moment he heard the shooting, the Berlin chief of police, Emil Eichhorn, an Independent Socialist, had sent out his special security patrols as was his duty—to what end it is difficult to say, at any rate for the security of the inhabitants of Berlin, however he interpreted that. Most of them, then, were very quickly on hand; they shoved their way between the sailors and the soldiers from Potsdam and then attacked the men from Potsdam.

This seemed to them to be the best means of guaranteeing Berlin's security.

More and more civilians from the awakening city became involved. As we said, the terrain had its difficulties. Fearlessly, men and women approached the positions taken by the government troops, for after all these were their own Berlin streets. They had a right to use them, to take their walks there, and to demand to know what was going on in them. These men and women debated with the soldiers, and were not to be shooed away by these fancy officers.

Also to be found among the government troops were those proud men of the Republican Militia who were getting higher pay, and who had got cold feet the evening before on Wilhelmstrasse. Now, however, they could use their legs, lay their rifles to their cheeks, and, if they wished, aim at the blue-jackets and their hangers-on. But when these soldiers began to move about among the sailors and the Guard Cavalry Rifles, and women began telling them all sorts of things about these men from Potsdam who were shooting although no one had done anything to them, they came to the conclusion that it would be better to join the sailors.

Which is what happened. They went over en masse to the sailors, as they should have done the day before in Wilhelmstrasse.

As we have seen, it was Friedrich Ebert all by himself who had pushed the button causing the hard-of-hearing flat-trajectory artillery and other cannons to open fire. The noise they created also awakened the three Independent people's deputies who were a part of the government, awakened them from a very deep and salubrious sleep. (Independents always slept well in those days; constant doubt and indecision tired them out so.) They took fright, for this meant back to work, back to doubting. They hurried out onto the street. The battle was already raging. Cannons were being fired in the center of the city. Could that be Ebert's doing? He was in charge of military matters. But what was the military? Something to doubt. One only needed to turn one's back and right away something happened. Things were bound to happen when one didn't know what was supposed to happen. They hurried to the Reichs Chancellery. All the way there, the situation looked bellicose.

They entered the Reichs Chancellery excited and frightened. All hell was breaking loose. Ebert's friends were sparing in their comments and did not appear to understand. There were numerous rumors about the course of the battle.

Ebert had just been called to the office of the head of the Chancellery. An officer had arrived, sent by General Lequis to deliver a message. Ebert stood there, a short man with a gray face who needed sleep, his head between his shoulders; before him stood the proud officer, who reported softly: "We cannot hold our position. Our troops are completely paralyzed. The rebels have mobilized civilians and women and children who preclude any military action. Either we proceed with negotiations, or . . ."

"Or?" Ebert asked, his heart pounding.

"Or we must withdraw from battle."

Ebert thanked him. He walked slowly to his office, where in addition to his two friends the three Independents awaited him. With a grim look, but without answering, he listened to the questions of the outraged Independents. His own friends were curious to see how he would defend himself. But he picked up the telephone receiver and asked to be connected with the War Ministry.

"Yes, Ebert speaking. Morning, Your Excellency. Thank you. I hear that at the moment the Guard Cavalry Rifle division is engaged in an attack on the stables and the palace. Yes, I've just received the report. Will you please see to it that these hostilities are discontinued. It is the wish of the entire cabinet. We want to avoid any further bloodshed, and therefore we are asking for negotiations. Negotiations, yes. Thank you."

A quarter of an hour later, a car began moving down Französische Strasse, heading in the direction of the royal stables. Inside sat one officer and one civilian. A soldier carrying a rifle with fixed bayonet rode the running board. A white flag fluttered from the bayonet. They drove up to the stables.

Colonel von Tschirschky and a representative of the government got out of the car. The negotiations were over in fifteen minutes.

Immediately afterward, several sailors, armed and unarmed, come out of the stables. No one fires. The government troops begin to pull back. By eleven o'clock a general retreat is in full swing.

The flat-trajectory guns roll as well, backward this time. They know nothing about forward or backward; they just fire away, mere flat-trajectory guns after all, dreadfully stupid asses, muttonheaded idiots that you can do with as you will. There's no point in leading them to slaughter, since they are only advance troops of steel and mere symbols of the others made of flesh. If you want something of them, then you must deal with the men standing behind them.

The Republican Militia, lacking a pure conscience, assembles and leaves the arena of its spiritual agonies.

At twelve noon, however, hundreds of armed civilians move in to occupy the stables. The whole area around the stables—all the way up Königstrasse, the Schlossplatz, Breite Strasse as far as the Mühlendamm—fills with people, civilians, sailors and soldiers, all of them of good cheer. New machine guns arrive. From the crowd come threats and taunts. The area is transformed into an army camp. The impression one gets here is not one of victory by the Potsdam forces.

The agreement arrived at reads:

"The People's Naval Division pledges to leave the palace at once, as soon as the agreement of December 18th is carried out, which provides them with office space in the royal stables.

"The sailors will be incorporated into the Republican Militia, which is under the command of the city commandant. The manner in which they are incorporated into the militia remains to be decided in a later agreement.

"The sailors pledge not to take part in any future actions against the government.

"General Lequis's division will be pulled back at once. The sailors and soldiers will return to their quarters.

"City Commandant Wels is to be set free at once."

On the government side there were two dead and two wounded.

The Naval Division had nine men to mourn, and countless numbers of them left the battle wounded, some lightly, some severely. In addition, there were twenty casualties from the ranks of the civilians who had joined in combat.

As Philipp Scheidemann was leaving Ebert's office, his hands across his back and taking the corridor in slow strides in search of his own office, he could not believe his eyes: there stood Otto Wels before him. But in what a state! A specter, his clothes torn, his countenance fallen, his hands trembling.

Scheidemann led him to his office, laid him on the sofa and called for some cognac, which slowly brought life back to the fainting man. Scheidemann had him lie back down, and ran again to Ebert to tell him Wels was there, but in what a state.

He found Ebert reading a train schedule. A map of the train system lay in full view on his desk. Ebert threw Scheidemann a quick, somber glance as he burst into the room with his news, and then he immersed himself once more in the timetable.

Scheidemann: "Well, what do we do with him?"

Ebert finally deigned to raise his head. "You've no greater cares than that? He'll recover on the sofa."

Scheidemann: "And then where shall I have him taken, what's to become of him?"

Ebert: "Wels is finished. We have no more use for him."

Scheidemann was thunderstruck. "No more use for him? Why? Because a couple of madmen wanted to kill him?"

Ebert examined him with unfriendly eyes and muttered, while turning back to examine his map, "Our concern now is not for persons, but for the cause." (By which he meant himself.)

And then he took pity on Scheidemann and folded up the map. "Perhaps we can take him with us, just so he doesn't fall into their hands."

Which had such an effect on the fully unsuspecting Scheidemann that he reached for the closest chair and sat down. He stared at Ebert, who with an inscrutable tranquillity was again thumbing through the timetable, and stammered, "Are things so—bad?"

It turned out that Ebert had already had the head of the Reichs Chancellery order a train for the government.

The whole government, Ebert said, was going to be evacuated from Berlin. The only thing not yet decided was the departure time.

"Lequis has left. The sailors and Spartacus will follow through. We can't stay here. The trouble is I don't know where we can stay."

They were beaten and on the run. There was no arguing with Ebert in the matter, as little as there had been the night before about the order given the War Ministry.

But while Ebert sat there brooding mutely at his desk, with that thick head of his and his arms crossed, Scheidemann, though frightened to death, suddenly had the impression that his friend had fallen victim to pessimism, as sometimes happens with fat men who must labor with their stomachs.

He tried to coax him. He did not react. His face did not light up. This could get dangerous for all of us, Philipp thought, for me as well. Scheidemann, who had just poured cognac down Wels, ran to see Landsberg.

He hastily confided his worries to him.

They sat down together with Ebert, taking his map and his timetable away from him. They worked on him for a full half an hour. Scheidemann pondered whether simply to put him on a fast or to dose him with Glauber's salt in order to save the nation.

At last Ebert was mollified. He sighed and gave in, but he also said, "Sooner or later we'll have to go anyway."

Scheidemann told him he'd feel better after two glasses of Glauber's salt.

Then they turned their attention to the half-dead Wels, who was no longer city commandant.

That evening, however, Ebert began to seethe with rage. His eyes grew red. He knew on whom he could unleash his anger.

He locked himself in his office and called Kassel.

General Lequis's magnificent troops, who were eager to disarm all Berlin on December 12th, and were expected to do so—even with heavy artillery they had been unable to deal with the sailors!

Groener thanked him for his call and said that Lequis had already given him the information.

Ebert: "And where do we go from here? What is our next move?"

Groener, cool and obliging: "First of all, we've seen to it that you are no longer locked up inside the Reichs Chancellery."

Ebert, bitterly: "That can happen all over again tomorrow. What else?"

Groener: "I can't predict anything at the moment. In all Berlin, by the way, we have only one hundred and fifty men, Herr Reichs Chancellor. Please take that into consideration. I repeat: one hundred and fifty. The High Command is returning to Kassel."

"Now that's just charming. I'm very indebted to Your Excellency for the information. To tell the truth, Your Excellency, I've had just about enough."

Groener, repressing a malicious laugh: "I can sympathize with that. Won't you join us in Kassel?"

Ebert (he's gotten me into this, and now he wants to leave me holding the bag): "Thanks. I'm just studying a map of the train system."

"Of Germany?"

"Yes, what did you think?" Ebert paused to digest the question. "I've been consulting with my friends how best to organize our resistance."

Groener: "I see. Well, what do you know! My congratulations. Perhaps you'll keep me informed."

Ebert, gruffly: "Seeing that we've been deserted on all sides."

Groener (without reacting): "I can understand, Herr Reichs Chancellor." (And he thinks: not a bad situation on the whole—he leaves, there's Red Terror in Berlin, people will have to rally round us; we're all there is.) "But where are you thinking of going, seeing it's Christmas."

Ebert: "To friends, near Berlin. I've been invited. I desperately need a holiday. I've not been out of my boots for weeks, so to speak. I owe it to my family. I'll see to it that the other gentlemen also make themselves scarce at the Reichs Chancellery. I'm leaving no one but the porter in the building."

Groener: "Hmm. But won't people get the impression that the crew has deserted the ship of state if your vacation lasts several days and includes the whole staff?"

Ebert: "No concern of mine. We're sitting on a powder keg. If they lock us in here tomorrow, nobody will be able to get us out. I'm going up the Havel, where the scenery's lovely, and I'm going to get some sleep. If Liebknecht comes here to Wilhelmstrasse, he'll find the place empty, and his efforts will be nothing more than a puff of air."

Groener: "But he'll be sitting in the Reichs Chancellery."

Ebert: "Then we set up a government somewhere else."

Groener (let him think that. I would like to tease him just a bit more): "Well then, what do you say to Kassel, Herr Reichs Chancellor? We've always gotten along well together till now."

Ebert: "To be frank, I'd prefer not to strain the relationship."

Groener (bravo, now I've got you to admit it, old friend; and the feeling is mutual by the by): "I understand."

Ebert: "Merry Christmas, Your Excellency."

Groener: "My sincerest thanks, Herr Reichs Chancellor. Have a restful holiday."

Karl and Rosa, Two Butterflies, Flutter Near

They fluttered nearer, the two butterflies Karl and Rosa—Karl a mourning cloak with black wings unfolded wide; Rosa shimmering brightly, her wings beating violently.

They played about the ponderous, inert log named Ebert and bounced off the spike of the helmet of the great General Staff.

From what lands had they come? What strange climate had produced them? They had something magical, foreign about them. It was the magic and the strangeness of a dream. Many there were who swarmed along in their wake, many who gazed at them in wonder, many whom they filled with terror and disgust.

Before the war, Karl Liebknecht was just as much an anonymity as Friedrich Ebert. But in 1914, Karl quickly made up for his shameful error of August 4th, when he had voted for war loans with the other Social Democrats in the Reichstag.

Hardly a week before, his Party had circulated a flyer:

"A summons! The soil of the Balkans is still steaming with the blood of thousands who were butchered; the rubble of razed cities and ravaged villages still smokes, starving men without work still wander the countryside, as do widows and orphans—and once again the fury of war unleashed by Austrian imperialism is preparing to spread death and devastation across all of Europe.

"The class-conscious proletariat of Germany raises its flaming protest against the criminal actions of these warmongers in the name of humanity and civilization. Not one drop of a German soldier's blood shall be sacrificed for the potentates of Austria itching for power, for the profit interests of imperialists.

"Comrades, we urge you to express your unshakable desire for peace at once in mass meetings of the class-conscious proletariat. World war threatens. The ruling classes who gag you, despise you and exploit you in peacetime now hope to use you as cannonfodder.

"We do not want war. Down with war! Long live international solidarity!"

So pealed the bell on July 25, 1914.

It pealed differently on August 4th.

"We stand now before the brazen fact of war.

"We are threatened by the terror of an enemy invasion.

"Today we are not called upon to decide for or against war, but to respond in defense of our country with all means necessary.

"A victory of Russian despotism, which has befouled itself with the blood of the best of its own people, would place this nation and its people, our peaceful future, indeed perhaps everything in jeopardy.

"We will live up to what we have always maintained; we will not desert the Fatherland in its hour of danger.

"In so doing, we feel ourselves in accord with the International, which upholds the right of national independence and self-defense for every people, just as we likewise reject along with the International all wars of conquest.

"Led by these principles, we endorse the requested war loans."

As the Party leader read this before a breathlessly attentive Reichstag on August 4, 1914, the house erupted in cheers, and Karl, too, voted "yes" for the sake of solidarity. But it would not leave him in peace until he recanted, privately and publicly, and until at last they arrested him, called him up to do fatigue duty as a soldier and sent him to the Russian front. On the Dvina, outside Riga, he was forced to shovel, digging trenches for the advance line.

"I am in Russia," he wrote Sonya, his wife, "but under what grizzly circumstances. I cannot describe my psychological state. To be without a will of your own, to be the tool of a power you profoundly abhor—and what interests that power represents!"

He thought a great deal about home. He was a restless, hot-tempered, passionate man. This marriage to Sonya, who came from the Ukraine, was his second. They had married three years before; he was consumed with love and yearning for her. His children from his first marriage, to whom he was devoted, lived with her.

"I want to build the happiest future I can for you all," he wrote to them from so far away. "To give you all the energy and sunshine there is. I love you as much as any father ever loved his children. Don't ever doubt that. Powers beyond my control have continually driven me away from my family."

Those "powers" were his idealism, which had driven him to do uninterrupted battle with society. His fellow citizens, the heirs of classical humanism, had long ago cynically turned idealism into a school subject for their children.

His comrades in the Party, the heirs of socialism, had made an organization with weekly meetings and dues out of it. But for Karl, Plato and Sophocles, Shakespeare and Goethe were still prophets who proclaimed a new humanity.

There were times there on the Dvina when he sank into despair:

"Sonya, it is dark all around me. Someone is singing. I am afraid I will lose you. So afraid, I'm crazy with fear. All of past history is alive to me, and I shall drown in it, if you do not lift me up.

"I love you so, and reach out my hands toward you. Love me, help me. I can do nothing without you. Everything disintegrates inside me."

Once he was lying outside along a hedgerow, this man of moods, resting during a supper break. Yellow blossoms of bedstraw waved above his head, against a background of deep blue sky. He thought again of "her"—how it had been that time "next to the cabbage patch surrounded by lupine," when "bliss overwhelmed you."

And finally they locked him up, after a scorching speech at Potsdamer Platz in Berlin on May 1, 1916. He had been granted leave. Finally, a public statement of principles—and then prison.

They put him in Luckau, an hour's express-train ride from Berlin, in a roomy cell. He found a porcelain stove and a large window that he could open himself, with a view of a large exercise yard with trees, and he jotted down:

> You've stolen the earth from me, but not the sky.
> And even if it's only a narrow strip that my
> Eyes can make out.
> Through wire grating,
> Between iron bars,
> Oppressed by heavy walls,
> It is enough
> To view its peaceful, radiant blue.

> You've stolen the earth from me, but not the sky.
> And even if it's only a narrow strip, cramped
> Through wire grating between bars of iron:
> It makes the very meaning of life,
> Quickened by a free soul, freer
> Than ever were you who think to destroy me
> Here in prison with your chains.

He kept up his strength in prison. He took care that confinement did not break him or bend him. He never knew despair—not in prison. He had no wild dreams, and carried on no spectral conversations. He took his exercise and cold rub-downs only at designated times. He made shoes and glued paper sacks, and all sorts of jobs held his interest. The cell made him keener and more determined.

And so the days passed. He was supposed to be in until 1920, four years. Patiently he checked off each day gone by.

He read whatever the prison library afforded, even Willibald Alexis and Theodor Fontane, "the Prussian poet of the nineteenth century, though descended from French ancestors. What do our idiotic nationalists have to say to that?"

Reports from Russia after the overthrow of the Czar—the negotiations at Brest-Litovsk, Lenin's peace policy—they excited and confused him just as they had Rosa. From the first, he rejected the notion promulgated by German socialists that Lenin and Trotsky—though formerly internationalists, socialists true to their principles—had become Russian opportunists, proving themselves common demagogues who for a transient moment of victory had deserted to the camp of the German imperialists. He knew that these Bolsheviks had no intention of following the example of a Scheidemann, a David, or an Ebert. But the news made him unhappy nevertheless.

"They're playing a risky game," he noted, "moving toward a peace that they would have been better off to let the czarists make. The government they'll be setting up in Russia will be the one the German Kaiser wants."

The war thundered to an end. In 1918 Karl was forty-eight years old. He did not know, even at the height of that summer, how things stood. At the beginning of September he wrote Sonya a letter meant for their anniversary—Sonya, the beloved of this middle-aged man:

"If I were a free man, Sonya, I would give you an edition of Milton for a present. We would sit down on the sofa and read the fourth book. And by evening I would be the Satan of the ninth book, "with rapine sweet bereaved . . .""

And then — he was released.

And now he had everything, Sonya, his children and the struggle against war, the Kaiser, the generals, against capitalism, and against the Social Democratic Party.

He gave himself to it completely. This was life, his life. No one could say of him that he had wasted his life.

His campaign slogan—he continued to be the impetuous and insistent youth—was:

> I cannot waver, but only dare,
> Nor reap the harvest—only sow and flee.
> I cannot stand the hot noon's glare;
> A dawn, and then the twilight's majesty,
> Such is my day."

For the moment he stood in the midst of the fray.

131

They Hated Karl and Had Wanted to Catch Him Early On

A man whom no one knew entered the editorial offices and asked for Karl. He was not there, they showed the man out. He came back, again to be shown the door. But now they told Karl about him, and he laughed and wanted to get a look at the man. When he appeared for the third time, Karl actually took him along with him back to his office. After a half hour he came out again with the man in a fine mood, and they said a friendly, even jovial good-bye.

In the office Karl laughed at his friends. "You're seeing ghosts! What was supposed to be wrong with him? That's a capital fellow, a sincere man, a poor guy down on his luck, but one I can't help, either, I'm afraid. You're crazy, all of you."

And afterward he made a point of saying to them: "A visitor like that is really refreshing."

The man did not come back.

But then one day, shortly after the disturbance with the sailors, Karl was heading for his office when an officer moving down the street with a small military patrol confronted him, grabbed hold of him, and called him by name. He declared that he would have to arrest Karl on orders of the Berlin city commandant.

It was lunchtime and the street was busy. Other people gathered around the group of soldiers and this loudly protesting civilian. Not a little surprised, Karl recognized the officer as the nice fellow who had been so stubborn about looking for him at his office and had finally managed to meet him. Karl reminded the officer of this conversation in his office. The officer said he was sorry, but he could not get involved in private conversations.

"But I have very urgent business myself at my office," Karl declared, "that is no private matter either. I insist that you first allow me to go to my office with my attaché case, so that I can inform the friends who are waiting there for me."

Among the people who had gathered there were sailors as well, sailors of the unemployed and perambulating sort. They entered into the conversation and suggested that since Karl seemed to be an affable fellow and was not even attempting to resist arrest, there really was no reason why he should not be allowed to go to his office. The officer had to give in (we recall these "difficulties of terrain" in Berlin, with which a short while before the Guard Cavalry Rifle division had also become acquainted). The soldiers accompanied Karl. Two of them took up positions at the door to the newspaper offices and two on the ground floor at the door to the building.

Karl, however, did not come back out. He was on the telephone. He was talking with police headquarters and explaining to Police Chief Eichhorn what he was having to deal with. Within a very brief five minutes, several speeding cars from Eichhorn's security forces hurtled up and placed the whole magnificent bunch of soldiers under arrest.

They were transported to police headquarters in patrol cars. The officer admitted that he had personally prepared and arranged Karl's arrest. That he had failed was exclusively the fault of the telephone. He had not included that in his calculations.

And what had been the point of it all? Why? On whose orders?

Oh, it wasn't a matter of politics. He didn't mess around with that. But a certain organization had offered ten thousand marks to any man who brought Karl in. The whole thing, the cynical fellow laughed, was simply a kidnapping.

He wanted to apologize to Karl personally, however, whom he had come to know as an amiable fellow.

The officer's name was von T.

From somewhere up the ladder of command, as was to be expected, came the order to let him go.

The revolution swallowed Karl body and soul.

After the affair with the People's Naval Division, on the day after Christmas to be precise, he spent a few hours with his family in the upper-middle-class apartment of that cultivated Berlin lawyer Dr. Karl Liebknecht; there he played songs for the children on the piano and sang for them. He sat down with Sonya in her room and together they read from Byron's "Don Juan."

She was a young, saucy girl, but today her manner was downcast, because she felt she was being neglected. She had thick black hair and animated black eyes that could cast open, tender and fervent glances. Her strong, healthy body with its full bosom was sheathed today in a warm, light-blue house dress. She wore a necklace of thick, green glass beads, and above her wrist on her left arm a wide bronze bracelet, which she stared at long and hard before casting an accusatory glance at Karl; the bracelet served in a sense as the springboard or the prompter's box for her accusation.

She pouted. "What are you running around for like this? Who are the people you always have time for? Not for me at least."

He loved this tone of hers. Jealousy was a barometer of love. Without jealousy, love lost its spice for him. And Sonya was untiring in employing the battle tactics of love—pulling back, attacking, yielding and again growing cold, a constant ebb and flow, seeking and fleeing, quarreling and reconciling. Now, as he sat beside her, he determined with some satisfaction what a sly and inspired idea it had been for him to marry just such a person. Just imagine, arranging it so that the disturbance in one's house never ceased, a permanent war, marriage as permanent war. But why not? Now she could not escape him, nor he her. It was a precious and dangerous situation. Average folks doubtless had other ideas of hearth and home.

There on the sofa he placed his arm around Sonya's hips. "What, for instance, Sonyischka, my mistress and lady fair, would we do if we had free time? Let us build some castles in the air."

She glowed. "Travel. It doesn't have to be the Ukraine, although you did once promise me that, to come home with me to Rostov. But it would be just as unpleasant there now as in Berlin. But to the mountains, to the Bavarian Alps."

"Skiing?"

"Wouldn't that be wonderful, Karl?"

He laughed comfortably and laid his head on her shoulder. "Of course it would. But let's exchange roles. In Luckau I often used to fantasize that I would spend my time with you here at home and everything would be lovely, with a few difficulties, but necessary ones, since we're both show horses who love to take the hurdles, and then, too, I'm—to quote Milton loosely—Satan, and shall tempt you."

She giggled. "with rapine sweet bereaved . . ."

"Now you're fantasizing, and tempting me to go off to the Bavarian Alps."

"Karl, the mountains, the trees, white snow. And no Berlin. Berlin would vanish, no longer exist. I have a right to that."

"What right?"

"I'll tell you, counselor. 'Spouses are obliged to conduct a life of matrimonial partnership.' Paragraph 1353 of the civil code."

He laughed. "I certainly was asking for trouble, wasn't I, letting my books lie open around here? But there's nothing about the Bavarian Alps in them, is there?"

"No, only a lot of impudence showing that men wrote the book. But I can insist on a life of matrimonial partnership."

This was how he loved to see her. She wanted him as her property, as her husband. She, too, had wanted to have a lover for a husband. He

134

was much older than she, had just come from a tired, empty marriage; but there was something adventurous, fantastic, out-of-the-ordinary about him; women flew to him. They conquered him and then they wanted to possess him as well. But he had eluded her, he was a politician, and what a politician; and then came the war and they threw him in prison; his savagery excited her, she loved him all the more and wanted to possess him all the more.

She laid her arm around his neck, looked into his eyes, those eyes that could be so veiled and intense.

"Karl, do we not really have a right to each other?"

This was magnificent: to each other! What a pussycat.

He was delighted. He was deeply in love, how wonderfully she could lie and twist words, a lawyer could take lessons from her.

"Tell me, Sonyischka," he said dreamily, "what all must I give up so that our castle in the air gets built?"

"Only the revolution, for a few weeks."

"Only the revolution . . ."

Sonya: "Your old Ebert-Scheidemann."

Karl: "My old sailors."

Sonya: "Your old red flag, your blue flag and your green flag. All except one flag."

Karl shook for laughter. "I know, your slip."

"And why not, Karl? You stupid Germans are all just like in that passage you read me from Hölderlin—fragments, not men."

She kept finding new arguments. It made him happy. He sighed. "So then, what should I do, Sonya? How should I manage it?"

"Come away. Tell them you're sick; and you are."

He flattered her. "Yes, sick for you."

"You're exhausted. Anyone can see that."

"And what if they say I'm a coward."

She stood up as if something had stung her, she thought she had achieved her goal. "I could scratch your eyes out! You—a coward? Who stood there on Potsdamer Platz in the middle of the war? Who had to hide out every night afterward because they were following him? Who is going to accuse you of anything?"

He: "And Ebert and Scheidemann—?"

"Forget those wretches."

"They would triumph, Sonya, and it would all have been in vain."

"Are you ever conceited, Karl. There will be others who will come after you, you know."

"Certainly. But at the moment every man is needed, Sonyischka."

(I'd love to get away with her a bit myself, why deny it.)

She stood there furious, next to a flower vase that she looked down at, searching for her thoughts. Now she quickly turned toward him. He reached up inquiringly for her hips.

"Stop it, Karl. I don't understand you. If you're trying to make friends with someone and all you get is one kick after the other, you finally let him alone. Since the war you've done everything humanly possible for the workers of Germany. You go to prison for them, you leave your wife and your children behind, you have no home. Just look at you! And what do they do for you? They didn't even let you in the hall for the Congress of Councils."

"Even Lenin had to flee at one point."

"Well then, flee. That's what I'm saying. What do you want with them if they don't want you? They're not worth it. Just throw the whole mess in their faces."

He leaned back in the sofa and crossed his arms. Those were dreadful things to say. They hit home. In his worst hours they were what he thought as well. He muttered, "Be reasonable, Sonyischka. There really can be no question of that."

"And why not?" She stamped her foot.

Karl: "'He who knoweth the truth but speaketh it not is indeed a miserable wretch.' I know that Ebert is playing both ends, Sonya, that he has sold himself and this nation to the officers in order to save his own neck, that the officers want to lead this nation into a new war. And that is why I do what I do, for you and the children as well. We have to leave our children an honest heritage. My boys will not fight as I did as soldiers in a foreign country, not knowing why and wanting to hide themselves for the shame of it."

She sat down beside him and wept softly. "Karl, come away, please. The Germans don't deserve you."

He caressed her. "To Russia?"

"Yes."

"That—is what I intend to do in the end. And then we'll finally get to Rostov, too."

And without even noticing it, they had slipped back into serious conversation.

And as she sat down on the sofa beside him, in her corner, he laid his head as always in her lap, stretched out, relaxed. He told her that they could take heart. He flattered her while he kissed her hands. He thanked her for the strength she gave him. She let herself be caught up in it. She hummed him a Ukrainian song that he loved. They hummed the refrain together, just like always.

Afterward he slipped back to his feet and played the start of the "Moonlight Sonata" by Beethoven, melancholy arpeggios, then the trills and defiant passages; they rumbled and thundered. She stood next to the piano. He declaimed as he played. "Though earth take alarm, only slaves fear the storm."

They walked arm in arm through the room. He had about him the high spirits of a child. Her heart flew to him. This was the man she wanted, to have and hold—.

"The Kerensky period of the German revolution is racing toward its end," he gushed. "I swear to you, Sonya, it won't be long now. And then we will have our revolution, a German one. And it will take a different course than the Russian one."

"How, Karl?"

"Let us first take power. In Germany everything depends on the rule of order. But that will no longer come via the military, but through socialism. We'll sweep the last resistance away, those bits of anachronism among us. You will see the red flag flying. Instead of obedience, a natural sympathy from man to man. It's only awaiting the signal. In this country with its sense of discipline we'll not need mass executions. Blood is the business of Ebert and his generals. We'll structure the productive energies. Everyone will be glad to work with us. We'll lift the oppression from mankind. The storm of socialism will blow from Vladivostok to the Rhine—and on across the Rhine."

She embraced him, blissfully. She was totally his.

He kissed her proudly. He was aware of her meek submission. For him it was a cloudless afternoon.

Ebert Hatches His Revenge

Crafty Herr Ebert, consumed by fear, hid out near Berlin and waited out the holidays with a parvenu who hoped to profit from the arrangement.

Wilhelmstrasse lay still as death. The Reichs Chancellery stood empty. On the telephone switchboard little round bulbs would light up and call out to be connected. But no one grabbed the plugs.

That they were all living on shaky ground was proved by an event that occurred on Christmas Day. An armed mob shoved its way into the trouble-plagued *Vorwärts* building and occupied it. In the course of the revolution, the building had been through frequent occupations. It knew, therefore, how these things went, knew that this too would pass. Anyway it was a holiday, no newspapers were being published in any case, and there wasn't an editor in the house. But the next evening, as these gentlemen came toddling up intending to take up the world's history once more, their offices were teeming with total strangers. A flyer was pressed into each editor's hand, declaring that their paper "had been wrested at last from those illegally controlling it" and that "the people would at last learn the truth they so eagerly longed to hear."

The gentlemen were unwilling to have this said to them.

Although accustomed to such occurrences, they were annoyed; first, because they had come to work in vain, and second: what was this eagerly awaited truth that these others were going to proclaim to the people? This they attempted to find out on the sly. But the others' lips were sealed. So the editors lodged a complaint somewhere or other and at once found "mediators." The conquerors of *Vorwärts* beat their breasts, declaring they would only yield to force, which force promptly appeared in the form of a few telephone calls saying: "You've evidently gone completely crazy, is that it? Who put you up to this latest bit of nonsense?"

Hearing this, the conquerors argued among themselves for a while about who had in fact put them up to this nonsense, then finally crept away without a word, and without having achieved any results.

The next morning, awakening slowly from its Christmas sleep, the public learned about the incident.

On the front page of *Vorwärts* the "Revolutionary Shop Stewards" proclaimed that "the senior editors had been taught a well-earned lesson" and that the "Revolutionary Shop Stewards completely understood the grudge the workers of Berlin had against *Vorwärts,* which had insulted all honest revolutionary circles in the most shameful way."

Then the snubbed and insulted editors came limping along after them to declare:

"We shall restrict our comments to setting the facts straight. We consider those circles to be genuinely revolutionary which wish to hold on to the achievements of the revolution." (They were thinking of Ebert and General Lequis.) "To those who are toying with the idea of civil war"—they were not thinking of Ebert and Lequis—"we shall continue to say that they are the corrupters of the nation."

Then the sorely mistreated Social Democratic members of the government themselves came forward, rubbing their rumps—and what were they groaning about?

"We denounce those who day by day fabricate stories about the crimes of this government.

"Those who know no other word except tyrant, while they themselves wade through blood. Who are fighting ostensibly for the revolution but in fact desire nothing but destruction, anarchy and terror.

"Those for whom the Russian chaos with its starving population is not enough, who long for yet another chaos—in Germany.

"Those who long for a 'world revolution,' and will achieve only one thing: the world's doom.

"Comrades, you must trust us with power. (Aha!)

"There can be no government without power.

"The cost of December 24th was incredible in terms of national wealth and national prestige.

"One more such day and we shall lose (our heads) our status as a nation with which others will negotiate."

Ebert dared once again to enter Berlin. But he got the kick in the pants he had expected: the Independents resigned from the cabinet.

They staged their resignation at a meeting attended by both the people's deputies and the Central Executive Council. Ebert's use of force on Christmas Eve and his subsequent defeat had given the Independents courage. They could not do much, but they could resign. They weren't going to be talked out of that. Like the princess in the fairy tale, they could also pose difficult questions—for example: "Does the Executive Council share our opinion that a socialist government cannot and dare not depend for its support on the generals and the dregs of the old army built on blind obedience?"

Moreover: "Does the Executive Council approve of the transference of the government of the Reich to Weimar or some other city of central Germany as proposed by Ebert, Scheidemann and Landsberg?" (The news had leaked.)

The Executive Council, Ebert's retinue, withdrew, but did not know what to answer. They returned and murmured some "hmms."

Since the king's daughter did not consider this answer sufficient, they withdrew once again. And when they came back, they murmured some more "hmms," cleared the phlegm from their throats with energetic coughs and admitted with a slightly foolish smile that the questions posed to them could only be answered after thorough consultation with the Council of People's Deputies, the Executive Council in consultation with the Council of People's Deputies, council counseling council, a veritable privy consultation.

And now the Independents blew their tops. They grabbed their hats from the hat rack and resigned.

Once outside, they explained to everyone what had driven them to this unprecedented display of strength. It was a truly ghastly tale to hear, and everyone had to admit that they really couldn't do anything but resign.

First there was that absolutely despotic order to the War Ministry given the night before the battle at the palace, that appeal to brute force. Then there was Ebert's dubious position over against the generals; it seemed he did not even want to complete the demobilization of the army; he wanted to retain armed power within the Reich—ostensibly in order to defend Germany against Poles and Bolsheviks, but in reality only so that he might not lose his officers. That was also why he was making more and more concessions to them regarding control over the chain of command and the use of insignia for rank.

And, finally, he apparently was not even thinking of carrying out the democratic resolutions of the Congress of Councils.

All who heard this, approached by those representatives of eternal justice, the Independents, agreed that it was outrageous. Yes, they must abandon such injustice to itself. This could not come to a good end. And if just punishment did not ensue today or tomorrow, then somewhat later. Readers of tea leaves, consulted in hopes of pinpointing this "somewhat later," expressed differing opinions, but they all counseled them to stand fast and not give in, but wait. That day is coming, definitely coming, we see it clearly before us, like some elderly gentleman, retired, standing erect, in civilian clothes, carrying a cane and a stiff hat. He can be depended upon.

Ebert, however, sank back into the strange melancholy and depression that had only recently caused Scheidemann to speculate: should we use Glauber's salt or not?

But it was more the workings of a bad conscience than of his liver. Ebert had looked the revolutionary beast in the eye. The Independents were deserting him in order to avoid his fate. They had washed their hands of him. Let the buzzards eat him.

He sat there not knowing what to do. His mood was not improved by a report that revolutionary cadres who now had the upper hand were gathering in Berlin in order to form a permanent organization.

BOOK THREE

Antigone and Ancestral Guilt

Merry Christmas

Christmas in Berlin; the first peacetime Christmas.

Lieutenant Johannes Maus, back home from war and a military hospital, was sitting in the officers' canteen at the camp in Döberitz, glumly watching preparations for the celebration. Two great fir trees had been set up amid much hullabaloo and trimmed with candles, silver paper, and bright-colored balls. It looked pretty.

If only he could enjoy it as well.

And while musing about the past year and what it had brought him he suddenly thought of Hilda; she's alive, living close by, why should I have lost her as well. And he went to his room and got ready to go see her.

She was living in Britz and working as a nurse in the hospital there. She had cared for him and his friend Becker for months on end in the last military hospital he had been in, this wonderful Hilda, but she had given her sweet beauty to Becker. Maus's friendship with Becker did not hold up much longer after that.

He made the trip in civvies. It was the day of the battle at the stables.

In her wing in Britz he was told she was not on duty today, perhaps she was in her room. She came downstairs, then, to the large visiting hall; he stood there happy and curious, she downcast. They did not talk long. She changed clothes and came back, wearing her ankle-length buttoned coat with her dark blue nurse's cap and blond hair. They walked through town together, on past the railroad station along a chilly boulevard.

They touched on the topic of Becker. Maus acted nonchalant. She said she hadn't heard from him in weeks. For the most part he had recovered, was walking, using his canes of course; she had talked with his mother on the phone.

It was on the tip of Maus's tongue to say something about "Becker's dreadful political blunders," but he stopped himself (the remark wasn't appropriate at the moment, and besides: what did he care about Becker?) and spoke about his military service, about the lively bunch he had joined up with. No, "Poland is not yet lost," was the general mood.

She nodded, apparently intrigued by his words. Young Maus was surprised and downright bewildered that everything was going so well. What a lovely Christmas after the last awful weeks, after the armistice and his bad luck with Hilda and then the frustration and the longing. And now look here: he was walking with her, he was alone with her, she was listening to him, looking at him. Incredible.

She spoke little. He had the feeling she wanted to be consoled. It seemed her friendship with Becker, who wasn't fully recovered, didn't make her exactly radiant either. The question arose whether they should stay here in town or if it wouldn't be better to ride into the city. It would soon be dark here, they would find a quiet spot in the city.

They rode to Berlin. Hilda gave a sigh of relief in the midst of the teeming humanity of the brightly lit Potsdamer Platz. She cast her first calm glance at her companion. Evening papers were being hawked, he bought one for her. The fighting at the royal stables had "been broken off," an "agreement inspired by the holiday had been struck," no more spilling of blood. Here on Leipziger Strasse there was no sign of fighting, the Schloss Platz looked pretty bad, people said, but no one went in that direction. (That morning no one on Moklen-markt paid any attention to the fact that shots had been fired. A piece of shrapnel flew right over the roofs and landed in the upper story of a building where a woman was going peacefully about her housework; and that bit of explosive from beyond neighboring roofs struck her, and she was dead.)

Maus and Hilda strolled down Leipziger Strasse and became engrossed in the shop windows. From the "Porcelain Factory" they went across the street to Wertheim's Department Store. Maus gazed at Hilda and admitted to her: "It's Christmas. Hilda, I feel like we're two poor lost chickens. I'd like to give you a little bit of Christmas cheer."

She lowered her head.

"What do you say, Hilda, to sitting down together somewhere and celebrating?"

Then she squeezed his arm. "Shall we go to a café or a restaurant?"

Christmas pastry was being sold in a café near Wilhelmstrasse.

144

Maus bought a huge stollen; meanwhile Hilda took a seat at a small round marble table among a crowd of people and looked about. He laid the package next to her on the table. They drank hot chocolate. They exchanged only a few words.

Maus could not take his eyes off her face—it was so very familiar and yet somehow constantly new, never completely candid, always enigmatically sweet and knowing. He admitted he was a lost man, just looking at her. He had fought against his emotions these last weeks. He knew it was hopeless.

"Hilda, we're going to have to go. It looks like they're closing."

She nodded. "I'd say so too."

Once outside, she turned her face to his. "Hans, shall we take a cab?"

"Where to, Hilda?"

"Hail a cab."

They found one at a cab stand on Kanonierstrasse. When the driver bent down to them with a questioning look, Hilda said, "St. Hedwig's Church."

Inside, she took his hand. "It's Christmas Eve, Hans. You'll come along, won't you?"

He was happy with anything she might do. They got out at the church. He wanted to wait outside with his package, to walk up and down the street.

But she said, "Come in. And sit down in a pew."

A few people were moving about in the half-light of the nave. You could see some of them in the pews. Two women were kneeling up front. Candles were burning at the altar.

He sat down.

He watched as she knelt before an image of the Virgin off to one side. Now she was praying. He was with her. He obediently folded his hands. At the same time he thought: My father or mother should see me now, I'm in a church, and a Catholic one at that.

But it is Hilda. What a miracle, what a gift, what grace. This morning, disconsolate and hopeless at the camp in Döberitz—and then the idea strikes me and I take the train to see her, and now I'm sitting here with her.

She stood up, moved along the altar, knelt for a moment, walked on further. At the side—between two columns—she disappeared.

He sat and sat some more, impatiently. He held the Christmas stollen on his knees like a baby.

He waited. After a quarter of an hour he became anxious and stood up. He looked around and walked to the front, in the direction of the columns where she had disappeared. She was nowhere to be seen.

He turned around, crestfallen. He walked back to his seat and sat down again. He tried to control himself. What was this? Was it all just one of her moods? Footsteps at his side. She entered the pew without looking at him or speaking to him. He made room for her. She knelt down, crossed herself, buried her face in her hands, whispering.

All at once the dreadful anxiety fell away. He felt he had arrived safely in port.

Now she crossed herself again and stood up. She nodded to him. They left.

It was pitch dark outside. The danger zone around the palace and the royal stables was not far off. It would be a good idea to move away from there. He guided her to the Gendarmenmarkt; there it grew brighter.

"I was so worried about you, Hilda. You disappeared."

"I went to confession, Hans."

"Oh."

She put her arm in his as they walked. After a while she said to him, "Two lost puppies, that's us!"

They were selling Christmas trees at the Gendarmenmarkt, Maus proposed, "Wouldn't it be fine, Hilda, if we two could just sit down somewhere like normal people beside a Christmas tree instead of wandering about like this?"

"Abandoned puppies like us? But if that's what we are, why then . . ."

"I'd like to buy a tree."

"What for?"

"We'll sit down next to it."

"Where?"

"Do you want to?"

She squeezed his arm.

He: "We've got our stollen already. I'll get something for us to drink."

She whispered, "But where, Hans?"

He: "I'll—I'll find something, don't worry. I'll go looking. You can wait for me in a pub."

He led her across to a large restaurant on one corner. They sat down at a table with their stollen. He left her alone.

Fifteen minutes later he stormed back in and sat down next to her, his face beaming. "I've got everything, everything, Hilda—the tree, candles, ornaments, something to eat and drink."

"But what are we going to do with it all?"

"I've even got a room for us."

She dropped her head, fell silent.

He: "Well, Hilda."

"What—what do you have in mind, Hans?"

He flinched. He pressed her wrist. "You still haven't forgiven me, have you, Hilda? I—lost control of myself just that once, and you still haven't forgiven me."

He laid his head on the table. "Forgive me, Hilda. I've had to suffer so much because of that."

She looked down at his head and closed her eyes. It had been back in November, as the military hospital was being disbanded, on the last day. Amidst all the general chaos he had forced her into an empty room as they were saying good-bye and had had his way with her; she had been unable to defend herself.

Her eyes filled with tears. She bent down and whispered to him, "Hans, it just came over me. It's all right. I trust you."

He raised his head and looked at her full of doubt. She kissed him, right there in the bar, kissed his brow, his eyes, his mouth. He murmured, "And I love you, Hilda, I love you with all my heart."

They sat there, the beer mugs before them. Arm in arm. Hilda paid the check. A cab was waiting outside with a little Christmas tree and a lot of packages.

Maus had managed to find a room in a somewhat questionable hotel on Lützowstrasse. The vulgar manager smirked as he carried in the tree behind them, set it up on the oilcloth protecting the table, having cleared away a tray and a water pitcher and two glasses from it by putting them on a chair. There was already a fire burning in the stove. He brought them some hot tea. Then he took his leave. "Merry Christmas and good night."

The double bed had been turned down for the night.

She had been standing by the window, but now she turned to Hans as the manager closed the door. "I'm going to twist your ears off, Hans. You've deceived me. This is for the whole night."

"Oh, we can take off whenever we want, Hilda."

There was another knock. The manager brought a jug of hot water. "To wash up."

Finally she took off her coat and cap. They began to open the packages and decorate the tree. Then he ordered her over to the window and made her look out. Meanwhile he lit the candles and busied himself at the table.

They stood hand in hand before the tree. Little red and green candles burned brightly.

Hilda wept bitter tears. He took her in his arms. She wept, her head on his chest. What a year it had been. Oh, peace on earth and good will to men.

He didn't even recognize himself. These few hours of this one day had made him a more serious, a more manly man.

She let go of him. She looked over at the table. He had spent a lot of money. On the table lay a gold wristwatch, a necklace, and a silk shawl, all for her. Plus all kinds of pastries and chocolate. He apologized for having had to do it all so hurriedly.

"Don't ask what you can give me, Hilda. You have already given me so much, more than I have ever received in all my life."

And slowly she realized how he was holding her in his arms; she had still thought of him as an impetuous kid, hanging onto her apron strings. It was quite a jolt. He aroused her curiosity.

They sat down, drank their tea, and tried the stollen. He put the wristwatch on her arm. She was to put on the necklace as well. She put that off till later. She was more interested in him. She asked him to tell her about himself.

"Actually I've only you to thank, Hilda, for being in Döberitz at all. I kept arguing with Becker. I wanted him to join me in the Spartacists; it's true, I swear."

"You told me once that you took part in an attack on police headquarters."

He laughed. "Back in November, that's right. Now we're preparing a different attack, a much more serious one. I've joined the other side."

"And do you always have to be fighting, Hans?"

He told about his association with the Reds. "There are some solid fellows among them. But there's no idealistic core to the movement. They don't know Germany. They don't recognize any religion. They just recognize themselves, the proletariat, and don't even know that very well. They keep talking about classes. It's a madness with them. They wear blinders. They want a new society, without classes. The crazy notions they have! A kind of heaven on earth. They'll look long and hard for the people to fill it."

"And what do you and your new friends want?"

148

"A new and healthy Germany. People at the top who know how to lead and that you can trust."

He noticed even while he spoke that although everything he said was correct and reflected his convictions, that—somehow things were no longer what they had been yesterday. A special kind of light had fallen across them. It came from Hilda. The ideas were not nearly so enticing for him as they had been.

She listened while they sat hand in hand before the candlelight. She thought dreamily: am I doing the right thing? Am I really good for him? Am I not fooling myself? It's the same thing now with Maus as—before with Bernhard, in Strasbourg—who's dead now, and whose spell I fell under. I threw myself at him, exhausted myself, and then recovered. Isn't it just the same as it was with Becker? What bliss it was to be with him, a submissive bliss like in that song that goes: "Since I saw him, I think I've gone blind."

Hans sliced and peeled an apple for her. He was chivalrous and tender. At times he seemed to fear that Hilda wasn't serious about all this. While he sat there and chewed, he would now and again glance at the floor as if he had noticed something to make him anxious. He stared at Hilda, frowning. She understood and said some tender words.

They embraced there in front of their tree in the grimy room of this hotel of dubious reputation. The strapping youth wanted literally to fall on his knees before her.

It was ten o'clock. She wanted to return to Britz. She had to be on duty by six-thirty the next morning.

"And isn't there some way I can see you tomorrow?"

She had two hours free at noon. It could be arranged. He began carefully to pack everything up. The tree and the apples were left behind. When the candles had been blown out and the light turned off, he whispered to her as he laid his hand on the doorknob, "Okay then, in front of the hospital, tomorrow."

He opened the door. The light from the corridor fell into the room. As she passed by him, she pressed against him. They walked down the corridor arm in arm. This was happening to him.

They crept down the stairs. But the front door was locked. They had to ring. What a shame; they would have loved to vanish without a sound. The manager arrived, grumpy. He thought it was new guests. He hardly looked at them.

On New Year's Eve day, Hans took her to see his parents. The legation lawyer was decked out in his old imperial medals. Maus himself appeared in uniform. Afterward Hilda stared at him in astonishment. "What a strange world it is. But then maybe my father would have the same effect on you."

Hans: "The old world, Hilda. Those medals are his pride and joy."

They were together the whole day. Late that afternoon, on the way to the train station, Maus slowed his pace as they walked along a side street near the Anhalt Station. He felt embarrassed. When she asked what the matter was, he pulled a small package packed in tissue-paper out of his coat pocket and ripped off the paper himself. But before he could open the little box, she took it away from him.

"I know what it is, Hans. And I thank you. But why did you do it?"

"What do you mean, Hilda?"

"The ring. Can't we just stay like this? Friends? Can't we?"

He gazed straight ahead. "Is that what you want?"

"Why not, Hans? You're in such a hurry. The holidays have been so lovely."

"Hilda, please, try to understand me. You can't shove back into uncertainty."

"But we'll go on seeing each other, Hans."

"But not the way I want, the way I have to have it. The sun can't say to the moon just go on your way, I'll illuminate you, you can depend on it."

They were standing beneath a lamppost. In its reddish light Hilda opened the little box. Two golden rings bedded in red velvet. She closed the box again. "They're beautiful. Beautiful."

She turned to Hans with a smile that took away his every care. "And why do you give them to me here out on the street? We were at your parents' and then in a café."

"I couldn't bring myself to it. I was afraid of what you'd answer. But I had to at some point. I won't be getting any more leave again soon. It looks like we'll be moving out."

"So this is a wartime engagement."

She had closed the box and put it now in her purse. She took his arm and pulled him along with her now. Suddenly she looked at him. "I'll take a later train, Hans. Where shall we go?"

"What would you like to do, Hilda?"

"To be with you for another hour. Let's go to that little hotel where we were at Christmas."

"No, no, Hilda."

150

He protested vehemently. But she held tight to him. "Why not, Hans?"

He hesitated. "It's so dirty there."

"I want to. Let's take a cab."

There was nothing he could do. He had to tell the cab driver the address, on Königgrätz Strasse. Away they drove. The stout manager opened the door, regarded them as if they were old acquaintances. He gave them the same room that they had celebrated Christmas in.

They were alone now. He helped her out of her coat. She was wearing a black dress with a small opening at the neck. His delicate necklace hung at her throat. About her hips was a silver brocade belt that ended in wide ribbons hanging down. Her dark blond hair lay combed smoothly and simply on her head, and was bound together in a large knot at the back with a jeweled hairpin stuck in it. Normally Hilda had a full, oval face with a healthy glow to it. The black dress made her face look thinner, her cheeks were pale after the long day.

He gazed at her with immense joy, and as he removed her coat he regarded how she stood there and how a smile played about her lips, a smile that he could never figure out: it was ironical, it was warm— and it was always accompanied by a very knowing look.

She sat down on the sofa. He did not dare touch her. She slid closer to him and laid her head on his shoulder. The box with the rings lay next to the water pitcher on the table. The bed on the other side of the room was pulled down. She took his hand. (It's a good thing I'm sitting on this side of him; his other shoulder was the one that was wounded, how often I've dressed the bandage.)

"You're so silly, Hans. Why can't you be content with our staying just as we are? Am I some ideal of yours. Men often make these ideals for themselves. I'm a human being, Hans, a sinful human being. You know that. I've lain in your arms once before."

"Stop it, Hilda. I forced you to."

"Hans, do you know why I wanted to come to this hotel? We're no better than the others who come up here off the street to embrace. Don't be angry with me. I want to hold on to the truth, nothing else. I went to confession on Christmas and told the priest just how I am. Are you any different, Hans? My dear Hans? Tell me."

"Hilda, my sweet Hilda, I'm not like the other people who come up here off the street."

"You didn't go to confession. You haven't examined your conscience. You haven't repented."

"Hilda, you know I'm not religious."

"Hans, do you know why I brought you here to this dirty hotel room? Because I know that things are no different for us than for the people who usually come up here. And if you want to give me a ring— then you must give me something else as well."

"Hilda, I love you."

"Come, my darling, look at me."

What was the vision she had of this man. She searched in his faithful anxious eyes, in those young, tense features (look, his cheeks are no longer as pudgy as they were in the hospital, he's gone through a lot).

Nor did all the memories of her earlier life emerge now, as they had once before when she had laid her arms around Becker's neck, that whole shadowy, sweet chain of events revealing what she once had been and what she left behind her. Here sat (no vision rose up within her) a serious young man waiting for her answer. He was not the infatuated Lieutenant Maus who had tagged after her in the hospital.

She laid her arms around his neck, joining her hands behind it, and asked, "Do you really want to stand alongside me before God? I feel deep in my heart that I'm good for you. But I cannot exist without God."

"What do you want me to do, Hilda? I'm not a believer, I've told you that. Do I not deserve your trust on that account?"

She let her hands fall from him. She said softly, "Oh, that isn't it."

And as they sat there, not saying a word, the mist cleared from before his eyes as well. He had clung to her, love had burned him. And now here sat a human being with the features of the woman he loved, a restless human being with its own anguish, not some magic Mona Lisa.

She played with his fingers. "And now Hans is thinking what a rotten creature she is. First she gets my hopes up and then she lays down her conditions. I'm not making any conditions, Hans. I only want to understand you. Look at it this way: when someone goes to a slave market intending to buy another human being and the person is standing there naked, he tests his muscles and checks him from top to bottom. And then there's me, what do you want of me? What am I to you? Who am I for you? My body (please don't be angry with me, Hans), you've already had that. Perhaps I pleased you and that's why you can't part with me. I'm—not blaming you for that. But these gold rings speak another message. They're made of gold, they shine, like little stars. They shine from another source."

She waited to see if his expression changed. With Becker, Maus's battle had not been for God, but against God. He had listened scornfully to Becker's confession of faith. Here everything seemed quite different. Here sat someone whose very soul and happiness were vital to him.

He whispered, "Hilda, tell mé what it is you want."

"Want? I don't want anything." She embraced him again. "I want you. Really just you."

"And I want you, Hilda."

"And I would like for God to hear what we say."

"Then He shall, Hilda."

She looked into his eyes. "Say that once again, Hans."

He repeated it.

She gave a cry and broke into sobs as she hung about his neck.

He lifted up her chin and kissed her.

They still had a half hour left. They were both happy and spoke to each other hand in hand.

She talked about Becker as well. She asked Hans whether what Becker's mother had said was true, that he had become religious. Maus confirmed it; but he had not liked Becker's brand of piety, and that was why they had argued.

"You mustn't think he's a coward," Hilda remarked, "for not joining up with a political party. It's simply not enough for him. But what is enough? He's become religious. That's strange. For him, that's strange. It frightens me."

"Why is that, Hilda?"

"He knows no bounds, never will. I'm an Alsatian, Maus, and I know you fellows from the Reich. When I think of Becker, and especially now with all his piety, he is the most German thing I know. That's how the people must have been who built our cathedral in Strasbourg. The cathedral is magnificent but it always frightens me a little. Do you know why I'm so glad to be a Catholic? Because it holds me, firmly and strictly."

He laughed. "But is that necessary for you, Hilda?"

Her helpless glance. "Yes, darling. And not for you? It's necessary for all of us."

She reached for the little box on the table and opened it. He took the rings out and put them on her finger.

Then they both had to laugh. The rings were too big.

"We're going to have to grow into marriage, Hans."

He helped her into her coat. She said: "But now let's get out of here. Hurry, hurry, and then damn the torpedoes."

In the Cave of Thought

Friedrich Becker emerged from the cave of his thoughts and looked about.

News swirled rhythmically about him like snowflakes. It fell on people from the newspapers. You could sweep it away in the morning but by afternoon there it lay again, and in the evening, before you went to bed, it fell again.

Becker was a man like millions of others who went off to war in 1914 without knowing why—because they had received their marching orders was why. He was out in the field until 1917, advanced from lieutenant in the reserves (as a teacher at a public academy) to first lieutenant, was awarded the Iron Cross, and was then on the western front. There he was struck down by a piece of shrapnel that entered one of his lower vertebrae, resulting in a month long paralysis of his lower limbs. His recuperation dragged on for some time in various different military hospitals, the last one in Alsace. From there he was transported back to Germany at the outbreak of the revolution. In Berlin he recovered, he could stand and walk again, although at first only with the aid of canes.

But once home, apparently as a consequence of his illness, he found himself in a serious emotional crisis that almost ended in madness: he felt that he was to blame for the war.

It was the beginning of January now, in the new year of 1919.

He sat in the warm study of his Berlin apartment, a tall, emaciated figure with an ashen gray face, his brown hair combed back smoothly, a man in his middle thirties. He had been supporting his head with his left arm, but now he let his arm fall to the table from which he had just eaten breakfast. He folded his hands on his napkin.

"You're going out, Mother? So early? To fresh deeds, oh my young hero? You're not going to stop for a rest while the year is new?"

She laid the simple, dark-green winter coat that she had taken from the closet over a chair, and shook out the fur collar.

"People need someone to help, Friedrich."

"Do they really, Mother? Or do we just imagine they do?"

"You're getting better, Friedrich, you're teasing. I would like to see you return to work again soon, at your school. It would take your mind off things."

"1919, two 19's; it sounds like the bong-bong of a bell. What do you suppose it's announcing?"

154

"That the war is over, Friedrich. That it's all over. That you're going to be well again."

"That's what the bong-bong of 19 and 19 is announcing?"

She was a robust woman in her late fifties, with a full, frank face. She pulled her black fur hat down over her thick gray hair and laid an arm on his shoulder. "Friedrich, we're going to send you off to school. And then . . . ."

"What then, Mother?"

"Then I'm going to get hold of Hilda. She's still at the hospital in Britz, I'm sure. She did you so much good when you were still in Alsace."

"You liked her, didn't you, when she visited us here?"

"Us? You. Gioconda, Mona Lisa."

Friedrich turned his head around to look at his mother as she buttoned up her coat.

"You want to blast me with a double-barrel, is that it?"

"So that you'll stop reading the papers. You'll not say no, will you Friedrich?"

"Why should I? She's the one who walked out on me, you know."

His mother left.

He sat there alone.

He stood up, pulled the belt of his blue robe tighter and sauntered into his study in the next room.

It smelled of smoke in there, the stove drew badly. Becker opened a window and let cold air in.

He had looked down onto this gray proletarian street only a few weeks before—and what a sight had greeted him! Out in the street an old woman and a ragged lad had been pulling along a child's wagon of firewood. He was still rejoicing now from his recent good fortune, and thought how everything, everything would change now.

For something extraordinary had happened. He, an atheist, a pantheist, a friend of Greek antiquity, a heathen, had returned to the faith of his mother—at the end of his crisis, which had the appearance more of an illness than of an emotional experience. He had emerged from his dreadful sufferings a Christian. Unbidden, as if it were a gift, healing had come to him. From one moment to the next he had found a great joy and was well again.

That had happened four weeks ago. Then—things changed slowly.

How insidious time is! It pretends to be blameless, with its sunrises and sunsets, the transit of the stars, seasons, rain, snow, warmth and cold. It's chief concern seems to be astronomical and agronomic. A day passes in the form of a few harmless hours—of which several are quite void of content— unobtrusively gets ready to depart, turns around at the door, gives you a brief, mocking glance, and is gone. Only afterward do you discover what had happened. You have misjudged time, as if she were a woman.

While she was strolling about so harmlessly with her parasol or her umbrella, lounging about so picturesquely, she has been plying a ghastly trade. She disorients, changes, and confuses human hearts, and not just the hearts, but everything down to the marrow and the bowels. She never gives you the chance to say, "This is me, this is most definitely me, and my name is Herr X or Frau Y."

Like some enchanting naked beauty who passes by a row of serious, learned and pious men, doing nothing more than throwing each a glance and a smile, so that those learned men are no longer learned and sink back to the miserable state from which they first began, standing now at the same stage as all the rest of humanity and bearing only the generic name "human being," "man"—that's how time works.

She appears unbidden, does not cause a lot of trouble, and joins you at your table. But if you think she's making small-talk with you, you're mistaken. She's like some police detective sitting beside a man who won't do his neighbor the favor of confessing. But the detective is patient. He says, "Don't exert yourself if you don't think of it right away, it will come to you soon enough." He stays there beside you, eats and drinks with you, follows you as if he were your own shadow. You are innocent. You know that and also know who it is you're dealing with. You think, go ahead, let him follow me, if that makes him feel good, what can he do to me, and even if he puts me through a meat grinder, he'll not squeeze guilt out of me.

But gradually you are no longer you. The shadow will not leave you. Since when are you always two people? Up till now you were only one, Herr X or Frau Y, weren't you? And you grow accustomed to your shadow, you tell him things in confidence just so you won't be frightened of him. He asks you this and he asks you that. You notice he won't give up, that he only wants to catch you up. You tell him whatever pops into your head. He applauds; it's working, things are going all right. And then you laugh, and since now you have the whole thing behind you, you want to do him a favor if that's what he really insists on, so you tell him, admit everything he wants you to— and he has you.

Friedrich Becker breathed in the fresh winter air as he lay on his chaise longue. Was he not already viewing his experience as if from behind some other past occurrence? What remained now of that great

156

moment, of that total bliss? Had it not all faded away? Had it been anything more than just a mood?

Yes, he was relapsing rapidly. All his assurance was vanishing. He was slowly approaching the state where phantoms encircled him, spoke to him and placed a rope in his hand. Those wicked, tormenting questions had started up again, the ones regarding the reason for all this misfortune —, where had the horrors of war come from, the long years of incomprehensible and disgraceful murder? How, in the midst of life, had there suddenly emerged a kind of life that, as a human being, you could only be ashamed of? How could it have crept into our peaceful and transparent lives? Oh, if only those ghastly, unanswerable questions did not start in all over again.

He read the newspapers to divert himself and to get his bearings. He tried to determine how things really stood in the world, and where he was himself to stand in it. He laid himself upon the glowing grill of daily news and policies. This got him nowhere, it only inflamed and burned him. His mother had recognized this.

And as he now directed his gaze across the way to the gray facade, asking himself in his despair, in remembrance of those glorious hours of fulfillment, "Did it truly happen, what I experienced then? Was it true?"—at that moment the question turned back toward him, walked up to him, spread wide its arms and brought him the answer: "It is true."

Without his having made any motion, the answer came: it is true, and he knew it was so. His face grew calm and smooth, his breathing became easier and deeper.

He looked over toward his desk. There in a niche between two little boxes stood a small crucifix. He realized, like snow melting in the sunlight, yes, it is the truth that transcends everything else, that surpasses all things visible and does not let them disintegrate. You reign above all time. Neither wars nor revolutions touch you.

He closed the window. His eyes once again took in his study.

What was to happen now? His mother suggested that he go back to teaching. How curious, to let everything go on as before. I'll go back to school and teach Greek and Latin again in the upper form. How am I supposed to imagine myself there at the lectern, drilling away at grammar and irregular verbs and the war and all the rest of it? And not to have any conclusions drawn.

Friedrich Becker wore his new experience like some ill-fitting piece of clothing. It was always slipping somewhere, or pinching him or interfering with him. Even if he had his confidence back, he could do nothing with it, and sighed and did not know how he was to move about with it. And if he lost it, he would wail and moan and feel like a fish out of water.

He sat, indecisive, at the window in the armchair his mother usually occupied when she joined him. He smoothed out yesterday's newspaper hanging over the arm of the chair. News, whirling about like snowflakes.

Then the bell rang in the corridor. He opened the door; it was his mother's brother, Eberhard Roeninger, come for a visit in Berlin. He had announced yesterday that he was coming. The broad-shouldered, full-faced man hung up his heavy fur coat in the corridor without further ado, braced himself against the wall so he could pull off his rubber boots, and then let himself be led into the bright living room. He sat across the table from his nephew. Again he inquired after Becker's health and whether he had not had enough of being sick by now.

He was a commissary official, from Cologne, and had the same round, friendly eyes as Becker's mother, the same definite way of looking that could become somewhat fixed and rigid. His temples and jaws revealed a firmness and strength of will.

"Our military hospitals," he told Becker, "are still not emptied out. There's a whole pack of them who won't get off our backs, unemployed fellows looking for pensions. We need bouncers more than we need doctors."

When Becker inquired what he planned to do in Berlin, he removed his glasses from a crushed black cardboard case, placed them on his nose, and cast a glance at the newspaper before him; his visit had to do with military supplies in his district. You had to record the stocks handed over by the troops at demobilization. And now voluntary corps and militias were being formed, you could truly say like mushrooms after a rain—most of them of course merely for the pay—and they were demanding equipment. All of them were demanding something; and partly the problem was that they did not have the supplies, and partly that they were most uncertain about what they ought to hand over, if anything.

He removed his glasses again and gave his nephew a piercing glance. "And now you can explain to me what is happening here with you in Berlin. In the Rhineland everyone says that if you keep on like this, we can't guarantee what will happen."

"You won't get much information from me, Uncle Eberhard. I've been sitting around here at home most of the time."

"Have you ever been to one of the Reds' mass meetings?"

"One, with a friend I met in the hospital."

"I can imagine you wanted to knock some heads."

Becker laughed.

The old man declared, "These people, here in our country—what a breakdown. Creatures like that wouldn't have dared show their faces under the Kaiser. And now they're making public policy."

He reached a hand across the table to take hold of Becker's arm, and said confidentially, "My boy, do you believe the people really take them all seriously—Ebert, Haase, Liebknecht, and Adolf Hoffmann? Don't people see that that shabby, vile bunch has no place in a civilized nation? The dregs of society—and we had a Bismarck, a Helmholtz, and a Schiller. It makes your blood freeze in your veins. They say we've been defeated. But others have been defeated before this, the French for example. I was a little boy in 1870. They also had people who wanted to misuse their nation's plight for their own purposes. But first of all, their Commune was not such a miserable and pitiful thing as this revolution here, and secondly the French generals and army were on the scene. And they knew what it was all about."

Friedrich could only call up murky memories of the transport back home in November. How sorry the German revolution had seemed to him then, as they encountered the first battery of revolutionaries on German soil—like some veterans' organization that had mistakenly raised its banner.

The old man raised a hand in protest. "Veterans' organization, well I belong to a veterans' organization myself. No, like a herd of sheep! And you can easily tell what sheep they are by the fact that those Reds set up guards to watch over the supplies and weapons, and they were so faithful in the execution of the task that, sure as shootin', the other side got the whole stock."

The old man was getting warm. He looked about the simple room. "So this is where your mother lives. She is a good, devout woman, like our mother. Little of that rubbed off on me. But let me take this opportunity, Friedrich, while I'm alone with you, to tell you how much I admired you during the war. I knew that you would pull through your illness. Your father is no longer alive, so you can take it from your uncle."

He thrust his heavy hand across the table, and Becker shook it.

The old man: "He who trusts in God, and goes through life roughshod, builds not on sand or sod. And don't let that bunch that are on top now alarm you. One day soon they'll be happy to be back where they started."

The old man slid his chair back and stood there in all his great, worthy amplitude. He strode out of the room, all the while continuing the friendly advice; he pulled on his rubber boots, worked his way into his fur coat with huffings and puffings, and departed.

"What do I want, really, Friedrich asked himself, as he walked back into the living room. What am I waiting for? For a sign from heaven? What do I imagine heaven to be? Have I chosen God to be my commander, the colonel of my regiment from whom I expect my orders? He can do very well without soldiers of that sort.

The more he thought about his strange uncertainty and perplexity, the funnier Becker seemed even to himself. All this trying to puzzle things out was childish.

Oh, what a learned man, what a doubt-tormented man you are, Herr Becker, what a burlesque figure you've made of yourself. Come to, stick your head under a cold shower. You ask yourself what a person who is a Christian does these days. Well, you're not going to find out sitting around here.

That noon his mother did not find the newspapers spread all over, instead she found her son Friedrich ready for an outing.

"I'm planning to go look up the school director after lunch," he declared.

She couldn't believe her ears. She hugged him rapturously.

"Mother, one of your heavy cannonades had an effect. At first I only intended to have a general discussion with the director. Now I'm going to agree to go back to teaching."

Then he told about his uncle and the lively hour he had spent with him.

And so that afternoon Dr. Friedrich Becker went forth, a man who had marched into the field in August, 1914, a man who for many months had lain gravely wounded in a military hospital and then had been plagued by a dangerous spiritual crisis—he went out now to test things, to find out what a man can achieve in these times after he has gone through war and returned home and does not want to forget.

The director, a gentleman in his fifties, received him in his elegant bachelor quarters. He was of average height, well fed, with a soft, full face and a head of thinning, dark blond hair. He greeted his visitor with surprise but with fervor. The man had visited Becker a few times during his illness.

They moved across a heavy pile rug through a high-ceilinged atelier furnished with busts, paintings, and exquisite furniture that served as the gentleman's living room. Becker apologized for dropping in like this and stated the point of his visit. He was told to take a seat on the delicate rococo sofa in front of the bookcases. The director—a refined, soft-spoken man of ingratiating courtesy—pushed a small cart of fruit, candies and cookies over to Becker and urged him to take something.

And, he whispered bending over to Becker, he also had a surprise for him.

He went to the rear of the room where there stood a massive table heaped with portfolios and sculptures, and returned with a stack of notebooks. "Just look at—what I have here."

Becker opened a notebook, a translation from the Greek. "What are these notebooks doing here with you, Herr Direktor?"

"Well, I'm teaching the course. I had to take over for Dr. Willmer, who at this moment is lying in the hospital with appendicitis. I am the substitute for the substitute. It's high time we got back to the genuine product."

"Then I've come at just the right moment."

"If indeed you want to step in, my dear colleague. You kill two birds with one stone—you help both the class and me. The only question that remains is whether you can manage it."

"Herr Direktor, here I am. I came here without assistance. I sit around all day in my study with nothing to do. If you'd like I'll bring a doctor's certificate."

The director, nibbling at a cookie and sitting in the other corner of the sofa, weighed the issue. "May I make a suggestion. We shall try it, unofficially. Come to school tomorrow morning, without any formalities. There are two hours of Greek scheduled for the senior students tomorrow, from nine till eleven. I'll leave it to you whether you want to teach both or only one hour. At any rate you'll find me somewhere in the building. And meanwhile you can prepare your application for reemployment, get the certificates, the papers from the military showing you've been discharged from the army and whatever else you have. Right. The citation for having received the Iron Cross as well. You'll have a place in our files once again." He laughed. "For in our world, dear colleague, that is the essence of human life. We wander from one filing cabinet to another."

Becker joined in the laughter. "So I can begin moving the papers."

"It will not be necessary for you to mention in your application that you have already made a trial attempt at resumption of your duties. I'll append that myself."

Everything was arranged.

The First Hour of Class

At 8:30 A.M., Becker drove up in front of the school.

He had left this sober red brick box in the middle of gray apartment houses on a narrow side street on August 3, 1914. The streets had been decorated with flags that day. Everywhere on the streets and in the public squares were uniformed men and troops of civilians, young men lead by noncoms, moving toward the railroad station to entrain—tension, excitement, intoxication in the city, and news of victory already, everyone wanting to be part of it—the barracks could not handle all the volunteers who appeared and stood in long lines.

The old building had survived the triumphs and defeats of war. It seemed to have drawn back into itself somewhat; it had gotten dirtier. The wing added on the street side contained the school's collections, its library and staff residences. The entrance led through a high iron gate, past the custodian's apartment and into the broad schoolyard, which was empty now. To the right stood the gymnastic apparatus, the jungle gym, the parallel bars.

For four years all this had been erased from Becker's life, and now his eyes took it in again. Was it all still in its same old place? Am I someone who has reemerged from the underworld and nothing more?

There lay the broad somber red brick building that made up the academy proper, ponderous and immobile. Becker's pace slowed as he crossed the schoolyard. The building, grave and menacing, was no different than others the state had erected in railroad stations, barracks, hospitals, prisons. He shrank back. Back into the yoke again?

His soft black hat pulled down on his brow, his blue-gray, heavy winter coat drawn around his long, lean body, both hands in his pockets, a stout cane hooked over his left forearm, Friedrich stopped at the bottom of the steps leading up to the school's entrance hall; he hesitated.

But while he was considering, his foot was already groping for the next step, his body moved upward. He was walking, he stood before the open door, and entered.

But as the rotunda vaulted above him and the double rows of white columns thrust around him like the tentacles of two polyps, the whitewashed ceiling glared at him with its dead eyes, he wavered— and then hurried to the wall to sit on a bench.

There he sat for several minutes, bowed down. Something here stirred the terrors of his recent crisis. He pulled himself together. To the right, the first hallway led off down to the faculty room. At a window beside the door to it stood a small table with rock samples; he bent over them, fossils with ferns from some primeval era. A thought announced itself to Friedrich, a thought of primal things, but he did not complete it. Becker entered the faculty room.

The central yellow table, the row of chairs to the left and right. He took off his coat, sat down, leafed through an education magazine. The bell rang: nine o'clock.

One teacher after the other came in, with or without exercise and text books; brief greetings. The director came over to Becker and shook his hand warmly. While they were standing there together, Dr. Krug appeared, the easy-going science teacher and Becker's old friend, who as yet knew nothing of Becker's decision. Krug was so touched at the unexpected sight of Becker here in these familiar rooms that he embraced him.

As the second bell rang, the director slowly climbed the stairs with Becker, past the bust of Pericles on the second floor, the bust of Bismarck on the third. Next to the assembly hall was the senior room.

The class, fifteen young men, rose silently as the director entered accompanied by an unfamiliar man, tall, pale and much younger. When the two of them had stepped up onto the teacher's podium and the class was seated, a student jumped up and placed a second chair on the podium for Becker, who thanked him with a nod of his head.

The director, distinguished in his long, black frock-coat, his face rosy, full, smooth and somewhat youthful, his thinning blond hair shining and parted down the middle, began to speak to his "dear friends" without taking a seat. He introduced them to their new and proper Greek teacher.

"Herr Dr. Becker, as you know from announcements made in assembly and from the school's prospectus, has brought great honor to the school. He returned from the field with the Iron Cross and, unfortunately, gravely wounded. The gravity of his wounds, now healed, has kept him from the classroom until now. My dear friends, make his reentry into the work of this school an easy one through your diligence and hard work."

The class stomped academic applause.

Becker accompanied the director to the door. As he returned to the podium alone, the applause thundered once again, only ceasing when he sat down and raised his hands.

The class spokesman, a tall, pale lad wearing glasses, came up and

163

showed him the list of students on the class roll; two were missing because of illness. Becker called out the names of each of those present. Each stood as Becker looked at him, nodded and said, "Thank you." Then he reached for the book the director had left behind for him and the lesson began: *Antigone* by Sophocles.

He had glanced through the text once again yesterday.

Since detailed reading of the play had been completed, the task now was to form some idea of the work as a whole. Becker suggested comparing *Antigone* to the two other plays from the same thematic group, with *Oedipus Rex* and *Oedipus at Colonus*.

A redhaired boy in the second row who talked rapidly in a high, squeaky voice spoke first.

There were women, it was true, in both *Oedipus Rex* and *Oedipus at Colonus,* but in *Antigone* a woman was the heroine. It became apparent that this heroine did not appeal to the redhaired boy. She broke the laws of the state, and during a war, moreover. And for a very private reason. In that light it served her right. According to Aristotle, one must feel fear and sympathy for the hero of a tragedy, while with such an unsympathetic heroine as this one that was out of the question. Besides which, there was the girl's fiancé (the young lad stubbornly insisted on calling Antigone a "girl," to the amusement of his classmates), the son of King Creon. That the king's only son should hang himself on her account was downright deplorable. The play was riddled with sentimentality.

As a result of this promising introduction, a debate arose. Only one boy took the side of Antigone, the "girl." She was courageous, he said, enormously courageous for a girl. But the "girl" was still damned.

Becker understood: this debate was meant in his honor. They considered it necessary to show off their manliness, and believed that they owed this attitude to him, the warrior returned home.

One of them praised *Oedipus Rex*. That was real drama. Oedipus had been guilty of wrong, too, but he had faced up to it and had executed his punishment with his own hands.

Now they waited expectantly for what Becker would say. This was his debut in the class. The tacit ovation given him by the discussion cheered him. He had credit to draw upon with the class.

"Let us talk about the tragic element in each of the three plays. What is Oedipus's tragedy?"

They repeated: he had been guilty of a great wrong, the murder of his father, marriage with his own mother, and that had resulted in punishment.

164

"Let us think about that," Becker suggested. "Don't tell me his deeds, but show me to what extent, if indeed at all, he was guilty. He is the man who committed the deeds—but is he also the perpetrator, the guilty party?"

They understood what he was aiming at: the Delphic oracle that preceded the crimes.

A large blond fellow in the first row said, slowly and softly, "It is not his fault. An oracle existed from a time before he was even born. It prophesied that he would commit both these crimes. As soon as he hears of that later, he does everything he can to keep from slipping into error."

The class was violent in its contradiction. "Precisely, but still he killed old Laius and married Jocasta, and there's no way he can get away from that."

The very self-confident redhead shouted, "Oedipus would be quite put out if you told him he wasn't responsible. Otherwise he would simply have let the matter rest and declared: how can I help it? Instead of that, he put his own eyes out."

The stolid blond lad in the first row, Heinz Riedel, asked after a short pause, "Please explain to me how he is supposed to arrange things to keep from murdering? His parents have abandoned him at birth because of the oracle. He grew up with a cobbler. He learned neither his own name nor that of his parents. Later King Polybius of Corinth adopted him and he considers him to be his father; and then he learns that he will murder his own father. He immediately takes the necessary measures, he does not return to Corinth. And then what happens but that out on a country road, at a narrow crossroads, he meets up with a man who is a total stranger, they get into an argument about who is to yield, the old man strikes first and Oedipus has the misfortune to hit back in just the wrong way so that the old man falls and dies. From Oedipus's point of view, it was a common brawl. He doesn't think any more about it."

The redhead, Neumann by name, calls from behind, "That would make it a mere accident. Which means the play's not a tragedy at all."

When the blond fell silent, Becker urged him on, "Riedel, you can't evade the question. Is there no guilt involved?"

Riedel: "It simply couldn't be avoided. It was fate."

Becker, who liked the warm, calm tone of the lad: "It simply befalls men. Does that mean that men are not guilty? Are the gods guilty, do you think, as the Greeks saw it?"

Riedel: "Above the gods there is *moira*."

165

Becker: "Correct, an inescapable fate. And that's how Sophocles sees it. Sophocles presents in his drama the total impotence of men when confronted with ineluctable fate, whose motives and meanings, whose relationship to themselves they cannot comprehend. As soon as Oedipus is confronted by this fate, he attempts to avoid it. But fate does not let itself be tricked. Oedipus has to go down that terrible path prescribed for him—he knows not why. He wants to do the best thing. But he resists in vain. You can see that most clearly in that segment of his life when he believes that he must flee from his father in Corinth, and does he ever flee him—only to meet up with his father out on the road he just happens to be traveling. And doom takes its own course."

The class was silent. They had moved on from the gleeful damnations of Antigone the "girl." They could see the situation with Oedipus, but they couldn't begin to deal with it.

"So that the question remains open—if we don't wish to speak of mere chance in the play—where, in our sense of the words, do guilt and responsibility actually lie. Human freedom, personal freedom, is the precondition for responsibility for us. That is the central reality of any deed. We would call a play a tragedy, I think, if a hero attempts something great and worthy with all his strength, but finds it requires more strength than he has. It is in that way that Prometheus does battle with the gods, or a fallen angel with the power of heaven—he is flung into the abyss. The deed for which they suffer is one they desired to do. The equation works. In *Oedipus* as you can see, the equation does not work according to our concepts. So let us research the matter: does Oedipus consider, as do a few of you, his deeds to be matters of chance?"

And in this way they slowly got around to talking about the shadowy events preceding the oracle and Oedipus's birth. A dreadful narrative emerges—about Oedipus's father, even his grandfather. And this same grandfather so long dead, it turns out, had received a warning from Apollo not to enter into a certain marriage.

He cast this divine warning, Becker summarizes, to the wind. "And to this wicked man, then, is born Laius, who was murdered, and to Laius was born Oedipus, who is forced to blind himself, and to Oedipus are born two sons, who slew each other, and this poor Antigone, whose tragic fate we were discussing earlier. One man, one single man, had been guilty of wrong in the past, as in the Biblical story of Adam. But this one wrong, the guilt of this one man, was grave because it was committed against a divine power. The suffering of the children occurs as a result of the guilt of the parents and grandparents. The children know nothing of this—but the curse is laid upon them and they destroy themselves."

The students sat there, uneasy.

Friedrich looked out into the class and shut his eyes. They were the children, the heirs, grown older now while others had been out there engaged in war. They had assumed the guilt of those older than they—and they knew nothing of it.

Two of them whispered at the back. Becker invited them to speak up.

Finally one of them said, "It reminds me of venereal disease."

Becker had to force the lad to explain himself. The young fellow's face turned red, and he explained that he had read that venereal diseases were passed on to the children, at least fairly often. That's why many children were born idiots.

Becker: "Correct. Another example of a result of some former event that does not restrict itself to a single person. That means that nature, so to speak, makes the family as a collective unit responsible for something, so that members of the family cannot avoid their connection with the others. In such cases we have a kind of inherited curse in the corporeal sense."

Still the strain lay upon the class. Becker was glad; they were protesting, they would not accept such a fate.

And now the tall, pale class spokesman turned around to the class, made a slight motion of his head, carefully removed his glasses from his nose, and while he carefully wiped them with a leather cloth, he calmly remarked, "I've also read that talents are inherited, and sometimes the tendency to commit crimes and certain other pathological tendencies."

A deadly stillness in the classroom. The class spokesman slowly replaced his glasses and stared ingenuously at Becker. Throats were cleared. Someone whispered with a giggle, "It's all fate. There are no more crimes, they can close the prisons. You could pull off most anything and blame it all on your grandmother."

The class spokesman nodded in agreement and said matter-of-factly, "That's my opinion, too. That's why we're on King Creon's side, too."

Becker did not understand this strangely underscored remark Schröter had made. The behavior of the class was very odd, and while he paged through his book as he thought about this, the redhead spoke up again, "So then it's all just like I said before. The person to blame is the one who's been up to something, and there's no way he can talk himself out of it."

Becker, uncertain of himself, had the vague feeling that it would be best if he moved away from the subject. Therefore he asked the class to open their books to the text itself again, they would return to the problem in the next session.

And so they began with the moving exchange between Antigone and the chorus. Antigone, condemned and being led off by the guards, sings her own funeral song:

"See me, citizens of my fatherland, setting forth on my last journey, looking my last on the sunlight—soon for me it will be no more; but Death, who hides us all from the sun, is hasty with me; soon I shall stand on Acheron's shore."

She sings of how she was to be a bride, and to what end she has come: "But the Lord of the Dark Lake will be my bridegroom." To this the chorus answers words of consolation, that are none:

"Yet I would give it praise, the way of your going: neither did sickness waste nor violence smite you. Mastering fate in this wise never has mortal gone down to Hades."

Becker sensed, as he followd their translation and added his commentary, that he had to struggle to free himself from anxiety. Now it was clear: Schröter's remark was aimed at the director. But how did he dare presume to do it, really, so coolly and smoothly, just like that. They thought they could allow themselves remarks like that right here in the classroom, a student speaking about the school director. Things must have come to quite a pass.

Concerning the Difference Between the Law of the Gods and The Law of Nations

During the break, Becker went for a walk with portly Dr. Krug in the schoolyard. The students from the senior class whispered behind their backs; Becker was the talk of the school today. He watched as a group of his pupils gathered around Schröter, the class spokesman. They were engaged in vigorous discussion. As Becker passed by with Krug, they fell silent.

Again the boom of stomping feet as he entered the classroom. They finished translating the great antiphonal chorus. The choir commends Antigone to her fate: "All too rash was your deed, unhappy maiden. Bolding daring even the throne of justice: there you fell. Alas, you must pay to the utmost, doom of your father."

But Antigone laments: "Then it is certain I must take this journey, for none befriends me. There will be no marriage-song; I may not longer even look on the sun. No one mourns my passing, none even weeps."

"And so how," Becker asked as they closed their books, "shall we deal with this now? Did you use the break to continue your discussion of the problems of classical tragedy?"

They smiled. Becker asked the class spokesman, this slender, delicate lad (he had something of the pretty-boy about him) to speak up. He balked, but then declared he had something to say for the whole class.

They had all been very glad that he had taken charge of their Greek class, some of them for one reason, others for another (followed by loud murmurs of agreement from several rows, then a sharp "psst"). They would be particularly pleased, however, if he would tell them about the war.

Enthusiastic stomping.

Becker asked them to show some consideration for the class below them, then explained that he would think about it. He would ask them to give him some time, the right moment would offer itself.

Again the start of stomping, but this was quickly suppressed. Becker paged through the text. What was the meaning of the mysterious reference to the various reasons why the class had welcomed his return? What were the murmurs and the "psst" all about? He would have to consult Krug about all this.

Now to return to their subject. There was no great enthusiasm at all for further discussion of Antigone. This war generation rejected the play as feeble and sentimental.

The class spokesman replied for the whole class. "Antigone really doesn't have our sympathy. One of her brothers bravely fought for his native city; he fell in battle and was buried with honors. As it should be. The other brother was a traitor who had assembled a great hostile army to attack his home. That would be the same as if now the Spartacists were to invite France to send troops here to do Germany in." ("Right!" came an echo from the classroom.) "And if Polynices, the rebel, falls in the attempt, then the Thebans are right in letting his body lie on the field of battle."

Becker: "And his sister Antigone?"

Schröter, the spokesman: "Should think as they do. She is herself a Theban and old enough to know what is happening. Even a woman should know that much. It wouldn't even have been necessary for Creon to issue a special edict. He did, however, and despite that, Antigone goes out to the city gate."

This was patently the general opinion. Sophocles had written a flop with his notion of fate and this heroine.

The class spokesman added in a smart-alecky tone that as an officer and soldier who had served in the field, Becker would obviously share their opinion.

The senior class hung on his words. Becker rubbed his hand across his brow and cheeks. He walked down into the class and leaned against the window sill, his arms crossed.

"You asked me to speak to you about my wartime experiences. In a certain sense I can keep my promise right now, even though I am not speaking directly of the war, by presenting you with my understanding of the story of Antigone. You do of course understand, I think, that as a teacher who defends his subject and materials, as a classical philologist, that I am not going to leave Sophocles in the lurch. But, it is more than just that.

"Before the break you could not reconcile yourselves to the Greek notion of fate and inherited guilt. It is, however, the central idea of antiquity. In pre-Christian times, man did not understand himself so individualistically, was not so conscious of himself as a person, as a self. Which is why the actions of a classical hero are so peculiar. The heroes of antiquity are literally struggling to be able to act at all. But they do not succeed. They do not succeed in latching onto their self and doing their deed. Now to Antigone. I'll grant that we can almost understand her without the ancient notion of fate, and that has also kept the play alive even today. She acts, at least at first, entirely on the basis of her feelings. The dead man is quite simply her brother. She is not about to waver in this feeling—and the king can decree whatever he likes. He is her brother and she has a sisterly duty to mourn and bury him. In following her emotions, she challenges the king, and willfully, knowingly disobeys the law of the state. She commits a wrongful act in our sense, she is guilty of a crime. Now let us look at the deed itself."

But at this point a full-grown, broad-shouldered and large-headed fellow in the middle of the class raised his head—August Schramm, the son of a left-wing district deputy in the neighborhood and himself active in a workers' organization, the "Red" of the class. He wanted to say something about Antigone's deed. He first made disparaging remarks about the play in general: "Prehistoric fables, patricide, blood-guilt, nothing but atrocity stories and dark superstitions."

Then he continued, "But Antigone represents a modern personality. She confronts a tyrant, and doesn't come to heel the way several people here would like. Her brother has fallen, and she is determined that he will be buried, and she won't be denied. If the king forbids it, that only proves what tyrants like him presume they can do. And it's all the same whether we're talking about a man or a woman. Though it's bad enough that there are no men in the city to do it."

Becker (he watches the icy stares of the others): "Antigone represents then, if I understand you correctly, the rights of the person, of the individual, over against the state?"

Schramm: "The political rights of the oppressed over against tyrants. And Sophocles takes her side. And if the play is so famous it's only because, like Schiller's *William Tell,* it's a play about political freedom."

The redhead interrupted (it was obvious that these two were implacable enemies): "Antigone is a female who doesn't have the vaguest notion what a state is. Her little brain cannot comprehend the fact that you have to get control of your feelings when it's a matter of the general welfare and that many people even sacrifice themselves for the state. She can only howl like a pampered poodle when her foot gets stepped on. Isn't it a curious idea to want to make a tragic heroine out of a person like that, who causes trouble to the world around her because of her feelings and is willing to endanger everyone else."

From the rear someone called out in agreement: "She's simply ridiculous."

Becker wrung his hands in exasperation. "It's getting worse and worse."

Laughter.

The "Red," Schramm: "Of course she's obeying her feelings. Wouldn't it be just dandy if she didn't react. She's not going to put up with a tyrant's brutality, and so does what she can. It's just a rotten shame that the chorus stands there singing dirges instead of wading into battle."

"A revolution, perhaps?" the belligerent Neumann suggested.

"Why not?" Schramm replied.

Neumann: "Schramm naturally wants to shunt the whole thing onto another track. Presumably Antigone doesn't do what she does because of her feelings, but because she has a definite political goal. I don't see any of that. She doesn't think about anything. Her sister Ismene is a lot cleverer."

Becker asked them to open their books again.

They read from verse 441 on.

The guards have just discovered Antigone performing cultic rituals over the body of her brother, and she is lead before Creon. The king interrogates her in the presence of the guards:

"You, then—you whose face is bent to the earth—do you confess or do you deny the deed?"

Antigone: "I did it."

At this the guards are dismissed and the actual interrogation begins.

Creon asks whether she knew of the edict forbidding the burial of Polynices as an enemy of the state. She says she did.

Creon: "And you had the boldness to transgress that law?"

To which Antigone replies: "Yes, for it was not Zeus made such a law; such is not the justice of the gods. Nor did I think that your decree had such force that a mortal could override the unwritten and unchanging statutes of heaven. For their existence and authority are not merely for today or yesterday, but for all time, and no man knows when they were first put forth."

Becker: "Here we have the core of the play. Antigone reinforces her opinion later in verse 518, after Creon holds up to her that her brother fell as an enemy of the fatherland. She does not yield, but answers: 'Nevertheless, Hades desires these rites.' Nor does she waver when Creon falls into a rage and and makes it clear to her that 'Your place, then, is with the dead.'"

Becker, back at his podium, concludes: "You can see therefore: Antigone is not following some blind impulse in doing this deed, but is governed by a universally recognized, moral and religious understanding. Antigone is not doing battle at all. She sees herself as an instrument. She is serving divine law. For good or evil she is bound up with it. And in so doing, without even knowing it, she is also initiating the end of the dreadful hereditary curse. She submits to divine law."

Schramm, the socialist, replied coolly and saucily: "We shouldn't blame the Greeks all that much for their religious notions. People back then simply weren't very rational. Without these fairy tales about Zeus and Hades, though, the play would be even better and much more suited to modern times."

"Suited to modern times? How?" the class spokesman asked mockingly. "All because of your revolution? Not even the chorus is buying that."

"Because they're cowards. They leave Antigone stranded. But the tyrant knows what Antigone means and acts upon it. And the tyrant's followers would understand her right away, too. They've understood her here well enough."

The spokesman: "Where?"

Schramm: "Here in this classroom. That's why you don't like the play."

The spokesman stood up and turned toward Becker, pleading for help, for him to protect him from political libel in the classroom. Vigorous stomping ensued. A less vigorous scraping of feet tried to express protest.

Becker waved this off; no one would think of libeling someone else in this classroom. He assumed that this had not been anyone's intention.

He grew very earnest. He praised the class for not understanding the play in simply aesthetic terms or as a mere exercise in translation. He wanted, however, to present them once more with the central conflict, and then they could go right on and take issue with it.

"How is a person supposed to behave in relation to the state, Sophocles asks. He doesn't make the answer easy, not as easy as some of you think it is. That minor, petty feelings have to yield before public necessities—he does not even bother to discuss that. Antigone, and please note this well, does not stand in opposition to the power of the state, in the person of the king, as just any private citizen, but rather she represents a principle, which is at least as legitimate as that represented by the king. You suggested, Schramm, that she was a rebel, and was calling for revolution. She is courageous, but no rebel. She is absolutely the opposite of a rebel. If anyone in the play is a radical, then it's—and don't be amazed by this—King Creon. You haven't noticed that fact at all? But of course, because by virtue of his indeed tyrannical will, of his pride in his victory and in being king, he believes he can dismiss sacred tradition, ancient facts of life. For in civilized Greece it was a fact of life that a family mourns and buries its dead. They had the duty to perform certain funeral rites and to honor the gods of the dead. Creon believes he can ignore these old rites of piety. He believes that once he has defeated and destroyed his enemies he can do with them as he pleases, even beyond the bounds of death. But there are bounds that are set by other powers. He has run up against supernatural powers. From them come the laws that no one dare undermine, and that are so strong that they can allow themselves to speak through the mouth of a weak young girl. For these invisible powers have inscribed their laws in the most secure of places, in the hearts of men. It is to such unwritten laws that Antigone appeals. All men know of this law, including Creon. He believes he can break it, and that Antigone must be condemned to death. But he himself learns a dreadful lesson."

They sat very still. No one knew what to say. They accepted this, but only lukewarmly. For the moment they did not know how to react. That was all so farfetched. They could agree, but to whom did it make any difference? Ancient burial customs, and a woman gets all excited about them and appeals to an unwritten law in her heart. It was kind of funny, actually.

Again the refined, smooth Schröter, the spokesman, raised his hand, resuming his steady, calm and cool voice, "Without wishing to impugn the validity of this doctrine of unwritten laws, I would nevertheless like to pose one question: Where does that get you? The state has to depend on something. It must work with cogent, written laws that have been established once and for all. It expresses the morality of its citizens in the paragraphs of a written code of laws. Under no circumstances can the citizens be given the opportunity, especially not during wartime, to claim that some divine inspiration has been imparted to them by which they can then bring disorder to the whole of civil life."

Even while Schröter was speaking, the blond boy, Riedel, indicated that he wanted to have the floor. But when Becker invited him to speak, he hesitated and sat there with a red face. Finally he managed to say that he had nothing in particular to add, he only wanted to say that Becker's explanation seemed plausible to him . . . He stuttered a few words, Becker nodded to him to encourage him, but nothing more came.

Now Becker declared that they would put the topic aside, and should anyone still have questions, he was available in the teacher's office. In any case, they would return to the questions involved in one context or another. He felt exhausted after this debate. It depressed him.

The spokesman and Riedel appeared afterward. It was curious how they stood there at the door of the teacher's office. Becker found them standing next to each other but pretending the other was not there. First Schröter came in. He asked whether they might have a short conference, if possible outside the school itself.

Becker asked him to come to his home later that afternoon. The class spokesman had made an unpleasant impression on him even in this short exchange of words. He had a strange, categorical way of asking for this "conference" as he called it—as if it were not a matter of a conversation gladly granted, but rather some sort of official matter.

Blond Riedel stood there with a burning face and began once more to stutter his thanks to Becker and to assure him that he agreed with him. Becker thanked the young fellow amiably. Riedel was sweating; he obviously had something else on his mind. He wanted to talk about something else. Becker encouraged him, but he could not get it out. The young lad abruptly ended the conversation, made a little bow, said "many thanks," and was gone without daring to look Becker in the eyes.

The director did not make an appearance that morning. Krug, too, was not to be seen. So when the large building was quiet once again, and the teachers and students were back in their classrooms (it really was a monstrous learning factory), Becker made his way home.

Life Emerges from the Books

His mother was not listening very attentively as Friedrich told her about school. Only after he had eaten and was about to return to his room did he notice that she was still sitting at the table. He turned back to her and asked what was the matter. She looked up at him despondently and sighed.

He sat down beside her, and she explained.

Among the people she visited, trying to be a good Samaritan, was a sick man, an old man who did not live far from here and was suffering from incurable stomach cancer. The man had had surgery, but without success. Jaundice had set in. He suffered great pain and needed morphine. He had continued to stay at home, and was being cared for by a nurse. But the nurse occasionally had time off, and today was her free day. The wife hadn't wanted to be alone with the sick man, and had turned to the Patriotic Women's Club for assistance, and she had been asked to go over.

"So I went. It was a depressing situation. He lay there in a large, darkened parlor smelling of iodoform. At first I didn't even see him as I entered with his wife. He had crept under the blanket. The woman went about in a white coat, like a nurse, but without ever touching anything. She did it just for herself. She was afraid of catching something. She wouldn't go near the bed, she left the room immediately, would touch the doorknob only with a cloth in her hand. I told her, 'Cancer isn't contagious, you know.' She answered that people had told her that, but she was simply afraid. She gave such huffy answers. She was a little, delicate woman with reddish hair, most of the time with a nasty look on her face as if she felt she had to defend herself. It wasn't easy dealing with her."

"A kind of cactus," Friedrich said.

175

"You might say. I had the impression that she was angry with her husband for being ill, just for that reason in fact. She simply let him lie there and avoided him. I wasn't sure whether she acted that way because she was really afraid of catching something or whether she was just saying that. At any rate she wasn't willing to take over even for the few hours the nurse had off. She told me when I was alone with her that she had turned to our auxiliary because the sick man 'was obstinate'—that's how she put it—and wouldn't have any other nurse. But that she couldn't manage herself.

"I sat in the room with the patient. It took quite a while until he crept out again from under his blanket. He didn't want any light. I don't know why. He wanted to have it continually dark. That's why he had crept under his blanket. As he reemerged, I saw his long, gray hair and his face all yellow as a quince. He asked me to get his glasses for him. I couldn't find them, and when I left the room to ask his wife where his glasses were, she was outraged; what did he need them for. They were lying in a buffet drawer in the living room. She had put them there. She gave them to me in their case and repeated—she's not a good wife, that woman—she didn't know what he would want them for.

"He simply could not see very well. And besides that, the room was dark. When he had put on his glasses, he hid himself again and wept. He is perhaps in his late fifties. His face is all dried up and a yellow like I've never seen before, almost blackish yellow. And his eyes are so unnatural because of the yellow, too. Oh, how sorry I felt for the man. I had to give him an injection. And then I had to bed him down again and change the sheets. He is incontinent. And all the while he wept from the pain, and was ashamed of himself—and right away back under the blanket. I didn't see his face even once more again before I left. While I was changing the sheets and looking for some cotton swabs, his wife showed me where they were, but then ran right back out again and locked the door behind her.

"Afterward I met their grown son in the corridor, a bank official. He looked like her. He did not go in to see his father. I heard them arguing for a moment in the living room about money. The son slammed doors. Then the nurse came and relieved me. She asked me as I was washing my hands whether the wife had helped me or not, and laughed. Then she asked me whether the son was there yet. 'Have they already been arguing? They do it every day. I'm happy when they've both been invited out and don't come home till late. Then at least it's quiet around here.'

"That's how people are, Friedrich," concluded his mother, nodding

176

gloomily. "I'll have to go there from time to time. The nurse doesn't want to stay on, not unless she has some time off at least twice a week."

"And you can take over for her, Mother?"

"If you had asked me that before, yesterday I mean, before I had been there, I would have said no, I'd rather not, that it would be too difficult for me. But today—when I think about that poor man. Maybe he's the same kind of person as his wife and his son, and is being punished for it now and is suffering. I want to give him support, Friedrich. I have to."

She took Friedrich's hand. "Friedrich, how difficult life is. But you know that already. Try to stay happy. It is un-Christian to give in."

An hour later—just when the mailman was due—something was thrown into the mailbox at the door, but without anyone ringing the bell. Becker's mother went out and brought Friedrich a letter, unstamped, apparently delivered personally, the address printed in fine Roman characters, as was the letter, on expensive ivory paper. Becker read it.

It was, without any postscript, without any signature, a poem by Stefan George:

The New Empire

When from the trampled battlefield you returned home
Unscathed by the scorching rain, by the hell of bursting debris,
The words flowed almost chaste from your lips, of duty done,
Of charges bold and rash, of labors that wearied and taxed.
Your shoulder lifted freer, because it was no more laden
With a hundred fates.
In your arm still lay the reflex of action and ready command,
In your soft, pensive eyes, the wariness of constant danger.
Because those so much older than you had fought back their terror,
There arose from you an energy of assured composure
As your youthful figure towered up and with easy grace
Swung down from the saddle.
The die of battle was cast far differently from what you'd dreamt.
Because the shattered army had laid down its weapons now,
You stood before me, saddened!"

Becker turned to the yellow envelope, looked inside, but found nothing more. Who was this? A student. At once he saw before him the face of the blond boy, Riedel. He feels inhibited. I don't know why. Now he writes this anonymously, disguises his handwriting, copies a poem. — I like the lad. He has some secret. What can I do?

At exactly five o'clock the bell rang—Paul Schröter, class spokesman.

An elegant young gentleman, he wore a stiff black hat, dark patent leather gloves, which he removed slowly, one after the other, out in the corridor. He then took off his well-fitting black winter coat, hung it up, and stood there in his smart frock-coat. His movements were very formal, and he permitted Becker, who had slipped out of his robe and into a suit in honor of his guest, to lead him into his study. He inquired dutifully after Becker's health. He then sat down when requested to do so in the chair in front of the bookcase. Becker sat near his desk.

Schröter made small-talk. He seemed to like to hear himself. He was personally very interested in Becker's war experiences. Becker could demand an entrance fee whenever he decided to spend an hour telling about them, the students would come pouring out of all the other classes. His father, a member of the parents' advisory committee, had suggested Becker also deliver the lecture in the auditorium for the adults.

Becker let the young man make whatever approaches he cared to and only replied with brief, courteous remarks.

At last his visitor broke off, looked down at his knees, pulled the creases of his trousers tight and gave his countenance a determined, pointed look. He declared that he had come to discuss a serious matter concerning the school, one about which Becker had doubtless already heard.

Friedrich was given a sharp, inquisitorial look.

Becker shook his head.

Schröter fixed him with his eye. "You haven't? Without wishing to be indiscreet, I'm sure the director called your attention to the matter when he gave the class over to you."

"My dear friend, what do you mean by this? Don't beat around the bush. Speak up."

Becker felt embarrassment creeping over him. He remembered the gossip that Dr. Krug had shared with him about the unusual "friendships" that the director maintained with several of the students. But why were they coming to him about this?

Schröter: "Really, that's quite hard for me to understand, Herr Dr. Becker, that he would say nothing to you—about why he wanted to give up the class?"

Becker: "I'm really not in any position, Schröter, to give you an answer to your strange questions. I'm amazed at you. You surely have not been taken with the notion of bearing tales out of school to me."

"The matter has long since gone beyond the bounds of mere gossip. Certain serious persons outside the school are already concerning themselves with the matter. It has even reached the ears of the director himself."

"Of the Herr Direktor, please, Schröter."

"Excuse me, naturally. I myself have been commissioned, as class spokesman, to make contact with the Herr Direktor and to keep him informed. I fulfilled my commission yesterday morning."

"I still do not know the nature of the matter at hand."

Schröter: "We had assumed that the Herr Direktor had informed you. We supposed that he suddenly recalled you from your leave, and we saw that as a result of my action."

"Who is we? And what was the nature of your commission?"

"I was asked to inform the Herr Direktor that if his friendly relations with students of the school did not cease, a public scandal would result."

Becker cleared his throat, stood up, and paced back and forth in disgust. The best thing would be to grab this kid by the collar and throw him out. He kept his distance from this clever and elegant hoodlum.

Schröter: "The Herr Direktor attempted to portray it all as harmless. He pretended to be outraged at such gossip, and declared that he would call to account whoever it was that was spreading such rumors. I explained that this was the point of my mission, that this was likewise our concern, and that we expected immediate steps on his part for the sake of the reputation of our school. He repeated that I could depend on that. He took the news with complete calm and thought it hilarious that I in particular (he meant it as a compliment) would be taken in by such rumors. He spoke of the abnormal imagination of some people, of the jealousies among students and so on. Then—no investigation followed, but rather he turned our class over to you."

"Does this concern students in the senior class?"

"One of them."

"You are mistaken at any rate, Schröter, in assuming that the Herr Direktor approached me first in the matter of my taking over the class. It was I who came to see him. He engaged me as a result of my own initiative."

The young gentleman smiled knowingly. "I see. You practically flew right into his mouth like a roast pigeon."

"Schröter, watch how you speak of the Herr Direktor. Have you no manners?"

The young gentleman did not stand up. A soft flush flitted across his face. He grinned in embarrassment and stroked his chin. He muttered something like "I beg your pardon," and gazed at the floor.

Becker, standing close to him: "Have you anything else on your chest? I will, as you might expect, inform the Herr Direktor of your visit."

Schröter, arrogantly: "I suggest you do. It will make no impression on him. He has already heard a great deal about this matter and has not moved on it. I came to you, Herr Dr. Becker, because we assumed he was hiding behind you, and that he was making a fool of you."

Becker: "That's enough, Schröter."

Now at last the young dandy stood up, standing there somewhat at a loss. He tugged at his necktie.

Becker asked him, "Who is 'we' if I may ask?"

Schröter threw his head back. "Oh, the class and a few people outside the school."

"That's very interesting. So that this is a regular campaign against the director, is it not?"

Schröter stood there, cleared his throat, and pulled himself together. He fixed his eyes on Becker as if he were a target, bowing toward it, and then walked past him stiffly as an automaton toward the door. Becker followed him slowly into the corridor. He watched Schröter open the hall door. He heard him descend the steps at a slow, firm pace.

In the living room, his mother sat mending at the table by gaslight, a sturdy, amiable woman, her glasses set on her nose. Friedrich sat down beside her. She nodded to him. "You see, Friedrich, you're slowly getting into the swing of things."

He told her about his visitor. While he spoke, she laid her mending aside, removed her glasses, and listened in horror. The director, that poor man.

"Mother, unfortunately there is something to all this. I've heard about it myself."

His mother, who had met the director on a few occasions, did not want to believe it.

At last she said, "You'll have to speak with him and lay it all before him. It's ghastly if it turns out to be true. He's ruining his life. He can lose his position."

"Mother, if it were a matter of warning, then he would already have changed one would think. Once, during a visit in my study, he hinted at it. He's apparently afraid. He's constantly afraid. But he keeps right on."

"Such a fine man. Friedrich, speak with him. Go see him, today."

"Today? He'll be very surprised."

"Go, Friedrich.'

He telephoned the director, who received him in his apartment that evening at seven o'clock.

He moved to greet Becker jovially in his black velvet jacket, gray trousers and elegant slippers. He wore a loose, black bow tie of the sort artists wear. He had remarkably small feet and hands. His dimly lit atelier was wonderfully cozy now after dark.

"So, your great day has come to a happy conclusion," the director said as he sat down at the table where a spirit-burner flickered beneath a samovar. "How nice of you to want to give me a report directly from the field of battle. Was it not too much for you, two hours right from the start?"

Becker was glad to take a cup of tea. The director lit a cigarette, they talked, everything went well. Then Becker began to speak about the visit Schröter, the class spokesman, had paid him that afternoon.

The director, calmly: "A bright lad, but perhaps a bit too clever, don't you think?"

"He came for a very particular reason. Someone had sent him. It concerns the gossip being spread about your friendly relationships with your students, but you know about that already. I don't rightly understand what Schröter wanted of me. He was suggesting, I presume, that you and I were in cahoots, that I was allowing myself to be misused by you and he wanted to warn me."

"Actually that was very nice of the boy. An expression of sympathy for you. He came to me with these stories as well. He takes his office as class spokesman very seriously, thinks of himself as a sort of guardian of morality, as the Cato of the academy."

A pause.

Becker: "I thought, Herr Direktor, that I had a duty to you, Herr Direktor, both a personal one and to you as my superior."

"You needn't bother about the superior part of it, my dear Dr. Becker. I find it touching that you are alarmed on my account because of this affair. I thank you with all my heart. My friend, you don't know the school now, what it's become since the war. We are in the middle of a revolution, and yet at the far end of a revolution. I am a patriotic man, but have nothing in common with the clergy and the church, and as a result I'm decried as an atheist, branded a freethinker, a libertine. And of course they attribute vices to me. It's an old method. An atheist is right away a sodomite. For those people any

181

means in their struggle is just, and I am unfortunately without any support. Since I would rather forego the support of socialists."

Becker: "I have heard about that."

Director: "So you know about that. My position is rather isolated."

He silently puffed on his cigarette.

The Director: "Did Schröter name any names?"

Becker: "He said that it concerned one student from the senior class."

The director made a disdainful gesture. "There you have it. Concern yourself with a student, show any human interest for him, become for him something other than a mere authority figure, and then—they'll string you up. Instead of their being happy that you've climbed down off your pedestal, that you're not just drilling students, that you care about the individual talents and interests of the students. No, they howl like hounds and are ready to bite you. Those people have only one notion of a school: make assignments and correct the homework. We're regressing, my dear Dr. Becker."

Becker asked sadly, "But where do these boys get such gossip?"

The director stroked his full, rosy cheeks and gave this serious consideration. "There can be several sources. The most probable is that at some point you've shown an interest in a student who neither understands nor deserves it, and out of pure wickedness he tells the others whatever he pleases. It can also be that one of them is jealous of another, wants to take revenge on me because I've found my interest poorly repaid and act reserved. What should I do with a young man whose sense of good taste I would like to form, but of whom I soon notice that he only wishes to boast about his visits with me or is secretly only interested in my cigarettes?"

"Is that the cause of all this?" asked Becker.

The director tapped his finger on the table in front of Becker. "I'm sorry that you've stepped into a hornet's nest. That's most certainly not what you went to war for, my dear friend, for all this sort of thing to reappear."

Becker swallowed his disgust. He thought of his mother: "The poor man, you must help him." But there he sits and he's lying.

Becker bent forward. He propped his chin in one hand and studied the arabesques in the carpet. The director smoked in silence.

Finally Becker asked softly, "Can I be of any help, Herr Direktor?"

He gave a genuine shout of joy. "There is the question. That's what I've waited for so long. Finally, someone on my side. Of course I need your help. For someone to demonstrate that he understands me and throws this gossip back at them. Just watch how they'll come back down once someone stands up to them, especially to people like that. It's all political agitation."

Becker: "And if I can be of assistance to you in some manner, I can also be absolutely certain that you're hiding nothing from me and that there is truly nothing behind all this gossip, correct?"

"My dear friend!"

Becker: "There are people, after all, who take special pleasure in young men, who love their company and who perhaps—also caress them, out of friendship."

"You see. That's my situation exactly."

"Young people can also be terribly mean. I observed that with this Schröter."

"You see."

"If it were just a matter of that, of conversations, small-talk—why not . . ."

"Why not? That's what I say. We'll not allow reactionary idiots to take this human right from us."

Now the director paced back and forth on his carpet with a militant expression, between a small bronze statue of a discus thrower and a tall, white reproduction of the Hermes by Praxiteles.

Becker followed him with his eyes. He said without intonation, "We're getting some clear, cold weather now. People are going to the mountains to ski."

The director seemed busy with his thoughts. "I see. Is that what people are doing?"

Becker: "I believe so. You once told me you like to ski, did you not?"

"That's true. But who has time for that nowadays, my dear friend?"

"Might you now use such fine weather to take a trip, to the Riesengebirge or the Black Forest? Perhaps to Todtmoos?"

"What makes you think of that? Ah, you mean I should—make myself scarce?"

"It would ease the situation greatly. And it would do you good. Go ahead, Herr Direktor, do it."

"Whatever are you thinking, Dr. Becker? What do you think of me? Is that why you came? I thought you wanted to offer me your assistance. Am I supposed to slip away? That would be as good as an open confession. Why, I might just as well put a bullet through my head right now."

Becker: "A vacation, what could be more natural?"

The director stood beside the table. He pulled the bow of his necktie tight. In the shadows, his cheeks were paler and gaunter.

"I beg you, let us drop this topic. I thank you for your goodwill. You don't understand how one has to handle this sort of people." He smiled again. "No, my friend, that you don't understand." He bent down over the table to Becker. "Sometimes one can even plug up their mouths with money. That shows the measure of their character."

He whistled through his teeth and tripped merrily along the row of his sculptures. "Your report was in any case of great benefit." He repeated for the third time, "Of great benefit." He was apparently thinking of something else, of something that heartened him.

But as Becker moved to go, the gentleman pulled out his watch. "Five till nine. You're going to call it a night already? Still convalescing? I won't hold you here. And it truly was a . . ."

In the entrance hall Becker passed a young blond man in a sailor's coat. The entry was half in shadows. Becker turned back to look at the young man, who also turned to look from the first landing. Who is that, Becker asked himself once outside. I know him, I know that face—but in a sailor's uniform?—

"They want me to desert you, my dear," said the director. "They want me to take a vacation."

"Take me with you. Why shouldn't you? I don't give a damn what my parents say."

It was Riedel, the blond boy.

Becker made his way home, the results had proven meager. How would he have managed such a conversation with the director in times past? He would certainly not have preached a sermon on morality— you don't interfere with other people's private lives—but first he would have laid out the difficulties for him in clear and no uncertain terms, telling him that the faculty could not simply ignore such rumors. And the Herr Direktor could then draw his own conclusions about the matter. Had he done nothing and had simply stayed on, then—why then the State School Commission would have had to concern itself with this embarrassing matter if the police did not first take matters into their hands. In times past he would under no circumstances have considered the affair anything more than an embarrassing incident.

But now—Becker was in torment, as if it were his personal problem.

His mother was waiting for him. She at once saw how worried he was. He stayed with her in the living room.

"He simply shrugged it off," Becker concluded. "Ultimately, I achieved nothing at all with him."

"And that's how you'll leave it, Friedrich?"

"What should I do?"

He didn't dare to speak of the meeting in the entrance hall, of his suspicions. The director made an appointment with me for seven o'clock and at eight he was expecting a boy. He is shameless.

"You're not helping him by treating him so gently, Friedrich. If that's how he is, then you must take a firmer stance."

Becker, still preoccupied with that meeting in the entryway, said, "He apparently wasn't even paying close attention to me, he pranced around his atelier and was thinking about—God knows what."

"You're not helping him, believe me. He should be ashamed to have such a vice, especially as a teacher. Friedrich, you're making yourself an accessory if you don't intervene."

"I'm slowly coming to see that too." The thought that that man was now sitting together with a student outraged Becker. "We'll discuss the matter. Tomorrow I have no classes, and after lunch Dr. Krug is coming."

"Friedrich, how timid you are. There's nothing to discuss. You're not going to ask this man Krug what you have to do, are you? You're not going to push it off onto him, are you?"

"Only just how one ought to proceed, Mother."

"Friedrich, that's not the correct way to handle it. You men with your procedures, conferences, discussions. What for? Simply go to the man and tell him it can't go on like this. With this vice you cannot remain at our school. That's like setting the cat to guard over the pigeons."

"He doesn't even admit he's done wrong."

"And you just sit there? You are certain that they've told you the truth, aren't you?"

"To my sorrow, quite certain."

"What do you mean, to your sorrow, Friedrich? I'm a Christian, too, and our Lord said: Judge not lest ye be judged. But many a sheep has to be separated from the herd."

"Fine, Mother. Please sit in with us tomorrow when Krug visits me, Mother."

She was not there when Krug arrived. Krug knew nothing of the events of the previous day and was horrified at the news.

"That they've drawn you into this the moment you appear on the scene! I have very simple advice for you: don't get your fingers burned on this one. The affair is dangerous. It can be regarded from several angles. Your position is very simple, you've not even been permanently reinstated yet. Forget school for now. It won't run away. If someone comes to find you, you're ill."

He opened his arms wide. "You are in a most enviable position. Of course politics is what's behind it. I'd love to make a bolt for it myself."

"But then, how do we make headway on this, Krug?"

"We? What headway? Other people will see to that you can be sure. My dear old pal, keep out of the line of fire. They'll be slinging mud."

"The question is whether I have a duty to intervene."

Dr. Krug, this most peaceable of men, this paragon of indolence, sat there with his mouth wide open and gazed at his friend as if he were a sea-monster. "If I hadn't just heard that with my own ears, I would have disputed that anyone had said it." The man should never have gone back to teaching again, he's really not up to it. "What's that supposed to mean? In a week the scandal will have broken anyway. It can't be prevented. I know the director, I assure you. He'll not dismiss his darlings. He's like an alcoholic. He can't resist the stuff. He knows the threat hanging over him. But it does no good. He's running into misfortune with eyes wide open. It's a tragic affair, Becker, a case study for you as a classicist. The man is not to be helped. No, damn it all, we let him have his head and make a wide circle around him. Happy the man who has not met the same fate. Because, just between us, the same abnormal—predeliction, let's call it, might have fallen to your lot or to mine."

"That's just what I've been thinking. And that's precisely why we must help him."

Krug, with determination, almost with anger: "Not I. Most certainly not I. If you feel drawn to behave like a fool, why *s'il vous plait, monsieur,* please I'll not say, 'After you, good sir.'— On the contrary! Keep your hands off, Becker. You'll incriminate the whole faculty. People would then say that our faculty . . ."

He stopped in mid sentence.

Becker: "But we wouldn't be taking the director's part."

"You know nothing about it. The reactionary rabble is hot on his trail, from the custodian on up—because he's rich, satisfies his appetites, because he plays the cello and dresses elegantly. He riles them. He doesn't fit into their scheme of things. He doesn't have much use for such nationalists. So then, that's sufficient. And then the poor unfortunate felllow happens to have a weakness. I looked into it. At his previous post he kept himself more in check. People whispered all sorts of things, but at the time the gossip was aimed more at a student. The revolution has apparently nudged him forward. The man has literally gone crazy. You can see that."

He pulled out his wallet and took a small lilac envelope from it.

"Just take a look at this, it's in his hand, as you will recognize. A— love-letter to a boy, perfumed paper. Kisses and longing, ardent yearnings. I was at his place one evening before my vacation, and on his tea table I saw a volume by Taine, "The French Revolution." He was reading volume two. He recommended the book to me and pulled down volume one from the bookcase. The man is pursued by misfortune. In that volume lay this letter. Signed: "Your puppy dog.""

Becker: "Nauseating."

"And then this page with a poem by Stefan George."

Becker took the sheet of paper and read the verses:

"Love deems the man unfit who e'er regrets,
For love endures, for just a glance, all pain,
And squanders, without thanks, great wealth and gems
And blesses in self-sacrificial flames.
Dear one. As that may be, your road to bliss,
Known but to you, grows dark at my approach,
And wounded I pull back. May fate ne'er lead
You to betray yourself against your wish.
Sweet one. Still more than this: that not a breath
Should ruffle your soft sport, I ban myself,
And suff'ring doubly, I depart, and tell
My grief to me—to this poor song of mine."

Becker gave him back the page. "A farewell poem."

"Yes. He's aware of something. He stands under an unlucky star. But now tell me: don't you think this man is possessed? He's itching for the boy. But the boy apparently already wanted to get away."

Becker: "There really must be an end to this."

Krug laughed heartily. "That's the male in you rebelling. We'll keep this letter to ourselves of course."

Becker: "I will go to him and force him to get away."

"Old friend, he'll just laugh at you."

Krug got up. "He will offer you a cup of hot chocolate and a cookie, and within five minutes you'll be talking about something else."

Krug took his leave in a good mood, having extricated himself from the affair. Even in the hallway he recommended his friend take his cue from a model worthy of his emulation.

"You see how easy it would have been for me to get involved, after this letter episode. Just what I needed! I'm not going to get burned with this. You've always been such a reasonable man up till now, Becker, avoiding politics—why should you suddenly get in over your head and interfere in a situation where you're not wanted, and where you cannot accomplish anything anyway. We all take our pleasure in our own way. Let him take his as he wants. And if he has his fun, well fine; since he must also know that it may very well mean he'll have to pay for it."

When his mother came in later and he was helping her out of her coat, Becker said, "What a shame you've come so late. Krug was here and he suggested . . ."

"To keep out of it."

"Right."

They went into Becker's room. His mother sat down by the window. "I know your old friend Krug. As far as he's concerned, half the world can perish if only his own life doesn't get disturbed. I have just spoken with the pastor about this affair, without naming names. He says that you must make clear to the man what danger looms ahead and what terrible wrong he is doing."

"But if he denies it all, what then?"

"This time tell him straight out. And if he still denies it," his mother gazed sternly before her, "why then, Friedrich, we'll have to talk about it once more. There's no turning back, you dare not make yourself an accomplice."

"You're so uncompromising, Mother. How can I bring myself to judge him?"

"Friedrich, you can do it. And you're not sitting in judgment over him. You must only avert, you must prevent him from causing, still further damage, and you dare not allow a libertine, a depraved man among children whom he'll corrupt."

How difficult it had all become for Becker. He felt the full weight of it as he sat there alone again in his room. How dare I presume to call him to account. What all haven't I done myself, not in that direction, but in the other. How can a hypocrite such as I look him in the face and accuse him of something. My worry ought to be that others won't sit in judgment over me. And even if I am truly sorry and condemn myself, how can I know whether I've been forgiven?

And once more he sat there uncertain of himself, wavering. To be so completely alone. Whom should he talk to, to his mother, to the pastor?

And in his restless pacing he found himself beside his desk, without having noticed how he got there.

He had walked onto the small rug, across which during his illness, his nervous breakdown, those visions, those ghastly phantasms had crept. On this chair his tempter had sat, the handsome Brazilian, and had incited his pride. On this rug the yellow lion had lain, ready to tear him to pieces if he resisted his evil advice. The tempter in a second form. And finally it was out from under the rug that the little rat had crept, squeaking and chirping, and he had had no more resistance in him and no one to help. The ugly rat had climbed up onto the bookcase and thrown down to him the rope with which he had felt compelled to hang himself from a nail in the wall, and so make an end to this whole, cursed, senseless, and infernal existence. He had been rescued; Hilda had raised him up, and afterward, as she has knelt and prayed for him, from one moment to the next, his eyes had been opened, and he knew.

He knew that this world is not cursed and not senseless, infernal. An eternal God has created it. And a saving God descended to it full of mercy, to show us that we do not have to tear and maul one another to pieces and that the Evil One has no power over us. We need not follow him, and we dare not. We have the duty to direct our gaze to things eternal and be still.

Becker picked up the small wooden crucifix from a niche on the desk and placed it out on its flat top. Directing his gaze fervently at the lowered head of the crucified deity, he whispered the Lord's Prayer, repeated it once, and then once again.

All the while an emotion grew in him, and his spirit grew more steady. And the verses of an old hymn that he had learned for confirmation came to his lips:

"Christ the Life of all the Living, Christ the Death of death, our foe, who thyself for us once giving to the darkest depths of woe, patiently didst yield thy breath but to save my soul from death, praise and glory ever be, blessed Jesus unto thee."

Now all humankind has been blessed and saved, because He lives among us.

There Becker stood and made his decision to go to the director once more and to convince him to resign his post.

The Hostile Camps

Greek class the next morning lasted from nine till ten. As Becker walked past the custodian's quarters, the custodian was sweeping snow from the walk. He turned when he heard Becker's footfall and said to him without bothering to greet him, "Herr Dr. Becker, the Herr Direktor wishes you to visit him at his apartment between ten and eleven."

Becker: "At his apartment? Is the Herr Direktor not in his office today?"

The custodian went on sweeping. "Can't say. Professor Wendig is standing in for him." Absolute silence as Becker entered the classroom.

He sat down, opened his book and cast a glance at the class. The class spokesman was sitting nonchalantly at his place, the lad had fine control of himself. Riedel was missing, that was a shame. Becker pointed at the empty seat.

"Riedel sick? Anyone know anything about him?"

Absolute silence.

Becker: "I see."

They know something, apparently more than I do.

The class had hatched a plot before he had entered. There was to be a theatrical production, a kind of kangaroo court directed against him. This Becker fellow has disappointed them. They had expected something robust, something heroic from a frontline officer. And then this man had shown up with his milquetoast speeches. As a frontline officer he was supposed to speak about the state and the Fatherland. And now the class spokesman had found out and told everyone that the man was linked to the notorious director, perhaps he was the same sort himself. During the nine o'clock break, the class spokesman had passed the word: not to cooperate in any way with this man, at every turn to present passive resistance and obstruction.

As Becker had entered, however, and opened his book, looking out into the classroom, the whole situation changed. There he sat on his podium, a tall, gaunt, and calm man, very serious, very pale, with a peculiarly severe face, a broad brow, deep lines around his mouth, apparently the result of long illness. To look at him was to travel in some distant, unfamiliar land. The seniors felt that. In looking at him they realized that a man is more than a visible object, that he is a symbol of what exists behind him. Something emanates from a man, he creates a magnetic field that in turn creates other magnetic fields.

Becker looked at the class. His eyes were eyes that had seen Satan. He gazed at fourteen young men intending to do something to him.

They're lying in wait, they don't want to accept me. Why not? They come here with old, rotten ideas, from homes that did not experience the war. These aren't young men at all, they are men from 1900 or 1910.

He began his lesson with the remark that they would take one last look at *Antigone* today. One historical note as a preface: The three plays of the Oedipus cycle, *Oedipus Rex, Oedipus at Colonus* and *Antigone* were not written in sequence. *Antigone* was Sophocles' twenty-third play, while *Colonus* was written when he was a very old man. By that time, at about age ninety, the poet had experienced a great deal in life, but *Colonus,* his last play, reveals no bitterness, as do the works written in old age by our greatest modern playwright, Shakespeare—for example *Timon of Athens.* Sophocles, although fully resigned to life, saved his tenderest poetry for *Colonus,* as Cicero would later say. The mysterious working of fate remains his central theme. The world is governed by eternal laws, and man—this is Sophocles' special point in contrast to his predecessor Aeschylus—suffers though he is not guilty. What we are left with is respect for and a holy awe of the gods who guide our destiny.

Becker did not realize just how much this statement annoyed the class, these big boys only held in check by his intimidating outward appearance.

They sat there unsure of themselves, gazing furtively at one another, until redheaded Neumann, the class quibbler, got up his courage and asked whether they might not return to a particular point regarding *Antigone.*

"Please do!" said Becker.

But Neumann really had little to say about it, only repeating his thesis that the teenage Antigone, this girl who had no notion of the state or the nation had unsuspectingly got herself mixed up in the headiest kind of politics.

Becker, who understood what this was meant to lead into, remained patient, only expressing his amazement that apparently everything he had said about "unwritten law" had been preached to the wind.

He asked, "Why do you stop your ears in order not to hear that? Why won't you accept that?"

Neumann answered jauntily in his clear voice, "Because we just don't see it that way. Because we reject this creature Antigone, because she has challenged us to do so. So an unwritten law is supposed to have descended from heaven! Anyone can say that, you know. It seems quite puzzling that only she knows about it. And a heavenly law about funeral practices? That just goes to show what an excitable woman can come up with if she's pigheaded."

The whole class laughed.

Schramm, the biggest boy in the class, the socialist, joined the ranks of his enemies and offered his two-cents worth in his deep, drawling voice. "There's something to what Neumann says there. Every age has its old wives' tales, and women are always especially susceptible to them. And why women, you ask? Because they are systematically excluded from public life."

"You can forget the moldy slogans," Neumann interjected. "You always think you're at some mass meeting."

"The Prince of Homburg," someone called from the rear. It was, it seemed, a catchword. Becker asked what that was supposed to mean. The class spokesman answered (this was all prearranged):

"The problem of the state and the individual, the state versus the individual or the individual versus the state, the Greek version is found in *Antigone. The Prince of Homburg* by Heinrich Kleist, which we are reading just now, provides the German solution. The prince does not obey an order, in wartime, at the battle of Fehrbellin. And even though he is victorious on the battlefield, he is condemned to death for taking the law into his own hands. And as a German he respects that decree without further fuss. He does not take refuge in som unwritten law or other."—Someone called out: "He wouldn't have gotten very far with that with the Elector!"—"He recognizes the sovereignty of the state and his own duty to obey. The Fatherland is for him, just as for his Elector, the highest good."

What good did it do Becker, seeing that there was an open conspiracy against him, to reject this comparison of *Antigone* and *The Prince of Homburg*. His explanation was greeted by the class spokesman with a casual remark: "Fine, then that's the Greek view. We have nothing more to say. It is alien to us, exotic. For us Germans, the Fatherland was, is and always will be our ultimate imperative, an absolute and total one. One that admits of no compromises."

Becker looked at the refined, intelligent class spokesman, this little lord who sat there giving nothing away. He restrained himself. This generation had learned nothing. When would they learn, do you suppose? What would teach them? How deep must the knife cut until they felt the pain. And without knowing why, he began to speak of the war, to plead in his own behalf.

"Let's take a practical example. None of us who went off to battle in 1914 entertained the question of divine right versus civil right. It was as if it were 1813, when the King called and everyone, everyone answered. We were men, we had sworn our oath of allegiance and now followed the colors. Of those I knew, there was not a single one who offered one word of criticism of the state, of our state, and thereby set himself off as an individual from the others. Not one of us hesitated to meet death for the sake of the state."

They sat silent now. First the stomping of one pair of feet. Then the whole class was stomping.

"We obeyed. The dichotomy of the individual versus the state had continually existed, however, during peacetime. It ought to, it must exist, since we are the bearers of the state. But at the outbreak of a war you have to be totally clear about your relation to the state, in order to know precisely that it is for this that I am laying down my life."

Becker now began to speak very softly, his eyes directed to the top of his desk. He stood now for the first time as a Christian among heathens, and was compelled to make his profession of faith, even if it led to martyrdom.

"It is a fearful thing to fall into the hands of the living God. That was demonstrated by this war as well. We stood here in Germany shining brightly. And so we went off to war. We entered the fray with all our strength, with all our will and knowledge, and collapsed, as a collective unity. Under such circumstances it is pointless and dishonorable to look for war criminals, as is being done now both at home and abroad. One reads that our former foes are preparing lists of names of the men actually to blame for this war. We are all to blame, young and old, those now living and those who lived before the war and took part in the war, on our side and on theirs. The whole nation, the whole world went to war, and has been punished."

Schröter cleared his throat loudly, and as Becker paused he interjected in a careless voice, "What is there to blame people for?"

Others, who had been cowed by now, nodded. "Yes, please, what is there to blame people for?"

Becker: "There you have the dark, puzzling question. You can see the punishment. The misfortune is patently obvious. Investigate the matter, however, and no one is patently guilty. As little as Oedipus was. But something, something beyond us, has proclaimed the verdict."

The class spokesman, to whom the whole class now turned, sat there stiff and erect, listening to Becker as if he were speaking to him alone. He puckered up his lips and spoke to Becker as if interrogating him.

"And who is this dark something supposed to be, this something beyond us, tell me please?"

His arrogant tone did not in the least anger the pale and preoccupied man, the teacher up front. He was already in the process of expressing the ideas coming to him now, and abruptly he began to speak of death.

"Behind the question 'state versus individual' or 'duty to the state and to unwritten law' there lies hidden the question of death itself. And that brings us directly to the central theme of the tragedy of

Antigone. Some of you have taken offense at the notion that a whole tragedy should be built upon the question of whether a dead man should be buried or not. To you it seems absurd that such an argument concerning a funeral should have such massive consequences. But to formulate it precisely for you: the theme of *Antigone* is neither 'emotion versus duty' nor 'duty to the state versus duty to heaven,' but rather, 'How is the world of living to treat the world of the dead?'"

The students looked around, several of them smirking. One of them whispered, "What a prig," while others were intrigued and had to follow the argument.

Becker: "The heroine of the play senses that death is something very important. And indeed: the real hero of the play is not she, but—the dead Polynices. The subject of the play is the claim of a dead man upon the living. A warrior has fallen. He has left behind no unsullied memory. This dead man does not become visible, nor palpable, nor even audible in the play, but he forces his way into the world of the living and finds an advocate in his sister Antigone. A woman takes up his cause. Just as it is woman who receives the unborn, those who are not yet present among us. Polynices is held back and cannot speak for himself, but he works through her, uses her body and her soul, and she cannot escape him. Nor does she want to escape him either. For what he demands are his rights. She speaks for him and presents his arguments for him. Support for his existence, care—that is what the dead man demands. We won't concern ourself with antiquity's conceptions of the existence of life after death. They imagined that the dead lived on as shades in the underworld. But antiquity was certain of one thing: man's life is not congruent with his visible existence. It transcends it. The ancients believed, as we learn from this magnificent play, that we should look beyond this visible existence of ours with fear and trembling."

(Just as Antigone takes up the cause of her dead brother, so have I taken up that of the many who fell, the many who died too young, who departed so totally unaware. I know that I serve them, I shall not forget them.)

And when now a quite respectful request came from the class for him to say still more about all this, he continued—in a manner that surprised them. He spoke, in fact, about the remarkably contradictory movements of our astronomical and spiritual cosmologies. With Copernicus our astronomical world had expanded; the earth, which before was but a few thousand years old, now had millions of years behind it, and one could no longer even speak of the size of the universe, since all concepts, all notion of numbers broke down.

"And in contrast to that, there is the shrinkage of our spiritual world. Man grows ever smaller, ever more unimportant. Evolution damns him to be a single species within a long chain of species. His mind becomes an organ of utilitarian purpose, a mere instrument by which he maintains himself upon the earth. And when death overtakes this human animal, why then his death cannot lay claim to much more interest than that of a calf or a blade of grass.

"But let us take a cool, firm look at things. In Sophocles' play, out there on the plain before the city lies a dead man, a fallen warrior. Is it only a rotting corpse? Is there no longer a Polynices? Antigone says and knows that he lives, he is leading another existence. He has not vanished from the realm of being, and he will not let her go, this brother of hers, and she will not let him go. She must show him honor and serve him, at least by burying his body. Nowadays we have other notions of life and death than did the ancients. But we know that we have only a brief, visible, corporal existence. And that we travel in a very small boat across a vast ocean. Call that ocean what you will, the beyond perhaps or merely death, at any rate it is not simply 'death as the final end, the nothing.' A profound verse from the Latin that you perhaps know in Luther's translation says, 'in the midst of life we are in death . . .'"

And then he added, changing his tone of voice—he had been speaking very softly toward the last, "Now, when you pose the question: How shall the state, indubitably a reality, deal with death, yet another reality, perhaps you will be more careful in answering it than before."

The young men had followed intently. They vaguely sensed that this was an experience from the battlefield. But some of them were annoyed, and were annoyed too at the idiots who were letting themselves be taken in by Becker. Keep this up, and they could lose the whole campaign they had planned.

Schröter, the class spokesman, suddenly declared in his clear, cool voice that this was not the point at all.

Becker: "And what then is the point?"

"Simply put, whether one has a clear concept of the nation and what one owes it. We have no need for spiritualism these days. The nation just needs men who will take up its cause."

"For heaven's sake, Schröter, what do you mean by that? And I hope, I sincerely hope, that you consider carefully what you say."

Schröter had stood up and had placed himself beside his bench just as he had stood at Becker's living room door before making his short bow.

"We had expected, Herr Dr. Becker, that you would provide clear precepts and points of view, especially concerning such a controversial theme as 'Antigone versus the state.' To our regret, we have determined that we cannot count on you. As things lie, however, I also feel it my duty to inform you that the class currently attending your lectures in Greek will go on strike should the director dare once again to enter this classroom."

It was an attack that fell wide of its mark. The class spokesman had simply let his shot fly blindly. Becker noticed at once that most of the young men sat there with their heads lowered, embarrassed. He remained calm and pulled out his watch. It was a few minutes of ten.

"You can leave the classroom at once, Schröter, and report to professor Wendig in the director's office. Immediately."

Without further ado, his head held high, Schröter obeyed. Becker had just enough time to dictate the homework for the next class when the bell rang.

He was aware as he left the room of the hang-dog look of the seniors. But he did not know that this was his last hour of instruction in the class. At the door he ran into Professor Wendig himself, who had been teaching in the adjoining room. As they walked together, Becker reported the incident to him. The professor listened worriedly. So things had gone now this far. Of course he would question Schröter and punish him accordingly. He asked Becker not to take this as a personal attack, it was not directed at him. It was an ambiguous, lukewarm conversation.

My Poor Brother

Slowly Becker left the building on his way to visit the director. Into what murky waters have I been thrown, he thought, after having barely begun to move among people again. Schröter's right, it's a controversial topic, "Antigone versus the state," but I'm not the one who broached the topic. And then there's the director; he stands there in my path and I cannot get by. Why have I been confronted with this? Are these temptations, trials?

But what should I do? Can I do anything else? Shall I simply forget it all? Shall I, too, prove to be a coward, and not give the dead the honor due them? They marched off blind and terrified. I was saved, and I know for what: so that I would not forget. In the midst of life we are in death.

196

The director himself opened the door, wearing a dark-blue silk dressing-gown and blue slippers. He looked frightened.

Becker saw him and thought: this is my poor brother. How mysteriously the meaning of things bursts through appearances. They put me in a schoolroom with *Antigone* in front of me, and now this careworn man stands before me, the image of what I used to be.

The director marched restlessly about his atelier, the room now in considerable disorder. He thanked Becker for the visit. The campaign against him was growing ever larger. This morning he had received an anonymous registered letter: if he did not immediately quit the field, they would lodge a complaint calling for his arrest. The police, moreover, had already been informed.

"I could hand over the letter to the police myself. It's simple blackmail, written apparently not by students, but by their families, third parties. But I would prefer not to turn it into a scandal. You understand, I'm sure."

This was followed by an endless monologue about the Mrs. Grundy's among the parents and teachers. If this were a school on the West Side things would be quite different. They would regard things in their proper light. It was a helpless lamentation, partly intended, it seemed, to divert his guest and prevent him from getting a word in at this point.

Becker thought: the man hasn't the slightest sense of awareness. He wouldn't be lost if he would make just one single move.

"How was the class?" the director asked suddenly, standing in front of Becker with his faded, childlike face, the few hairs on his head in disordered strands.

Becker thanked him for asking. "Nothing special. Riedel was absent."

The director put his left hand to his chest. "Riedel—was absent?"

He was a broken man. "What's happened. Did someone say something? No? But something has happened, I'm sure. I knew nothing about it. They've done something mean and low. And the boy, for godsakes, he wouldn't go and . . ."

He sat down in the armchair nearby and whimpered. There was no longer any point in lying.

"Help me, Dr. Becker. You're the only person who's taken my side. Dr. Krug has left me in the lurch as well. I'm not such a damnable and despicable human being, that . . ."

He directed his despairing eyes toward Becker and held out his hand to him. Becker took it. He pressed it tight, worked it, while he whispered to him, "Couldn't you go to him, to Riedel? I'll give you his address. Someone has to find out on the sly what's happening. Could you do it?"

Becker: "When was he last here with you?"

"Yesterday, after nine o'clock. I'm sure he went home from here."

"Perhaps he has received a similar registered letter, he or his parents."

"That's it, you're right, Dr. Becker, and then what? What has he done? Why didn't he come to me?"

"Maybe his parents wouldn't let him go to school and he's sitting at home."

"They're keeping him in, right. They've locked him up. What are they doing to him? Or maybe he's wandering about. He's run away. My dear little boy, my Heinz."

"Herr Direktor."

The man wept. "What law have we broken? Do you understand? I don't. I have never understood and never will."

"Is Riedel—your only friend?"

"Heinz? Yes, he is."

"Calm yourself. I'll go see if I can find the boy. But you must get away from here, as fast as possible."

"Me? No, you're wrong. Then there would truly be a scandal."

"If you stay, there'll be an even bigger one."

The director: "I can't go. Just look at all this, my collections, my portfolios, my sculptures. I'm supposed just to leave it all here, leave it behind. I'll not go into exile. I've committed no crime."

He interrupted himself and listened. Somewhere in the background there was a scratching sound, and someone moved. "Excuse me, please."

He hurried to the rear and vanished from the atelier. Soon afterward Becker heard a scream, a voice of happiness—it was the director's—and another, softer voice of woe. That was Riedel.

Becker sat and waited. It took a long time. He pondered whether he ought not to go. The whole thing was embarrassing, almost unbearable. But he contained himself. From behind the door the director appeared, beaming and laughing; he spread his arms wide and called out, "We've got him back, our runaway. Nothing has happened. I can breathe again."

The happy man sat down beside Becker, whose lips were tightly pressed together—but he noticed nothing. "I wanted to bring him in here to you, but the lad is ashamed of himself. He's only a child. His parents really did receive a registered letter with similar suggestions in it, which resulted in one devil of an argument. That's when he ran away. It was definitely the wisest thing for him to do. He didn't dare show up at school either."

"And what's to happen now, Herr Direktor?"

He tied the belt to his dressing gown tighter. He was completely his old self again. He took a mirror and a fine-bristled brush from his pocket, and carefully put the part back in his hair. Earnest, confident, and amiable, he said, "Oh, it will all work out. We'll not let them rob us of our sleep. We'll not panic, which is what would please some folks. These righteous citizens, these gentlemen of the vestry here who've been pushed to the fore by a few parents. They think I'll take flight at the first little wink of an eye. I'm an abomination to them, an atheist, a Greek. I can understand how they feel. But why should I yield to them? I've nothing to reproach myself with. Go ahead, ask Riedel. I'll bring him in here for you."

"Please, don't. Why do that?"

"As you like. You can convince yourself. The poor boy is completely beside himself. The first victim of those rabble-rousers. He's trembling. His father slapped him. He's got welts on both cheeks. It must have been terrible."

Becker softly: "So there you see what damage you've done."

"What? What damage I've done? His father is the same sort of miserable philistine and hypocrite as the person who wrote that anonymous letter—and a family tyrant besides."

"I can listen to no more of this, Herr Direktor. I beg you, stop talking like this. You can see what terrible misfortune you've brought upon the young man. You've got to let him go, for once and for all."

The director, downcast, unsure of himself, and apprehensive: "But why? We have a friendly, warmly human relationship."

"You know very well that this is more than a matter of a friendly, human relationship."

"I insist that it is a matter of simple friendship, to which I have every right."

Becker was enraged. "Then—I'll have to go."

"Please don't. Do sit down, please."

He came after Becker and held him tightly by the arm.

Becker stayed.

The director stood before him, an indecipherable look on his face. "What do you think I should do?"

Becker: "Come to a decision, an honest one. Give up your relationship with Riedel."

Without answering, the director turned back to his atelier. At last he cleared his throat and whispered as he paced, his face to the floor, "You believe we can avoid a scandal that way?"

"You will take a leave of absence for illness. You can go to a sanatorium somewhere. There was already something of a scandal in the classroom today."

"Because of me?"

"Yes."

The director, bitter: "I see. That too. As the old have piped the tune, the young sing the words. Well, I am very grateful to you, Herr Dr. Becker. You can't know how obliged I am to you."

Becker stood there watching the man, how he was turning it all over in his mind and moving about with tiny steps. Becker took a deep breath. More than likely the director was thinking about the boy outside.

"I would like to have a word with the boy, Herr Direktor."

"That you shall. That's very kind of you. What—do you want to say to him?"

"We'll see."

The director looked unhappily at him, a look of profound sorrow, of pain on his face. So now it would happen. He begged, "Don't hurt him. I know I can depend on you. What is all this? The very heavens have fallen upon me."

He still hesitated. He looked again at Becker. Then he departed. At the door he said, "You won't upset him, will you? He's already completely beside himself."

Becker did not answer.

It took several minutes before the director appeared again, Riedel right behind him. The tall, blond boy hung back at the door, his head lowered, his face flushed. The director laid an arm around his shoulder, soothing him and pulling him into the room. Becker walked over to him and gave him his hand. He asked the director to leave them alone for a few minutes. The director gave him a worried, reproachful look. But when there was no change in Becker's stern face, he shrugged and smiled wanly. "As you wish. I'll wait in the next room until you call me." He shuffled wearily from the room.

Becker, alone with Riedel now, pressed the young man down into an easy chair before he could even open his mouth. "Riedel, I know everything. You can speak openly with me. Your father has struck you. Has he often done that?"

"No. Father has always been good to me."

"What does your father do?"

"He's in insurance. He was a captain during the war, at an army base."

"Your mother is good to you too?"

"Yes, I'm the only child at home. My older brother is still in a military hospital, he lost a leg."

"And why is he still there?"

"He still has some shrapnel somewhere in his hip that they want to take out."

"Well, I'm sure it will turn out all right. I know of similar cases. I lay in a hospital myself for a long time, and as you see, I'm walking again. Riedel, what is going to happen to us now? The director is very fond of you. But you know that such relationships lead nowhere."

Riedel held his hand before his eyes. "I know."

"Can't you help yourself?"

Riedel lifted his head. He whispered, "Me? Sure, why not?"

He put his index finger to his lips and made a gesture toward the door.

Becker: "I see. Then all the better. I'm glad to hear it. Shake hands on it, that that's the truth."

Riedel did. Becker's firm handshake answered him.

Becker: "Then we'll have to turn this matter over in our minds. You could change schools. That's difficult in the middle of a semester. It would be better to take private lessons for a while. I'll speak with your father about it."

Becker was pleased with the fervent, grateful look the boy gave him as he pressed his hand firmly between both of his own.

Riedel whispered: "Help me, Herr Dr. Becker."

Now Becker asked the director to come back in. When he saw the boy sitting in the armchair, his gaze directed away from him, he realized at once what had been going on.

They spoke earnestly and impersonally. The director told them that in the meantime he had telephoned the doctor. He would be going to a sanatorium. He was feeling poorly. He spoke so loudly that Riedel, who had not turned his head back, had to hear. But Riedel did not react.

The director sighed and inquired with a forced nonchalance, "And so you'll take care of our young friend here in the meantime, won't you?"

Becker promised he would go see the parents and, as well as he could, put everything back on an even keel.

"Let us hope so. I know that you can be depended upon. I'm sorry that you had no sooner returned to society than you had to be confronted with all this bother. I only hope it hasn't put too much of a strain on you."

He pressed Becker's hand. He extended a hand to Riedel as well, who, after glancing at him shyly, took it and then let it go again at once. Riedel hurried to the door ahead of Becker; he was taking flight.

At the door to the atelier the director stood in his blue dressing-gown and watched them go.

The door slammed. He turned back to the room.

They had been sitting there just yesterday evening, on the sofa in front of the large yellow floor lamp, what a wonderful twilight mood there had been to the room, the Hermes of Praxiteles had shimmered its soft white, they had been reading shoulder to shoulder, just twelve hours ago:

> —"That you are lovely, makes the world spin.
>   If you are mine, I'll cause it to spin.
> —That you are lovely, holds me spellbound till death.
>   That you are my lord, leads me to danger and death.
> —That I am lovely, perhaps you think that's true.
>   That I am yours, I swear to you is true."

Yesterday evening, just twelve hours ago . . .

Glimpses

The conversation with Herr Waldemar Riedel, former captain in the reserve and now an insurance agent, began stormily. This robust man with a stern, red and pimply face, with fixed, slightly glassy eyes—he liked to drink—was in a foul mood and absolutely not inclined to listen to Becker. At first he thought Becker had come more or less to express the sympathies of the faculty, and to inform him that they had broken all ties with this director of theirs. Instead, the man seemed to want to mediate the affair. He apparently wanted to hush the whole thing up for the sake of the academy's reputation.

But he wasn't going to get very far with that with Herr Riedel.

He would put an end to this filthy stuff, he declared to Becker, and it was all the same to him what trouble that caused. He wasn't going to let anyone talk him out of it.

He grew gentler when Becker, who had been through a great deal this morning, braced himself on the table and asked for a chair. He apologized; he wasn't quite steady on his legs as a result of his wounds.

At that the former captain in the reserve recalled that Heinz had told them about a new Greek teacher, a first lieutenant with the Iron Cross, who had returned badly wounded. This was the fellow then.

In a completely different tone of voice he inquired, as Becker seated himself, whether Becker had been laid up in a hospital for a long time, and where. He spoke of his other son—the doctors were still puttering around with him—and of where he himself had served, mostly in Belgium. He sat down at the table with Becker, called him "comrade" and pounded his fist energetically on the table, urging him not to let himself be misused. How could a man try to protect such a bastard as this director.

Gradually—he kept starting his tale from scratch—he grew maudlin, returning again and again to his other son who had lost a leg and still couldn't come home yet, and now this had to happen with his other boy. Finally, bending over the table and with tears in his eyes, he confessed his greatest care, that this morning he had hit the boy—who had been seduced, of course, and was totally innocent in the affair—something that had never happened before. Heinz was his pride and joy. His hand had just—slipped.

At the sound of this loud lament, a woman entered, an equally large teutonic figure, much younger than the tormented Waldemar Riedel, her face serene. She shook Becker's hand and greeted him warmly as her husband introduced him as his "comrade," a "first lieutenant, wearer of the Iron Cross, just returned from the field." She had also heard about this sensational new Greek teacher from Heinz.

She immediately put fruit and a bottle of brandy on the table, and was delighted to hear—something the father had not asked about— that Heinz had been found and that Becker had spoken with him. (Neither asked where, both of them assuming it was at school. The mother had really been afraid that Heinz would do something to himself because of the letter and the blows from his father.)

Her husband, she explained, had become so upset this morning, first on account of the letter, and then perhaps even more so because of the episode with the slaps. He wasn't even able to go to work because of it.

"Yes," the father admitted mournfully, though already mollified, having poured himself a schnapps. The mother drank one too, relaxed now, peaceful and jolly, peeling an apple for Becker. "Heinz has some big ideas in his head. He wants to join the navy. He's always been interested in the sea. We haven't talked him out of it yet. Germany doesn't need a navy now, without the colonies. And then I certainly don't want him sauntering about in a navy uniform, on account of those outlaws from Kiel. I say no to that."

In due time they were in complete accord with everything Becker suggested. They didn't want to enrich Berlin with yet another new scandal, and they certainly didn't want their name connected with it. The boy should be taken out of school.

And when Becker, correctly predicting how the parents would react, informed them that he had brought the boy along with him, that he was waiting downstairs in the entryway—they were overjoyed, and the father at once stormed down the stairs to fetch the boy. Becker then took his leave from the family reunion. Heinz was a quiet, serious boy, who was terribly ashamed of himself and wept as he hung on his father's neck.

Frau Becker had kept dinner waiting for Friedrich. He had to tell her everything. She sighed with relief. He was in a good mood. Everything was going well, and even the class would work out as soon as the details were arranged.

The next day, Becker had the day off. Dr. Krug came to him with great news. The director had suddenly taken ill—the story was "appendicitis"—and had been taken to a clinic, and the senior class boy, Riedel, who had been involved in the affair, had been taken off the rolls by his parents.

For a few minutes Becker was overcome with an almost sinful pride; that's what I accomplished, that's what I arranged. But he was alarmed at catching himself at it, and spent a rough half hour in self-reproach.

His mother, too, had good news today.

She had been taking care of her patient, and could report a certain success. She could find no peace at the thought that that poor man lay there abandoned in an atmosphere of hate, and would thus spend his last earthly days before death. She had taken it upon herself, following a fruitless conversation with the patient's wife, to get him out of that environment.

This had proven enormously difficult. The first resistance had come from the patient. For when she suggested that he might prefer to be in a private clinic where she also helped out, she had absolutely terrified him. It was quite incomprehensible. Her question had only resulted in making her patient even more timid, so that he now crept under his blanket and hid from her as well. He whimpered that he did not want to go anywhere, he didn't want to die.

Frau Becker was once again given the opportunity to consider how people reacted to their own death. Very few acquiesced to it if they were conscious. Death came most easily for those who freely cast themselves into its arms or who died by accident. Even after a horrible life full of awful disease, people clung to existence. There must be then, despite everything, something lovely about this life. Added to that there was the fear of the unknown, of the darkness of death.

Frau Becker sat beside her patient's bed and thought in her pity: How can I help free him from his agony?

She went to work on his doctor, whom she knew well. He found her suggestion to abduct the man an excellent one. A clinic was the only appropriate spot for a poor creature like that. Moreover, he treated patients in the very clinic that Frau Becker had in mind, and received (though this he did not tell her) a certain percentage for every patient that he had admitted there.

The doctor disclosed these plans to the patient's wife. And she replied with a flat no. Curiously enough, she did not want to have her husband kidnapped, despite her fear of infection. Why not? What advantage was his presence to her? Frau Becker could not understand it. The doctor, being an experienced and cynical man, explained to her, "The lady doesn't want her toy taken away from her. She teases him, she torments him—she gets herself upset over him, she's afraid of him—but if you take that away from her what has she got except her son, with whom she quarrels, it's true, though not enough for her? Besides, the woman is afraid that the patient will feel better in the clinic—a thought she cannot bear. For how could he dare to feel better? I've known those two for years, a good fifteen. If he were to go to a clinic and, given the circumstances, start to feel better, it would bring the woman's whole world collapsing down upon her. I'm convinced that somehow she's got the notion that this illness serves her husband right, and she can't stand the idea that he might get away from her. Atavistic ideas, aren't they? It's only right that he should suffer, and that she should do her part to help him.

"And the craziest part is," the doctor frowned and wrung his hands, "that the patient is in full agreement. Looks like a full-fledged madhouse, doesn't it? There's a kind of subterranean understanding between the two."

Frau Becker found this so gruesome and unnatural that she could not believe it. The doctor could explain it however he liked. All the more reason, she said finally, if that's the state of things, for me to get this man out of that hell.

"Hell," the doctor replied, "is the right word. The two have damned themselves to it. There you have human nature. If people aren't getting skewered, tortured and roasted, they don't feel right. And now they go and make a great fuss with their revolution, thinking they'll achieve something if they give people a bigger parlor and better wages. Good God! They ought to have a look at the fine folks who've already experienced such good fortune. They live in elegant houses, have servants, and scratch and tear each other's eyes out in another way. Because they're not about to give that up. That belongs among their inalienable human rights, and exists as an unwritten law; only that, it would seem, makes life bearable."

At which Frau Becker could only vigorously shake her head, of course. The doctor's professional cynicism was something quite new to her. But when she protested, predictably enough, he was pleased, and patted the soft hand of this old "brave idealist." She talked the doctor into speaking with the woman once more, and brought another woman in the same apartment house into the conspiracy. This woman croaked loudly about the man's serious condition, predicting such awful things that the wife finally consented, for she didn't want it said that she hadn't done everything possible for her husband.

And so the man was placed in the clinic. She was allowed to visit him only for half an hour every other day (to break the habit, the doctor mocked). Frau Becker could now manage things just as she pleased. And she got her way. The head nurse at the clinic, who was a friend of hers, let her have a free hand. She often said, "Frau Becker should have been a soldier in the Salvation Army."

And in fact the man was no longer hiding under his blanket. A wise and watchful nurse was placed on duty during the day, and she conversed with him. That hadn't happened with this man for months. Ebert and Scheidemann, and the wonders they were performing between them, in part with, in part without the generals, amazed him mightily. He was perhaps the only man in Berlin who wanted to know who Ebert really was. The miracle of the German revolution made him forget his illness for half a day. They performed a fake operation on him. Sometimes he thought he would get well again.

This was the news that Frau Becker was able to offer her son when he proclaimed with what success his efforts on the director's behalf had been crowned.

They were both happy. Frau Becker laughed as she told what tricks she had had to employ in order to keep her patient in the clinic. The wife didn't dare get the notion that her husband was really improving. The cynical doctor had been quite correct in his diagnosis. The wife had draped herself, of course only in gestures and bearing, with the weeds of the mourning widow and she seemed to like the role. The patient had caught on to this, and the minute she would open the door he would begin to complain. He groaned and whimpered and pulled the blanket over his head, and she departed.

Frau Becker, with her robust optimism, also saw Friedrich's success as her own work. She now wanted to convert Friedrich to her own doctrine that one needed only to trust and believe and everything would turn out all right, provided that the desired results were good in themselves.

Becker fell silent at this song of triumph; it set him to trembling. He stopped his ears against it. He considered it blasphemy.

And was it not just a week later that the director was found badly beaten out in a suburb of the city? And did they not shortly thereafter have to pull Becker himself and an unconscious Heinz out of a burning building into which a hand grenade had been tossed? And what became of Frau Becker's laughing cancer patient and his wife, who had already draped herself in widow's weeds?

BOOK FOUR

The Challenge Is Made and Accepted

The Serviceable Noske

Noske was a tall, lanky man with steel-rimmed glasses and a low brow. He walked slightly hunched. He came from Brandenburg and had worked his way up from lumberjack to town councilman, journalist and Reichstag deputy. But his unique work was yet to come.

As Ebert sat there gloomily in his office in the Reichs Chancellery after the unfortunate affair with the People's Naval Division and the resignation of the Independents (they've left me to public scorn, the rats are deserting the sinking ship, they want to unmask me as a traitor, as the stooge of the officers, and together with Liebknecht they're going to present the German people with the revolution that will bring us all true happiness), he was suddenly illuminated by an idea.

I'm still the representative of reason in this land. I'm still right in rejecting this revolution. I've joined forces with the generals, true. But let someone show me what else I should have done to save this nation from chaos. They surely know that I am right. But they don't dare admit it publicly. They're afraid of the radicals. Liebknecht is a madman, a dangerous lunatic, he can't help himself. But what about the others, Haase and the rest of the Independents. With them it's nothing but treachery and politics. They want to isolate me, so that I truly have no choice except the generals, and then they want to point their fingers at me and say: see what sort of fellow he is. But they're going to be badly deceived.

And the rage rose up in him and with it came his illuminating idea. The name of Noske occurred to him. I need a bloodhound.

Ebert reached for the telephone and had himself connected with Kiel.

"Gustav, you're coming to Berlin. Yes, right away, today or tomorrow at the latest. You've got to come to my aid."

Noske replied that he had expected this call, he read the papers too, after all.

And he got out his suitcase.

They had sent him to Kiel at the beginning of November, 1918, in the interests of public order, which he was to establish. But just as he arrived in Kiel, the first train cars, draped in red bunting and crammed with jubilant sailors, were leaving town with the news of the uprising, carrying that same uprising with them across the nation. Noske turned gray and green with rancor. He went to work, hoping to calm things down. But then the fire he hoped to quench, the revolution, broke out with dreadful violence in Berlin and other cities, with such violence that no ordinary methods for extinguishing it were of any help. And then a great miracle happened. The revolutionaries did not liquidate Noske, any more than they liquidated Ebert and his generals. Instead, they made Ebert first people's deputy and Noske governor of Kiel. Noske's amazement knew no bounds. He was the governor of the revolutionary government. "Ha!" he cried, "if a miracle like this is possible, then there will soon be some others." And immediately he called officers to him in order to inform them just how he interpreted his miraculous office.

Vice-Admiral Souchon and the top brass of the naval station gathered on a gloomy November day in the station headquarters, in the chief of staff's office, to listen to this lanky man from Brandenburg who looked like the editor of a small-town paper and not at all like a bloodhound. He acknowledged the recent grievous events in the Reich and felt it was not necessary to underscore that he was not to blame for them. But in any case, he and not someone else had been named governor. He regretted having to see men like Souchon and his aides before him now in this situation. He asked them to submit to the inevitable, for to the extent that it was within his power, etc., etc. They looked on in amazement, the saving miracle had happened, the miracle of 1918. Afterward he rejoiced that he was in command of 6,000 men, for although he had never even been a soldier he had always taken great pleasure in things military.

All over Germany, some remarkable events were taking place at that point, and in Kiel one occurred under Noske that we wish to speak of here:

On the island of Alsen, made famous in the Danish-Prussian War, there lived a village schoolmaster, normally a peaceable man, but now gone quite wild. He thought that a genuine revolution had broken out in Germany; reading the papers had misled him as it had many others.

212

Since no one else appointed him, he named himself the ruler of the island of Alsen. The wild little man had the fantasy of ruling autocratically on the island of Alsen, in the midst of the sea, of governing and of allowing no one else any say-so in the matter, even if that someone were Noske in Kiel. What new policies he wanted to introduce on Alsen he did not make public. But he did at once break off all diplomatic relations with Germany, declaring that he wanted to introduce a new national language in order to underscore the separation. In fact, he envisioned an independent Alsensian language, which did not as yet exist. The creation of this language was costing him great effort, since it dared not be either German or Danish, but in every facet true to Alsen, which lay embraced by the sea. And so he sat there on the beach searching for this language, listening to his nearest neighbors, the fish, and without betraying to anyone his secret he came up with the idea of taking fish from the sea, since water tended to swallow up all sounds, and then listening to them. His problem was: how can you understand fish, since they are constantly moving their mouths; and how can you get fish to talk out of water? He did not solve his problem. So he set his sights on a still higher goal.

Besides this wild little man there was a small population of fishermen on Alsen for whom he was too revolutionary, and who therefore turned to Noske in Kiel, begging for his help. Gruff and uncivil as he was, he sent a couple of soldiers over and had the wild man arrested and locked up, and, adding insult to injury, not in a prison but in a military hospital, where they put him to bed and fed him with sleeping pills. They simply assumed he was crazy. He resigned himself to the inevitable and slept on and on. And when he awakened, he found himself in the same situation as before and broke out. Soldiers again marched to Alsen's beaches, captured him, locked him up, and again gave him sleeping pills. He resigned himself to the inevitable, slept on and on, came to himself again, and broke out again. The Alsensian revolution was not to be crushed. Noske had now had enough. He put the wild man in prison. If the man thought so much of the German revolution, then he should be made to realize that for a German revolution you needed two, one of whom was Noske.

The man sat in prison. There was a good possibility he would be tried for high treason, secession from Germany, introduction of a foreign tongue, etc. A court-martial was given the files, and its hair stood on end when it learned of the fish language that this Alsensian criminal hoped to introduce. It was high treason. And doubtless even worse: high treason on the high seas.

The wild man's wife appeared at the prison; she had had to take over his job as schoolmaster on the island of Alsen. She had one child and a game leg, those were her total assets, and she had only recently come to both. The man was deeply touched at her visit, and stirred by her humanity. And when the child began to scream, the wild man listened. He realized that the mother understood the child merely from its screams. This impressed him. It touched upon his problem with the fish language. It meant he could drop that project and introduce the language of infants instead. No speech, but rather screams, bawling. In fact, you could make yourself understood by bawling—and that was revolution.

The woman said she could go to her parents in the vicinity of Dresden. The man flinched at that, and then agreed. He wanted to study the language of infants in peace. The revolution required basic planning. Postponement is not abandonment. You had to bawl. Noske gave him his blessing and let the man out of prison; at once he was lost among all those other folks in the outside world who were imitating infants.

And so, thanks to Noske's leadership, the Alsensian revolution came to nothing.

The other revolution, the grand German one, would do no better—that he swore.

Noske set up an effective striking force in Kiel by allowing no sailors to join, only soldiers and noncoms on active duty, not that he turned down naval deck officers; and he called the whole thing the "Iron Guard." He did not reveal for whom he thought these troops were being held in reserve—when just then Ebert called from Berlin.

Noske went, and for safety's sake he took along with him Rear Admiral von Trotha, who just happened to be in the vicinity at the time. However this had nothing to do with naval matters, but with something much more important.

Ebert admitted him to his Wilhelmstrasse office, had him take a seat, and praised him highly for not allowing the dangerous Kiel battalion out of town when shortly before Christmas they were all set to come to the aid of their Berlin comrades in the People's Navy. Noske said modestly that that was the least he could have done.

Ebert: "Gustav, now listen to me. They recently locked me up here inside the Reichs Chancellery, and I was released only by a miracle. Our friend Wels was beaten half dead; the military forces at our disposal then went into operation on my orders, with what awful results you are aware. And had we not called off the battle, it would have been a total defeat. And now the Independents have deserted as well."

Noske gazed in wonder at the fat little man before him, there was something soft and sniveling about him. Ebert, sitting beside the lanky lumberjack, lamented, "No one knows what these Independents are up to. Will they join forces with Liebknecht? Do they want to tear our party apart? They reproach me with having called in General Lequis without asking them first. But I'm in charge of military matters."

Noske: "Fritz, you don't have to apologize to me. We know those fellows well enough."

Ebert: "We're beaten. And if they join up with Liebknecht we have nothing to counter them with."

Noske: "I'm of an entirely different opinion on that. It seems to me you're all in a muddle there."

Ebert, softly: "Fine. And that's why I've called you here. I'm pleased that you think so. I need help. I want you to look around and see what can be done here. Gustav, we've got to be prepared for the worst, make no mistake. Now for starters, go over and have a talk with Colonel Scheuch at the War Ministry."

Noske went, and a gray-bearded noncom latched onto him in the reception room and asked him how he liked Berlin. Noske, without giving it a second thought: "Berlin? Enough to make you vomit."

Thereupon Noske sat down with Colonel Scheuch in the War Ministry, and they made a quick survey of all the troops at their disposal in the Reich. When they had finished, Noske left, and in the ministerial reception room they met up with an officer whom Scheuch introduced to the governor from Kiel as an adjutant of General von Märker, the founder of the new Volunteer Rifle Corps in Westphalia.

Later, as they sat in Scheuch's office, this same officer asked Scheuch to repeat the name of the gentleman the minister had introduced him to. Scheuch: "That's Noske, Gustav Noske, governor of Kiel. Ebert's right hand now it seems. You'll probably be dealing with him shortly. — But why are you so silent today, my friend?"

The man cast him a questioning glance. Scheuch encouraged him to speak up.

First Lieutenant von R.: "Begging Your Excellency's permission . . ."

"Please, please."

"I'm shocked."

Scheuch: "By what?"

Von R.: "By—the sight of this Herr Noske."

Scheuch: "The man did a good job in Kiel."

"Your Excellency, I've just come from General von Märker's camp. As Your Excellency knows, we're working away day and night, in selfless devotion, officers and men alike all of us with just one thought: Germany, our Fatherland."

"Go on."

Von R.: "And then—Noske, this creature. You expect me to go back with news of that?"

Scheuch: "My dear friend, whom are you telling? I sit here slaving away too."

The right corner of von R.'s mouth was pulled down caustically, he squinted. "I don't know how my comrades will react when I tell them about Herr Noske."

Scheuch: "Don't tell them anything. Clench your teeth. Patience. By the way, how's your father doing? Back on his estate again?"

"Thank you sir, very good, sir."

"Give him my greetings when you write him." A pause, very softly: "Perhaps I'll see him myself when I return."

"You're leaving, Your Excellency?"

Scheuch: "Yes. I'm too old for this. It's different for you young fellows."

And there Noske sat with Ebert again.

"Fritz, you Berliners are a complete riddle to me. What are you all so upset about? Because things didn't work out at the royal stables on Christmas, even though you were so poorly prepared? And what else is wrong? Who's harming you? Do you know what it all looks like to me? Like the English during the war. Whenever they made a successful attack, the first thing they wanted to do was beat a hasty retreat. That they could have managed a victory was quite beyond their comprehension. That's how pessimistic they were. The French practically had to use force to make them realize it."

"You must explain that to me, Gustav."

Noske: "For example, you're rid of the Independents."

Ebert: "And what's so wonderful about that?"

Noske bent over to Ebert. "That you really are rid of them, that you can make your moves now all on your own. And in two or three weeks we'll speak our piece with them."

Ebert shook his head, grumbled and waddled back and forth behind his desk. "And whom do we have on our side? Who's going to stand with us? People have already accused me often enough of having gotten too mixed up with the officers' corps."

Noske laughed loud and heartily. "Let them. Why not? Aren't the officers Germans?"

Ebert: "Not so loud, Gustav. You don't have to tell me that. But all the same, you needn't have any illusions about them either."

Noske, cheerful and sure of himself: "I'll not get upset over that. I'm a long way from turning gray on their account. I've found enough respectable, honest men among them, patriots with whom we can work. Besides which, Fritz, you use what you can find. Or do you want to put things in order here by using Spartacus and the Independents?"

Ebert sat down, murmured several "hmm's" and gazed once more at his lanky friend. "All right, Gustav, fine, that's settled. We'll give it a try. Let's get to work. You'll stay here in Berlin, that's sure, and not go back to Kiel. We'll put you in the Cabinet. I've talked about the idea with the others already. You'll take over military affairs. I'll still be in charge. But, Gustav, that means making a clean sweep of things."

And Ebert's face was distorted with savage hatred. Noske's face mirrored his. "I can promise you that, Fritz. We'll lay into them. I've had it up to here myself."

A few days later the government of the Reich issued a proclamation: "The paralyzing discord has been ended.

"The government has been newly reorganized as a single unity.

"It recognizes only one law for its actions: the welfare, the preservation, the indivisibility of the German Republic, regardless of party.

"And now to work."

Noske rolled up his shirt-sleeves.

The inspection of military formations began.

These were the fragments of the battered colossus that had been the Imperial Army, its soldiers and weapons. For we are cobblers. We'll take our leather wherever we can get it. It will suffice to make a pair of boots with good, firm heels to crush them with.

In the near future we will have the reserves of the 17th and 31st Infantry divisions and of the Guard Cavalry Rifles at our disposal. There was the Iron Brigade of Kiel, the National Rifle Corps, countless civilian and semicivilian squadrons, the Republican Militia, the Resident Defense Corps, the Hülsen Volunteers, and, as the capstone—Märker's brand-new Volunteer Rifle Corps built around iron discipline. That was the phoenix that had risen up out of the ashes of the old army. They all were aching to fight, to strike out at whomever you asked them to: at Poles and Bolsheviks, at Spartacus or whomever.

Noske worked from dawn till late in the night.

After the unfortunate incident with Wels, the post of commander of the City of Berlin was vacant as well. As far as Noske was concerned, only a high ranking, active officer could be considered, at least a colonel.

"Easy, easy," Ebert tried to cool him down. "A colonel? The next thing I know you'll suggest a prince. Gustav, it's still 1918. You've got to leave something for us to do in 1919."

And so they agreed on a sergeant major from Potsdam by the name of Klawunde. But Noske couldn't refrain from naming Marks, a captain from the General Staff, as his aide.

During the days that followed, the victims of the battle of the stables, sailors and civilians alike, were buried; as usual, a massive demonstration resulted. Flyers were circulated among the participants in the procession and among the passersby in the streets down which they marched. One of the flyers read:

"Liebknecht and Luxemburg are befouling the revolution with their shameful deeds, and endangering all its achievements.

"The masses dare not sit back and watch for even one minute as these criminals and their hangers-on paralyze the work of the governmental agencies of the Republic, pushing the nation ever closer toward civil war and throttling the right of free speech with their filthy bare hands.

"They use lies, slander and force to tear down whatever stands in opposition to them. Their insolence in playing the role of rulers of Berlin is unbounded."

That is what the gentlemen of the Social Democratic Party wrote. The "Citizen's Council," however, let loose as follows:

"The Christmas offensive of the Spartacists leads only to the abyss.

"The naked force of this criminal gang can only be met with force.

"Do you want peace? Do you want freedom? Then see to it that this armed idler Karl Liebknecht is no longer a problem."

To the accompaniment of such music, the victims of the revolution were borne to their graves.

Spartacus Is of the Opinion That Things Are Not Yet Ripe

As the old year came to an end, Spartacus delegates from all over the Reich decided to meet in the Landtag building on Prinz-Friedrich-Albert-Strasse to consult about how they might tighten their organization and further the cause of the revolution. For it was their opinion that they had a word or two to say about such matters. But what resulted was not a word or two, but several—and unfortunately very diverse ones.

One hundred fourteen persons appeared, of whom eighty-three were delegates. The Party leadership served up a long introductory lecture in which they got all their wishes and latest slogans off their chest.

"The bloody illusion of a global empire under Prussian militarism has been expunged on the battlefields of France, and the gang of criminals who began the World War and immersed Germany in a sea of blood, deceiving her for four long years, has finally been defeated."

(Palpable nonsense that not even the French nor the English believed. You only needed to open the window and stick your nose out and ask any officer who chanced to be passing by, or even General Märker himself, and you could hear something quite different on the question of Germany's defeat and the expunging of said illusion.)

"Our society is confronted with the choice of either erecting a capitalist system with new wars, chaos and anarchy, or erecting a socialist society that alone can save mankind."

For which reason they desired immediately to carry out:

"Disarmament of the police, officers, soldiers and all members of the ruling class. Confiscation of all weapons and munitions by workers' and soldiers' councils.

"Arming of the entire male proletariat.

"Formation of a Red Guard to defend against counterrevolution.

"Abolition of military discipline.

"Formation of revolutionary courts of justice.

"Trials for war criminals.

"Immediate confiscation of all foodstuffs.

"The final abolition of all independent states and the creation of a unified republic.

"Cancellation of all public debts, with the exception of war loans, up to a predetermined sum.

"Expropriation of all landed property, with the exception of small holdings, all banks, mines, major industries and commercial corporations, control of all modes of transportation.

"Spartacus is the social conscience of the revolution. Kill it, cry the secret enemies of the proletarian revolution—the capitalists, officers, the anti-Semitic press and the Scheidemanns who like Judas Iscariot want to sell the proletariat to the bourgeoisie.

"Spartacus will seize power, alone, by the incontrovertible will of the majority, of the proletarian masses of all Germany, who must first adopt both the goal and the tactics of the Spartacists. The road is long. The victory of the Spartacus League will not come at the beginning, but at the end of the revolution. It is identical with the victory of the millions who make up the socialist proletariat.

"Let us be a thumb pressed in the eye of the bourgeoisie, a knee pressed against its breast."

In order to pass resolutions about these and many other matters, one hundred fourteen people from all over the Reich had gathered in the Landtag building in Berlin, of whom, as we noted, eighty-three were delegates. And what the presiding committee thought and wanted, they had just heard. What they themselves wanted, however, was something quite different.

They wanted simply to strike the blow. They wanted to get the stranded, mucked-up German revolution afloat again. For a dreadful racket could be noticed coming from Russia. This was the work of Nikolai Lenin.

He and his Bolsheviks were toppling the walls and underpinnings of the old society.

On Lenin's behalf, little Karl Radek had appeared to study the terrain. The Russians respected, but also feared German erudition.

Karl Radek, Karl the Small, with his thick head, monstrous spectacles and his dashing sailor's beard, looked about attentively, and was especially interested in Karl the Great, Charlemagne, Karl Liebknecht. Because the essential question was truly one that worker's delegations from the Reich had posed: First: were they going to let the revolution get bogged down? Second: if not, was it their belief that they must first slowly create a terrain from which to do battle? Third: did they realize that before that could happen they might be overrun by the counterrevolution?

Which side was Karl Liebknecht lining up on?

The battle was joined, and the fronts were clearly separated by a single point: to participate in elections for the Constituent Assembly or not.

That such a question would even arise upset and outraged most of the delegates. Had not the *Rote Fahne* continually branded a constituent assembly as the instrument of counterrevolution? And now they were supposed to discuss the issue? Incredibly enough, even Rosa, the great herald in battle, advocated participation, not all too clearly, but clearly enough.

Radek stood in one corner of the hall and listened to Karl conversing with the delegates. They sat down to talk with him. He consoled them. "Just wait a bit; Rosa will explain the whole thing in her speech." That still didn't please the worker delegates. They didn't need anything clarified. The conditions for the revolution in Germany were considerably better than those in Russia, where there was nothing but broad steppes and farmers, and here there were cities and industry and a schooled and organized working class. Why shouldn't what had worked in Russia work in Germany?

Little Radek watched his Karl. What would he answer? He was working very hard to avoid giving a clear answer. It was not pleasant to have to listen.

When Karl became aware that Radek was listening, he shoved his arm under Radek's and they walked off together.

Karl: "What do you think? Why do you look so grave, Radek?"

"Me, grave? You're not out to offend me, are you? Why should I look grave? My countenance must be acting independently."

Radek thought: Why are you asking about my looks when you know yourself why I'm making such a face.

Karl: "Where's Leo hiding?" He meant Jogiches.

Radek (aha, you want to get your information from him, but you'll not find out anything there either): "I'll take you to him, he's sitting there at the desk."

Jogiches interrupted his letter-writing as the two approached. Radek vanished at once. Karl quietly told him all about the conversations that had taken place.

Leo: "Do we participate in the elections or not?"

His worried face did not relax, his eyes remained clouded. He asked Karl straight out, "And you, which side are you on?"

Karl thrust his hands into his pants pockets, stretched his legs out onto a chair and gave a whistle. "Frankly, I go to bed at night and I'm for the elections, and when I wake up the next morning I'm against them."

Leo nodded (interesting, so you think that what we're dealing with here is a matter of psychology): "And what's your decision after dinner?"

Karl laughed aloud. "You're right. But that's just how things are with me. Don't you feel the same way? The only one who remains firm and knows what she wants is Rosa. But for that you have to be a real theoretician like she is." He cast a glance at Jogiches, at the severe face across from him that showed no sign of amusement and had bent down over the sheet of paper again. This was Rosa's mentor, the falcon, the most exacting and clear-thinking one among them. Karl suggested lightly, "Lenin was right, you know. Revolution is not just a matter of calculation, there's also an art to it."

Leo stared at him in amazement. "Revolution an art? Lenin said that? Yes, well, he can afford to. What do you say to that? Mysticism?"

Karl threw his head back with a laugh. "Not really, Leo. I hope you don't think I'm crazy. I only meant that somehow revolution has some similarities with the arts in several respects; for example, will, planning and inspiration all play something of a role, and because you also have to stay very much in contact with your medium, with the human masses, so that something can properly develop."

Leo, cold and indifferent: "For that you probably have to be a real artist like Lenin."

"At any rate," Karl said, "I like the notion."

Leo, bent over his papers, said no more. (We can't change you, dear Karl, I can see that. We can make no more of you than what you are, our beautiful, colorful banner. Just so you don't do anything foolish!)

The delegates surrounded Rosa, that little, energetic woman. Karl joined the group. They were attacking Rosa: "There's something rotten with you people here in Berlin. First you say one thing, then another."

Rosa: "And what do *you* want? The dictatorship of the proletariat by tomorrow morning? Fine, I'll join in with you."

"There's no way to figure you out. You don't even know yourselves what you want."

Rosa: "Where do you get that? We know very well what we want. Only we don't scream it from the rooftops. Just stop and consider for a moment who is for us, and who is against us. We have every legal authority against us, the government and the Executive Council. We have, you say, the masses of the people, the proletariat on our side. But they're not yet fully certain what it is we want and who we are, and they're not well organized enough. You've got to understand that. Don't delude yourselves, you'll end up paying for it. You have to be patient, otherwise you'll endanger everything. You can just imagine how the reactionaries behind Ebert are simply waiting for us to strike a blow and expose our weakness. But we've already made enough stupid blunders."

"And so now you want to make one more really stupid blunder and join the Constituent Assembly. The word across the nation is that some of you are thinking just like the bourgeoisie and that all you want is to be deputies again and make hour-long speeches."

"Aren't you ashamed of yourselves?"

"Well, somebody's got to tell you. There's no point in a constituent assembly for us, none at all. We'll get nowhere with a lot of hot air. We know who has something to gain from that: the reactionaries. Lenin knew about that too. And that's why he broke it up right away. Once you let them start talking, they've got a foothold and we're the losers.

Rosa: "Got a foothold? It takes someone to let them do that."

"What is all this? We've got to take advantage of the situation. Now's our chance. There'll always be risks involved."

The session begins. Elections to the Constituent Assembly are on the agenda. The leadership counsels caution, the delegates give their opinion. The vote: of the eighty-three delegates, sixty-two vote against participation in elections.

The leadership is outvoted. Incredible joy in the hall.

A pause.

The leaders meet and try to calm one another. They are alarmed. Jogiches is a broken man. He says to Rosa, "Maybe the whole idea of founding the Party was premature. People just aren't ready for things. A party doesn't begin by shoving its leadership aside."

Karl seeks out Rosa. The impression he leaves is that he is completely unworried. He doesn't say it, but she can see it at once: in point of fact he's glad with the result of the vote. Karl is always there, it seems, when somebody is dying. He soothes Rosa. "Pour oil upon those wild and troubled waters, Rosa. You still have the last word. We'll have them all in our hands again, you'll see. I expect you to accomplish it all."

She knows that he's not being candid with her and asks directly, "That's what you expect of me, Karl?"

He quotes: "Gather all your forces together, the passion and the sting, our task this day is to move the stony heart of the king." And he made a comic gesture in the direction of the delegates.

She is amazed: the man quotes poetry at a moment like this. She sits down by herself, spreads paper out before her and takes a pencil in hand so that no one will disturb her. But she's trembling. She cannot calm down. Strange, how I tremble. My mind is clear. What has upset me so? And only now does her mind comprehend what her emotions have already taken in: Leo is right, this is a dreadful defeat, the fate of the entire revolution may depend on it. Because what will happen if they really do strike the blow they intend to strike, without us, even against us, as weak as they are and so disorganized—once people find out about it and provoke them into action?

The hour for Rosa's speech has come, for her swan song.

What's wrong with Rosa?

Doesn't she see the victory they've won, that the revolution was won on December 24th, and that this has left Ebert and his general trembling. Doesn't she understand that they now have to take up pursuit of the defeated foe?

She is so clear-headed and exact, even now, a sparkling and profound mind. She sees it all—and dismisses it. She doesn't believe. It's against her theory. She doesn't believe in victories and defeats that do not come from economic upheavals. The great upheaval has not yet arrived. The country has not yet been seized by it. The situation is not yet ripe. If this were a true upheaval, according her dogma, the command centers, the generals and the government would topple along with the capitalist economy. You don't have to topple them separately. An earthquake is not concerned with traffic signs. But the proletariat will accomplish this grand and genuine upheaval, and with it will come the liberation and fellowship of all mankind. The proletariat must work toward that goal, prepare the way for it.

The delegates watch this little, pale old woman. Even those who do not agree with her watch with love and shock. They know that she is a flame that has been burning for decades. But now she is exhausted and frail. Prison has weakened her, as have these hours here in the Landtag building. She speaks, it's a topic she knows. She speaks the perfect truth. Karl Liebknecht and Jogiches are sitting there among the delegates, though not beside each other, listening. Radek has found a seat way at the back. Rosa's voice rings out loud and clear:

"We dare not repeat the delusion of the first phase of the revolution, the one from November 9th, thinking it sufficient for the success of the socialist revolution to unseat a capitalist government and replace it with another. We must undermine the government of Ebert and Scheidemann by revolutionary class struggle, at every step. The November 9th revolution was above all a political one, whereas it must primarily be economic. It was likewise only an urban revolution. The countryside is as good as untouched by it all. If we are serious about wanting a socialist revolution we've got to direct our gaze to rural areas.

"History will not make things as easy for us as it did for the bourgeois revolutions. But the November 9th revolution wasn't even a political one. Only a few superficial changes were made. There is a straight line running from Imperial Reichs Chancellor Prince von Baden to Imperial Reichs Chancellor Friedrich Ebert and to Imperial Secretary of State Philip Scheidemann, behind whom Hindenburg stands as unyielding as ever, ready to come forward at any moment. It is not enough to topple one official authority and replace it with a few dozen new men.

"We have to work our way up from the bottom, and that corresponds to the character of our revolution as a mass movement, striving for goals that affect the basic substance of the social order.

"Down at the bottom, where the individual entrepreneur stands in confrontation with his salaried slave, down at the bottom, where all the leading organs of the ruling political clique stand in confrontation with the objectives of rule by the working class, by the masses, that is where we must seize the reins of power from our rulers, bit by bit. I believe it is healthy for us to have a good, clear look at the difficulties and complications this revolution brings with it.

"I do not presume to prophesy how long this process will take. Which of us wants to calculate such things? What should we care?

"If only our lives are long enough to bring us that far!"

She had spoken. They had let her speak. It was just like old times; Rosa, the friend of all, Rosa, the strong warrior.

But the majority of the delegates realized: "They're trying to shelve the whole thing. She points to the grand and ancient highway to revolution. And it's not here yet, and must still be built. This isn't ready yet, and that isn't ready yet. That's what Rosa says. But if everything isn't ready yet, then maybe the sailors in Kiel should have forgotten the whole thing and we could have let Wilhelm stay in his palace."

They argued with her. Rosa reiterated that the comrades were making their radicalism all too easy. The elections for the Constituent Assembly would take place whether they liked it or not. Even Karl seconded her on this, slightly miffed as he asked if perhaps his work or that of others in the Reichstag had been really quite so meaningless for the working class.

Rosa begged them not to keep harping on Russia. Finally she grew more explicit and was not afraid to say, "The Spartacus League is in fact not a party that wishes to rule the working class or to gain power through it. The proletarian revolution can only achieve clarity and maturity step by step along the Golgotha route of bitter experience, through defeat and victory."

It was a rejection of all rash action. Rosa knew she was preaching to deaf ears. But they had come to a dead end. Something had to happen to unify them.

The little Russian with the immense glasses, Lenin's emissary, was the man of the hour. He unleashed storms of applause when, without naming Rosa or the others in the leadership, he spoke of the dictatorship of the proletariat. Only the erection of a proletarian dictatorship could save Germany from its foreign enemies. Only the spread of the world revolution. The Russian proletariat was just waiting to join its German comrades in a battle at the Rhine against Anglo-Saxon and French capitalism. That filled all their hearts with joy.

Rosa listened from the rear, where she stood hunched against the wall. This man was as clever as they came, and he spoke up for his Bolsheviks. She thought of friends there who had been shot and killed. Ghastly.

Then came Karl. Radek's fanfares had called him forth. As always he let himself get carried away. The goal of international communism could only be the destruction of the capitalism of the Entente.

"Clemenceau declared that he would burn Paris to the ground if he could save France by doing so. And likewise we Spartacists must proclaim that if need be we will lay Germany in ruins, so that from the ashes of the old Reich a new and great nation may rise."

With wild cheers they voted to join the International Communist Party, whose main contingent was the great, victorious Bolshevik Party, and whose German wing they wished to be—communism across the entire continent, from Vladivostok to the Rhine.

Leo tapped Rosa on the arm when it was all over and whispered, "Thanks for your speech, Rosa."

She asked him to find a cab for her, she wanted to go home.

"You're not feeling well, Rosa? Isn't Tanya around?"

"I sent her home. It went on too long."

She sank down next to him in one corner of the clattering cab.

He gave her his heavy scarf. As they drove down the Königgrätzer Strasse, she looked at him perplexedly and muttered, "What's going to happen, Leo?"

His wrinkled face twisted into a faint smile. "The question is, what are they going to try now?"

Then he said in his typically earnest and cool way, "We're having the same troubles with our conference that Ebert is having with his generals. We called the conference and it ran away with us."

"And what will it all come to, Leo?"

"Do you know anyone in southern Germany?"

She closed her eyes. "Why do you ask, Leo?"

"You never know. I can give you an address. And Karl should take a look around for something for himself and his family."

She sat there in her corner, a heap of misfortune, and he snapped at her just as he always used to, "Rosa, pull yourself together. You'll demoralize others as well."

"I'm so weak, Leo."

"All the more reason for you to get away soon."

She sat alone in her wretched hotel room. Tanya was not there.

What is this? Why do I let myself be treated this way. Leo is back to playing the archangel with the flaming sword. He takes his anger out on me. Am I to blame if the others won't listen to reason. Tanya came in at last. Rosa clasped her tightly, shaking as if from the cold.

"Is the conference over?" Tanya asked.

"Yes, thank God."

She stood breathing against Tanya's breast, with her eyes closed as if she wanted to go to sleep. Then the telephone jangled loudly. Tanya ran to it. It was Karl calling from the hotel lobby. He asked whether he could come up. Rosa said wearily, "Let him."

He entered full of excitement.

"Rosa, what are you hiding for? You vanished like a bolt of lightning. Nobody could find you."

"It's eleven o'clock. I was tired. Pull the curtain, Karl, please."

"I wanted to talk to you after the session. Leo was gone too."

Rosa: "He brought me home."

"I see. What does he have to say?"

She was half lying on the sofa. "That we should get away, go somewhere in southern Germany."

"But why? Not now, surely."

"You heard me, Karl, we ought to go to southern Germany. Soon, he said. He would give us some addresses if needed."

Karl sat down next to her. "What's wrong, Rosa? He said that?"

She shrugged. "You know all that yourself."

"No, or—yes, I do understand. He's afraid they'll now do something stupid here. Did the vote really get to you that much? But why? We're a revolutionary party. We ought to be pleased that our people are so active. Let them go ahead and kick the traces once in a while. I let my children get away with things at home too. It's fun to do it. Do you know the poem by Richard Dehmel that goes:

> 'My son, if all your father has to say
> Is, as a son you should obey,
> Tell him nay, tell him nay.'"

She gazed at Karl. The educated man was quoting again. He took a new tack.

"Leo may be right after all in saying that we're a little ahead of ourselves in founding the Party. For the most part, you know, people thought they had been convened here solely for the purpose of preparing battle plans for the future. Really splendid when you think of it."

"Karl, may I quote something for you? From our introductory report, a document you know well. 'Spartacus wishes to assume power only on the basis of the unchallenged will of the great majority of the proletarian masses throughout all Germany, who must first accept both the goals and strategy of the Spartacists.'"

He sighed. "I would be very happy, Rosa, if we could put these theoretical debates behind us once and for all. All this week I spent talking with Radek about putsches, dates and mass uprisings. People want to see deeds."

Rosa, "Is that right?"

Karl: "Of course, and if they can't get deeds with us, then perhaps with others, or they'll just forget the whole thing, which would be the worst of all. Ultimately they'll simply turn their backs on us because the whole thing just seems too silly."

Rosa had sat back up, she was full of energy again. Her face betrayed nothing as she said, "Karl, you remind me of Lenin."

"Of Lenin, why?" (He guessed something nasty was coming.)

Rosa: "Distantly."

Karl: "Go on, please."

Rosa: "Lenin forces his people to follow him, and you—your people force you to follow them."

She laughed heartily. He answered with a grand theatrical gesture, "I would hope that I have nothing else in common with Lenin, otherwise I'm afraid you would eat me alive."

He laid his head on her shoulder and said wistfully, "Your reproach doesn't upset me so very much, by the way. First, no one is forcing me. And second, what would be so awful about following the masses? When speaking, I've always had the impression that my truest and soundest ideas came from my contact with the people. The masses inspire us."

Rosa, coolly: "Please, please, don't let me interfere with your source of inspiration. But of course what interests me is what you great artists are about to impose on us. You're the true democrats now, you and your delegates."

"Rosa, don't joke. You're only hurt because those people didn't go along with you. They're just common everyday people, doers, that's all."

Rosa: "Which means that we can chuck our intellectual exercises. They want to follow their feelings, their stupid feelings."

Karl stood up with a sigh. "Rosa, I repeat, you're wrong. I believe there's something to be said for the reason of the masses."

Rosa: "That's what I said. You're Lenin in reverse. He said no to the whole Soviet Congress and got his way. You really do remind me of him."

Karl paced up and down the room. That's the way women are. Rosa watched him walking about. She thought: first he sighs, then declaims, then convinces himself how unjustly he's being treated. And suddenly her anger burst forth.

"Don't think for a moment, Karl, that I'm going to put up with some Lenin or other who comes along with mass executions, not from you or your comrades in the Party. I would hope you're not assuming that. You and your sixty delegates."

"For heaven's sake, Rosa."

She was furious. "It's clear, after all, what sort of plans you will forge once we've abdicated and theory no longer matters, just the so-called will of the masses, with you as their high priest. But don't fool yourself, Karl. I'll say no, and I won't be alone."

He stood there dumbfounded at this outburst. Still out of control, she hissed at him, "I promise you, you're not going to have your way. There will be no uprising here, because it's a stupid idea, asinine, because it's impossible, because we are the future, because it would be a betrayal of the working class and because the man who leads it would be a traitor to the working class, and I don't care if that is you with your sixty delegates."

Karl, his shoulders dropping, let it all roll over him.

"So now I'm a traitor to the working class. Anything's possible. Rosa, let me assure you that I did everything I knew how to change those people's minds."

She remained firm. "Then that's where you're weak. You're always boasting how you can always sweep them along with you."

He gave a forced smile. She's overwrought. "I had better go, Rosa. I hope you recover quickly from all this."

He turned his back and strode out the door; she followed him with a fixed stare. He was virtually running now.

Her eyes, still directed at the closed door, grew clouded. There was a pied piper dancing there, playing his flute and turning back toward her. He was taking a narrow path across the meadow at the base of a mountain. Many people, men and women, were following him. And Rosa had to join them. The mountain opened up. They entered.

And as they crossed the threshold, the mountain closed up sound-lessly behind them.

The Eichhorn Affair

On January 1, 1919, the same day on which Rosa concluded her great speech with "I do not presume to prophesy how long this process will take. Which of us wants to calculate such things? What should we care? If only our lives are long enough to bring us that far!"—on that same day two Berlin newspapers with close connections to the government, *Die Politisch-Parlamentarischen Nachrichten* and *Vorwärts,* launched an attack against one Emil Eichhorn, accusing him of dishonesty and wasting public moneys, and moreover of being an agitator for civil war.

This harmless Herr Eichhorn (the name means "squirrel"), had the misfortune to be the Berlin chief of police. He had been placed in that post during the fine days of the November revolution by our minister of finance. He could not see that there was any reason for him to resign. Quite in contrast to the minister of finance himself, who felt a strong pull to leave his office for his paintings, greenhouses and the stock exchange. Those who urged Eichhorn to resign and at the same time made such accusations could point to the precedent of the Independents in Berlin and throughout the Reich, who had themselves resigned their posts when their people's deputies left the government. But that was no argument for our Eichhorn. He did not want to hand his post over to "the murderers of the workers." This usually so mild-mannered man also often preached the necessity of uniting with the Left and cursed this "revolution in house slippers." Not for a moment did he dream he would ever be forced to pull on a pair of jackboots.

Once the pressure was on and he did not depart, showed no inclination to do so, the Central and Executive Committee took up the matter—which overnight had become "the Eichhorn affair." This good-natured man, convinced of the rightness of his position, was at a loss to know what to think. In the Executive Council they asserted—and as we know one can assert all sorts of things, an assertion is always more effective than its refutation—that in addition to his official salary he was receiving a thousand marks a month from the Bolshevik intelligence bureau "Rosta." Even those who wished him well had to admit that the word "Rosta" was as good as proof of guilt. It burst among them like a bomb.

On January 2nd, therefore, we find a very perturbed Berlin chief of police riding in a carriage from Alexanderplatz toward the Prussian Ministry of the Interior, where he is to be subjected to an interrogation about how it happened that he, counter to the general inclination of Independents to resign, was resisting—he alone, Eichhorn. And what was the reason behind this egregious lack of resolve, whence this spiritual defect?

He was at once received by Minister Hirsch. This gentleman, in contradistinction to the minister of finance—banker, horticulturist, patron of the arts and Independent—was merely a Social Democrat, and therefore he could continue unimpeded to concern himself with his visitor and the reason for his visit. He led him with avowals of affection into a large room where the members of the Executive Committee already sat waiting to wring Eichhorn's neck.

The Executive Committee had armed itself with a thick portfolio, from which, like Pandora from her box, they drew nothing but abuse and vexation for Eichhorn, this guest who had come all the way from Alexanderplatz just to see them. Each of them reached into his pockets and conjured up a new grievance. They were more than Executive Committee members, they were executive magicians.

Eichhorn denied, resisted.

He said he would not stand for this. He had not come here for this. Would they kindly put away their portfolios. He alone could manage stunts like this.

The executive magicians saw that their magic wasn't working. He was obdurate, and they would have to find other means to proceed. They then accused him of several things straight out. They boldly asserted, for example, that he was not willing to let himself be forced out of office. He had an unnatural relationship with Alexanderplatz. It was a perversion, a heresy. They declared that they were going to have to burn him at the stake for it.

Eichhorn, sly man that he was, directed their conversation to another topic. Yes, he was fond of police headquarters, because he had been placed there by the revolution to defend a socialist republic.

We have met this frightening argument once before, advocated in the Ministry of Finance by the naval division. We saw the results of such arguments: a public auditor's reason was immobilized, so that he ran to twelve bureaucrats whose mouths went dry upon hearing these same arguments, causing them to demand water from a firehose, resulting in the occurrence of countless complicated things, some with lasting effects, which, despite the speed at which they happened, lost none of their improbability. And here too, in the Ministry of the Interior, such words caused dreadful mischief. The minister of the interior and two of the Executive Committee members did indeed want to break Eichhorn's neck. But this madman from police headquarters had uttered the phrase that robbed them of their reason, causing them to fall into delirium.

The minister of the interior was named Hirsch. That his name meant "stag" had never occurred to him; he had always just assumed that that was what he was called. Now he cried out, like the stag for the quickening stream, naturally, and he sought it in the room. Not finding it there, he asserted that he had lost his head, it was gone, simply vanished. And the Executive Committee, taking alarm, ran about and searched under the tables and chairs, asking where their minister's head might be. And then he gave another cry; he'd found it, there it was. And what a curious and interesting sight it was: there was the minister leaping and cavorting like a stag at play, emitting various screams and cries, turning his antlered head about in all directions to rub it against the antlers of other stags and butt them.

Eichhorn—what could Eichhorn do? He retreated. He made a leap to the right, the enchanted stag followed. He made a leap to the left, the enchanted stag followed. The committee members stood there amazed, gaping and running about with empty portfolios. What could they do? Eichhorn called to them, urging them on: "You can kiss my ass. The revolution put me in this position to defend the socialist republic."

The phrase had been spoken yet again. Their reason was immobilized, their throats were parched, their stomachs turned topsy-turvy, and the only thing left to them was the recollection that they were members of the Executive Committee.

And so now they began to turn slowly about their center, with indescribable calm and regularity. They turned so slowly because they were gazing at all the things yet to come. Then the turning accelerated, faster and faster. Already they had toppled the chairs that Eichhorn and Hirsch had vacated.

Eichhorn himself was now seized with it. He no longer knew how to save himself from the stag. The atmosphere was too charged. His distress now managed what the Executive Committee's portfolio had failed to accomplish. And he grew little legs and a pointed nose. With a swish, a monstrous tail grew out of his back, and with it he now battered the stag about the mouth.

The committee members spun about in silent delight.

The tumult awakened the entire Ministry. It was, as we noted, January 2nd, and the bureaucrats had arrived at the Ministry hoping to sleep off their New Year's hangovers. They listened at all the doors, finally found the right one and saw it all. Still inebriated, they immediately wanted to participate, to turn about, to jump and cavort. But it turned out they were too old for this. Their cold brains could no longer comprehend tangible realities and follow them in a natural fashion. There was nothing for it but to stand there and be amazed at all the uproar.

And behold, the spell was broken. Eichhorn grew long legs again, the great bushy tail wound back up, perhaps to be whisked out again on some other appropriate occasion, and the Executive Committee members gave up their spinning about, apologized, first to one another, then to all present, and sat back down. The minister sought his chair, found his head in the process, and remarked that someone had beaten him severely about the mouth, but was soothed when those present assured him that this could be remedied.

And so now they moved on, the spell having been broken without achieving any concrete results, to a sober consideration of the matter at hand.

The socialist minister asked their invited guest, Emil Eichhorn, chief of police for Berlin (who had made himself unpopular by his actions during the fighting at the royal stables and just in general), "I cannot figure you out, Herr Polizeipräsident. You've been in office since November. That's a very, very long time. During that time, as every novelist can confirm, a great deal of water has flowed down the Spree. But you're still there. How is that possible? What's happened to you? Are you defying time itself? Do you plan to outlast the elements? Why don't you go? What is there within you that resists? Have you seen a doctor? Do you know Freud's work? Did your grandmother perhaps ravish you as a baby and are you staying in office now out of protest? Is that the reason? Your grandmother will undo all that. We'll use all the influence we have at our disposal."

Eichhorn remained silent. Hirsch nodded. "Resistance, plain and simple."

He began anew. "It's hard to make rhyme or reason of. You're the only one still sitting there at police headquarters. Don't you feel lonely, isn't there something wrong with your social conscience? You've declared yourself independent of the Independents. Can you continue to bear such a life? Doesn't it break your heart? It ought to break, truly it ought."

The Executive Committee members confirmed this, it ought to break.

How did Eichhorn react to these paternal remonstrations. In a vulgar, common manner. He answered, "Herr Prussian Minister of the Interior, I beg you to allow me to decide how to interpret my relationship to my political party. You truly cannot expect me to relinquish my position now after you've accused me of irregularities in this fashion."

Only a lunatic could talk like this.

The minister slapped his hands together. "Dishonesty, wasting public moneys, one thousand marks of Bolshevist bribes a month—good heavens, that upsets you? We only said it because it is the truth. We did not wish to offend you by saying it. You're really pathologically sensitive, Herr Eichhorn. Now, perhaps it will facilitate your decision if I inform you that I intend to relieve you of your office."

Strangely enough, Eichhorn only grinned at this news, and replied that the minister could not fire him under any conditions.

Reproachfully Hirsch inquired, "Why not?"

To which Eichhorn replied: "Why, because the revolution put me in office in the first place, as I have already informed you several times."

"He won't let go of that," the minister sighed and threw a despairing glance at the committee members. One of them was struck with the notion of asking Eichhorn what he thought of the Constituent Assembly.

Eichhorn clicked his tongue and said dreamily, "It's fine, fine. Don't you think so too?"

All that was left to talk about now was the weather and the price of coal. This conversation was pursued without difficulty.

Whereupon they took leave of each other, each wrapped up in his coat and silent, to weigh all these things in their minds, recalling the poet's words:

> "Dare I still let hope impel me,
> Gleams yet light from my life's star?
> Must such sorrow overwhelm me,
> Can my pain itself not tell me
> Whether she is near or far?"

The Stone Starts to Roll

In order to facilitate Eichhorn's decision in light of the scene just described, Hirsch, using the official stationery of his ministry, informed him two days later that he, Hirsch, Prussian minister of the interior, was dismissing him, Eichhorn, chief of police for Berlin, from office as of today's date, January 4, 1919, and that on this same date Eugen Ernst would assume said office of chief of police for Berlin.

"That takes three," said Eichhorn when he read it, "and I see only two, Hirsch and Eugen Ernst."

He betook himself down Alexanderstrasse to nearby Schicklerstrasse, where the central office of the Independents was to be found. He was thereby demonstrating the feelings of solidarity that the Ministry of the Interior wanted to deny him.

This morning constitutional was a fully inconspicuous act, but it represented the first step toward an armed uprising, leading to that ominous mountain that had opened before Rosa's eyes after Karl's visit and then settled down dark and heavy upon her and so many others.

Soon, then, there was Emil Eichhorn sitting in the central office of the Independents showing them the letter he had received from Hirsch. And like bees around a fragrant tree, they gathered, buzzing and humming, and soon they were joined by the Revolutionary Shop Stewards, as though by the biggest, fattest bumblebees. And there arose a grand and mighty buzzing and humming. And there were thick swarms of Spartacists from the newly founded German Communist Party. They whizzed over with bells clanging like the fire department. They had transformed their jaws to sickles and their forelegs to hammers in witness to their fondness for the Soviet Union. They rustled, they swooshed, they clanged, they hammered and they sickled around Emil Eichhorn, and Emil sat there in their midst and smiled as only Emil could smile, thinking that this was quite a different feeling from what he had felt when he was with Hirsch.

They clung to the letter, sucking from it. They transformed it into honey and bore it across the city. And by Sunday it had become flyers and all Berlin knew the news.

"Attention, Workers, Party Comrades!

"The Ebert-Scheidemann government has escalated its hostile activity against the revolution to the point of a vile attack directly aimed at the revolutionary working class.

"It is attempting to force Chief of Police Eichhorn from office by underhanded means.

"The Ebert-Scheidemann government wants to establish a tyranny opposed to the revolutionary workers of Berlin.

"With the aid of bayonets, the Ebert-Scheidemann government hopes to reinforce its power and secure the favor of the capitalist bourgeoisie, whose disguised agent it was from the very beginning.

"Show these tyrants that the revolutionary spirit of November has not been extinguished.

"Join us in a momentous mass demonstration.

"Today at 2 o'clock, Siegesallee."

This was signed by the Revolutionary Shop Stewards of Major Industries, the Central Committee of the Social Democratic Electoral Union, the Independent Socialist Party, and the Central Office of the German Communist Party.

They rustled, buzzed, hammered and sickled, and Emil sat in the middle, smiling an embarrassed and gentle smile.

They were unable to surprise short, fat Friedrich Ebert. He no longer fell for mass demonstrations. His Gustav Noske was running faster than the revolutionaries.

On the day of the planned demonstration, January 4th, Noske was able to present his boss, Friedrich Ebert, with a strong contingent of the rifle corps that General Märker had mustered in Westphalia, which had just arrived and was now waiting at a camp in Zossen near Berlin, ready to be reviewed and put to work.

Zossen lies 30 miles south of Berlin. Ebert and Noske drove out in army cars.

There at the camp there stood in formation, in closed ranks—what a balm, what a surprise after the dreadful days before Christmas— there stood genuine soldiers, mustered by General Märker, the old African, an officer who had served under three kaisers. General Lütt- witz was in command. It was a dry, cold day. They stood on the hard- frozen sandy ground. The "Present-Arms March" rang out. Their military boots beat heavily against the soil of the mark, which received these blows like pats of love.

Clad in field gray, wearing steel helmets, the Rifles marched past Friedrich Ebert, their faces gray, immobile, hewn in stone.

It was the first time in the history of the nation that Prussian troops had paraded before a civilian. They did it with shame and loathing.

Ebert, in his heavy winter coat, held his top hat in his hand. His head was freezing, but he was warm inside.

Beside him stood his friend and aide, comrade in politics and suffering, tall Gustav Noske with his low brow and steel-rimmed glasses.

They both had only one thought: at last.

The Eichhorn affair fitted wonderfully into the mopping-up plans that were afoot—for the third time. After the mess that had been made of the troops' entry from December 10th to 12th and after the dreadful failure of Lequis at the stables, Berlin was to be mopped up.

When on that Sunday, January 5th, the bees, wasps and hornets buzzed and showered Berlin with their flyers—"Join the mass demonstration against the government on the Siegesallee"—Noske strolled out of his office at the War Ministry, Leipziger Strasse, walking calmly in the direction of Wilhelmstrasse. This time he was off to visit Wolfgang Heine, the minister in whose company he hoped to find the future chief of police for Berlin, Eugen Ernst, a man awaiting his swearing in with all the fear and expectation of a bride. At the moment, to be sure, there were only endless masses marching through the city who did not want him there. He could not understand why.

Gustav Noske, who had General Märker and his Camp Zossen troops behind him, who from a distance resembled Lenin during his nightly walks about the Tauride Palace in Petersburg, watched these singing, marching masses, through which he had to wind his way to get to Wilhelmstrasse. He climbed the stairs to Minister Heine's, where Eugen Ernst sat in bridal excitement and where Lieutenant Anton Fischer was likewise to be found, a man left behind by ex-City Commandant Wels.

They talked and talked, and frequently glanced out the window to see whether some of them might be headed toward Wilhelmstrasse. But they weren't. The masses were stubbornly making for the Siegesallee. Noske suggested they close the window. He had caught the sniffles in Zossen, and he wasn't going to let his fine sniffles be ruined by Spartacists.

Lieutenant Fischer, a versatile man who had headed the office of police intelligence at one point, said he knew this man Eichhorn to be a totally good-natured fellow with whom you could talk—he had definitely been dragged into this affair against his will. He, Anton Fischer, offered his services; he would drive over to police headquarters and bring Eichhorn to reason. To which Heine replied: that was not going to be easy. Hirsch at the Ministry of Interior had been badly bruised in one such attempt. The man had a thick skin.

Fischer, confident of victory, said, "I'll talk with him."

And he invited Eugen Ernst to come along. Maybe Ernst could then stay on and take over his new job.

Wolfgang Heine let them go, and Noske was only too happy to do so.

It was increasingly difficult to force a way through Alexanderplatz. Eugen Ernst was greatly grieved at this. So many people gathering to prevent him from entering. If only he could just talk to them for one minute.

They fought their way through to headquarters, which was surrounded by a great wall of people. Did Eugen Ernst ever feel faint!

Anton Fischer continued to smile and acted cheerful.

"It's not really so bad. First they'll rally, and then afterward they'll all go home."

He took the downcast Eugen Ernst by the arm, the bride he was about to barter.

Inside headquarters, things did look highly dangerous. There were whole wagonloads of machine guns on display; young people were gathering to be issued rifles. Trucks were arriving at the gate with squads of men and machine guns to join the demonstrators outside.

"We mustn't be intimidated," Anton Fischer muttered, who had turned pale himself, and tightly pressed the arm of his treasure.

Everywhere in the building there was the noise, the atmosphere of battle. This was not a police headquarters, it was a mobilized camp, a fortress preparing to defend itself.

In Eichhorn's office the police chief took one look at Eugen Ernst, whom they had brought in to him, and remarked that he had no need of a successor. Negotiate? About what? Voluntary resignation? Anton Fischer should not make himself ridiculous. Fischer appealed to Eichhorn's amiable nature. No one wanted war, why should he?

"Why should I? I don't want it either. Why do you?"

"We?" said Anton Fischer in horrified amazement. "Why do we want war?" He looked at his friend Ernst. "We simply want to crush the workers' movement here in Berlin and put Ernst in office while we're at it."

"But the office is occupied," Eichhorn mocked him and leaned back in his chair. "You can see that with your own eyes, Herr Ernst. You'll just have to wait. Perhaps you'd like to go downstairs in the meantime and take part in the demonstration. If you give a good account of yourself there, perhaps I can do something for you."

The tumult in the building grew. Even Fischer now realized that an agreement with Eichhorn would not be possible. So the two of them took flight through a side door. For they had learned just in time that Karl Liebknecht, Däunig and Ledebour were in the building as well— and apparently Lieutenant Dorrenbach too, the rabid commandant of the sailors. And they were absolutely sure they didn't want him to catch sight of them.

"Locking up Dorrenbach," Anton Fischer swore as they crept away, "is going to have to be your first official act."

A trembling Ernst promised it would be.

In the meantime, Gustav Noske had taken a walk down Unter den Linden to have a look at the commotion. He went past the dispatch office of the *Lokalanzeiger* and the Russian embassy. People filled the central promenade and the sidewalk on his right, while more of them swarmed up from the rear. They surged toward the zoo.

What in the world did these people think was going to happen at the zoo? Karl would speak, and Däunig and Ledebour, to be followed by the second and third string. They would get cold legs and feet and not much more. The ones with rifles up on the wagons knew better what they wanted: to give other folks a shove toward disaster. But we'll put a stop to the plans of this Eichhorn fellow.

Noske stood at Opernplatz, at the equestrian monument to old Frederick the Great. He looked across the bridge toward Schlossplatz and his amazement knew no end. It was black with people, with here and there a red flag. Really quite astonishing how many they can mobilize. High time we did something to stop it.

And finding himself lined up with others on the sidewalk, he had the good fortune to see Karl Liebknecht drive by in a car from the Brandenburg Gate. He had most certainly been out to inspect the Siegesallee to see if it was to be his personal victory boulevard. His car halted now at the monument, they would not let him through, he must speak. There it is, there he stands, without a hat, a fanatic, a madman, the poor numbskull he's always been. Once again an impassioned speech, nothing new to figure out about him, they hadn't lost anything in losing him. In the Reichstag I once told him across the table that I considered him a buffoon. He paid no attention. This time I'll be a bit clearer about how I tell him. He seems to have given up his pacifism; at least he's learned that much. Old man, it's not going to help you.

Those two, Ernst and Fischer, should be back from headquarters by now. Or perhaps they've been held there. That would be a good joke.

And lanky Noske walked along in his winter coat (it was much too short for him, but it was a favorite, this coat of Noske's), once again in the direction of the Brandenburg Gate, to Wolfgang Heine's ministry. And when he entered, he learned at once that the two of them were already back.

And there they sat next to one another, Lieutenant Fischer and Eugen Ernst, whom nobody wanted to buy, and as might be expected, they both had worried faces.

"May I offer my congratulations?" Noske asked, not letting on.

"In a certain sense, yes," Heine laughed, who was playing the observer in all this, "since they're both back safe and sound."

"Let's be happy for that much," Noske agreed, and shook their hands vigorously. "Did you have a difficult time of it?"

They both began at once to tell their tale of horror about Alexanderplatz. But Noske waved them off. "We know all that already." Since there was no other topic for conversation, and the two, Fischer and Ernst, were just sitting around useless and discouraged, he pulled Wolfgang Heine off to one corner. (Now Heine was not too comfortable with all this either, not as a man of jurisprudence, for law was an item tht no one decided during a revolution; but, he thought, that will change, someone will be the victor in any case, and whoever is victorious will need law.)

Noske whispered to Heine, "Look at those two schlemiels sitting there, wouldn't you like to slap them first on one side and then the other? I can just imagine how they acted at police headquarters, how Anton Fischer gave Eichhorn a good talking-to: wouldn't be please, please step down. We should never have allowed him to go. Now it looks as if we're weakening and we're trying to put out a feeler. That's what they'll make of it."

Noske saw his own officers against him on this, and he grew angry.

"Well, what's done is done, Heine. Throw both of them out, tell them to go eat lunch. They'll probably be able to manage that well enough. But enough backstairs politics."

He left, clapping his two idiotic negotiators on the shoulder.

And where was Friedrich Ebert at this point? He wasn't tucked away in the Reichs Chancellery. That was wise. It took a while for Noske to find him in the private home of a party comrade. There he sat, mute and somber.

Noske was all self-assurance for him, and began to report about the abortive mission of the two comrades at police headquarters. But Ebert interrupted him.

"Eichhorn refused. Of course."

He had also seen the protest demonstration and knew that half the city was on the march. He cursed and grumbled, wondering where the Social Democrats were—weren't there any left in Berlin? Noske replied that they would get aroused in due time, and why disturb folks out for a walk. But Ebert was not buying. He was upset by the size of the demonstration. He remained restless and mistrustful.

Noske started again then with his Märker and his Iron Brigade, and Ebert growled that they were too few; what were they against hundreds of thousands? They would be overrun easy as pie. It was the same farce they had had before Christmas. He didn't even dare go back to the Reichs Chancellery.

Indeed, Ebert's rage cast him back into his old blue funk. He thought: the one bunch won't help me now and the others will hunt me down.

They ate and discussed. Where should the government spend the night? Ebert couldn't go back home to Treptow, not tonight. What would become of them? The guardians of the state, its governing authorities, had become a little gang of crooks to be locked up.

"What a fine government we are," he said with a venomous look at Scheidemann, who had arrived to take him to a meeting with Banker X. "Here we sit. I told you we should have moved to Weimar or Kassel."

Scheidemann looked from Ebert to Noske and from Noske to Ebert. He sat down in his coat next to Ebert, still holding his soft hat in his hand. He looked at his hat, at his good soft hat, which had been his constant companion and served him so well. The hat gave its perplexed owner no answer, the poor hat had no talent for that. "Do you think," Scheidemann said, turning to Ebert, "it's too late for Kassel or Weimar now?"

Ebert would have loved to smash him into little pieces. Noske took his leave.

As they drove along, they buried themselves in the upholstery of the back seat, and Ebert could only repeat angrily, "What a fine government we are!"

Whenever they were forced to stop at a cross street and light fell on the car, there was a chance an incident might flare up.

The banker discreetly greeted the peoples' deputies. They were safe inside his elegant villa.

They made phone calls and ate and drank, both quite well. Evening approached. They learned that Wilhelmstrasse was still open, but that the first incidents had occurred. The *Vorwärts* offices had once again been occupied, and this time the Mosse Building, the Ullstein building, and perhaps a few others as well.

Ebert mulled this over and passed the news on to Scheidemann.

"We made the same mistake we made with Wels and his sailors. Attempting to dismiss Eichhorn so rashly was our mistake. Noske can't offer us anything but promises."

Scheidemann: "But you were in Zossen, you saw it all yourself."

Ebert: "What did I see, what are you talking about now, what do you know? Were you there?" You may not have a bad liver, but you've got the brain of a chicken. "How many are there, of our people? And where are they hiding? Noske and his phantom soldiers have forced us to make decisions that will cost us dearly."

Scheidemann raised his arms. "There's danger in everything." He was afraid, but he hoped he might talk some courage into Ebert.

Ebert, however, just made things worse and worse. He fumed, "Nobody needs to tell me that, but I've got to face the music; I'm the one who is in for it first and foremost."

Scheidemann whispered in desperation, "Well, I'm still here too after all." But this was whispered so softly that no one heard it, and since he didn't have his hat with him he said it to his beloved boots, recently resoled, which had borne him so far and would indeed bear him much further still.

A gloomy evening. The banker led them to their rooms. They were provided with a bath, fresh linens. On each of their night tables stood a pleasant nightcap, sugared lemonade. Ebert gazed at it, touched— lemonade. He had to laugh. In principle he welcomed this course of events, and there was danger in any case.

The Decision Is Made for an Armed Uprising

Ledebour and Däunig unleashed their speeches on the masses from the balcony of police headquarters. New throngs came marching up Kaiserstrasse.

Liebknecht was informed that Fischer and Eugen Ernst had been there and had tried to negotiate with Eichhorn. They had tried to wheedle him into resigning voluntarily. The peaceable Eichhorn himself told him all this. And when a balled fist hadn't worked, they had then tried to get their way with sweetness and light.

But Karl viewed the matter entirely differently. When he heard about it in the midst of this hour of battle, he knew at once what they were planning. They wanted to sneak into headquarters through the back door, wanted to lure Eichhorn away from the proletariat so that he would hand the red fortress over to them. A dirty way to do things, but it was what he had come to expect from those fellows.

He was supposed to speak, and he wanted to speak. He could not keep to himself what he had just heard. He wanted to expose their treachery. He stepped out onto the balcony; they recognized him from down below, the crowds clustered together, Karl's voice rang out.

And now they learned from his lips what new plot had been hatched against the working class of Berlin, how neatly contrived and how carefully executed; but it had misfired, repelled by the implacable stalwartness and class-consciousness of Emil Eichhorn. The more Karl got wrapped up in this event that had taken place behind his back in response to such a tremendous demonstration by the proletariat, and the more he spoke of it, the more monstrous seemed to him the cunning and deceit of his enemies, of these Scheidemann types who had throttled the metal workers' strike while the war was still on. Eichhorn was received with shouts and jubilation as he joined Liebknecht on the balcony.

Rumors of what had happened were passed along out on the streets from one parade segment to the next. They heard what miserable tactics the government was forced to try in order to hold onto its power. And now one delegation after the other arrived at police headquarters in search of a leader with whom they might speak. Again and again, speakers had to appear on the balcony to calm the masses and assure them they would retain police headquarters.

"Down with the government, down with the government!" was the unceasing shout.

They wanted battle. Liebknecht had aroused the masses. Now they had caught fire. You could see them burning. The leadership locked itself inside one of the rooms at headquarters and discussed things. For a long while nothing was resolved. They wanted to fight, probably they would have to fight. But what forces did they have at their disposal? It was the same question Ebert was asking himself at the moment.

An overwhelming majority of the workers of Berlin, they concluded, was behind them. Even those who still wavered would have their eyes opened now. They could likewise depend on the Berlin garrison—at least that was the assurance given by several soldiers' council members who had stationed themselves in the building. They declared that every soldier would take up arms to topple the government of Ebert and Scheidemann, which intended to give the officers all their old privileges back and had allied itself with the reactionary Volunteer Corps. Then they received news from Spandau fortress, that no less than two thousand machine guns and thirty pieces of artillery were available for the use of the workers of Berlin. And a store of munitions was also nearby in Frankfurt on the Oder.

They debated. A constant stream of new representatives from workers' and soldiers' councils, sailors, envoys from various parties and factory delegations kept arriving.

"We cannot, dare not yield," was the conclusion of every speech. The masses would become uncertain and then desert them if they did not now summon their courage.

They were continually interrupted in their discussions, for again and again one of them would have to go out onto the balcony and make a speech. The hurrahs and boos kept up without end.

243

Liebknecht and the others who had discussed Eichhorn's proposal on Schicklerstrasse the day before had to admit that things had developed in a way that went far beyond anything they could have predicted yesterday.

(And while they pondered and discussed, they dimly sensed that they were no longer the masters of events.)

Eichhorn, the quiet, harmless lord of the manor, sat off to one side while these honors were heaped upon him; and he, the martyr, accepted them with a grave and ever more dumbfounded mien, laying them to one side unopened, so to speak.

After a while there was no getting around it as they sat there in their debating chambers, they had to decide.

The decision read: Armed resistance to Eichhorn's removal, and overthrow of the counterrevolutionary government of Ebert and Scheidemann.

BOOK FIVE

The Revolution is Lost Even Before the Battle Begins

Rosa Begins Talking to Herself Again

Both natural and national history are concerned with diverse entities and phenomena, such as stars, countries and states. Laws and a secret meaning that one is obliged to search for give them form.

The founder and preserver of this world, however, is so great and beyond all earthly measurement, that even these splendid phenomena and entities do not exhaust him nor diminish his power. He infuses himself into the smallest, tiniest things, even into the fates of those who know nothing of him and his ways and who would seem to do battle with him. But his ways remain, whether they recognize them or not.

After the conference at the Prussian Landtag, Rosa felt as if she were dying of thirst. She knew what work she had to do. She knew what orders she had to give. But that was all a matter of routine. She did not mourn, she did not rejoice, she hardly felt the urge to help others. What had become of all her feelings?

It was not simply because of the conference, or that her comrades had chosen another path. Just when her own energies were dwindling, just before the final whistle, so to speak, she had thrown herself into the German revolution, and now she saw that it would come to nothing.

She was plagued with fainting spells. There were times when she broke down completely. Everyone who had known this white-haired woman who had once been so active could see it: something had happened to her.

From time to time they forced Rosa, just because she was Rosa, into some immense hall packed with people. She was made to speak to the thousand-headed throng and pour out to them emotions that she did not feel. The hall filled her with dread. When the applause rushed through her, she shrank back and was overcome with tears. Then Tanya, who was standing close by with her coat and scarf, would take her by the arm, and they would leave. She would accompany her incredibly exhausted friend home, only to rush into Rosa's room and plead with her: "Do you have to stay here, Rosa? What should we do? It's not good for you to stay here. And every night we have to move to another hotel. What kind of a life is that."

"Right," Rosa nodded, "not a very nice life."

"Come with me to Breslau," Tanya begged, her eyes sparkling with yearning.

"And what is there in Breslau? Still just your Schweidnitz Cellar, right?"

"And all the streets and shops, the bars, I know them all, I know so many people there."

Rosa smiled. "And the fresh carp and Silesian ambrosia."

"Silesian ambrosia? Have you ever eaten it, Rosa?"

"No, you know I'm not much for gods and heavenly food, Tanya. There's no ambrosia and no heaven for me."

Tanya put her hand to her mouth in alarm.

Rosa did think of Breslau, however. Of the women's prison, of the courtyard and of the heavy wagon with its load piled high and Rumanian oxen pulling it in through the gate, and of the coarse driver, that young soldier who beat them over the back with the butt of his whip, unmercifully. The blood ran down the flanks of those black, meek-eyed animals.

Rosa wept.

"Why are you crying, Rosa?"

"We'll make that trip to Breslau, just as soon as I have a little more free time."

How happy that made Tanya.

"It wasn't so bad there, Rosa, was it? Over in the men's wing was where my Michel was in prison."

"In two or three weeks, Tanya. We'll rent a room somewhere."

Tanya hugged her, blissfully happy.

At the editorial offices, Leo Jogiches walked up beside her.

"Tired, huh, Rosa? Sleep badly?"

She shrugged.

He: "We're all sleeping badly. You've got no monopoly on that. By the way, all sorts of things have leaked out from the conference."

"I can believe that."

"We should have postponed the meeting. They carried on like a local anglers' club."

Rosa: "What's Karl doing? Did you two argue?"

Leo: "He's not worried about anything. My only hope is that he'll lose his voice soon. Before the conference you could still talk with him. Now he's completely swept away with it all. He's really a very dangerous man."

"Is he out speaking in the factories?"

"In the factories, in the barracks, on the street, everywhere where there are two people standing next to each other. He beats the drum, he preaches—as if this were a crusade. Was the man always like that, Rosa, always so totally without self-discipline? We would have known what to do with him in Russia."

"Oh, but, Leo, that's just how Karl is. Of course we've always had difficulties with Karl."

Leo, gloomily: "Of course, you say. And now you see where it leads."

"But I have no doubts about Karl. We can always pull him back in again. I remember moments during the war with him, when we were agitating . . ."

"You can leave out the lyric poetry, Rosa."

"I beg your pardon."

Leo was already walking off. "And be careful, even more than before. Noske is sitting out in Dahlem and assembling his troop of volunteers; that's a gruesome bunch. Be careful. What are you writing for tomorrow?"

"Nothing about these latest events."

"Good. As factual and remote as possible, write about Persia or China. But be careful, Rosa, and in case you're not planning to leave, make some travel plans."

"Thanks, but no thanks. See you, Leo."

Evening. She had been at the office for hours—but actually only to avoid going home. Because once there she would start musing again. And now there Rosa sat, on her hard, shoddy hotel sofa.

A white gas flame burned on the ceiling. Along the walls stood a pale yellow wardrobe, a dark coat tree, a metal wash-table with a basin and pitcher, a towel draped over the chair next to it. The middle of the narrow room was occupied by an old extension table covered with a checkered tablecloth. A red armchair stood in front of it. There was no heat. She sat on the sofa, her hands in her pockets, her scarf and coat collar pulled up high.

I should leave Berlin. Yes, Leo's right. I can't accomplish anything here. I'll soon be getting on his nerves. So that is what it's come to. This is the famous freedom I longed for while I sat in my cell.

The gas flame pitched its song higher. Rosa looked up.

This is my home. In the prison there were trees, birds, titmice, crows, and I waited for the revolution as if for the dawn. The news all came from Russia. And then here, too, there was a revolution, a German revolution. And as she started to think of it, she fell asleep.

Rosa was freezing. She moved about. But her shoes banged on the wooden floor. It was late. So she sat down in the red armchair at the table and looked up at the singing flame.

And the other thing? What had that been about, the thing with Hannes?

At the moment his name came to her, she had the unpleasant sensation that her body was changing, that she was losing the ability to sense her own body. She grabbed hold of her arm in order to feel it better.

What is all this with Hannes? Why shouldn't I think about him. But as soon as she thought of him intentionally, she felt nauseous. She ran to the corner and drank some water. That's strange: why do I feel nauseous when I think of Hannes? And in the next moment, she knew why. She saw the bleeding mass of flesh, the corpse. She saw how he lurched toward her bed, his head hanging down, the forehead blown away, the eyes burst, the mouth gaping, and the black blood dripping from his mustache. She put her head in her hands.

Phantasms, hallucinations. I went crazy, prisoner's psychosis. The doctor said it was hysteria, a semiconscious state. I'm glad that's behind me. I don't think I'll go back to Breslau after all.

Rosa started to turn down the simple bed. But she was dazed, and she had to sit back down on the sofa.

And suddenly, as she sat there apathetically, rage surged up within her: I don't want this, I don't want it, I don't. I want to tear it out of me. It's witchcraft. That's what it is. I'll have myself dissected by students in anatomy labs.

And suddenly she smiled to herself. Something that comes from Hannes, from my Hannes, buried so long ago. How far back that all lies now. What a strange story. Hannes, right, he's not coming back. Whatever has become of him. At the end there, he really had his own way and came dancing up to me with his corpse. How funny. But I left him in the lurch again. I didn't want to do what he wanted; I had too many things planned: freedom, the German revolution. Oh my. How gloriously he moved, like a cherub. He had black clouds above his head, beneath his feet the sea raged and icebergs forged their way through him, and the whales rose up from the water and blew their spouts. One time he wore a plumed hat, he had been fighting at Fehrbellin against the Swedes three centuries ago, what a magnificent, reckless spirit. But he never arrived at his goal. He's like me. Something always forced him back.

Where is Hannes now? I have no more energy left to call to him. The song is over. He's destroyed and has rotted away now. They had, it seemed, done everything they could do together after all.

Rosa shivered from the cold. She pulled her legs up onto the sofa and lay back.

There is something evil about the world, no one can convince me otherwise, something that prevents us from becoming what we are, that teases us and finally tosses us away in a corner. That's what I call evil.

And if there is anything in this world that is true besides man and nature, then it is the evil that pursues us. Satan, our Lord, there you have him, the force that always seeks evil and creates the good, as Goethe says. That creates the good, what nonsense, thanks but no thanks for that goodness, floating bubbles, the illusion of false reality.

I don't want to meet anyone else in this world; I'm not interested in any foreign vistas. But I would like to encounter him once more, this archevil, this lord of all villains. If I could nab Satan, then I'd gladly leave this life. Just to get hold of this governor of our fate who makes life such a miserable mess.

Come on, you tyrant, you beast, you cowpuncher. Come out of your swamp. For the first time in my life I'm praying. I pray for you to come. I have the right to see you. You must show yourself to me and answer my questions. My whole life was nothing, a constant struggle, a struggle and more struggle, and nothing achieved, and it's all a trap and an illusion of false reality and floating bubbles, even love is. Come on, you beast. You exist. I confess it before you. If you also possess pride in addition to your wickedness, then appear.

Rosa dragged herself to the table and laid her head on the cold oilcloth, sobbing. Then she walked over to her bed at last and slept for a while.

When she awoke again in the dark, those nights in Breslau came back to her, the guards at the window—and Hannes once again.

Those were only thoughts, figments of my imagination. Why are thoughts nothing? Why is only a chair something? Why is only a mattress something? Why is only my hair something, my fingernails when I trim them and toss the trimmings away? Even in the trash can my fingernails are still something. Only my thoughts are supposed to be nothing, even though I can encompass heaven and earth and all mankind with them. Plato, Shakespeare, Beethoven—nothing; but horse manure, that is something.

I was fond of Hannes. I loved him. He was my life. And why can I not have him again?

She lay there half asleep and turned over on one side. She felt the warmth of the bed.

And then he came in, in boots and spurs as an army doctor and almost took me out of my cell. What a story that would have been if he had succeeded: I'm lying there dead as a dormouse on the floor, and next to me sits an army doctor and no one knows how he got into the cell. He can't tell them himself—Hannes never was very fast with repartee. They arrest him then and imprison him for the murder of Rosa Luxemburg. A cheap tale of love and passion.

She laughed into her pillow and fell asleep.

In the wee hours she crept from her bed, completely exhausted. She felt better out in the room at the table, in her clothes. Memories of Berlin ran dimly through her mind. She let her head sink, drunk for sleep.

In the middle of the table was a brass ashtray. On its rim had been placed, strangely enough, a shepherd and a small goat. The connection between the shepherd and the ashtray apparently consisted in the fact that the shepherd had a pipe in his mouth.

Although this shepherd was small and made of metal and soldered to an ashtray, now in the twilight he managed to free himself. He assumed normal size and candidly confessed to Rosa that he was the devil of whom she had been speaking a while before.

She did not want to believe that.

He said oh, but it's true. It was unusual for a shepherd to be the devil, he would admit that, but shepherds were busy in many fields and they were respectable people. Mostly he guarded ashtrays, but of course that was not his only profession.

Rosa wondered what there was about ashtrays to guard.

The shepherd: "What? As a revolutionary you ought to be able to figure it out. I observe what goes on in this room. My goat loves the smell of cold ashes."

"Ugh," Rosa said and shuddered.

"Yes, it's true." He had straddled the goat now and was riding around the table. "The animal is not used to this, but he is my goat I assure you. The people in this room are normally busy fornicating or hatching some crime or another. I ascertain such things."

252

Rosa: "And then?"

He rode around the table excitedly.

She repeated: "And then? After you have ascertained all that?"

The goat didn't want to go on. It bucked. He dismounted. Rosa asked once more. He gave the goat an ill-tempered kick, at which it simply sprang back up on the table onto the ashtray. The shepherd said, "You see, that's how it behaves."

He made a couple of other remarks. It turned out that he was not really the devil, but only a simple shepherd who had wanted to have some fun with his audience.

As she reached for the ashtray, he was already standing on the rim with his goat and not budging. He had been found out.

I'm glad, Rosa thought after having drunk a cup of coffee, that I have that prison madness behind me.

She felt no uneasiness now when she thought of "him." What a shame, really, that I have no souvenir of him. What a shame that I tore up his picture. She rummaged in her drawers, looking, so she thought, for a handkerchief. But she already had a handkerchief. It must not be the right one, it wasn't large enough. She didn't know exactly herself what the right one would be. She went on rummaging—until she ran across a blue dress scarf.

And as her fingers touched the small scarf, a great sweetness passed through her.

She cried out, "Hannes, is that you?" and slid to the floor.

Rosa Takes a Coach to Her Fairy-Tale Castle

From that morning on, she knew that the affair with Hannes was not over yet.

She upbraided herself violently and discussed the matter back and forth with herself. What does "dead" really mean after all? Can something that exists become nothing? From the proper point of view, don't I have a duty to him just as before, to obey the precepts of reverence? The ancients believed in that, it's self-evident when you come down to it.

And so one noon she left her office, pretending that she was feeling weak; everyone believed her. She could not get home fast enough, close the door behind her, cast aside her hat and pull open the drawer. And now for the blue scarf.

She sat down on the edge of the bed and held it in her hand, all the time saying to herself: who can say I'm crazy. I'm fully in possession of my faculties.

There he sat on the chair by the table.

She knew it without even looking up. Finally she whispered, "Hannes, is that you?"

She dared not raise her head, however. She heard a soft, strange sound coming from the table, it terrified her. Though she was still in her clothes, she threw herself on the bed and pulled the blanket up over her. But the sound continued.

Then he spoke. "Why did you call me, Rosa, and now refuse to look at me?"

She shivered under the blanket.

"I didn't call you, Hannes, really I didn't."

"Is that right? Should I go then?"

It was ghastly, there he was. She was not hallucinating, because she could see what was in the room.

"Hannes, I thought you were lost for good."

"Aren't you just the least bit happy, Rosa, that I'm here? I haven't heard from you for a long time now."

She came out from under the blanket. "Since that last time. Forgive me."

He gave a brief laugh and fell silent. She was afraid, still unable to comprehend that he was there. She said, "You're not going to hurt me, are you?"

"Really, Rosa."

"You won't hurt me?"

"Rosa, how can you?"

There was such a mild tone in his voice that she was moved. Slowly and carefully she pulled the blanket away from her face, let her legs down, and sat up, though with her head still lowered and without looking at him. With no sign of impatience, he asked, "Rosa, do come over here."

So she stood up and walked to the other side of the table where there was a small wooden chair, but kept her eyes to the floor like a sinner. He had to beg her to take a seat and then grumbled cheerfully, "Rosa, what a farce for me to have to ask you to sit down. I'm not the host here."

And as she sat there at the table she realized that the unbelievable was happening—it's Hannes, Hannes is there again. She didn't have to go to Breslau to find him, and what else had she wanted to go there for anyway—he hasn't disappeared and no one has taken him away from me—she rejoiced, and life streamed through her once again in a way she had not felt it for a long time, the warmth of life, something she hardly remembered, the delightful joy, the good cheer, the drive. And it welled up in her, and at last she trusted herself to open her eyes. And there he sat, alive and well across from her on a chair at the table in her room. He was wearing his usual gray-blue uniform jacket. He sat back in his chair (it must be sorcery) in a comfortable position, his back against the blue woolen scarf that she had thrown over the arm of the chair as she had hurried into the room a while ago.

And she could not contain herself, and pulled her chair over to the narrow side of the table next to him, and as she did so she gazed at his clean, dark blond hair combed straight back; how it shone. It was hard to realize that this was a dead man.

And then there she was sitting at the table with him, he had not moved. There was something strange, however, about his unusual calm. And now she directed her eyes to his face. And it was—all the doctors in the world could say what they wished—it was his old strong-boned face. He bore a certain resemblance to Leo Jogiches that she had never noticed before, but Hannes was less grave than Leo, yes, his was a mild face. How smart his trimmed mustache looked. And there was that same broad nose of his, the strong chin and the good, thoughtful expression.

His eyes reached hers, his old familiar eyes, but more radiant, more glowing than ever. And it seemed to her as she let his gaze enter and descend into her that she was meeting Hannes for the very first time, had never seen him before, heard him, touched him, and as if this were indeed her first love stirring within her, that fascination, that earthquake that overthrows mountains and valleys and lifts up new depths.

She began a conversation with Hannes that no words can express. She kept staring at him, the enchanter and the enchanted. The quivering of a somber sweetness ran through her body, accompanied by the certain knowledge that she was totally ruined and lost. The terror of love hovered over her.

During a pause in the conversation she was amazed as she looked down at herself, but only for a brief moment, for after a first fright she found that she was wearing, as if to celebrate the occasion, a light blue muslin dress with embroidered pink flowers, and that a delicate gold necklace was at her neck, and that in her lap lay a new black handbag bearing her initials "R. L." in silver.

She could not resist the temptation. She grasped at the handbag, opened it and found a little pocket mirror. And as she glanced surreptitiously in the mirror she saw that she was so very young and beautiful, she had never seen herself so beautiful. And she knew at once: that was love, that's what love does, and I have him to thank for that. But it was as if she were drugged by it. He smiled at her. He seemed to guess what was worrying her.

"It's really unnecessary, Rosa," he said with sudden excitement, "to always have to sit around the table here in your room."

And he stood up and made a comic bow to her; she took his arm, and so they left the room and descended the hotel stairs. The most amazing thing, however, was what Rosa discovered in the hotel lobby. She was no longer limping. She convinced herself conclusively with a look at the wall mirror: she was walking proudly and erect and was totally symmetrical. He smiled down at her, proud of his victory, or so it seemed to her. She understood what he meant: the power of love and of thought.

In the lobby (in a fuzzy way she was aware that she had apparently checked into an elegant hotel, at least it was not the shabby one at the lower end of Friedrichstrasse) she handed him her room key. He laid it on the desk in front of the porter and ordered a coach for a trip to the lake. She broke in, "But Hannes, you don't know anything about this area. There are nothing but city streets here."

But he laughed and the porter did too. An open coach pulled up, for though the weather was cool, it was sunny. And they were in Zurich, as she soon discovered, and riding down Rämistrasse, and then along the lake for a while between rows of trees. The view of the mountains in the distance was enchanting, she had missed it for so long, the air was wonderful, and what a joy to sit in an open coach with him and to get away from all the hubbub of the city. To bury yourself in a large city, what a hopeless, foolish thing to do. He thought so too. You had to decide to act at some point, he said.

She had all sorts of things she wanted to say, and slowly she got them out. Why had he not come before this? She had needed something like this for so long now. Where had he been hiding?

He smoked his cigarette (she noticed his golden cigarette case) and answered evasively the way a busy man does when he does not want to burden others with his cares.

"You're so elegant, Hannes. Where do you have all this money from? We're staying in a fashionable hotel. This ride is costing a great deal as well."

"I was rather shabby back then, you mean. That's true. I wasn't getting anywhere that way, you noticed that. There had to be some changes made."

"And what have you done?"

256

He laughed long and hard, so that the driver turned around to look. This coachman had an unusual red beard, she had not noticed it as they had gotten in, a mighty, flowing beard of golden red that billowed down over his chest. The man laughed heartily along with Hannes. And Rosa saw now for the first time how the two magnificent horses, sorrels, almost the same color as the coachman's beard, were wildly leaping about. Rosa repeated herself, somewhat embarrassed, "Yes, what have you done?"

"You always think in such a middle-class fashion, Rosa. Like that doctor of yours in the infirmary in Breslau who wanted to convince you that you were suffering from a semiconscious condition, when the semiconsciousness was really inside his own head. We have other possibilities open to us, of course." He let out another proud laugh. "You saw how even there in your cell I could go on long journeys. You pointed at a spot on the map with your pencil, Narvik—and there I was."

She opened her eyes wide. "I was aware of that."

"There must be some advantages to being dead and not weighing in at a hundred and fifty pounds anymore. It took me a long while to realize it. At first I wept for those hundred and fifty pounds, absolutely had to have them back. You know what the result of that was."

"Yes, and then?" she asked anxiously. They had left the promenade along the lake and were speeding down an endless, tree-lined road, one tree after the other.

"Either you have a body and the amenities and discomforts of that body, or you have none. The least that my sort can demand is to move about freely. After that unfortunate incident in Breslau I realized all this. And so then I decided to start anew, in my own sphere. And that is how you see me now."

"And what is this new path?" she asked nervously.

"You are assuming it's something bad, just the opposite: it's something quite necessary. You must always attempt things on your own, you dare not just be pulled along. That is what freedon of the will means."

She was enthralled. "That's just what I think."

He: "Every reasonable person realizes it. At some point everyone gets hung up, and if he doesn't come to a decision and tear himself loose, he's done for, finished. I now stroll about in the world, now here, now there, a man without a country, but I manage."

They had just driven by a small pavilion. The coach stopped with a sudden lurch.

Rosa: "And you still found time to think of me?"

He gently assisted her down from the coach without answering; and although he did not pay, only gesturing dismissal to the coachman instead, redbeard up there on his seat had already given the sorrels free rein, and away they went, disappearing almost at once in dust and vapor.

Hannes accompanied her as they approached the locked pavilion. It was a small, interesting building, rococo perhaps, at any rate very old, with a peculiarly sloped roofline and oval windows that looked like portholes, while the stairs up to the door were grown over with grass.

"I bought it very cheap from the former owner," said Hannes. "The little house sinks a bit deeper into the earth each year, in fact two floors are already hidden below ground level."

"Do you live here?" she asked in alarm. (She thought: he's a dead man, and the dead live underground.)

He pulled the bell beside the door. An old woman opened it, and at the sight of Hannes she gave a small cry of joy. She was so charming and so uncommonly lively, despite her age. She had a thick gray mustache on her upper lip, round gray eyes, they were true cat's eyes. Whatever was wrong with her hands—she was wearing gray gloves—could not be determined. And this was Hannes's housekeeper.

They went inside. He gallantly led her to her boudoir. She was delighted as she gazed at herself in the massive mirror. In her pale blue dress she resembled a dancer in a painting by Watteau (or was it Fragonard?) that was one of her favorites.

Hannes entered, but in point of fact he looked so very different that when she first saw him in the mirror she did not recognize him, and as she turned to look at him she dropped the little silver comb with which she was smoothing her gray hair. Had she not known from her inner feelings that this was Hannes, no one else but Hannes, she would have thought him a stranger. He was—at least it seemed so to her, although that was ridiculous of course—larger and more powerful, more agile and yet more erect in carriage than Hannes. He had the energetic traits of a medieval condottiere. Hannes generally had more of the look of a naive Swabian about him, and a certain awkwardness. This was a man of quick decisions and deeds. In informal clothes now, he was dressed like a pasha, with wide green breeches bound by a silver belt, and a sky-blue jacket with ruby-red buttons.

"Can it be you?" she asked enraptured as she lay in his arms. "Can it really be you, Hannes, and can this be me and is everything really so different? Am I dreaming? Tell me yes. That I'm only dreaming. If I were to tell all this to that fat doctor in Breslau he'd simply laugh in my face."

"Let the idiots and philistines say what they like, Rosa. Don't you suppose people like that would have laughed just as much at the idea of x-rays if someone had told them about it thirty years ago? You can't teach an old dog new tricks."

"And what are you really, Hannes?"

"You can embrace me, you can see me, Rosa. *Cogito, ergo sum.* I kiss, therefore I am."

"How you've changed and grown, Hannes?"

He laughed and nodded. "You mean since my death, is that it? Yes, who can really change and grow here on this rotten old planet? You've experienced the same thing. On earth we tramp about as if we were walking in glue, getting stuck everywhere."

"Yes, it's our misfortune."

"But afterward things are different, Rosa, when you have a free hand and can carry out your own decisions. Because what people lack is not the plans and the good intentions, you know. So now you see. You have to dare to experiment. You can do no more than perish in the attempt."

He carried her in his arms. How strong he was. She realized to her amazement that she was wearing long white stockings and brocade shoes with high heels. That was a sign that her hip problems were truly behind her now; her whole life long she had only been able to wear low-heeled shoes. He cradled her, swung her about like a child, and showed her the chandelier, and it was indeed a rarity. When he blew on it, the chains from which it hung came alive and changed into lizards that carried the lamp down toward them. They could turn the lamp about as well, and as it circled it began to glow, giving off the tones of some strange music.

"It's a musical clock," Rosa giggled, enchanted.

"It's not a clock at all, it's simply a lamp," he laughed. "You'll get used to these rooms and to the way I live soon enough. The furnishings here aren't so mechanical as they are on earth. We're just at the start of our acquaintance, if I may put it that way—now that I no longer come to you, but rather you to me."

"What silly notions I had then about dead people, Hannes."

"But I did, too, Laura. This is our first rendezvous, and the first stage of our experiments."

"My name is Rosa, Hannes."

"Rosa, why do you want to be called Rosa, haven't you had enough of Rosa? Haven't you already tried everything using Rosa, and were things really so very exciting with her? I'll also gladly dispense with Hannes."

It was their wedding, a real marriage this time, and how very different from the first one in prison with the icy shade who wanted to warm himself on her, with that poor broken warrior. This man was warm, hot and bewitchingly handsome, and gave of himself, nor did she hold herself back.

The ecstasy, the intoxication robbed her of consciousness.

Had he already left? She heard his voice at the door: "Laura, I'll not forget you. Have courage. Have courage."

She thought dreamily, "Courage? That I've never lacked."

Tanya had been hammering on the door with both fists for quite a while. Finally something stirred inside. Rosa fumbled at the lock. Apparently she wasn't having any success.

Finally she pulled back the bolt and opened up.

Tanya saw at once: Rosa was distracted.

It took almost a quarter hour, as it always had before, until she could converse. She was brought to the office and telephone calls were made. While Rosa washed her face, Tanya made hot tea. They drank it slowly together. Slowly Rosa thawed out again. She ate some cookies that Tanya was proud of having found.

"How long was I away from the office?" Rosa asked. "What time is it?"

"You were gone barely fifteen minutes," Tanya said, "they begrudge you every bit of rest, although everyone can see that you need it. But I'm taking you with me to Breslau, Rosa."

Rosa stared into her cup. "To Breslau? We'll see."

She patted Tanya's hand. (Courage I've never lacked.)

The Mysterious Suitor Presents Himself

Rosa was still a candle burning at both ends. She raged against Leo and against herself. Treachery ruled the world. Floating bubbles, the illusion of a false reality, and once you realize that, it's all over. Suddenly the thought came to her again: that is what evil is, that is the devil who rules this world. In the past, people had sold their souls to the devil. If only I knew how to bring him here. I would love to do it. He is the only thing that really exists.

What was all that a few days ago? I was in Zurich. I was dreaming. Sure. Or maybe not? But what else could it have been? Of course it was a dream. It was the same state that I was in when I had Hannes with me in prison.

Her thoughts were already running away with her.

Hannes was wonderful. What he said was the truth, from start to finish. You get caught in the glue of this earth. Took the words out of my mouth. He is right, too, not to bother with me anymore, because what can I offer him ultimately?

She was caught up in the memory of that adventure in Zurich. She laughed. All of a sudden her name was Laura. What had she gained by that?

Hannes, moreover, had behaved so strangely. I would have sworn it was another man. He wanted to perform some sort of experiments. How he had changed. That was not how he used to be. The way he simply called a spade a spade. I would like to see him again. I was supposed to take courage. That I have. Anything is better than this life.

She entered her room, and at once she bolted the door behind her.

And even if he is Satan incarnate, I want him. He's right, I want to throw myself in his arms. She took out the blue scarf.

No, it was Hannes after all. They went hand in hand through the streets. He looked as naive as she could ever have wished. He wore a flat peasant hat in the Black Forest style and shining boots. His black jacket with its shiny brass buttons stood open. He looked ever so smart. Except that he stubbornly called her "Julia." She called his attention to the fact that her name was Rosa. He apologized, he was wool-gathering. She felt sorry for him and squeezed his arm. Ouch, he cried. She had not intended to hurt him. And then she poured out her heart to him, about what had happened last time and how she was forever plagued by doubts.

"Hannes, here we are now peacefully together, and you're my boy-friend, and so now you can tell me in all honesty and candor how things stand. First, whether you really exist and we are really here together, and then, whether you are Hannes and not someone else."

He looked at her anxiously.

"Yes," she went on, "Hannes, is it really you, really? Are we dreaming now? When we were in Zurich together recently and then afterward as well, I had my doubts."

"Why?" he asked, visibly distressed.

"Because everything that happened was so fantastic. There must be some reason for that. You're dead, Hannes, but I will follow you and I'll not forget you. I'll bring you more than a few flowers and thoughts and all those things that other people bring the dead. I'll bring you my self. I am devoted to you, and bound up with you like two doves tied on a single line. But you arrived in Zurich in such a rush and left just as quickly. We loved each other. I might just as easily have been dreaming."

"In all honesty," Hannes answered, "I can assure you that we exist and that you're not dreaming. What's bothering you is the constant problem of weight, of pounds. People are always looking for the weight of things. Weight looking for weight. If I wanted to make a joke of it, I'd say, burdens of a feather flock together. But we actually do exist, really."

"As spirits," Rosa said.

"Of course, as free beings."

"I understand," she whispered uncertainly.

But he was certain. "It simply all depends, if you believe you're dreaming or hallucinating, on the way you go along, and how much of you is here and whether you're a part of it. Just look: you called me and brought me here. Not everyone can do that."

"Yes, Hannes," Rosa snuggled tenderly against him, "I can no longer stand life on earth. I can bear it no longer. I've been cast aside like a hunk of old iron. I follow you about like someone lost following one who knows the way. And now tell me, are you really you, Hannes?"

This question had a powerful effect on Hannes. He pulled himself up straight, casting aside his ingenuousness and ease. His eyes radiated energy. He pressed her arm forcefully.

"I am the one who knows the way, the leader, and you shall follow me. Let that suffice for you, Julia. And so we can forget, once and for all, all these needless conversations about whether I exist or don't exist, about who or what I am. Let us go forward. One must have courage. One must perform experiments with oneself."

And already they were galloping across the plain, both of them on black steeds of some small Belgian breed. Rosa sat on a man's saddle. She had never ridden before, but it presented no difficulty, and she thoroughly enjoyed it. There were so many things she had had to forego in her life on earth. Now she was being rewarded for having been faithful to Hannes, for following into his realm of death, which wasn't nearly so bad as people said it was. What was the basic difference between it and normal life? That was hard to say. Actually only that it was more beautiful and really worth living for.

262

Hannes suddenly began to speak in Polish. So he could do that too. A gifted man. Now, in fact, he had a certain resemblance to a Polish friend of Rosa's from the old days of desperados and daredevils, many of whom had been executed.

"What's wrong with you, Julia?" he cried out at a crossroads. "Stay closer to me. We still have an hour's ride yet."

She spurred her horse. "Where are we headed, Hannes?"

He cursed. "Just see that you keep up."

They halted at the edge of a wood near a railroad track, and tied their horses to trees. There was a shack where three men, obviously rogues, were sitting beside a bull's-eye lantern, smoking and playing cards. She thought of the smugglers in Bizet's *Carmen*. But these rogues were not singing. Hannes spoke to them.

But, sure as anything, this was not Hannes.

It was another man, a totally different man.

As soon as he had ended his conversation with these rascals, during which he had several times pointed at her with his thumb and used the name Julia, he came back over to her (she was still standing, not wanting to sit down on the greasy bench where the three rogues had thrown their dufflebags). She confronted him straightaway.

"Who are you really?"

He: "Are you afraid of me?"

"No. Who are you?"

"Guess. Who do you think I am?"

Rosa: "At any rate, I don't think you're Hannes."

He: "What a good nose. You're afraid of me."

Rosa: "No, I'm not."

He: "Say that once more."

"No, I'm not."

He: "Wonderful. I like that."

He embraced her in front of the three men, who were vastly amused. She wanted to push him away, and pounded on his chest. But now he was a strong giant of a robber, clad in sheepskin, with a beard already gray, sunken cheeks, and coal-black eyes that shone like two mournful stars. He gave off an intense, gamy smell. Without effort he pulled her to him and forced upon her as many kisses as he wished. He held her hands tight. She could not even wipe her face, and had to allow it all the while she wept and screamed.

"You're not afraid," he was mocking her again; he bit her lip.

"No, I'm not," she shrieked.

"Wonderful," he said, laughing and picking her up in his arms.

She begged, "Don't hurt me."

He: "We did it once in Zurich, and you liked it then. These fellows know that you're my wife."

"Let me down, please. I'll obey you."

He whistled through his teeth. "A man likes to hear that."

And he carefully put his doll back on its feet. Then he motioned for the rogues to disappear.

"What would you like then?" he asked.

"You're not Hannes."

He: "I thought you were going to obey."

"Yes. But first tell me who you are."

"Guess, my little pet."

"Since when am I your little pet?"

"Since I decided you were."

He had eyes in which she could lose herself, wild and sad eyes.

She: "All right, who are you?"

"Guess."

"A robber, someone up to no good."

"True."

He let her gaze at him. Mockery played at the corners of his mouth.

"Why are you laughing?"

"Because you have such a refined way of speaking."

The laughter spread out now across the whole bearded face. His eyes grew small and squinted in delight.

Rosa: "What are you then if you're not a robber? Where did you get the notion to be Hannes?"

"Yes, just how did I get that notion?"

She shook him. "Who are you? Where did you get the idea, you lout? Why are you meddling in my life?"

He was shaking with laughter. "You called me, you know. Have you forgotten? And so finally I could not leave you all alone."

He now underwent an immense transformation. His jacket, which she had grabbed by both lapels, was left in shreds in her hands, the tatters caught fire. She screamed and cast the burning pieces away.

But there he stood burning before her, a single flaming fire.

He caused the walls of the shack to go up in flames, and the gigantic, darkly smoking glow licked upward into the night sky.

Rosa fell to the grass unconscious.

He lifted her up and set her at the side of a ditch. He did not speak. She looked up at the railroad tracks, where a train with lights in its windows was speeding by. He pointed at the train as it passed them. "To Warsaw."

264

She edged closer to him. She studied his face.

She whispered, "You are Satan."

He taunted her. "Fairy tales. There's no such thing. There's no Evil One."

She whispered. "I know."

He: "Come, come, little mouse."

Rosa: "You are he."

He: "Well, go on. You want to argue with me, it seems. You wanted to confront me."

She: "Where is Hannes? What have you done with him?"

He laughed so violently that the tops of the trees swayed as if in a storm. "Me? What did I do with him? He was my friend."

"You liar, you pursued him till he could find no peace. He wanted to live again. What you have done to him is the same thing you have done to me my whole life long, lured me on, deceived me, lied to me, and hunted me down."

He could not stop laughing. "Me, me, it has to be me. You're wide of the mark there, you are. You are both my friends. Otherwise I would not have concerned myself with you. You'll just have to turn to someone else for help."

Rosa stared at him. His black eyes returned her gaze. She let her arms fall.

"Then it wasn't you."

"Truly it wasn't, Julia, not me. I've only come to console you and to enlighten you because I feel sorry for you, sorry that such an intelligent person has such false ideas about me, ideas that originate among the common folk. Those notions are for your Tanya, not for you."

"Then tell me, what is true?"

He tapped her ironically on the chest. "No matter what, you'll be staying on with me, my little mouse."

"If you'll be my friend."

"Blood of your blood."

"I can't believe that."

He caressed her shoulder. Her clothes fell from her. But she had no reason to feel ashamed.

She was a small creature with strong, goatlike legs, muscular and covered with black hair, and she smelled just like him.

He looked down at her with satisfaction. "I've been waiting for this for a long time. I knew that sometime you would want something else besides going whining after your blasted ideals. I knew that at some point you would want to take a peek behind the curtain."

Rosa: "Yes."

He: "You're made of good stuff. You're proud and you're aware of things. You can think. There are no limits for you."

He no longer restrained himself. Any child could see that he was Satan. Rugged curved horns grew from his brow. A coat of smooth, shiny hair covered his taut body. The light from a nearby signalman's hut fell across his brown animal body.

"No limits," Rosa admitted.

"No humility."

"None."

He puffed out his words like clouds of smoke. They ran side by side along the railroad embankment. When they came to the signalman's hut that served as the source of the light, he stood up straight beside the crossing barrier.

He smoked heavenward, grayish brown and tall.

His dark wings spread out toward the horizon. And Rosa too had stood up straight now in the smoke.

He looked down at her. His eyes glowed like furnaces. They gave off a weird, flickering glimmer and molten light that flamed up and then died back down. She saw his malice, his scorn, his strength, his unbending cruelty.

Slowly they began to fly.

January 6: The Revolutionary Committee is Formed

The leadership spent the night between Sunday, January 5th, and Monday, January 6th, at police headquarters. They were aware of the seriousness and dangers of the situation. They weren't in a tight corner yet, but they could foresee that Ebert would not yield in the Eichhorn affair any more than he had yielded at Christmas with the sailors. He would force things to a crisis as he had then by calling in General Lequis, although there had been no need. The man ran amok; only he knew why. They, however, had the masses behind them. Quite unexpectedly a massive sword had fallen into their hands. Georg Ledebour had participated in the discussion, a dependable fighter, an honest man, a hothead, not without theatrics and a revolutionary romanticism. Lenin would have grinned at the sight of him. He spoke, and when Karl Liebknecht had spoken as well, things were clear to everyone there: there was no more pulling back. The masses were already breaking loose. The masses understood better than their leadership.

While the first scuffles were occurring out on the streets—revolutionary raiding parties were advancing on the newspaper offices belonging to Scherl, Mosse and Ullstein, actions directed by no one but intended for starters to gag the lies of the press—they moved from police headquarters to the royal stables, so as to be nearer the center of the city and also remain in closer contact with the People's Naval Division, which was indebted to the masses for the victory of December 24th.

At the stables a crucial decision was arrived at. From the "representatives of the revolutionary working class" they created a "Provisional Revolutionary Committee" consisting of thirty-three members. The steering committee was made up of Ledebour, Karl Liebknecht, and a certain Paul Scholze.

At once they formulated the text of a proclamation that was printed early on January 6th:

"Comrades, workers!

"The Ebert-Scheidemann government has made a mess of things.

"The undersigned Revolutionary Committee, representing the revolutionary workers and soldiers (Independent Socialists and German Communist Party) hereby declare that government deposed. The undersigned Revolutionary Committee has temporarily assumed the reins of government.

"Support the measures taken by the revolutionary committee.

"Berlin. January 6, 1919.

"The Revolutionary Committee.

"Ledebour, Liebknecht, Scholze."

And with that they showed the masses that the die had been cast. Their intent was to force indecisive supporters to desert, to terrify the bourgeoisie, and above all to call the rest to arms.

They were in full swing. The morning of January 6th dawned. They would begin to march today.

Today they would set their trap and place the noose around the neck of corrupt Prussian militarism.

Today they would drive the nails from which they would hang the carcass of the mighty, floundering, bloodthirsty creature that wore a spiked helmet on its head and a monocle in its cynical, ugly face.

But as it turned out, the judges and executioners would stumble into the very trap they had laid, would get wrapped up in the noose they had tied. And the perpetrator of the crimes, believing that his own last hour had come, would use this moment to leap forward and tie the noose tight about the neck of his judge and executioner and

267

string up his struggling victim—his victim once again—with all the energy in his practiced hands, string him up, and all with the assistance of the friends of the court. The court was made up of the current republican government, put in office by the revolution, of the ruling Social Democrats whom later generations would curse. The German revolution would hang by its own rope, and with it, though invisibly, millions of other people living in Europe, Asia and Africa.

Morning had come, and it was time to proceed to execute the plan that night had given birth to.

There were several hundred armed men gathered in the courtyard at the stables, and they received orders to advance on the War Ministry on Leipziger Strasse and demand the surrender of the building. One of these men was given the proclamation composed during the night as the legitimation for this maneuver.

About three hundred sailors boarded the trucks, each of them carrying a machine gun, and through the quiet city they sped, down Breite Strasse, across the Gertraude Bridge and Spittel Market into Leipziger Strasse, all peaceable, middle-class streets unaware of the spectacle they were participating in, the first unnoticed scene of a profound tragedy, at the end of which a good number of these very same buildings would go up in flames. The trucks, too, were peaceable as they drove on, bearing their sprightly three hundred sailors, seeking out the building they wanted to take over, the War Ministry. It was an old, elongated, nondescript building with smooth walls, windows, and doors.

When they had sprung from their trucks, someone rang the bell and someone else came to open up for them; and there they stood, a battalion of sailors, guns on their shoulders, their leaders demanding to be led to see the minister of war or one of his deputies.

They let the troops in, seeing they were not to be trifled with, led them along the long corridors until they came to the office of Undersecretary Hamburger. They entered. When that gentleman demanded to see their authorization, a sailor showed him the piece of paper they had given him stating that the government of Ebert and Scheidemann had been deposed and that the Revolutionary Committee had temporarily assumed the reins of government. They knew nothing of all this at the War Ministry. The leaders of the sailors demanded the surrender of the building.

The undersecretary was a civil servant, and certainly did not want to take responsibility on his own for such an action. He apologized and declared that in such a situation he must first consult with his colleagues in the Ministry. The sailors had no reason for objecting to this. He should go right ahead and do his consulting.

He went into the adjoining room and spoke with other civil servants who were no less dismayed than he. What should they do? Make telephone calls, of course, to find out what was actually going on. But the sailors were not about to give them much time. It was an outright assault. Then the civil servants read the piece of paper once more, and because they were bureaucrats they at once detected a formal error. Three men were supposed to sign it, a place had been designated for Ledebour's signature but he had not signed. No, that was out of order, they could not comply with it. And Hamburger, accompanied by his colleagues, went back to his office, where the sailors were patiently waiting to assume control of the War Ministry.

Furrowing his brow and pointing to the piece of paper in vexation, Hamburger indicated to them what was wrong here and why. The paper had not been signed properly. Why anyone could come along and demand the surrender of the War Ministry.

"Please see for yourselves, Ledebour's signature is missing."

They saw that it was and had to admit it. One of them declared that that was merely because old Ledebour had not been able to hold out all night at the stables and had gone home.

"I'm terribly sorry," Hamburger answered, "I can understand that fully. But if you want something done, then you must stay the course. At any rate, without that signature it's no go."

He resolutely gave them back their piece of paper. They cursed the whole damned mess. They did things in such a slipshod fashion at the stables, they couldn't even write up a petition properly. And they would have to drive back and forth a second time.

They all leaped onto their trucks once more with martial energy, weapons in hand, machine guns menacingly aimed toward the streets. They roared off.

At their rear, however, in the War Ministry, all the telephones were being put to use. Alarm was sounded in every direction. Several hundred Social Democratic workers had been waiting in front of the Reichs Chancellery since the night before, and at the Reichstag building was a detachment of recruited soldiers. They hurried over at once.

But a half hour later, when these guileless sailors came rumbling up again from the Spittel Market, one imposing truck after the other, armed with rifles and machine guns, and wanted once again to present their piece of paper because it was correct now, and Liebknecht had signed as a proxy for Ledebour, things looked very different on

Leipziger Strasse. The sailors got their first surprise on Dönhoffplatz, because from there on something was up, people were swarming everywhere. And then came the War Ministry and they could not even get close, and the trucks had to stop and they had to get out. They looked about. The situation was clear. If you wanted to accomplish something here, you'd have to fight to do it.

They attempted once more to get through by peaceful means. They declared they had written orders for Undersecretary Hamburger.

"We want to see Undersecretary Hamburger."

"What Hamburger, who's Hamburger? How about salisbury steak?"

What a screwed-up situation. Damn them for messing things up like this, sending us here with a scrap of paper twice in a row, just so we could look ridiculous. The fellows in there look like they're ready for most anything. But shoot? Why should we? That's not what they sent us here for. So the indignant sailors stood there next to their trucks and debated. And then they cursed Hamburger, that ever so refined gentleman who was no better than a crook and who had made suckers of them. But that didn't get them anywhere either. So they took to their heels again and raced back to the royal stables for a second time. They had been had. At the stables they jumped down off their trucks, cursed loudly as they crossed the courtyard, and reported to the central office, intending to toss their scrap of paper back onto their desks.

On the streets, new flyers were being distributed. This scrap of paper read:

"Workers, soldiers, comrades! You demonstrated what you wanted with overwhelming force this past Sunday, striking a deathblow in response to the last, infamous machination of the bloodstained government of Ebert and Scheidemann.

"But now we are involved in greater things.

"All counterrevolutionary intrigue must be blocked. Therefore: leave your factories.

"Appear in masses today at 11:00 A.M. on the Siegesallee.

"Our purpose is to establish and implement the revolution."

The three revolutionary organizations had signed this.

The sailors crumpled up these flyers and threw them to the ground.

The demonstrators march past the royal stables. Cries of "Long live the sailors, the heroes of the revolution!" while the guards stand smiling at the gate. Some strike up the "Internationale." The "Marseillaise" rings out.

The unending throng is on its way to the zoo, bearing thousands of red flags. They sing, they shout, and they fall silent. There are many more of them today than yesterday, there are many truckloads of armed men as well. The whole city is on the move. For today is January 6th, the day on which the noose will be readied for the infamous Prussian militarism. Today they will drive the nails from which to hang the carcass of the bloodthirsty creature that wore a spiked helmet on its head and a monocle in its cynical, ugly face.

Noske Offers His Services as a Bloodhound

On Fasanenstrasse, in the banker's home, First People's Deputy Friedrich Ebert is served an excellent cup of morning coffee, which refreshes him. For despite a first-class bed and absolute quiet, he has slept poorly. His old comrade his undersecretary appears and reports what measures have been taken. We have sent a message to all the factories we could reach, asking the workers to take to the streets in defense of the government because Spartacus was threatening to use force against it. This message (they were no longer in control of *Vorwärts*) has had a certain effect, he says.

The old comrade has also brought a "red" *Vorwärts* along, the one now being printed on Lindenstrasse by those pirates. It demands: the counterrevolution is to be disarmed, the proletariat of Berlin should take up arms; moreover, they are to form a Red Army, all socialist workers' and soldiers' councils are to be united in joint action, the councils are to seize power, the present government is to be abolished. "From now on this newspaper will be a pioneer on the road to freedom."

(What wouldn't I give, Ebert thinks, if I were a free man myself at this point.)

Gustav Noske is announced. This useful man enters, taking long, powerful strides. His look is bright and cheerful. Ebert asks at once, "Have you read *Vorwärts*?" (The man is known to be slow at finding things out on occasion.)

Noske answers, "No. I haven't the time."

The message they had sent out has had a surprisingly good effect, they hadn't really known how many people stood behind them. They've been streaming into Wilhelmstrasse since six this morning. On Leipziger Strasse, sailors had tried to occupy the War Ministry. But they had come a cropper there. Our people were already waiting out in front.

Ebert mutters listlessly, "Tremendous." (What a rosy optimist Noske is.)

Noske: "So, let's get over there."

"Where?"

"Wilhelmstrasse. By the way, some armed bands have attacked the main railroad offices, and the supply depot as well. But we're not making it easy for them."

Ebert: "Just how do you suppose we are going to get to Wilhelmstrasse? And what would I want to go to the Reichs Chancellery for anyway? To get myself locked in again?"

Noske calmly continues to give his report. "They have, as I said, occupied the military engineers' barracks and a portion of the Reich printing office. There's all sorts of action around the Silesian Station."

"Dreadful."

"And that's why we have to go to the Reichs Chancellery. I just came from there myself. There's no danger. Executive Officer Suppe, a reliable man, is holding the building."

Ebert turns with an inquiring look to his undersecretary. He has already gotten up out of his chair. He wants to go along with this idea. So Ebert has to as well.

"All right," Ebert says to Noske. "I'm depending on you."

They drive in a closed car. Ebert is calmed by the sight of the people on Wilhelmstrasse, from Unter den Linden as far as Wilhelmsplatz. He softly repeats his astonishment: "What do they expect of me really?" Once inside the Reichs Chancellery, as he enters the familiar rooms and is greeted by loyal comrades, his old self-assurance returns. Enough experiments. He pulls himself together. These people expect me to do something. All right then, let's go to it. If those fellows out there want a fight, we'll give it to them.

He sits down at his desk. It's to our advantage at least that the Independents aren't here anymore.

Soon the lanky Noske shows up again. He is the man of the hour. He announces some bad news: the minister of war, Scheuch, has resigned.

"Makes no difference for us. I called in Colonel Reichert from the former Fourth Guard Regiment, a very energetic man."

"Colonel Reichert? And what sort of ideas does this colonel have about the present situation?"

"I just had a long conversation with him. He'll be here soon. We had quite a laugh about what those sailors did this morning. Hamburger at the War Ministry is the hero of the day. We should award him our first medal for rescuing the German republic. Unfortunately a lot of other things are at sixes and sevens. Lieutenant Anton Fischer from headquarters, you know, the fellow who tried to handle Eichhorn to no effect, an overzealous fellow—well he went over to the royal stables this morning and hasn't come back."

Ebert mutters, "They've locked him in of course." (There you have it.)

Colonel Reichert had himself announced. Noske introduced him; they sat down together.

Reichert remarked, "Lieutenant Fischer, yes—no one sent him to the stables. If he had asked, we would have warned him against it. He should have learned his lesson from his earlier experiences at the stables."

Ebert: "I would think so too."

And then the colonel laid out what measures he intended to take: concentrating all available units—the barracks troops, the militia, the Guard Cavalry Rifles—and making an effective striking force out of them. To that end, he has drawn up an order under the terms of which the government and the Executive Committee would commission General von Hoffmann to command these troops.

Ebert's reaction is silence.

The other two realize at once that this has to do with General von Hoffmann.

Ebert plays with his beard. He thinks: a general, precisely what Liebknecht and the Independents want, as proof that I am relying on the generals. We could at least be cautious enough to keep up some appearances.

He replies in a deliberate manner (he wants to go easy on Noske) that they have to go undercut all of their opponents' arguments, every objection they might make. Of course one must also take into consideration the workers loyal to the government.

"Naturally the executive power should be placed in the hands of experts. It's obvious that an officer should be put in the top spot. But perhaps not the highest officer. I was thinking," he paused to ponder and look at Noske, "I was thinking of you, Gustav."

"I'm sorry. What did you say?"

"What would you say to doing the job yourself? Your credentials are impeccable, you're a civilian, an experienced parliamentarian and now a people's deputy."

Noske glanced at Colonel Reichert, who had caught on at once. He did not betray what he thought. They need officers, but they should not be seen. I understand. We'll take care of the rest. He slowly folded up the paper with the orders he had drafted, his face frozen, and suddenly said obligingly (we'll stomach everything, we'll stomach worse than this, but we'll not forget it when we hand in our bill), "Excellent. I second the idea without reservation." He bowed to Noske. "It is of course the most natural thing to do, especially since you're already here and have learned the ropes."

Ebert: "Gustav, you've got to see that we can't put just any old major or noncom in such a position."

The colonel nodded, fully convinced. "To tell the truth, that is the suggestion that I had expected."

Ebert: "Well then, Gustav?"

Noske sat there, tall and erect. "Makes no difference to me. If that's what it has to be. I'll not shirk my responsibilities. And ultimately, someone has to be the bloodhound."

Ebert smiled. He shook his hand. "An honest man's" (a bloodhound's) "word is as good as his bond."

Like a wall, the workers stood in front of the Reichs Chancellery. From time to time they would raise a cry. The irrepressible Philipp Scheidemann happened to be in the building. Unable to withstand temptation, he opened a window and spoke.

He thanked the people who had come to create a living wall around the Reichs Chancellery.

"You've demanded arms," the cheery gentleman shouted, "and you shall have them. We will call out the entire population of Berlin, and I can guarantee you we'll not press umbrellas into their hands."

What a wonderful scene that was, the speech had paid off. What a shame that he couldn't tell the people inside about it right away. But they were all such blockheads. And besides, ever since his proclamation of the republic in front of the Reichstag on November 9th, Ebert had lacked all appreciation for Scheidemann's orations.

The Revolution on the March

Once the revolutionary workers had set out on their march, their numbers exceeded all expected bounds.

Later, when it was all over, eyewitnesses reported:

"What happened on the streets of Berlin in those few days was perhaps the largest proletarian uprising history has ever known.

"We doubt that such mass demonstrations as these occurred in Russia. From the Well of Roland to the Victory Column, the proletarians stood shoulder to shoulder. Their ranks reached as far back as the zoo.

"They had brought their weapons.

"They unfurled their red banners.

"They were prepared to do anything, to give anything, even their lives.

"It was an army, a new army for Berlin, an army of two hundred thousand men, unlike any Ludendorff had ever seen.

"It stood and waited.

"It waited for the signal."

Yes, hundreds of thousands surged toward the zoo amid incredible hurrahs and curses, with music and songs, from every quarter of the city.

The broad stream carried with it thousands of undecided souls.

The middle class, the peaceable citizens who stood along the sidewalks of the streets through which these masses rolled, huddled together and thought: here go the judges and avengers, the sword of judgment has been raised.

The broad Siegesallee through the zoo was engulfed by the masses.

The white, petrified ranks of Brandenburg and Prussian margraves, princes and kings kept silent in the background. There they stood as proxies for the accused on their pedestals between rows of bare trees, and they awaited the indictment that would be brought against them. They could not deny the guilt of their fathers.

The plaintiffs had appeared in full force. But where were the judges? Who was the chief justice? Who would pronounce the verdict? The masses were there, where were their leaders?

They are not to be seen. They are not there. Or when they do come, they make a speech and vanish again at once. What is happening, what are they up to?

During the night, the leaders moved from police headquarters to the stables in order to be among the masses. Yesterday everything was clear. Today it all has changed and things are eerily confused. A demon has put on the mask of Reason and walks among the leaders and whispers in their ears, "You're crazy. What you plan will only cause bloodshed. You're driving the nation to civil war. Haven't you had enough war? Stop it. It's still not too late."

On Schicklerstrasse the Independents are sitting in their offices imagining themselves to be clever men who have slept on an idea. This is what Liebknecht's call to arms has got them. They clap their hands together in dismay.

But this isn't what they had intended at all. This would mean an armed uprising. Certain hotheads apparently wanted to present them with a *fait accompli*.

Incredulous, they studied the proclamation issued by the three men, Ledebour, Liebknecht, Scholze. They wanted to assume the powers of a provisional government. An honest-to-goodness revolutionary committee. Their hair stood on end.

Each Independent looks at the other. No one had intended this. They had not wanted to watch Eichhorn get fired with their hands in their pockets. Hands in their pockets—but does that mean grabbing a rifle? They wanted to warn, admonish, threaten if need be. But shoot?

Each looks at the other. Today is Monday and yesterday was Sunday. How can there suddenly be revolution and civil war today when there was none yesterday—for no reason, with no need for it, without our intending it. We surely have a thing or two to say about this. Elections for a constituent assembly are only two weeks away. That's the correct thing; that's the orderly way to proceed. They had slept in their beds last night and would be sleeping in them again tonight, they would indeed. Whose idea was this to interrupt the course of world history?

So they sit there on Shicklerstrasse and come to a conclusion: no one wants an uprising. And in case one should nevertheless occur, those here present will raise their hands and solemnly swear that they have washed their hands of it.

Haase is not there. And without Haase they are skittish.

The vote is unanimous.

But what do they want then? They avoid the question. They don't dare look that question in the face. But an old member of parliament, Bernstein, asks it. He finds—he makes a little speech—that it is not sufficient to wash their hands of it. The Independent Party serves no further purpose. The Party fulfilled its mission in the war. He wants to resign from the Party. (He speaks only of the Party, not of the present situation.) He wants to return to the old Social Democrats. Bernstein is an honest man. He wants nothing to do with revolution, nor actually with all that socialist stuff. The whole thing has lived past its time, he is a revisionist, and a return to the Social Democrats is the least of what he wants.

They listen to Bernstein, dejected, depressed, and with secret envy. They watch him go to the door and leave. They find the appropriate slogan: Protect the proletariat from rash actions. That's a good slogan. What consolation is there other than in good slogans. But there is another word that must be added, it cannot be avoided. That word is "mediation."

The day is rainy and dark. But the great masses outside are caught up in the intoxication of revolution.

Revolution echoes in all their cries, in the blast of their bands, in their songs and in their silence.

They are filled with the anticipation of great events.

At the royal stables, the revolutionary committee is in session. They pass on to Liebknecht the gloomy rumor they've heard about Schicklerstrasse. He climbs into a car and hurries off to the Independents. He is recognized along the way. A roar of jubilation: Revolution! Revolution! He waves, his car has to stop. There are cries of: "Let him through. He has things to do."

He has things to do. On Schicklerstrasse he ends up in a ghastly, nearly suffocating debate.

They accuse him of being a dictator. Cowardly and weak themselves, they attack. They refuse to be towed along in his wake. He raises his arms in protest. What is all this about him? Isn't the point the revolution? And is it not already happening?

The men gathered here don't want that. These men don't want anything to do with it. How are they different from the middle class or the socialist chauvinists? They want to stab the revolution in the back, and that's why they are attacking him personally.

He protests, he rages. He pleads with them. "Just open your windows. Listen to the people singing. Go out on the streets. Come with me to the Siegesallee and look at the masses of people. What's all this debate? The masses have already decided."

They don't want that. Every one of his arguments hits home, and so they shout him down all the more. "You had no right to issue such a proclamation. Either we're part of the ad hoc committee or we're not. Your own friends in the Spartakus League have rejected that idea."

Liebknecht had no choice but to pull himself together, grit his teeth, and permit them to pursue certain political actions right away: open discussions with the other side—although their opponents would only conclude from this that they were quarreling or thought themselves in a weak position. He succeeded in getting them to agree that if here should be negotiations—which he personally was against—they would not surrender in those negotiations, either in fact or in theory, positions already won by the masses. Ebert and Scheidemann and their government were to resign, Eichhorn was to be confirmed in office, the buildings of the major newspapers were to remain occupied.

A negotiating team is named. They request a certain freedom of action. Their primary wish is to establish a kind of armistice, and so prevent bloodshed.

Liebknecht gets nowhere, even though he cries in rage, "We're offering them an armistice? That's incredible. Offer them an armistice, when they can't even strike a blow?"

They attempt to calm him. When he speaks and rages, the hearts of the Independents beat as one with his. He is himself a piece of the revolution. But unfortunately what is beating in their breasts is not a heart, but a pendulum. They reproach him, "You want the same unity of action we do, don't you? The whole proletariat in closed ranks?"

He speeds back to his stables in despair.

Whereupon the people on Schicklerstrasse go back to their discussion. They elect to the negotiation committee an ever so learned and dependable man, Kautski. The gentlemen then express their wish to proceed to Ebert on Wilhelmstrasse. They are urged to hurry.

And ignorance, cowardice, treachery and criminal impotence, clad in the robes of theory, trustworthiness and wise prudence, set off and going, straight to the task at hand (the murder of the revolution.)

The Negotiators on the March

Early that afternoon they appeared on Wilhelmstrasse and were received at once.

Yes, with open arms, with magnanimity, Friedrich Ebert received them personally into his formidably guarded offices. For the news of their arrival had heartened him greatly; it was more than he would have dared dream possible. Here they came again, his beloved Independents, who had turned their backs on him after the incident with the sailors. They had wanted to pack him and his generals off to the desert. And now the rats had returned to cling to the reputedly sinking ship.

Before they could even open their mouths, he understood that it was savage Karl Liebknecht, now his new ally, whom he had to thank for this visit. It was clear that these gentlemen were fleeing before Liebknecht and the masses he had set in motion, and were seeking succor with him.

And behold, they had already figured things out and now submitted their so-called proposals to him. He hardly listened. The music itself sufficed. He sat there comfortably and said little. He had put on the mask of moderation and common sense, and if he was thinking anything, it was how far has Noske got by now?

They offered as their platform the establishment of an arbitration commission whose task it would be to begin negotiations to prevent and suspend all hostilities.

Ebert nodded in agreement, naturally. Once the negotiators had determined that, as was to be expected, a spirit of reconciliation reigned on the side of moderation and common sense, and that they were in fundamental agreement, they rode home to the central office on Schicklerstrasse.

And how they did rejoice.

Now that they had what was very much like firm ground beneath their feet, they could turn to the Revolutionary Shop Stewards and share with them the Independent position. They attempted to unsettle them, to convert them to cowardice, weakness and ignorance, to convince them to participate in the negotiations, in their subversion, in their crime against the nation and world peace.

The Masses Stand in the Streets

It was afternoon now, the mass demonstration at the zoo was long since over.

The bands had played. The songs had been sung.

But the masses stood there, and stood there some more.

The plaintiffs were standing there. The court proceedings were to begin.

They had been called. They had come and were on hand.

They knew what was expected of them.

The bare branches were silhouetted in hard, sharp lines against the grayish white of the sky.

The hours passed. Always those same trees. Between the trees were the same mocking rows of marble statues, the margraves, electors and kings of Brandenburg and Prussia.

Fog crept up from the Spree. It turned colder.

Here and there a group would raise a song once more. But they were tired by now, and the songs did not last long.

They laid their banners on the ground. They made room for themselves so they could squat down. In the midst of the masses, there on the pavement, they made camp. Some of them had brought along something to eat; here and there a sort of picnic was arranged.

Now and again the masses would divide and form narrow alleys through which troops wound their way, either in retreat or to move out into the neighborhood to search for provisions.

They stockpiled their weapons.

Some of them, sensing that something must be done to improve the general mood, began to sing battle songs. That worked for a while, people amused themselves, sang along. But it did not last long.

Arguments arose. Everyone talked at once.

Many people were already getting sullen. People gathered in groups to decide what should be done. They sent people over to other groups to find out what was happening there. The answer came back: "We don't know anything." Others said they simply had to wait. "Don't get excited, you've always got to wait for Prussians."

Small patrols moved out in order to make inquiries of their own, to have a look at Alexanderplatz and discover in the city center what then really was happening, why there was no one to be seen and why they had been left to stand around in the street like stupid apes.

The masses were already drifting off. The first to leave, early in the afternoon, were the armed troops who marched in closed ranks to the battle zone near the newspaper offices in order to join the combatants there.

More and more people began to stir on the Siegesallee. The great mass lost unity. As it grew dark, larger and smaller processions wandered through the city, still incredulous and yet alarmed that nothing had happened, an armed proletariat with neither plan nor goal, pitifully abandoned by its own leadership. On the Siegesallee the disintegration spread. Things grew totally confused.

Walking toward them, from Unter den Linden, came a tall, elderly man wrapped up in his civilian overcoat, the fur collar turned up, a soft hat on his head, steel-rimmed glasses on his nose. Beside him was a younger man, also in civilian clothes, but who carried himself like a military man. They walked through the Brandenburg Gate, heading for the Victory Column. The tall pedestrian was the commissioned bloodhound, out viewing the masses he was supposed to hunt down, Gustav Noske, people's deputy, who had just left Wilhelmstrasse after having been named commander of the governmental troops and governor of Mark Brandenburg. The younger man in civvies beside him had been assigned to him by Colonel Reichert.

The sinister flood of demonstrators rolled past them, a jumble of armed columns, disparate clumps of soldiers, throngs of women and bands of civilians trotting along like social clubs.

The troops marching in closed ranks toward Moabit prison would regularly halt in front of the headquarters of the General Staff to give vent to their hate with boos and calls of "Down with the Generals!" Noske stood and watched. When one such procession stopped to roar the "Internationale," fists raised at the silent windows, Noske whispered in his companion's ear, "We'll soon cure them of their impudence."

The two pedestrians entered the deathly quiet building. On hand were von Hammerstein and von Stockhausen. The minister of war had informed them by telephone that Noske was coming.

They took seats in the large planning room, the middle of which was taken up by a massive table laden with globes, atlases and books. The walls were still hung with melancholy, the maps of the General Staff for the Russian offensive. The building had several windows that looked out on the street. Demonstrators could still be heard marching by, and to add to their misfortune they could hear the shouts from below twice over—there was an echo.

Noske remarked that the building was not an ideal place to work.

The officers confirmed this in resigned voices; they had likewise noticed the fact.

"Especially because of the echo," Noske observed.

The young captain laughed, "General Staff headquarters ought to ring with an entirely different echo."

They turned at once to the question of finding a place from which to work, not in Berlin, but not too far distant either. One gentleman suggested they would be best off in one of the suburbs to the west, and he offered his own residence in Dahlem, where, not too far from him, there was also a nicely situated school, isolated, easy to defend, in the middle of a friendly population. Noske at once demonstrated that there had been no mistake in naming him, and that he was a man of action and quick decisions. He decided in favor of Dahlem.

The officer explained, "It's the Luisenstift, an academy for girls above the age of twelve."

Noske laughed with him. "That's just what we need. We're all over twelve, I presume."

They telephoned ahead and informed the girls' school of their visit. It was already evening when they drove out. The building was in an excellent location, the rooms were usable; the directress agreed, since there were no paying boarding students these days anyway.

They went to work at once. Colonel Reichert sent out a Major von Gilsa to assist Noske. The building was outfitted as the main headquarters for the commander of governmental troops. And wagonloads of engineers and telegraph operators came rumbling up.

It was still Monday, January 6th.

All-too-clever Lieutenant Anton Fischer was still stuck at the royal stables. They had posted a guard in front of his room.

Late that afternoon Liebknecht appeared, measured him with his

281

wild eyes and sat down on a chair. Fischer waited expectantly for what might happen now.

Liebknecht asked what Fischer was doing here at the stables. Probably the same sort of thing he used to do at police headquarters, spying and trying to persuade people, right?

When Fischer answered that he had only been looking around, since the stables were still under the control of the chief of police, Liebknecht nodded.

"So to speak. So to speak. But you've made one mistake. It's no more under *your* control than is police headquarters."

Fischer: "Your people have suggested I declare in writing that I have resigned from my post at police headquarters. I won't do that."

"Do as you please. Your government won't exist tomorrow."

Liebknecht stood up. Fischer saw that he was ashen and that his face was twitching. He left without a word, slamming the door behind him.

Karl Radek, with blue-tinted glasses, a full gray beard hiding his own goatee, was also prowling about in the twilight along Unter den Linden, moving against the crowds returning home.

Several times someone spoke to him. Radek pulled back. Suddenly a man buttonholed him, tipped his hat and said, "I see you don't recognize me. Don't you recall our meeting at Habel's Restaurant?"

Radek did indeed recall it, and he smiled with relief. He had taken part in a dinner of Russian Whites at Habel's Restaurant on Unter den Linden, disguised of course, as a Russian refugee, and this man had been there as well and they had walked a bit together afterward, during which the fellow had proven himself to be an asinine clown.

"You're out taking a look at this folderol," observed Herr Motz, who was indeed an idler, a parasite, and who had been given his invitation to the aforesaid dinner, by the way, by someone else. "It must have a strange effect on you. Of course you are reminded of your own revolution. Fortunately this here has nothing to do with you."

"That's true," Radek agreed with a grateful sigh.

"There are many people coming from abroad to have a look at our German revolution. Such discipline. With my own eyes I saw how a fellow wearing a red armband on Pariser Platz screamed at another man for tossing aside the paper his sandwich had been wrapped in. Magnificent."

"That's true," Radek agreed, since as a Russian he did not have a large German vocabulary at his disposal.

Motz: "They'll obey, too. Though of course there has to be someone there for them to be able to obey. And that's something they didn't count on with their whole revolution. If they chase off the people they're able to obey, what then becomes of their revolution, for all their discipline?"

Radek played naive. "But, sir, did you not see the armed men? And the many trucks with sailors and machine guns?"

Motz: "Of course I did. And what did you notice? Nothing at all? I noticed something. That you kept on seeing them. They were always the same trucks. They're driving here, there, and everywhere until they run out of gas. What else can they do? They don't know where they're supposed to drive to. Any man who's served in the army will support what I say: discipline alone isn't enough. You need officers, too. And they've chased those off. There you have the symbol of the German revolution. People who don't know how to drive get into the car and throw the chauffeur out."

"But, sir, the idea was to lead a revolution against the officers."

Motz, coldly: "But that's just what won't work. You have the proof before your eyes."

"Unfortunately it worked in Russia."

Motz: "You find yourself at present in a highly civilized country. And that's the reason for still another phenomenon, the fact that no one here likes any sort of uproar, except in the theater and at home in the family. The theater and the family are uproar enough for Germans. And personally I am content with other people's families. Our theater doesn't amount to anything. Do you know Confucius?"

"How do you mean?"

"He was a Chinese sage who set up their state. In China people pray to peace and law and order. In China peace and law and order come directly from heaven. All we get from heaven here is rain. So you can well imagine what a difficult job of it Ebert has when he wants to achieve the same thing the Chinese have by pasting posters on the walls."

Radek: "People hardly bother to read them."

Motz: "Quite correct." And then he added, "Our ideal is China. Tell your friends who can't stand things in Russia to go directly to China instead of coming to Berlin. Write them—if your postal service is still functioning."

Radek: "It's still functioning, sir. Why shouldn't it function?"

"I figured because of the Bolsheviks. But, please, I didn't mean to offend, it's your country of course. The only thing I know about postal matters in Russia, by the way, is that the railroad cars use wider track than ours do."

"But the post office can still function despite that."

Motz: "To be sure. On the contrary, it can function better. The wider the railroad cars, the more stable they are."

The conversation lurched to a halt—it was not clear whether this was because of complete agrement or complete disagreement.

Radek wanted to pump his Berlin companion for information.

"You're a member of the middle class. What does the progressive middle class here think about the war and the role the officers and junkers played in it?"

"Good things," Motz answered.

"How so?"

"Excellent things. We think about them the same way you and your friends think about the Czar. That's why we're such natural allies. We'll get over our differences of track width on the railroads."

Radek thrust his hands in his pockets; he was speechless. Did the man think he was a fool or was he just a jokester. He repeated his question.

"You think good things about the war?"

"But of course. Don't you? The course it took was an honorable one. You can't demand more than that from a war."

"And the devastation? And the millions dead and wounded?"

Motz: "So what? What else do you expect from a war? Births, maybe?" He laughed heartily. "Then you'll have to send an army of young ladies out to fight the soldiers. But two armies up against one another, with cannons, rifles and machine guns—why, there can't be anything but dead and wounded. That would be contrary to nature."

Radek: "Hmm. And you're not afraid of a new war?"

Motz, decisively: "Absolutely not."

Radek: "What do you mean in saying that? My guess is that if you keep the old military in power here, you will very soon have another war."

Motz, blithely: "My opinion precisely. A war of revenge."

Radek: "Well then, and you are amenable to that, you, as a representative of the progressive middle class?"

"Naturally. We have enjoyed a first-class education in our schools, sir. The German school is at its pinnacle. We have read our great historians. Wars are always a possibility. We don't want people to get the notion that possibilities can be made impossible."

Radek: "They could, however, get the notion to do away with the old caste of officers and aristocrats."

284

Motz, outraged: "But what would become of us then? Why do that? To what end, for what purpose? What a step backward that would be for us. And what would we gain in return? These grim reapers here maybe? Just look at them, I beg you. They're limping home now, the stillborn things. They can't manage anything."

"Sir, it is always possible that one can be deceived. Our experience in Russia was quite different."

Motz pressed his hand in sympathy, while he politely tipped his stiff derby with his left hand, baring his high, pointed head.

"Russia tried for centuries to learn from Germany. They never did a very successful job of it. But perhaps they'll manage yet. Your mass executions are most promising."

A People Forsaken

It is still Monday.

It is dark now. Rain is falling. The last contingents are leaving the Siegesallee. The masses were not impatient. But now it is clear: they have been forsaken. They stream back into the city in loose segments. They wander about. Some of them gather in front of the *Rote Fahne*. They cluster in front of police headquarters, seeking some explanation.

Some of them begin to toss their weapons to the ground anywhere where there is a dark shadow, or lay them against a wall and leave them there. Then they go and sit down in a bar to get warm. They return to the neighborhood pub from which they had departed early that morning. Their local group leaders are there. They all wear the same sullen, ill-tempered faces.

They scoff: "Do they want us to go back to the Siegesallee tomorrow morning, too, and freeze our feet? They're on the wrong track there. We're not their trained monkeys."

But everywhere there are also young men, still armed, who come to the decision that they should join the ranks of combatants at police headquarters and at the *Vorwärts* office.

The revolutionary committee is in session at the stables.

Many people come, many people go.

At least something was actually happening in those chambers. People slept. People argued. People wrestled. People departed to get some rest and then do battle again.

Karl and Ledebour were the official leaders. But everyone looked to Karl. He had already been to Shicklerstrasse, however, and he knew how things stood with the Independents; and from his own group, from the newly founded Communist Party, how many were with him? Not one of their leaders. And then came the accusations, the objections, the angry protests.

He was Laocoön in the grip of snakes. He did not succeed in freeing himself. This was the first government of a German republic, a government against the generals, junkers and industrial barons—and against the next war. The nation stood behind him, but they were rolling boulders in his path and would not let him lead.

Radek, back from his walk along Unter den Linden, looked about the rooms. Perplexed, anxious faces, heavy smoke, heated words. Radek moved close to Karl and watched his friend. Karl was caught up in debate like everyone else. He wrung his hands, drops of sweat stood out on his brow.

Whereas in Petersburg, as Radek knew, Lenin had stood up, set his mouth in a gentle smile, waited patiently for a while until the others had talked themselves out, and then hurled his arguments against them, against the idiots, romantics and sentimentalists—and at that they had all fallen silent.

Radek pulled Karl off to one side. He only shook his head wearily. "You see how things stand. They've all deserted me."

"Oh," Radek replied coldly, "that's not how it is at all. Up to this point, I hope, nothing has been left undone. But if we stand still, stay where we are, then it could get dangerous. Then we would have our abortive putsch, and Rosa and Leo would be proven right."

Karl wiped his brow and his mouth. He stared ahead absentmindedly. He whispered, "I haven't any ideas. I can't think of anything else. I can't do it all alone. You all won't help me."

Radek, remorselessly: "Convince them. Defeat them. It depends on you."

"Please, my dear Radek, what are you talking about? I've been fighting all day, since last night. What else do you want from me?"

Radek saw that he was completely worn out. He suggested that he go get some sleep somewhere in the building, if only for an hour.

Karl could not decide, he was no longer capable even of that much. He begged Radek to leave him alone. "You think I should lie down?"

Radek shrugged. "And why not, if you need the sleep?"

But Radek knew exactly how things stood.

When late that evening the dreadful news came in that the masses had dispersed and small bands of troops were wandering about the city, they were still sitting there helplessly in their smoke-filled room, not knowing what was up and what was down.

They were told that the Revolutionary Shop Stewards had held a joint session with the Independents, a few members of the Spartacus League had been present as well. And the Revolutionary Shop Stewards were also now supporting the idea of negotiations, having voted in favor of them, sixty-three to ten. And six Independents and six stewards had been to see Ebert this evening to negotiate.

Karl stood against one wall of the noisy hall and looked about. Now, at this very moment, those shameless wheeler-dealers would be knocking at the door of Wilhelmstrasse and begging for fair weather for the nation. Even though they had not dared the least action, had undertaken nothing of importance, if one excluded the attacks of those small heroic troops who had barricaded themselves in the newspaper offices and in the engineers' barracks. Karl's arms and legs were stiff from the long hours of sitting. He walked along between the tables. All eyes followed him. Many of these people were devoted to him. They saw how exhausted he was. They pitied him.

Out in the cold corridor he paced about a few steps and took counsel with himself. What should he do? How should he go about it? For such an appeal he needed a large audience, that's where he felt himself in the right environment, where he would awaken, could excite others and stir them. Nothing worked for him here in individual conversations among these quarrelsome people who didn't want to do anything, who had brought along their fixed opinions and sought to establish them. He was seized with alarm and almost grew faint when he realized this. What was lacking here in this building was a man who could silence them. He was not the man, but where was there such a person?

When a messenger from the fortress who was just having a look around approached him in the hall, Karl hid himself for the shame of it all in a second-floor room usually occupied by Lieutenant Dorrenbach. (But Dorrenbach, happy man, had not been seen here the entire day. He was out there at his station where the fighting was going on. A man to envy.) There was a telephone in the room, and Karl called home. Sonya came over within a quarter of an hour. The young woman, a black fur hat on her head, pale with cold, in a fur-trimmed winter coat, flew into his arms.

"Oh, you smell like tobacco. And how you look, Karl! What's wrong?"

She was dismayed when he did not answer. And when he raised his head and showed his weary, vacant face, she threw aside her hat, laid her coat across a chair and pulled Karl to her on the sofa. She asked no more questions. She talked about whatever came into her head, about the children, what they were doing, how they were playing with their Christmas toys. When she told a funny story about one of the children, she had him. His eyes shone for several minutes, a smile passed over his lips, and he took deep breaths. He was under a great deal of pressure. Finally he began to speak, he talked about the mess they were in, how everything was falling apart, about the gruesome tug-of-war. And as he talked, he suddenly got his wind. He leaned back, his face showing his anger, and hurled a whole cascade of accusations and charges.

"I know, Sonya, what most of the people here lack: the war. Yes, the war. They don't know what war is. Or they have already forgotten it. They have no courage. They don't realize that a man must dare, and dare again, because he has no other choice, and that that is the situation in which we find ourselves. And that means you don't count your words, that you don't probe at your own weakness. You don't worry about death. They talk about bloodshed, whole grand speeches about it. We'll be shedding our own blood at the same time, you know." She listened to him, the man who yesterday had been a pacifist. "What is all this stuff they're preaching, theories out of books, economic laws and so on? All of it nonsense. They don't want to act. They're weak in their spines and knees. Always move ahead slowly, build from the base up, first wait until things have progressed out in the rural areas, wait until the Social Democrats and the petite bourgeoisie have caught up with us—it's ghastly, such unbearable claptrap, and all at the very moment when the counterrevolution is arming itself and already preparing to take us off to the gallows."

He shook his head and muttered, "No, this is not the way to do things."

She asked him anxiously, "How should they be done, Karl?"

She was not accustomed to his speaking with her about political matters. She was not pleased at this new turn. It was not a good sign.

Karl: "Either you want to do something, and then you simply have no fear and take whatever comes, particularly in a situation like ours; or you let things lie where they are. These damned bunglers and cowards. They can't see, they can't feel, and they stopped hating a long time ago. When what you have to do is want to act. You can do nothing else, you have to act, if you don't want to be a traitor."

What could she say to this? Apparently they were not following him. Actually that was all to the good. But how could she bring him around and entice the old Karl out again?

He continued to grouse, he was really only talking to himself. "Pussyfooters, hucksters, petty politicians. An idiotic yowling about death and bloodshed. If only I had a hundred reliable men behind me."

He balled up his fist and waved it in front of him as if he had no idea where he was.

"I'm afraid for you, Karl."

He rasped, "I'd make short work of them. Hang the traitors from the lampposts. Bloodshed, ha! What's history without bloodshed."

"Karl."

She let go of him and covered her eyes with her hands. She leaned back against the wall. Only now did he look up at her and recognize his Sonya. His face relaxed and assumed a mournful look. He took her hands and laid them to his brow. He thrust his head to her breast and lay there with his eyes half closed; after a while he sighed, "It's unbearable, Sonya."

"You've taken on too much, Karl. Your nerves won't hold up."

He sat up straight and said, this time really talking to her, "Sonya, they're all deserters and traitors. The people outside are magnificent, and we're deceiving them, betraying them. Shame on us; I could rip my guts out, we can never again dare show ourselves to them. They've offered their blood, and we won't be able to save them. What a disgrace, an ineradicable disgrace. I would like for the earth to swallow me up. And these fellows here who call themselves my friends, these sly dogs, these learned men, these pussyfooters and wait-and-see-ers, these scribes and Pharisees, you should see and hear them, just how stupid their cleverness is. Animals, without hearts or ideals. They call themselves socialists, but they're half-wits. Line them up against the wall, for the sake of mankind."

He marched about nervously. She thought: how can I keep him tied down here?

He: "I'll lead the masses without them. I'll go to them. I'll stand in the midst of them. We'll fight on without compromise."

She followed him and embraced him. With an ardent look, she offered him her mouth. He brushed a kiss across it and smiled at her distractedly. She let him go. He had totally lost his bearings.

He kept on talking about all sorts of things; she could find no way to approach him. She was unhappy with the way he paced about so pitifully, muttering curses. And then she faltered in front of him, and she was displeased with herself. Suddenly it was clear to her that the life of this man wandering about here, her Karl's life, hung in the balance, and she held tightly to him, threw herself about his neck and wept.

"Don't you think of anyone but yourself, Karl? Don't you think of us, of me and the children?"

He stroked her hair, gave a brief laugh, and patted her jokingly on the cheek.

"Don't I do that, Sonya? Don't I really? Why I do that all the time."

He was obviously not aware of what she meant. She wept and pulled away from him. Now at last he began to speak in a detached and serious fashion, giving her advice for whatever might happen. She should not be afraid. The children should be kept at home as much as possible. He would send her a note now and then. But she was not to allow herself to be questioned by anyone.

As she went back down the stairs, she sobbed uncontrollably. He had not spoken one kind word to her. And he was not concerned in the least about her, he was way in over his head in politics, as if nothing else even existed. Down below, on Breite Strasse, she became outright angry with him, and would have loved to have run back and thrown a tantrum. She was burning inside just to give him a good shaking. But that did not suit her either. She was offended. She pouted. She would not lower herself.

When she was gone, he asked himself why he had bothered to call her. Just to give her instructions? No, she was supposed to refresh him. Give him courage. Her presence had always excited and animated him. But this time—there was none of that. Why not? He had treated her badly perhaps, had let himself go. What a shame. A shame that she had left so soon. But perhaps she would turn around and come back.

To get some exercise, he wandered up and down the corridor and descended the first turn of the spiral staircase.

There, on a dimly lit landing along the wall stood an old sailor, frozen, his hands in his pants pockets, regarding him with suspicious eyes. Karl walked past and paid no attention to the man. The sailor followed him out into the noisy and brightly lit courtyard. Once there, the man walked over to a group of men standing between two wagons and motioned with his head toward Liebknecht, who was pacing back and forth bareheaded.

The men approached him and barred his path. Karl looked up.

One of the sailors greeted him and gave his name: Masterlitz. Dr. Liebknecht probably did not recognize him as yet, but he was now the

commander of the People's Naval Division, now that Lieutenant Dorrenbach had been relieved of command and was no longer to be seen
around this place.

"I see, I see," replied Liebknecht and crossed his arms. "That's news
to me. I knew nothing about this."

"This here is Sergeant Grundke, who's working with me."

"I see. Pleased to meet you." He gave both an attentive look. "I
wish you a lot of luck."

"Yes, and we just wanted to say to you, Herr Dr. Liebknecht, in
case you've come down here to make a speech to our people, that we're
not going to put up with any more politics at the stables."

"Is that right. Sounds better and better. No politics? How do you
plan to manage that?"

"You'll see what we mean. We've declared ourselves strictly neutral."

And now the older sailor who had followed Liebknecht into the
courtyard put his two cents in. "Comrade Liebknecht, I'd like to give
you some good advice, you and the other guys up there. Hit the road
as fast as you can if you care anything about yourselves. We've had
enough of you around here. We've already got rid of Lieutenant
Fischer.

Liebknecht: "On whose orders?"

"On my orders," declared Masterlitz.

The older sailor was getting tough. "This morning some people
sent us over to the War Ministry with a scrap of paper from the
Revolutionary Committee, you'd signed it yourself. It wouldn't have
taken much for shooting to have broken out. And that's enough of
that. That's the last straw."

"Right," the commander said, clearing his throat and clapping the
other man on the back to calm him down. He spoke as decisively as he
knew how. "As sorry as I am for it, Herr Dr. Liebknecht, I'll have to
insist on it, and this is not meant as being directed at you. But in view
of our neutrality, we can't put up with you and your Revolutionary
Committee any longer here in the building."

Sergeant Grundke was a bearded fellow with a full, amiable face. In
a conciliatory bass voice he remarked, "Comrade Liebknecht, you
know that on Christmas we made an agreement with the government.
We're going to have to hold to that. That's the least that the government can ask of us if we don't want to risk everything."

Liebknecht nodded. Ah, they were afraid they were going to lose
their pay and the chance to be integrated into the Republican Militia.

At least they were candid. Quite instructive. No, you couldn't have a revolution on that basis.

He stood then and considered. Then he quickly went back upstairs to the conference room, to the debating club. He had control of himself once again. He was calm and determined. They should learn the news from him.

He noticed with pleasure that the news alarmed them. They said, "And now this!" One of them cursed loudly, "Just so that these rascals from the Naval Division can get their pay—that's what we fought for on Christmas, is it?"

And in their bitterness and rage they thought of funerals for the victims of December 24th. Honored as heroes of the revolution, sailors and civilians, and what had they really died for?

They had been shown the door, tossed out. Without stopping for a moment, they gathered up their papers. They were ashamed to look at each other, ashamed of their earlier quarrels, and wanted to get out of this house full of traitors as quickly as possible.

Our good Eichhorn, the chief of police, the innocent root of all evil, was among them, and he made a suggestion. He invited his comrades to try again over at police headquarters.

The invitation was accepted without a second thought. They wanted to move there, the whole Committee of Thirty-Three—and for what, why for what else?—to continue their deliberations. They were at the end of their tether. They felt like some chronically ill patient: the suffering goes on, if only some change would occur, for better or worse.

It is late evening, night actually. They move across Kurfürsten Bridge, down Königstrasse. The street is deserted, dimly lit. On the right side of the street, this straggling band of men walks in the direction of the Rathaus, many of them carrying portfolios under their arms, some of them smoking and chatting, some with their heads gloomily sunk to their chests, a few of them just trotting along.

This is the homeless German Revolutionary Committee.

Last night they were ready to take over the reins of government. One day has intervened, just one single day, but what a long, long day it was, a day that never got filled up, a dreadful, fateful day.

It lay behind them now. No, it strode on up ahead of them and forced them to follow it, and it would turn about on its heels and thrust up its arms and throw them to the ground.

Liebknecht exchanged a few words with Eichhorn. Then no one spoke any more. Before them lay Alexanderplatz, broad and deserted, murkily lit, and on the right the somber red building of police head-quarters. Karl shivered from the cold, he had had nothing to eat all day.

"And so we return; I'm awfully tired. I would just as soon stretch out somewhere on the ground. Otherwise I'll simply keel over. I can't go on. Sonya was here. Why did she run off like that? Everyone is leaving me in the lurch. What a damned rotten day. It's deep in my bones. I've got to toss it away. A damned rotten day, from morning till night."

Midnight on Wilhelmstrasse

It is midnight.

Till this very hour, from noon on, the negotiating committee, six representatives from the Independents and six from the Revolutionary Action Committee have been waiting here on Wilhelmstrasse. Now the door to the radiantly bright Reichs Chancellery is opened to them. The people inside had plenty of time. Only the weak have no time. From Noske's central headquarters, and from some other well-informed quarters, had come the advice not to hurry, to hold off. (Naturally they have not gotten terribly far with things out in Dahlem, they've just managed to get a roof over their heads.)

At noon there had assembled within these lovely, warm rooms: cowardice, weakness and betrayal, clad in the garb of erudition, dependability and wise prudence. Which is to say, the emissaries of the Independents had gathered around Friedrich Ebert, and he had received them personally, and erudition had been graced with a pleasant glance, dependability had received a worthy nod of the head, wise prudence could boast of having been given a warm handshake. Now— the midnight committee was referred to Philipp Scheidemann, a man who remained friendly and noncommittal under all circumstances.

The twelve of them at once submitted the glorious ideas they had come up with in the course of the long hours of the day now past, and adorned these ideas with the title of "Basis for Negotiation," to wit: cessation of hostilities on both sides; no further advance of troops on either side; removal of troops brought forward by both sides; and no amassing of weapons and ammunition by either side.

I keep hearing "on both sides," thought the alert Philipp Scheidemann, and if I'm not mistaken they repeat the phrase on purpose. He was Philipp the Brilliant, also Philipp the Oily, the Obliging, who had been given the job of getting rid of them. He would have to find nits to pick in these suggestions. He thought, how do I find the nits? They speak of this, they speak of that; he cannot find the nits.

However, as we have said, these were pleasant, warm rooms, while outside harsh winter weather and revolution reigned, and Philipp sat across from his petitioners, the grand prince. The situation pleased him, revenge is sweet. He kept the discussion going, still looking for the nits; but they wanted concessions. He was most certainly Philipp the Forbearing, but he was not so very forbearing, and besides, he had been charged with an assignment.

One could see just by looking at him that at the moment he was taking a vacation in some southern, perhaps a Moorish castle, half stretched out on a luxurious divan. Three odalisques with glowing eyes—taken from some cigarette advertisement—had just been scratching his beard and had been scared away by these midnight visitors. The Munich painters Stuck and Makart were waiting now in the anteroom to paint him in oils and syrup.

"What?" he said to the twelve messengers of the Bedouin tribe cowering there on the mats beneath him, awaiting his pleasure. "You speak of a cessation of hostilities on both sides? But who could desire that more than I, than we do? We are not hostile. How could anyone ever get the idea to present us with such a demand? We have long since fulfilled it. We are the representatives of peace and order. Peace is the cry that is raised hourly by this government."

He closed his eyes. One could literally see the government entering in the form of several chancery bureaucrats so as to blare the hourly cry of "peace."

It turned out that in making this remark he had walked into a hornets' nest, which was what he had wanted to do. They began to protest. And so he could no longer remain Philipp the Kindly. He had them submit their arguments, and worked them over with a blunt instrument until they were horrible to behold. A tumult arose as a result.

"I beg you," the protest came from the one side.

"Please," the word from the other.

"I would like to remark,"—one side.

"But let me finish what I was saying,"—the other.

"That's what you say. But I . . ."—the one side.

"Let us return to the main point again,"—the other.

"And what is that?"—the one side.

"The occupation of *Vorwärts,*"—the other.

The contradictions bounced off each other in those lovely rooms, crackled and exploded.

Scheidemann said, "Please, by your own admission you are against acts of violence. Is the occupation of *Vorwärts* an act of violence or not?"

Philipp beamed, he had found the nit, now he had it; it was a whole nestful of nits.

They countered: "Is the firing of Emil Eichhorn an act of violence or not?"

Philipp: "It is an official act."

"An act of official violence."

One side: "Gentlemen!"

The other: "Ladies!"

One side: "But good sirs!"

The other: "Most honored guests!"

They took deep breaths. Philipp scratched his head. The strangers began boring at another point.

Covertly Philipp wound his watch. Good heavens, it was past two. How quickly the hours flew when benevolence, kindness and the picking of nits were the keynotes. He yawned. This was the signal. This was Philipp the Decisive. No more benevolence now, no more consideration. In his high tenor he observed:

"There is no doubt of the goodwill on both sides. But what are you offering us? We want to see actions. Without first retracting the occupation of *Vorwärts* you have not proven your goodwill."

He stood up, pale and exhausted, weighing each word. "We can only enter into negotiations when particular conditions are met. The first precondition is the liberation of the newspaper offices."

There he stood now, Philipp the Just, grieved and dignified. But the strangers did not see this, or pretended at least that they did not. They acted outraged. They practically threw a tantrum.

He was bringing that up now? He should have told them that right from the first. The Provisional Committee, under the aegis of betrayal, weakness and cowardice, would have maneuvered in quite another fashion.

Signaling his regret, Philipp opened wide his arms. It was not his fault. But when it came to freedom of the press, this republican government would not be toyed with. No, it would not retreat one single step.

It was now three o'clock in the morning. He sighed, he could sympathize with how upset the others were. But they should now break off and resume their negotiations at 11:00 A.M.

He stood alone now in the wide corridor. They had departed, taken flight. The galleries applauded. He looked up, laid his hand to his heart and bowed. He begged their pardon, but he was really much too tired for an encore. Thereupon little puffs of cloud and chambermaids bore him away. He lay there limp, his arms and legs outstretched, enjoying this abduction to the seraglio. They shaved his head and polished it till it shone. They did away with his beard and painlessly pulled several rotten teeth. Full of wonder, several birds—robins and nightingales—flew over, perched themselves on his lower lip and gazed into his mouth, into the throat from which he had enticed such magic songs.

Then they undressed him, and as they did so a metamorphosis occurred. Instead of his clothes, they hung him outside the door to air. He pointed out to the geishas the mistake they were making. But it was already too late. They had bolted the door at once, and he could see through the keyhole how merrily and elegantly they were dancing with his clothes inside.

He hung by a thread. He fluttered in the wind. There was a ringing in his left ear. That must be Friedrich Ebert thinking about him, perhaps about rescuing him. And then the storm broke with a roar, Philipp gave a scream. The thread broke, and he entered into eternity as a piece of string.

Midnight on the Siegesallee

The broad pavement lay in shadows. All along the wide, empty Siegesallee at the stroke of midnight, the margraves, electors and kings gave a crack of their marble joints and went for a walk. They always went for a walk at midnight. But today they were excited, something had happened here on the boulevard, they did not understand it.

Albrecht the Bear, close to the Well of Roland, could not be kept on his pedestal even before midnight. He thought that there had been an invasion of Slavs. They had broken into the fortress and had entrenched themselves nearby. He climbed down to go seek help.

Now when marble statues awaken, a great deal depends on whether they have been correctly erected or not. Expressionist figures, for example, have a hard time of it, and are constantly in mortal danger because of their unnaturally long and sinuous limbs, which are hard to

296

manage. Albrecht the Bear, that valiant old warrior, realized once again as he clambered down from his pedestal that something was wrong with him. He limped, he limped dreadfully. He had never limped in all his long life. How could he have survived such battles otherwise? But for the sake of perspective, or out of error, the artist had left several inches off his right leg. Now Albrecht stood down on the ground all askew; he jerked up his left leg and sank back down on his right. How was he supposed to storm in attack and begin the battle? He howled with rage; the living do whatever they please with the dead. But he regained control of himself and hobbled away.

"Sound the alarm! Fire, fire!" he shouted. He had a colossal chest, the artist having made up there for what he had omitted in the legs.

It is difficult for a living person to see the world through the eyes of a stone figure. Albrecht the Bear galloped down the boulevard, and although he had run this way a hundred times, he was amazed at how all his fellow sufferers, his colleagues, were still sleeping in their long, immobile rows. What were those fellows doing up there? The Slavs had invaded, and there they sat up on their pedestals and didn't budge. He bellowed, "Hello there! Fire! Alarm!"

The first to leave his balcony was Friedrich von Hohenzollern, the burgrave of Nuremburg, whom the artist had supplied with large ears that amplified every sound, making his life of stone a bitter one. He heard Albrecht the Bear shouting, and being a nervous statue in a very foul mood, he accosted him: What was there to scream about so?

Albrecht hopped up on his left leg as if sitting on a perch and bellowed, "Jazko von Köpenick. Fire, I say, fire! Man the decks. Batten the hatches. The Slavs are here. They've crossed the Havel. The Slavs have invaded."

Friedrich was astounded. "What do you mean? What Slavs?"

"Jazko von Köpenick! Ho, I say. Man the decks. Batten the hatches."

Friedrich of Nuremberg gazed at this fellow swinging his sword about. He blew up at him. "You're drunk. There are no Slavs here."

Albrecht lowered himself onto his left leg in surprise, stared at his companion, and gave him a shove on the chest. "Jazko, Jazko von Köpenick." And then he ran on, roaring loudly. The afflicted Friedrich covered his ears.

And now the others crept down from their pedestals and came waddling and bumbling along, while Albrecht went on down the center of the street, bellowing and hopping. They tried to get used to their legs, to bend and turn, to lengthen or shorten them. The poor

297

things groaned and bewailed the condition in which art had left them. They sighed or cursed, each according to his character and to the nature of the rough treatment he had suffered. And there beneath the trees of the Siegesallee there appeared: Albrecht Achilles, Johann Cicero, Joachim the First, Joachim the Second, Joachim Friedrich, Johann Sigismund, Johann Georg. The whole family tree, the whole historical register had set itself into creaking, cracking motion, raising a fuss and all wanting to know what had happened here today. For they all felt something had happened and were worried. They attempted to get away from there. But moving in marble is always difficult. From a bush there came a screeching voice.

"Au secours, au secours, aidez-moi, je vous en prie! Will no one come to my aid?"

This was the Grand Elector, who had got his full-bottomed wig caught in the branches of a tree. Two gentlemen ran over and whacked off the branches with their swords, so that Friedrich Wilhelm could then finally climb down. But one of the chopped-off branches was still caught in his wig. The enraged Elector made a grab for it, and suddenly there he stood, bald—a momentous change, truly, and much less electoral—and he was terribly embarrassed. He angrily sat down on a bench, holding his shiny pate and moaning, "I've had enough."

General Derfflinger had been affixed to this bench. Although fully incapable of life himself—since he consisted only of a head, chest and left upper arm—he took pity on the Elector and tried to get him to put his wig back on, otherwise he would catch cold. The Elector, however, only cursed, "No, I've had it up to here. Who were these asses who couldn't even chop a branch off correctly?"

"Your ancestors, Your Majesty, your forebears."

At that Friedrich Wilhelm hunched over in total dejection.

Meanwhile, in the middle of the boulevard, a great deal had been happening. King Friedrich of Prussia was walking out there in solitude and splendor; true, he was short and tilted, but he wore a long, heavy, trailing royal cloak, and in his hands he bore his crown. He gazed down at it in delight, grinning as if it were a cake that he would like to bite into. Others might think him crazy, but that made little difference here. This king did not ask why the others were upset. He simply ogled his cake.

As Albrecht the Bear arrived at the upper part of the boulevard, still screaming of fire, he bumped into a thin gentleman with a long, pointed nose who barred his way.

"What are you shouting about, man? Why are you carrying on so?"

"Jazko von Köpenick," Albrecht groaned breathlessly, and pointed back toward the Well of Roland.

"Remove your hat when I address you, you unwashed peasant!"

In reply, the dumbfounded Albrecht could do nothing really but take hold of his helmet and remove it. But standing there, helmet in hand, while Friedrich barked at him "What's your name, and what's your business here?" the old warrior lost his temper. "Who? Me? What is my name? You dirty cur, you old sot, you old lady with that pigtail of yours."

And he clapped his helmet back on and raced off, swinging his sword and shouting, "Fire, Fire! Sound the Alarm! The Slavs! Jazko von Köpenick!"

Gentle King Friedrich Wilhelm IV, of more recent times, smiled at old Fritz, who stood glaring malevolently at the old, screaming warrior.

Old Fritz remarked peevishly, "What good is all this afterlife if all it amounts to is being gaped at during the day by unwashed schoolboys and nannies and having to put up with that racket at night?"

The younger Friedrich Wilhelm IV: "Posterity holds no pleasures. As forebears and erstwhile regents we are charged to stand around here on our pedestals. And I'll grant you, it's a bit like being monkeys in a zoo. But we are responsible for the state, and even after death we are its embodiment. Marble brings considerable discomfort with it, I'll admit. But consider the others, those who simply died straight out. They have to go through a very complicated process of rotting and purging. That's not so lovely either."

Old Fritz: "Have you any idea, worthy sir, what occurred here today?"

"I think," answered gentle Friedrich Wilhelm IV, "that it was a display put on by the common rabble, a street revolt. That old idiot there, the one who's screaming about the Slavs, is mistaken of course. The residents of Berlin have not holed themselves up, they simply went home some time ago."

And now a shade came swishing down from the Column of Victory. Yes, the stony figures had been joined by a veritable shade. The marble statues recognized this creature at once by its unencumbered movement, by its flowing contours, by its occasional phosphoresence and ah! by the heavenly regularity of its limbs. The shade flew between the marble giants and out onto Charlottenburger Chaussee. They surrounded it, they confronted it and asked it what was happening, where it was headed, whether it knew anything.

It whispered, "I simply wanted to see what the others were doing, my friends who were here today at noon."

Friedrich Wilhelm IV remarked jovially, "Go to bed, my boy. Your friends have long since gone home, as is only proper, and so what brings you here?"

The transparent creature whirled about, throwing its arms into the air, and answered, "We are fighting. We are the judges, the avengers. We stood here the whole day long, and now we will fight."

"Who are you? And what are you fighting for?"

"We fight here in the streets, where else? For the revolution. Against the junkers and the officers and the rich. Against the war criminals. For the people."

"I see, I see," remarked gentle Friedrich Wilhelm IV, an expert in matters of revolution. "My son, it takes two to do that. And the Hohenzollerns are still around I presume."

"The Hohenzollerns? Good lord, man, what's wrong with you, you must have a screw loose. Wilhelm and his whole tribe are gone, to Holland. They lost the war, and how."

"Nonsense. Don't even listen to this fellow," grumbled Friedrich II. "Let's dismiss him."

The shade: "Since when is that nonsense? I was in the war, you know. I should know, I'd say."

Old Fritz mocked: "But now you've been shot and killed."

"For the revolution. And that is better than for war."

The scrawny king raised his cane. "You've been shot and killed, fellow. You should thank the fates for that. Otherwise I'd see that you were hanged."

The shade whisked across the pavement and fluttered away.

He fluttered in the direction of the Brandenburg Gate. And it did not take long—the flabbergasted statues went on talking about the incredible news—before there came a rustling and a scraping from the city. The muddled sounds of a great throng of people approaching, it grew louder. You could hear the clapping and the stomping. The regular beat of marching steps accompanied by the roll of drums and the whistle of pipes became clearer and clearer.

The marble princes listened with joy. These were the battalions, the Prussians, these were their soldiers. They were coming from the city to greet them and honor them as a result of the excesses of today's mob. At the sound, the stone figures flocked together from all sides and hurried toward Charlottenburger Chaussee, surely the site of the parade, and they gazed in excitement toward the Brandenburg Gate.

And there they came. Did they ever, and so many of them! There were so many that they could not all march down the road at the same time. And so they marched on top of one another in tiers, some on the asphalt, some on the heads of the first, the next tier at the level of the trees, and some who were above the treetops. And they surged through the Brandenburg Gate into the gloom of night, and they were all shades, ghosts, dead men, the fallen soldiers from the regiments that had marched back into Berlin on December 10th, 11th and 12th—they had returned with them, unseen and unsung. The Guards, the Field Artillery, the Infantry, the Guard Reserves, the Rifle Battalion Graf Yorck.

And now they were leaving the city. They were retreating. They had accompanied their comrades, who had worn lilies of the valley in their buttonholes and lustily sung, "Home again you'll start anew, live again as you once did, find a wife so fair and true, and Santa Claus will bring a kid."

The shades did not sing. They followed the heavy, dull thud of the drums. The cavalry sat atop their horses, the field artillerists followed behind their cannons, the infantry placed one foot behind the other. Forty-eight men strong, the Cuirassier Regiment had marched in on December 10th, all the others lay out there in France, on the banks of the Aisne. Now they came, all except those forty-eight.

They marched on as best they could, one without an arm, the other without a head. Many of them glassily transparent—that was because their bodies had been totally ripped apart by grenades. Next to them strode a ragtag group of civilians and sailors, no better off than they.

Marching in solemn step they approached, their flags waving. They spread out to the right and left on the Siegesallee; those on the ground took over the space where the assembled revolutionaries had waited all those long hours during the day. Bands played: "And now adieu, dear native land." Several bands tooted a strangely distorted version of the "Hohenfriedberg March."

The moment they came to a halt—the ones on the pavement, the ones on their heads, the ones at the height of the treetops and those higher still—the music broke off. A long roll of the drums followed, a strident sound, repeated three times.

A clear military voice was heard:

"Attention!"

The order moved from troop to troop, from bottom to top. "Attention! Attention! Attention! Attention!"

Followed by: "At ease! At ease! At ease!"

The commanding voice rattled:

"Comrades, we have left Berlin. We came with our regiments to receive the honors due us and to assure ourselves that the war, though lost, had come to an acceptable end. We are now departing. We shall hold our court-martial. Prosecutor, what do you have to say?"

At the crossing of Charlottenburger Chaussee and the Siegesallee a headless cuirassier sat mounted on his horse. His head rested on the pommel of his saddle. He affixed it now to his lance. Then the head began to speak, booming so loudly that it could be heard everywhere and causing the lance to swing back and forth so that two men had to hold tightly to it.

"This government, its leaders and civil servants, is an absolute disgrace. They praise us and then ban us to the void, for they are without honor. Infamy reigns, avarice ransacks, the billyclub rules. They have done this. They have destroyed Germany. We fought this war in vain. Comrades, we have been misled."

At that, the head plunged from the point of the lance and landed with a thud on the pavement. They tossed it back up to the cuirassier.

The commanding voice:

"Attention! Attention! Attention! Attention! Gather up the flags! Throw them to the ground! Set a torch to the flags!"

The cloth of the flags took flame, the woods crackled.

The commanding voice: "Three salutes above the graves of our flags."

The volleys burst.

The command: "Throw your arms in one pile! Throw powder on! Lay the fuse! Everyone back."

An explosion, a flash and a boom, a heavy black cloud of smoke, glimmering with red, rose up.

They massed together again.

The command: "Forward march! Forward march! Into your graves. Woe to the living! Woe to the traitors! We shall return. Into your graves."

And they soared up into the flaming red sky and dispersed amid dreadful screams and groans.

From the ground below came the howling of voices: "There they are, the guilty ones, the criminals. Grab them, they've been hiding, give them a beating."

For as they were flying off, they had discovered the white, stony figures who had crept into the bushes out of fear. But they had seen them, and now there was no escape. From all sides the savage hordes of shades came thronging, the judges and avengers, swooping above them.

"These old men, our forebears, those proud men, make mincemeat of them!"

And they hurled themselves at the stone figures from above, from all sides, they hung on them like clusters of grapes, and tore at them, strangled them. A silent wrestling and drubbing began. How can shades damage municipal marble statues? It is difficult enough for them with living men of flesh and blood. But they could do a few things, as was obvious here, to make their lives, or in this case their deaths, difficult. They terrified these monuments who fled before them. But, of course, the shades were faster. The statues tried to climb the trees to get away, but shades were already perched up in the branches, and if one of them did scramble up, they flew into his face and cast him back down. To make their flight easier, the margraves and electors tossed away their emblems, weapons and armor so that soon the lawn was strewn with shields, swords and royal regalia.

One band of ghosts danced about with the royal cloak of Friedrich I. The King, who had been snug inside it, now stood pitifully beneath a tree, his face to the trunk, terrified. They bombarded him with his crown and scepter. Friedrich was by nature a puny, misshapen ruler, and this escapade taxed him sorely. He swore to himself: if I ever get out of this misfortune alive, I'll never mount another pedestal. I've truly earned the right to be dead at last.

And scrawny, sharp-nosed Friedrich II, king during the Seven Years' War, who called himself "the Great" and during his lifetime had been an active atheist and admirer of Voltaire—how he was paying for all that now. He was forced to run about under the trees, fleeing shades who were making sport with him. They held out his cape and he had to hop over it. They made him turn somersaults and shoved him around until he fell breathless to the ground. Then, however, the trumpet for the shades' departure began to sound, the drums rolled urgently and the last of the shades arose and fluttered off. Their cries dwindled away.

The stone figures picked themselves up from the ground, caught their breath, and looked gloomily about. A nasty joke had been played on them. They howled and wailed like old women, collected their tattered clothes and tried to put them on again—their arm and leg guards, their swords, their armor, their medals.

But how was marble supposed to go onto marble? It had been quite a trick just to tear the stuff off as they fled the shades. How was it all supposed to fit together again? But they managed. It stuck on, clung to them. It might almost be called a miracle.

They really were quite a sight now, our margraves and electors and kings, these statues already plagued with artistic faux pas, the way they dragged themselves back to the Siegesallee. Ah, what a defeat it was. Each of them lugged along his pile of ornaments, the ones that would not fit at first try or kept falling off, causing them to bend down again and again to pick them up. And how difficult all that was for a marble statue one can just imagine.

But strangely the return to their pedestals did not go so badly, not as badly as it had looked at first and as the princes themselves had assumed it would at battle's end, with all the ponderous emblems of office that they now cursed for having to be worn constantly, day and night, and what for? Why for schoolchildren and a few tourists from the provinces. But quite unexpectedly, they felt refreshed and more nimble now. They were more supple, more elastic. The massage that the ghosts had treated them to had done them good. They were almost of half a mind, as they neared their pedestals and looked up at them, simply to stay where they were, to have done with that whole boring business of standing around up there, to go instead for a walk in the city, in Berlin, to go to a café or a bar—they had heard so much about such things from passersby, but none of them knew anything more definite about them.

But then Victory screamed down from her column, "Twelve fifty-eight, twelve fifty-nine, one o'clock. Attention! One o'clock, one o-one."

Victory from the Siegesallee, gilded bronze and adorned with classical wings, was a living clock; and they were afraid of her, of the way she would fly down among them, thrashing about with her palm branches and laurels, beating them and driving delinquent strollers and sleepwalkers back up onto their pedestals. So the old gentlemen hopped back in place with unusual elegance. Some of them leaped back up cheerfully, enjoying their new agility.

"Enough," cried Victory, "or I'll soon come down there."

Some of them, moreover, had climbed up onto the wrong pedestal, but there they obediently remained; and so it happened that during the next few days several princes stood with the wrong dates written beneath them—but no one noticed.

Albrecht the Bear, the bear-wrestler, who, if that is possible, had understood even less of all this than the others, sat perched for quite a while after curfew on the first step of his monument, listening for sounds from the city. He was still preoccupied with the Slavs and Jazko von Köpenick. Then, too, he was worried about his short leg. Finally, unable to resolve it all, he took a firm hold of the edge of his pedestal and clambered up. He was a robust fellow.

He was in a hurry. He heard whispers. That must be Jazko's scouts.

With a jerk there he stood up top, casting a sidelong glance down below.

It was a soldier and a girl who did the cooking for a family on Regentenstrasse. They were returning from a widow's ball. They embraced as they sat on a marble bench, then moved off into the dark.

Albrecht the Bear modestly froze stiff.

BOOK SIX

The Hour When the Dead Hear the Voice of God

The Rousing Call to Revolution

"The hour is coming, and now is, when the dead shall hear the voice of the Son of God: and they that hear shall live, and the others shall not live."

But one need not descend to the dead to meet ghosts.

War and revolution were the rousing calls of a supernatural voice. Who heard them, who noticed them?

In these weeks of revolution, the voice gradually dwindled away.

Satan

They slowly flew off together, Rosa and Satan, beneath the sable sky of night.

He said: "We live at the border between heaven and earth, between day and night. We have chosen this place so that we may easily move about in both directions. You have done well, Rosa, to decide to join me. You have taken up with the stronger side. You no longer expect things that don't depend on your own actions."

Rosa: "What do you do?"

"You should ask what I do not do. I must bring order to a world that others have made a botch of. My friends and I have our hands full doing that. It is easier to create something new than to make amends for mistakes. He, the other one, simply plunked down his creation. He thought that he could create the universe with the means at his disposal. It got stuck in the planning stages. What did he want? Peace? Harmony? But he created the world from nothing, and time and matter became part of his plan but did not fit the plan. His error was patently obvious, but he did not want to see it. He saw the error in his world, but did not want to admit it was there. And certainly not to me, whom he had likewise created. He would not let himself be convinced. And so I and others of his host conspired against him. And when he caught on to our plot, he attacked me and struck out against me with all his might, not in order to improve his world, but to throw us into the abyss."

They were flying above black clouds. They came to rest on one bank of clouds from which bluish lightning flashed.

Rosa: "What did you do then?"

"My dear child, you have so many questions. For a long while I did nothing. I asked myself whether I even still existed. You have no idea how much power he possesses. Look about you, look at yourself and at me and at the cities and mountains and seas. That is all from his hand. He has the power to destroy me completely. He did not use it. He let me live. A small tremor of his will would have sufficed for me to vanish for all eternity, as if I had never been here. He contented himself with chaining me in the abyss. And as I came to . . ."

When he fell silent, Rosa, who had been watching with delight as the flashes of lightning played across his bold, terrible face, repeated what he had said. "And as you came to . . . ?"

"Then I started to think things through from the beginning, and I realized first that he had not destroyed me—I did not know why. It might mean: he doesn't want to destroy me. And it could also mean: he recognizes me for who I am, which is as good as saying that he now admits the error in his creation. In any case he shall be made to feel that I am here. I went to work. I noticed the chains that bound me. And that was the second thing: I burst my chains asunder, freed my comrades, and pulled them up out of the abyss. We entered his world. Not his heaven; not that, of course. We had already had more than enough of that."

"And he allowed you to do it?"

Satan smiled.

"That would be saying too much. Tolerated it, is better. He accepts me along with the rest. He acts as if I don't bother him. I am a necessary evil. Though some have claimed that there's been a discussion between him and me, it never happened—as is understandable, since we had already had every conceivable conversation long before, when I had stood before him."

"Do you long to go back, to him?"

No answer.

They flew on through the night.

310

Satan, savagely: "There is no longer any connection between him and me. I do not wish to speak with him. He knows where my place ought to be, but he denies it to me. He suffers no one beside him and he can bear no contradiction. But I have kicked against his traces. That is unforgivable. No one could get me to take one single step in his direction. I bear my fate and I know my duty. He knows who I am and what deeds I perform, but he lets me be cursed and slandered. You humans have the wrong idea about me, because you are incapable of imagining what the world would be like without me. Your opinion does not matter to me, for what I do, I do for myself, and against the others. But I search for confederates. And you must begin now to see more clearly, because you stand at my side. He created you last of all. Man is the weakest link in his creation. The battle is waged for men. Have you heard of paradise?"

Rosa: "Naturally."

Satan: "And what do you know about it?"

Rosa was pleased.

"You're testing me. You know all of this much better than I, from having seen it with your own eyes. It was a splendid garden named Eden, with many trees and animals that all played together, the wolf with the lamb, the vulture with the dove, and did not hurt one another. And Adam and Eve lived there as well. And in the midst of paradise stood the tree of the knowledge of good and evil. And it had been forbidden for men to eat of the tree of knowledge. Otherwise they would die. And then the snake came, who was more cunning than all the other animals of the field, and said to Eve, "You will not die at all, for on the day when you eat of it your eyes will be opened, and you will be like your creator and know good and evil.' And afterward they ate from the tree, both of them, Adam and Eve, and then they were driven from the garden, and since then cherubim stand watch over paradise with drawn swords to guard the way to the tree of life."

Satan enjoyed listening to Rosa's report. His laughter had interrupted her several times. Now he said merrily, "And so that's how your pretty tale ends, and now the cherubim are standing before paradise for ever and ever and won't let you back in, is that it? Yes, that's how he wants it told. That's his propaganda. You can believe me, Rosa, the facts are different. Man was not driven out of paradise. He went all by himself. They had had enough patronizing. I admit that I was involved in their enlightenment. It was a pitiful thing to behold, Rosa: a magnificent garden with human beings inside, but they were not allowed to be human beings at all; instead, they were some odd, meek species of animal without feathers or fur, under the

311

trees, in the grass. But they might just as well have been perched up in the trees with the birds and apes. I only had to look in their faces to realize how things stood with them. They were one big question mark. There was something buried within them. They were my poor oppressed brothers and sisters. He was abusing them with his power. These creatures couldn't even rebel. I spoke to them on many occasions. Finally they took fire like tinder. They couldn't stand their paradise in quotation marks any longer. They ran away. I had freed them. It didn't take any cherubim to keep them out of it."

Satan gazed straight ahead in silence. He sneered. "Ha! They didn't even thank me. To this very day. They accepted my liberation of them, but I am still their seducer. The other party befuddled them with his fables. He couldn't lure them back into paradise. So at least he made their life on earth a bitter one.

Rosa: "You are my friend. Now I understand you. You are blood of my blood."

"And now let's have no more yammering because you haven't succeeded at this or that. I have not succeeded at a lot more things. But I'll not do him the favor of whining. After every defeat I reply with an even more caustic no, battle on and offer still greater resistance."

"Satan, I am yours. My life is coming to a close. What should I do?"

"At last. Rip the sentimentality from your body. Don't dote on moldy emotions. Steel yourself, steel others, make them hard, obstinate. Teach them to laugh, cynically if need be. They should fear nothing except their own reproaches at having failed. They can go ahead and curse me for all I care, if only they have me in their hearts. Destroy those foolish illusions about peace and harmony drummed into them by others, by their priests and poets. He wants to make you weak and tame. He begrudges you your having me. Show him what a human being is, what human dignity means, what makes a human being human: pride, wit, energy. And though he may throw down a hundred towers of Babel that you build for yourselves to live in as you choose, do not so much as pause before beginning with the hundred and first.

"What can he do, that other party? Look at me. I can storm across the emptiness of space. I am involved in wars, in politics, in the vital, open life of the world. He has to hide in churches, with old ladies and priests whispering in his ear. He could not destroy me, he had to hold his tongue and make a place for me in his universe. Don't slacken or let others slacken. Whoever chooses to despair, let him despair. Sift mankind, give them riches to lose, and if they are weak and perish in the loss, then let them perish. Sate them with lust for the earth. Enflame the lusts and passions in men and women so that they bring child after child into the world after their kind. Go into their universities, praise critical intelligence, praise expediency, praise science."

A greenish yellow ray of light showed Rosa that they were nearing their new home.

She looked back at the earth. A sharp pain went through her. But only for a moment.

In the Vital, Open Life of the World

As Friedrich Becker left the classroom—for some unexplained reason he was distracted and plagued by melancholy thoughts—the old mathematics teacher who was standing in for the ailing director spoke to him in the corridor, and as they slowly walked down it and then descended the stairs, he invited Becker to join him for a few minutes in the director's office. He would not keep Dr. Becker long.

Once in the office, the gray-bearded man with twinkling eyes inquired in some detail after Becker's health, whether his duties at school were not preventing him from reporting to the military hospital for treatment, whether he was forced to take long rests after each class, and so on. Having received satisfactory answers, he praised Becker's considerable energy, but then at last he observed that yesterday, upon assuming his official duties, he had noticed a minor formal irregularity in the matter of Becker's resumption of duties and he would like to correct that.

Becker's sick leave was, in fact, for all intents and purposes at an end. But not officially. Officially Becker had not yet resumed his duties.

Friedrich confirmed this, saying that this had indeed only been a trial period that he had undertaken upon consultation with the director, and one, as he had said, that was doing him good. He would at once make an application for reinstatement, including the proper papers concerning his military discharge and his medical certificates, all of which he would hand over to the mathematics professor within the next week.

"You've taken a load off my mind," said the mathematician. "Do that, do it at your leisure. It is not urgent. You know how slowly the official wheels turn. Or at least you'll discover the fact once again. That didn't change during the years you were out in the field. And so here you are, and when I stop to think that you were already in the field in 1914, were critically wounded, were still walking about on crutches last November and are still under medical supervision, and how you are already back at your job in January, why then I can only say: I admire you. In all honesty, I do admire you."

Becker bowed slightly and seemed to wish to get up. But the mathematician took him by the hand and asked him to remain a bit if he was not urgently expected elsewhere. He had only broached the subject because the people at City Hall, the provincial school board, were interested in the matter.

"Just by chance, there was a telephone call yesterday from City Hall, inquiring about the health of Dr. Willmer, the Greek teacher for whom the director was substituting. I answered that for the foreseeable future Dr. Willmer would scarcely be able to resume his duties. And since we had officially reported the illness of our Herr Direktor, they inquired further how things stood with our Greek courses. I told them how things stood, mentioning your name, and they were very much taken aback. They knew nothing about you. The director had reported nothing about it. He must have forgotten."

Becker: "Hardly. It was, as I said, arranged between the director and myself for me to assume duties only on a trial basis, and depending on the success or failure of that trial I would then prepare my application for reinstatement, whereupon the director would pass the entire matter on to City Hall."

The mathematician raised both arms. "No, no, my good colleague, that's no way to do things. You surely must have misunderstood the director. He simply must have forgotten to turn in a report, of course. You would not want to incriminate our Herr Direktor of such an arbitrary method of installing new faculty, now would you? No, that is most assuredly a mistake on your part."

"As you please. But how does the matter stand at the moment?"

The professor: "Incredibly easy. We have been very happy, Dr. Becker, that you were able to step into the breach, so bravely and at just the moment when the director expressed his desire to step down because of illness. It all worked out wonderfully. But at City Hall they insist upon doing things by the book. They do not wish, as I read things, to expose themselves to any risks in this trial period you have planned. They told me on the telephone that they would first like you to present a written report with all the documentation, your discharge papers, medical opinions, etc., and then for me to send these papers through channels. Your request will be granted, as a matter of course, but, my dear colleague, first I need to have it in my hands, and you must therefore provide me with it."

314

"It'll be done. It is their wish, then, that I not continue on as before with my unofficial trial period?"

"Please, my dear colleague, let us have no misunderstanding. You know what red tape is like. No bureaucrat ever leaves out a step in the process. And they only want the best for you."

Becker looked squarely at the mathematician, who had patted him on the knee. "Do these reservations have anything whatever to do with the affairs of the director?"

"I can only respond with a direct and simple no. I have told you the true reasons. Nor, in general, is there anything exceptional about the matter."

Becker stood up. "So that until I have fulfilled this obligation, I should disappear from the scene here, is that right?"

The mathematician stood up as well. "Please do not be bitter, my good colleague. Have a good rest, continue to enjoy your break, and let us see you from time to time."

As he shook his hand, he whispered in his ear, "Don't be in all too great a rush. Teaching nowadays is no picnic."

Out in the corridor, Becker stopped a student and asked him to go look for Dr. Krug. The lad returned quickly. Dr. Krug was teaching a class, but he had a message for Dr. Becker: he would stop to see him at his home after lunch.

Portly Dr. Krug, the physics teacher, already knew all about the matter when he arrived at Becker's study. What he had to say confirmed Becker's guesses and fears. The assumption was that Becker and the director were involved with each other. Moreover, there had been denunciations against Becker from the class.

Krug said, "Apparently you spoke too openly during your Greek class about the state and nationalism."

Becker: "I have the task of explaining Sophocles' thesis that an unwritten divine law transcends the laws of the state."

Krug shook his head in sympathy. "Oh, so that's what you explained—and more than likely defended as well. Nowadays one shouldn't even touch on such ticklish questions in any fashion. You are also said to have expressed your disdain for *The Prince of Homburg*."

Becker shrugged. "And if I did?"

"There you have it. That's how you see things. You got the class upset and you got their parents upset. And the parents' advisory council is running around protesting. That is its function after all. And then the matter gets discussed in faculty conference."

"Was there any talk about the director in the conference as well."

315

"Some very cautious things were said. Our mathematical boss would not allow any real discussion to take place. He suggested that you yourself were not satisfied with your trial teaching period, and that for the time being a substitute would be brought in. My dear Becker, my dear war hero, it is much more difficult to earn one's laurels on the civilian than on the military front. Courage in civil life goes by quite a different name than out on the battlefield. You cannot expect decorations. Don't write up your application right away. Let a couple of weeks go by, until some grass has grown over the affair with the director. And keep all this in mind for later eventualities."

"What do you mean by that, Krug?"

"I don't need to explain that, my dear friend. You should keep it in mind. But I have no great hopes that you will. Cats will go mousing, come what may."

The affair with the director continued to develop.

In the best of health, the director walked about an elegant sana-torium in the western suburbs, was visited by two physicians, had a few minutes of polite small-talk with each, permitted his body to be lightly massaged mornings and afternoons, was subjected to hot and cold showers, which he enjoyed, and was considered for ultra-violet therapy. At noon they wrapped him up in warm blankets and shoved him out onto the veranda, where he could lie and watch the bare trees and the gray January sky for two hours. It was very taxing. The gentleman was a man of physical pleasures, of a jovial, impulsive temperament. He had been spoiled and pampered. This situation was not to his liking.

It was clear to him that he had been done an injustice. There had been petty jealousies among the senior students; they were jealous of his friend, young Heinz Riedel. Perhaps Heinz himself had let a few imprudent words slip—setting the whole lower-middle-class rabble, this pack of nationalists and parsons, parents and teachers, into action against him. Philistines standing in judgment.

What was he doing here? What sense was there in his sitting here. What was he waiting for?

And then the man thought of young Heinz Riedel. What were they doing to the boy right now? No one would protect him—while *he* had fled to a sanitorium.

So the man bewailed it all. He could not tear one thing from his heart: he could not forget how they had sat together that last time in heavenly contentment in his atelier reading poetry.

And when the third morning dawned, promising yet another empty day of massages, showers and a view of the gray sky, the man knew that he could not bear it. The mania, the yearning, unmerciful love itself pursued him. What torment. He knew where to heal this pain. And it was not in a sanatorium.

"Why am I sitting here and burning up inside?" the man groaned. "Why have I banned myself from his presence as if I were an ascetic, a penitent, which I certainly am not? Why have I knuckled under to the mob instead of taking up arms against it? I hate this vulgar crowd, this filth from the streets. Here I sit locked in a cell, while out there my poor Heinz is wandering about helpless."

There was a rage in him hotter than love—like the torment some-one feels who has been denied his morphine or opium. It was a hunger for poison. Divine laws have been written in man's heart, but nature has filled it with savage passion as well. The director stood there like a drunkard in front of a barroom. He had to go in.

During the morning consultation, he avoided asking the doctor in charge for permission to leave, which would have been permitted. But why get bogged down in that and cause all sorts of discussions.

Downstairs, at the entrance, he told the doorkeeper that he in-tended to take a short walk, which was noted with a nod of the head and an entry in his book.

Then the gentleman, with his hat and coat, was out on the street, feeling like a prisoner who against all expectation has made good his escape. He had nothing with him except his wallet and a volume of poetry as a memento and vade mecum for Heinz.

Where should he go? To Berlin. Like an arrow he flew toward his target. In the train (how splendid that I am free, I'll go get the boy and we'll journey to the mountains together) he considered where and how he could meet Heinz.

He had the address with him. It was near the school.

Before he went looking for him in Berlin, he bought himself a small suitcase on Dönhoffplatz, some underwear, a toilet case, and a bath-robe. He added a few books as well, and thus appointed he drove to a large hotel patronized by salesmen, not far from the school and Heinz's apartment. He took a large room, nothing fancy and not as high-ceilinged as his atelier, but bright, comfortable and quiet. Here I'm a free man, master of my own decisions. I'm no longer young, let me live at last as I want to live.

And he happily said to himself: "Actually I've arrived at my goal against my will, and unencumbered by official duties, I can enjoy the beauty of human existence."

Ah, enjoy. The fever raged within him. But he called it neither fever, nor poison, but human nature. It was nature itself, he said, that drove him and urged him on, and how should he, a man who adored the glories of nature, rebel against her powers.

It was 11:00 A.M. Where was Heinz? The director lurked about for half an hour in the small side street where Heinz lived, in front of the apartment house with the number forty-two. Impatience consumed him. He wandered back to the hotel, anxious and unhappy, and up in his warm room he thought once again of the boy and how he would like to be together with him there and he knew no way, until the idea came to him (it has to be, it can go either one way or the other, I'll dare it) to write a note asking Heinz to come to see him at two that afternoon. And, in case the note came into his hands too late, it could also be that evening between seven and eight. The gentleman did not forget to name the hotel and add his room number.

He slipped the note into the volume of poetry that was meant for Heinz, carefully wrapped the book, and handed it to the porter with instructions to deliver the book at such and such a place, for the son of the family. He should say that the book had been found in a classroom and belonged to the boy. It was a stupid, poorly thought-out story. He realized that himself, but nothing else occurred to him. One must spur the horse on, hold the reins loosely and then take the hurdles—death and the devil.

The porter did what he was asked to do and delivered the book; the boy's mother took it and laid it in the dining room on Heinz's chair.

And when at one o'clock the boy came back home with his father, who had taken him with him to his office to try to awaken his interest in business, he found the package lying on his chair, and his mother told him what she knew about it.

While his parents sat down, Heinz tore open the package, and a deep red suffused his face.

His father asked what was wrong. Heinz answered evasively and said he would put the book away. He muttered that it was a book of poetry that he had left lying somewhere. His father, however, asked him to give him the book. During the meal, which was eaten in silence, the book lay next to his father's plate where he had put it.

When Heinz had gone off to his room, his father, upset by his recollection of the repulsive affair, set to work reading the poems. But before he even began—he had merely opened the book—the note, which the boy had not even noticed, fell into his hand. He read it to himself, and then with the boy's mother.

In his initial rage he wanted to storm up to the boy's room. The mother managed to hold him back.

"Heinz doesn't know anything about this. You can see that; otherwise he would have taken the note out."

They deliberated about what should be done. The director was plainly pursuing the boy. The fellow was a barefaced seducer, and he was supposed to be a teacher, a school director. The father poured down one brandy after the other. He marched wildly back and forth. Now they had something in their hands to use against the fellow, hard proof. The man lured boys up to his hotel room, his boy. They could go to the police with this.

Boiling over with anger, the father declared at last, "I'm going over there myself. That will be a surprise for him, a big one, that I promise you."

His wife tried to prevent him from going. But there was no talking to him. Shortly before two, he set out.

The director was sitting happily in his lovely, bright and warm room, decorated with flowers and made a bit more personal by his own perfume. He was wearing the blue silk robe that he had purchased that morning. At two, there was a knock at the door.

No one in the hotel heard the cries of help he uttered. His visitor left the hotel unnoticed.

At about three o'clock the switchboard in the hotel flashed his room number. The operator plugged in and heard an indistinct, soft voice asking for someone to come up. The light signal stayed on, but the gentleman did not answer. Neither did he hang up.

As a result, the operator gave a message to the waiter for the floor. He found the door in question cracked open and the guest lying in the middle of the room, under a table on which a vase full of flowers had been knocked over; the water trickled down onto the red carpet, forming a puddle. The telephone, a small table model, lay next to the guest on the floor. He was still holding the receiver cramped in his right hand. He had apparently pulled the phone from the table to the floor with him.

The waiter bent down to the gentleman, whose eyes were open. His eyes, however, were swollen and black, his whole face was swollen, and from one corner of his mouth a bright, foamy stream of blood ran down his chin. The man was conscious. He gasped for breath and begged the waiter, who was about to ring the alarm, to remain quiet. He wanted him to send the manager up.

He soon appeared along with a porter and the waiter. The three of them lifted the moaning guest up onto his bed; there he lay, breathing with difficulty and not moving in the least. He blinked with his eyes for the manager to come over, and whispered that he did not wish the police to be notified. He knew the perpetrator. He had been attacked. He begged them to remain silent. But he would like a doctor to come.

The doctor, summoned from a neighboring building, was there in a few minutes with the manager. It proved impossible to examine the wounded man there. They could not even sit him up because of his pain. Apparently it was a case of broken ribs, perhaps of internal injuries. Besides which, his nose and a front tooth had been broken. It was a case of unbelievable savagery. The man refused to give any information, and in his condition they dared not press him. He whispered with the doctor and gave the sanatorium as his most recent address, saying that he had left just this morning. He begged the doctor to telephone the doctor in charge. He would prefer to be hospitalized there rather than in the city; there was a surgical clinic nearby as well. This was how they determined the man's identity. At first the doctor resisted transferring him to the clinic, since the transport alone would take half an hour and would be too hard on him. But the guest insisted on having his way. And so the transfer to the hospital was undertaken, after the wounded man had been given a large shot of morphine.

Thus the director left the hotel to which he had been driven by his uncontrollable yearnings. And thus he returned to the suburb he had left in such bliss, like a prisoner making a successful escape. The head physician soon appeared at the surgical clinic, where several complicated rib fractures were diagnosed. The right lung had been punctured. The director was in critical condition. He had no close relatives in Berlin. He asked that a friend, a certain Dr. Friedrich Becker, whose address he gave them, be notified.

We note the date: January 5th. It is the first day of the massive street demonstrations undertaken by the proletariat of Berlin in protest against the planned dismissal of the Independent chief of police, Eichhorn.

Slowly and gravely, Becker and his mother were returning home from church. The sermon had been preached on a verse from Isaiah: "And what will ye do in the day of visitation, and in the desolation which shall come from far? to whom will ye flee for help? and where will ye leave your glory? Without me they shall bow down under the prisoners, and they shall fall under the slain. For all this His anger is not turned away, but His hand is stretched out still."

They sat down silently to breakfast. Becker was now without a job. The doorbell rang. His mother brought him a telegram. It was signed by a clinic out in the suburbs. Becker was asked to come see the director, who was in critical condition.

Becker read the telegram in horror, his mother standing beside him. His mother said at once that he had laid hands upon himself.

Becker: "I don't think so. That's not in his nature. Even at the end, he took the whole affair far too lightly."

He looked up at his mother. What a dreadful thing, how incomprehensible human existence was.

Friedrich immediately started out. He managed to find a cab to take him to the train station; it was hard to make one's way through the streets, they were clogged with demonstrators. At last, early in the afternoon he arrived in the suburb. The doctor reported that the director's condition was not hopeless, but there was concern because of the internal injuries.

What had happened?

No one knew. The man had not wanted to say anything till now. He had been in a hotel in Berlin, where for unknown reasons he had registered under an assumed name, had been attacked by an unknown visitor and left in this condition. The gentleman wanted to hush everything up, but the police were already investigating the matter.

Becker then heard that the director had in fact been residing in the sanatorium close by and that only yesterday morning he had gone into the city, apparently for this rendezvous.

Becker entered his room. The nurse whispered at the door, "He has difficulty speaking. Please stay only a few minutes."

The director's face was not visible. He was wearing a white mask with slits for his mouth and eyes. Becker could not find the sick man's eyes behind the mask, but it appeared that he could see.

As Becker, shocked by this, took a seat on a chair by the bed, one of the hands of the sick man reached out to him from under the blanket. Becker pressed it, the hand would not let him go. When the patient made a gesture with his head, Becker bent down to him and heard the disjointed words.

"Thank you, thank you. I'm not doing well. The man wanted to kill me."

Becker: "His father?"

"Yes. I wanted to see the boy."

Becker sat there, a broken man.

The sick man would not let go of his hand. "Give Heinz my greetings."

Becker nodded.

The sick man repeated, "Greet him for me."

The last cramped squeeze of his hand was meant for the boy.

Out in the hall, at the door to the room, a man Becker did not know, carrying a coat and hat, spoke to him. He showed the badge on the reverse of his coat lapel and said, "Police."

In the office of the physician on duty, then, Becker had to report everything he knew about the affair. His information confirmed what the police already suspected. The officer reported that thus far they had undertaken no action in the matter. The director wanted to keep the whole thing hushed up because of circumstances with which they were all familiar. But it could hardly be left at that. And besides, why, to what purpose? The matter was already known all over the district— and as far as official considerations went? The director certainly would not be considered again now for his former position.

Becker remarked that the director's intention before this misfortune had been to disappear silently from the scene.

The officer jotted this down in his notes and shrugged.

Days of Visitation

When Becker returned home after dark and told his mother what had happened, she wept. What a calamity had befallen the director, and Heinz's whole family, father, mother and son.

"But what could I have done, Mother?"

"You, Friedrich? You could do no more than what you did."

"Perhaps I should not have separated the two of them."

"You had to do that."

"Or maybe not have gotten involved at all. Would it have turned out any worse if I had not gotten involved?"

"Friedrich, the Lord is the judge. His hand is stretched out still. What shall we do on the day of visitation?"

They sat silently beside each other.

Eros, the victor in battle. There upon his bed of pain lay that refined, highly cultured man, an expert in antiquity, a worshiper of beauty—and his life had fallen to pieces, for he had made passion and lust his masters. They had shoved him over the edge of the cliff into the abyss. What had he known about himself, with what had he identified himself finally, but with Eros, with sweet lust and passion, to which he yielded himself up. They had led him on according to their own law.

Monday, the dark day of January 6th, has come, the day that will decide the fate of the German revolution. The nail will be hammered in, the noose will be tied, the rope they want to lay about the neck of that evil monster called Prussian militarism slung. But the judges and avengers will themselves dangle from that noose.

Becker does not leave the house. He trembles as he awaits bad news. His mother is out doing errands.

The doorbell rings. Becker opens the door: Heinz. Becker brings him to his study.

Becker: "You know what has happened?"

Heinz: "The police were at our house."

"And?"

Heinz: "First they questioned my father and then me."

Becker: "And you told them the truth, didn't you, Heinz?"

"Yes. — Dr. Becker, I came to ask you how he's doing."

The boy's lips quivered. How anxiously he looked at Becker.

Becker: "Would you like to see him?"

Heinz, very softly: "I'm not allowed to."

He wept.

Becker: "Now, now, my boy, what is it?"

Heinz: "Father had been drinking, he didn't want to kill him. And Mother says that I brought this whole disaster on the family."

Becker: "You? Then I did too. Don't listen to that. Your mother doesn't mean it that way. She's only afraid."

"Will he—live?"

"I hope so. We must pray that this cup may pass from us."

Heinz: "Please tell him that—I think well of him."

"I will, when they allow me to speak to him again."

Heinz: "Could I come with you tomorrow, Herr Doktor?"

"Of course."

Becker sat there alone again.

I could use some help now myself, someone to comfort me. Not long ago a voice would speak to me sometimes, a pleasant voice half in a dream, half waking, for many long weeks, after my illness. In Alsace and then later too. It was Johannes Tauler, the old man from Strasbourg, the wise preacher. He knew the right words, he was my patron saint. He stood here behind me, too, when it was a matter of life and death, when I no longer wanted to go on living because I did not know what I should live for. He led me through the gate of dread and despair, tenderly, and delivered me from evil. Now—now he has deserted me. Why, my teacher? You watched over me like a father watching his child as it swims, so that it learns the motions without drowning. Support me now, my teacher.

The doorbell rang. Again.

He flinched.

It couldn't be his mother. She would not come till noon.

What was coming now? He did not get up.

The bell rang again. He got up, moved toward the door, opened it.

Outside stood Hilda, in her nurse's uniform.

He put his hand to his chest and leaned against the wall. His heart was beating wildly. (I've not been deserted, I have been shown a sign.) She entered quickly, closed the door and embraced him. He was white as chalk.

She took him by the arm and led him to his study; she made him stretch out on the chaise longue. But soon he sat back up, regained his natural color and he stroked her hand. He said that this was quite a surprise, that she came by so seldom he had not expected to see her again.

She took off her coat and cap and sat down beside him.

Becker: "I'm having some rough days. Every time the doorbell rings I am terrified."

And he told her about the academy and how he was feeling, and about the director.

"And so I was just sitting here, waiting and thinking: what is going to happen now, what will strike me down next, and then there you were, Hilda."

He took her right hand. "Your hand. It has hurt me many times, when you bandaged me in the hospital. I was really terribly afraid of you. When I heard your dispensary cart coming down the corridor and you'd come in with your pincers and shears. And would always find one more little splinter in the wound, and then another one—this won't hurt, you'd say, and then it would be over."

Hilda: "And now you're well again, Friedrich. You wouldn't believe how healthy you look."

"Teaching that class was good for me. And now here I sit. I was just now dreaming about my guardian angel. I didn't realize that he had already been thinking about me and had sent you here."

She could not look him in the eyes. She was trembling. How can I do this to him? I can't tell him.

"Why are you so still, Hilda? Too much work?"

"I was just thinking of something."

Becker: "Of what?"

Hilda, after a pause: "I've seen Maus again."

"Oh! I'm glad to hear that. So I'll hear some news about him after all. He was so violent when he said good-bye to me that time; we hadn't agreed about politics. Does he still despise me?"

"Friedrich, Maus is simply going his own way. He's stationed in Döberitz, with a volunteer corps."

"What did you say. With a volunteer corps?"

She nodded. Becker crossed his arms. "There you have him, big as life, our stormy Johannes Maus. That's him all over, pure Maus. I assume, Hilda, that you realize what lies behind it? Or more precisely who? You, always you, Hilda. I've known it for a long time. But that last time, when we finally quarreled, he admitted it himself. He let loose with his truly dreadful hatred of me, hatred on account of you, because I had stolen you from him, yes, really, because I had deceived him. It was very bad. For the first time I saw what our whole, endless discussion about politics had been about. Only about you. He was unable to free himself of you since we left our hospital beds in Alsace. And do you know what I thought of after he had gone? Of the hero from the legend of the holy grail, who was poisoned by the wound from a lance and can never be well again. Only the touch of the same lance can heal him."

Hilda listened intently. "Did you say that to him?"

"No. I thought of it only afterward."

She said, "I see." (I'm going to speak up soon now. Maybe he suspects something. I simply can't hide it from him.)

Friedrich, calmly: "And so in his madness he joined up with the volunteer corps, right after trying to persuade me to accept radical ideas of an entirely different sort, ideas he was as good as wedded to at the time. Maybe wedded is something of an exaggeration. And how was he when you saw him, Hilda? Why are you so quiet?"

"I found him—depressed. He wasn't at all happy with himself. He came out to Britz to see me at Christmas, quite unexpectedly."

"And you talked with him. That must have done him a world of good."

"Me too."

"You? Wasn't seeing him again like that, meeting him, some-what—difficult?"

Hilda: "On the contrary. Everything that day happened, both for him and for me, as if it had been decreed and preordained. He came out to Britz. I was off duty. We were both expecting to spend a sad Christmas."

"You celebrated Christmas together?"

Hilda: "Yes."

"And then, Hilda?"

"He was happy. And so was I. I was too."

Hilda reached out to Friedrich with her left hand. "There, Friedrich, I'll not hide anything from you. There's the ring. We're engaged."

That was the blow.

Neither of them spoke.

He hunched over, resting his elbows on his knees, laying his chin in his hand.

"Why, Hilda? Why?"

She did not answer.

He: "Why didn't you come to see me? What happened between us?"

She: "Nothing. Nothing happened, and nothing has changed, Friedrich. But—I want to be with him. I want to, I have to, I'm determined. Please don't be angry with me about this, Friedrich. I saw no other way for myself. I look at you, Friedrich. I know you. During those days when you no longer wanted to live, I wept for you as I've never wept in my life for a human being, and I prayed for you. We went through a terrible time together, Friedrich, my dear, my beloved Friedrich. It was more terrible for me than you knew, and than I can ever tell you. For I was a poor, miserable creature. Friedrich, I'm not leaving you. But let me have him."

He sat there bent over his knees. "And is Maus happy now?"

He sat up, letting his glance rest on Hilda, groping for her hand.

And as Hilda sensed this gentle touch, it all broke loose within her. Tears of joy streamed from her eyes. She could not hold back the tumult within her. She threw both arms around his neck passionately, hugged him and kissed his mouth and cheeks. She wept and thanked him and stammered. He let her do it.

When she had quieted down, she looked him in the eyes and said (he has given him to me), "He's not a little boy anymore, Friedrich. Oh, I'm so happy. He became a man almost overnight. You wouldn't recognize him now. The look on his face, the way he carries himself, the way he talks, it has all changed—as if the bad luck he's known had slowed down his development. Friedrich, I need your protection. I am weak and alone. Friedrich, you'll let me have him, won't you, Friedrich? Please give him to me."

She was so torn by all this that she had thrown herself on her knees before Friedrich.

"Stand up, Hilda. For heaven's sake."

"Tell me, Friedrich, that I'm not a heavy blow to your life the way the academy and the director have been."

"Come, Hilda my love, stand up, sit down here closer to me. You see, Hilda, I could reply with some pretty phrases now, to calm you and to keep all this brief. But to tell you the truth, I don't really comprehend it all yet, what you've told me. It hasn't reached me yet. And as long as you're sitting here beside me, it won't. —Hilda, forgive me, it's almost enough to—to kill a man."

"What should I do, Friedrich?"

"Don't let yourself get confused. Stay honest. Let us see you from time to time. My mother has always said you look like the Mona Lisa. No, I don't comprehend it. Forgive me, I'm not a hero."

"May I come back soon, to see you again?"

He: "Whenever you like."

He stood with her then out in the hallway and put out his hand to her. But she did not want to go. She threw herself at him. They kissed.

He let his arms fall and begged: "Go now, Hilda, go. I'm still so—overwhelmed."

He accompanied her as far as the landing.

She ran down the stairs.

She had once run downstairs like that before in Strasbourg, in her own home, when the man she had once loved, poor unlucky Bernhard, had embraced her again. She fled from him because she sensed that she would lose herself body and soul to him, would lose herself over and over, and it was happening, and it would not end—until she had torn herself away and he had hanged himself. Now she was completely free. She had said good-bye to Friedrich, and he had let her go.

Hilda walked down the long street, not consciously aware of anything. And when she stopped at one point and looked around, she could not figure out where she was. I'm in a different neighborhood. I have all that behind me. I have already left him.

She waited for a trolley, but there weren't any because of the general strike. Finally an empty cab drove by, it took her to the train station. As they drove they heard shots. The driver had to go a great distance out of their way. Afterward she stood there on the platform in the cold for a long time, waiting for her train.

In Britz, in the hospital, she ran to the telephone at once. During the train ride she had had this conversation that she now wanted to have with Maus a dozen times.

"Hans, I'm free now, really free. Come to me."

She got her connection with the camp in Döberitz. They went

looking for Maus. While she stood there in the little upholstered booth and waited, she carried on the conversation with him in her mind, but without him.

"It's me, Hans, Hilda. You're there at last. I've been talking with you for two hours now, repeating the same thing."

"What is it, Hilda? What's wrong with you?"

"I went to see Becker in the city. His mother had called me here. I had to tell him everything."

A pause.

"I had to. Everything is fine now, don't worry, Hans, don't be so silent. Come see me here, now, right now."

She sobbed into the telephone as she carried on this imaginary conversation, the receiver in her hand, and she waited. He did not come to the phone; once again there came a crackling sound. She went on: "I'm terribly upset by it all. I still haven't come to myself. I got lost out on the street. Tell me something lovely. Kiss me, Hans. I can't live without you."

Now the telephone operator at the camp came back on to tell her that she should hang up. The lieutenant had been given the message and would return her call himself in fifteen minutes.

She hung up, and suddenly she felt her mind eased and much better. It was as if she had spoken with him. The mad chase was over. She had found herself again. She had followed Friedrich Becker out of the military hospital. What terrible things had happened to her since then. But then Hans Maus had come along, a simple, honest lad, and he was good, just plain good. God had sent him to her. She pressed his ring to her lips while she stood there in the phone booth. He was her husband, her defender. The phone rang. She picked up the receiver and greeted Hans with a bright, cheerful laugh.

"Hans, Hans, oh my dear, at last, my love. I've been hanging here on the line for half an hour. I've been waiting for you, why, why because I simply wanted to be with you, there's no real reason other than that, but don't run off just yet. You're so far away, Hans, you're acting like the man in the moon, and I'm no astronomer, dear Hans. You'll be going to Berlin soon, you say? You're moving out? Yes, there's some shooting here too. There's no reason to go to Berlin, there's no sense in that. You were afraid because I was calling so late? You had such a funny feeling all day? But why, Hans? You're clairvoyant, but you're seeing the wrong things. There was nothing, absolutely nothing. Don't run off. You have to hang up because it's an official phone? Well, we'll just see about that. This is an official

328

conversation. You're my boss, my commanding officer. You should give me orders about what I have to do, what I should do and what I should not do. I have been given personal orders to kiss you and hug you, and I don't know how I'm supposed to do that over the phone. Hans, you rascal, don't hang up. I warn you. When are you coming here?"

She was unutterably happy.

It was not just simple ecstasy. She whispered prayers of thanks as she went up to her room.

She had not felt like this for an eternity, so free and fine, so at peace with everything, not during the war, not before the war, maybe during her schooldays, as a teenager.

She danced about the darkened room in her bare feet before she lay down to sleep, letting herself fall into bed. She blew kisses out into the dark countryside without thinking of any particular creature, but of all the people out there, both near and far. Of Hans, of Friedrich, all the way to Strasbourg, to her father.

BOOK SEVEN

Police Headquarters;
or, The Black Swan Takes Flight

The Dust before the Gates of the City

When Hilda had gone, Becker stood in the corridor as if turned to stone.

He paced back and forth in his room, his arms crossed, holding his chest.

Everything had become unclear.

He stood on the small throw rug beside his desk, where in the days of his darkest battles the demons, the rat and the lion had attacked him. Becker sat down at the desk chair. Here I am again. I'm at your disposal.

But things were different now. It turned out that he was not the lost man of those days who had to expect his help to come from outside.

Even as he sat there, quietly, his eyes closed, his arms on the desk, he felt how the convulsion within him subsided. A ray of sunshine fell through the window onto his brow. He opened his eyes and sighed. Such pain on Hilda's account. Why had she done this to him? Impossible to conceive of her not being there anymore.

His left hand had touched the little book that lay on the desktop, the New Testament. He opened it, and it was the Second Epistle to the Corinthians by the apostle Paul.

"Thrice was I beaten with rods, once was I stoned, thrice I suffered shipwreck, a night and a day I have been in the deep; in journeyings often, in perils of waters, in perils of robbers, in perils by mine own countrymen, in perils by the heathen, in perils in the city, in perils in the wilderness, in perils in the sea, in perils among false brethren; in weariness and painfulness, in watchings often, in hunger and thirst, in fastings often, in cold and nakedness.

333

"Who is weak, and I am not weak? who is offended and I burn not? If I must needs glory, I will glory of the things which concern mine infirmities."

A voice pierced his heart and did its work, soothing, insightful and touching, as it had done two thousand years before. And then the lament:

"And lest I should be exalted above measure, there was given to me a thorn in the flesh, the messenger of Satan to buffet me. For this thing I besought the lord, that it might depart from me. And the Lord said to me: my grace is sufficient for thee, for my strength is made perfect in weakness."

Becker stared straight ahead. I am still too rigid and too expectant. I am still without real weakness. And therefore more sufferings must come upon me.

But Mona Lisa had left. He bled. Again he gave himself over to his pain and recalled the old scenes of Hilda in the hospital, of her saying good-bye to him and bending down to kiss him—Hilda, how he had met her on the street below his apartment—Hilda here for the first time in his apartment—Hilda in this room as she wrestled with his demons, pleading, kneeling and praying, in tears.

And she would be there no longer. She had saved him, but for what?

"Ah, my brethren, lest I should be exalted above measure, there was given to me a thorn in the flesh. And the Lord said to me: my strength is made perfect in weakness."

In that moment Becker became aware of the fact that faith and Christianity were not as easy as it had seemed to him from time to time. The path to God must always be prepared anew, and was always being blocked again. He sat there and stammered, "Heavenly Father, Creator, who guideth all things. Thou hast sent this to me as well. I have received it from thy hand. Behold how I struggled. Ease my torments. I am thy child, thou art my Father. Lord, I submit myself to thee."

After that, his dismay had not completely left him, to be sure, and his study was not free of the terror of her farewell. But it was no longer dismay alone that was within him. Where is there a pain that is not mine also? Where a grievance that does not grieve me too?

And then young Riedel appeared again. Becker had given him permission to come whenever he pleased. The whole Riedel family was quaking, hoping that the director would live. The nurses out at the clinic had promised Becker they would telephone him in case the patient's condition worsened. There had been no news. They were uncertain. Becker said to the boy, "It's still early. Come on, we'll go out there."

They arrived toward noon. The nurse greeted them. They thought the visitors had come because of their telegram. They had sent a telegram. The patient was not doing well.

She led both visitors in to him. The sick man's bandages had been removed. He was a terrible sight. His nose was thickly swollen, as was the rest of his face clear up to his forehead; it had turned a blackish blue and was shiny, apparently from some salve. There were bandages from his lower lip to the tip of his chin.

The patient was conscious. He breathed with difficulty and in pain. The injuries to his ribs had brought on pneumonia. Becker gave the sick man his hand, which he pressed for a long, silent time.

Then the director held Heinz's trembling hand. Becker stepped back. He saw the blissful look in the sick man's eyes.

"Save me, Lord," Becker pleaded at the window, next to the surgical table, "save me and do not leave me to the judgment of evildoers. Judge him and be gracious unto him, thou who letteth not the sinner fall. Help him on his way."

The nurse whispered, "You have to go now."

On the way to catch their train, Becker had his hands full with the desperate boy. Heinz walked the whole way weeping, his head lowered, his handkerchief in his hand. What had he brought about? He was to blame, he said. He didn't even dare to go back home. They would put his father in jail, and the director . . .

In Berlin, Becker had no choice but to accompany the boy home. He spoke with his mother and the father, who vacillated between outbreaks of rage and misery. When he heard how the director was doing, he broke down. Husband and wife both wept. The man protested that this was not what he had wanted. He had only wanted to give the director something to think about, but all the alcohol . . .

In the midst of all this noisy misfortune, the pain young Heinz was feeling left him. The lad had to calm his mother, and they were afraid his father would lay hands on himself.

The next morning the boy was already at Becker's by eight o'clock, hoping for news. They went to the nearest post office together and telephoned to inquire. The clinic answered: "Unchanged, critical."

They debated the matter back and forth out on the street. Heinz was deeply grateful to Becker when he decided, "We'll go out."

They could see when they entered the patient's room: he was doing better. The director's face was badly swollen, but he could see more clearly. Becker first let the boy approach the sick man's bed. Heinz gave the director the flowers he had brought. Although Becker stood nearby, he could not hear a word. It appeared as if neither spoke a word. Then the boy rushed past him toward the door.

Becker sat down beside the sick man, who thanked him most warmly for all his attention, his trouble and everything else. "You are a genuine human being, Dr. Becker, a genuine human being."

Then he said that he did not want to get well again. "The doctors have been having me breathe oxygen and are giving me camphor."

Becker was amazed. "But you're mistaken. You're doing well. Don't talk so much."

The director smiled. "Why not. The end is approaching." He gazed up at the ceiling. "My life, my life was lived solely for beauty and love."

He was dreaming apparently. He turned his face, it's expression strangely serene though the lips did not move, toward Becker, who had risen to go. He managed to give a friendly smile, but he could not keep his eyes in focus and soon drowned in general bliss.

Late that afternoon, quite exhausted from the trip, Becker was lying on his chaise longue when it seemed to him that someone was pacing back and forth in the corridor before his door. Maybe he or she was trying to read the name plates. But then whoever it was stood still and knocked, hesitantly.

Who was knocking? There was a doorbell after all. Perhaps— Hilda. Perhaps Hilda had strayed this way again.

Now the knocking was more resolute. Becker called to his mother, who had heard nothing.

In the obscure gaslight of the top landing, she saw blond Heinz there before her, standing like a beggar with cap in hand, head lowered. He asked if he could speak with Dr. Becker for a minute.

Becker's mother could not understand the boy's diffident manner. She hesitated, she wanted to question him first, but then she let him in.

Becker got up the moment the boy's gaze fell on him.

What had happened?

Heinz: The police had come to their apartment while they were eating and arrested his father.

The tall lad said nothing more than that. He stood with his cap in hand, his head on his chest.

Becker: "Come here. What's happened?"

Heinz did not move, he let his head droop still lower. The director had died today at noon.

The boy had held it back until then. Now he sobbed loudly. He held his left arm before his face. His shoulders jerked, you could hardly hear a sound. Frau Becker came up to him from one side, pulled a chair over to him, stroked his hair, and took his cap out of his hand. Becker sat on his chaise longue, bent way over.

His mother patted Heinz's hand. "Your mother is alone at home now?"

He wiped his face. "She is with my aunt, her sister, out in Charlottenburg. My aunt came and got her."

Frau Becker: "And your mother will be staying there?"

Heinz: "Father told her to, before he went away."

"And what about you, Heinz? What is to become of you?"

"I have the key to our apartment."

Becker had not spoken. Now he stood up, and they watched him walk across the room with slow steps. His mother and Heinz followed him with their eyes.

He stood silently before his desk. Then he placed the crucifix in the middle of the desk where they could see it. With a slightly hoarse voice he said, "Mother, Heinz, let us remember the dead."

They stood up.

Becker folded his hands and lowered his head, they did the same. No one said a word. And then they whispered the Lord's Prayer with Becker.

Becker went over to the boy and laid his arm around his shoulder.

"You'll stay here, Heinz. You've had to run around enough as it is."

It occurred to his mother that with all the confusion at home he had probably had nothing to eat. Heinz protested, but not loudly enough. It was decided that he would stay. They would eat their evening meal a bit earlier. Becker excused himself from his guest and went with his mother into the living room. They could not let the boy stay alone in an empty apartment, and neither could they send him out to his aunt, who had enough to do already with the mother. Frau Becker was of the same opinion, and they went back to the boy to invite him to stay as their guest for a few days instead of living in the empty apartment.

The lad, completely helpless, acquiesced in everything.

After their evening meal, Frau Becker, active as ever, took it upon herself to go find the aunt in Charlottenburg. She was the wife of a furniture dealer. But Frau Becker did not immediately encounter the husband himself in the large, dreary apartment stinking strongly of tobacco.

The lady of the house sat down in the cold parlor with Frau Becker, but left the doors wide open, ostensibly so that some warmth could seep in. Then she called her sister, Frau Riedel, and Frau Becker could not believe her ears when she heard the woman say, "There's someone here from the Welfare Department, on account of the boy."

Frau Riedel did not prove very friendly at first. Frau Becker's plans did not suit her; and why should they? Heinz was a big boy, he wasn't afraid to be alone in the apartment; in fact he could come out here to Charlottenburg, for after all, she could look after her son herself.

But her sister had something else to say.

"You can't look after him. It can only do Heinz good if he's under someone else's care for a while."

And she added in a loud, resounding voice, "You should know, Frau Becker, that in our family we have nothing to do with alcohol. The men brought the habit back with them from the war. From the bases. Out on the front lines they might have had other things to think about."

At that, a large, bald-headed, beer-bellied man in shirtsleeves showed himself at the door, as if on cue, shouting gruffly into the room, "They would have shot us down out there for sure—which would probably have suited you better."

After this statement he pulled back into the darkness again.

The wife of the furniture dealer gave her sister a jab with her elbow. "Did you hear that? Still playing the big man."

The result of this unpleasant visit was that for the time being, in any case, Heinz would be allowed to stay with the Beckers, if that was what he wanted to do. Frau Becker was extended no thanks for her offer.

In the meantime Friedrich was talking with the boy in his study. They were both sad and dejected, especially without Becker's lively mother. Friedrich read from the Forty-Second Psalm, reading its ending aloud:

"My tears have been my meat day and night, while they continually say unto me, Where is thy God?

"When I remember these things, I pour out my soul in me: for I had gone with the multitude, I went with them to the house of God, with the voice of joy and praise. Why art thou cast down, o my soul? and why art thou disquieted in me? hope thou in God: for I shall yet praise him for the help of his countenance.

338

"I will say unto God my rock, Why hast thou forgotten me? why go I mourning because of the oppression of the enemy?

"As with a sword in my bones, mine enemies reproach me; while they say daily unto me, Where is thy God?

"Judge me, O God, and plead my cause against an ungodly nation.

"O send out thy light and thy truth: let them lead me; let them bring me unto thy holy hill and to thy tabernacles.

"Then will I go unto the altar of God, unto God my exceeding joy: yea upon the harp will I praise thee."

Heinz sat there silent and listened. He looked over at Becker with large eyes. "You believe in God? The director—didn't believe."

Becker: "Perhaps he did. It just never occurred consciously to him. And all the more then should we believe, and think of the dead and pray for his soul."

Heinz: "Do you think so?—Why do you believe in God?"

Becker: "Because He exists, Heinz."

Heinz: "Where? Why? I don't know anything about that."

Becker: "You know, Heinz. You simply haven't asked yourself about it. You ask other things many people about so many things every day, or they ask you, and you never get around to asking yourself. But with a little peace and quiet you would come to know what it is you know."

Heinz: "I have peace and quiet, Dr. Becker. I have peace and quiet now. But where is God? I don't see him and I don't hear him."

Friedrich: "That may be. But your eyes aren't content just to see and your ears want to do more than just hear. You think and you feel, too. Is this book here only a book that you can perceive with your eyes and your hands? For your eyes it's a black rectangle, for your hands it has a certain weight. Is this book, which is a black rectangle and has a certain weight, nothing more than that? I open it to a given page. For my eyes, the page is sprinkled with irregular black marks. That's all. But it is also a text: 'There is a sword in my bones, mine enemies approach me; while they say daily unto me, Where is thy God?' It's this psalm."

Heinz: "That's true. But where is God here in the world or in our lives?"

Friedrich: "You can't find him?"

Heinz: "No. I've always thought the stuff in church was just so much talk. The other fellows did too. Our—fine director once said he preferred to believe in . . ."

Becker raised his hand.

"Enough of that, Heinz. Don't go repeating things about him after he's gone. He said that perhaps, but he knew better. You'll find God and you'll discover him in spirit—since only in spirit can you discover him—when your eyes are opened and your hour has come. Then you will recognize a lot of things more clearly and better, just as you now recognize that this page is not just a white rectangle with black marks on it, but a psalm and words that are directed to you in spirit: 'As the hart panteth after the water brooks, so panteth my soul after thee, O God.' And then, Heinz, you'll see flowers, too, the same ones you see now, but not as botanical subjects, and the multitude of animals, but not as mere zoology, and the stars, but not just as astronomy, and your self and your fellow human beings, but not as mere objects of biology and medicine. You'll see instead that everything that is, bears its sign, just as these letters have their meaning, by which they become a text. And then you can find a miracle in every movement of a head. And only then, when you think of your soul, through which you experience and perceive all this, is the great mystery there, and you are not the master of it, or only in very small measure."

Heinz whispered, "Have you had such experience, Dr. Becker?"

Becker: "All that and much more. But one needs so much time for it, my dear boy. And it will not be granted you without misfortune. Without suffering and misfortune, you can grow along with the animals and the plants, but you'll never be a man. Suffering separates us from the rest of nature."

They both sat there silent. Suddenly Heinz jumped up. It occurred to him that they knew nothing about the director's funeral, when and where it would be. At once they put on their coats.

Becker said, "Here we sit talking about him, and forget him. We are his closest friends. He has no relatives in Berlin."

Out on the street they looked for a restaurant, since the post office from which they could have telephoned was closed. Finally they found an empty pub, and Becker called the clinic. They answered that they knew nothing about a date for the funeral. The body had been impounded by the office of the prosecuting attorney and had been taken to the morgue in Berlin. Becker and Heinz wandered back home in alarm. It was actually quite understandable, what they had been told, but they had not thought of it. Early the next morning, two police officers appeared at Becker's door, the same ones who had arrested Herr Riedel the day before. They were surprised to find Heinz there.

It turned into an extensive interrogation of Becker. They treated the "First Lieutenant, sir" very respectfully. Afterward, Friedrich and his mother had to make a declaration about the presence of the boy.

Since Heinz happened to be there, they also questioned him again, alone. They expected him to give evidence about certain things he knew nothing about. After the two officers had left, he sat there in the living room defiant and angry. He told Becker that two senior students had slandered the director and said nasty things about him.

Becker let him get it out of his system.

Then he said, "I myself once saw you wearing a sailor's uniform. Why were you wearing it in the winter? For love of the revolution?"

Heinz blushed. No, the director loved the uniform. But nothing had really ever happened between them. They had only eaten, read and talked with each other. Once the director had laid his arm around his shoulder and patted him.

Becker nodded and sat there in a brown study.

The boy: "Do you think I should have told them more, to help exonerate my father? But if it's not true, what then?"

"Heinz, I wasn't suggesting anything."

"The police said, too, that my father must have had a reason to go after the director like that, and that what I had told them couldn't be the whole story. But there wasn't anything else. First of all, I can't accuse the director of things that are lies."

"And secondly?"

The boy bit his lip.

"I'm not defending my father either. I'm a free man. I'm still a minor in the eyes of the law, but I know what I must do and what not to do. I can defend myself all by myself if someone wants me to do something I don't want to do."

Becker: "I see. I see."

Heinz: "If my father beats up the director, well that's his affair. He didn't have to beat him up on my account. I was already willing to break off with the director. When I got that letter, I would have gone to his hotel and calmed him down. We would have come to an understanding. I had noticed right away what the director's tendencies were. I wasn't angry with him on that account. But I wanted to leave him."

In the Footsteps of Antigone

They made their way to the morgue.

On the street Heinz asked, "Why does Frau Becker leave so early in the morning? Does she work?"

Becker told him about her charity work.

The boy found that very admirable and useful.

"Just look at my father, how he's got into the habit of drinking. He's even got my mother to join him, because he needs company. And when he drinks he gets so furious. The doctor has had to come a couple of times because of his problems with his stomach and his nerves, but he can't stop it. And then he gets furious about everything and curses the Spartacists and the republic, but he won't listen to anything about his drinking. And then sometimes he works himself up into such a terrible rage, like on the day after Christmas, late in the evening. Just because my mother took his bottle away from him he knocked over the whole Christmas tree with all the candles burning on it, so that the carpet and the curtains caught fire, and even his own house-robe that Mother had given him."

"Did you tell the police about that?"

"No. They didn't ask me about it. And I don't want to make him out to be too bad, after all. It was in just the same sort of rage that he went after the director, and then he claims that it was for my sake. That he did it for my sake. He killed the director for my sake . . ."

The boy clenched his teeth. And so they made their sad way by bus to the morgue on Hessische Strasse.

"He is lying here in this building," said Heinz.

They asked in the office for permission to see the dead man. They were friends of his. The official had to inquire of someone else, and came back with the information that the body had already been autopsied and put in its coffin, and that it was unthinkable for them to reopen the coffin.

Then Becker inquired what would become of the body now, when the funeral would take place.

The official looked in his book.

"Yes, we'd like to know that ourselves. The body has been released by the prosecutor's office. The deceased has a brother in Frankfurt am Main, we've informed the man by telegram. At the moment we're still waiting for an answer. If we don't have one by tomorrow, then the funeral will be arranged from here at the expense of his heirs."

Heinz got involved. Would it not at least be possible to see the coffin.

"If that's important to you," said the official.

He called an elderly man from down the hall who was busy sweeping, and the man led the two visitors down a stone stairway to the cellar where the bodies were kept. The coffin number was twelve hundred eleven.

There was an extensive cellar area, icy cold, filled with a sweetish odor. Small lightbulbs were burning from the ceiling. In niches along the walls lay bodies stacked in tiers on wooden platforms. You could see only the yellowish white soles of their feet. Out on the floor were the closed pine coffins.

The old man searched for number twelve hundred eleven.

"This is it," he said and stepped back.

Becker bent down and touched the coffin lid.

Heinz held his hands before his face.

"Let's go," he whispered after just a few seconds. They climbed back up the stairs.

In the corridor Heinz ran away from them, holding his hand to his mouth. The guard laughed. "Happens to a lot of people, they can't take the smell." Friedrich gave the man a tip and had him take him back to the office once again to make certain they would notify him in case the director's brother did not reply. In that case he would take over the burial arrangements. The official took down his address and said that he would call early the next morning. The cost, as he had said, would be covered by the estate.

As Becker and Heinz walked through the gardens at the front of the building and got some fresh air, it seemed to them as if they had just ascended from the underworld, and that this was the upper world and they had had to leave that poor shade behind them. What could they do for him? How could they render him a kindness?

Becker explained what he had arranged with the official with regard to the burial.

Heinz said resolutely, "We'll take care of it ourselves. I'll pay for part of the costs. Yes, I will, I've saved up fifty marks."

Becker patted him on the shoulder.

Heinz: "They've laid him in such an ugly coffin."

Afterward he added, "I'm certain no one from school will come."

"Yes they will, Heinz. I'll be there."

"Yes. That's enough."

They remained together till noon, but with a certain tension in the air. When Dr. Krug turned up, and Friedrich asked him if he wanted to attend the funeral, Krug at once said that of course he would. And when Friedrich warned him that doing so could result in some unpleasantness, Krug remarked nonchalantly, "We'll let that come as it may. The intention is clear: make life for everyone who isn't a monarchist and a reactionary so miserable that they leave the school. The throne and the altar are united as always. Well, they won't have it so easy with me. I've got my connections, too, if need be, but more on the Left. Becker, it wasn't this bad before the war. They're spying on me in my own physics class."

He declared he would be there even if the funeral took place during the morning. Friedrich warned him once again—Krug was going too far. But the plump, easy-going fellow stuck to his guns. He was annoyed.

The next day brought with it the unexpected.

When Heinz called at the morgue in the morning as Becker asked him to, he was told that they did not know anything new. When he went back and got Friedrich to speak with him, he was given the same vague answer from two different people—and then finally the strange news that by mistake they had been given the wrong information yesterday when they were told that the prosecutor had released the body. In fact, the prosecutor had not issued any order of the sort.

And what was the reason for that, Becker inquired.

They had no way of guessing that. Perhaps the prosecutor had not yet been handed the coroner's report, or the report did not satisfy him.

They both returned home in amazement. Dr. Krug was already there, pacing up and down the street. He had kept his morning open. He had been upstairs and rung Becker's bell. He wanted to know what was happening.

Up in the apartment, when Becker reported to him the strange seesaw of information he had received, Krug expressed considerable interest and with a mysterious smile pulled a newspaper from his pocket. There in the local column it said that an autopsy had been carried out at the morgue on School Director X., who had been beaten to death in his hotel. Since the director had no relatives in Berlin, close friends had taken over the funeral arrangements, which would remain private.

Becker and Heinz were amazed. Everything was public knowledge.

Krug grinned.

"Yes, but there's some even more peculiar news. This morning, before I had even gotten ready to go out, my landlady brought two grave and elderly gentlemen in to see me. I think: either they are detectives and they want to arrest me, or they've brought me a challenge to a duel. I figured the latter was more likely, since there were two of them and they made such solemn faces. I could already see myself out in Hundekehle with a revolver in my hand. Though I hadn't the least notion, by the way, whose honor I might have offended this time. And then one of them start in—they refused to take a seat, that's part of regulations—and makes a little speech about the director and about his double life as a school official and wastrel, about which I had already been informed. They were members of the parents' council of the school. The parents' council was profoundly shaken by these events that were now public knowledge. But they hadn't the slightest intention to generalize. They had unqualified confidence in the faculty as a whole. And then your name was mentioned, Dr. Becker. You had already gotten mixed up in this embarrassing affair in a way that was quite difficult to fathom, but about which there could be only one possible opinion: severest condemnation. But now they had also learned that you were concerning yourself with the funeral arrangements. That was why they had come to me, as your friend, so that I might inform you that such an act would be seen as a direct challenge, and the public would in no wise regard it as a demonstration of respect for the dead, but rather as an endorsement. What do you say to that, Becker?"

Friedrich only grumbled. He had wrinkled his brow.

Krug: "As far as that goes, the whole debate is pointless. The prosecutor has not, as you say, released the body yet."

Becker: "Hmmm. Those folks are in a hurry."

Krug: "The spokesman introduced himself as an officer in the reserves. He spoke to some extent as your comrade-in-arms. It was well known that you had returned from the battlefield severely wounded, and apparently you had not gotten used to the new circumstances in your life."

Becker: "They only want to prevent me from further recklessness. What did you answer them?"

Krug: "I said I was just getting ready to visit you in order to tell you I wished to take part in the funeral."

"And what did the gentlemen do?"

"They were speechless. You can imagine. A lightning bolt out of the blue. Then they became very formal, whispered to one another, clicked their heels and vanished as noisily as a whole armed battalion."

Becker: "That's the same gang that sent the class-spokesman, Schröter, up here to see me that time. They won't give in. It's not enough for them that the director is dead. Their hate extends beyond the grave."

Krug: "Right. They want it all."

Krug took his leave, but was back again inside of two minutes.

"The whole pack of them is down below; hurrah, they're coming!

They pulled up in a cab, but they appear to have the wrong address, they're looking next door."

Becker: "Heinz, please, bring the gentlemen up here."

Krug: "Please, let me do that. It's a shame that I can't be here after I have done that much."

Downstairs, Dr. Krug gave instructions to the two gentlemen as they emerged from the neighboring building. They did not seem particularly delighted at meeting him here. The spokesman presumed to remonstrate with him. "You gave us this address yourself."

Krug: "Enough, good sirs. You didn't even ask me for it. Good day."

Becker asked Heinz not to show himself, so as not to complicate the situation.

The gentlemen rang the doorbell and asked whether they had the honor of speaking with First Lieutenant Dr. Becker.

Becker, who acted as if he knew nothing about all this, inquired whether this were something about insurance.

No, they had something to tell him, something—it was not possible to do so here in the stairwell.

"Please, come in."

In the living room, the two gentlemen introduced themselves, hats in hand. The older one, bald-headed, who stubbornly addressed Becker as "Herr Comrade-in-Arms," rattled off the same litany he had given Krug. To which Becker, who was still standing himself, replied: "To what do I owe your interest in this matter? Why are you so concerned about me? During the war, during my illness up to this very day, you have not shown any sign of your concern for me."

The gentlemen cleared their throats.

The older one declared, "The affair of the director is the talk of the town. It is our duty as a parents' council to think of the reputation of our school. We would like to prevent the academy to which we send our children from being the object of further gossip. In a discussion of the matter, it was determined that now that this misfortune has occurred, the affair must be made the starting point for a—shall we say—a cleaning-up operation. Until now, Herr Dr. Becker, we would not directly involve you in our operation, as a front-line officer and a patriotic man, nor initiate you into matters concerning the general climate at our school. We regret that deeply, and that is why we have come to see you personally. We would like to call your attention to the fact that when we learned of your intention to take part in the director's funeral, it was as if we had been struck by a thunderbolt. We

346

cannot believe that it is your intention to disturb the parents of the students even more than they have already been disturbed. We need unanimous assurance on the part of the faculty, also for the sake of the general public, that incidents of this sort are not only to be condemned, as is perfectly obvious, but that the faculty is willing to grasp hold of the root of such evil—to cleanse our school of all manifestations of decadence and decay."

This was said by the older of the two, who might have been the owner of a large wallpaper and linoleum store. The younger one could have been a tax official. The bald one, the older one, implored Becker to go have a look at Alexanderplatz right at this moment, where civil war was in full swing.

The younger one, although apparently not an officer, appealed to Becker in a spirited tone. They must stand together, having fought together out there on the front shoulder to shoulder, to prevent the total disintegration of the nation, for which fight unity and firm principles were needed. Under the rubric disintegration of the nation was just where the director affair should be placed as well. The outrage of the parents was immense.

Given the garrulousness of these gentlemen, Becker had plenty of time to formulate his answer.

He now bade them be seated. Suddenly he found it unbearable to allow his visitors to dominate the conversation in this fashion.

Becker: "I would like to show the deceased such honor as I feel I dare not deny him. As a man beside whose deathbed I stood in his last days, he has a right to that."

They were sitting around the table; the gentlemen were holding their hats on their knees. The bald one nodded: perfectly understandable, quite estimable, but there were special circumstances in this instance requiring that personal feelings be set aside.

Becker: "What special circumstances?"

"Well, the monstrosity of the affair itself and the outrage of the parents, who are awaiting some reassuring sign on the part of the faculty. That means but one thing, at the very least: demonstratively not to take part in the funeral."

Becker: "Even while the murdered man was alive I attempted to deal with the matter."

"We are aware of that."

"Then there is no necessity for me to add anything else. No such sign is necessary in my case."

The voluble bald man: "Herr Dr. Becker, all respect for your feelings. But you have a duty with regard to the public that you cannot ignore. No one would understand why you alone should appear at the funeral. People would merely conclude from it that you very consciously choose to act in opposition to the rest of the faculty."

Becker, calmly: "Please let me worry about that, and also about defending myself before the general public and officialdom."

The bald man: "But the parents' council itself represents the interests of the general public, and official interests as well."

Becker: "True. It does appear to me on the basis of what you've said, that primarily you represent interests extending beyond the purview of the school itself. To be quite frank, I have the feeling that the affair with the director was quite opportune for you."

The two gentlemen looked at each other. The younger one began to get up. The older one held him back and, after an extended clearing of his throat and pursing of his eyebrows, said, "Perfectly true. Only too true. It was most opportune for us. We have known for a long time what we have come to and how things stand with us. Such a clear example could only be of use to us, serve to unmask things so that no doubts are left. Because we know that Germany cannot get back on its feet if such evil is not disclosed, not before the abscess has festered and burst."

Becker, still quite calm and completely sure of himself: "And you consider yourselves, and those whom you represent, at the academy and elsewhere, you consider yourselves—pure and clean and without blemish?"

"What does that mean?"

"I mean, so free of blemish that you begrudge a poor man who has paid for his mistakes with his life, the presence of a friend at his grave."

"We want to serve the general public. I repeat. For that purpose we can demand that each individual make his sacrifice and suppress even the most notable of his personal feelings."

Becker (I'm slipping completely into *Antigone*. King Creon will be here soon to have me arrested): "There is neither a public nor a general interest that could deter me from showing a poor man the last token of my affection."

The two gentlemen had risen at the same time that Becker rose. They exchanged glances and marched to the door. The older one, the voluble bald man, felt it necessary to turn around once more to assure him, "You will soon have some contact with that general public, Herr Dr. Becker."

* * *

348

As the door slammed behind them, Heinz entered. He had heard it all.

Becker sat there highly enraged, immobile, with a pale, hard face, harder than Heinz had ever seen it.

Those who had just departed were the righteous ones. They had left, proud and sure of themselves. And a man has been lost. A lost sheep from the herd, a human soul, a soul worth just as much as the ninety and nine righteous men. We neglected to do our duty by him. I wonder if our prayers will come to his aid? Anger, veritable hatred consumed Becker totally. Without moving, his eyes dry and his expression rigid, he sat there in front of Heinz, who took fright. The boy tapped him on the hand, he was afraid while Becker continued to sit there in enigmatic gloom. Then all at once the demon departed from Becker. He ran his hand over his face, stood up and led the boy with him into his study.

Heinz was cheerful. Becker had told them both where to get off.

Friedrich: "And all the while I didn't dare let on to those two that we're not sure we're going to have a funeral."

Heinz: "Be careful, they'll play some trick or other on us."

Becker: "I would guess so too."

Heinz: "It's a disgrace that he's still lying there at the morgue. If they don't give him to us soon, I'll take him out by force."

"How are you going to manage that."

Heinz thrust his hands in his pockets. "I can't do it alone."

"I'm here too, you know."

"No, I can't use you for that."

He considered.

Becker: "What've you got in mind?"

Heinz: "I'm thinking if we do get the casket, where do we take it?"

Becker: "I have a somewhat less crazy idea. It is noon now. We'll go over to Moabit and I'll ask around until I find the prosecuting attorney handling the case."

Heinz: "But he's forbidden anyone to do that."

Becker: "All the more reason."

They took off. Becker was ready to meet great difficulties just in making inquiries about the precise officials to deal with. But things went surprisingly quickly, and after a brief wait he was let in to see the prosecutor, a businesslike, serious gentleman. The man had the portfolio brought into him, because, he said, Dr. Becker, whose name he recognized from the documents, probably wanted an official statement about the matter. He was amazed when Becker presented his request.

"But the body has not been impounded."

"That is what they told me at the morgue."

"But I assure you, there must be some mistake. The body was impounded only until we received the coroner's report. When were you there?"

Becker: "In person, yesterday. But I telephoned this morning and was given this information."

"Strange. Wait a minute."

He reached for the telephone and had himself connected with the morgue. After a short conversation he turned to Becker. "Apparently you spoke with the wrong person. Go on over there and demand to speak with Director K."

Becker walked slowly through the Palace of Justice. Everywhere in its massive corridors he met groups of people waiting to get into particular rooms: witnesses in cases, family members and the curious. And the director had now gotten caught up in this machinery of justice after his death. Now the day had finally come before which he had hidden himself in fear his whole life long.

Heinz, who was told to stay outside the main entrance, came running over from the far side of the street. The building had disgusted him. He cursed when he heard that the body had been released all along. But Becker admitted that he was gradually gaining respect for their opponents.

Becker: "We'll get over there right away. But you stay outside, otherwise there'll be a fight."

Heinz: "I'll come to blows with somebody about this thing before it's over."

They had Becker wait out in the corridor. The constant reply was that Director K. was busy. Then the official who had dealt with Becker yesterday came down the corridor carrying some files. Becker walked up to him: how long would it be until he could speak with Director K.

The official: "I can't provide you with any information about that, but what do you want, really. You were here just yesterday."

Becker: "In the meantime I've been at Moabit, and the prosecutor told me that the director's body has been released."

"I see. Well then I'll have to go find out about that myself."

At that, he went to his office, and Becker was forced to wait for a considerable time once again. Then the official called him in, acted friendly enough, seemed embarrassed and stiff and explained that there was a dreadful uproar here at the morgue, as might be expected, because of the revolution—new corpses daily that needed to be identified and autopsied. Becker could not see what this had to do with his problem and what had in fact happened. At any rate, the man informed him, he was quite obliging now, that the whole matter had now been set in order, and that Becker need only get in touch with a funeral parlor and arrange the details.

Becker and Heinz, informed now that they had no reason to meet with Director K., who was ostensibly busy with no letup, took counsel out on the street about what to do, and they decided to notify an undertaker at once. They spent yet another hour in the vicinity of the morgue, and personally supervised the removal of the body. Heinz had to convince himself personally that it was coffin twelve hundred eleven that was shoved up onto the wagon. The afternoon was filled with nerve-racking formalities.

On the morning of Friday, January 10, the burial took place. They stood side by side in the dim light of the small room—besides Becker and Heinz there were Becker's mother and Dr. Krug. Four wreaths lay on the coffin—no priest, no organ. The clergyman whom Becker's mother had asked to attend had refused on the grounds that the dead man would have placed no value on his presence.

So the man who loved beauty and joy was lifted from the catafalque at exactly nine-fifteen, and carried out of the room by stocky men in black. Becker walked with his mother, Dr. Krug next to Heinz.

The dug-out rectangle and the fresh mound of earth indicated the spot. The joyful dance on earth had come to an end, the lover of the transient show now gave himself over to it completely, let it do its work.

After they had thrown three handfuls of dirt, Becker spoke a prayer aloud. His mother and Heinz murmured along, Krug stepped to one side. Only when the men shoveled earth onto the coffin did Heinz break out crying like a little boy, so that Becker's mother took him in her arms. Then came the epilogue. Led by the cemetery guard, two men walked up quickly to the freshly dug grave, and before the members of the funeral party knew what was happening, lights began to flash. They were being photographed. Just as quickly, the two men turned around and vanished.

Krug: "The press. I expected that."

The mother: "They're hounding the poor man even beyond the grave."

Krug: "This time it has less to do with him than with us."

Heinz was amazed that anyone knew that the funeral was taking place at that hour.

King Creon

They remained together in Becker's apartment for a bite to eat. While Heinz helped Becker's mother, Becker talked with Krug.

"It hurts me to the depths of my soul, Krug, to see you in your present company. I've been outlawed. Wasn't this an imprudent move on your part?"

"That's my affair. You've given me inspiration, Becker. The visit by those two musty men from the parents' council got my dander up. I said to myself: that's how it's going to be, I'm not going to quit the field for that bunch."

"I'm glad you're not sorry."

"Good lord, man, what do you take me for? What have I done to deserve that?"

Becker, sitting on his chaise longue, was depressed. He was still wound up in the funeral.

"And so now we've buried him. What did he achieve with his death? Remember, Krug, what we were like ourselves—to be sure, not just like him, but close enough. He sought and found some justification for himself among the Greeks and the philosophers. But ultimately, what is this beauty, this joy, this love that he was so enthusiastic about and for which he went to his death? What is it? He acted as if it came from nature, as if it were the true state of nature. But I think that's not the case. It all seems very human to me, and human not in the good sense. What is behind such urges, whether you take this man or that; is it really nature? How much of it is really instinct, an organic drive, nature in the sense of hunger and thirst? A person tries to entertain himself, looks for excitement and variety, thrills and tension. That is the way with everything erotic. I would guess that not ten percent of our eroticism is from nature, by which I mean, truly instinctual, organic. An instinct is there, but we reshape it into our eroticism and add the other ninety percent ourselves, making the erotic a grand human thing, perhaps a habit or maybe a vice, a human thing, a matter of the mind or a product of the imagination. Second nature, if you will. But we leave our mark as the party responsible."

This gave even Krug something to think about. He replied that there was some truth in that. He was only slowly learning that now.

Becker: "Who is going to help you see it, when half the world has conspired to turn this product of man into his second nature? Look at our literature, the theater, lyric poetry, not to speak of music, of the opera. Everything revolves around the thing to which they give the name 'love.' If only it were just lust! But it's all merely cultivated. Am I boring you, Krug?"

He shook his head vigorously.

"I've known for a long time that we civilized men are exploiters of nature. We don't just rob the earth and, under certain conditions, our fellowmen, but also our own natural dowry to use it for our own purposes. Apparently we couldn't go on living any other way."

"What did you say? We couldn't go on living? But are we alive like this? Think of the director. He was driven by his instincts, and then was swallowed up entirely by his passion."

His mother knocked—the food was ready.

"Nevertheless, I hope," Krug replied as they went into the next room, "you're not going to develop into a misogynist."

Afterward, when both Krug and his mother had taken their leave, Heinz was left behind with Becker, who had lain down for a rest. Heinz said something about wanting to go over to the cemetery to take some flowers.

"Do that," Becker said, holding the *Odyssey* in his hand. "Here in the eleventh canto, Odysseus thinks of the dead as he continues his long sea voyage. He goes down into the underworld and sacrifices animals, and then the shades approach, the souls of the dead, wanting to drink the blood from the pit."

Becker let the book fall.

"That's the notion the Greeks had of the dead."

"And what is their existence really like?" Heinz asked softly. "What do you think?"

Becker, just as softly, as if the dead were listening to him: "My idea is that those who have left us have not yet exhausted life once they have ended their earthly pilgrimage. This life is so filled with dreadful accidents. The last word has not yet been spoken."

Heinz put his hand to his face again. He shook his head and suddenly began to weep bitterly. He ran off, and as evening fell he had not come back.

A worried Becker went to the Riedel's apartment building the next morning and made inquiries. From the doorman he learned that the boy had in fact spent the night there, but had left early in the morning.

"A clever man," the porter remarked. "He's out looking for work. That's how they are nowadays."

Disturbed, Becker returned home, where a surprise awaited him. The school had sent over a whole bundle of telegrams, all of them addressed to Becker at the academy. His mother was waiting impatiently for him.

"Let's have a look," he said in amazement.

There were congratulations from a "Group of Progressive Berliners," who greeted him as their "fellow citizen" and a "brave warrior against medieval prejudices."

One telegram, signed by a Free Socialist Cultural Club, shouted, "Bravo, forward to storm the Bastille."

A "League for Sexual Reform" congratulated him on his manly and unflinching stand, and expressed its hope that they would soon have the opportunity of greeting him personally in the circle of their membership. "You can count on our total support in your struggle."

The telegram from an attorney, to whom the deceased "had turned when his back was to the wall" and to whom he had dictated his last testament. He regretted not having heard anything about the funeral. Besides the telegrams, two letters, one a thick one; the return address on the envelope said Dr. Krug. The letter contained a newspaper. The evening paper had published on its front page the photograph of yesterday's graveside scene. Becker, Krug, and Heinz, seen from the front, Becker's mother with her back turned. Beneath it stood their names, and the whole thing was headlined: Funeral Services for Director X. at G. Cemetery.

The other letter contained an official document, a short note from the hand of the deputy director of the academy. If his health allowed it, Dr. Becker should report tomorrow morning between ten and twelve to Herr School Inspector Y. at City Hall.

"Wait a couple of days before you go," his mother advised. "In the meantime things will have quieted down."

Becker: "They want to interrogate me. The two men who were here to see me have blown the whistle."

He was likewise very concerned about Heinz. He asked his mother to look to see if Heinz were hanging about the area if she got anywhere near the cemetery.

"But, Friedrich, he's not going to prowl around there like a dog."

Becker: "It's only a notion I had. But where can the boy have gone?"

He pulled out his watch. "I'm going to be on my way. I'm going to City Hall, but before that I'll have a look at the cemetery."

"Friedrich, you're on the warpath."

"People are attacking me. I'm not going to let them get their ugly way."

"You're upset."

"And why shouldn't I be, Mother? If you had seen those two men, those two self-righteous men, you wouldn't act any differently. Mother, do you recall how upset you got the first time you saw that man with cancer being mistreated by his family. You didn't rest either until you had gotten the man out of that house."

She smiled sadly. "True, I didn't rest."

"And was that the wrong thing to do, Mother?"

"The man is back home again now. Yes, at home. He was doing very well at the clinic. But he insisted he be taken back home."

Friedrich shook his head. "And his family is mistreating him as before."

"The wife treats him especially badly. I arrived as she was accusing him of compromising the family and embarrassing them by letting himself be admitted to the clinic. But do you think they really want to live in peace? I had thought so. But that's not how it is. The doctor is right: this man requires his daily squabble. That's the point of his life. He makes himself miserable and shames himself in order to apologize to me for making a mess that I have to clean up; but he simply couldn't bear to be readmitted to the clinic, the peaceful, quiet clinic. I would like to visit him more often. But I can hardly do that now. I would have to belittle myself in front of that woman. She's celebrating her triumph. She's been proven right. Isn't that discouraging? But you just can't let yourself get discouraged."

She couldn't convince Friedrich not to go to City Hall at once. First he went by the cemetery, where he found fresh flowers on the grave, almost certainly put there by Heinz. But no trace of Heinz himself. Where had he gone? He definitely hadn't gone off to see his mother. If only he doesn't go after someone from the academy.

In this nervous state, Friedrich arrived at City Hall, and was immediately admitted.

The school inspector, an older man of medium build with a full gray beard—he wore very thick glasses that apparently did not give him full sight nevertheless—was sitting bent over documents at his desk; he was wearing a frayed black morning coat with leather-patched elbows. He expressed surprise that Becker had come so promptly and that he looked so fresh and healthy. He had assumed he was very ill from the description given him. To one side of his desk lay the newspaper with the photograph of the funeral.

The gentleman pulled his chair closer to Becker, his face only a hand's breadth distant. He seemed to take a lively interest in his visitor. He corrected his mistake, as he inspected Becker's face from all angles: he wasn't quite as healthy as he had first thought him to be.

He now began in a querulous tone, "What is actually wrong with you, Herr Dr. Becker? What is the point of what you are doing in the matter of the deceased director? You know the details of this ghastly affair, an assault on a student by a teacher, seduction of a minor, etc. What, indeed, are your real intentions? Tell me clearly, once and for all."

Becker, annoyed by the man's officious gaping at him, could not find his first sentence right away. The inspector, whose head was right next to him, almost on top of him, forged ahead, pressing him hard.

"You must have some notion of what you were doing. The affair has raised an awful lot of dust. I'm sure you've read the paper. As a teacher who wasn't hired by the public school system just yesterday, you must have had some idea of how your official supervisors would react to your conduct." As a symbol of the probable eventualities, he made large circles in the air with a heavy blue pencil. "In whatever we do, we always keep your reactions in mind."

Now Becker was ready, and he answered.

He had known the deceased. He had also heard of his tendencies, and even when the director was still on the job he had been in contact with him, advising him to take a vacation. Nevertheless this terrible thing had occurred.

The inspector growled, "I see, I see. A vacation would not have served our purposes much."

He was microscopically close to Becker's face now, breathing on him. "And then?"

"Nothing more. I have nothing further to report, Herr School Inspector." Becker turned his face to one side.

"Well, well. You did go to his funeral yesterday. That's in the paper. Here is your picture. You recognize it. The senior student, Riedel, the boy who was involved in the affair, was there as well. Let me see," he picked up the paper, "yes, you, Riedel and Dr. Krug, and your mother as well." He shook his head. "The whole thing leaves a strange impression. I've been told that you personally covered the expenses for the funeral. You'll surely be reimbursed for those. But what is one supposed to think of all this? Speak openly. What is the point of it all? What did you intend?"

He pulled back from Becker, scratched his beard and began speaking before Becker could utter a word, his blue pencil lifted as before.

"Do you in any way approve of the director's actions? Or were you in any way induced or forced to take up the cause of the deceased? No one compelled you to get involved, and surely not to such an extent. Moreover, you were on leave, and without our knowledge and without our permission you took up your old position—though that's only a tangential matter, that wasn't your fault. But all the same, you get actively involved and go to war against the whole world. You've just returned from the front. We know that the men who were out there are not happy with a great deal that is happening here. As they should not be. But this sort of filthiness . . ."

"How do you mean, Herr School Inspector?"

"Your behavior, however you may account for or explain it, even if the man were your closest friend, is unacceptable. You were an officer, and have distinguished yourself in service. Such an affair is not worthy of you."

Becker: "Was I invited to come here, Herr School Inspector, in order for you to tell me this?"

"I am not finished."

"If you wish, I can immediately tender my resignation."

"But not a word has been said of that."

The bearded man crawled back to his desk and buried himself in his documents. He wallowed there, flipping pages. Turning back to Becker, he muttered, "You've caused us great embarrassment. One really has no other choice—. One would only like to know what's going on in that head of yours, that you would provoke such a scandal, and why, in such an absolutely clearcut case, you have chosen to take on the whole world, the school, the faculty and the parents."

Becker answered (who is this man, who are these officials): "I have not taken on anyone, neither the general public, nor the faculty nor the parents. I knew the deceased. He paid for his sins. When he died, I could not deny him the same respect we show to everyone who departs this life. He died as a man with his weaknesses and vices, which in his case were especially dreadful. We all have our weaknesses. We two have other ones. And then the director was dead. I had no intention of continuing to dwell on his infirmities. We stood on the same level. I had no advantage over him, and had to recognize him as my fellow human being. If others chose to exclude themselves from his funeral, that is something for which they must answer. It is for me to pray to God for his poor soul."

The inspector, who had edged up close again as if he wanted to get his answers at the source, jerked back. He could not believe he had

357

heard correctly. He held his lips as if he were ready to give a whistle. From where he sat he first looked askance at Becker, blinked, and since he still could not see Becker all too well, he held the back of his hand up to his nose and appeared to want to count the hairs on it. He really did whistle softly now.

Suddenly he remarked, "Hmm, hmm," and then, "I see, I see." He asked if by chance Dr. Becker knew the chief school inspector.

Becker said he didn't.

The man: "No? But he told me that he knows you. Wait just a moment."

The man seemed to be totally perplexed. At the door he turned around to Becker as if to assure himself that this was a man and not some hallucination. But once again, from that distance he could not see him so very well, could not make a decision in that regard, and so gave up and vanished.

It took ten minutes before he appeared again, in a good mood, his hands in his trouser pockets. He whistled softly and moved past Becker, nodding his head, and then sat down in his chair as if in triumph.

"So then, Herr Dr. Becker, here we are again. The chief inspector has been fully informed. He does know you, by the way. So now you can come with me."

They passed through several offices, then entered a librarylike room where they were met by a robust, dignified gentleman with gold spectacles, who, as the inspector withdrew, took Becker by the hand in a friendly way and led him over to a leather armchair next to his desk. He himself sat jauntily on the corner of the desk.

"You're not aware, Dr. Becker, that we are acquainted? No? Through your good mother. She works in the same patriotic women's club as my wife, and I have often had the pleasure of greeting your mother in my own home, if only very briefly. And how is Frau Becker? And how is your health, Dr. Becker? Excellent. You're looking quite well, not enough fresh air, but otherwise hale and buoyant. Ah yes, youth finds a way. We old folks don't have things so easy."

A pause.

The chief inspector: "Yes, we've been concerned about you, Dr. Becker—first of all, because you've been working at the academy without having notified us of the fact, but we'll not speak of that. And then, yes—and then. You've probably seen your picture in the paper. You're all the news, a kind of celebrity. Has anyone interviewed you yet? No? That will happen. So then, you can now give me your first

358

interview. Tell me about the entire affair in as much detail as you can."

Becker acted perfectly naturally. The chief inspector, who sat down at his chair behind his desk while Becker spoke, watched him attentively. Finally, after a long pause to consider, he said, "So then, you're not denying the culpability and reprehensibility of the director's actions lying at the core of the matter? That brings us a major step forward. Nonetheless, as you can see for yourself in the papers, this was the impression that was given to the public. Especially after this spectacle with the funeral. We were terribly concerned. People were asking us: what is with this man? And now we are at least clear as to your motives, and in that sense relieved. That makes me very happy. Very courageous of you, Dr. Becker, the way you turn your views of man's duties, including those we owe the dead, into deeds. Personally, that pleases me. Impresses me."

He extended his hand to Becker. They stood up. The audience seemed to have come to an end.

The official: "Here is a man who brings something else back home besides coarseness and savagery—courage. We can use that here now, in every area of life. That the battlefield taught men that, delights me. Just look, Dr. Becker, what's happening right here in our immediate vicinity on Alexanderplatz. Civil war, a war among the men we have educated, or should have educated, with all of whom we shared the same set of principles, the duties we owe our fellow citizens and our Fatherland. It is a censure of our whole educational system. Something is wrong: either our principles or we ourselves. The latter appears to me the more probable. And then you simply go bravely to work, doing what you must do, all by yourself. You walk right in," he laughed, shaking his head in amazement, "and bury an old sinner. But that is not the point. The result has been a scandal. That makes no difference to you; you only note that it is the case. Fine. Excellent. It only gives you a little shove on your way. Or at least it should give you one. I'll tell my wife all about you."

Becker directed his gaze at the chief inspector. "Since the civil war has led you to think that either our principles or we ourselves are of no value, what conclusions do you draw from that?"

The clever man laid a hand on Becker's shoulder.

"You see, there you are. Drawing conclusions, right off. That is the courage I was talking about. I don't know, dear friend. I would like to learn from you. A civil servant does not have things so easy; he can't exercise the rights a private person can. I know, you're a civil servant, too, a teacher. And you dare to do it nevertheless. As I said, very rare. How very much I would like, as a private individual, to affirm what you have presented here. Without qualification. From my heart of hearts. But just remember what building this is that we're in, what office I hold. 'But things are jostled hard in such narrow quarters.'"

He spread his arms with a comic look of terror. "It isn't just the parents and the teachers and the school bureaucracy and the newspapers. Beyond that are—the ministries. I am but a drop of water in a great sea. It's been a pleasure, Dr. Becker. Many thanks. And my regards to your mother."

The nearsighted inspector was soon back in the office of his boss, who had rung for him and was now sitting there pondering.

The chief inspector: "You're right, my good colleague, it's a hopeless case. And yet what an attractive fellow, very attractive. And it almost shames me to say it, but he won't do. He brought this back with him from the war, in addition to his wounds, this sort of courage, this refusal to yield on principles. Reminds me in fact of Michael Kohlhaas. Some of them take off for the Baltic wars wanting to prove what patriotism and the Fatherland mean, and others—insist on burying their dead. He was, by the by, an excellent teacher."

The inspector: "They say he had a nervous breakdown."

"Is that right? Nothing in his file about that. In fact, a little taste of that sort of a breakdown wouldn't do any of us any harm. He's following the path he believes to be the right one, and since he has no intention of taking other advice, there's nothing we can do."

"And what measures do we take?"

The chief inspector: "We can take comfort in the fact that personalities of that sort always find a certain satisfaction within themselves. We," he shook his head gloomily, "we simply have to let him go his way. It would be dreadful if we found it necessary to make a formal request for his dismissal."

Becker stood on the steps facing Königstrasse and pulled up the collar of his coat. A piercingly cold wind was blowing.

An attractive man, the chief inspector. He'd like to do the right thing, but not desperately. He'll not defend me against the hue and cry.

But going down the stairs, Friedrich was no longer thinking of his own situation. What had happened to Heinz?

It worried him.

Becker felt drawn toward Alexanderplatz; but moving up Königstrasse, he found his way blocked at the railroad station.

You could hear shots. Becker's anxiety increased. Something dark lay upon Becker like a heavy burden. He had emerged from City Hall, but there was still that murdered man, that poor sinner whom they had buried. And his story had not yet come to an end. What were his intentions for Heinz, would he not let him go even now?

Becker rode back out to the cemetery again, brought a bouquet with him, and laid it next to Heinz's. He wanted to mollify this dreadful corpse. He begged him to show mercy. He prayed long and fervently for the peace of that poor soul.

As Becker left he was literally dizzy. The visit to the grave had not freed him at all. He was all knotted up inside. Something was not right with Heinz. He had to rescue him.

After January 6th

For this is now the hour when the dead shall hear the voice of the Son of God, and they that hear shall live, and the others shall not live.

January 6th has passed. This Monday with its dreadful painful spectacle, with its cast of hundreds of thousands who gathered, waited and stood ready for battle on the Siegesallee and then wandered about forlorn in the streets of Berlin, has come to its end. It has sunk into the past. People let it sink.

Now the hour of the black swan has come.

The black swan has begun to move. It flies soundlessly, its neck outstretched, its wings spread wide, its little feet balled up beneath it like paws. With an easy beat its wings bear it forward.

Karl was unable to halt the disintegration in the ranks of the revolution. Now he was alone. And he took hold of himself again. He was the man of lost causes.

The negotiating committee, the execution committee, was hard at work. As arranged, they found their way back to the Reichs Chancellery at eleven the next morning, and spent hours in a discussion doomed never to shift out of neutral. The Revolutionary Shop Stewards stood fast. There could be no question of the release of the newspaper offices, which the government demanded in the name of "freedom of the press." They would not, they declared, begin with a capitulation. The newspapers were not a matter for negotiation. They said frankly—for the atmosphere was so bad that it could not have been ruined any further—the government apparently wanted to meet force with force.

Their speeches made no impression on the government. It stood by its demand: first release of the newspapers, then negotiations.

As the negotiating team appeared on Schicklerstrasse that afternoon with this result—that is, with empty hands—the people there understood: the situation was serious. They were facing a catastrophe.

And then a whispering began among the Independents, the way one whispers when one wants to send out the signal to flee. One dare not make the issue of the newspapers the central issue. The gentlemen crossed their arms, furrowed their brows and cleared their throats: "uh-hmm, uh-hmm!" While they walked about, they began speaking of higher views, and of the real goals of their actions (which was to go home), whereas the newspapers played a subordinate role (indeed). They postponed these negotiations, which had in fact been none at all. They had the feeling that they would be able to speak louder tomorrow morning.

But the men in the government were doing just that today. They had no need to discuss the matter. They differed from their opponents in one important way: they knew what they wanted. A certain Herr B., a majority Socialist and editor for *Vorwärts*—that newspaper that kept getting away from them—had used the night between January 6th and 7th to occupy the Reichstag building and the Brandenburg Gate with a force of forty men, something the revolutionaries had neglected to do. (No, the revolutionaries had not forgotten it, they simply had so infinitely much to discuss, one with the other—and all the while each quarreling with himself—that they did not even get around to thinking at all.) While it was still dark, Herr B. sent for volunteers on trucks and by morning he was able to announce the conquest of the Reichstag building and the Brandenburg Gate, which encouraged such a massive flood of volunteers to join his troops that a whole regiment, the Reichstag Regiment, could be mustered. The War Ministry sent over Colonel G. to serve as its military advisor.

Already by January 7th the revolution had lost one of its own few conquests: the central railroad office. Pioneers stormed the building and "cleared" it of Spartacists, as they put it. This was in point of fact a breach of the agreed-upon armistice. But no one was bothered by that. Since who was there to protest against it?

The objections, moreover, which the revolutionaries raised against the suddenly neutralist People's Naval Division, convulsed nothing more than the air. What did you expect from sailors? Were they supposed to go to great expense merely to retrieve a position already lost? They had had enough of that. What was the point of these eternal references to the splendid battle for the royal stables and of statements proclaiming that the sailors formed the avant-garde of the revolution. That was behind them. Really, you could go around playing the avant-garde of the revolution for weeks on end without being it—and so they decided once and for all to be what they were. They had just finished taking up arms for higher pay; and now they were neutral, and were waiting for the permanent post that had been guaranteed them. The "Ladybugs" went even further than these sailors. The "Ladybugs" declared at once and with no provisos that they would remain faithful to the government for better or for worse, and offered to serve as its guards in the northern parts of the city.

Then on Wednesday, January 8th, whole segments of the security forces up and deserted the unfortunate Herr Eichhorn, placing themselves under the command of Charlottenburg police headquarters and of the municipal commander of Berlin.

That same Wednesday, at around three in the afternoon, the negotiators approached the Reichs Chancellery once again, for the last time, with knees shaking and their heavy portfolios in hand. This time they didn't even dare mention the subject of breaches in the armistice agreement. They immediately humbled themselves timorously before the government, offering to take several steps backward. They were prepared, they declared, to hand over the bourgeois presses if the government and the Executive Council would agree to begin negotiations about the other questions, including the occupation of *Vorwärts*, immediately upon the completion of their doing so.

The representatives of the government, and cold fellows they were, knew that these people had nothing to offer them. They were simply amazed that these gentlemen were still at it and seriously thought that they would deal with them. The negotiators, with the sweat of fear on their brows, received their answers: "No, either freedom of the press or . . ."

And then finally the negotiators understood. They had to have it beaten into them with cudgels. Silently and grimly they packed up all their long-since superfluous documents and left the Reichs Chancellery never to return. They had done what they could, they muttered darkly, it was not their fault. History would judge this matter differently, etc.—world history is the world's court . . . , and "John, John the gray goose is gone" and "Tell me why the stars do shine."

They disappeared in the dark, not without having first issued the following proclamation:

"We no longer see ourselves in a position to continue our mission;

nevertheless we assure both parties that we are ready once again to take up our task as negotiators, since we hold it to be our duty to avoid bloodshed."

Thus spake the rabbit to the vulture as the latter grasped it in his talons: "Woe to you, for I am blameless if blood is shed here."

Quite apart from these protestations and the honest love of peace shown by the negotiators, on this same Wednesday afternoon the armistice, already bent, crushed and mutilated several times over, was now once again broken with a vengeance. Even the greatest lover of peace had to ask himself whether there was in fact still such a thing as an armistice. For ultimately what differentiates an armistice with so many fractures in it from no armistice at all, or put another way, from war? This time it was the Guard Fusiliers who took their rage out so brutally on the armistice. They had designs on the Reichs Printing Office. A pack of workers from Schwartzkopf Industries had barricaded themselves inside. The possession of the Reichs Printing Office was of great use to the revolutionaries, since contained therein were some eighteen million marks in paper bills, and they had even greater designs, since they were in control of the plates as well. With the Reichs Printing Office behind you, you didn't need to act as pitifully as the sailors had in December for the sake of a few lousy marks. All the world knows that if you want to make war, you need cash, and the revolutionaries had it, for a few days, and then they didn't have it anymore. And even during those few days they had only appeared to have it.

For they couldn't get at those lovely millions. Why not? The bills were lying in the cellars, and the revolutionaries didn't have the keys; and no German revolutionary would stoop so low as to break in and steal. Those nasty bureaucrats in the Reichs Chancellery had the keys; they would not hand them over. Everywhere bureaucrats were making things difficult for the revolution in Germany, impeding its march toward victory. The revolutionaries spent the whole time they occupied the building coaxing, begging, pleading with the bureaucrats to please, please open up the cellar. The gentlemen did not want to. They showed them the keys, but they said, "We're not opening up." Enough to drive a man to despair.

The revolutionaries tore out their hair and strewed it in bunches along the streets. But it did not turn into money. At one point Emil Eichhorn, the current chief of police for Berlin and the notorious root of all evil, appeared at the building and declared that even he too needed money—argent, bread, wherewithall—at once, he had several thousand men to feed and pay. Tempter that he was, he urged the heroes of the Reichs Printing Office to get him the money. But they stood firm, they would do nothing illegal. And after all, what did Eichhorn know about the bureaucrats of the Reichs Printing Office and how stubborn they were?

But finally this team of workers took fright. They had elected a civil engineer to be their commander, and he was advised by a certain Herr R. Both men were already bald from tearing out their hair. And when Eichhorn happened to make the remark that if this was how things looked and how they stood then he didn't know how he was going to be able to hold headquarters—why then the civil engineer and his adviser lost their courage, their hearts were in their boots. And they saw visible proof of all this when, on the evening of January 8th, shots were fired outside, some of them even hitting the building itself while all of Hausvogtei Platz nearby, along with its confectionary stores, seemed to explode at once. For at that moment, a chancery official by the name of Schulze had set things in motion, having sworn that he would take the Reichs Printing Office that very day. What drove him to do this, no one knew, but it had come over him, and it was reported that he had been made a lieutenant, not a bad idea it would seem. As a lieutenant at the head of the Guard Fuseliers—as many of them that is who were still around—he stormed the building. The revolutionaries, bickering among themselves and, as we noted, in a miserable state, handed over their arms to the intruders; they really didn't know what to do with them anyway. They said: let Lieutenant Schulze see how he was going to get around those old bureaucrats. They were happy to have him conquer the Reichs Printing Office. Lieutenant Schulze praised the civil engineer and his adviser for their integrity, and even the bureaucrats shook his hand.

The shooting out there on Hausvogtei Platz, however, lasted on through half the night. This gunfire came from the weapons of the former occupation troops, from a number of weapons that had been leaned against the trees as the men fled—automatic weapons, which, angered at not being used, discharged themselves.

Fat little Ebert sat quiet and content all the while, and had the glad tidings brought to him. There was no one any longer taken with the notion of locking him in or chasing him off. That itself was great progress. He observed with some amazement and satisfaction what was going on outside, and with even greater amazement and satisfaction what was not going on. He decided the moment had come to speak to the people. He spoke:

"Fellow citizens!

"Spartacus is now using every bit of strength it has to wage war." (Ha, ha, all its strength—they're being run off like rabbits, but we must keep chasing them down until they lie dead.)

"Their intent is to topple this government." (Nobody can accuse me of not having a sense of humor.)

"The people are not supposed to be allowed to speak." (How fine. I mean that in all seriousness. That's why our main demands are "freedom of the press" and "democracy must take its stand against dictatorship," and whoever maintains the contrary will have to take pointers from Gustav Noske.)

"Where Spartacus is in the saddle, every form of personal freedom and security is abrogated, "(Proof: they locked me in here)" the press is suppressed, transport brought to a halt.

"Have patience just a little while longer.

"Force can only be met with force. The day of reckoning is near." (How I wish it were already here!)

He pulled open a drawer. The thick train timetable shone up at him. He took it in his hand with satisfaction and apostrophized the object:

What all has happened in the time since we last conversed, O precious timetable. Scheidemann came tripping in here and talked me out of my trip. He thought the whole problem was with my liver. Yes, the worm has turned. Now I'm no longer in search of you, precious timetable, I am only looking for my blue pencil, so that I can underline what needs to be printed in caps in my speech.

Thursday, January 9th. Ebert's henchman, the lanky Noske, stepped in. Ebert greeted him.

"Hello, my friend. What's happening in Dahlem? How are you coming along with your girls' academy?"

Noske, who has not even had the chance to press his hands against the seam of his trousers and report: "Your Majesty, the horses have been saddled, the battle can begin," has his reservations. Quite a few things are still lacking. But all the same he assured him that the blow to be dealt the radicals this time will be so powerful and so definitive that those long dead would now have to admit that they hadn't any idea of what it meant to be dead.

That sounded comforting. But when, please?

Noske pointed out the turnabout in affairs that had occurred since Christmas, when that smart-aleck Lieutenant Dorrenbach had pressed Noske so hard:

366

"We'll extract the thorn painlessly. By the way, yesterday Major von Gilsa and I had a look at that boarding school for girls over twelve that's been put at our disposal. Conclusion: we'll shortly be ready to advance on Berlin and execute the disarmament we've promised right on time. We must be absolutely sure before we move."

"Of course," Ebert replied, thinking back on all the previous lovely, miscarried plans. "I'm of the exact same opinion. We cannot yield now. They won't give us back *Vorwärts* . . ."

Noske: "And if they do give it back. . . ."

Ebert, soothing him: "No, they're not going to give it back, and— yes, you're right, even if they did, we must make an example of them once and for all in the interests of stable government, especially in the eyes of other countries what with peace negotiations at hand."

Noske: "Correct. The foreign component is something my officers remind me of every day. Those gentlemen are literally overawed by the Red Terror. They're just burning for the moment . . ."

"To do what?"

Noske: "Why, to restore their lost honor."

Ebert raised a finger. "How? At whose cost? Be careful, Gustav. I've told you often enough."

Noske: "I know them like the palm of my hand. They're honest men and concerned patriots."

Ebert: "We too, you and I are too, and the next thing you know Liebknecht will stand up and say he is as well. But as far as the officers go, they've always wanted to have a monopoly on patriotism. And afterward they'll present us with a hefty bill for services rendered."

Noske, who knew this line of argument from Ebert, shuffled uncomfortably through his documents and then continued, "All right, Fritz, we have determined that we are in command of the Guard Cavalry Rifles, Captain Pabst is mustering a full corps right this minute. In Zossen, as you know, we have the Maerker troops, our pride and backbone. Fritz, I think I can guarantee you that the next time our troops march into town, which I am preparing for now, it won't be the pitiful scene it was last time, with men in top hats standing around the Brandenburg Gate and telling you what you're to think and what the officers think and what the citizenry thinks and what the workers think. You won't be standing around out there at all. You'll be here sitting quietly in your office, and you'll get a telephone call from me once we've got the whole thing nailed down tight."

Ebert listened to this with great satisfaction.

Noske: "Moreover we have my own personal brigade, sixteen hundred men, absolutely dependable, all of them mad as hell at this so-called revolution."

"Are they for the republic as well, however?"

"But of course. My people especially hate the sailors who started this whole monkey business, and if I let them loose on the sailors then you can be certain that it's sailors they'll go for. I've had them brought in from Kiel in small doses. They didn't want to release them there. But now they're quartered out in the Mark. The farmers are mighty glad to see them; they're all soldiers to the man, noncoms and warrant officers, an elite troop."

Ebert: "I see."

Noske: "At their head are experienced front-line officers. You know that the 'Ladybugs' are seeing to the security of the northern part of the city. Besides which we have got hold of the Residents' Militia and commissioned them to see to things in the western suburbs. Not everything is working perfectly. We've turned down all Independents, but now many of our own comrades don't want to work with us again."

"Why not?"

"They're sensitive. It all seems too reactionary to them. Everyone has something to take exception to."

The black swan took flight soundlessly.

The slow beating of its wings took it forward.

At police headquarters, Emil Eichhorn brought the Revolutionary Committee to order.

They would not disband. They could not disband. They did not know what would happen now. But nothing was working now either. They were as perplexed as ever.

Karl Liebknecht and his friend Pieck held fast to the idea of an uprising. The Russian emissary, Radek, appeared in the building and pulled Karl over to one side: they should abandon this fight. They had met with defeat, just as the Bolsheviks had in September 1917. There was no help for it, they must proceed accordingly.

Karl: But they had not really even begun to fight.

And Rosa came to attack Karl, too, her old comrade-in-arms. She did not mince her words. She struggled passionately with him for the central issue in her life. But it was also Karl's life.

What were her arguments? She accused him again and again of having abandoned Party discipline, and this time it was not simply a matter of discipline being broken by a reactionary group like the Social Democratic caucus in the Reichstag in 1914, but by a revolutionary

368

cadre in the midst of battle. Karl was acting like some middle-class individualist who wanted to have his own way.

And so Rosa fought Karl, with her tongue and with her mind. But when she had cast him to the ground, and he sat there quietly, pale, his cheeks sunken, haggard, his hair turned very gray, things took on a different look. This was not how a middle-class individualist would look, someone who stubbornly wanted to have his way.

Karl admitted all the miscalculations, the lack of planning and the dangers in their enterprise, but he admitted it with a shrug of his shoulders and without drawing any consequences. They were amazed. They sat up, paying attention but no longer arguing. They looked at him and recalled May 1, 1916, when Karl marched at their head, so sure of himself, so fearless, a pillar of fire by night.

What was this? They did not understand him. He was no theoretician, but ultimately he must understand the reality of the situation. Gradually, as they watched him wander about and speak with others, they understood:

He had chosen this position and would not yield. He understood just as well as they and Radek the dangers in their situation. But he was sticking to what he had done. It was out of the question for him to pull back. He would not yield to reality. The people had risen up, he would not leave them in the lurch. Rosa sensed that he despised this reality she was holding up before him—just as much as she did ultimately. He would not flee before some shabby reality.

The black swan flew and slowly bore itself forward.

And how did things stand with her?

Did she not have to envy him?

There Must Be Heresies Among You

Karl could not be halted.

His place was no longer in the debating chambers (which he hated more than ever) but out on the street, among the men occupying the newspaper offices and everywhere else in the city where the rebels had barricaded themselves. He ran to the most dangerous spots in order to show people they had not been abandoned. He brought them all the same encouraging news, and above all he brought himself.

But plenty of news was trickling through—that at such and such a place people had deserted, that the leadership was not united and that negotiations were underway again. Yes, even Rosa didn't believe the action would be victorious, so it was said. And in fact, one day Rosa's secretary appeared at the *Vorwärts* building, sent by Rosa personally to give the combatants an idea of how things looked, and to urge them strongly not to let things come to a final choice. The fighters listened in virtual disbelief to this young woman Rosa had sent them, but then they went at her something terrible, cursing her and giving her a drastic message to take to Rosa. When Karl showed up later on, he found the whole building in such an uproar that it was all he could do to calm people down. He had no choice, although he himself was outraged at what had happened, but to explain it all as though the young secretary had misunderstood what was said to her and had gone far beyond anything Rosa had told her to say. The people should not, said Karl, be taken in by fibs and tall tales. They knew their Rosa, didn't they?

He could only speak out openly against Pieck, Dorrenbach, and a few others, complaining bitterly about their intrigues, and that now even the leadership of the Party was betraying these brave and enthusiastic warriors, hoping to harm their morale. Oh, he seethed, these theoreticians, these appeasers and parliamentarians could not get back to their desks and their lecterns fast enough. Revolution? Bah! Those in charge were philistines.

He wandered about without a roof over his head.

He knew just as well how things stood as the three wise men of his party, which was no longer his party. But he also knew what the wise men did not know, that this was a dreadfully crucial moment, and that so long as a spark still glimmered the great conflagration might still break out, and that all was not yet lost for the proletariat.

When, during his wanderings, he happened to run into Rosa and Radek in a bar on the Untere Friedrichstrasse, he sat down with them. Rosa started in with her usual violent accusations: when would he finally give in, just how far did he intend to push things, wasn't this enough? He did not even respond to her unending indictment about his breaking Party discipline. Tormented as he was, he pulled himself together and begged her, urged her, even pleaded with her to be consistent and apply the thesis she apparently took for absolutely proven, her unshakable principle, her battle-cry "you must work from the grassroots up," to the Russian revolution.

"Are you condemning the Russian revolution now, too, Rosa, which you can't make disappear from history by saying that it's no revolution because it's illegal or illegitimate and runs counter to your theoretical demands?"

Radek pricked up his ears.

"Karl, I'm sticking by my demand. We're not going to risk the fate of the proletariat. That's our fundamental principle. We'll not permit some general to lead a putsch only to become a tyrant later."

Karl, dully: "Tell that, please, to Radek, Rosa. Let him answer for me."

Radek put his hand in front of his face and grinned. She noticed it and threw him a caustic glance.

"Up till now we've always observed the principle that the proletariat should be organized democratically and that its undertakings should reflect a clearly thought through plan. You know that you don't have that—I'm not even speaking now of democracy—you have nothing but little splinter actions. That's supposed to be the proletariat? I see nothing but gangs, and I don't even know whether there aren't other people mixed up with them who aren't even proletarians. But I fear the worst."

Karl: "It's not a mass action yet, that's true. It's unnecessary for you to tell me that, and unfair for you to say so at this point. If we haven't overthrown the government yet and haven't achieved our other goals either, why haven't we? Because you are standing off to one side and sabotaging us and pretending to be the bigshots who know everything better than others."

Rosa, sharply: "We're not acting on emotions, that's all."

Karl: "And where are my emotions?"

Rosa: "Oh go on. You simply let yourselves be provoked into action."

Karl bent over the table to her. "And even if that's true, Rosa, please be reasonable now. If someone has typhoid fever, will he get better if someone else says to him: you shouldn't have drunk that water, you know. I told you so. What's the point of that? But last Sunday, when last Sunday the whole city of Berlin was set in motion, was that just a provocation? And on Monday? Afterward, you yourself wrote in the *Rote Fahne* that ten thousand proletarians from Berlin were wandering about without leadership, tens of thousands were bubbling over with the spirit of revolution—you spoke of the spirit of revolution, you see, Rosa."

"Karl, how gladly I'd like to help you, if only I knew how. It's our cause too you know."

Radek listened mutely, his head propped on his hand. Karl went on complaining about what was the point, what did Rosa want to accomplish with her accusations. Karl wasn't seeing the total situation, she said, and therefore should not be giving orders. And so all this talk was in vain and superfluous.

Radek gave a sigh when the two stopped speaking. "Karl, nothing's going to help. We've got to pull back."

Karl: "I wouldn't even think of it. I'll tell you both once again—and pass the message on to Leo, please, because I don't want to see him—that you are acting against the express wishes of the Party convention, and that you did not honestly come to my assistance when things broke loose. You'll have to answer for that some day before the judgment of history."

Which made Rosa furious all over again, so that she began to rage, "Your operation? You go off on your own and then afterward you scream about our betraying you? Karl, get hold of yourself."

He crossed his arms, laid his head back and countered her with the Pauline dictum: "Oportet haereses esse"—or there must also be heresies among you."

Radek and Rosa exchanged glances. He was a patent megalomaniac.

Karl, his hat pulled down low, his coat collar turned up, his face to the floor, hastily left the bar. (I cannot delay, but only dare, I cannot reap—only sow and flee. I cannot bear the noonday glare, dawn and twilight are enough for me.)

The worst days came after January 8th.

Rosa found herself on the horns of a dilemma. Party headquarters, under the leadership of Leo Jogiches, commissioned her to write the official disavowal of the uprising for the *Rote Fahne,* denouncing the occupation of the newspaper offices. They wanted to block once and for all any future denunciations, with their dangerous consequences for the party and its leadership. Because at Party headquarters, people were sure that this putsch begun in such a thoughtless and unprecedented manner would cost many lives. And so Rosa was given the task of representing the official party line. And behold, when they opened the *Rote Fahne* the next day and read Rosa's article, they found something quite different on its pages. It was open palace revolution. She had not been able to bring herself to follow her orders. She stood firm when Leo confronted her with it: no, she could not write against revolutionary workers, against the occupation of the newspaper district. Whether it was being directed well or badly, whether headquarters approved or not—they were revolutionary workers taking up the struggle in a dreadful situation. And besides that, the movement had sprung spontaneously from the masses.

Leo wrung his hands.

In the meantime, the throngs freshly recruited for the "Republicans" were occupying the northern part of Wilhelmstrasse, including the Reichs Chancellery, and were gathering at its southern end, while lying in wait and eyeing the editorial offices of the *Rote Fahne*.

In the early hours of January 9th, they fired on the building with machine guns. But they did not risk storming it because nothing was stirring within, and the attackers took this for a strategem of war intended to lure them into a trap.

But when they had waited the whole night long, and morning came without anything having changed, they took courage and pressed their way into the mysterious fortress—and found nothing inside, absolutely nothing living, nothing even suspicious. But at the top of the stairs (the offices were on the fourth floor), they ran into a woman who was attempting to slink by the advancing soldiers. They seized her and interrogated her. She gave them evasive answers. They led her back downstairs and took a look at her in the daylight. And they called over an officer, and then it became clear they had made a good catch, it was none other than Bloody Rosa.

They escorted this personage, protesting vehemently, maintaining cheekily that she only worked there, to the main entrance, and placed her under the guard of several soldiers while they continued their search of the rest of the building.

The news of Rosa's arrest spread like wildfire through the vicinity, and a large crowd of people assembled in front of the building. An hour passed and then another, and the prisoner, amid frequent pokes and shoves, stood there in the portal (the door itself was closed) awaiting her fate. Finally there was a commotion in the streets, cars drove up, the main entry was opened, and the soldiers who had been carrying out the search upstairs came rumbling down the stairs and ran out to report to their commanding officers. This left the prisoner alone, and she used the moment to slip out through the soldiers unnoticed as if she were a resident of the building, and then proceed on past the cars and across the pavement to the other side of the street, where she disappeared into the crowd at once.

The soldiers, who had just announced the tremendous news of Rosa's arrest and had turned around to go fetch her, found the entrance area empty and no Rosa in sight. They stormed up the stairs and back down again, they thundered at every door, they crept about in the attic of the building, even searched the roof itself, but there was no Rosa.

She had never been there at all. The prisoner had really been just a secretary in the editorial offices, was considerably younger than Rosa and without the least resemblance to her; the only thing was that she had a Russian accent.

While the bamboozled soldiers went on complaining and cursing among themselves and being cursed by others, the poor sacrificial lamb, the secretary, recovered from her fright in a restaurant in an adjacent street. And when the young woman moved on to search for Rosa, she found her not far off, in another pub, where she was conversing happy as you please with her comrades. Rosa had already heard the rumor that she had been arrested, and she found it terribly amusing. Now she learned who had suffered in her stead, and she consoled her assistant, beginning to grow more thoughtful when she learned how the pseudo-Rosa had been treated. The secretary complained that several times she had been afraid she would not get out alive. Moreover, Rosa herself had been standing in the crowd across from the building, and before the cars loaded with officers had driven up, she had walked up bold as brass to the guards posted at the entrance and had tried to explain to them that they were wrong in doing this, that instead they should start shooting and take over the offices themselves. The soldiers who were guarding the pseudo-Rosa at the rear gruffly made her move on.

They now set off and walked across Belle-Alliance Platz. As they were crossing the square, Rosa could not be prevented from joining one of the groups of people busy discussing things and taking part in their debate. Her companions had to drag her away by force.

Reluctant and anxious, Rosa let them lead her away. She had only begun to recognize just how much danger she was in from the secretary's report. They escorted her to the home of a friendly doctor near the Halle Gate. Deep inside, however, Rosa still did not understand it all clearly, first of all because she knew no fear for her own person, and second, because she did not really believe the situation to be that dangerous. For in Warsaw and in Russia she had been through quite different straits, and this was no real revolution, only a little putsch, and a civilized one at that, a revolution in kid gloves. And in the background she heard the whispers of her theories and her pipe dreams: we'll soon have all this behind us.

She was taken in by the friendly doctor and given the guest room. The building was near the Halle Gate, and Rosa was now hidden, her daily search for a new room and her anxiety over being discovered during the night at an end. People meant well by her here. Her companions were satisfied as they left her behind.

There she stood, staring out the window. Suddenly she was torn away from all this. She found herself on an island. She was on vacation. The sounds of a lively household surrounded her. She was weary, exhausted. She could not organize her own thoughts; she threw herself on the bed and slept for several hours.

During the night she thought of Karl. She had attacked him. She was sorry for that. He was out there now, hard at work, wandering around somewhere busy with the rebels while she lay here in bed sleeping. She envied him. She turned on the light and wrote him a note that she would have a courier deliver the next morning, telling what had happened at the *Rote Fahne* offices and how she was doing.

While she sat there in her warm room the next morning after breakfast, she gasped for fresh air like a stranded fish.

At last Tanya came.

What was going to happen to Tanya? She would be housed nearby.

"You'll have to come here often, Tanya. I'm back to where I was during the war. I've been locked in and can't move about."

"Rosa, how awful you look. This isn't good for you here. We were hoping to get away. You promised me."

"I know, to Breslau. Ah, Tanya, when I think of Breslau and how all the world still stood open to us then, we dreamed and hoped—it was as if we were young again." She wept. "And how long ago was that? Two months. In those two months I've aged ten years."

"Rosa, you're not well. This is no life for you here."

"Tanya, think of our prison. I can't wait to get back to Breslau."

Tanya: "You and your crazy prison."

Rosa: "We went through a lot in prison. It seems to me that it was more than I've experienced outside it. Do you remember the great central courtyard, the trees, and the birds?"

"The trees were part of the insane asylum."

"And in the evening the crows flew out to sleep in the fields. I translated. There were wonderful moments."

Tanya: "Yes, we went through a lot in prison."

On Thursday morning, on that same January 9th, at the same time the soldiers on Wilhelmstrasse thought they had arrested Rosa, workers from AEG and the Schwartzkopf factories gathered in the open air at Humboldthain to discuss what was happening with the occupation troops in the newspaper district and to debate the question of negotiations and the disintegration of the movement.

Another committee was elected, which was supposed to get in contact with the all-too-familiar central headquarters of the Independents. The committee did what it had been bidden to do, and of course after discussing the matter, the decision was made to retreat a few more steps in order, as they expressed it, "to pave the way for an end to fratricide." The basis for negotiations as they envisioned it: armistice, evacuation of *Vortwärts* even before negotiations began—in return for nothing more than the government's assurance that they would carry on these negotiations in the spirit of socialist reconciliation and that they would fill the post of chief of police for Berlin only in consultation with the Independents.

But who was supposed to accept these new proposals. The government, which bore the name Ebert and Noske and planned a mopping-up of Berlin? Or Eichhorn and Liebknecht? Ebert and Noske did not regard their submission as sufficient, and Eichhorn called the project an out-and-out capitulation. There the negotiators stood, not knowing what to do now. And a delegation from the Löwe factory came up with the idea of simply going directly to the people at the *Vortwärts* building (and thereby demoralizing them). The workers from Löwe cheerfully advised their colleagues simply to leave *Vorwärts* behind them, for the future was dark, very dark.

To which the occupation forces answered that they would rather be buried in the rubble of the building than surrender.

One day later, on Friday, Spartacus and the *Rote Fahne* ended their call for demonstrations and armed struggles. All the streets were clear, and the government felt strong enough to declare that it would no longer put up with any further demonstrations from now on, and that every mob would be countered with brute force. It spoke to the striking Socialists in the same way the imperial government had done in its day. Furthermore, the Socialists on Wilhelmstrasse made broad hints about the "dishonest tactics of the Independents."

Our good Independents felt that they must really protest such statements. But there was no need for that. Every insider knew that they were not dishonest. True, they weren't completely honest either. They were neither the one nor the other, because they were nothing at all. Who could assert anything else about them? The only sure thing about them was that they had a party headquarters on Schicklerstrasse.

And now that they were back to negotiations and discussions, old tempestuous Ledebour could not resist, he had to take part as well. He wanted to do his part to save the revolution. And he spoke with Richter, the chief of police in Charlottenburg, and something very strange happened to him in the course of their conversation. Richter spoke with him in frequent, lengthy and long-winded discussions, and Ledebour did not notice—just as he normally did not notice much— that the government appreciated the length and long-windedness of these negotiations, for in the meantime they could quietly go about playing their game. And then suddenly they no longer needed to talk and they simply threw Ledebour in the clink. Yes, unmoved by his lily-white innocence, they had Ledebour arrested in the apartment of a friend named Meyer, a former editor for *Vorwärts,* and they did it on the very same Friday that they had been engaged in serious negotiations. That was really unreasonable and a dirty trick, Ledebour thought, one that stank to high heaven. He couldn't, wouldn't believe it. It could not be true.

But it was true; he was locked up. And he had to control himself and wait for the day when he would be freed and could appear in public. And then his words would be thunderbolts that would smash this government and its lies.

The Storming of Vorwärts and the Massacre

But troops were already assembling in front of the *Vorwärts* building. These were not all the handpicked troops with which the new German republic was to be founded, but only a sample of them, Noske troops.

Major von Hoffmann was supposed to storm the building with his Potsdam companies. He studied the terrain with an expert eye and discovered that to storm it would be difficult because of the many courtyards, wings and cross passages. It could not be done without heavy artillery, but that would cause considerable damage to the building. Which was why he recommended negotiations. That outraged the governing Socialists. There would be absolutely no negotiations. They insisted on bombardment, despite damages to the building. They nobly declared that even if Mosse, Ullstein and the other newspaper owners stood to suffer during the attack, they were not to be given preferential treatment. Nasty-minded folks, however, suggested that they only wanted revenge, to wipe out completely these cheeky Spartacists. At any rate, the order to storm the building stood.

Major von Stephani had heavy artillery brought forward.

The black swan was flying. The hunt for Karl was in full stride. The pursued man was constantly on the move in the area around Belle-Alliance Platz so as to be near his child of sorrows, the editorial offices of *Vorwärts.*

He had a hard time finding a roof to sleep under. Even the most obscure hotels turned him down. Once he showed up in the south of the city at a cheap boardinghouse. In the middle of the night, however, the landlady knocked and woke him. She could not have him there. She only took in "respectable people."

Friday evening they brought him the news of Ledebour's arrest. Rumor had it the old man was being mistreated. Karl was not afraid for himself, but he knew that his family would worry about him. That same evening a courier was sent to Sonya with a handwritten message:

"Darling, I hope you are well and not anxious about me. You will soon see me and I'll send you word daily. Wasn't X. at home early this morning? I send you warmest kisses and embraces, darling. Your Karl. Kiss the children, tell them their father sends his love."

All through these days, the Party's grand inquisitor, the man who decided what constituted true revolution and what false, old red-headed Leo Jogiches, sat in the Party offices on Friedrichstrasse, ignoring the false paths taken by the enthusiasts he had already condemned. He wrote letters and received letters. He managed the organization in the Reich and gave out directives. He did not let others notice how much this putsch upset him, filled him with spite. He suppressed his rage at Karl, who had done this to the Party. His struggles in Poland and Russia, imprisonment and flight and long years in exile, had dug deep lines in his face. The Russian revolution had been ruined and bungled by his old enemy, Lenin, that putschist. But here in Germany, in the land of Karl Marx, there would be a classic socialist revolution. Leo stood guard over that, and nothing else concerned him.

And when on the day the *Rote Fahne* was occupied and the secretary from its editorial offices who had been mistaken for Rosa came bursting in on him and told him what had happened to her, how she had been handled and how they had made her stand there in the doorway for hours on end, he only made an annoyed gesture, reaching for the letters she had in her hand but had not given him. And instead of answering her, he took them out of her hand and ripped the envelopes open. After casting an angry glance at her, he began at once to read them. It was clear to the grand inquisitor what had to be done now: get out of this mess as quickly as possible with no damage to the Party.

The occupation forces at *Vorwärts* and in the other buildings were now only a pitiful remnant of those enthusiastic and mighty forces that had marched on Monday. They were fanatical men and women, young and old, all deeply touched by the great rousing call of the revolution, gladly willing to fight for the sake of humanity and to sacrifice themselves. There were strangely excited and intense figures among them, believers; believers in this world and utopians who dreamed of eternal peace. And though they were weak and they were few, they towered miles above the miserable figures of the little philistine Ebert and the wooden Noske with his mercenaries, who would soon raise their cudgels and smash them.

Even on January 9th, the *Rote Fahne,* though with only one lung left and its throat shot open, thought it could manage a trumpet call. It counted up the successes that the revolution ostensibly had to its credit throughout the Reich. It boasted: "The government is calling for volunteers at its meetings. This is proof that the counterrevolution can no longer depend on its own troops. They need volunteers to register for the bloody work of mowing down socialist workers. The government has thereby publicly proven its weakness. Its defeat has been halfway sealed."

And then the *Rote Fahne* (where is its home, where will it pitch its tent today or tomorrow) gives the negotiating committee, which is still on its way to a mass meeting in Humboldthain, a proud message to take along: not to deal with the Ebert Socialists as equals. "Today's power is the power of the fist. Today's task is to reconstitute the Executive Committee under the slogan of down with Ebert and his hangers-on."

The government received this final negotiating committee with interest and amazement (is it possible, do these people live in Berlin or on the moon?) and assured them indulgently how much it appreciated and admired the attitudes and motives of the committee. And there should most certainly be negotiations—when there was some free time. But they had to realize that a government cannot leave the settlement of these disagreements to a group of private citizens. Moreover, further delays in the matter were not feasible. The delegations retreated before all this official phraseology.

Wilhelmstrasse couldn't get its way fast enough. They put Noske to work. They called him to Berlin on the 10th and questioned him, and he found them all eminently impatient; something had to happen. They were not pleased with the news coming in from the Reich because they had oh such weak nerves and an ever so bad conscience. And there were even some of them who suggested that one should build bridges of gold for their defeated enemies, they were after all Socialists and workers, and the shedding of blood, all were agreed, was something heinous. That was more than enough for Noske. He pinched himself.

He wanted above all to prepare everything carefully, to do precision work. But if they started talking to him, their bloodhound, about bloodshed and such, then he would show them a thing or two. He wasn't going to let them spoil the text for his sermon. And he got in touch with his staff in Dahlem and issued the following command: the Iron Brigade from Kiel and several other mobile units were to start moving toward Berlin that very night.

That same night, von Stephani polished off *Vorwärts*. Lindenstrasse 3 was an extensive complex of buildings, and the *Vorwärts* building was located on the courtyard furthest back. But the rebels were still holding the buildings at the front.

After blocking off the whole terrain for some blocks around, the major had 10.5-cm cannon brought forward and began firing at the complex. Later he added heavy machine guns. The rebels knew what a bombardment with heavy artillery meant. But they assumed that an extended, unsuccessful seige in the middle of Berlin would prove dangerous for the beseigers themselves, as had been the case at the stables at Christmas. To hold their position, the rebels had been hard at work the last few days. They had accumulated as many weapons as possible. They could indeed match Noske's guard when it came to stamina and courage. But there were so few of them, and as far as their arms went, they had just requested light and heavy machine guns from their friends at the Spandau Arms and Munitions Works. But they were still waiting for them on the day the encirclement began. Among the defenders were the young workingman's poet Werner Moeller and the writer Wolfgang Fernbach. Both had been on the staff of the "red" *Vorwärts* that had been published there. Just two days before, Fernbach had written: "To Arms!" He had said that the government was condemned to death. The masses would carry out their revolutionary will. "We are called to arms by our belief in the victorious ideals of our brothers, to execute the judgment of history against their murderers."

Things turned out differently (at least for now).

The heavy artillery and machine guns of Major von Stephani did their job. Then he had his soldiers form ranks in the courtyard of the dragoon barracks and gave them their orders: "Shoot anyone who comes out of *Vorwärts*." Like a medieval captain, he left the enemy fortress at the mercy of his troops.

And when the cannons and the machine guns had done their job, the men seeking a truce, among them Moeller and Fernbach, emerged from the bombed-out building. Von Stephani had them informed that he demanded an unconditional surrender. The truce party, Moeller and Fernbach among them, were then led behind the ranks of the attacking soldiers to the courtyard of the dragoon barracks—and were there beaten to death.

The soldiers felt they could legitimately do this because of the major's orders; and the daily press, in both the morning and evening editions, had branded the revolutionaries as criminals who had placed themselves outside the law.

Even while the evacuation and search of the *Vorwärts* building was in full swing and the rest of its exhausted defenders were being marched to the barracks with their hands above their heads, a division of soldiers paraded up Friedrichstrasse to pay a visit to the grand inquisitor. He could not ignore these soldiers. They arrested him, and young Eberlein with him.

Leo found an opportunity, while getting himself ready to go, to whisper to a comrade who happened to be present that she should pass the word to Karl and Rosa for the two of them to get out of Berlin just as quickly as possible, and head for southern Germany.

The Seige of Police Headquarters

The revolutionaries' hatred of the bourgeois press was immense. The lies and the malice of such stupid, mercenary journalism infuriated them; and thus it happened that their first attacks had not been directed against military targets but against the strongholds of the hue and cry, the newspaper offices.

The houses of Mosse and Ullstein were still being defended by the occupation forces, weary to death now, on the 9th and 10th, Thursday and Friday. They fired from windows and doors, protected by furniture and rolls of paper, and they fired from the roofs. The government's troops, at their head the Reichstag Regiment, attacked from buildings along the side streets and from the steeple of Jerusalem Church.

The defenders at Mosse took heavy losses. They did not have any long-range weapons either. And so on Thursday evening they had to send out a truce party asking for a cease-fire, so that they could care for their dead and wounded. This was granted. The occupation forces asked for an armistice at six-thirty, and while hostilities ceased, Lieutenant Bachmann turned to the government to learn whether the occupation forces could be assured of mercy if they surrendered. Once he had been given such assurance, his decimated and exhausted forces at Mosse laid down their arms and abandoned the building. Ullstein was stormed at about the same time.

*　　*　　*

Gustav Noske, however, marched with a part of his troops to a demonstration that noon, just as he had promised. Frightened spirits were to be cheered, the irresolute frightened, and Spartacus was to get the message that its last hours were near.

Rain poured down on a dismal, depressed Berlin. But from Dahlem Noske came with his parade of three thousand men, the troops of civil war, equipped for heavy marching; and they had machine guns and cannons and whatever else they needed, even flamethrowers.

It was not easy to understand what had motivated Noske, with his poor posture, a civilian unfit for service, to set himself at the head of the battalion next to Colonel Deetgen. People in the western part of the city did not comprehend it; they would gladly have done without Noske, he did not add any color or charm to the military parade. People in the eastern part understood better. Noske wanted to demonstrate by being at their head that this was not a march of the counterrevolution, because in fact he was among them. Whether that argument carried any weight, in the east, is another question. At least there were no hurrahs or shouts of joy in either the east or the west. The comfortable and peaceful population of the west watched these rain-soaked and powerful troops with interest, with wonder and with a certain satisfaction. To the extent that people gather in such weather, from Dahlem to Potsdamer Platz they were amazed that there were still (or once again) such troops and that a people's deputy was leading them. But he must know what he was doing. They paraded along Potsdamer Strasse in the old, familiar and celebrated march step. The brass bands did not let themselves be bothered by the masses of water. They defied the elements, tooting and drumming and thumping all the more. They were grieved as well by the fact that a civilian was slouching along up ahead.

Now Potsdamer Platz opened up before them, that cursed spot where in 1915 Karl Liebknecht had uttered his first revolutionary cry in the midst of war. It had all started back then with that cry, had ended with the overthrow of the imperial Reich. The kettledrums beat forcefully and the pipes piped shrilly, to chase away that memory and wipe out the shame, at least musically.

They marched down Leipziger Strasse. Over and over again the people of Berlin asked themselves: "Why is Noske walking next to that colonel? Does the colonel need a nanny?"

And then, "Left face, march!" into Wilhelmstrasse, directly to Friedrich Ebert, so that he too could have some enjoyment from all this. He only needed to walk to the window now and open it. Speeches were superfluous. Everything ticked like clockwork, and soon it wouldn't just tick, but boom.

The noble gentlemen in the Reichs Chancellery all shook hands, first each others' and then their own. It was raining, but sunshine follows the rain.

And already glimmering gloriously there on the darkened horizon was the Constituent Assembly, where, we will wager, Friedrich Ebert will be elected president. And it won't take the efforts of a soldier named Spiro, rather the entire nation will do the job.

Having completed their parade, the troops worked their way back out of the city again, leaving behind them for the moment a declaration directly from Noske's hand for all those who, because of the rain or for whatever other reason, had not been able to be present:

"Workers, soldiers, citizens!

"Today at one o'clock, three thousand men armed with heavy artillery and machine guns marched through Berlin and Charlottenburg.

"The government has thereby proven that it has the power to carry out your (he means: its) will.

"Thieves are plundering automobiles in the east of the city.

"The last pretense of it being a political movement that we are dealing with has been unmasked.

"Thievery and plundering have revealed themselves to be the sole and final goal of this uprising."

There you had it. It spoke from the hearts of many, especially of those who had always said that was the case. Those people only wanted to steal. Actually, it was very decent of Noske and those other Socialists in the government, who were everyday sorts of people, to undertake some measures against it. You could see that a people's government had some effect. We're living in Germany and not in Russia. The working classes of Berlin read the message very gloomily. In their hearts was the dream of a unification of all socialist parties. Some of them complained: "That's where disunity got us." Others grumbled: "We've got Karl and Rosa to thank for this. They've made this mess." But both the former and the latter let their weary comrades at *Vorwärts,* at Mosse and Ullstein, go on battling alone and be decimated.

And now the storm broke around the red brick police headquarters. The Reich was aflame with rebellion.

In Stuttgart the Spartacists conquered City Hall and disbanded the city council.

Hundreds of thousands of workers went on strike in Westphalia.

In Dresden the revolutionaries tried to storm the *Volkszeitung*. The attempt failed.

In Bremen a socialist republic was proclaimed.

And Kurt Eisner (an Independent in his own fashion, former editor-in-chief of *Vorwärts* and since November 1918 prime minister of Bavaria) attempted to throw himself against the tyrants in Berlin in the name of European peace and in the interests of the working class (and because he recognized the same old Prussian militarism that had just been defeated as standing behind Ebert and Noske). He sent a telegram to the government of the Reich (that was all he could do, being an Independent):

"We have followed this deadly civil war with ever increasing alarm. It must end if all Germany is not to be destroyed. Berlin's example has a demoralizing effect. It has brought forth an epidemic of diseases, and the only remedy is a government founded on the trust of the people, one that includes all socialist parties and is determined to assist democracy and socialism to its victory in Germany. Everywhere in southern Germany there is a growing anger with Berlin. Already shadowy figures are calling for a fratricidal civil war even here."

"Incorrigible old gas-bag, what a charlatan," Ebert said in a bored voice as he tossed the telegram onto his desk.

"A rascal and a traitor," Noske the Bloodhound growled beside him. But for the moment he could not bite the man in Munich.

Lieutenant Schulze and the Security Force

At police headquarters there were great piles of arms in reserve, but there was a shortage of chiefs and Indians. Emil Eichhorn himself, the chief of police, had already deserted the field. He had taken off for parts unknown, if you can call the Bötzow brewery in Friedrichshein unknown.

And as the lord, so his lackeys. Eichhorn's famous security force, weakened already by desertions, marched away in closed ranks on Sunday evening. They had lost courage, these six hundred men, and there were various "factions" among them. So they marched out of headquarters, and since they had to find quarters somewhere (because they did not choose to disband, what would that get them?), they crossed over Alexanderplatz and went up Münzstrasse, and there on their immediate right stood an army barracks. And they had spotted it. It was the Alexander Barracks, named for a Russian czar.

But inside this barracks were soldiers who sported anything but a czarist mentality, for, at least in part, they had declared themselves to be Spartacists. And as our sad, homeless security force now marched off from police headquarters, six hundred men strong, they were sent kindest regards from those nonczarist Alexandrians and bidden to approach yet nearer.

And when the security force had approached yet nearer and reported how things stood with them and how ragged and sore of heart they were, the non-Alexandrians took pity on them and handed over to them the entire drill hall. They could bed down there and need not lose heart, and could give themselves over without hindrance to the conflict in their souls.

But in front of the building housing those insecure security forces a guard was posted, which meant that the former Eichhorners had been locked up. They noticed this, too, but accepted the fact. They took it upon themselves. They paid no attention to it. They considered it nothing less than a stroke of fate. They were not interested in the entire campaign. They wanted to be neutral just like the sailors and to sleep. They left their weapons right out in the courtyard.

Now among the Guard Fusiliers, among the so-called "Ladybugs," there was a wild fellow named Lieutenant Schulze, an ambitious and unemployed man who was determined to have a part in the German revolution, but had constantly been hindered from doing so. He was thus a very different man from the Eichhorners—especially since a determination to play a part in the revolution at that point was far less evident among the revolutionaries than among the counterrevolutionaries. It grieved Lieutenant Schulze on that Sunday evening that so few men were under his command. A grand total of forty men from the 2nd Guard Regiment were his, plus twenty czarist Alexandrians. That was not enough, you couldn't make much of a show from that—even the revolution could defy them. There could be no question of seizing police headquarters with these sixty men. Haste was in order. For quite apart from everything else, other troops might show up at any moment, beat him to the punch and seize headquarters first.

What does one do in such a situation? That's what Lieutenant Schulze asked himself. And being a determined man, he set his sixty men in motion and used them to get hold of a trainful of machine guns in Reinickendorf. He knew that there were machine guns in Reinickendorf, and so he simply marched out and got them. (By which he once again proved himself radically different, this time from the occupiers of *Vorwärts*, who had sent a messenger to Spandau with a slip of paper asking for machine guns, and then, of course, waited for them in vain right up until their tragic end.)

Not that these machine guns and rifles (including the men to man them), so generously donated by the Guard Field Artillery Regiment, gave Schulze's little band all that much of a chance for life. But Schulze's courage and appetite grew. The thing could be done.

And then late that evening, as the capstone, he heard the news of the six hundred men of the security force who had floated away from police headquarters, disheartened and leaderless, and had settled in at the Alexander Barracks. It was dark now, and the assault really ought to be made by night, but Schulze still did not have enough men. Moreover, police headquarters was an incredibly rambling sort of place, considerably larger than the *Vorwärts* building with all its wings and additions. It took up almost an entire block. How was he, Lieutenant Schulze—with sixty men, a section of machine guns and a few rifles together with the men to man them—supposed to manage it? Like Diogenes with his lantern, he went in search of men.

He ran down Alexanderstrasse, and there he bumped into a fellow named Dräger, who told him in confidence, man to man, that he was a leader of that very security force that had left police headquarters that same day, drawing a heavy line between themselves and Eichhorn. But his men were a rotten bunch, he said, and could not come to any decision. They had now simply gone to bed, six hundred strong, in the middle of a revolution, and the Spartacists in the barracks had just locked them up. There they were now, locked up in the drill hall, and he, Dräger, was running around in the dark here on Alexanderstrasse and didn't know what to do.

"What?" Lieutenant Schulze asked, who was so amazed he couldn't believe this (were the roasted doves flying straight into his mouth?), "locked up? Taken prisoner in battle?"

Dräger: "You kidding? You don't know them. They just walked right in on their own. And now guards are posted outside."

Schultze: "And what about their weapons? What did the men do with their weapons?"

Dräger: "They just laid them down out in the courtyard."

And Schulze laughed out loud, overwhelmed by a mixture of extreme rage and immense delight, directed at different objects: at the security force, because it was six hundred men strong and had let itself be locked up and left its weapons in the courtyard, and at the Spartacists, first simply because they were there, but also because they had locked up the security force for him. It was enough to make a man scream, which he did. Matters would have to be mended, absolutely. For Schulze, the remedy could only be having these six hundred men take part in the assault on police headquarters.

Dräger was dumbfounded. But he couldn't convince Schulze otherwise. There in the dark of Alexanderstrasse (the street lights had been shot dead), the lieutenant gave him what for: "We'll carry it off."

And Schulze, who always worked with the smallest contingents, went and got his three score men, with whom he had accomplished so much already, equipped them with his freshly confiscated machine guns, and taking his place at their head amid a bellowing of countless commands, headed off to the courtyard of the Alexander Barracks without further ado.

Quick as a wink, a colossal exchange of gunfire ensued. Who was shooting at whom was not clear in the dark. All that was clear to each of them was that he was shooting and therefore this was war, and each of them moved quickly, after each shot, to load up again and get another one off so he wouldn't fall behind. This went on for quite a while and made for a whale of a battle. In the dark all cats are gray. Both sides profited from that.

Gradually the gunfire dwindled for lack of ammunition. And then too, they wanted to see what the results were.

And it turned out, as Lieutenant Schulze shone his flashlight around the courtyard, there weren't any Reds there at all. Perhaps—and this was the cause of considerable debate afterward, and the matter has never been clarified to this very day —there had been no Reds there at all, and Schulze's three score men had been the only ones shooting, and their own shots in the dark had so terrified them, made them so desperate, that they could not stop. It was a good thing that none of them was injured in the process.

At any rate, Schulze breathed a sigh of relief as he looked over the large courtyard and surrounding territory and not a single Red was to be seen (of course all of them had bolted and fled, most probably to join Emil Eichhorn at the Bötzow brewery). He breathed his sigh, and now he could go to work and tear down the drill-hall door, which was riddled with holes.

It was incredibly close inside and warm, and people were lying on straw and snoring in a many-voiced chorus like frogs in a bog.

The six hundred doughty soldiers of the security force, having now renounced revolution, were sleeping the sleep of the just there on the straw.

In the glare of the light, Lieutenant Schulze stood at the wide-open door and roared like a desert lion into the grim darkness of the room. Did that man ever have a pair of lungs. The security force leapt to its feet, to the extent that it did not hold to its tactics and go on sleeping.

Schulze screamed.

What did Schulze scream?

He screamed: "You are free. Get up."

This caused great anguish among the soldiers of the security force. It perplexed them. They had, in part, listened to the shooting outside the way one listens to the rain when one is sitting high and dry, and they had thought: how fine it is to lie here in the drill hall while outside guards are posted who'll not let anyone in; we couldn't have managed things better, and tomorrow morning after we've had coffee we'll go out in the courtyard and collect the dead.

For Lieutenant Schulze to be standing there at the door pitilessly screaming "Stand up!" was unwelcome news for them, and they got up only very slowly, one after the other, rank upon rank so to speak, and said to each other as they dusted the straw off: "Free, he said. What does he mean, free? It takes two for someone to be freed."

But that was not Schulze's opinion. He didn't ask anyone about it. He wanted to capture police headquarters before anyone else did, and that was why they had to stand up.

He was not unaware of their contemplative mood. And he got madder than hell, and he kept screaming at those "lazy bastards, I'll get you moving," until they all toddled drowsily out into the cold courtyard with rancor in their hearts. He vented his feeling with further curses.

"You're just like all the rest. Except for a handful of tough men, the entire German nation is made up of goldbrickers."

A dreadful curse followed, which was swallowed up in the general noise.

As the "lazy bastards" now assembled again in the poorly lit courtyard, they were handed the weapons from which they had parted with such pleasure. How had they ended up like this, what sort of trap had they fallen into? Couldn't the Reds have guarded them better? The cowards had fled, had left them in the lurch in order to save themselves. It enraged the soldiers of the security force just to think of such a dereliction of duty. Lieutenant Schulze was quite right when he cursed the goldbrickers. That pack didn't deserve success, they would have to be handed it. And so the six hundred arrived now at a motive for fighting again: they wanted to pay back the Reds for having delivered them over to Lieutenant Schulze.

The merciless lieutenant, however, did not so much as ask about their motives. He ordered the companies to get in formation and bawled at them: he would now give them the opportunity to recapture the police headquarters they had deserted. And so now they knew their hour had come, and they sighed and resigned themselves to the task. They found themselves in a frightful pickle. They marched against the Spartacists with deepest bitterness.

But the Reds who had fled, those absconded guards, were watching all this from nearby buildings. They did not notice the mental anguish of their prisoners, it is true, only that Lieutenant Schulze had assembled them in the courtyard and rearmed them. Then from roofs and windows they started shooting at these renegades whom they had dealt with so mildly. The whole livery-barn district appeared to be in an uproar as the six hundred men left the barracks courtyard. But the Reds were unable to prevent their departure.

It was already 4:30 A.M., and Schulze's field artillery, donated by the Guard Regiment, began to do its work. They were stationed in several streets. The battle was on.

Things grew serious. Under the cover of artillery fire, patrols and commandos approached the building from the side streets. Hand to hand combat developed. Rebels were hiding in the cellars and apartments of the houses in the vicinity and dealt out considerable losses, both from the rear and on the flanks of the unsuspecting attackers as they moved forward. They fought on Wadzekstrasse and on Kleine Frankfurter Strasse.

Things grew more bitter. Hand grenades were tossed. At about six o'clock they had worked their way forward in close-action combat as far as police headquarters, and were firing on it from the narrow Kaiserstrasse. The effect of this heavy bombardment was enormous. Machine guns were flung to the side, gun crews were killed or chased off. Both Kaiserstrasse and Elisabethstrasse were badly damaged.

They moved in on headquarters under the cover of artillery fire and machine guns that had been affixed to cars.

Morning dawned. It was Sunday, January 12.

Private Matters amid the Thunder of Cannon

About a dozen typists were clattering away at their machines in the rather large, bright room. Now and then one of them would stand up, a sheet of paper in hand, and whisper with another one. Lieutenant Maus had been offered a chair by one, but he preferred to gaze out the window at the rainy Leipziger Strasse and pace about a few steps in his restlessness. He was on orderly duty with the staff in Dahlem, and early this morning he had been sent here to the War Ministry with a written report and was now waiting for the answer.

A clerk came out of an adjoining room, looked about and asked him if he was Lieutenant Maus. He was wanted on the telephone.

To his astonishment the call was from Britz, from Hilda.

She apologized for disturbing him while he was on duty again, but this time it was something really important. Becker had just called her and asked her for help. He was terribly upset, but didn't want to tell her why. He was so insistent that she had finally told him where Maus could be found. When she had inquired in Dahlem, they had told her where Maus was at the moment.

Maus replied good-naturedly that the people in Dahlem had been exceptionally cordial to her. What was it that Becker wanted?

"But that's what I don't know, Hans, and that's why I'm calling you ahead of time, so that you won't get upset when you hear from him. I'm so afraid for him. He seemed to be downright feverish."

Maus: "Let's just wait it out. Thanks, Hilda. You're at home, right? I'll call you again the minute I hear."

"Keep calm, Hans."

Maus waited close to the phone. And sure enough, within a few minutes he was asked for once again. It was Becker. He begged Maus's pardon, but this was an urgent matter and Maus could be of assistance.

"Gladly," Maus answered. "What's it all about?"

He was happy to hear right off that it was nothing to do with Hilda. Becker asked to meet him, right away. Maus replied that that would hardly work. But he would inquire how long it would be before they were done with him there. He was able to tell Becker to expect him within an hour, wherever. Becker suggested City Hall on Königstrasse. And so they met there. Tall, gaunt Becker was walking back and forth in front of the City Hall steps beneath an umbrella, in his winter coat and soft, black hat, when Maus drove up in a cab and picked him up. They drove together to a café on Spittel Market. Only then did Becker unburden himself.

It was a strange story that Maus heard.

What had happened to Becker was this:

He had said good-bye to the ostensibly friendly chief school inspector at City Hall and had gone out onto the street when the thought of Heinz took hold of him. He had wandered uneasily up Königstrasse, looking about to see if he might not run into the boy by accident. He stopped, hopeless, on Klosterstrasse, and decided to drive out to the aunt in Charlottenburg where Frau Riedel was staying. Perhaps she would know something. It wasn't likely. But Becker had to go. A grim feeling, a terror that the dead man had not come to rest and was reaching out his arms for the boy, drove him on.

When he gave his name at the door of the Charlottenburg apartment, the lady of the house made a face. She told him to wait in the hall until she had fetched Frau Riedel. Heinz's mother was outraged: how dare he show himself here—what did he want. She broke into tears. He was probably the same sort of scoundrel as the man who had seduced her son.

Becker explained calmly that he wanted to find out about Heinz, who, as they had agreed, had first stayed with him at his apartment, but who had now disappeared without saying good-bye, and he was not staying in their own apartment either.

Frau Riedel (who only now closed the apartment door behind her): "Then he's just bumming around. I want nothing to do with the hooligan." She moved her teary face closer to Becker's. "He was here yesterday. I don't know what he wanted really. Acted as if he wanted to comfort me, brought me flowers. And then the boy started talking about . . ."

She had to walk back into the room and sit down. The aunt gestured for Friedrich to follow. Frau Riedel sobbed, sitting at the table.

"That hooligan has brought all this misery on us. He gave evidence against his own father, he admitted it, against his own flesh and blood, his father who loved him. Our other son is gravely ill and in a military hospital. Heinz was our baby. For him his father got into this terrible trouble. And now the boy, his son, his own flesh and blood says: the director didn't do anything to me. That's all a lie and made up. That's what he said to the detectives. He told me himself. He's a murderer, that's what I told him. If he talks like that and does that to his father, we don't want to hear anything more from him. Let him go ahead and be a bum. That suits him fine."

Friedrich stood out on the street, greatly discouraged. And as he wandered about Savigny Platz, he had to stop at a bar under the loop of the tramway in the station, just to sit at a table and get hold of himself and think this through. Where was the boy? He needed to ask God to watch over this helpless young man, hounded here and there. Friedrich could see Heinz wandering about, sitting on park benches, probably hiding in doorways now to keep out of the rain, sleeping in waiting rooms, likely enough.

391

Friedrich remembered an old saying that comforted him now: "God, who created you without your help, can also help you without your asking."

Berlin is so incredibly immense. Look for Heinz? Where?

Becker, his anxiety increasing, sat down in the tram, intending to ride back to the neighborhood of his own apartment. But underway he heard shooting and he got out at Molkenmarkt.

And there was City Hall again. Little groups were clustered on the stairs despite the rain, debating.

What was driving the boy on? The cemetery, the grave, those last words of longing the dead man had spoken to Heinz? But we prepared a grave for him and laid wreaths upon it, and we prayed for him. We left nothing undone. Where is Heinz? Oh what a dark world. How little I can see of you.

Becker walked up and down the street, walked down side streets, came back again. He walked in circles.

Even when he was still alive, I begged the director to keep his hands off the boy. He wouldn't listen to me. He won't do it now either. What voracious and perverse forces fill this world. But I'll not let it happen.

The rain fell in torrents, Friedrich was forced into a dark entrance hall on upper Klosterstrasse along with a dozen other people. He shoved his way to a back corner. He was desperate, suffering.

How can I find him in the huge city of Berlin? I haven't a clue, not anything to start from. God only knows where he is. But how am I worthy that God should stand by me, look upon me, as I stand here, and should show me his grace and rescue me from my pain? How can I ask him to cast his eye upon me, here in this entry hall? How vain and grand I was to those men at City Hall who questioned me. How can I presume that God will see me?

How can I show thee, thou great, omniscient God, how poor and desperate I am, and that I submit myself to thee and desire only thee! How can I prove myself worthy just to be thy creature! Receive me! Turn thou to me, who knoweth all things and comprehendeth whole universes at a glance. Lord, I get thee for this favor. At one time I knew only one single stern world, come together by accident, where power and meaninglessness ruled. I did not recognize thy life, the reflection of thy light and truth, within it. Now behold me here, in this entryway, in this corner, here on this street. Almighty, all knowing God, thou wellspring of truth, help thy servant.

The rain had let up, people left their shelter, and Becker too went his way. He had walked so much he could feel it in his legs, but he still did not know what to do.

On the corner stood a newspaper boy who held one out to Becker. Becker reached in his pocket automatically, paid for, and took the paper. And there stood the headline:

"Crisis at Police Headquarters Nears. Eichhorn Flees."

Friedrich's eyes soaked up the black letters and the black lines became bars, prison bars across a doorway, and through the bars he could see into a courtyard at police headquarters, and in the glass-roofed courtyard Heinz was walking beside other young men, they were dragging planks or something similar. Becker stood bent down over the paper, still next to the boy who continued to shout, "Extra, extra, Eichhorn flees!"

Becker folded up the paper now, thrust it into his coat pocket, and began to move. The scene had faded again and his eyes were taking in the events on the street, but within him everything was still empty and stone-hard, as if he were dead. Then slowly his conscious mind began to register again; Friedrich noticed a street sign, he remembered where he was, in the vicinity of Königstrasse again, he was still walking around in circles. And now the vision that he had just seen came to him again, he took the paper from his pocket, read "police headquarters." Heinz had been walking around in there behind that barred door; he was dragging something with the help of other young people.

What should he do about that? Nothing. It was a vision, a fantasy, a delusion of sorts, his imagination. There lay within him, deep in the recesses, a mighty animal that leapt out of the dark, hoping to cast him to the ground. It said: Heinz is at police headquarters; you saw it yourself, you know it.

He walked faster now. I know nothing. It's as if someone were trying to trick me.

But the wild animal sprang forward once again and said: you saw it, Heinz is at police headquarters.

Because of a new heavy rain shower, Becker had to stand in another house entry. The vision, the phantasm, the unwanted notion disturbed him. It prevented him from thinking and examining the real possibilities. But he felt so helpless, he sighed and had already resolved to walk away in despair, to look for a cab and simply ride home, when once again he thought of the all knowing God and he cried out to him in need.

Afterward he felt freer and more sure of himself. And when the vision of police headquarters came to him again in this gentler mood, he inspected it and said: perhaps it is a possibility. Why not? He could really be at police headquarters, although I don't know what he would want there and what could have driven him to join the rebels. It's not very probable, it doesn't fit him, but if he was desperate and without a roof over his head, just wandering the streets, he could have ended up there. Maus did something similar when he was so desperate.

And suddenly Becker knew: yes, that's how it was, and I have received this as an answer. He no longer doubted. He breathed more easily and was thankful.

Now he began to circle police headquarters, but this time with conscious intent. It was about four in the afternoon, and he soon determined that you could no longer get into the building from any direction. What to do? When he saw the military patrols, he remembered Maus. He had enlisted in one of these units; maybe he was right here in the area. Maus could help.

But at the tobacco shop where he was about to go in and make his telephone call, he was struck anew with uncertainty. He wanted to call Britz. But what should I say to her, how should I explain to her? It's all so nebulous what I'm up to here.

His hand still on the doorknob, Becker hesitated, but then a customer pulled the door open from inside and so forced Becker to enter. He still could not decide, and wanted to disguise his intent by simply asking for a pack of cigarettes. But there in the corner (how unfortunate, he thought) stood the telephone booth, its door open. He glanced at it, and the clerk who noticed his glance asked: "Telephone?" Becker found himself answering, "If I might," and then he was in the booth and talking with Hilda and asking her for Maus's address.

Now here he was sitting with Maus in a café on Spittel Market and he presented his request. It was about one of Becker's students, a senior, who had done something enormously stupid. The young lad really hadn't been involved in politics at all, not in the least (Becker said this while his heart tightened with despair within), and now the boy had become suicidal, you could say he was driven by suicidal desires, and had got himself involved with the Spartacists after having had an awful row with his parents.

Maus asked: "A love affair?"

Becker: "There's some of that involved."

Maus, thoughtfully, with a serious smile (we know all about that): "And now the kid is inside police headquarters and can't get out. Okay, what do we do?"

Becker had noticed while speaking of the topic just in general, that Maus knew nothing about the affair with the director or of his own role in it, about the funeral and so on.

Becker: "There's no way even to approach the building, it's blocked off from every direction."

Maus: "Of course. I've been told that the assault will come today or tomorrow, and they'll probably begin soon with the bombardment, which means some fragments may come zinging by. That is the reason for the area being cordoned off."

At Maus's suggestion they got up and left. It had grown quite dark; evening, Sunday evening, the rain had stopped and they went on foot toward the east. Maus was glad to give his opinion.

"You're not going to get the boy out. You'll just get yourself in a hell of a mess. At best you'll manage to get yourself in one way or another, but most definitely you won't get out again."

Becker said he had to do something, he couldn't just stand around and do nothing in such an awful situation.

Maus: "As you like. I can only warn you. All right: whatever I can do to help, I'm at your disposal. It won't be my fault."

They walked for quite a while, until they had reached Landsberger Strasse via Münzstrasse. There they turned up Kleine Frankfurter Strasse, and then at the corner of Kaiserstrasse Maus told his companion to wait. They had come this far only with the greatest difficulty, and got through only after long negotiations with the guards.

Becker had to stand there in the dark for a half hour and wait next to a guard. Finally Maus rescued him, hooked an arm in under his, and pulled him away a few steps. He spoke very gravely.

"Hell, Becker, stop and think about this whole thing one more time. Nobody wants to get involved. Nobody wants to risk his ass. The whole thing is much too risky, and besides it's a purely private matter. What's all this private stuff at this point. If you want to do something and want to be pigheaded about it, then you'll have to be answerable for it. You have to see that as soldiers none of us wants to get involved with this."

Becker: "I know." (Things had begun to take their course, there were no more questions and no more doubts.)

Maus: "What are you really after? The boy's stuck inside. He's had his way. Let him alone. He can't get out, and you won't be able to force your way out with him either."

Becker: "Maus, you'd use force to hold back a total stranger if you saw him standing on a bridge ready to throw himself into the water, and if he were down in it, you'd dive after him to try and save him."

"True, I'd do that, unsound as the decision is. All right, now listen, old friend. I have spoken with the unit commander here. They're not letting so much as a cat in or out. Your private affairs don't interest anyone. So it won't work that way. You've got to assume a role, at least appear to do so."

"What does that mean?"

"You've got to take over a mission. Either openly or secretly, however you wish or however they instruct you, you'll go over to the Red side. Do you know, by the way, why I'm helping you, Becker? Apart from everything else, because without your having lectured me for hours on end there in your study, I would be on that side myself right now. You remember how I was—lost and devastated, just like that kid. You could get in from the other side, from the back of the building, from where the tram tracks are. It's worth a try. No one from our side at least will shoot at you. What you're supposed to tell the other side and what they'll have to say and how they'll treat you— that's another matter."

Becker: "I don't know the terrain. Is there no other possibility?"

Maus: "Of course. Straight ahead, across the street. With a white flag."

"As a one-man truce party, then. To negotiate what?"

"That's your business. We're not negotiating over anything. But maybe they'll think we're willing to negotiate with them. They'd love to, I'm sure. At least they'll let you in on that basis." Maus laughed. "Maybe, though, they'll say to you: How nice of you to come, good sir, you've saved us a walk ourselves, because we're about to surrender unconditionally as it is."

Becker considered. "They would permit me, then, to go over carrying a white flag?"

"Without any message. Is that sufficient for you, and are you willing to accept the consequences?"

Becker nodded.

Maus took hold of him by the shoulders. "But when a suicide is about to jump from the bridge, you grab hold of him. Like this, and now what should I do with you? Shall I give you a shove?"

Becker, warmly, "Dear Maus, I'm not feeling suicidal. If you're willing to do your part to help save a poor boy, then you're doing a fine thing. I'll never forget you've done it."

"All right, come on. I'll take you in to the unit commander. Explain to him what you intend to do, short and sweet. I've vouched for you. It may happen, of course, that the Reds will mow you down despite your white flag. You understand that?"

"Completely."

Maus took hold of him once again. "Becker, you're crazy. Does this kid really mean so much to you? Let him learn his lesson."

"Maus, let me do this."

Beneath a burning lantern they exchanged a long glance while they shook hands. Maus's eyes asked: did this thing with Hilda hit you as damnedly hard as my bad luck with her did me?—And Becker's eyes answered: no, believe me, I'm not lying—and so now let me go.

The guard led them now into a house on Kaiserstrasse. There in a vacant store, behind the lowered venetian blinds, an old sergeant major had set up his headquarters. They saluted one another. The unit commander said to Becker:

"It can only be to our advantage that you're willing to volunteer to report to us what's happening over there. You can figure out for yourself what's essential for us: the number of men, how they're armed, how they're positioned, the general mood. Your first job is to get across and tell them your personal problems. You have no commission from us. Maybe you'll have good luck. I'd be very surprised if you did, though. What makes you so weary of life, Herr First Lieutenant? You don't imagine, do you, that the Reds are going to give you back your prodigal son, even if everything does go smoothly? But as you wish."

Becker asked whether he was being allowed to go over as a sort of truce party.

The unit commander laughed, "Sort of one, yes, if that's sufficient. Because if the fellows over there take you for a truce party with your white handkerchief, when you've once said your piece they're going to realize there's something rotten in Denmark. I can only promise that you'll not be fired upon by our side while you take your nighttime constitutional. And in case by some chance you should manage to get out with the kid, which I personally don't even include in my calculations, then move fast. I can't guarantee anything for two hours from now."

Becker thanked him. They gave him an improvised white flag, which made the unit commander laugh.

"We don't have any prettier rag than that one. We're not equipped for truce parties. Lots of luck on your trip."

Maus and Becker threw a last glance at each other.

Inside Police Headquarters

The line of guards opened for Becker. In his left hand he carried a flashlight whose beam he directed up at the white flag.

He was able to walk part of the way down Kaiserstrasse, as far as the corner across from police headquarters and then to cross the pavement without any problems, when someone from the other side shouted, "What do you want?"

Without thinking he answered: "To talk truce."

After a pause, someone shouted: "Up the right side of the street, first door."

Becker walked slowly. Not a shot was fired. From Alexanderplatz and from somewhere behind him there came the crack of gunfire, and further in the distance was the confused, dull noise of a great city. But he crossed this zone in total stillness.

At the door indicated, he stopped. They opened it almost at the same moment. They let him enter and barred the door again. He was blinded by the light of the flashlights directed at him. He could see several soldiers, but they quickly blindfolded him, pressed his hat in his hand, and led him away like that. They went down long corridors, up steps, another corridor.

Along the way he heard the voices of the people he passed. "What's up now? Where did they get that tall bird? Another spy—they're going to interrogate him. Why the big long conversations? Lining them up against the wall makes more sense than interrogating them. Lord, he's carrying a white flag. The latest fashion! Let him wipe his nose with it."

They were standing still now somewhere. A knock. A door opened. Becker was shoved into a heated and smoky room. They took off his blindfold.

While he was being led along, his eyes closed, he had repeated to himself: it's beyond my strength, I'm not the one who's walking down this hall, I don't know what I'm doing, I don't understand it, I don't comprehend it. I'm sinning against God, against my self, my mother and everything that's important to me. I'm not crazy, it's much worse than that: I'm shooting craps, I'm gambling my own life away. During the war, during that one attack, I leapt up out of my trench and ran forward with my men behind me, but I could die then, it was done with premeditation, I was a part of a larger whole, I knew what I wanted. Now I don't know. I'm looking for Heinz, I assume he is here—but why should he be here, he could be anywhere. Have I fallen into a trap? Lord, save me, let me not perish here.

He found himself in a rather large office. A kerosene lamp was burning on a table covered with a green cloth where two soldiers sat. They both had distrustful, working-class faces and were watching him. Becker saw five men standing behind him armed with rifles, two in sailor's uniforms, three in civvies.

What did he want?

Becker gave his name. The moment he spoke, his self-assurance returned. He explained. It didn't even occur to him to tell a lie.

The two soldiers looked at one another, and then looked at him.

They repeated their question. He answered once again. They repeated after him: then he wasn't sent over as a truce party and had only come to look for some young kid who was part of their garrison.

Becker confirmed this.

One of the soldiers at the table crossed his arms and leaned back, the other propped his head in his hand and stared at Becker. No one spoke.

Becker: It was all just as he said it was. When he had applied to the unit commander on Kaiserstrasse about the matter, they had let him come across at his own risk, all on his own, with a white flag so that no one would shoot. He hadn't come to negotiate anything.

The smaller of the two soldiers, a gray-haired man, said, "You seem to think we're dumb kids, if we're supposed to believe that. Or are you just trying to have some fun with us."

The other one: "Did you guys make a bet or something about how easy it would be to get in here? That that would be easy as child's play with us?"

Becker swore that that was the farthest thing from his mind. They could believe that he wouldn't put himself in such danger just for fun. What he cared about was finding young Riedel, who had joined up here.

At least Becker avoided telling them that he wanted to get the boy out. But the old soldier laughed aloud now: "This gets better and better. And I suppose you intend to take him back out, is that what you think?"

The younger one, a broad-shouldered, robust man, stood up and walked over to Becker. "You're a spy."

Becker was about to reply, but the man screamed: "Shut your mouth, man. You idiot. If you're going to talk with us, you're going to have to think up another story, I can tell you that."

While they blindfolded Becker's eyes again, he heard people saying: "We've got to put a stop to this. This morning there were those two we just caught up with as they were trying to get out, and now this guy. Well if that isn't the limit, he's playing the fool."

He was led out into the corridor and held there for a while. Then they took him to another office, smaller than the first one. Here an acetylene lamp was burning on the table, and it filled the air with an acrid odor. A sturdy sailor was stomping back and forth, his hands clasped at his back. Several civilians and another sailor stayed in the background. Becker had to tell the whole story once again to this pacing sailor with heavy bags under his eyes, a melancholy lower lip and a generally mournful look about him.

The mournful sailor, who apparently knew the whole story already, was as amused by it as his friends, and they all listened scornfully but with considerable pleasure to this tall civilian that had been dragged in.

What then, the presiding sailor inquired, might be the name of this young man whom Becker was seeking, running after and whom he just had to visit? Heinz Riedel? Might he not also go by a different name, in case it should turn out there wasn't any Heinz Riedel in the building?

The others grinned. The presiding sailor studied Becker—he was a real treasure-house, he had to have more fun with him.

"Then he could perhaps go by another name," the presiding sailor repeated.

The audience laughed out loud. Becker could not answer.

And now they tightened their ropes around him. If this Heinz was not to be found here, then it would be proven to them that he was a spy, just like the others they had captured. What luck that the melancholy (though for the moment, good-humored) presiding sailor did not ask just how he knew in the first place that this boy prodigy was to be found here. Of course he did not ask, because it was ninety percent certain that this was a spy he had before him. The presiding sailor stood in front of Becker and stared him in the eyes.

"Now I'm going to take you completely seriously, old friend. We are now going to let you play your role to the bitter end. We're not going to do anything with you but give you two men who will go down into the courtyard with you where our new comrades are, and you can search for him. If the lad is not there, then you can tell us yourself what you deserve as a reward for your conjuring tricks."

At first the two men wanted to bind Becker's eyes again. But the presiding sailor motioned for them to forget it; that was completely superfluous, what was the point. And Becker realized then that he was not to be let out again. (Why hadn't he thought of that before—but what had he really imagined would happen? — Had he believed they would let him go with the boy? — Perhaps he would have been better off not to have said anything about the boy.)

The great, glassed-over courtyard of police headquarters, to which they now descended, was a veritable war camp. Tremendous noise filled the space, car horns, hammers, commands, shouts. The arc lamps up above and the lightbulbs along the walls had been covered. On the floor, groups of men completely in the dark alternated with others garishly illuminated.

Becker walked with his two companions among these ghostly groups, wagons and platoons. He searched about. But how, among so many people and by this murky light and with everyone running back and forth, was he supposed to recognize anyone? One of the soldiers accompanying him called out from time to time: "Heinz Riedel! Is there a Heinz Riedel here?" No one paid them any attention. Outside they could hear the ack-ack of machine guns.

As Becker threaded his way through the courtyard with his guards from back to front and no one responded and night was beginning to fall, he recalled the whole long day that was behind him now—how it had begun with the telegrams at home, how he had gone to City Hall, and then the telephone conversation with Hilda, his meeting with Maus and now this search for a desperate young man, and all of it the result of the ugly affair with the director. The wickedness, the evil was not receding, and everyone was doomed to perish because of it, he too. With his head lowered, Friedrich strode on, like a man condemned to death. I was mistaken, nothing more than simply mistaken. I thought he might be hiding out here. But what was I thinking. I'll pay for it now.

As they turned around to head back, a sooty young face gazed out at them from a truck parked near a barred gate. Several people were mounting a heavy machine gun up on top of it. A slender figure in a sailor's uniform slipped down from the truck, ran up to Becker, gazed up into his face, and raised both arms.

Becker jerked back. He did not recognize the greasy, excited face, and they were in shadows besides.

But Heinz flung his arms around him and shook both his hands, and was so happy that he laughed. "Dr. Becker, what a surprise this is. You're here? I didn't know that."

Both soldiers stood close by and listened. One of them laid a hand on Heinz's shoulders. "You know this man?"

"Who?"

"This fellow here."

Heinz: "What's wrong? What business is that of yours?"

"And you're Heinz Riedel?"

"I am."

The soldiers: "But then why didn't you answer when we called your name?"

"Me? I didn't hear anything. We were up there hammering away mounting that machine gun."

The soldier: "I see. And what's this fellow's name?"

"Becker."

"His first name?"

Heinz: "Friedrich. What's wrong?"

At that the two soldiers had a talk, and then one of them declared to Friedrich, "There's some truth to the whole story after all." At which they left the two of them standing there and went their way.

And indeed, from that moment on, no one bothered any further about Becker. Apparently the two soldiers made their report to their commanding officer. But he would hardly have paid it much attention, because the general situation was growing more and more dangerous. Probably he only shouted at them: "Forget that bilge, let me alone." And for him, as for the two soldiers, and for everyone else in the place, the case was closed. For now it was a matter of life and death.

Heinz quickly grabbed his friend by the arm and led him over to the wall close to the stairway. Others were camped there already; they were apparently getting some rest. Becker was supposed to wait for him there, he had things to do.

Becker was happy for the moment to be left alone. He felt weak, he couldn't stay on his legs any longer, but it was not just because of simple exhaustion. He sat on the ground, perplexed, shocked, and he thought about it all and asked himself: but can that really be Heinz? It really isn't possible, it isn't possible at all.

And in this courtyard filled with the noise of war, Becker could do nothing but sit there in the shadow of the wall and thank God, the creator and preserver of all things, the father and trustworthy friend of mankind. He begged for forgiveness for his constant doubts and for the grace to trust all the more. And again he gave thanks and held his hands before his eyes as tears welled up. This gift of tears had also been granted him by God.

402

Then Heinz rushed up, sat down beside him and embraced him once again. But now there was something else to be amazed at. What had happened to Heinz, to this young sailor? You really had to ask yourself, was this Heinz, this determined, serious young man? Becker felt disoriented and unsure of himself.

For what had he come here to do? He wanted to save a desperate and confused boy about to do something foolish. But here was this self-aware man with bright eyes—why had Becker risked this path into the lion's den? Did this young man even want to be rescued by him? The whole thing was beginning to have something comic about it.

(As serious as the situation was, it had considerable resemblance to what was happening at the Alexander Barracks, where at about the same time Lieutenant Schulze was trying to rescue the six hundred men of the security force, who were sleeping peacefully and wanted nothing better than to go on sleeping.)

At the portal across from the streetcar line things were more or less quiet. There several men lay on straw that had been spread about and slept; Friedrich and Heinz crouched beside each other. Heinz beamed at Friedrich.

"Dr. Becker, I still can't believe that it's you. That you've come here too. I can't tell you, Dr. Becker, how happy that makes me. For you it must have been quite another kind of decision than it was for me. The last thing I would ever have expected."

Becker was deeply moved, and at the same time agitated and unsure and at a loss for what to answer. He brought the conversation around to Heinz's mother and asked how Heinz himself had gotten the notion to come here to police headquarters, to the Spartacists; he had never mentioned any such intention before.

"No, I never did," Heinz laughed. "I couldn't have, where would I have got an idea like that? I didn't know anything, only my school, my home and a few pals. I went out to see my mother in Charlottenburg. I wanted to have a good talk with her and comfort her."

"Heinz, your mother told me everything."

"About my ingratitude and wickedness and so on, the shame of it all, right? Tell me straight."

"It's all right, Heinz."

"I know, I took it all in. But what was I supposed to tell the police? Lies? Heap yet more shame on the director? I won't do that. I can't help it if my father got carried away like that. It's a ghastly thought for me just to think that it was my father who went and beat the director to death, a man I was fond of. I was fond of him, and have much to thank him for; I, at least, won't forget him, even if they all sling mud at him. Mother called me a murderer because of my statement and chased me away."

Becker: "I know, Heinz."

"So I ran here. Angry up to here. And full of hate for all the meanness people have shown and because of the funeral, because of the cowardice of the faculty who wouldn't even show some sign of sympathy when their own director was beaten to death. Not one of them even sent a card to him in the clinic. Not one of them dared, and you're supposed to learn something from them? I didn't want to go back. It was all right with me that my mother had thrown me out. But I didn't know where to go."

He halted. Becker waited.

Heinz: "It's not easy to find work, Dr. Becker. I have fifty marks in the bank, but my mother has the bankbook. No money. I asked people on the street where I might find work. Someone told me on Brückenstrasse that you could sign up at the Reichstag, the pay was good, I could be a soldier for the government."

New people arrived, most of them armed, and threw themselves down on the straw. They didn't know each other. They squeezed together.

Heinz whispered: "We've got to call each other by our first names. Otherwise we'll be out of place here."

"Sure, go ahead, Heinz."

Heinz: "Thanks, and I beg your pardon, Friedrich."

"And how did things go from there, Heinz? How did you get here."

"Then there were some people standing on Blumenstrasse, arguing, and I stopped to listen. And all of them were cursing Ebert and Noske and saying that it would be just like it was under the Kaiser, and that if they could they'd bring the Kaiser and his officers back again. And one woman swore and said that it was already happening in her grade school, that the teachers were worthless and people didn't have anything to eat and only the profiteers were getting fat. And so I thought: why should I go to the Reichstag and fight for them? I had already heard from other people how corrupt and nasty they are. And now here they were trying to play the superpatriots. And so that's why I came over here."

He took Becker by the arm. "And I was right, wasn't I? You just have to take a look around at what kind of men and women these are. I've never seen people like them. And now you're here yourself, Friedrich. I can't tell you how happy that makes me. Have you been here long?"

"For about an hour."

"I can hardly believe they let you through, but it's splendid, and now I'm just that much happier to be here. And you can shoot a gun, we need people who know how. I don't."

"They haven't asked me to yet."

"Tell them yourself. And you know how to command. Wait, I'll come back with a couple of my group."

Becker: "Please, Heinz, don't tell anyone who I am."

"It wouldn't make any difference. But however you like."

When Becker sat there alone again, his shoulders drooped. A total defeat, a disgrace like none he had ever known, a bit of buffoonery.

And why, for what? To save Heinz. It was like his mother's attempt to tear that sick man from his evil wife, and there he was once again in her clutches.

But he had been led here, to this place, he had indeed. How was he supposed to understand that?

The shooting had stopped outside. Becker listened intently. That there was no shooting was not a good sign. Something was up. If only Heinz didn't come back now and see him in his misery.

But Heinz did return, and Becker was spared nothing.

Heinz brought another young fellow with him, a small lad with long hair. Becker found his way again just by looking into the face of this kid here in the dark. Both boys were loaded down with bread and beer bottles, and without ceremony sat down beside Becker on the straw. They spread out all they had on the ground. Both lads were sweaty and thirsty. They went on whispering as before.

When Becker turned down a bottle of beer that Heinz offered him ("Thanks, Heinz, those are rations for the men who've been working hard"), the other boy, who had a noticeably high voice, urged him to drink. Becker should go right ahead, they had plenty in reserve. Heinz introduced him: "This is Minna, Friedrich. She works as hard as two men."

Becker gazed at her in astonishment. It was a girl, or a woman, wearing a worker's shirt and cycling pants. Her hair fell disheveled into her face. She had a straightforward, proletarian face and small, lively, searching eyes. She chewed her bread and broke off a piece for Becker, which he took. Only now did he notice how faint he felt, he hadn't had anything to eat since that morning. She watched him.

"You're an intellectual. Did you study with Heinz?"

Heinz nodded: "We're good friends."

Minna, who said her last name was Imker, said, "We don't have many intellectuals here. There were more at *Vorwärts*. They wrote the propaganda there. Do you know Moeller or Fernbach, Comrade Friedrich? No? They got clubbed to death too. No use fooling ourselves about what's waiting for us if they get their hands on us. There's not a bit of humanity in them."

They sat there in silence. Minna gave Becker another piece of bread and smiled.

"Hungry, huh? I can imagine. There's no work for intellectuals either. I'd only like to know what the intellectuals expect from capitalism, because they don't seem to want to let go of it, even though the capitalists just use them as shoeshine boys. But I'll give you the answer, Comrade Friedrich: because the intellectuals are a long way from being so intelligent. And they're cowards besides."

She took a swallow from her beer and snapped the cap shut again. She sat there limp, her shoulders rounded, her legs pulled up to her.

"Tired?" Heinz asked.

Her shoulder shrugged and a few rapid twitches passed across her mouth, giving him his answer: what are you asking for, you know that already.

She peered with trusting eyes at Becker. "My brother was at *Vorwärts* too. He was in the war for a whole year." She breathed heavily. "And you, comrade, why have you come so late and why haven't you brought others with you? We need people. It took you long enough to see how things stood."

Becker looked helplessly toward Heinz.

Minna: "Just kind of keeping out of harm's way, I suppose that's it. Well, maybe more will join now, because they'll see how those guys are living it up and how they've treated our friends at *Vorwärts*. Maybe they'll still join, maybe. It's plenty late in the day."

Heinz: "Minna, he's been sick, from war injuries."

Minna: "I can see that. Who came back from the war healthy, I'd like to know. And what they'd love to do most, if they only could, is get us into another war tomorrow. Get up, Heinz. Our time's up."

She stood up, Heinz took another long pull at his beer. Someone was snoring loudly close by. Minna said to Heinz, "As soon as we're done with that doorway, you two go up on the second floor and have them tell you what you're supposed to do next. There's rifles and ammo in the cellar."

She turned to Becker, brushing her hair back behind her ears.

"Do you think it's all over with us, too, Comrade Friedrich? Karl was here yesterday and kept on saying: 'Stick to it, don't slacken, the revolution is growing all over the Reich, and in Berlin things are getting better for us, the whole working class is banding together since the murders in the dragoon barracks.' Karl didn't come today. Rosa has never been here at all. And they say Eichhorn has gone off. I don't believe it. They should blow the head off anyone who tries to save his dirty hide."

She gave Friedrich her hand. "Bye. I'll send Heinz over as soon as we're done."

The Crisis

Becker could only wait, so he eased himself back down and sat alone. The girl despised him. What pain there was in her brow, in her small eyes, around her lips.

He talked to himself: I'm getting worse from minute to minute, I'm lost. They're going to hand me a gun now and I'll have to shoot. His hands seemed to fly. He didn't know what was happening to him. He buttoned his collar, but more than anything he would have liked to throw himself to the ground and rip his own chest apart.

Heinz turned up sooner than expected to say that the command post on the second floor had issued orders for them to find a free window on the third floor. They were to take up a position there. Heinz whispered archly, "I cheated. I told them we could both shoot a gun. I'll get the rifles now."

When he returned with two rifles and ammunition, Becker took one of them from him without a word and trotted up the stairs behind him. A great many people, men and women, were moving up and down the stairs. Outside, the stillness reigned as before; the artillery had been brought up into position.

On the third floor, Heinz and Becker asked for directions. They opened a great many doors. The offices, large and small, were all more or less occupied with armed men. They found a narrow file closet with a high window that looked out onto Alexanderstrasse.

Becker suppressed all thought. He acted mechanically. He tried to shut out everything else and act like a soldier in battle who has a specific mission to fulfill. Because he had no choice. Occasionally, spontaneous thoughts and questions arose inside him against him will. He was brought back to reality by the painful sensation of having gotten himself caught somehow, he wrenched himself around and turned with his rifle out toward the street.

They stood at the open window and watched the far side of Alexanderstrasse, which was still unoccupied even now, a row of multi-storied private homes from the roofs of which there had been gunfire just a while before. They were told that they should keep close aim on the intersection of Kaiserstrasse and Alexanderstrasse. It was clear that the attack would come from there. Becker thought: what would Maus and the sergeant major, the unit commander over there in Kleine Frankfurter Strasse, say if they knew that I'm standing here on the third floor of police headquarters with a gun in my hands and firing in their faces. And that for that they let me cross over here, and that this is the result of my adventure. It is my fate to perish here, dishonored and disgraced, a more miserable creature than if I had been killed in the war, and it was on account of the war that I tore my own heart out and have gone down this path, and now here I stand acting in contradiction to everything that I am as a man.

How is that any different from suicide?

And a whole conflagration of terrible thoughts flashed up within him. Why had he not died back then, when in his helplessness and desperation he had put the noose around his neck. If only he had done it a second time. The whole rescue, the healing, the light and the knowledge, all of it lies. Because he could see it now: he had battled his way through all the terrors of the past months only to end up here now, at this random spot with a gun in his hand, to fire it and fall.

In the meantime, another Becker had been studying the situation militarily, and had told Heinz that there was no point in standing here gaping out the window. They couldn't see anything from here, they would have to move further north. He suggested that they work their way up the corridor to their left.

And so they left the narrow file closet, wandered up the long hall and ended up in a room with a lot of tables and cabinets where most of the windows were already occupied. The room had been divided by the cabinets into two halves, and Becker and Heinz finally found a free window after a search. As they had seen the others doing on the other side, they shoved filing cabinets over and used them for cover.

After a while they could make out large charts and graphs on the walls in the darkness. In the cabinets were stored plaster casts of human skulls, criminal cases, a grisly exhibition. Apparently they were in the workroom of the criminal investigations division.

They flung open the window and discovered that they were now catercorner from Kaiserstrasse. To their right and left stretched Alexanderstrasse with its black housefronts. There were lights blinking on Alexander Platz.

Heinz wanted to know how you use a rifle. Becker said he could hardly learn that in fifteen minutes, he'd be better off to forget it. But

Heinz insisted. So they threw themselves on the floor behind a cabinet and by the light of a flashlight Becker demonstrated to his friend the use of a rifle and several grips. Heinz listened intently and got the knack of it.

My life has been destroyed, Becker thought. I have fallen irredeemably back into war. It is 1917. And I'm thinking that I can save myself. And I was depending on the mercy of God.

There was a loud boom. The artillery had thrown its first grenades into the building from the other side. Somewhere machine guns rattled. Heinz got himself into position and took aim. He could not be held back. Becker gave him instuctions. From the windows next to them, people were firing wildly and without any clear notion of their object. Now there were calls for ammunition. Heinz put his gun down and ran off.

Then Becker set off as well. He wanted to have a look around the building. If he was going to have to fight, he wantd at least to know what was happening and what he could accomplish. Slowly, but with a firm step, he went down the corridor. He descended the stairs. The noise from the courtyard rolled up toward him. And then there was the open yard itself, the same scene as before, people swarming about, wagons, gear.

Becker was just about to force his way forward when there was a dreadful crash, an explosion, deathly stillness, terrible screams.

A grenade had fallen into the yard close to the street. There were calls for help, people rushed over to where the damage had occurred, the source of harsh screams and mad shrieks of those who had been hit. Worker-medics ran to the spot with their stretchers, people making way for them. The screams let up and then began again.

They moved past close to Becker with their first ghastly find: on the stretcher something without human form lay in a huddle of clothes and blood. Then followed stretchers with the prone forms of whimpering men. Two men dragged a soldier away by the arms and legs, his head dangling down. And who was it that a large, gray-bearded soldier was carrying in his arms, all by himself; carrying the body, he wept and begged: "Let me through."

The blood from the light body seeped through onto his shirt and trickled down his trousers and boots. You didn't need to search for the path to the cellar, a broad, bloody puddle showed the way. At last a stretcher came toward the old man. They took the body from him, arranged it carefully and quickly moved off.

"Are you an intellectual? Did you study with Heinz? We don't have many here, there were more at *Vorwärts*. And you, comrade, why have you come so late? It took you long enough. Just keeping out of harm's way I suppose."

It was Minna. Those were her cycling pants, that small face, waxen pale now, the long dark hair.

"It took you long enough. The intellectuals are a long way from being so intelligent."

Already the same noise filled the yard as before. Becker stood there at the same spot where the gray-bearded soldier had carried her past him.

Why am I standing here with my mouth hanging open?

He went into action, climbed the stairs.

She sacrificed herself. And you're hiding, aren't you ashamed? I wanted to rescue Heinz. That was nonsense.

His brain was working wildly and chaotically, but his emotions were running ahead of his thoughts.

The way she shared her bread with me, the way she checked me out so disdainfully. She knew me better than I know myself.

I wanted to rescue Heinz, but he had already understood before I did. These are poor human beings. They're searching for help. They don't know what else to do. And whatever they do, whether they're mistaken or not, they are my brothers and sisters, they are like me, and I am no better a man than they.

Becker had arrived at the top corridor and had to lean against the wall to catch his breath. It had all become clear to him. The fog had lifted.

This is good here. I'm at the spot where I belong, among creatures created by the same God who made me. Heavenly Father, and here I thought I had been deceived and that thou hadst forsaken me. Forgive me my fears and my doubts. Let me live no worse a life and die no worse a death than this girl.

Men raced past him carrying rifles. Heinz emerged from the large hall, looked around the corridor, recognized Becker, who had not been able to get his bearings. Becker greeted Heinz as if he were meeting him for the first time. Heinz could not understand this sudden warmth. He asked Friedrich what was happening down below, whether there were many wounded. Becker changed the subject. They went to work with their rifles at the window.

Now Becker started shooting, though it had been a long time since he had had a gun in his hand. While he did so, and while giving Heinz instructions, he said, "I have a confession to make to you, my boy, one that will surprise you. Do you know why I came here? On

410

your account. Only on your account. I was convinced after I left your mother that you would do something to hurt yourself."

"And then what?"

"I thought that you were desperate, and I looked for you here and found you, too, and wanted to rescue you."

Heinz threw his weapon to the floor. "And—so you didn't even want to come here, to join us? I figured you had had enough of them just like me, after all those dirty tricks with the funeral and even before that. I was so happy to see you here."

Becker: "But I am here, Heinz, you see. I only wanted to tell you because I could no longer keep it to myself. I've learned some things here."

"Just like me, Becker. Minna explained it all to me. A person like her is better than any lecture or book, isn't that right, Friedrich?"

Becker: "Come on, boy, let's not chew the rag."

And now the tension grew in the room, for the rat-a-tat of heavy machine guns was getting closer to the building. Once in a while there was the sound of a cannon being fired, but they did not hear any direct hits. Becker moved over to the men at the next window and warned them. They should keep back from the window as long as nothing was moving down below, it was enough if one of them kept watch. They discussed the idea. Now they could see cars down on the street corner, and alongside and in back of them a few men. Becker pulled his rifle to his cheek, aimed and shot. Next to him a gun rattled wildly. The cars across the way stopped, then advanced slowly. They had spotted the row of windows from which Becker was shooting. Down below, people ran back and forth.

Suddenly there was a crash of thunder. Then were was a wail that came at them, a whistling and grating and banging, iron on stone.

Everything in the room was blown apart, cabinets and cupboards lay shattered across the floor. A thick white dust filled the room.

Outside, masonry dissolved and tumbled down the facade. One window casement was torn away. In the ceiling above the window a wide hole gaped, mortar trickled down through it.

Nothing moved in the room. The largest load of stone had struck the fighters on the left. But Heinz and Becker lay buried under mortar and wood as well.

When Becker came to, he was laying on the floor on his stomach, and he felt a terrible pain in his right hand. He pulled it out from under him with great difficulty, only to discover that it was caught in a rifle barrel that had been broken off. His fingers were pinched between the barrel and the stock. He freed them slowly with great agony, his middle fingers hung down smashed. Then he rubbed the glass splinters from his forehead, chin and the back of his neck.

Meanwhile people near him began to get up, moaning, working themselves free and calling out. Becker set about to dig out Heinz by using his right elbow and good left hand. He couldn't see him. He felt faint himself, and while he worked he noticed a great, heavy headache growing.

He had no flashlight. The night sky offered little light. The piercing pain in his hand was awful, blood dripped from it. Becker called to Heinz. Once he thought, since nothing moved: maybe Heinz isn't here anymore, maybe he's gone off to get help. Becker burrowed among the wooden planks of the cupboard and shoved bundles of files and documents aside. The grisly plaster cast of a suicide's skull became visible. It must have been someone who had leapt from a window and smashed his right eye and mouth into a flat plane, like a flounder.

Now Becker could see cloth, and a leg beneath it. There lay Heinz, unconscious.

Coughing, dizzy and half faint himself, Becker worked away. He cast clumps of stone and boards to one side, underneath he could feel Heinz's chest. Just a few more boards and he would have the face free. Now he rolled him over and pulled him from the mass of debris.

Heinz's face was pasty wet, presumably with blood. His chest lifted, but Heinz did not answer him. Now Becker had to go over to the men at the neighboring window. They had freed themselves, were kneeling on the floor, groaning and calling out. Becker, although reeling himself, helped one man up. They swayed arm in arm out into the corridor, but then the man could go no further, and fell stretched out, moaning loudly, right in the middle of the hall.

While the building trembled from further direct hits, Becker staggered painfully back down the corridor until he came to the top of the stairs, where wounded men were sitting. A robust woman took one look at him, grabbed him by the arm and helped him down the stairs. She led him into the cellar. There a small first-aid station had been set up. Becker's right hand was crudely sterilized, then quickly laid in plaster and bound up. They looked for splinters on his head and neck. They gave him something to drink, but he urged them repeatedly to go look for more men still lying up on the third floor. He was bedded down on straw next to others. He could only give vague instructions about which room he meant. He lost consciousness again. But people went looking.

At last they stumbled over the man Becker had brought out into the

412

hallway on the third floor; he was screaming. Not far from him a door stood open, and when they shone a light into the room they found it totally in ruins. They found Heinz just as Becker had left him. They dug out the men from the next window position, but none of them showed any vital signs now. They dragged Heinz into the corridor, for artillery fire was increasing and shrapnel was landing in the ceiling. Medics came with their stretchers.

Heinz was unconscious. They put him in the cellar next to Becker, who sat up for a moment as they laid him down. But he fell back immediately.

The Fall of Police Headquarters and Its Epilogue

The security force, although six hundred men strong, had no choice when confronted by Lieutenant Schulze but to march as Schulze commanded them.

Indeed, this lieutenant went about dealing with his locked and bolted box of treasure differently than did the Red civilian engineer who had sat in the Reichs Printing Office with his men and couldn't find his way into the vaults with their millions. The good bureaucrats wouldn't give him the key; they had their instructions and held to them—which was the reason why Emil Eichhorn, the chief of police, did not get his money, and why the revolutionaries' automatic weapons had to discharge themselves on Hausvogtei Platz all on their own, because no one wanted to fire them, and why they were so bitter in censuring their erstwhile owners. Lieutenant Schulze did not ask the security force, he fetched them out of the Alexander Barracks, gave the order "Forward, March!" and not one of those Prussian hearts could resist.

When four-thirty came that morning, his forces spread out along the streets around police headquarters and approached the building under cover of artillery fire.

They fought their way up Wadzekstrasse and Kleine Frankfurter Strasse. They threw hand grenades into the cellars. At about five forty-five, the guns moved up onto Kaiserstrasse and bombarded headquarters from in close. The effect of their artillery fire was enormous: machine guns were sent hurtling off to the side, their gunners killed, wounded or chased off.

The men under seige resisted doggedly, as though crazed. They knew from what had become of *Vorwärts* what awaited them. They kept on firing from all the windows of police headquarters and would

413

not surrender. Kaiserstrasse and the streets adjoining it were badly damaged.

Things were rough inside. A fellow named Braune was in command. His troops were melting away. He risked leaving the building, walked up to the nearest White guard and demanded to be led to his commander, that is Lieutenant Schulze. Braune told Schulze that he had just come from the Reichs Chancellery on Wilhelmstrasse and had been given permission to surrender the building and depart with his people.

Schulze wanted to see that in black and white, he would only accept unconditional surrender. Braune did not take kindly to the idea, he asked for ten minutes to consider it, and they allowed him to return to police headquarters under a white flag.

Finally, after ten minutes, a man came out of the building with the same white flag. But instead of going across the street to Schulze, as had been arranged, he turned down a side street and was seen no more. But this was not Braune. They caught him later; he was simply a fellow who had seen the white flag lying there in the building and for private reasons had gone his own way with it shortly before the final whistle.

As the morning of January 12th dawned, the storm troops moved in on the fatally wounded building behind cars on which machine guns had been mounted.

The people inside were ready. Unarmed men, arms raised, emerged from the building and declared that they wished to negotiate. They had no leader. They were urged to elect one and then to await the conditions of negotiation. These were provided and they read as follows:

Surrender of police headquarters. Surrender of all weapons. The entire occupation force to be taken captive and imprisoned at the Alexander Barracks until they could later be brought to trial by the government.

Despite death, destruction and exhaustion, these conditions caused a violent argument inside. There were many who swore they would fight to the end. They said it would be better to be shot in battle than to be clubbed to death in a barracks courtyard by the Whites. They did not even get around to choosing a leader or arriving at a decision. The attack on the building showed no signs of letting up, and so several of the men disarmed those of their own comrades who were unwilling to give up. And now a sombre group of warriors, unarmed, their wounded with them, emerged from the building and declared that they accepted the conditions of surrender.

414

The victors entered the courtyard. There were still shots being fired inside, and it was not clear at whom, but some of the most embittered men were firing at their comrades who had deserted them. There was an incredible tumult in the covered yard. There were the screams of the wounded, the bellowing of the enraged men who felt they had been betrayed, the wails of desperation and of terror before what awaited them.

Lieutenant Schulze had a stentorian voice. He managed to make himself heard. He announced that he would at once have any man executed who was still firing. That worked. The shooting stopped, the noise subsided. They began to put things in order.

Close to a hundred and fifty men were still found in the building; they were brought to the courtyard and searched. They had to hold their hands over their heads, and were made to keep them there for the march to the Alexander Barracks. This was not done without brutality.

As they marched up Münzstrasse by the light of dawn, escorted by the Whites, and were led into the courtyard of the barracks, the whole neighborhood around Münzstrasse, Schönhäuser Strasse and the livery-barn district was in an uproar. People felt an immense hatred for the government and for the White troops that it was making use of. There was a constant flash of gunfire from the low houses surrounding the barracks. The victorious troops had to illuminate the side streets with floodlights. But for a long time they could not subdue the popular rage, for people knew that their brothers and friends were being martyred and murdered inside the barracks.

The explanation given later was that the bodies found lying in the barracks courtyard were the victims of previous battles.

BOOK EIGHT

The Murder of Karl and Rosa

At Halle Gate and in Neukölln

Saturday evening, while the attack on police headquarters was in preparation, the doctor's family with whom Rosa was living near the Halle Gate was sitting in the dining room. Dinner had just been put on the table when the doorbell rang and Werner, a young worker who served as Karl's courier, appeared and stood whispering with the doctor for some time at the front door. Werner asked whether it was safe here and then disappeared, only to reappear a half hour later with Karl, who was looking for a place to spend the night.

Karl, his face gray and his cheekbones jutting out even more than usual, took off his dripping muddy winter coat in the entry. His boots were caked with clay. The doctor led him to his bedroom and had him take off his clothes. Karl washed and dried himself. In the doctor's bathrobe and slippers, he appeared in the living room and greeted Rosa, for whom he had a little present in his hand—the note she had written him, reading: "Karl, come back, all is forgiven." Waving the paper before her face, he smiled softly. "Thank you, Rosa, that was sweet of you."

She tore the note from his hand. It was like a knife in her heart to see him like this while she was sitting so comfortably in this bourgeois living room. She grabbed his hand. "Don't be angry, Karl."

After having taken a look at the little room where he would spend the night, Karl then returned to the others and admitted that he was hungry. They had already set a place for him. They all sat down to eat. Karl reached for the bread basket and began to stuff himself—and once again the doorbell rang, violently this time.

They all stood up at once. Rosa pulled Karl into her room. It was the courier again. Again he whispered with the doctor in the hallway and then he was led to Karl. Trouble was brewing. A comrade had just

419

told him that spies had the doctor's address. Karl and Rosa would do well to get out of here as quickly as possible.

Neither more worn nor more upset than usual, Karl appeared once again in the living room and went to work again on the bread. Being hunted, having to keep moving—they no longer made any difference to him. He chewed calmly and was glad when the doctor's wife carefully prepared a thick sandwich for him. He hadn't had one in a long time. Rosa pressed him to go get his clothes on. But he ate. He suggested that she precede him, which was necessary in any case. But where should they go? They discussed this with the courier, for whom the doctor had poured a glass of beer, and Werner suggested Neukölln, at the home of a reliable comrade.

They accepted the invitation at once, and Werner and Rosa took off while Karl made himself comfortable. With a grateful smile, he announced that for once he had to stuff himself.

Then the courier came back and told him he would have to leave the richly laden table. Karl had to change his clothes. But he would not part with his muddy, wet hat and coat, they were old comrades-in-the storm; he would not betray them, and they would not betray him. He did not trust the doctor's clothes. He left in an amiable mood, refreshed now, and waved as he thanked them, "Good-bye—and so it's off to Neukölln.

It was not far.

In the darkness, he entered a tenement and climbed the stairs to an apartment in a side wing. The comrade's wife, an energetic, serious lady, made room for Karl in her living room; Rosa had already taken over the one bedroom that was not let out. The woman was proud to have Karl and Rosa in her home. The man was still at work. She could not be talked out of setting a table for her guests first thing. Karl beamed. The feast was to continue. Werner, the courier, had to stay as well.

The night passed in perfect quiet. This was the night of terror from Saturday to Sunday, when police headquarters was surrounded, bombarded and stormed.

The couple disappeared early that morning. About ten o'clock a copy of *Vorwärts* was shoved under the door, and shortly afterward the courier appeared, from whom Karl and Rosa learned all the latest news.

Yes, this was the end, the finish. Why hide the fact. Rosa wept as the courier reported what he had heard about how the prisoners were treated on the way to the barracks and what had happened there. Karl stood there, white and slumped. He shuffled over to the sofa, where he sat down.

When they were alone, Rosa wept for a while silently to herself. She glanced over at him. He did not speak. Then she went to her bedroom.

She could hear him pacing back and forth in the other room. And when she once had her tears under control she went in to join him, her face red from weeping. She watched as he moved back and forth, his hands in his trouser pockets. She sat at the table, her lips and cheeks trembling, even her shoulders, and said, "Karl, be honest, tell me yourself, did it have to be like this?"

He did not answer.

Rosa: "We predicted it all. All of it. You wouldn't listen."

He stopped, sighed and said softly, "No."

She was paying close attention. "You still stick by it even now? Karl, that can't be, I can't bear it. I'll not stay another minute under the same roof with you if you just stand there and have nothing more to say, not a single word."

"Please, tell me what word I ought to say."

"You have to ask? Karl, are you a czar, or are you Napoleon, dragging the workers into his war for his own goals and leaving them lying there on the battlefield—and if it was a defeat, why then it was just another defeat?"

"Rosa, the cause of the proletariat will continue amid defeats. You've said that yourself."

"That's not how I meant it. Men have died, Karl. You drove them to their deaths."

"You're a monster, Rosa."

He pounded on the table.

"I am? Then what are you? You, the man who has them on his conscience? Stand still for once. You can't run away from yourself. I, no, we demand that you account for these deaths. I have fought for the proletariat my whole life long, and you had better believe I won't be silent before you now. We tried to convince you, we came to you with our facts and our arguments. We showed you how things stood, within the working class and among our foes, and what immediate preparations we needed to make."

Karl: "I know, the Constituent Assembly."

She would not let him interrupt.

"Any child could have seen what was coming. Your own friends, your Party. The great masses were not with you. If ever there was an example of a putsch, of an arbitrary stunt, then it was what you've done. You still don't realize what damage you've caused. You're as good as blind. But you'll realize it soon enough perhaps. Karl, I don't know how you can stand to live with yourself."

He was standing at the window, and he made a faltering, resigned gesture with one hand. "Don't say that, Rosa, not that too."

Then, as he sat down at the table across from her, his eyes directed at the tablecloth, she had a chance to gaze calmly at this man, her comrade in suffering and in arms, this fugitive, half-starved, in his filthy, rumpled clothes, with fallen cheeks bristly with a growth of beard.

He pulled his bloodless lips apart. "They fought bravely. What's going on now is the brutality of the Whites."

She wrung her hands. "To have them in that situation, that they had to fall into their hands."

He motioned for her to stop.

"Our dear friends who've fallen in battle and who are now being clubbed to death, Rosa, our good comrades. It's hard to sit here, Rosa. Why am I sitting here? What good am I doing here?"

He began to pace again. "What ought we to do, Rosa? What do you advise? What ought we to do?" He stared ahead in torment, frowning.

She said angrily, "Leo suggested toward the end that we ought to go to Frankfurt am Main."

"I know."

"And what have you taken into your head now?"

Karl: "I'm not going, under any circumstances."

Rosa: "I agree."

He turned around to her on the far side of the table and nodded.

And when she saw how his face had changed, suffering, grave, with his fixed stare, she thought of the dead and the martyred, and she began to sob for anger and pain, and had to hold her hands to her eyes. She didn't want to look at him.

"What shall we do, Karl?"

He: "They'll try the shabbiest trick of all. They want to try us in their middle-class courts. They'll renounce the revolution that put them at the helm. They'll slander us as common criminals, convicting us under some legal clause or other. That's how it is, Rosa. That's why we must show them that there's still a revolution. We are staying here."

Rosa: "Do we write anything?"

Karl: "We've got to spoil their fun. We can't let them get away with it. The *Rote Fahne* will continue to be published. We'll tear the mask from their faces day by day. Ebert and Noske are not to be allowed one peaceful hour. These murders are on their heads. We have taken on as our opponents a pack of murderers, beasts, wolf-men.''

Rosa suddenly felt faint. Karl saw this and took hold of her hand. "You're not feeling well, Rosa."

Rosa: "I'm not as strong as you are."

And without explanation she crept back to her room and threw herself on the bed.

There in his room he did calisthenics as though he were in prison. He needed the physical exercise. He did knee-bends, he stretched his arms and pulled them back in; he kept it up for a quarter hour. Then he planted himself at the window and watched intently what was happening down in the Sunday courtyard.

Around noon, Rosa came back in. The atrocities at the barracks had given her no rest.

"Karl, they're *les Boches*. I figured it out. There you see what the Belgians and the French were talking about. We weren't treated like that even in Russia under the czars. They didn't dare touch us. A prisoner was considered a sad case."

Karl: "Rosa, the Whites act the same way all over the world."

"No, they're *les Boches* who deported Belgians, sadists who show their brutality when they see no one there to resist them. Born sadists who take pleasure in watching others suffer."

"Nonsense, Rosa, you're talking like a patriot from the Entente. These people have been brutalized and ruined by the war. And add to that the cruelty with which Prussian junkers and officers love to give orders and that comes with the privileges they enjoy. Crush that class, and you've almost got your peace right there."

"I've said the same thing myself often enough. If only I could believe it, Karl."

"What do you think it is then?"

"Your Germans have war in their bellies, all of them, from top to bottom. The elimination of a class won't help either. You can create any society you want for them, they'll wage war. And Karl, once you get these barbarians, with or without their monocles, into heaven, then they'll organize the heavenly hosts and wage war against God himself."

(She did not know how this metaphor suddenly came to her, the excitement of the moment stirred it up within her.)

He laughed: "I assume that war is already in good hands, in Satan's."

She stopped, unsure of herself, and looked for the words, for her thoughts. She had lost the thread. How had she come to speak of the battle of the angels against God, and now Karl to speak of Satan. She repeated herself (and for the moment freed herself of her insecurity): "Well, Karl, what can you do with creatures like that? That's why pacifism is useless here as well."

Karl, calmly: "So then, now you're for dictatorship, a new sort of steeled man must be created."

She flinched. What was that? How had he come up with that? She answered, uncertainly (did he notice how insecure she was?): "Thanks, but no thanks, for that sort of man."

Karl remained gentle. "So then, pacifism is useless, elimination of warring classes doesn't help; what does help then, Rosa?"

She wiped her tears away. "Nothing at all. No, nothing at all."

He nodded. He understood. She was a desperate, nervous woman; he had had such conversations before.

Early that afternoon there was a familiar knocking at the door of the apartment. Rosa looked through the peep-hole. It was Tanya, who had come from the doctor's at Halle Gate and brought clothing for Rosa as well as a package with tea, sugar and cigarettes. When she had made tea and set the kitchen table as best she could, she called Karl in, who wanted to hear the latest news from Tanya.

They could not expect a great deal of Tanya. She said that everything was very quiet in the city, because it was Sunday, you know, and she had not ventured over toward Alexanderplatz. Everyone was happy that the shooting had stopped, there had been a lot of ruffians, in cars, who had been robbing people.

Karl asked in a resigned voice whether she had seen these robbers. No, that she hadn't. But she'd been told about it.

Karl: Those were officers in civvies trying to spread panic.

After tea, he left the women alone, and the moment he closed the door, Tanya at once began to whisper: "Can he hear us?"

Rosa: "What's up?"

Tanya pulled her to the window.

"See that you get out of here. They're going to do something to you. Why are you always hanging around with him? They are already cursing you more than they curse Karl. Rosa, they're ready to kill someone just for putting in a good word for you."

"Okay, and what am I supposed to do?"

Tanya pointed toward the door. "What's he intend to do?"

Rosa: "Nothing. We're here for now. We smoke cigarettes and drink tea."

Tanya: "He's to blame for everything. Why do you hang around with him? Let him go his way. You're not going to stay with him, are you?"

424

"Why not? He's not doing anything to me."

Tanya: "He can stay here then. But you have no reason to."

"How do you know that?"

And then the white mask gazed at her with such a deep and long look that it seemed to Rosa as if she were being hypnotized, and it was a knowing look—the cell, Hannes.

"Come to Breslau, Rosa. This is no place for you."

Rosa, after a pause: "And—how do we get there?"

Tanya grasped her hand in delight.

Rosa: "I can't go by train."

Tanya: "We'll think about that."

Tanya got ready to go. Rosa held her tight by the arm.

"Be careful. Don't blabber with people you don't know. You know that if you say anything about me, I'm lost."

Rosa sat alone, in a jumble of emotions. It seemed to her that she had dared to make a first step. Just by allowing Tanya to say that sort of thing about Karl.

She heard him pacing in the next room. She was afraid. But nothing had happened after all.

When the afternoon had crept by, Karl's courier appeared again. News? Yes. Karl's oldest son had been arrested.

Rosa lit the lamp in her room. Karl had taken the news hard.

"They're taking hostages," he said.

He only began to improve when their hosts arrived. They brought newspapers and they all ate together.

Late that night, after their hosts had already gone to bed, he came in to see her once again. That pleased her. They talked about Sonya and his family. Karl was afraid that Sonya would lose her head, that she wasn't equal to such things. Who would stand by her? Once Karl declared that it would be better for his family if he surrendered. They could expect the absolute worst from the Whites. That thought was unbearable for him.

Rosa was beside herself. Was he crazy? Or did he believe that they would treat him kindly? If they were such beasts, it would not change them in the least if he surrendered. And what sort of effect would that have on the proletariat?

He muttered that it was only an idea.

But she saw that he was preoccupied with it. She talked to him, gave her arguments, ones which she did not believe herself. She could not bear the pain. When he had left her room, she turned the light off at once and groped for the little table with its rustling newspapers and sat back down.

Ah, sweet night. Not to know of anything else.

Her shoulders and knees began to tremble.

She found she was walking slowly across a frozen river. The ice floes crackled. The ice was not yet solid. But there were a lot of people walking on it.

She climbed up onto the riverbank and sat down on a bench on the promenade. She was seventeen years old. And here came another girl scrambling up after her from the ice, her skates still on her feet. It was her girlfriend B., with rosy cheeks, loose black hair, her fur cap in her hand. She tottered up to the bench, where at once she began to giggle and tell Rosa something.

But as Rosa looked into her green, radiant eyes, she thought, "Why are you doing this? Why have you gone to such trouble? I recognize you, don't you know?"

And sure enough, young B. took hold of the back of her neck, and pulling at the full head of hair from the back and up over her face—her entire scalp—she tore away the whole fresh, girlish face with its nose, mouth and ears, and dangled the bloody plunder, laughing, but without changing the tone of voice.

"I'm so happy, you know, because we haven't seen each other for such a long time. What are you doing hanging around so long on earth, Rosa? How can you stand it? I've been dead for ever, ever so long now."

She had let the scalp fall onto a mound of snow, and sat there all prim and proper, her legs crossed, still wearing her skates. She unbuttoned her sporty winter coat. She had pulled her fur cap way down over her face so that the others could not see the skull.

She giggled.

"Yes, Rosa, I was already dead by the time they put you in jail in Warsaw. I read about it in the newspaper, and I thought to myself: why does she allow them to do that, what does that get her? She must know how dangerous that is. And here you are still alive. That's funny."

Rosa suddenly felt as though she were a hundred years old and had long been dead herself, and had only just now come here to listen to all this once again and to sit here on the Vistula, on the promenade, on the bridge that had been blown up, and to see what had become of everyone.

"Living carefully and dying cheerfully," young B. whispered. "Means you've spoiled the devil's work."

And she reached down to the scalp and its girlish face and threw both it and her hair up into the air. As it flew it caught fire and fell back down in a shower of sparks like a rocket.

Rosa shook herself. "I don't like you, you ugly beast. I know you, you were always like that. Be on your way."

Then young B. stood up, pulled back her coat and showed beneath it her naked young body, her breasts, her navel, her pelvis, her legs. But as the light of day fell upon it and she did a teasing little dance before Rosa, the flesh melted and steamed off the bones. Her abdomen and chest emptied themselves, and the skeleton in a woman's coat and with a fur hat on its head hopped about yodeling—when a great, white hand shoved it to one side.

And bent down over Rosa from behind—him.

The skaters skated away and were lost at once. They massed themselves out on the ice behind her and grew small as flies.

It was he, but he did not speak.

Finally, he said:

"What's the problem, Madame Lübeck? What's wrong? Still deep in thought? Everything still unclear?"

He came around to the front of the beach, walked up to her.

He was as gigantic as last time. He accommodated himself to his environment. At night he formed himself into dark cloud masses, now he stood there grayish white against the bright background, and only his contours and external outline were visible, and the dead eyes of pride, so wide open, the sharply chiseled mouth, its static smile, the iron shoulders, the frightening biceps.

He was an angel, the anti-god. He spoke:

"My advice to you, Rosa, was to give up your illusions. It seemed that you had accepted that advice. I told you to accept things as they are and not to submit your will to anyone else's. That proves that you are a human being. Whatever eludes you shows you your own weaknesses. Your limitations reveal your failings. But you will accept no weaknesses and no limit. For I have made you free. Do you understand, Rosa?"

She whispered, "Yes."

He: "There is nothing finer than a benefactor of mankind. You and those like you have found your occupation. Death and destruction flower along your paths as along no one else's. You are my friends and helpmates, because you sow more hope and harvest more despair than anyone else. And so you make the field free for me."

Rosa: "Is there such a thing as progress, Satan?"

"There is, and you are in its service. There is progress, but no peace. The goal and the path, you know them both. And there is no room for either emotion nor scruples. You must be made of steel."

He let loose a laugh. "And no sympathy and no mercy."

(Rosa thought of her friends who were being slaughtered, and of Karl in the next room, and she wept silently.)

Satan: "Death to emotion. You are slaves, free yourselves. Think of the goal. You must make a place for yourself in this world, despite the others, as I did. You are my blood. Do not disgrace me. You have reason and your will, no one can resist that, not even him. Don't humble yourself with emotions, don't let them make a fool of you. That's how he toys with you."

In his anger, Satan bore her high above the white ice. She hovered there in his arms. She was dizzy.

He raged: "You are free, don't you finally understand? Because you keep on whimpering, I don't know for whom, but you deserve to be hurled into the maw of the other one. You have all deserved my leaving you right where you plunked yourself down, in the trees, as half-apes. What's all this whimpering? Do you want to go back to your nest and crack nuts? Still want that paradise just beyond the roofs?"

She complained, "They are clubbing my friends to death."

"So they're clubbing. Why not? There are all sorts of things going on in this world. There are cherries, there are apples, there are plums. Why not death? Why not pain?"

He was furious. "You cry-baby, you sissy. When you're lying there dead, I'll not even bend down to pick you up."

He let go of her, kicking her with his foot as she fell.

She hugged the table tightly. She moaned aloud. Karl called out from the other room, "Rosa, what's wrong? Aren't you well?"

He came in and turned on the light. "You fell asleep over the papers."

She stood against the wall and sobbed convulsively. In dark fear, and for the dead. At least in front of Karl she could do that freely.

Through her mind a desperate thought wandered: "I'm riding like a witch to Walpurgis Night again."

Four Hundred Dead Men All in a Row

Monday morning, January 13th, the day after the fall of police headquarters. The government of the Reich thought it could allow itself to issue yet another call to the German people—and this was being studied by the officers of the Guard Cavalry Rifle Division after a hearty breakfast in the Potsdam officers club.

428

One of them, in a leather armchair, his legs stretched out comfortably, his pipe in his mouth, held the paper and read it aloud for the others.

"A call to the German people!" (Gentlemen, doesn't that grab you when Fritzie Ebert says "German people?" I ask you. Whoever feels touched, raise his hand. No one? Well look at that.)

"After a week of severe disorder, life returns to normalcy. The loyal troops of the government have succeeded—(succeeded, he says, there we are right back in the same old mess, and since when are we the loyal troops of the government? No comments, please, just keep on reading!)—have succeeded" (Good lord, man, you don't have to serve up all that old hash for us. Fine, so I'll skip that part.) "Misguided fanatics, together with certain dubious elements of the city—" (wait, a pause, please: who is who? Who are the misguided fanatics and who are the dubious elements of the city? The ones like Ebert and Scheidemann? They're what? You leave that to me. Laughter. Who are these misguided fanatics? — I suppose Liebknecht. Ebert and Scheidemann as misguided fanatics, not with all the goodwill in the world. — Fanatics never, misguided is more like it. Only do you know who misguided them, huh? We did. Yes indeed. Excellent. A peal of laughter. Attention, three laughs in honor of their speaker, ha, ha, ha, that's it. Please, not so loud, gentlemen. The walls have ears. — But damn I would really like to find out once and for all what these crazy men, together with the dregs of the city, have been up to, what they've instigated. Yes, sir, read on.)

"Met with the resistance of the people, especially of the working class" (There you have it. That's a lulu. Doesn't that strike you funny. Soon we'll have no choice but turn the cannons around in the other direction. We're playing the role of his shoeshine boys, and then he goes ahead and gives us a kick. What alluring prospects. Still all that alluring? You're a sweetheart.)

"And so on, and so on. I can't bring myself to say it. A rehash of the same old atrocities, the ravages of criminal acts (looks like they copied it out of some suburban paper, for granddaddy sipping his coffee). The hogwash ends with the following hope: 'the hope, that this victory will open a new chapter in world history for the benefit of our people and of all mankind.' (Hilarious. The seizure of *Vorwärts*, the fact that the Socialists have got their *Vorwärts* back, is supposed to open a new chapter in world history. Looks to me like they've gone off the deep end. And it's not sufficient for the German people to rejoice, but all mankind has to get into the act. All mankind is supposed to profit from the Socialists' putting out their greasy old rag *Vorwärts*—Chinese, Eskimos, Hottentotts and Jews. — Let them have it, comrade, their hope in a new chapter in world history. That chapter's coming. But it will be written by us, and the call to the people we compose will look different than this.)"

The noble gentlemen were angry because others had beat them to the conquest of Berlin, and because it looked as if just in general one ought not to show one's face in Berlin. Which was why, for instance, Noske had personally marched in the parade. But what could they do to counter? Play along with them? Out of the question. Their motto remained: don't let them push us out. By the way, Lieutenant Maus was sitting here as the guest of these gentlemen. He had been sent on a mission to these troops and was then invited by the officers to stay for breakfast.

A rough morning for young Herr Maus. The memory of the scene in Becker's sickroom will not let him go. His work with the troops is no longer any fun. Something of Becker has apparently rubbed off on him.

He is my friend after all, and this is how they treat him in front of me. And what will Hilda think if I just go ahead and quietly volunteer my services here as if nothing has happened, without drawing any conclusions from it all?

Oh, the troubles of the Germans!

Monday morning in Neukölln, Karl bravely declared that if nothing new happened in the course of the day he would go for a walk in the streets that afternoon. Why not? Neukölln was the securest place in the world. It was certainly more secure than Finland, where Lenin had hidden in his day. Karl joked that he was safer in Neukölln than he would be in jail.

He stomped around the parlor like an impatient foal.

He repeated to Rosa, who wasn't convinced it would seem, "We're going to show ourselves this afternoon for our comrades. Why be so cautious anyway, Rosa? What do you expect for the future? We'll be locked up for a long time. We can then study the question of whether, and if so in what way, the prison system of a republic differs from that of an empire."

He even cheered Rosa up, and together they prepared a fighting article for the *Rote Fahne,* which made the morning fly quickly. The courier brought newspapers and reports. They were still busy with them when the courier, whom Karl had told about his grand plans for the afternoon, reappeared.

Alarm. Nothing would come of their lovely walk. This new hiding place of Karl's and Rosa's had been discovered. That at least was the word Werner had—Karl's young courier, whom he trusted implicitly.

Karl shook his head. You could live more securely in Finland than in Neukölln, and while they were discussing the matter, Rosa's secretary, having finally found her way out here, arrived only to learn that they must take up their wanderings yet again. As always in such situations, Karl was completely unflappable.

What Rosa and her secretary managed get out of Werner regarding the cause for such alarm, however, did not wholly satisfy the two of them. A man who worked in the intelligence bureau at the headquarters of the municipal commander, a reliable Spartacist, was supposed to have whispered to him that they knew where Karl and Rosa were. He had mentioned Neukölln. And they also appeared to know the street as well. In any case, word had leaked, and this was no longer a safe spot.

Rosa had her doubts. How could it have leaked? They had not stirred from the apartment, and no one had seen them come up here. Werner shrugged, and said he was only warning them. If they wanted to test it—that was their business. He had warned them at least.

"That's enough, Rosa," Karl interposed. "Let's put our minds instead to where we go from here."

It then turned out that the secretary could play the role of guardian angel. In her purse she carried the keys to the apartment of the R.'s in Wilmersdorf, where she herself had put up for a time. She had kept the apartment keys in reserve, for an emergency, she said. The R.'s were reliable Independent comrades.

When Werner the courier heard the word Wilmersdorf, he agreed at once. Wilmersdorf would be secure. Rosa did not share that opinion. Wilmersdorf would be a bad place. Neukölln was much better, much more secure. Neukölln was a great deal more dependable than all the Independent apartments in other parts of town.

Karl laughed at this argument. "Rosa is a tough fighter and a conservative by nature." Rosa was outvoted and had to acquiesce.

Then transportation was arranged, again in two waves, first Karl with the secretary, who unlocked the apartment, then Rosa with this courier, whom she followed reluctantly. She had said to Karl with some annoyance before they left, "We should have stayed right here, and then spoken to our comrades in Neukölln this evening."

Karl laughed good-naturedly. "We'll get our chance, Rosa. You've got to help yourself, little mouse."

("Little mouse," she repeated dreamily to herself as she descended the stairs. Who called me that here recently? But in her haste she could not remember. Only her mistrust and uneasiness increased. Where's Tanya? Why has she deserted me like this?)

As they drove, Rosa declared openly to the courier that she was doing this for Karl's sake, so that she could stay together with Karl. She couldn't see the point of all this, and she was not at all comfortable with the idea of middle-class Wilmersdorf.

But when she arrived with Werner, Karl had already taken possession of his room and he gave Rosa a tour. It was a pleasantly furnished room, but nothing special. He declared: "I am lord of all this realm, were his words to Egypt's king, I confess it gives me pleasure."

The occupant of the apartment, Frau R., led Rosa to her room. Really, as far as living went, this was more comfortable than in Neukölln.

Had she been satisfied with her cicerone, asked Karl.

Rosa pulled herself together and shook Werner's hand.

Karl retreated to his room. He was calm and cool when he departed. In a quarter of an hour, however, he came back to Rosa, *Vorwärts* in hand, his face distorted, looking grim, tugging at his mustache. While he spoke, his nostrils distended. There was something sullen and savage in his expression.

Vorwärts, which they had lost right along with police headquarters, had published a little poem with the title "Proletarians," the final verse of which read:

> "Four hundred dead men all in a row,
> Proletarians!
> Karl and Radek, Rosa and Co.
> No show. No show.
> Proletarians."

"Listen to that, Rosa. What do these bastards want, these paid scribblers and hacks? And why do they print that stuff? It's a denunciation. We're not lying there with the rest of them, we're missing in the ranks of the murdered men, without us that long row of murdered men just isn't as much fun. They're calling for a repeat performance. The beast hasn't murdered enough yet. They're foaming at the mouth to get us. Why? Because they're traitors and stand there exposed in front of us. That's why they send their bloodhounds and their wolfmen against us."

Rosa: "Karl, throw the paper away. Is that news to you?"

But Karl couldn't get over it. He grieved for the dead at *Vorwärts* and at police headquarters, and now nothing could stop the beast.

"What have we worked for, Rosa, for what?"

432

That was the same song she herself had sung in prison.

And with visible horror he spoke once again of the new type of men that he met among the Whites everywhere now, with faces like those of jackals and wolves, men of unspeakable malice and cruelty, the garbage of war, the last degeneration of mankind.

"These wolf-men are a departure from nature. They're lower than animals, purest degeneration. Because civilization is part of nature. Reason has been given to us so that we can shape and order our relations with each other. But they use it to ruin nature itself."

And he raged on, argued, and while he paced back and forth he began to settle his accounts with his own pacifism.

"Rosa, the only ones to profit from our love of peace were the scoundrels. To them it looks like we're just castrating ourselves, and they like that, we're easy prey for them. If Leo Jogiches wants to rant and rave about the Bolsheviks and Lenin's dictatorship, I'll not join in. There's nothing to rant about. If you don't want to be murdered and have everything disappear down the gullets of the wolf-men, then you can't do without dictatorship. I know you think otherwise, Rosa, but I hope that at least you see what a dead-end street pacifism had brought us to."

Rosa remained silent.

He raged: "They want our blood, these semihumans, these nonhumans, these cadavers, these ghouls, in the hope perhaps of at least coming back to life themselves that way. But they'll get poisoned on us."

He sat down at a small, brown piano and propped his head on the closed top. She watched him from the side. His face muscles were quivering. He lifted the lid covering the keys and banged at a few notes, then more. He sat up, and slowly his doodling became the mournful aria from the *St. Matthew Passion* by Bach that she had often heard him play in better days.

While he played, she quietly left the room, a broken woman. She did not turn on the light in her room.

If only sleep would come soon.

A Message from Hannes

"More cares?" he mocked. "Always these worries and woes, my darling. You're tormented by what you think you owe others, is that it? Ah, those sweet emotions. And you, where are you? What do you owe yourself?"

Karl was playing in the next room.

He: "He's putting his whole soul into it. Listen, what nobility of soul, what a glow, what a great soul that must be. Go in to him, Rosa, cheer him up, dance for him, I mean metaphorically of course."

"Satan!"

"Yes, the lord, the leader and liberator of mankind, Lucifer the bringer of light. And you have sworn me your allegiance, Rosa. You will die soon. No offense intended, but I can't use you like this."

She murmured, "I know, I know."

He: "Don't go making scenes like some nervous little female."

Satan's voice was very close to her. "Rosa, to the barricades, charge! Do you want to hold on to this miserable world?"

Rosa: "I despise it just as you do. I don't want to hear anything about any emotion."

He: "You don't need to worship me. You don't even need to swear to me. Swear to yourself."

As she lay there on her bed she thought: I am not afraid of the death of which he speaks. When I'm dead, I'll not lead the beggar's existence that Hannes does, standing before other people's doors and knocking. I will be happy to be without this sad body. Truly. He's right, everything here is misbegotten, and we had these bodies hung on us to humble us and to keep us from being critical. But now the hour of liberation has come.

She was awakened during the night by a humming sound. She sat up. The humming was very close to her. She decided the proper thing to do was to stretch out and listen quietly to the sound and determine where it came from. It was a mysterious noise, a melodic rustling and soughing that from time to time almost took on the character of a song. She thought in her dreamlike state: that's left over from the music that Karl was making yesterday.

But now she jerked up; she could differentiate words and sentences.

She had not thought of Hannes, last of all of him, and certainly not in connection with this peculiar sweet voice—but who else could it be?

"Hannes?" she called.

"This isn't Hannes," came the answer.

She sat up and looked all around the dark room. But she could not make out anything. The sweet rustling and humming and wafting continued. She had to lie back down and stretch out again.

"Is it you, Satan?"

"It isn't Satan."

It sounded too furtive and too tender for that. She gave herself over to the wordless sounds, without any further questions. Then she began again:

"Wouldn't you like to tell me who you are?"

"I've come with a message from Hannes."

Rosa: "Why didn't he come himself?"

"He is far away. He cannot come. If you call the name Hannes, he can no longer hear you."

Rosa: "How do you mean? What's he doing? Why can't he hear? I don't understand. He was everywhere and could always come, why not now? What glorious wanderings he made. He knew no boundaries. Time itself did not hold him back. He fought old battles all over again. But he always returned to me. I loved him, loved his proud spirit. He shone through the centuries."

The voice: "Where he now sojourns, he lies on the ground and wrings his hands."

She shrieked: "So that's what you've done with him. You finally brought him down. I should have known. That's why he no longer came to me."

The voice: "Whoever lives, strives for perfection, bends back upon his origins to the primal cause and wishes to be perfect. Rosa, I have brought you a message from Hannes."

Rosa: "What does he say?"

The voice: "This is the message Hannes sends you through me:

"I could not speak with you that time. I was being pursued. But not by anyone else. I was chasing myself. I could not separate myself from this world, and you were holding onto me. And so I went back to find myself, and to begin all over again what had ended so suddenly and so bitterly. But each time, I didn't know why, I was thrown back. I was not permitted a new beginning. Life had been lived. I screamed, I was desperate—and I tried again. And did it many times over.

"Then I stopped immersing myself in distant centuries and I no longer wandered across the earth. I investigated my own life, what was behind all this, why I could not get any further, what was pushing me away. I investigated my own life, trying to learn why this was happening to me and why I had to despair like this. I went back through the years of my life and found guilt and weakness and error and failure.

"I encountered the guilt of yesterday, and the day before, and the day before that. Oh, Rosa, like a tree that has blossomed and withered, that's how I stood there and then bent down and picked up all the faded petals, trying to recognize myself in them, and I wept. Oh what misery, all that way back.

"It was a different way I took than the proud path of earlier years.

As I strode by, the good and evil deeds rose up from the ground. I had to bend down to them and look into their gray, vanished faces. I was doomed to look in their faces, in the name of justice, at the bidding of the powers of heaven.

"Because it was a judgment. It was judgment, Rosa. When I had looked them in the face and recognized them and named them, they rose up and joined me on my way. They crept along behind me. Sometimes they were already standing, and had been—waiting for me for a long time and were rescued at last when I came and led them away.

"And when you take hold of them with both hands and try to speak to them and they surround you at an intersection, that is when the great pain and suffering begins. The regrets, the lamentations. And you begin to sing a song with them as you go down that long, long road, a song of wandering, and they sing along, belting it out, and each new one that rises from the ground sings along, and each verse of the song ends with: 'Oh, if only I had, oh if only I hadn't. Oh if only I had, oh if only I hadn't.'"

Rosa: "Justice, did you say? Heavenly powers?"

"That is the message Hannes sends.

"He asks me to say:

"And as I went along it became clear to me what was happening. This was the dying. For I had not yet died. The regrets and the suffering, they were dissolving me and tearing me apart and nothing remained of me.

"And so, despite all the torments, I began to feel better, better than I had ever felt on earth. The further I went, the better I felt. It was no longer even a matter of feeling good. It was a gathering up, a resurrection."

Rosa lay there under the spell of the voice. She struggled to free herself of its power.

"You said something about justice? About heavenly powers? What does Hannes mean by that?"

The voice: "Justice and heavenly powers."

Rosa rolled over on one side. "You've beaten him down, humbled him that's all. Hannes goes back and is sorry for his sins and errors. What sins? What's he talking about? In his scrawny little life? A young doctor from Stuttgart, he's only making himself ridiculous. You've driven him crazy. He has nothing to regret, only things to make up for. I know that for a fact. What did he have with me? He wanted to travel, later, to Switzerland and Italy. After the war, and then he was already dead. And he found his way into my cell, dirty

436

and hungry and thirsty, looking for the life that he had never even had, and now he no longer had a body either, and he held onto me, and I was supposed to give him what I didn't even have myself. He wanted to devour me. But he was ten times more real and fair than now."

The voice: "Rosa, be careful. You don't have much more time now."

Rosa: "You've driven him crazy. Hearing you, even though I don't know you, I can only say that if you're not telling me fairy tales and this is the truth, then Hannes is making himself ridiculous, and so are you in bringing me this message. You'll meet him again I'm sure, oh worthy stranger. Give him my regards, and—tell him that I hadn't thought he was so stupid and foolish and silly."

The voice: "I accepted this job as a messenger—for your sake, Rosa."

She rose up as if he had stung her, her eyes trying to penetrate the darkness, and she hissed, "Now go your way. I said, your way. You'll not dare to try to visit me again, I know. And now let me see you. Show yourself to me."

The voice vanished.

Rosa could not sleep she was so angry and upset.

Guard Rifles and Spies

The next day, January 14th, the Guard Cavalry Rifle Division, which had set up its headquarters in the Eden Hotel near the zoo, was finally able, now that the auxiliary troops had prepared the way, to set about disarming Berlin (and getting revenge and demolishing the Revolution).

Noske announced this event to his dear Berliners with the following words:

"Yesterday's occupation of the Moabit area of the city has been followed today by the entrance of a considerable number of troops into the city. They have come to free us from terrorist repression.

"All public assembly in the streets is forbidden.

"For the immediate future the municipal long-distance telephone lines will be used entirely for military and political purposes."

There had long been organized spy rings in Berlin. They were employed by official and unofficial agencies that generally had a great deal of money to spend. For the moneyed circles that stood behind them knew they were investing their money well—for the investigation and neutralization of criminals, traitors and Spartacists. As far as the Anti-Bolshevik League went, founded by Russian nobles and barons who had lost their palaces, estates and power, they had no greater heart's desire than to capture Lenin and the robbers and murderers allied with them as quickly and thoroughly as possible, to capture—to hang, to torture, to throttle, to behead, to shoot down, to drown, to poison, to torpedo and to blow up, and then to gather up the physical remains, whatever there was to be found and collected, and to row out onto the open sea and to feed them to the sharks. As long as this enterprise, which had been thought through to the tiniest detail, could not be carried out—because of the great distance between Moscow and Berlin and because of foreseeable difficulties and the resistance which those concerned would offer to such attentive treatment—they were content to busy themselves with goals that lay closer to home: the pursuit of Karl, Rosa and Radek, for example. A price was placed on their heads, and they constructed a nest of spies that was a sight to behold (but of course was not allowed to be seen).

Who was Karl's courier, this soldier named Werner? And where was Tanya hiding?

Tanya knew what she wanted to do. Rosa was in danger, and she had to be gotten out of Berlin, that is, to Breslau. A young woman who is weak and receptive to manly attractions cannot avoid finding companionship in Berlin. Tanya, although she had been warned by Rosa, found many friends, the latest a serious, coarse man, just the sort she liked, who seemed to be of the same stamp as her deceased Michel. Realistic personalities like Tanya's do not, however, open up so easily. She would only give her heart away after certain trials and proofs. She danced with Kasper (that was her friend's name), they drank and made love. He thought she was Rosa's housekeeper; he had seen her with Rosa often enough, but she told him that she was now out of work and that she wanted to go back to Breslau.

He wanted to know what was so difficult about that. She told him that she was a poor train traveler. Which he did not believe. Instead, he bet her that he could go riding with her in the trolley, second class, around town for a whole hour, and that she would get off just as perky as when she got on, and with him for company, perhaps even perkier.

That might be, said Tanya stubbornly. But she would much rather go by car. There were always so many guards and criminals standing around in the station, and they checked you out on the train, and she didn't want to have to show her papers.

Her perceptive friend could see that without his spectacles. As far as checking went, he felt just as she did. Yes, he declared, he would like to think it over, how they might arrange for a trip to Breslau by car.

"And with a reliable chauffeur, too," Tanya demanded.

"Agreed. That's a matter of course. For how many people?"

"For two."

He slapped his thigh. "So I'm coming along, Tanya."

"What makes you think so?

Kaspar: "First, because I'm arranging for the car. And second, you can't assume that I'd hand you over to some other gentleman for such a long trip. My girl, you know yourself that you need somebody to protect you."

The white mask made a dubious face: "Kaspar, I'm afraid nothing will come of that."

He: "What a shame. Why?"

Tanya: "I'm traveling with a lady. We can see each other once we're there. But we'll talk about all that, Kaspar, once you've got the car, a big car. I don't want to travel such a long stretch in a little one, and then we've got things to take along with us, too."

"Of course," replied Kaspar. Would the lady also have a little pocket money did she think?"

That, Tanya said, gesturing her disapproval, might be as it may, first the car and then a dependable chauffeur.

And so Tanya made her preparations to get Rosa out of Berlin. But then she no longer saw her Kaspar for days on end. And when he did reappear on the scene—elegantly dressed and already tipsy early in the morning—to share with her the happy outcome of this affair and to ask her when the lady might want to board the car, she suddenly could not reach Rosa, since unexpectedly both of them, Karl and Rosa, had left their really safe apartment in Neukölln without letting anyone know where they were going. The people who rented the apartment were themselves amazed when they found the nest empty late that evening. If the two had been safe anywhere, then it had been there. Tanya was afraid, and tried to find out where Rosa was—had she been arrested, abducted?

Karl's courier, the coarse, loyal Werner, took a more direct approach.

He was sly and deft in what he did. Up till now, the spy rings knew only that he was tied in with the Spartacists. They pressed him hard and tried to interrogate him. But he had fun leading these fine folks around by the nose. He was true to his principles, Karl had not been mistaken about him. Only when they came to him with offers of large sums did he waver—and take counsel with himself. When would such sums ever fall in his lap again in his whole life? Slowly he discovered that these were solvent organizations, all working hard for the same goal: to get Karl, Rosa and Radek—a Citizen's Counsel of Berlin, the Reichstag Regiment, Section Fourteen of the Auxiliary Service and the Anti-Bolshevik League.

On the morning of January 14th, Werner brought Karl and Rosa letters and newspapers. They asked him whether there was anything new, but he knew nothing. Instead, he looked about the apartment of the R.'s and told Karl that they were really well here. Did the apartment have several exists? Karl was gratified to see Werner studying the apartment for himself. When he came back from his inspection of the rooms, Karl and Rosa were already sitting in the living room with their papers. He stood there for a while at the door to the corridor, however, and let his gaze pass over both readers. He uttered a brief "good-bye" that the two of them, immersed in their papers, answered with only a short, half-audible "good-bye" and "fine, Werner."

And he was already racing down the steps.

They both read in the *Rote Fahne* the article "Calm Over Berlin" that Rosa had written yesterday in Neukölln.

"In the midst of battle, while listening to the victory sirens of the counterrevolution, the revolutionary protelariat must give an account of what has occurred, must measure these events and what has resulted from them against the larger scale of history."

The article spoke of political unrest among the soldiers, who were allowing their officers to misuse them. (Rosa sighed while she read this text again. When were things ever any different: a Prussian soldier who wouldn't obey!)

The rural areas had not been touched by the revolution at all as yet. What was lacking was a unity of action. And then came the detailed analysis, the part she had already underlined in her major speech at the Party convention (which they had paid no attention to, and their inattention was the reason for all this misery, in Rosa's opinion): the economic battles were still in their preliminary stages, and those battles were what fed class struggle.

"The contradiction arising from the fact that our task is growing ever more critical but that there is no connection between the task and its solution in these preliminary stages is the reason why the individual battles of the revolution have ended in out-and-out defeat.

"But revolution is the only form of war where final victory can be prepared for only through a series of defeats."

Karl laid the paper down and nodded: "Good. Those are your ideas."

440

"But not yours, even now?"

He hesitated. "Perhaps. That too. Certainly we're moving foward in a series of waves."

Suddenly he stood up, looked about uneasily and started to pace. He said, "That all just confuses me, Rosa. Now don't get angry. What you've written there is true and it's not true. How does our cause stand? For the sake of orientation, let us go back to the outbreak of the revolution. For four long years, junkers, officers and industrialists led a war into which they had driven this nation, and millions were left dead on the battlefields, and everywhere there was hunger and despair. That was the case in Kiel, too. That was the point of departure. What did the sailors want? The same thing we wanted in May 1916 on Potsdamer Platz: no more war, the overthrow of the government, of the regime that had led us into this misery.

"Please, Rosa, correct me: am I wrong or not?"

Rosa, the cool head, listened: "And then?"

Karl: "That was the starting point, and we have moved away from it. We have overburdened our cause, loaded it down with ideas and ruined it in doing so. We have wanted too much and therefore achieved nothing. We didn't carry out the first step correctly: the overthrow of the government and the regime. We only made a start at it, on our tiptoes so to speak, and then immediately ran off. We imagined we could get away with it. Our ideas would not give us any rest. They drove us on. A lack of realism. What you've said here, Rosa, about developments in agriculture and about preparations out in the rural areas, that's all fine and true. But later. At the moment we needn't discuss it, because we're still stuck at the point of overthrowing the government and the regime. Ebert, Scheidemann and the generals are still the old government, the old regime, and we've managed to get no further. It was wrong to urge programs and theories on us when we had not yet finished that job. We first have to bring the open drive against war and its instigators to completion, and that is the first step of the revolution—and it has not been taken yet."

Rosa: "We were perfectly right to come forward with our programs, right away."

Karl: "No."

Rosa: "Yes we were. Because the war emerged out of the social order of the past as an inevitable natural process. And that was why at the end of the war we had to go to work revising that social order, and that means carrying out our revolution."

Karl grit his teeth: "No."

Rosa: "And I repeat, yes."

Karl: "If only you would finally learn to follow, Rosa."

She gave a resigned laugh. "Gladly, Karl. I do follow, you know. But don't you see, haven't you noticed that we're sitting here as prisoners? I warned you. How can you claim that I'm the one who was blind? These events have confirmed my theories. But what do you hope to prove with this criticism of yours?"

He, unswervingly: "We had the most magnificent platform in the world, and were sitting in a position that won't be offered us again, with an imperialist war that had been lost, and in losing it, our natural enemies, that is the enemies of socialism, had compromised and ruined themselves to the point of bankruptcy. We only needed to make full use of this situation and do whatever was necessary for the moment. But to do that radically and totally and completely, and to forget the theories and programs and concentrate only on what the situation and the moment demanded, something every reasonable person in the country could see. Every patriot of whatever class—apart from the junkers and officers—would have had to agree with us. Throw out the Hohenzollerns and the pack that stood behind them. Our momentum would have been tremendous. We had several hundred thousand with us on January 6th. And with those slogans and with that goal millions would have joined us. With them on our side we could have done everything. Because we would have represented democracy, the overwhelming majority of the people. Instead of that we limited ourselves with our theories and dogmas. We narrowed ourselves down to a sect. Lord, what have we done! That's why we're still standing here at the beginning and will soon be thrown back behind the starting line. I don't want to accuse you, Rosa, but you didn't do us any good with your doctrines and textbooks, not when there was nothing written about our situation."

Rosa, mildly: "I know your impatience with theory, Karl. I'm just waiting now for an open confession that you are a Blanquist."

He sat down gloomily and summarized: "All for nothing. We can never make it up again. The whole thing ruined to its very foundations."

She suppressed a smile of sympathy.

"No need for despair, Karl. Generals always have things easier than we. They have a standing army with back-up troops and can march out to face their enemy, whom they already know, vaguely at any rate. But for us everything, at least on our side, is unfamiliar and unclear. It's all in the process of becoming something. You don't know how many are following you, you have difficulties making preparations just for tomorrow. No wonder then that proletarian revolutions stumble from defeat to defeat. But we don't want to be generals either."

442

He asked her abruptly, "Rosa, you're not for a dictatorship à la Lenin are you, or have you changed your opinion?"

"I don't understand you."

Karl: "It seems you have decided totally in favor of democracy, for a constituent assembly, parliament, etc. You don't even want to impose our proletarian rule on the nation as a whole, not before we are quite certain and assured that we have the majority of the masses behind us."

Rosa: "Well?"

Karl: "Was that a form of democracy when you—you, Leo and the others—did not honestly respect the decision of the majority at the Party convention and openly sabotaged it instead? Leo would have loved to expell me from the Party."

She sighed. "Oh, Karl, please, is this really the time to dig up that old quarrel. I also believe, by the way, that had we participated in the course of this battle it would not have changed anything."

His mouth twitched with bitterness. He let it go at that.

She knew that he was for Lenin, but that he did not dare admit it. Because nothing had stood in the way of his playing Lenin himself. It was better not to touch the subject.

While they were still sitting there leafing through the papers, Rosa unexpectedly let out an "ah!" in the midst of her reading. She threw the newspaper on the table, breathing audibly, planted her hands on her hips, ready for battle, and with an almost cannibalistic expression she gazed at Karl, who now looked up at her.

"Karl," she shouted at her unsuspecting fellow-reader, "will you give me a moment of your time?"

He felt in his bones that nothing good was coming, and before he knew what was happening the thunderstorm struck. One of Karl's secrets from the grand days of January 5th and 6th had come to light, in *Vorwärts,* which in this latest issue had published the document that Karl and drawn up with Ledebour and Scholze appointing themselves a revolutionary committee and provisional government.

Rosa screamed. She demanded an explanation. She did not think it possible.

Hearing all this, her secretary came in and stayed to watch the whole scene. Karl dodged and twisted, but he could not save himself, for the facts were out in the open. Bloody Rosa waved her *Vorwärts* and raged away in her top form from the old days.

What Karl submitted for his exoneration was that they had needed such a document for purely practical purposes, in order to supply themselves with weapons for instance. This did not pacify Rosa. The fact remained that he had wanted to play dictator with these others and had set himself up as a government, had acted arbitrarily. He was unmasked.

Karl turned to the secretary, begging her for support by shyly asking what she thought about this. But when she also took Rosa's side, he retired from battle and said sadly, *Et tu, Brutè,* and patiently bore the lightning and thunder.

Finally Rosa calmed down, at least externally.

Werner the courier appeared once again that afternoon at the apartment in Wilmersdorf. He had nothing to report, but he was in a good mood and assured Karl over and over again that they had really been lucky in finding this hideout. No one would suspect they were here. They were searching everywhere.

This short visit encouraged Karl so much that he once again began to talk about going for a walk, tomorrow or the day after. At any rate, he wrote a courageous article for the newspaper, and Karl and Rosa made jokes about their situation: how Noske and his mighty Guards had marched into Berlin, everything freezing at the sight of them, while they lay hidden behind his back and shot their arrows like Paris shooting at mighty Achilles before Troy.

Karl and Rosa had not moved beyond the law, and what revolutionary does not enjoy that feeling?

Out in the world, people were audibly distancing themselves from them.

The Independents behaved in their customary fashion. They declared that they, of course, had had nothing whatever to do with that fantastical Revolutionary Committee, which had met at the royal stables and called itself the provisional government.

However that did not prevent them, they added in their conversations with the Central Executive Council, from insisting on adherence to the goal of the movement, which was (not the toppling of the government, nor the revolution iself, but) the question of the chief of police for Berlin. Since Eichhorn had now fled, they demanded that this post be occupied, if not by an Independent, then at least by someone who had been approved by the Independents (which meant he could be the government's man).

The Executive Council did not even deign to answer this request. Its reception was equally cool to the request of these same German politicians that the government be dismissed and replaced by figures who had compromised themselves somewhat less. The Independents were thinking primarily of men from their ranks who could indeed have shamed children with their innocence, and were therefore the most suitable candidates for governing Germany after the war.

In sum, people wanted to put this unrest behind them as soon as possible. The elections for the Constituent Assembly, scheduled for the coming Sunday, should be protected from all danger; and after that nothing stood in the way of peace and an ordered state of affairs throughout the country.

The Cherub

When Rosa had been lying in her darkened room for a while that evening, a vision emerged from the shadows, grew brighter and brighter and stood then before her as a shimmering cherub.

She remembered at once the magical form that Hannes had once taken on in her prison cell in Breslau, and she greeted the figure without alarm, although also without any particular friendliness.

"Well look here, it's Hannes. So you've decided to drop in again."

But unlike Hannes, this vision was not transparent, nor did landscapes and mountains move across it and around it, but it stood there rigidly, an oversized figure made of light, in white robes and with broad wings lowered, illuminating the whole room.

"I am not Hannes," the voice said.

"Oh, it's you, the messenger. Hannes still can't come. He's still using ambassadors. Oh, but he's gone elegant."

"Hannes has asked me to tell you . . ."

Rosa: "I'm just infinitely agog, Your Royal Majesty, to hear news from him. What high position, what place of honor does he hold that he can afford to send such a distinguished mailman?"

"Hannes has a message for you."

She interrupted him: "Why does he even bother to condescend at all to a poor little female like myself? We were on friendly terms in the past. At one time he was happy just for me to let him into my cell and find a place inside this old, used body of mine. Once he even wanted to elope with me."

"Rosa, I have something to report to you from him."

Rosa: "I'm listening, Your Excellency. But can't you empathize with my finding Hannes's behavior somewhat remarkable, considering our earlier confidences, in that he has to deal with me through third parties? What have I done to fall into such disfavor?"

"Rosa, will you listen to me?"

Rosa: "No. I protest. He's a low cad. How does Hannes know that I—that I—have any further interest in him? He should not assume it just like that. He thinks that I'm just licking my chops, waiting for his report of how His Highness is feeling. He's mistaken. I don't want

445

to hear from him. I can dispense with every message he has for me."

The cherub did not move.

Rosa: "And I don't want to see you either. I told you yesterday. I already know enough about Hannes and his ridiculous penitence and the rest of that asinine nonsense. He's just showing off for you. There's nothing to it. Do you know Stuttgart? What can be so remarkable about him? Yesterday you had the impudence to tell me that you had come for my sake. And that's when I threw you out. I'm telling you now that if you don't leave at once I shall take my lamp here and throw it right at your head."

And when he did not move, she grabbed the little electric lamp from where it stood on the chair. But before she could throw it, he had grabbed her wrist. Her hand went lame, the lamp thudded to the floor.

He laid his right hand across her breast and bent his face down to hers.

Breathless, speechless, she looked into the supernatural beauty, a shadow of anger skitted across it.

Then he moved back again and said, as if nothing had happened, "Rosa, I have a message to give you."

She: "Tell me what it is."

The cherub: "Hannes has told me to tell you this. For he is far away from you and it is no longer in his power to speak.

"Come, Rosa, is what Hannes calls out to you. Hear the call to true life, to eternal life.

"Come, you need not despair. Hands are stretching out to you, arms want to lift you and hold you.

"Grace has been poured out upon you, as rich as sunlight."

She lay there tense.

She whispered: "Go on, oh glorious one—oh glorious one."

The cherub: "So you are listening? Only those who have begun to be still within themselves can hear me. Souls demanding their own power cannot hear me.

"Hannes, who is no longer bewildered by phantasms, Hannes, who has been released from the maelstrom has this to say to you:

"We are not lost, Rosa. You called out to me before. And this time I have come. And if ever there was love for me within you, as there is now in me for you, so accept gladly what I say to you and do not separate yourself from me.

"Ah, what roads I traveled, Rosa, after I left you that last time. I knew then that there was no way back. I had already wandered backward, in penitence and contrition and under the eyes of judgment. The road that I now was going down, where did it lead? I did not know. I wandered across meadows and through beautiful, broad and blustering forests. I thought, here I shall find my home. And I looked about me; this was not it.

"Then came groves where brushes and nightingales sang gayly, and above which eagles circled in the blue, and the groves were filled with a sweet scent, and springs gushed forth, and deer stood by my side as if in a fairy tale. Was this the place, I asked myself? Should I stay here? This was not the place.

"I did not know where to go. I could not find my way home. I was going in circles. There was no road before me.

"Then I sat down in the grass and wept still hotter tears than before and mourned and tore myself up inside. I hated the joyful airs of the birds. The thrushes and the nightingales frightened me. I wished that an eagle would swoop down from heaven and bear me away."

Rosa: "Hannes, my dear Hannes, what happened then?"

"There were brooks that flowed alongside the path, they were all full of tears. Few trees grew there and they gave no shade. There was nowhere to rest from the burning of the sun. And the birds in the trees proclaimed bright pain and woe.

"And then of a sudden there was a heavenly garden. You could see the silver white gate from far away. And as soon as you noticed its glitter you knew that that was the goal you wanted to reach.

"I wandered for a long time until I stood before the silver white gate. It towered up to the sky. To the right and left, trees swayed their high tops. They grow there in that heavenly garden, and when you look up at them you feel yourself blessed because you know they are growing in that heavenly garden."

Rosa: "What are you doing there, Hannes, what are you up to, there on the road before that silver gate."

The cherub: "It is I, the messenger, who is speaking to you for Hannes.

"I saw him standing there and I went to him and comforted him. I raised him from the ground and spoke to him. The gate was not open for him, his hour had not come nor has it yet come.

"He stands there full of longing, waiting, his eyes never leaving that silver gate which does not move. But his heart is full of constant joy. I can hear him speak:

"How can I describe the sweetness that draws me on? On earth there is the burning sun, how can I describe the sun that shines and warms here, causing flowers to shoot up, but also dispelling all death. How meager was the body. How heavily the body lay upon us with its earthbound burden.

"Rosa, did you not tell me about freedom, and that you were

fighting for freedom? Rosa, what can a human being know about freedom? He must wander from one jail to the next. And did not I myself believe that I was free when I could do whatever I wanted? But I did not want what I should have wanted. It was not *I* who wanted something. Who did want it then? Who was passing himself off for me, for my ego? I did nothing; I felt and rolled about like a man in a vat full of stones who has been shoved off down the face of a mountain."

Rosa opened her mouth: "Oh, say nothing against the body, Hannes, do not forget so quickly. Don't be unfair. Have you forgotten it all? Even if it was not everything, Hannes, it was something. It was something just to live, and to wear clothes and to breathe and to eat and to drink. Even if we do not walk through paradise here, what miracles the earth still offers! Hannes, look at me, how I am suffering, pursued like a common criminal and threatened by murderers. But even that cannot wrench my love of mankind from my heart, nor how the thrushes and crows made me glad, nor the pussywillow buds on the boughs."

The cherub: "You're not speaking now to Hannes, Rosa."

Rosa: "If you are his messenger, then go and tell him:

"Hannes, I was afraid of you when you came and wanted to rob me of my body, my sick, old body. But that pleased me more than what you are now doing, when you do not come and only carry on about heavenly peace. Hannes, you are an incorrigible Württemberger. Even in death you're straight from Stuttgart, that's how morose you are. Hannes, believe me, you have gotten completely off the track. I don't want to be to blame for that. You tried to make use of me twice, the first time you wanted to escape with me, the second time you wanted my blood. Try me a third time. The grapes hang high sometimes, but perhaps not too high. But I don't like the way you are now. The physician has suddenly become a theologian. Come, let me see you again now the way you were before. I'll fetch the scarf, our magic scarf."

The cherub shimmered, but did not move.

She groped for her purse lying on the chair, and sighed as she drew out the magic cloth and threw it over the arm of the chair. She spoke without taking any notice now of the cherub:

"What's the point of all this drivel you've had passed on to me, and why do we need third parties? Here, this is for you. I did not think that I would ever need this scarf again. The chair stands ready. Come, Hannes, don't let them confuse you. And even if you are ice-cold once again, so let me warm you and drive that silly humbug from your head.

"See, this is what I want of you and what you still want of me, why should we pretend—you, a doctor of medicine and I a Marxist. I want to lie in your arms and on your breast. I want to melt away in you and not be able to find myself again for all eternity."

And behold, in the glow of the light emitted by the cherub, Hannes was sitting there. He had come, she had accomplished it.

He sat in his usual civilian clothes, just as she had known him during consultation hours. Even the wooden stethoscope peeped out of his jacket pocket.

"Forgive me, please," he said with a slight nod toward the white figure, "for not being able to withstand such enticement. The temptation was too strong, and in the end I will be forgiven, since after all I was still only standing *before* the gate to the heavenly garden.

The brightness in the room dimmed. Only by a vague aura did the cherub still reveal his presence.

Rosa screamed for joy. She embraced her Hannes and pulled him to her. She pinched his arm and whispered in his ear (and sure enough, that was all possible with him now, he had rounded himself out since his last botched attempts).

"You've cut and run, have you? Magnificent. Congratulations."

He, gallantly: "When someone calls the way you do, what else?"

"But where have you been hiding. Is that all true, what he's been telling me. Now tell me, what sort of tales are these? What's with this mailman? Can't you open your mouth for yourself?"

"Of course I can, darling. I wanted to, too. But—I was embarrassed. And when someone else offered to do the job for me, I was more than glad to let him."

"Isn't that splendid," Rosa said indignantly, "You didn't even give him the order yourself."

Hannes: "Give him the order? Absolutely not. I didn't object. But certain people can't get their goal fast enough, and have to interfere in everything and stick their noses in."

Rosa: "Then everything he has been telling me is nonsense, is that it? All this about penitence and brooks full of tears and the rest of the stuff?"

Hannes let loose with a scornful laugh. "But Rosa, did you have any doubt of that? I hope that you didn't let him pull your leg for a moment. He's just ad-libbing so he can make me look ridiculous."

Rosa: "Now if that doesn't take the cake! And you let him get away with it?"

"Don't get so excited, child. In the dead state, one can do some things, but not a great deal. You see, I've arrived in the nick of time nevertheless, and have spoiled his fun." Hannes gazed about the room.

"But, Rosa, it seems you are living in straitened circumstances. The room is small. Anyone with a bit of tact should notice that when you have a visitor he ought to withdraw."

Rosa: "You took the words right out of my mouth. First he tries to swindle me, and then he stays on cool as can be." She called out, "Hey, you sir, Mr. Swindler, Mr. Sharper, what do you suppose you're doing sticking around here? Do we have to remove you by force?"

Hannes became outraged. "The sensualist enjoys watching love scenes. Fine manners those are. No longer satisfies you, good sir, to be involved in the action yourself, is that it?"

The pale glow was immobile.

Hannes made an awkward bow, swinging his arms and bending low before him. "As you wish. Your Majesty has your moods. Your Majesty will note, however, that I have made myself fully independent once again and can do without your pious training." To Rosa: "Let's pay no attention to him. He catches on slowly, grade-school education."

He threw his arms around Rosa's body; she was sitting up in bed now.

"Come on, Rosa, let's pretend he isn't there. Let's not begrudge him his pleasure."

"I want him to leave," Rosa whispered.

"But why?" Hannes laughed, "if it's fun for him, just that much more for me."

And he covered her face with kisses.

But the moment the breath of his mouth touched her, her body went rigid, and she knew in a moment that it was not Hannes, the poor, unfortunate Hannes who had taken a bloody departure from Russian battlefields to find shelter with her. This was Satan, the mighty sorcerer, the worker of wonders who ruled human hearts, who brought lust and torment, the lord of victory and defeat, the restless pursuer who is not broken by any misfortune, the iron warrior, the mocker, the defiant one, the pride and vigilance of mankind.

And she recognized him—how delirously happy she was.

And as she took him to her and made herself known to him—how deliriously happy she was.

Young, slender and free, as if newly created, she slid down from his lap. And in this guise he paraded her before the mute, blushing, mournful cherub.

"The game can now begin. We report ourselves present, Your Execellency. You may take your pleasure."

He lifted Rosa and bore her in his arms.

The room trembled. A white flame burst up.

Rosa lay on the floor.

But there was no longer a room.

The brilliant white cherub, unfurling its immense wings, was hot in pursuit of Satan. The beating of his wings raised a windstorm and the forests began to rustle.

Satan constantly changed his form. He sat upon a judge's chair in the city, wearing a black robe and handing down decisions. The courtroom listened to him. But the white wings rushed in upon him. The judge spoke no more.

Satan walked as a farmer behind his plow. The rushing sound approached, the horses shied and raced off across the field. The farmer had vanished.

He clucked as a hen in the barnyard. The chickens fluttered into the air. The horses whinnied and bumped against their stalls. And where was the hen now?

Satan was hiding in the dungheap as a mouse. And when even that availed him nothing and the dungheap went up in flames, he gave up these metamorphoses.

He rose up to a great height as a cloud of black smoke and flew off beneath the heavens. The chase slowed. The black cloud crossed mountains and lay upon glaciers. In the wilderness of the mountains the conversations between the hunter and his game rumbled.

"Why are you going to all this trouble?" Satan shouted, "You slave! What payment do you expect from your master? Is a good word from him sufficient, a merciful word? I'll write out a recommendation for you attesting that you've proved yourself to be a well-behaved drudge. He'll let you keep you job."

The cherub: "You sinister liar, you poisonous soul, you seeker for revenge. When will you finally lay down your arms?"

"I flee, you're quite right. But it is ten times better to flee as a free man than to conquer as a slave."

"Satan, our brother, child of our father, in the name of your eternal suffering when will you lay down your arms? You are fighting the eternal. You are beaten, you are devoid of life. You lie before the gates of our native city as a corpse, and no one comes out to bury you and do you last honors."

"Then I have fallen in honor, and that is enough for me. You'll not make a fool of me, slave. You are speaking with a lord. But you are wrong when you think that I am alone and that no one has come out to me, to celebrate me. Just listen."

A howling and a raging approached; out of the darkness between heaven and earth where Satan has set up residence and from whence he makes his raids against what is above and below, there came a thronging host of the lost and the damned to greet their lord, whose voice they had heard coming from the mountains.

"Am I alone?" Satan rasped gleefully as they surrounded him, so that he was now hidden from the eyes of the cherub. "Here is the realm of freedom. There are still free creatures who cannot be touched by outside force. Pluck up your courage, brother, do not let him misuse you. Join me."

The screeches and mockery moved off. The blackness swallowed it up.

Rosa lay on a meadow, in green grass. She lay there stiff, her face twitching with pain.

As the shimmering cherub descended to her she spoke to it.

"Where is he? What did you do to him?"

He: "You know who he is."

"Yes."

He: "Rosa, control yourself. Say nothing. You think that you are clever and understand all things, but you only know what lies just at your feet."

And while the cherub spoke—he was once again an oversized figure of light, in flowing white garments and with broad and lowered wings—his magical humming began again out of which his words emerged like a song. The sound swelled and receded and surpassed every charm that the other one had ever conjured up.

"You are not as clever as you think, Rosa. For if you were clever, you would know that you are only a human being, and that your eyes only see some few things and that your ears hear but little. Listen now, ears. Eyes, see."

Again he laid a hand upon her chest. But she closed her eyes and held her ears tight. She did not want to see or hear, because he was trying to confuse her. She took her hands away, only to thrust them before her face again.

He sang, "Hear, ears, hear what you have never heard till now. Eyes, see what you have never seen till now."

She thought, he's not going to succeed. I am me. There is freedom. And she moaned and let her arms fall and looked up.

The supernatural beauty.

"Oh splendid one. Let me look upon you. Stay. Do not turn from me. Let me gaze at you, splendid one. Who are you? Oh forgive me that I barred your way to me."

The cherub sang: "And what will happen to you now?"

452

Rosa: "If ever I was hungry, never did I eat and become filled as I am now. If ever I was thirsty, never did I drink and have my thirst quenched as now. What difference does that make. I have lived to experience this moment."

"What will happen to you now, Rosa?"

Rosa: "Like a child at its mother's breast, I cling to your glory and will not depart from it."

"I demand a price."

"Any price you wish. Only do not let me go."

"I demand your self, your proud soul."

"Take it."

"I demand repentance."

Rosa: "I feel it. I have never known it."

"I am nothing. I am a messenger of the great creator, a shimmer of his glory, a breath from his body."

"I did not recognize you. Do not let me go. Have mercy upon me. I do not want to go back."

Among the Wounded

No matter how he contrived it, Lieutenant Maus could learn nothing that Sunday morning about what had become of Friedrich Becker. Maus had spent the night with his parents in Bellevue, had gone then early that morning to the War Ministry to learn any news about police headquarters. He heard that the fortress had fallen. But where was Becker? Friedrich had promised to give him word immediately about the upshot of his adventure, either by telephone or telegraph. He had not been heard from, and from hour to hour Maus felt more burdened and more guilty of the crazy affair.

When there came no word from Becker either in Dahlem or at the War Ministry, Maus had to unburden his heart, and he called Hilda, who calmed him down to be sure; but apparently she was also afraid herself, and she suggested that Maus personally get over there and make some inquiries—which is what Maus already had in mind. But while underway it occurred to him that neither he nor Hilda had thought of the most obvious solution—Becker was at home of course.

And ten minutes later he rang the bell of Becker's apartment, it was going on eleven o'clock, and very soon someone came running hastily down the hall and opened the door and sprang back—Becker's mother in her coat and hat.

"Dear God, Herr Maus. Forgive me. You frightened me. Please come in."

And there in the entryway she told him that she was expecting Friedrich any minute. She had been up and looking for him since early that morning and had not been able to find him, and could not understand it at all. Yesterday morning he had gone to City Hall, quite against her wishes, to the school board, on account of this dreadful affair with the director. He had gotten himself involved with something quite terrible there, and people were so mean. She had just been to see the chief school inspector. Becker had definitely been there, and everything had gone quite smoothly, but the chief inspector could not tell her anything more than that. So where was Friedrich? He was apparently looking for Heinz, whom he had been so worried about. Did Maus know Heinz? He was one of Friedrich's students, but unfortunately involved in the affair with the director. He had been living with them after the whole misfortune had happened.

"And evening before last Heinz suddenly went off and left no word, and Friedrich was terribly upset. I was out to see Heinz's mother, and she admitted that Friedrich had visited her yesterday afternoon and had asked about Heinz's whereabouts. And that's the last thing I've heard of him. Where can he be? Did Heinz go off somewhere, perhaps, and he's gone off after him? But why hasn't Friedrich given me even some token sign of where he is?"

Maus realized that she knew nothing about police headquarters.

He sat down with the excited woman there in that living room which he knew so well. He did not understand what this misfortune was that Frau Becker was talking about and what had been the consequence of it all for Friedrich's school director. She had to explain the whole affair to him, and she gave him all the details. It did her good to talk, since for the moment she could not do anything and hoped that Maus might give her come clue.

The report she gave Maus, so innocently offered, had a devastating effect on him. And on top of it all, Frau Becker showed him the telegrams that had come pouring in the day before, sent anonymously, some of them congratulating Becker for what he had done, and a great many of them abusive and threatening.

"The world is such a wicked place," sighed Becker's mother.

Maus saw right through the whole thing. He had slid right into these slippery matters without a single suspicion. Becker had not uttered so much as a syllable about it, downright malicious.

Maus could not stand to stay in that apartment another moment. He promised Becker's mother, who didn't want to let him leave, that he would send her news the moment he learned anything.

In his dismay and outrage, he could think of nothing else but of sharing all this with Hilda from the nearest post office. He told her with great anger, increasing even as he spoke, about what good old Becker had gotten involved in.

Hilda had read about the affair, but that Friedrich was involved was news to her, and it was completely incomprehensible to her that Friedrich would drag Maus into it.

"What do you intend to do now, Maus?" she asked in concern.

"Most of all I'd like to go out to Dahlem and tell my comrades about this whole affair."

"Don't do that, Hans, please. You'll have to do that soon enough. First talk with Friedrich. Things may be different from what his mother has told you."

"But I read those telegrams with my own eyes, the ones they sent him. Hilda, even if there's nothing to it and he's innocent, which I would gladly believe, how can he have gotten me involved in such a slimy affair when I'm in active service? How could he do that?"

Hilda admitted all that, but begged him not to do anything yet, and after some discussion she had calmed him down (he called it all a filthy mess and spoke of Friedrich's treachery) to the point where he said that for now he would simply go back out to Dahlem and wait there quietly for whatever happened next. Becker's fate was absolutely of no importance to him.

And then Hilda had to urge him again not to be so hard. He stuck to his guns: the best he could offer was to let the man stay stuck where he was. But she would not yield, and continued to maintain that it was all so uncertain. And now she succeeded in getting Maus to promise he would undertake further steps to ascertain where Becker might be. Maus acquiesced, though against his will, so that he too might be able "to shed some light on this dark and dingy affair," as he put it.

Hilda begged him really to listen to Becker once he found him, and to send her news at once; and no matter what (since she had the afternoon off), she would be on Potsdamer Platz at four o'clock, at Siechen's, and then they could talk for an hour.

That poured oil on the stormy waters.

Maus drove over to the Alexander Barracks, where, although he was in uniform, he was admitted only after extensive formalities. (Uniforms were distrusted at that point; there were a lot of spies running around in uniforms, on both sides.)

The robust unit commander to whom Becker had reported on the previous evening remembered the whole curious affair exactly. He was interested in how things had gone and what the result had been. At Maus's request, he sent for a list of the prisoners taken, and then after a minute or two he spread his arms wide and said, "There you have it. The man's not on the list. They've shot him. That's it. I told you it would happen."

That proved a shock to Maus after all. He inquired whether all the names were in fact on the list.

"Absolutely all of them. By which I mean all those that we could nab. We don't have the names of the dead. You'll have to go to the morgue to get those. There you'll see the results of all this madness."

The officer was so convinced that Becker had been shot that he did not even point out that there were wounded men as well, and Maus did not think of that himself. But as Maus wandered in confusion around the barracks courtyard, uncertain of what to do, he called out to a guard posted before the drill room, asking him where they had locked up the prisoners; and the guard, who was happy to engage in conversation, replied, "Yes, well if the fellow in question isn't on the list, then he's probably not in the drill either. But he could have been wounded, you know, that's in case he wasn't killed, and we've got a whole bunch of wounded who were transported to Moabit Hospital. Besides that, the Spartacists carried off several of them themselves, but they're keeping them hidden."

Hearing this, Maus drove to Moabit Hospital, feeling a lot more merciful than he had an hour before, and with the most heartfelt wish that Becker might still be among the living. And almost as soon as he arrived at the administration building he learned that he was. Dr. Friedrich Becker was among the prisoners lying in Pavilion X.

The unit commander at the Alexander Barracks, whom Maus called at once, was amazed and congratulated him. "He was hiding among the wounded, you say? Well, what do you know. Must be some sad story behind it all. Why didn't he report to us? What's wrong with him?" "Ah, you don't know yet." "Well, and now you want to get your hero out of there right away. We'll arrange that first thing. But you have to promise me as a way of thanking me that you'll have the man come here to me as soon as he's back on his feet, and tell me in full detail what he went through there with the Reds."

And within half an hour, written permission had arrived from the barracks for the immediate release of Dr. Friedrich Becker, and Maus, who had requested that he be taken to the ward, had a brief conversation with the ward physician, a stout and obliging surgeon who was happy to give him information about Becker's condition—a slight concussion, wounds to one hand, general condition excellent—but looked Maus up and down archly when he expressed the desire to visit the patient. In that get-up, the lieutenant would be better off not visiting the pavilion. The gentlemen in there had something against such a uniform, you see. That difficulty could be removed, however, easy as pie; he put in the order by telephone that Becker's bed be shifted at once to an empty private room at the entrance to the ward. Then he personally accompanied Maus past the posted guards.

Becker lay in bed, and had just turned to gaze out the window to get his bearings when the two men entered. The doctor shook his hand and took his leave at once. Becker smiled at Maus.

"Two surprises. I was just wondering why they pushed me over here, to an interrogation I assumed, and now you come in. And I presume I have you to thank for this change of room, do I?"

Maus sat down and gazed at his friend, whose forehead and temples had been bandaged and whose left hand was wrapped in a heavy dressing. An ice-bag hung above his head from a string; he had pushed it back up out of the way. Maus asked him how he was feeling.

Becker said with a grave and quiet expression that he had a couple of bumps and that he was still a bit befuddled, as if coming out of an anesthetic. But he was most concerned that his mother be sent word. Would Maus do him that favor?

Maus: Becker could do that best himself.

Becker: "I think not. We're behind barbed wire here."

"You can leave, Becker."

"Me? No. I'm still clearheaded enough for that. I'm a prisoner. As a nurse told me just a while ago, we're not just patients here in this building."

Maus: "Things have been arranged. I've spoken with the unit commander who received you yesterday evening. You're not counted among the prisoners, most definitely not. I don't think we'll have to send your mother word. By the way, I visited her just a while ago in any case. We'll just drive there in an ambulance or a comfortable car, however you wish."

"I see. I see. You spoke with the gentleman from yesterday evening. What did you tell him, Maus?"

"The truth, which I had trouble enough ferreting out myself. That you were lying here, wounded, in the hospital. At the news, he was kind enough immediately to send an adjutant over with a written request that you be released."

At this Becker's expression did not change at all. He laid his good right hand behind his neck and calmly said, "My sincerest thanks for all you've done. My mother was terribly worried I suppose?"

"She appeared to be."

"Well, now that you're here, Maus, and have some rank around here—could you perhaps do me a favor and inquire at the nurse's station or from the doctor whether Heinz Riedel, that's the boy I wanted to get out, is here as well? We were wounded at the same time."

This was that filthy affair that Becker had dragged him into. Grudgingly, disgusted, Maus stood up (he was also annoyed at the cool manner in which Becker had thanked him for his troubles). Out in the hall, the head nurse he asked pointed at once to the ward: there lay Heinz Riedel, a very young man. His condition was of great concern. It was a matter of a serious skull fracture. Thus informed, Maus went back in and sat down beside Becker to give him the news.

Becker: "Oh, what a rotten shame. But he's still alive. That takes a weight from my heart. Thanks so much, Maus."

At that their conversation came to a halt.

Maus was once again burdened with the impression this repulsive affair made on him. He could not look Becker in the face, and so he asked in a detached way what he intended to do, whether he wanted a car or an ambulance ordered up for the ride home.

Becker shook his head and let his hand fall down on the bedspread.

"Thanks. Neither one nor the other. I'm staying here."

And what was that supposed to mean now? (The blood rose to Maus's face.) "This is a ward for prisoners. If you need to be treated and want to stay in the hospital, you only have to have yourself transferred to another station."

"Nothing of the sort, Maus. It's not for me to want anything. You're operating under false premises. The unit commander who ordered that I be set free was not correctly informed. I am by rights a prisoner like the others. I was in police headquarters, and I took part in the fighting."

Maus froze. "Becker, you're crazy."

Becker: "I understand that that alarms you. But I cannot deceive either you or the gentleman back at the barracks. I repeat, I took part in the fighting."

"But that's perfect nonsense. How did you manage that? And why, for heaven's sake? What have you in common with these fellows? Enough of this madness."

Becker: "I showed Heinz how to handle a rifle. We both took up an observation post together at a window on the Kaiserstrasse side. That's where we had our luck, too, when a grenade hit."

458

Maus stammered, "What happened? Please, explain this to me, would you? Were you interested in the battle from a military point of view? What sort of awful joke is this."

Becker: "I'm sorry, but I can't do anything else. Do you have a few minutes, Maus, to hear me out?"

"For that, I most certainly do."

"I don't want to offend you. I know that you cannot forgive me. You should not have reached out to give me a hand."

Maus: "Get down to cases."

Becker: "I'm not a Spartacist, nor is the boy. But in my search for the boy I ended up among these people, and I began to see things differently and more precisely. It had nothing to do with my political opinions. I saw the helpless situation these rebels were in. On top of the misery of their working-class lives, they had had the further misfortune of having run after muddle-headed ideas and then being betrayed."

Maus, repressing his anger (but he contained himself, he was afraid he would fall into his old wild state, but he thought of Hilda, to whom he would have to answer).

"Don't give me any lectures about these people. I want to know what's wrong with you. I've got a right to hear that."

"Then you'll just have to listen to what I'm saying. I'll keep it short. When I went over there, my only intention was to get Heinz out. But once I was inside I was horrified when he ran into my arms thinking that I had come not for him but to join these people. But then I began to move about among them and I looked and I listened. And I saw, too, how they went to their deaths. That is the point, Maus. Either you understand me in this or you don't understand me. I saw only these poor people standing up for what they believed, because they did not know anything else. There are things, Maus, that one learns with great difficulty. I, for instance, am having trouble learning to be a Christian. I constantly fall into the error of believing I've got hold of Christianity and can walk around with it as if it were a book I'm carrying under my arm. But that's not how it is. My Christianity is like a tropical rainstorm. The ground dries out again a short time afterward."

Maus: "I really have to interrupt you, Becker. You've been telling me the most monstrous things, and as an explanation you give me theological remarks that don't interest me and seem to be absolutely superfluous. You'll have to excuse me, please. The facts are, as I and anyone else would see them, as follows: I helped you get across to police headquarters, you had come to me because you wanted to get a boy out of there who had got in by mistake. Instead of which, you fight for them over there, along with him. I find that monstrous. I repeat: monstrous. You broke your word, you betrayed me. You now seem prepared to make your role at police headquarters public. I don't know why. Perhaps you're thirsting for fame, for a martyr's crown. But with all respect for your courage in confessing your sins, I'd like to call your attention to the fact that I'm involved in your little game. Without any misgivings, I put myself at your disposal, and as my thanks I find you intend to ruin me."

"Calm down, Maus, you're so upset. I'm going to ruin you? Why? No one would ever think of making you responsible for my deeds. You had every reason to assume that as an officer, once there I would do exactly what I promised I would, and for which you lent me a helping hand, and nothing more."

Maus: "Fine, let's assume that. And beyond that you have nothing more to tell me? How you treated me nevertheless? How do you figure this whole affair? You're an officer, you're a teacher. You're also a Christian, so you say. But don't you have duties and principles as a Christian that forbid you from fighting on the side of Spartacus and from breaking your word?"

Becker: "My hope is that you'll forgive me; if you'll have only a little patience."

Maus: "I can do without the theology."

Becker: "I'm speaking of the circumstances. You often used to accuse me of being nothing but an intellectual, an observer without heart or will who was only intrigued by ideas. That's what they reproached me with there in police headquarters, too, right away. I don't know why. A person always gets thrown in with the rest of his class. Well, that makes no difference to me now. But then the bombardment began, and the dead and wounded were dragged by me, including some that I had just spoken with—simple, brave people, civilians, a young girl was among them as well, common, everyday people, you know them by the hundreds, the grass that grows upon the earth. But at that moment I was not seeing the grass. I was not even an observer. I was really and truly locked up inside my head, just as they had accused me of being. What a way to be a Christian. I experienced it all anew. Once again I had known nothing of what it meant. You aren't a Christian on the basis of principles. You have to give up principles and a lot of other things as well, throw them away, let go of your whole ego and follow your heart. And finally, in the process, as bitter as that may be, you must not—please forgive me— be afraid of the consequences."

Maus had crossed his legs and arms, and was hardly listening. Rage

460

was eating him up inside. He thought: what a blessing that one man can't look into another man's heart. Otherwise he could see inside me now. But Maus struggled with himself, his face was distorted with an unnatural smile. Finally he had to release these emotions, and they were formed into words.

"Once again, let me say I have no interest in your religious opinions. But if this is supposed to be Christianity driving you to do such acts, then I'll admit that I thank my creator that I've been taught otherwise. Let me put the question to you now, Becker, short and sweet: Do you accept the release I've brought you, or not? You realize that you could keep all this information to yourself. You gain nothing by being locked up. You save me a great deal. Your mother as well, I would think."

Becker: "My thanks for your goodwill in the matter. Don't worry, I'll not cause either you or my mother difficulties. I can't change any of this. Let me hold to my decision."

Maus pushed his chair back and left without saying good-bye.

In an attempt to calm himself, he walked about for a while in the hospital garden. Then the thought occurred to him that he should give this news to the unit commander. He had to report in to him, since the matter would come to him sooner or later.

When he provided that gentleman with this information from the telephone in the administration building, the man first laughed heartily and then expressed his sympathy to Maus, "We got taken in by him, and how. Seems to be a crazy character. Gone off the deep end I suppose."

But the amusement of the old soldier at the barracks did not last long. Gradually he realized what this meant. Then he let out a roar and began to call it a filthy mess, worse than anything he'd ever heard of. He had Maus, who was trembling now, repeat all the facts to him once more, and then made a formal request for him to remain at the hospital. He would come over there himself.

A quarter of an hour later he appeared, livid with anger, accompanied by an adjutant, and with a brief nod to Maus who followed in his wake, he strode across the garden to the prisoners' wing, where the patients immediately began to assemble at the door.

"Chase them off!" he shouted to the guard. "Where's this fellow?"

Without knocking, he entered the private room with a firm step, placed himself beside Becker's bed and stared at him, not saying a word.

Then he erupted. "Are you the former first lieutenant Friedrich Becker who yesterday evening asked my permission to cross over to police headquarters in order to get a young boy out of there?"

"Yes."

"And what did you do instead?"

Becker: "Is this an official interrogation or not?"

The officer roared, "This is an interrogation. You've made a fool of us."

"If this is an interrogation then I would like to request that I be questioned in a calm and orderly fashion."

The soldier's full face was red with rage. He had not considered it necessary to remove his cap. Now his voice broke, his eyes popped out of their sockets.

"What did you say? What presumption! Orderly? You scum. You bastard."

And he grabbed hold of Becker by both shoulders and shook him. Becker tried to push him away with his right hand, when the soldier attacked him a second time and gave him a hook under the chin that threw Becker back and left him lying motionless.

Then the soldier left the room with his adjutant, walking past Maus who had remained at the door; and he snapped at the head nurse, "That man is a prisoner. He's not to be released, is that understood?"

The two of them stomped off. Maus slowly followed.

The Release of the Prisoner

The doors to the ward had stood wide open, but not a prisoner was to be seen. When the station door slammed shut behind the visitors, however, the room came alive.

The rumor of what had happened passed from mouth to mouth. No one had understood before why their comrade had been wheeled into the private room. Now it was clear: the man was in hot water because he was a former officer. They were going to make an example of him. They wanted to take their revenge on him. And immediately they all understood: the Whites wanted to liquidate him. An incredible uproar spread through the room, a babel of voices.

Outside the door to the private room, the grave head nurse conversed in whispers with several older nurses, some of whom had just come down from the second floor. And at once two nurses went into the private room, and then something happened for which no one in the ward was prepared: the bed with their mistreated comrade was rolled back into the ward. The nurses, it seemed, had the same misgivings as the patients, and it appeared they thought the man would

462

be safer placed among his comrades than in the private room.

A glad "Aha!" greeted them as they wheeled the bed down the aisle. The nurses smiled proudly; the head nurse stood at the door and kept an eye on the procession. Several patients at the front sprang up out of their beds and limped over to her and shook her hand. She shooed them off however, and sent them back to their beds.

Now Becker's bed was back in its old spot. From right and left they called to him. But he could not answer. His head, thudded from the blow, was full of dreamy thoughts and confused visions.

For almost a half an hour, Lieutenant Maus sat alone at the table at Siechen's on Potsdamer Platz, waiting for Hilda.

It looked as if she had missed her train. That meant she would not be there for another half hour. It had been a dreadful Sunday for Maus, one blow after another: in the morning the search for Becker, then the ugly revelations about the affair with the director that his mother had made, and now this ghastly incident at the hospital.

It's possible, Maus thought, that when they hear about this at the barracks they'll march over and do Becker in, just like that. What can I do? How did I ever get the notion to take this straightway to that crude unit commander?

Poor Maus was feeling very shaky. Nevertheless, all the while he was offended by what Becker had done. It had been disloyal in any case. But of course sometimes certain things could have priority over others, and then you simply had to do what you had to do. But that did not make it right all the same.

At last Hilda arrived. He only had twenty minutes left before he had to report for duty; he couldn't spend all day with these private affairs. Hastily he reported the whole thing to Hilda. She asked as many questions as she could, and although he could not stay, she had the whole evening off. There was nothing for it. She accompanied him in his car out to Charlottenburg. He grew less excited as they drove. Whatever it was that he was accusing Becker of, vanished. And what remained was only anger and a grim outrage that the officer had dared to touch Becker.

Maus had not yet sent word to Becker's mother as he had promised he would. Hilda took on that task. And as she drove back and Maus was no longer sitting beside her, she perceived the whole situation clearly. Something had to happen at once. It could be that they would lay hands on Becker yet today. Hilda had heard about the executions of the truce party at *Vorwärts* and of the gruesome mistreatment of prisoners. Everyone at her hospital had been talking about it.

At Friedrich's apartment—what memories rose up to greet her as she climbed the stairs where she had first embraced Becker after their return, and here was the door which she had recently closed behind her, leaving him leaning there rigid against the wall—inside, in the living room, she first repeated everything that she had learned from Maus up to the point of Becker's and Heinz's being brought to the hospital.

How good it felt, watching how his mother took the news: her deeply grateful expression, how she nodded and wept tears of joy.

"My son, he is my son. He is truly my child. He wanted to rescue Heinz, and then there he was among those poor people and he stayed."

But her expression and her carriage changed when Hilda moved on to the second, terrible part of her tale, holding nothing back not even what they had every reason to fear. A man in danger of his life, her son Friedrich threatened—they had been right in turning to his mother. She was an energetic woman who was accustomed to acting quickly. She declared at once, "We're going to get him out of there."

The women sat there and discussed the matter. There could be no question of a normal release through official channels. Friedrich was a prisoner like the others. Frau Becker thought clearly, and with a rapidity that surprised and impressed Hilda. Friedrich had to be admitted to the private clinic where she often worked. She knew the head nurse, and Friedrich would not be betrayed there. As for herself, Frau Becker said, she could get into the hospital gardens as a visitor and lead Becker out, perhaps with Hilda's help, both of them, as if they were visiting him. The question remained: how to get Friedrich out of the ward? The pavilion was under military guard.

As a nurse, Hilda could offer some advice here. Friedrich would have to be ordered to have a special examination perhaps, or to have some surgery performed, and so brought to the operation room. They would have to figure out a way to smuggle him some civilian clothes, a hat, a coat and shoes, so that he could walk out unnoticed as if he had been released. Hilda then improved on her own idea.

"He's suffering from a concussion. When they're severe, X rays are taken. He could be brought over to the X ray room. That has the advantage that you can take him over there at almost any time, since they take X rays at all hours."

Frau Becker searched her own memory and realized that she knew one of the administrative officials of the hospital. He could provide them with the connection to the X ray department. She would telephone the man at once.

"An elderly man," Hilda said dubiously, "a bureaucrat, he won't want to touch it. At all events, we'll need the assistance of a nurse in his ward. I'll simply appeal to one of the nurses, perhaps to the head nurse. They must all be perplexed at what has occurred."

"How are you going to manage that, Hilda, without some connection?"

She took Hilda along with her to the private clinic that she intended to use. After a conversation with the head nurse, Frau Becker introduced her to Hilda, and Hilda was allowed to listen in on a telephone conversation this head nurse had with a nurse at Moabit Hospital, with whom she had worked at one time. Hilda was able to arrange a meeting with the other nurse at once.

An hour later she discovered this refined and delicate lady standing at the main entrance to the hospital, waiting for her. Hilda filled her in as they walked back and forth in front of the hospital, and then finally entered. This young lady, however, proved to be much too skittish to take part in the plan herself, and the only thing she was able to do was to bring a nurse out to Hilda from the prisoners' ward and wish her luck. The delicate nurse, from the obstetrics ward quickly took leave of the two women she had brought together.

The surgical nurse, with whom Hilda now walked up and down in the twilight of the garden, proved to be a difficult case, but for other reasons. She was extremely mistrustful, and thought someone was trying to set a trap for her. She was just about to head back to the ward and sound the alarm—because what was afoot here was an attempt to kidnap a prisoner, get him outside somewhere and then beat him to death. So that Hilda had to go to a lot of trouble proving her identity with a letter to her from Frau Becker. And then she had the happy idea of taking off her wristwatch. "Here, show this to Herr Becker, please. It's my watch, he knows it well from the times I've taken his pulse in the military hospital when he was under my care."

There was an H. engraved on the case of the watch, and its silver bracelet bore an enamel representation of Strasbourg cathedral. The mistrustful woman went back to the ward with the watch, had a talk with Becker and two other nurses, and then she came back outside again. She was wild with enthusiasm.

They led Hilda off to the dormitory, to the room of one of the nurses, and there they arranged all the details of the kidnapping. But it could not be carried out until early the next morning. Hilda made one last round to inspect things, passing with the others through the garden and then into the X ray wing. Then she departed. She had to get clothes for Becker. They were all afraid of what might happen that night.

*   *   *

Hilda stayed with Frau Becker until morning. She had managed a half day's leave of absence from Britz.

At the hospital, the prisoners had arranged among themselves to keep watch and raise the alarm the moment anything suspicious happened. The two nurses on night duty appeared frequently in the ward, which was illuminated by blue light. Becker felt the tension. He knew from his conversation with the nurse who had shown him Hilda's watch that there were plans to rescue him. But everything that now made him happy and grateful was overshadowed by the memory of little Minna in her cycling trousers. She had given him a piece of her bread to eat, she had spoken softly and sadly, and then she was carried off, ripped to shreds. And over in the private room, that soldier had bent down over him and struck him.

One should not throw oneself as a sacrifice to evil. Even Jesus did not come simply for the sake of peace, but to cast a flame onto the earth and divide neighbor against neighbor for the sake of God. We dare not let ourselves suffer helplessly, simply bearing evil, when God himself came down from heaven to do battle with the demon.

Help me, Almighty Father, thou who hast led me thus far, allow me yet a while to live that I need not be ashamed in my hour of death, with nothing to show but repentance and despair. —

At about nine o'clock, Hilda pulled up to the closed doors of the prisoners' pavilion with a stretcher from the X ray station. She was wearing her nurse's uniform. She rang, simply replying to the guard who came up to her, "I've come to get a patient for X ray."

They let her in. Someone from the X ray station had already notified them that they were ready to begin the X rays of the skull fracture.

The whole ward watched intently (while the two nurses accompanying the patient gestured for everyone to keep calm) as Becker was laid on the stretcher and nicely tucked in. When someone covered up his face, he sat up straight, and then he saw how people to his right and left were beaming at him—it was their victory. But he was sorry that he had to be separated from them.

The doors to the building had been left open. The guards watching the entrance looked back into the ward. In the customary fashion, one nurse at the front, one at the rear, they rolled the little cart out amidst deepest silence. The guards did not leave their posts at the entrance until the door had been securely locked again.

They pushed him over to the empty waiting room of the X ray station, and Hilda helped him get dressed.

"You pirate," Becker whispered to her, "how do you even know that I want to be set free?"

He stood shakily on his feet. She put her hand over his mouth. He gave her a determined look. While she buttoned up his coat and helped him stick his wounded hand carefully into the pocket, he gazed down at himself and then straightened up. "I'm the fallen Achilles whom they are putting into his armor."

She did not understand what he meant, but she understood his glance, and she comprehended better than Maus why he had gone over to them and left them now only with difficulty.

He even permitted her to kneel down and tie his shoes and then finally to set his hat on his head. The nurse accompanying them had taken her leave in the meantime. Hilda herself disappeared and came back in a few minutes in inconspicuous civilian clothes, the dark green winter coat she had worn as she had walked through the main entrance a half an hour before. She embraced Friedrich and told him to take courage. While she kissed him, she laughed, "Do you really believe, Friedrich, that I've torn you from my heart because I have decided to take Maus instead? I was able to save you once before, my dear man. Don't begrudge me a second time. I'm not doing it without a reason. It makes me very happy to know that you are alive."

And now they left the X ray wing, he leaning on her arm. They wandered without anyone's noticing along a row of hospital buildings to the rear entrance. This was where delivery wagons came and went, and where patients left the grounds—only as corpses after autopsy.

As they approached this rear entrance, its doors flung back wide open, two military cars drove in slowly, closed cars with officers inside. Becker looked the other way. Afterward he nodded to Hilda: "The interrogating committee."

The porter did not want to let them out. This was not a public entrance. But Hilda was determined. "You can't expect us to go all the way back to the main gate. This gentleman is in no condition to do that either."

The man stood there, hesitating and cursing, "They all got the same sad story. But I'm not getting myself in hot water, 'cause I have my orders."

And now Hilda dipped into her purse and pressed some hard cash into his hand, whereupon he sent them on their way with a wave of his hand. "Okay, get a move on. Quick."

A car stopped directly in front of the exit; in it a nurse, a young woman from the private clinic, sat waiting. Hilda introduced them in the car.

As they rode, Hilda folded her hands and murmured a prayer of thanks, her eyes closed.

He asked: "Where's my mother? I thought she would be along?"

Hilda: "Friedrich, you're really a greenhorn. You don't understand a thing about conspiracies. You'll not be seeing her too soon."

He was given another surprise when they got out at Potsdamer Platz and then slowly turned down Bellevue Strasse.

"What's all this, Hilda? You're taking me the wrong way."

But both women were in high spirits; they had won, indeed they had. Hilda replied, "If only I had a little more time I'd take you to a café now to celebrate. What do you think?"

He walked along erect, holding onto Hilda's arm. He felt just as she did: how wonderful it was to have escaped. What bliss just to be alive. There was the square with its teeming humanity. The trolleys and cars drove merrily up and down. The traffic cop was up in his tower in the middle of the square, giving signals; on one corner people were selling flowers and newspapers.

What are they thinking, what do they know? Each of them is doing whatever it is he intends to do at that moment—climbing onto the trolley, crossing the square, standing at a store window and looking at the display.

And this varied scene, this crazy life goes on here today just as it did yesterday and would tomorrow. At Jostin's people were sitting at the little marbletop tables, smoking, drinking and feeling fine. They held their newspapers before their noses, and what terrible things were printed there, all of it happening a quarter hour away from them. They'll read about me this evening. The wounded were lying in Moabit Hospital and in the barracks the prisoners were waiting for the blow of the club.

They stopped before a shop on the corner of Potsdamer Strasse. Hilda began to speak to Friedrich.

He stared out at the square.

Jeremiah saith:

"Lift up thine eyes unto the high places, and see where thou hast not been lain with. In the ways hast thou sat for them, as the Arabian in the wilderness; and thou hast polluted the land with thy whoredoms and with thy wickedness.

"Therefore the showers have been withholden, and there hath been no latter rain . . .

"Wherefore a lion out of the forest shall slay them, and a wolf of the evenings shall spoil them, a leopard shall watch over their cities . . .

"The whole city shall flee for the noise of the horsemen and bowmen; they shall go into thickets, and climb up upon the rocks . . .

"And when thou art spoiled, what wilt thou do? Though thou

468

clothest thyself with crimson, though thou deckest thee with ornaments of gold, though thou rentest thy face with painting, in vain shall thou make thyself fair . . .

"For I have heard a voice as of a woman in travail . . . saying, Woe is me now! for my soul is wearied because of murderers."

Hilda took him by the arm. They crossed the pavement into Linkstrasse, where cars were standing.

He had been rescued. But he had no peace within himself. They had caught him off guard. He forced himself. He said an affectionate goodbye to Hilda, who hurried off to her train. He kissed her on both cheeks and bought her a little nosegay. She was walking away now, and turning at the corner once again, smiling, Mona Lisa, laid a finger to her lips and was gone.

At the private clinic they put Becker to bed at once. The doctor examined his head and his left hand. Here his name was "Herr Schlossmann." The head nurse had chosen that name, meaning "man in the keep," because he really did belong under lock and key, she whispered with a smile.

He really did not get to see his mother.

Because this was a well-planned escape.

Immediately after Friedrich and Hilda had left the hospital, four military men had climbed out of the two cars that had driven past them at the entrance; they had come to interrogate prisoners. And the unit commander immediately flung open the door to the private room, intending to begin with Becker.

The room was empty. They called the head nurse, who replied that the man had been transferred back to the ward because that proved easier for the night guards. Hearing this, the gentlemen entered the ward, and the unit commander asked, "All right, where is his bed?"

The young nurse on his right asked, "Whose?" and then answered that he had been transferred to the X ray unit. At that the unit commander ordered him brought back at once. He didn't care whether the X rays had begun or not.

The head nurse, who really knew nothing about the attempt, called at the other unit without any suspicion—and learned, that no one there knew anything about Becker's being X rayed. No one had telephoned from the X ray unit to order that Becker have an X ray taken or be treated with X rays. And no one had brought him in.

The head nurse was terrified as she brought this incomprehensible news to the officers. The men gave her a stern look and, without uttering a word, went to see for themselves. But he really was not at the X ray unit; they returned in dismay, and no one in the ward knew anything—the gentlemen could swear as much as they liked. The "fellow" had vanished.

The gentlemen next bellowed in a torrent of rage at the guard, who explained that a nurse had come with a cart and had told him she wanted to take the man to the X ray unit. — Why hadn't he asked for some sort of notice, an order, a written request? — The man said nothing. She had told him, that was all.

Their curses were to no avail. They were confronted by a puzzle. The only thing that was clear to these men was that the other prisoners here in the ward knew something. How could they get it out of them? The unit commander finally entered the room, set his fist down on the central desk with its vases of flowers, fever charts and thermometers.

"Which one of you knows anything about this?"

No answer.

"Whoever knows anything, speak up. No need to be afraid."

. No answer.

"No one of course. Nothing but innocent angels. Bandits! No point in asking. Well, we'll set your ears on straight here shortly."

The gentlemen stomped out and closed the door behind them. At once there was the sound of mocking laughter.

The unit commander tore the door open in a rage, "Who laughed?"

Deadly silence.

"Who laughed? I'll ask you once again. Filthy pack! If no one answers by the time I count three, you'll all catch it. One, two, three."

He banged on the desk. "You'll catch it now."

He marched out hastily, cursing these "rotten kids" and banging the door.

The gentlemen could forget their questions. Because the matter was already in the hands of the civil authorities.

That afternoon, two detectives appeared at Frau Becker's; she had wisely not gone out that day, but instead had her neighbor in for a visit all morning. She knew both detectives personally because of her involvement in a project for ex-convicts. The two men wanted to make a search for Friedrich.

The mother was dumbfounded. She was looking for him as well. And in reply to their questions she gave a detailed account of what she had done the day before, and this morning, and of her attempts to find Friedrich. The gentlemen did not at first have much to say, but then finally they were prepared to allude to his having been taken prisoner at police headquarters. The clever woman (exulting to herself—her son had dodged them then) refused to believe this news. And when the gentlemen, using the arts of their detective trade, suddenly told her the whole truth, more or less accusing her, saying that they assumed she had participated in the prisoner's escape; she simply wept. How could they believe that of her? She wept real tears. But they were tears of joy. The gentlemen, as we've said, knew the lady well, and now put their detective arts aside and undertook a kind of search of the apartment, declaring that they were especially interested in Spartacus literature and homosexual magazines. But there proved to be only classics—Greek, Latin and German—in great numbers, plus religious tracts. They took down the address of Becker's only friend, Dr. Krug, and then shook hands with the man's poor mother. Frau Becker just kept shaking her head. She did not understand her son. Had it really been he who had been fighting inside police headquarters and who had been delivered at Moabit Hospital? Might it not have been someone using his name? That didn't sound like him at all. He had no connection with any political party. And who could then have freed him from the hospital? She couldn't believe any of it. It hadn't been her son Friedrich.

The gentlemen admonished her to calm herself. It was he, they were sure. Politics were making everyone crazy. But things often looked a lot worse than they were.

From which Frau Becker realized that they were not about to begin a wild police hunt for Friedrich.

And so the day ended with an incontrovertible victory of the Whites, it was true—but among their laurels they found some thorns.

The Morning of the Last Day

When Rosa entered the living room that morning—Karl was alone, he had already drunk his coffee with Frau R.—he stared at her in surprise.

"What's wrong?" she asked.

Karl: "You're radiant. Literally, you're radiant."

She sat down at the table, took the brightly embroidered cozy from the coffeepot and poured herself a cup.

"Frau R.'s already gone shopping? I've overslept, Karl, I'm sorry."

"Don't mention it. You slept like a log. We had a long talk. Werner was already here as well. Did you have pleasant dreams, Rosa?"

"What makes you say that, Karl? I think you're trying to tease me."

"No. I'm glad that you look so fine. When the children get up at home looking like that, they always tell me they've had sweet dreams, and sometimes they can even remember what about."

Rosa, as she drank: "A person can be happy just to have had a good night's sleep. I can do without the dreams, Karl, because the life we're living is beginning to take on a lot of the qualities of a dream."

"Oh," he replied as he stood up, "it seems to me more like hard work, much more like reality. We're doing our fighting while lying in ambush, and they're moving heaven and earth to catch us. But—'Him they'll never catch, our free Father Rhine.'"

"What did Werner have to say?"

Karl, at the window: "It's wonderful how you sit there, Rosa, and ask: what did he have to say? If only I could sleep like that just one night. I'm basking in your sunshine, literally. Werner brought me the article I wrote and warned us once again that there are all sorts of rumors and that we have to be careful."

"I'd rather you read me your article, Karl, I don't like his croaks of doom."

He took the *Rote Fahne* from the table and read at the window:

"Oh, gently.

"We have not fled and we are not vanquished.

"Even if they bind us in chains.

"We are here and shall remain. And victory will be ours.

"For Spartacus means fire and spirit, it means soul and heart, it means the will to revolution, the act of the proletarian revolution.

"And Spartacus means all the misery and the yearning for happiness and all the determination to fight of a class-conscious proletariat."

"Because Spartacus means socialism and world revolution.

"The long road to Golgotha for the German working class has not reached its end, but the day of salvation nears."

She listened, her head propped in her hands. Now she came over to him and squeezed both his hands warmly, tears in her eyes.

"How true, Karl, how true that is, what you've written. Yes, that is Spartacus, and it was never anything else. I'm glad that you said that: all the misery of the proletariat and its yearning for happiness and its determination to fight. We'll not let them put us off with fine words, not let them placate us. And then, how brave it sounds, the echo of the ancient declaration: and even if they bind us in chains, victory will be ours. Perhaps from that they will finally realize what the class struggle means for us: much, much more than just a struggle of classes."

472

They sat down beside each other on the sofa, he laid the paper down and threw his head way back, as he always did when he cast his gaze upward to speak before a great crowd. His brow was furrowed as he said:

"What do we care if they call it class struggle and want to brand us with the term. You have to have solid ground under your feet as a jumping off point. We take our name from the poor whom we lead. But what the poor want, and what the poor are fighting for, the term doesn't say that. Spartacus. We are an army of prisoners and are doing battle against our slave overseers. What our army wants is as old as the world, and that is why it ought, must and shall continue to fight until victory, even if it takes longer than history itself." He was quivering. "'And though this world with devils filled should threaten to undo us, we will not fear for God hath willed His truth to triumph through us: the prince of darkness grim, we tremble not for him; his rage we can endure, for lo! his doom is sure, one little word shall fell him.'"

"Wonderful," Rosa whispered.

"And the end of the hymn goes—and they can't call this class struggle, you can even sing it in church, and I learned it in school: 'Let goods and kindred go, this mortal life also, the body they may kill. God's truth abideth still, his kingdom is forever.'"

They sat there in silence.

She brushed his sleeve with her face, still unchanged and serene. "Can you forgive me, Karl. I've often been hard on you. But you were right. We should have gone with you. We didn't trust enough. Something was lacking in us. We were too busy calculating things."

He nodded gloomily. "You've always calculated too much, from the very beginning. Figuring and figuring. Do you remember still those November days and our meeting on Sophienstrasse? I think you sent out exactly seventeen invitations, seventeen. And afterward people were standing out in the street, and we had to set up another meeting at the same time. We always underestimated our strength. On January 5th we had it all in our hands, and on the 6th we could have marched . . ."

He let his head fall in resignation and covered his eyes with his hand. "The world will never forgive us."

And after a pause he stared fixedly at her. "Was that our test, Rosa? It was the test. That was it. Woe to us."

The black swan was flying. It bore itself forward, head outstretched, its little feet pulled up backward, with slow beatings of its wings, moving toward its goal.

Karl continued:

"And back then, way at the beginning, at Busch Circus, the soldiers' councils demanded: the parties of the working class should take over the government proportionately, the Independents along with the Socialists. The officers put that bug in their ears. And the motion was passed, and that way the Whites were able to solidify their position, protected by those cowardly, faithless Socialists. They could go on right on double-crossing us with no one to hinder them: up front they were defending the republic, so that they could arm themselves in the background and when they once felt strong enough, attack it. It was easy to see through their game. Foreign countries would help them play it. Because the gentlemen in Paris and London are not just nationalists and capitalists like the ones here, they're also stupid, infinitely stupid. How are they going to escape the next war now? What a vision of the future, Rosa."

It would not let him be:

"How I hate that snake, Prussian militarism. Because it is a snake, you know, not an eagle."

Rosa patted his hand. "Please, Karl, that's enough."

He: "We've been condemned to sit here. I'll not bear it for long, Rosa. I told Werner just a while ago. I'm only waiting for Pieck."

Rosa: "What in the world are you up to? You were just talking about inevitable catastrophes and now you can't sit still for a few days and want to run right into their arms."

He marched about the room. "Maybe I do. If they have their road to follow, I have mine. I've never said that we have to creep back into our mouse holes. Not into mouse holes, Rosa. We didn't do that even in the middle of the war."

"Karl, this is worse."

"Pooh, we have our elbow room, we have a clear line to follow. They will hold their elections for a constituent assembly. Then they will lock us up, and we'll sit in prison, convicts just like in the war. But that will be dangerous for the republic, and it will have a tremendous effect on our cause, more than during the war. Just let them try to make martyrs of us. They'll have no choice but to pardon us very quickly. And then—but I'm not going to give up the battle now, not for a moment. We must get to southern Germany after all."

She asked him in disbelief, "So now you want to go to Frankfurt am Main?" She couldn't follow him, he leaped from one idea to the next.

"I don't know, it's something to consider, but better in prison than sitting around here in Wilmersdorf. Do you know what I'd like, Rosa? Shall I tell you?"

474

He sat down beside her at the table, and his face was full of that old boyish insouciance.

"To put it precisely: I—would like to play checkers."

A checkerboard was lying on a bureau nearby. He put the men in place. "Checkers is a game of freedom."

But after the first few moves, she heard a humming, a sweet humming, it swelled to a mighty chord and bore all her thoughts away. She fell face forward onto the checkerboard.

He had his hands full with her, for there was no one else in the house. And when she opened her eyes again, as she lay on the sofa, he was sitting on a chair at her head.

He teased: "What a competent person this Rosa is, a very clever woman, a scientist, a discoverer of new ideas about the accumulation of capital and about imperialism—and this rare woman sleeps like a log, dreams delicious dreams and in the middle of a checker game topples over in a faint like a teenager. That would make a pretty poem, Rosa."

She sat up, her face was soft and warm, though deathly pale, and she was smiling gently to herself. "I really was dreaming."

He was enjoying himself. "This time, Rosa, I've got the facts. I was watching you while you lay there. You were in pure ecstasy."

"Ecstasy?"

Karl: "Or in rapture. At any rate, a most enviable condition."

She looked at him tenderly. "Hannes, it was really true."

He burst out laughing, he was enjoying himself immensely. "Rosa, you just called me Hannes."

She laughed with him, without any alarm. "I'm sorry, it just came to my lips, it's the name of an old friend. Yes, I'm still a little bit sleepy," and she turned to him, her face close to his, and he could tell that she would soon fall into another faint. "Karl, do you know how I feel? Not so brave as you, and I couldn't join you now in a demonstration on Potsdamer Platz. But I feel very rich, as if I had won a huge lottery, had hit the jackpot."

He repeated it after her, with pathetic exaggeration, "The jackpot—all social questions solved."

She lifted her right hand in earnest. "I have the feeling, Karl, that we are going to lead long, long lives yet."

And she opened her arms to repeat it. "Long, long lives." (He was afraid she would topple over any moment.)

And then she pondered a moment and out of the blue her lips said: "By the rivers of Babylon, by the rivers of Babylon, there we sat down, yea, we wept."

Karl: "And then?"

She: "What?"

Karl: "When we remembered Zion."

Rosa: "Oh, oh," she had a mouth full of tears and sobbed, "to be able to shed these tears, shed whole brooks of tears."

"Come," Karl said resolutely and took her by the arm, "lie down now for an hour. At least we can manage that, since there's no one demanding work from us."

He led her to her room, she lay down on the bed. While her face remained gentle and relaxed, the tears ran down her cheeks.

Karl Wallows in Milton's Paradise Lost

The officers of the Guard Cavalry Rifle Division at the Hotel Eden near the zoo.

They were happy to be in Berlin at last. They were graciously being permitted to do their job as real soldiers.

The officers burrowed among the newspapers in the comfortable and cozy reading room of the hotel. One of them had run across Karl's article "Oh, gently" in the *Rote Fahne*. He laughed.

"The fellow is getting soft. His knees are trembling."

"Yearning for happiness," what a riot. "He'll find his happiness, the red bastard, if they ever get hold of him."

"They're already hot on his heels. The brave hero is hiding out somewhere."

"I can well imagine that a decorated soldier just home from the front who gets a look at this mess here might beg a chance at this hero as his reward."

"There are a lot of them eager for him. He has lots of suitors."

"As far as these democratic swine go, they may be fat, but they stink, too."

"Quite puzzling, you know. Money doesn't stink."

"Where does the stench come from then?"

"Shouldn't we go ask the Jews?"

"My problem is that I can't really understand what the people here in Berlin have against us so-called reactionary nationalists, or whatever name they give us. If that's clear to any of you, raise your hand. Where do you find democracy if not among us?"

"That's enough talk about democracy, you're not in Paris, you know."

"Why? People want to hold elections, to get themselves popular representation. Why there are no better representatives of the German people than their officers. We represent the German people, not with some pretense of feelings and a big mouth, but with our whole existence, with body and soul. Who are the monkeys going to elect? Why the fellow who talks the biggest blarney, time and again. And so I conclude: the German people are being duped by these elections out of the democracy to which they have a natural right."

"That's correct, my good friend, as far as it goes. But all the same we're going to have to present our demands as well."

"But not wih a lot of hot air."

"Certainly not."

The older men in their lounge chairs were talking softly and smoking.

"*Vorwärts,* and Backward, and Freedom, and Freeloader, and the Morning Pest, the Doily News, Old Auntie Voss—that's the names they have for these dogs that do all the barking and biting at each other."

"And I say—just let them be. The whole pack has got all these big ideas. They don't even notice that we're sitting here and that we're going to have to clean up their pigpen for them."

"No unnecessary press releases—just let them be. Stupid people never learn anything anyway."

"Quite true. I just think that when you see a fellow, all cheerful and fit as a fiddle, heading right into your ambush, that you should at least keep him in a good mood until the last moment."

"Yes, sir, you should make him feel ven better. Yes, for my part, my optimism has been reawakened since we're back again in Berlin. I think, the way Comrade Friedrich Ebert is going about things, he's going to have his national army, get it right from our hands. But what this national army is going to do—with him as well—that's a question one shouldn't put all too precisely to Comrade Friedrich Ebert."

"Definitely not. Except that the Entente is not so wild about this army."

"But there are whisperings that the other side is human too, that they sometimes err as well, and that they don't notice everything. And besides, we're certainly preferable to the Reds. The first thing is to give Berlin a thorough combing and brushing with no interference, and then to put him in a bathtub, so that he can wash all the red off, and then fill the tub with fresh water and throw the whole Reich in."

On the afternoon of January 15, 1919, the day that would be Karl's and Rosa's last, the first visitor Karl received was his friend Wilhelm

Pieck, and then later Werner appeared, his courier. He looked the same as always, but then Karl could see neither into his heart nor his breast pocket. In that pocket he was carrying a wad of money, the first payment. He was feeling fine. Now he could live a free and easy life. And why not? Karl and Rosa were going to get caught in any case, if not today, then tomorrow, and if not through him and with his help, why then through others, and why shouldn't he earn something for it, seeing as how he had worked so hard for them? There really ought to be a reward in it for him. There was already a whole bunch of people who wanted to snatch the booty away from him. But now he had it made. They were going to pull it off this evening. He had only come up here just to convince himself that his sheep were still sitting prettily in their pen.

He put on a show again, warning them, advising them not to leave the house. They promised. He would be back tomorrow morning.

He tripped merrily down the stairs. I'll be back tomorrow. Tomorrow you'll be sitting in prison in Moabit, and I'll be sleeping in my fine down bed. And then I'll buy myself a dress coat, white gloves, leather boots, a walking cane, and on every finger I'll have a girlfriend. Ah, my lad, my lad, that's what I call milk and honey. It's not wrong either, since they're going to be caught anyway. And there's no reason not to bleed and milk these fat moneybags, these capitalists and their organizations. If Karl knew about it and were even slightly reasonable he'd be sure to say: stick to your guns, Werner, stick to your guns.

As this day drew to its close, Rosa retired to her room for an hour or so, to stretch out before setting to work with Karl on their next article. At this point Tanya appeared, very much in a hurry, and she knocked at Rosa's door.

Rosa leapt up, and while she was putting her hair in order, the idea crossed her mind:

What will I say to Karl now if he asks me again what I was dreaming? I don't remember anything this time either. Just as in the Heine poem: "And I've forgotten the words."

How can I describe the sweetness, Karl, that drew me on and fulfilled me? It is not life and not death and not even dying. It is another existence.

How can I describe the sun to you that shines there, melting all the ice and even you yourself? It is as if you were molting and your skin was simply cast away.

How can I describe the light to you, which is neither white nor brightly colored—is it light at all?—in which you are bathed and in

478

which figures move and approach you and lay their arms around your neck and assure you they had been expecting you.

How can I describe the freedom that you feel. Freedom, yes, freedom, the very thing about which we have fought so often. We have entered the realm of freedom. There is true freedom there. It lifts you up and bears you on the wings of yearning for happiness that you wrote about. —

But Tanya knocked louder. Rosa called for her to enter, Tanya switched on the light by the door. She looked searchingly at Rosa, but saw only a clear, almost loving, friendly face.

Tanya came over to her quickly and told her in whispers what had been arranged. Everything was going like clockwork. She had the car. — "What car?" — "The car to take us to Breslau. You didn't want to go by train." — "Really, you've got one?" — "Yes, and a reliable chauffeur. And if you like we can get away tonight." — "Why at night? That calls attention to itself. Come back tomorrow." — "When tomorrow?" — "In the morning, and now tell me the whole thing once more, every detail."

Tanya shook her head. "But there's not so very much to tell, Rosa. You can't wait, don't you understand? There's so much talk."

Rosa: "But who's paying for the car?"

Tanya: "Let me worry about that, Rosa. You don't have any money, I'm able to help out, that's all."

Rosa: "All right then, Tanya, you'll come back tomorrow morning. Thank you for everything, it makes me truly happy that you think of me. I thought that since you hadn't been here you had deserted me just like the others."

Tanya: "Tomorrow morning then, Rosa. My friend, the chauffeur, is waiting for me at the Halle Gate."

Rosa: "Ah, Halle Gate. Greet Halle Gate for me. Till tomorrow then, Tanya."

Rosa found a taciturn Karl in the living room. He frequently looked down into the dark courtyard. It was clear that he was raging against being locked in like this, and it always grew worse with nightfall. She waited for him to calm down. That happened now, as it always did with him, abruptly. He was standing at the bureau, and he reached for a book that was lying there. He walked over to Rosa with it.

"Sonya sent this to me yesterday. Do you know it? One of the first presents I gave her after my prison term. I had promised it to her from my cell. *Paradise Lost* by Milton."

Rosa was surprised.

"I know the title. I've never read the book. *Paradise Lost*." (The words came to her again: "By the rivers of Babylon, there we sat down and wept, when we remembered Zion.")

Karl walked about the room with the open book in his hand.

"A magnificent work, Rosa, belongs among the masterpieces of English literature. In the center of it stands Satan. It is a product of imagination. But ultimately, what does the expression imagination mean for a real poet? What a true poet senses are not sensations, but revelations, whether he intends to or not."

"What does he reveal? Whom does he reveal? Himself?"

"Naturally himself, too, somehow, but that's not the point. He reveals something that is within every human being, by turning it into figures that can be interpreted symbolically. Milton describes his Satan here in such a way that you are swept away by him, fall in love with him. We could learn from him how you need to react in defeat."

Rosa: "Tell me, Karl, what does this Satan do, how does he act?"

Karl: "He is an angel, a great, overpowering angel who has rebelled against his creator. He cannot bring himself to kneel and scrape. He cannot serve, he cannot adore. He is a master himself. It may be that he overestimates himself—he does indeed overestimate himself—but that only makes him that much more tremendous, makes him a tragic figure, one that we humans can comprehend. This is a Satan made of the same stuff we are, so that we can hardly imagine a better description of what human dignity means. In fact, it is essentially a man who stands there opposing God. His creator has tried to deal with him several times. But Satan cannot serve, the rebel in him keeps on growing until the Lord realizes he's got to have the law laid down to him, which then occurs on a cosmic scale. The apostate angel, now the avowed anti-god and Satan and leader of the demons, is picked up and hurled head over heels down through the universe, into the deepest abyss, along with the others whom he had incited—and a great many evil spirits. The Lord—I'm sticking here with Milton, who had a much more robust idea of God and Satan than did our pale humanist Goethe—the Lord wanted to try again with his apostate Satan, even in hell. He needed only to humble himself and he would have been received in grace again. But he met every exhortation with an ice-cold no, so that the Lord then drew off from him once and for all and left him where he lay, an outcast. Pardon would have made this creature only prouder."

Rosa: "And so what happened, Karl? He sat there in his hell and pouted. What could he do in hell?"

"He pouted, Rosa. But he did not sit still. He had a certain freedom of movement."

"How is that possible? Why did God let this evil being into the world?"

Karl laughed: "I'm neither Milton nor a theologian. You don't dare ask me too much; you've always been too curious. Perhaps because the Lord was not afraid of him and knew that he could throw him back down at any moment."

Rosa, preoccupied: "I can imagine that. It would have been in his power to cast him off again."

Karl was glad that Rosa was so interested.

"Interesting, isn't it? Tremendous stuff, as I told you. Reminds you of the Greek sagas about the Titans who tried to battle with Zeus. He buried them under huge boulders after the battle, but they then spat out their fire as volcanoes. Or if you like, you can think of the gods of our own age, of the kaisers, the dictators, the field generals, the governments and capitalists who want to tread on the people, but with our help those people have become the proletariat, and the earth beneath the feet of these lords has gone up in flames and been turned into a sea of fires. What I wanted to say, though, was, once exiled from heaven and now a resident of hell, what does Satan begin to do, now that it is clear to him that he has a certain amount of freedom of movement? This is where Milton starts his story.

"Satan sneaks into paradise and sees the first humans, Adam and Eve, totally innocent, watches the wonderfully gentle way they make love, sees how they deal with the plants and animals—and he is pale with envy. He realizes that this has been created by the heavenly one, this bears the mark of his hand. And it has been denied him. He cannot bear the feeling."

Rosa: "He begrudges them their happiness?"

"Right, begrudges them precisely this kind of happiness, this un-clouded bliss of the blessed, this innocence. The sight of this first human couple excites him. It does not awaken any regret at his apostasy. Rather, since he could not do anything against the Lord himself, here at least he can do something."

Karl marched in long strides about the room.

"Rosa, how true those torments are that the devil feels at the sight of those two, through the bars of the palace gate, so to speak."

Rosa: "Proletarian envy? Is the proletariat envious of other people's property?"

Karl: "You're right, envy would be the wrong word. But the proletariat has been denied something they rightfully deserve."

Rosa: "So that Satan still desires his heavenly bliss just as before."

Karl: "But without wanting to subjugate himself. But bliss comes to no one without subjugation."

Rosa pondered this: "Strange. Is that certain?"

Karl smiled. "I don't know, but Milton thought so. It is a divine condition that a free creature such as Satan simply cannot accept. And that is why Satan is the epitome of the free creature. And there at the gate he decides to do something that is evil and glorious at the same time—not some simple seduction of the two, a temptation to do evil—but something much more refined. He will open the eyes of these two innocents to themselves, so that they become conscious of themselves and are truly in charge of their lives. That is why he inflames in them the passion to eat from the forbidden tree. In the form of a snake, he whispers the wish into Eve's ear. She passes the message on to Adam, they break the command. And with that, both of them become conscious of themselves, and everything they now see and feel, they see and feel with their egos, and with ah, what human tones and with what an incredible increase of sensation. The intoxication of the love they now experience as they recognize, greet and embrace each other; Adam and Eve, Eve and Adam. He holds her in his arms and bemoans each day that he spent in this garden with her and failed to enjoy with her the pleasures of this love. You must read it, Rosa, to see to what extent Satan succeeds in his task of making Adam into Adam and Eve into Eve, the task of enlightening mankind, and how only in this way, Rosa, do these humans become like him. And of course the innocence is gone, and the endless merriment has vanished, and in their consciences they have exchanged it for shame, for suffering and pain, plus sickness and death. It is no longer a paradise, but it is not hell either. It is human existence."

How at ease Karl was parading about now with his book. It was clear that he took pleasure in assuming the pose of Satan. He spoke of Satan and of paradise, but he felt and saw Sonya in this Eve, just as he had thought of her while still in his cell.

Rosa replied only with yes and no, apparently not sharing his delight. He described in dramatic style the magic and the beauty and the power of Satan.

"This proud fallen angel," he continued, "reminds me in many ways of Lord Byron. The radiant, all-powerful Lord had cast him into the deepest abyss with his rebel hosts, but although his neighbors might howl and moan, Satan uttered not a sound. Now he has become the total antagonist. Among the common people he is called the tempter, and that he is, because he is always and everywhere underway, poking at the weak spots in the creation of his foe, of which there are unfortunately not just a few. What is imposing about him?"

Rosa sat up. "You tell me, Karl, what it is that pleases you about him."

482

Karl: "His constant protest. Nothing rattles Satan. He does not soften because he has been denied the right to participate in the wonders of the world. No punishment alters him. The anger of God against him does not diminish. But Satan's 'no' is also infinite."

Rosa: "A destroyer."

Karl: "To sustain oneself against every outside power, and never to bow. The Lord himself is somehow in love with him, despite everything. He could eradicate him from his creation, but he doesn't. Why not? He lets him be, he gazes upon him and realizes that the whole of creation is good, and this Satan, too, is from his hand. He reminds me, Rosa, of Spartacus in ancient Rome. The hordes of slaves had cast off their chains. Storming in attack, they could not be held back. Rome had to defend itself. It was a confrontation of equals."

Then Rosa could no longer contain herself, and she broke out in wild laughter.

"Well then let's not call ourselves Spartacists any longer, but Satanists."

He, calmly: "Why not? We'd sure give the philistine mob a scare with that. That would suit me just fine. It would please the masses of the people less, perhaps."

Rosa laughed and laughed (he thought, hysterically): "I think so, too, Karl we'd better stick with 'Spartacus'."

He waved his book, slightly annoyed (his session with Sonya had been disrupted): "In any case, there's something enthralling about this Satan; he can serve as an example for us."

But she could no longer listen to all this. She turned around, bent over with laughter. He became frightened. Was something going to happen to her again?

Between spasms of laughter she managed to say: "Yes, Karl, that's it. We can use him for our example."

And she spread her arms wide, threw her head way back (complete hysteria, he thought, greatly concerned) and called out in happy bliss: "I will give him the message the next time I meet him—Karl, the Satanist."

He sat down at the table. Immersing himself again in his favorite book, he shrugged and said, "You simply don't have a feeling for literature, Rosa."

10:00 P.M., at the Hotel Eden near the Zoo

Karl was at his best. As he stood up, he bent his right arm as if to show off his biceps and again gave a recitation: "Though with every power in strife, hold to life." And then he finally closed his Milton.

His friend Pieck showed up, and they discussed the situation. Karl remained firm: he would not let himself be chased off, he wanted to show the revolutionary working class that the battle would go on.

Around ten, the doorbell rang. They weren't expecting anyone. Perhaps it was Werner, the courier?

It rang again, and then again. Now someone was beating at the apartment door: "Open up. Police."

A small troop of soldiers had come up the front stairway, led by Lieutenant L. and an innkeeper M.; they had been sent by the Wilmersdorf citizens' council.

Pieck, a stocky, intrepid man, opened the door. He was shoved aside at once as the soldiers pushed their way in. They selected Pieck first, and asked him his name. He gave it to them.

Karl and Rosa were quietly sitting beside each other on the sofa behind the table. All the papers had been pushed aside in time, their roles assigned.

Who were they, the leader of the troop wanted to know. Karl seemed taken by surprise and stood up. What was the idea, forcing their way in here like this? Who were they? This was their apartment. They wanted to see their identification.

They answered that they had been sent by the Wilmersdorf citizens' council and were looking for Karl Liebknecht and Rosa Luxemburg.

"This is my apartment," Karl said resolutely. "My name is R. You may search the apartment. There is no one else here. Besides which, the Wilmersdorf citizens' council has no right to dispatch people to other people's apartments. I will notify the police."

But his protests and his self-assurance did not prevent the soldiers from searching his pockets. And in his haste he had forgotten about that. They found a handkerchief with his initials, and in his breast pocket were letters addressed to Dr. Karl Liebknecht. He did not let this dissuade him; he insisted that he was R., whose apartment this was, that he had been assaulted in his own home in the most outrageous manner and then subjected to a search of his body. This was a breach of domestic peace.

In the meantime, other soldiers under the leadership of the lieutenant had been looking around the apartment, and in the process they had stumbled upon the frightened Frau R. in the kitchen. When the lieutenant asked her who she was, she answered, "Frau R."

He said: "I see, I see, you're Frau R. I thought the other woman in there was. But you're Frau R.?"

"Yes," said the woman, simply terrified.

"The situation is this," said the lieutenant amiably, "we don't want to do anything foolish and arrest the wrong person. The man inside says that he's Karl Liebknecht. But it doesn't look at all like him. Could he be your husband perhaps?"

Frau R. trembled. "My husband? That's certainly not my husband."

The lieutenant: "But he might have come home while you've been out here. He might have come up with us. You can't be sure if you were out here in the kitchen."

Her hands fluttered. "I—I don't know. My husband left."

"I believe everything you say. Pull yourself together. You're not to blame for what he does."

The woman wept. "We're not Spartacists. Someone had a key to our apartment and . . ."

"Tell us all that later."

She had to follow the lieutenant into the living room, where Karl was just explaining that he had been lent this suit by a friend, and apparently Liebknecht's letters had been left in safe-keeping with his friend.

"That's Liebknecht, right?" the lieutenant asked.

The woman nodded. At that, Karl gave up.

The man grinned at him in mockery and made short work of things. "And now let's move, otherwise you'll be in trouble. You've kept us waiting long enough."

He reached for his coat, someone plunked his hat down on his head, and he followed them.

After this, Rosa was searched. With her it went quickly. She admitted everything.

They were first transported to a beer hall, where this citizens' councilman had his headquarters. When the lieutenant telephoned in his report to the Guard Cavalry Rifle Division, they were given orders to bring them to the staff at the Hotel Eden.

When they arrived at the Hotel Eden, everything had been prepared for their reception down to the smallest detail.

The first car brought Karl. As he entered the hotel, his hat still on his head, his hands in his pockets, two soldiers standing at the door hit him over the head with their rifle butts. He stumbled, bleeding. They led him into Captain P. He was denied any dressing for his wounds.

Soon afterward came Rosa and Pieck. They were received by the soldiers of the division with threats and curses. While they led Pieck off to one corner, they pushed Rosa in to see the same Captain P., who looked at her briefly, jotted down her name, then nodded to the soldiers. They knew what was to follow.

A sailor was standing at the hotel exit. As Karl was being led out, he struck him to the ground with his rifle butt. The soldiers dragged him into a large military van that had pulled up to the hotel. Several officers, one of them a sharpshooter, climbed in.

Karl was shoved back into a corner of the van. He managed to stay upright, but sat bent way over.

Purr — purr — purr, went the motor, the wheels crunched, the car began to move. It was not yet midnight.

Blood ran down over his ears and dripped onto his coat and the floor.

The officers were in a good mood.

Lordy, the man's bleeding. What's wrong with that fellow do you suppose. He's not feeling well. He's making a mess of the whole floor. I believe something has happened to him. But if he doesn't stop it right now I'm going to get awfully nasty.

Gently, gently, he's an elderly man. He's been wounded some-how—that happens with all these street disturbances here in Berlin. Nowadays your very life is in danger. We have to report this to the police. Liebknecht is to blame for all this, Liebknecht, blame, Liebknecht, blame. And Rosa, his red sow.

Purr — purr — purr, around the corner, into the black zoological gardens. Oh lovely wooded groves. Who made your trees so tall? And Liebknecht is to blame, Liebknecht, blame, and Liebknecht is to blame.

Sir, we shall indeed have to sue for damages if you don't start behaving yourself. Will you please stop spilling this wretched bilge all over everything?

Give him a shove, see if he can stand up. Hey, he can stand. Let's get him out in the fresh air, let him walk around a bit. Halt, driver.

Get out, fellow! — They wrenched Karl up — he was only half conscious — and pushed him out of the van. He fell down off the running board, but scrambled to his feet. They were at New Lake.

Run, fellow. Can't the guy run? Give him a kick, then he'll feel better. Hey, no pretending you're tired now. You probably want to jump into New Lake. Help, we've got a suicide here. Ha, ha.

The shots cracked. Karl had already been weaving like a drunkard. Now he fell over softly and lay there. They bent down over him. They finished him off with another shot.

The car pulled up slowly to them. What shall we do with him? We can't just leave him here. Shot as he attempted to flee, that much is clear.

Four men dragged him into the van. Let's go, drive on. Where to? I have an idea, a magnificent idea: the first-aid station at the zoo. We'll bring him in there, we're such nice people, samaritans, found him on the road on our way here, bleeding. We're so worried, do you think he can be saved?

Purr — purr — purr. Bright streets, the Kaiser Wilhelm Memorial Church, shiny cafés, the zoo, the first-aid station.

One man should get out, whoever can make the gravest face. And don't make a lot of fuss. My name is John Doe, and I don't know from nothing. Nurses and aides came out of the station with a stretcher. The doctor inside was just bandaging up someone who had had the worst end of a brawl.

Forward, business is booming today. Berlin, how it weeps and laughs. Halt, heels together, hands to the sides. Herr Doctor in your white coat, Herr First-Aid Kit, here is a man we found out in the mud in the park. Almost ran over him, someone threw him out onto the road, the Red scoundrels. Seems to be dead, too, or is he still alive?

I see, I see. Unknown man, found in the zoological gardens. Doesn't look to be in such very good shape, either. Head wounds. Let's have a listen for the heartbeat.

Sorry, but we're in a hurry. The man's in the best of hands. We think we've done our duty. G'night.

Out of there, to the car. Congratulations, went smoothly, like butter. We're rid of him. Unknown man found on the road in the park, a hard nut for the detectives to crack.

If need be, we'll say we shot him while he tried to get away. Flat tire, we had to get out, he tries to hoof it, so as was our duty we made use of our weapons.

Please, after having first called out three times.

Naturally, after having called out three times, and then begging on our knees, please stay here with us, it's really quite lovely here you know.

And then down Kurfürstendamm to the Hotel Eden.

Rosa had seen him bleeding as the soldiers led him off. They will club him to death, they've already begun.

The soldiers held her tightly, she screamed, "Let him go, let him go."

The soldiers struggled with her. And while they did, Pieck crept unnoticed to the other side of the lobby, and pulling up his coat collar and with a cigarette in his mouth, he walked jauntily out the door, past the guards, right behind two soldiers who were leaving.

They shoved Rosa back. She was frantic. "They're beating him to death."

"Shut up."

They pushed her jaw shut from under her chin. She could only moan and throw them mute glances that glowed with her rage. They laughed. "She'd just love to bite off our noses."

The soldiers were infuriated when they found out that Pieck had disappeared, they looked for him in the lobby. She stood there under guard and waited, seething at this outrage.

— Weren't you the Rosa who drew away from me and submitted? Waded up to her knees in heavenly bliss? How fine it is that you've lived to have this experience. This cup shall not pass from you, you shall drink it to the bottom. It will help correct your heavenly opinions. You have no answer? I hope that as an intelligent person you now can see through that dreadful hoax and are able to differentiate between dream and reality.

She did not understand his daring to speak out in the light of day. Didn't the others hear him?

She thought: they will take me off to prison, and the first thing I'll do is raise the alarm on Karl's behalf. They have mistreated him. I'll demand an investigation and that the guilty be punished. What an abominable bunch of murderers, beating a helpless prisoner.

— Weren't you the Rosa who wanted to betray herself and me to the Lord of Justice? Well, you have your justice tangibly before you now, just as you have experienced it a thousand times in your life. It will be tested out on you, so you can learn it well. Just don't have any illusions about prison and making official complaints. They'll snuff out your candle, just as they're doing with Karl's. And that will be the payment for all your troubles. Rosa, under what banner do you wish to fight and fall?

She did not answer.

— Weren't you the Rosa who begged: O glorious one, do not depart from me, I don't want to turn back? Well you're back again soon enough, out of poetry and into prose. But prose is just your stuff. Now you see what magical bunk this world is, a bungle, trinkets in all their glory. You'll no longer get any ideas about pouring perfume over it now."

She did not answer.

— Do you think you'll be taking the five steps to the door? I have a

vague premonition that you'll get to the door, Rosa, but in what a
state. My voice will be the last thing your ears will hear. Be quick
about it, Rosa, make your decision, so that we can have a party for you
when you arrive, which is only proper for one of our own. We will
receive you with royal honors. You will be greeted by the greatest
intellects of mankind at the banquet we shall be giving in your honor.
Don't tax yourself. Let it be, be you, only you. I am Satan, the Lord of
the World. —

The van had pulled up to the hotel, they had delivered Karl and
now they climbed out. They were in a good mood, the second delivery
was to follow. They waved to the guards.

The guards let Rosa pass. Lieutenant V. led her out of the hotel. She
had passed through the door. Several soldiers were standing outside,
and on the right stood one all by himself in front of the others, and she
felt compelled to direct her gaze at him. He drew her on magnetically.

Because—she recognized him.

Dear Sonya, they were beautiful Rumanian oxen, used to their
freedom. One of the beasts was bleeding, looking straight ahead like a
child in tears that doesn't know how to escape its torment. But that is
how life is, Sonya. Despite everything, we have to accept it, brave and
undaunted.

The soldier with the young, red face beneath his steel helmet was
waiting for her, his rifle resting on the ground in front of him, both
hands on the barrel. He was stocky, flaxen-haired, and had a little
moustache. On his right cheek, just above the cheekbone, was set a
blood-red, star-shaped scar like a funnel. It was Runge, the sharpshooter who had never been able to do anything right in his life. But
this time he would.

He saw her coming toward him. Where have I seen that waddling
duck with the white hair before?

And he raises the rifle by its barrel and swings it high over his head
and lets the butt fall like a hammer on her skull.

His face undergoes a change. It grows indistinct and broader and
powerful and black. He spirals up into the air.

He stands there, a shadowy mass of clouds before a radiant background. Only his contours can be seen and the sharply chiseled mouth
with a cynical smile playing about it; the wide-open, defunct eyes of
pride; and the awful muscles of his arm, the iron shoulders; the fallen
angel of hate, who grabs her hair and pulls at it.

She spits into his tyrannical face. She tries to tear herself away and
screams her loathing at him: you have no power over me.

And now the soldier, his legs spread apart, has already drawn back his arm for the second heavy blow. He swings the butt over his head and slams it down on her skull with such impact that it cracks, and like a slaughtered animal she falls to the ground with the butt. She lies there like a sack, and moves no more.

He picks up his rifle again and turns it, checking to see whether the wood has cracked. He nods to the other two who are bent down over the mute, black body, and says, satisfied, "It's all in one piece."

They grab the lifeless woman by her shoulders and legs and toss her into the van. Soldiers and officers climb in behind.

Purr — purr — purr, went the motor. The wheels crunched. The van pulled away. It was after midnight.

The soldiers in the back pulled up their legs to avoid the blood that was running out of her and making a puddle.

Where to now? Who knows? Too many questions get too many answers. Where to? Out to where Mother Nature makes things pretty and green. But in winter nature's not green. Where it's pretty, where it's dark.

Forward, driver, step on it; give it more gas, next gear.

Bloody Rosa, the red sow, there she lies, they can rejoice.

The car rattles and shakes. The horn blows and screams at the facades of the buildings.

The hosts of the damned and wicked are lured out by the noise. They cling to the car and are ready to prepare the banquet for her. They turn with the spokes, howling, yelping, cheering among the tires.

The Landwehr Canal, to the next bridge, let's not make life difficult for ourselves. The poor child is going to bleed to death. We should do something about that. There, here's—a bullet. And there's another. That makes two, by my arithmetic. And now you're dead, and that's what should happen to you all, all you swine and Jews, the whole tribe. Now you'll no longer be able to open that trap of yours and spit your poison, you snake. To the next bridge, into the water, dilute the poison.

Fish, she'll learn what she never learned before: to keep her mouth shut.

Stop here, gentlemen, come on, grab hold, no pretending you're tired. The old cow will go to school with the fishies. Get the baggage out of the van. Over the railing. Swing it. One — two — three, there she goes. Plop, down she falls, and we'll see her no more. Cheers, cheers, and mud in your eye!

It is the Liechtenstein Bridge. They breathe in the icy night air and light their cigarettes. They stretch their legs and then climb back in. And let's sing, as long as we're out in the open air, a lovely song in honor of the deceased: "It would have been so lovely, it didn't have to be." Chorus please: "It would have been so lovely, it didn't have to be."

Driving off, slowly, on out of the zoological gardens. And now we'll sing: A hunter from Kurpfalz, he rode into the woods one day, and shot the game so fine, whatever crossed his way."

Streets, bright cafés, the zoo, on past the first-aid station—no, worthy Herr Doctor, we have nothing to deliver this time around, didn't want to put you to a lot of bother, everything's been well taken care of—to the Hotel Eden.

Gentlemen, back already? We're happy to report that the mission has been carried out. Everything go smoothly? Completely, except for the mucked up van. Well that can be repaired with a little determination.

Handshakes and laughter. And now for a nice healthy drink.

They celebrated till the next morning.

Near the bridge, two bums had been lying under coats and rags, trying to get a little sleep, since they had not been able to find a solution to their day-long discussion about what to do with the rabbit they had been kicking in a sack beside them. They did not want to kill it at any rate until they were clear about how it was to be divided. For each of them maintained that the bunny was mostly his, meaning, of course, that he had been the principal participant in its illegal acquisition.

They heard a van pull up on the bridge across the way, heard the tires crunch and stop. Several men got out, in the darkness they could not be identified any better. They were carrying something. They tossed it in one swing out over the railing. Then they spat in the water, lit their cigarettes and drove off. You could hear them singing.

"They threw somebody in the water."

"What do you mean? I didn't hear nothing."

"If I say they threw somebody in, they threw somebody in. I saw it with my own eyes."

"Where did you say you saw it?"

"Up on the bridge."

"On the bridge? Then I must have seen it too."

"Yes, you sure could have, man. But if you're laying there on your stomach, how you gonna see anything. That's how they did it, and splash into the water."

"All the fibs you've told me today. But you're not gonna get away with that one."

"Well now, let me tell you something."

And he turned around, ready to make his point clearer. And then it happened.

What happened was that the sack with the rabbit opened—he had been holding it shut by lying on it—and the rabbit strolled out. The man noticed this at once, jumped up as fast as he could and went roaring after the animal, which took no notice of him, however. The other one started cursing him.

The rabbit jumped thoughtlessly down some steps to the water, his warder in hot pursuit. And because he was drunk and there was no railing on those stairs, he stumbled wildly right on past it and into the water. He paddled around, crying for help.

And then the other fellow up on the bank got scared. He left everything there at the water—the rabbit, the empty sack and his friend—and made tracks.

The cold water in the canal sobered the fellow up, if not completely, at least enough that he understood what was happening; and he swam and bellowed. Strangely, he could not find the stairs again. Finally, people came running out of the houses along the canal and down the steps, where they all but stumbled over the rabbit; but it got away. They got the rescue boat untied and managed to get hold of the man.

He shivered from the cold, dripping and bellowing, and still not really sober. He wanted his rabbit.

Then his rescuers ordered him to shut up or he'd really be in trouble. They would throw him right back into the water. Not another word about a rabbit. They wanted to call the police to come and get him.

Then it became clear to him that they didn't understand, and he tried to make them understand it all: his buddy had made off with somebody's rabbit, and besides that, people had thrown somebody into the water from the bridge, and that had caused an argument, and then the rabbit had hopped out of its sack, and so on. They understood nothing of this. Then the police came and put an end to the drunkard's lamentations. They drove the fellow to a hospital, less because he had fallen into the water than because he was shaking so badly that they assumed he was delerious. They had to struggle a long time with him just to get him into the car.

The rabbit whose fault all this was, however, was sniffing away up there; and after everything had calmed down, it ran about on the grass until it found the sack in which it had been carried away as booty. It lay down on the sack for a nap, and it was spotted in that state the next morning by a housemaid out taking the family dog for its morning walk. The dog and the cook chased the animal for a while, until the cook tripped over it, pressing it into the ground and squashing it a bit; but she was able to grab it alive and kicking by the ears and wave it triumphantly in the air.

And so the source of all the strife, the rabbit, was borne to the next restaurant on the corner, where they paid cash for it.

It was a fat animal, slightly damaged. Ah, if only the two bums who appeared the following afternoon and searched sadly about the bank of the canal but found just the empty sack—although they noticed the pleasant odor coming from the inn on the corner—ah, if only they had known that this smell of roasting meat was coming from their own rabbit. It had already departed this life, and in its present condition—even more than in its previous one, where it had only been the cause of strife—it was giving gladness to human hearts. But to other hearts than theirs.

BOOK NINE

The End of a German Revolution

A Government Unchecked by Terror

As you will recall, the government had fought for freedom of the press. In the negotiations during the battle it had declared with full vigor that as a democratic government it could not negotiate anything away. Now victory was here, and the newspapers, unchecked by terror, were therefore allowed to report on Thursday, January 16:

"Karl Liebknecht and Rosa Luxemburg, the leaders of Spartacus, fell victim yesterday evening to the rage of the people. After their arrest in Wilmersdorf, they were delivered to the Hotel Eden, where they were literally torn to pieces. The terrible course of events, gruesome in every detail was as follows:

"When the rumor began to spread in the area around the Hotel Eden yesterday evening that the two Spartacus leaders had been captured and delivered to the staff of the Guard Cavalry Rifle Division, thence to be transported to Moabit, in no time a large crowd of people gathered in front of the hotel, cursing and swearing at the two captives. It was past eleven o'clock when the two were led out under heavy military guard. The crowd, however, fell upon them and tore them away from their attendants. Unknown persons began to beat them. They were absolutely torn to pieces. As the body of Rosa Luxemburg was thrown into a car, one man leapt onto the already moving vehicle.

"There is no trace of the whereabouts of Rosa Luxemburg. During the night, Karl Liebknecht was delivered dead as an 'unidentified man' to the first-aid station at the zoological gardens."

The middle class, including a great many members of the Social Democratic party, heaved a sigh of relief. The deed, gruesome in detail to be sure, was nevertheless an act of self-defense. The middle-class press did not think it necessary to hide its satisfaction. One paper wrote: "Justice of the lynching mob—but almost a judgment of God."

This was not the opinion in other quarters. Ebert's own undersecretary and People's Deputy Landsberg walked around the Reichs Chancellery in distress as the news spread. Landsberg went so far as to declare: "The cabinet will not survive this." Gustav Noske, not content with events up to this point and with even greater deeds in mind, found that statement a gross exaggeration, and one could see that he, at least, would survive it. He could weep no tears, he said, for those two. They were to blame for this civil war. A sad way to go, yes, a sad way to go; but as leaders of the pack they had to be rendered harmless.

And Philipp, Philipp the One-and-Only, Herr Scheidemann, the optimist, on whose heart as on the empire of Philip II the sun of his good temper never set, what did he have to say? Eternity, into whose jaws he had disappeared as an insignificant thread, had opened its giant mouth again and released him as the whale once released Jonah, letting him loose among the living, on loan as it were, allowing them to rejoice in him a while longer. The confusion with his clothes that had occurred on the night of the victory dance over the revolution had finally been revealed. For although his clothes were a match for him in every way—they could dance, stroll, rustle elegantly and supplely and deferentially follow every mood of the perfumed bayaderes, courtesans and partisans—it was the bald head that was missing. They did not have a bald head or a noble beard at their disposal, to say nothing of the "magic flow of his speech, the squeeze of his hand, and, ah, his kiss." And therefore eternity once again opened its giant maw and released him.

To learn something of the inner life of a German statesman, one had to have been in attendance at that silent meeting when Philipp first found his clothes again—on their hangers now, hanging by a new thread. And what did Philipp, returned now to earth, have to say about the news of Karl's and Rosa's murders?

The mirror of his bald head rippled. He had said it all along. It could have been predicted. Who sows the wind shall reap the whirlwind, and he who has never eaten his bread with tears is a lucky man.

Then his voice choked with the tears of deep emotion. They were about to dismiss him from the witness stand when he indicated that he had something else on his heart and had this entered in the record:

"I genuinely regret the death of these two, of Rosa Luxemburg and Karl Liebknecht, of Karl Liebknecht and Rosa Luxemburg. I regret the death of each of them, not because they were my friends, but, on the contrary, because they were not—as any one human being mourns two others whom he has outlived, who have had to pay that relentless cutthroat, Death, his due. And yet, and yet, with each new day they called for the toppling of this government. Now they are themselves the victims of their own bloody tactics."

Touching silence, clearing of throats, handkerchiefs, curtain.

They searched Liebknecht's apartment. As expected, they found Russian propaganda and correspondence that led the Reichs Chancellery to take the offensive. The government sent a note of protest to Moscow in which it claimed that irrefutable proof had come to light confirming that the insurrection in Germany was being nurtured by official Russian moneys and supported by Russian agencies, and that official Russian agents had taken part in it. The government protested most strongly against such interference in internal German affairs.

Then—several facts began to seep through.

Since the Hotel Eden was located in the center of Berlin, there were people who knew that the hotel had not remotely been surrounded by a crowd that evening between ten and midnight. Rosa's car was not attacked at all, but had instead gone its way undisturbed through the empty streets of the area late that night. The two had not been grabbed away from the soldiers there on the street and then struck down and dragged off. There wasn't anything to the statement that they had been abducted by the mob. Instead, some people had heard the soldiers at the Hotel Eden say that Karl and Rosa were to be summarily executed.

And now the workers of Berlin and the Central Executive Council took up the matter. They employed every means to get at the truth. The government, however much it resisted and pretended to be deaf, was put under pressure. (It was in an awkward situation. Because whom did it have to thank for the mopping-up of Berlin, which had thus far gone so well, and with whom was it going to undertake the mopping-up of the Reich?) But it had to comply with the mounting of a rigorous investigation. The government was heard to say:

"These two people doubtless caused grave harm to the German nation. But an act of lynching justice such as was carried out against Rosa Luxemburg, it appears, is prejudicial to the German nation. In Rosa Luxemburg's case, laws were apparently violated; and in the case of Liebknecht further explanations are necessary to decide whether the rule of law was observed."

Karl Liebknecht, the "investigation" revealed, had been shot as he attempted to flee while being transported to prison. There had been a flat tire on the way, and for that reason the prisoner had been requested to get out. He had used this as an opportunity to escape, thus forcing the military men accompanying him to make use of their weapons.

And in promising that a second rigorous investigation would be initiated concerning these doubly dark murders—dark from the night and dark from the silence of all those involved—the government declared that unfortunately it was bound by law not to allow anyone to evade being tried by his proper judge.

And thus it turned out that the proper judges for the accused officers, in a process to which the government was bound by law, were the officers' own comrades-in-arms.

This is called a court-martial, based in this instance on the premise that dog won't eat dog.

The public, however, though it had swallowed a great deal, would not accept this, not even under the banner of newly won freedom of the press. There were people, whole groups of them, who dared speak out, despite such newly won freedom of the press. And under such pressure the government took one step back, but that was to be the last, you understand, and arranged for, or secured, the addition to the investigation of two members each from the Central Committee and the Berlin Executive Committee. Presiding over the court was the Guard Cavalry Rifle Division.

Representatives of the workers of Berlin, who wanted the truth (why, really? What were they going to do with the truth after all? They already knew so much without making the least use of the knowledge), submitted motions, and the motions were denied by the man in charge of the investigation, Judge Advocate J., as was to be expected. Whereupon the workers stormed out noisily, as was to be expected. Their retreat was reminiscent of earlier processions held under those lovely red banners. The text to their noise was:

"We demand a regular civil trial.

"We publicly refuse to take any further part in this investigation,

1. because our demands have not been met by the government,

2. because despite repeated motions based on the testimony of witnesses, the known instigators, perpetrators, and their accomplices have not been placed under arrest,

3. because it is therefore possible for said perpetrators to flee and

4. because the danger of a cover-up exists."

This declaration from the members of the Executive Committee who had participated in the investigation but were now resigning from it, concluded:

"Before the proletariat of the entire world, we have refused to participate in a trial that allows all traces of the deed to be erased and permits the murderers to evade the arm of justice."

What manly words. But to repeat our question: What did the members of the Central Executive Committee want with the truth, since they had been unable to do anything with so many other truths thus far, and since ultimately it was their own government that stood behind this "trial by comrades," the government they had put in the saddle and supported—and still supported?

The end of the story is quickly told. After determining that Rosa Luxemburg had been struck down by two blows of a rifle butt and that she had fallen unconscious to the ground, whereupon an officer had put a bullet through her head, whereas Karl Liebknecht, escorted by six armed men, had been shot from close range, the presiding officer of the court demanded that the four officers who had fired the shots be sentenced to death for manslaughter.

The court declared them not guilty, although it admitted that certain evidence indicated that there had been a conspiracy to commit the murder of Liebknecht.

Lieutenant L., however, was confined to barracks; Lieutenant V., who had escorted Rosa, was given two years in prison for "infractions of guard duty" and "removal of a body" (he preferred, however, to go to Holland using a forged passport, and was later pardoned); Runge the sharpshooter, who really could do nothing right, actually had to go to prison, as was only reasonable, for two years on a charge of attempted murder. Sitting there in his cell, he discovered that big wigs are not the best sort of folks to deal with.

Gustav Noske, the man assigned to the office of bloodhound, confirmed the sentences, this time in his capacity as "commander of troops in the Mark," after an opinion was jauntily handed down by both civilian and military courts that, should the matter be taken up in court again, there would be no severer sentences laid down.

Rosa's corpse washed ashore in May. The funeral for the two of them in Friedrichsfelde was attended by tremendous numbers of the workers of Berlin, turning into a demonstration almost approaching that of January 6th. It was made up of the same masses of people as then, only that now they had it easier than in January. They did not need to argue and debate about what should be the object of their march. This time the goal was clear.

They marched to the cemetery.

The Clean-up

Leo Jogiches, the old red-haired conspirator, who had been released from jail again, was a broken man and you could not recognize him. He used the days after the death of the two to follow the tracks of the murderers. He gathered testimony and even managed to get hold of photographs of the murderers at their banquet celebration at the Hotel Eden. This did not prove healthy. He was arrested again in March, and this time he was shot dead at police headquarters by a detective named T.

Hot-tempered Lieutenant Dorrenbach, the former leader of the erstwhile People's Naval Division, who had locked up First People's Deputy Ebert in the Reichs Chancellery just before Christmas, ran right into the open arms of this same detective.

Dorrenbach did not survive his meeting with this lethal detective either.

Friedrich Ebert, however, no longer held the modest office of a people's deputy, a position still tinged with the red hue of revolution. He had succeeded in wiping off the last traces of this rouge and stood now at the culmination of all his wishes. The Constituent Assembly had laid upon him the comfortable middle-class toga of president of the Reich.

There was a little drop of wormwood in his wine, however, when on January 18th, the day of the founding of the Reich by Bismarck, the men who now should properly be closest to him released the following statement:

"We believed that the imperial Reich would last a thousand years. And now? Hardly half a century later, we are back in the old misery and have sunk deeper than ever before.

"Germany could only be defeated because it was disunited.

"In the last analysis it was the social democratic venom of the International and its disavowal of the state that made the Reich defenseless.

"How painfully wrong were those who optimistically laughed off the danger of social democracy. It will continue to be a danger to us in the future. We will not be healed unless we subdue the spirit of social democracy."

Ebert did everything to pacify these grousers. But he could not make things right for them.

They swamped him with declarations of sympathy in public, and in private they attacked him. After Karl and Rosa, they did away with Erzberger and Rathenau and many hundreds more.

The revolution died a slow death.

Friedrich Becker Leaves Prison

When, three years later, Friedrich Becker left prison—a tall, grave, slightly bent man with a full brown beard, wearing the same clothes he had worn the day he secretly left the private clinic where he had been hidden and turned himself in—no one stood at the gate to greet him.

Who was there to come? He had rejected all political help during his trial; his mother was ill and had not visited him for months now; Hilda and Maus, a young married couple, had long ago moved to Karlsruhe; Dr. Krug had been transferred to Magdeburg—and young Heinz Riedel, where was he living, what had become of him? The trolley pulled away, heading for the heart of Berlin. Becker looked about attentively, enjoying the cool March sun, the streets and the traffic, the conversation of the people on the platform. He got off before reaching his destination and strolled across Alexanderplatz.

He had become more even-tempered and calm, reconciled with himself and the world. He could have had no better stroke of luck than to be sentenced to prison.

He moved past the gloomy, red brick police headquarters and looked down Kaiserstrasse. He inspected the facade of the building and checked the windows. At which one had he stood that night with Heinz? The facade was without a dent, the damage had been repaired long ago. The mighty iron gate, barricaded that night, now stood wide open, and you could pass through without anyone stopping you. But he did not go into the courtyard. He stayed by the stairway at the entrance, letting his gaze wander the wide corridors, thinking of those good people back then.

Then to his mother's. She was lying down. They were glad to be together. She was about to move to her brother's home in Cologne, and she wanted Friedrich to come with her at once. But that was too hasty for him. He would not be talked into it. After she had departed, he bounced around in Berlin for a while with no job. He had lost his position at the academy following a disciplinary hearing. He searched for Heinz, and learned from his mother that after serving a short sentence, Heinz had joined the revolutionaries in central Germany, had fought with them there as he had here, and had been killed in battle. His unhappy parents (the father was pardoned after serving two years) had had his body brought back to Berlin.

During these beautiful spring days when everything was renewing itself, Becker often sat beside his grave and that of the director. He asked himself:

"Do I owe it to them to sit at their graves like Antigone, to bring them flowers and pray for them? Am I doomed to Antigone's fate—simply to raise a lament for the dead? Antigone's burden was a terrible destiny from the primal past, just like the fate that weighs on these dead men here. It lies upon us all, which is why we cannot live in peace with each other. We have been driven out of paradise, and drive ourselves to war and crime. But more light has come into the world since the time of Antigone. The curse has been taken from us. We can breathe. God is not malicious, and does not lead us to murder at the crossroads."

He ran his hand across the grass on the graves. He loved these dead men because they were creatures like himself. He would also go down that same path. He loved their death, because God had sent it to them.

His lease ran until October. So he sat alone in the half-empty apartment. He was busy with a multitude of thoughts. He did not touch a book. He was not even in any condition to open the Bible, that was too overwhelming for him. It was sufficient to know that the old book was lying there.

When Dr. Krug came to visit, the easy-going, portly scientist hardly recognized the gentle, bearded man who opened the door to him. It was a surprise like the one that had greeted him when Becker, the skeleton, had returned home from the war. But this time the sight of Friedrich shocked him even more.

Becker consoled him: his sentence had been much too short; he could have used a couple more years. But the prison officials were hard-boiled bureaucrats. They had brutally chased him out into freedom.

"And what about you, Krug? What are you doing with your freedom? How do you deal with it? Give me a hint."

Krug told about his not exactly comfortable surroundings in Magdeburg. He cursed the idiots and reactionaries there.

Becker nodded, it was the same old story.

"You make things too difficult for yourself, Krug. Your expecta-

504

tions are too high; they're false expectations. Do I, the classicist, have to summon you, the scientist, to be realistic?"

They eased into conversation. Krug had sad things to say about the new conditions in the country, about Germany's internal troubles, about the peace treaty, about the League of Nations that didn't amount to anything—and how it had been heralded, till you had even come to believe in it!—about the eternal struggle between England and France, and other rivalries, about the dangerous Russian dictatorship, which had grown stronger despite all expectations, and about how America was again letting Europe go its own way.

Becker: "And all that upsets you. But why limit your worries to just a few countries. There's more than just America, Europe and Russia. You could talk about China. And then there's India and Polynesia. But you know your geography just as well as I. And you will find the same turmoil everywhere; now here, now there it's worse than in some other spot. I'll grant, the danger zones shift fairly often. But why should salvation now suddenly come from America? You can be certain the people over there are in the same boat we are, and the people there are just like you and me and the people in Magdeburg. But that's how we always do things, we presume that other people can manage it. One person is always shifting the burden to someone else. Don't take things to hard, my dear Krug. Don't spread your worries out over things that are too far away. A person only moves within a certain orbit after all, and you should be content to manage that. The only question is whether that's what one is doing. And there's the rub."

Later on, when Krug would not admit this, Becker said that you could not expect to do things one hundred percent. "Let's be content that we have life here on this earth. Our existence is the human bridge between heaven and hell, and it doesn't like holding the middle position."

At one time Krug would have protested against such a comment, or have let it pass with a shrug. Now he understood better. He replied that then one had no choice but to lay down one's arms and despair.

Becker looked at him for a long time, as if examining him.

"It would be a good thing, Krug, if you had come that far. Then you wouldn't be so concerned about America and Russia. Then real help might be offered to you, sources of help that dig deep into the despair. Our world, by the way, is not the only one, you can be absolutely sure of that. I remember your telling me about dark rays that have been discovered by modern physics, rays that do not shine, but under certain conditions cause other things to glow. I was very excited back then when you told me. Let's take those rays for instance. We, with our bodies, our senses and our brain, move only in the realm of certain rays defining our living space. And that means the whole visible world with the continents and structures we recognize. But this visible world is only a fragment, a half, a quarter, an eighth of reality, maybe only just an apparent reality. In any case, it is absolutely certain that this world in which we move and which we call "the world" needs supplementation. And correspondingly, what we experience with our senses and conscious mind is not the whole of life, and our thoughts are not the totality of what I would call real thought. Why do we clutch to this fragment so frantically? The wild notion that things don't function well here is fully unjustified and ill-considered. How should they function in a fragment? This is no whole cosmos. The cosmos is an illusion based on the wrong facts. On the other hand, however, we do recognize its beauty and laws, its order and harmony and our own instinct for those things; we see that it all is but a reflection or a shimmer from the rays, to use the terms of physics, that stream into our sphere from somewhere else. I think we must interpret this beauty and harmony, and the happiness that we occasionally find, as a clue and an invitation, perhaps even as a road to be taken. You're right, Krug, we don't have it easy here. But that is no reason to lay down our arms, to use your phrase."

Krug tried very hard to follow this. He gave it his best. He was even eager to learn something. He replied, "Let's assume I am able to follow you, Becker, logically follow the process of your thoughts. And I want really to try to put myself into the constellation of your ideas. How could I apply them in the midst of my own little bit of misfortune, in Magdeburg, in any physics class at the academy?"

Becker laughed along with him. "I really don't know. But now be honest. You have not yet put yourself into the constellation of my ideas, nor accepted them. Don't deny it. I know, you're groping, there is something there. But once you're really that far along, then you'll answer the question for yourself.

"I remember my own condition during the time I was recuperating, toward the end of 1918, the beginning of 1919. Perhaps you can remember as well. I was back on my feet and was in control of myself. I could march about quite handsomely. But one thing wasn't functioning: I didn't know what to do, where even to begin. I read newspapers by the ton and kept up with current affairs, as they say. Where was I to grab hold, where was I to find my place? You know my views. I'm a Christian. But what should I do as a Christian? The question that I raised for myself was the same one you're asking: "What do I do in my misfortune there at the school in Magdeburg? Finally—I simply began to act. The questions were getting me nowhere. And then it turned out that, although I was merely going to work at a school, just as you do, that I was being kept busy, that much was demanded of me, richly so, almost more than I could manage or respond to. You know all that, and then I simply got rolling. And now here I am coming out of prison, and I'm still rolling as before."

Krug: "Because you're a Christian, Becker. You know the point, the center from which you are acting. But what am I doing?"

Becker: "Who are you, Krug? Do you know who you are? Have you ever plumbed that question? Try it, try it seriously. Find out where it really takes you. That's when help will come."

"I know—those sources you spoke of. And what are they really?"

"I'll keep to the image of the dark rays. They're useful in helping us understand ourselves. For it's the same with human beings as with all the rest of the visible realm. You ought not believe that you're simply what you assume yourself to be. The human being, in the sense that anatomy and physiology and psychology teach us about him and present him to us, does not exist at all. That is no true human being. That's only a fragment of humanity. The visible and describable human, the one accessible to our thoughts, seems to me more like a sediment, a precipitate in a test tube. He is the end of the chemical process, and inert, at least to a certain extent. It takes a great deal of hard work, and also those sources of help, to bring him back to life."

Krug pondered this gloomily. "And this hard work takes the form of desperation, is that it?"

Becker patted his knee and laughed at this fat, easy-going man who gazed at him so mournfully. "I don't want to get you all involved in the wrong activities, Krug. Don't plunge headlong into the melee if you don't feel the urge. Don't deal too brutally with yourself. But I don't think that's what we have to fear with you."

The other man sighed. Becker wanted to change the subject, but Krug appeared to be hard hit indeed and would not pull back. Finally, after having listened to Becker, he said, "Well, what's going to happen to you now, Becker? I get a bit scared when I hear you talking that way. What is going to happen when as a Christian, since that is what you feel you are, you are let loose on mankind in the same way as back then in 1919. You know the results of that yourself. Your life could get pretty topsy-turvy, don't you think?"

Becker squinted whistled a tune and stroked his beard.

"Do you think? No need to fear. In the end everything has its own specific gravity. Why should you be afraid for me? I'm not. If I dive into the water, I'll not sink one inch deeper than natural laws allow."

Krug shook his head. "Fatalism. A man can sink. You can never know ahead of time. Here you sit in this half-empty apartment and will have to get out soon. Don't you want to move near me? We'll find something that suits you."

Becker embraced him. "My very best thanks, Krug. We'll stay in touch. I'll think of you when things are going badly for me."

He took a position at a private school, and was equally a joy to the students and an abomination to the teachers, and even more of the latter to the accrediting committee.

He did not hold to the teaching plan. He seemed incapable of doing so. There were long conversations in the classroom between him and his students. He spent some of his private time with them, even got involved in their own home life. This resulted in certain difficulties, and he had to be let go.

He changed schools often, among other things because of the poor scores his students made on tests. But he did not change. He was of no use for regular classroom instruction. He was given unimportant positions as an assistant, just to keep him busy and employed, since the students and a few teachers were fond of him.

And then traps were laid for Becker.

The first snare—quite improbably for Becker—was: women.

The First Snare: Women

Krug really did have to come to Becker's aid. He was called to Berlin, not by Becker himself, but by the head of the school where Becker worked and where Krug was known to be his friend.

It turned out that something had happened to Becker that they had never expected from a man of his sort. It was fully incomprehensible. He was living, as the outraged director of the private school told Dr. Krug with genuine regret, "a wild, debauched life." He was running around with women, had come into sums of money that certainly didn't come from his salary as a teacher, and no one knew of any other job he might be holding. Krug could not believe his ears.

But it proved true. This time Krug found his friend, with whom he was at last on a first-name basis, neither so gentle, nor so sure of himself, nor so even-tempered as at that first meeting. Becker had indeed fallen into the hands of some beautiful women, relatives of students. He was giving them private lessons, and they visited him at

508

his home. Becker spoke openly and candidly about it, admitting everything to Krug. He was living now in a fairly large, furnished studio near Oranienburg Gate.

He said, "It's true. Someone told you about it? They object to it, do they? And you? Do you think I'm doing wrong as well?"

Krug: "Oh, you've got the wrong notion about me there. You ought to know me better. On the contrary, it pleases me. Before the war, neither of us was overly fastidious. Only your employers, if I may call them that, are not pleased. There's been some gossip, I take it."

Becker: "Pooh! What do you think, Krug? This interests me."

This time it was Becker who directed uncertain and gloomy glances at his friend. Krug shrugged.

"If other people make no difference to you, your employers and so on? But they are worried about you, I can tell you that. That is why they wrote to me. They mean well enough. People can't figure you out."

"I think I can understand that."

And then he confessed to Krug how things stood.

"Ever since I was wounded, I've not been around women at all. You know that. First there was my physical infirmity, then soon afterward I was in prison, and after that it didn't matter to me. In the schools and wherever else I happened to be, there were always some who wanted to attach themselves to me. I did get involved with a woman at one point because she was so insistent, and she was good, too, but I could just as well do without it, and I did. Then things changed. Other women started pestering me. They pretended to listen to me. They had me tell them all sorts of things, things that should have been just as important for them as they were for me. But they listened only at the beginning, or pretended to. Afterward they had other ideas, which is to say, as they themselves put it: me. They laid traps for me. I stumbled into them without any suspicion, at the start. But as I said, later things changed. I must have tapped certain wellsprings inside me that were not too healthy. There are all sorts of things in each of us. And then I couldn't get free again, and it became a real temptation and a total reorientation of my life, and I yielded; I didn't even know any longer how to resist. And that's where I'm stuck now."

And he smiled sadly at his friend. "And all of it goes by the name of Friedrich Becker."

Krug: "And what—do you intend to do? Is it what you want? Have you gone too far? Are you in over your head? If you are, that's beyond the point of simple pleasure."

Becker: "Pleasure? A disease. But it's there inside me, I've always known it was. — But the arguments are already lining up inside me."

"What arguments, Friedrich?"

Becker, who was dressed quite elegantly and now had a well-trimmed beard, played with the end of his bright silk necktie.

"I know that these women are lovely and exciting little creatures, nothing more, idle and luscious. First they let me tell them fine things, uncomfortable things, and afterward they thank me and take their revenge by degrading me to the status of a kept man. All the while they give their own wicked will free reign, and degrade themselves beyond what they already are, or better, below what they already are, demonstrating it for me and gloating over it. What is all this? I know it is not simply wickedness; for them it's a kind of admission, a hidden confession. Amid all the shamelessness. It is already mixed up with its own punishment and the desire to be rescued."

Krug: "Well, that does seem to be something out of the ordinary. I cannot really speak to it. A crude fellow like myself has nothing to say to such subtle matters. But when all is said and done, why not, if you enjoy it, and if they do, and you're getting value for your money?"

Becker: "The wretched thing about it, Krug, is that I don't enjoy it. And that is hideous and I can't accept it. That's how hungry I am for it, Krug. These women have infected me with their own baseness. I am in the same situation they are. There's no pure fun in it. We're dancing the cancan on an altar."

Krug remained cold. "But why not? There you have it, nature has rebelled inside you and has chosen this way to do it. You've overburdened yourself and have suppressed too much. You were close to forcing yourself to be a monk. That was the mistake, and here you have the bill to pay."

Becker groaned, "How true, that's how it is. I've been telling myself that. Go on, Krug."

Krug laughed aloud. "What else should I say? Keep it up, if it's not going to ruin you. There's a great deal to be said for it. You were out on the battlefield for years and then sick and then in prison. And finally you're back again, and naturally you want to be a full human being. Well, my boy, I can only shout bravo! It's the return of the troops from the front. And this time not at the Brandenburg Gate, but the Oranienburg one.

Becker tried to laugh with him, but it was a weak attempt.

Krug: "And how inconsistent you are, Becker. Here you are complaining, and not long ago it was you who gave me a lecture, a philosophical, theological lecture about how our world was only a

510

fragment—and you're certainly right about that—and how we human beings only touch the truth fragmentarily with our thoughts and hardly know what is actually happening inside us. And so here we are—apply it to yourself. You were trying to make yourself into a fragment of a man. It didn't work. Instead, you have tapped something inside you that is also a part of you. Now you only need to have patience. You're on the right track. Things will straighten out."

Becker waved this aside. "On the right track, you say."

Krug, eagerly. "Yes indeed, right in the groove. And women are among the most wonderful products of this world. You used to know that, too."

Becker: "Products of this world. Certainly it would be sinful to despise them."

Krug spread his arms. "All right, then."

Becker: "But that's precisely not the point. You don't understand, Krug, it's something else. There are two parts to every enjoyment: first the natural delight, the pleasure, and secondly, what the mind does with that and makes of it. Krug, I don't feel the natural enjoyment. I don't find anything of the desire in me that I once had."

Krug: "You're just toying with it, I understand."

And then Krug saw something dark flicker in Becker's eyes, something that alarmed him and reminded him of the awful days when his friend was battling his demons. At the same time, Friedrich's face took on a tormented look.

"A person shouldn't be so arrogant, shouldn't pretend he's an angel. Why not admit it when you find yourself in an unworthy situation. I didn't want to hold back from all that. I wanted to expose myself to the temptation. And then I let myself go completely. I just stormed right on in."

Becker dug his fingers into his own arms, his face was distorted. He went to the window.

Krug asked him, "What's wrong?"

Becker, softly: "I wanted every temptation. I didn't want to resist a single one of them, do you understand? I'm no St. Anthony. I don't want to be a saint. I abandoned myself. I risked myself. I wanted to determine my own specific gravity. I—don't want to limit myself to this fragmentary world. I want to annul my own death. I want to plunge into action, into total and real action."

Krug was unable to respond to that. He did not like to see Becker like this. Finally he said, "Pull yourself together, Friedrich, you're fantasizing. You really shouldn't be allowed to be alone with your own thoughts."

"But then tell me what I'm supposed to do with my life. Play the role of private instructor, make a little music, read? I wouldn't even consider it. I hope God will understand me. He must know what I want and what I must do. He took more joy in the wicked, sinful publican who smote upon his breast in the temple and would not even lift up his eyes to pray than in the pious Pharisee."

Krug: "Do you smite upon your breast?"

Becker: "I'm glad you can ask that, Krug. You've learned. I enjoy having you as a friend."

And the elegant man paced about the room groaning, and then sat down and groaned some more.

"I'm having a bad time, Krug. I don't smite upon my breast. I don't pray, either. I've let that slip as well. A man has to destroy himself, Krug, otherwise he doesn't amount to anything. Yes, that's how it is, and here I stand. But where has it all gotten me. These women already notice it, they're afraid of me. This is not what they intended either. But it drives me on, I've dropped the reins. I've bolted like a horse that's shied, and don't know how to stop myself. I've got to run as far as Satan himself."

He was whispering this to the floor. Krug was getting scared.

"I must see what becomes of me. I don't really care. If only I could finally let go of myself. It's not even the women anymore. I'm still seeing them only to hide myself among them. But it's all useless."

Krug visited him often, tried to soothe and divert him. But he could change nothing at this point.

It was high time for Johannes Tauler, the old man, his guardian spirit and teacher, to look after him.

One gray and gloomy morning as Becker arose, shaved, powdered, looked at himself in the mirror and wished he would die, Tauler walked up behind Becker and looked over his shoulder into the mirror, a very old man in white robes. He spoke:

"Where to, my child?"

Becker voiced the thoughts in his mind as he laid down the towel and began to rub oil into his beard (but were they his thoughts that he uttered?):

"Whosoever will come after me, let him deny himself."

"Do you think that is what you are doing by tormenting yourself? You ought to deny yourself, but in a different way from what you are doing. You ought to sink deeper and deeper, sink down into the unnameable abyss, where all things lose their designations."

512

Becker looked into the mirror. "That is my path. That is what I want."

The image in the mirror:

"You must break your form, dissolve your image. But lost as you may be, you should not lose the essence of life, the life that is above all life."

Becker: "That is my path. That is what I want."

The white vision:

"The creature prevaileth not against himself as creature. Be careful, Friedrich, do not wrestle so savagely with yourself. You do not yet know who it is that is wrestling now. Snares are being laid. Calm yourself, from scalp to toe. Let peace pervade you. Calm yourself, your thoughts. Look upon the solid ground, whose name is God. Speak his name with me."

Becker did so.

And then Becker made another visit to the cemetery in Berlin. Suddenly he could pray again, and he prayed at the graves of Heinz and the director.

He greeted them and told them how much he loved them, and that he would take to the road as a wanderer.

Friedrich's Wanderings

Friedrich's mother was still living in Cologne when he one day appeared at her door. His wild Berlin days were behind him. He now looked like a tramp. She was appalled at his appearance, could hardly believe it possible. She took him in and cared for him as best she could. Slowly she grew used to him again, but wept a great deal, for she began to know him once again.

He told her all sorts of things. He had never found a better audience. She tried to urge him to take up his old profession as a teacher. That would be good for him and he would find himself again, if only he would pray and ask for God's help, and if he would start working again, the way a man should.

She said this to him often. It was not clear whether he listened. As far as the praying went, he replied to her at one point:

"If only it were that easy, Mother. Some things suit one person, some things another. I have to do what I have to do. Pray? Don't I pray? God is not a human being, or a ghost. Words don't affect him. Sacrifices don't reach him, only those who sacrifice."

His mother pleaded with him (she did not understand all this) not to talk that way. But he repeated what he had said, and added:

"God does not stand in opposition to us, although we are his creatures. He permeates us and prepares his way where we least expect him. His will is always done, and all we must do is let that happen. He cleans up the messes we make, takes care of our aberrations and our sicknesses. Because we are constantly dying, constantly falling away. He deals directly with us. He works within us. And what am I supposed to do then? Only present myself to him, be open to him, allow him to come to me."

His mother pressed his hands, unhappy, wishing that he would not speak this way. She did not like Friedrich in this state. There was something strange and closed-off about him. He spoke as if he were talking in the shadows to a wall.

He said, "What difference can a word make, Mother, or a short prayer? We know who we are after all. We dare not forget that God made us in his own image. That we always remain bound to him. In the final sense we are not devils, nor do we wander this earth as a rebellious band of Titans. Rather, we receive the light of his sun, and we sprout and blossom in its light. If we live, we live only through him, you see, and so what does a prayer or an act of sacrifice amount to, Mother?"

"That's awful, Friedrich," she cried. "You never heard that from me, nor have you ever read that in any Bible."

He looked astonished and smiled, "Then I must have formulated it badly. I don't mean that you should make mankind prouder and more vain than it already is. For a long time I was truly savage and impatient. I fought it. I think I've calmed down now. What have I said, Mother, to alarm you so? Just as Jesus yielded himself when they tore the clothes from his body and even ripped the skin from his body with their whips before nailing him to the highest cross, that is how we must strip away all the weakness and wickedness, and our pride and vanity above all, so that we can present ourselves before God. We must present ourselves not just in words, but in everything we do. Surrender is the word."

That sounded better already. She assured him that surrender was fine, but love was better still. And whoever loved God should rejoice in his world and participate in it, love his neighbor and take up his burdens. Why was Friedrich wandering about like this. If only he would go back to his job. Since she would not stop harping at this, he promised to do what he could. But it did not sound hopeful.

He stayed with her, and she noticed a great many strange things about him. He had a dreadful addiction to loneliness and a tendency to spin out his thoughts nervously to himself, whispering and gesticulating as he did so, his expression constantly changing. But also one could often find him, in contradiction to his own words, praying. He would stop somewhere on the street and go into a church, there to have it out with God, as he described it.

Young people who met him would invite him home to speak with them; some of them formed a group around him, and that pleased his mother very much, for he was a teacher after all.

But after a while he pulled back from his friends. He would tremble when he came home from conversations with them, and had to isolate himself for days on end. When he began to feel better, he sat down with his mother once again, and it came out that people, as he put it, were demanding too much of him. He could not deal with it. He couldn't.

The situation across the nation went from bad to worse. These were the inflation years. Everyone felt that the country had been betrayed and was being exploited by people in power. They stole money from the pockets of the little people and paid their debts by depreciating the value of the mark.

The government, still under the direction of the ill-fated Ebert, the embodiment of all the weakness and insufficiency of the nation, let things take their course. The outrage cried out to heaven. People tried to defend themselves, but the old tricks by which the revenge and punishment of revolution had been held back (in order, you see, to maintain law and order—without admitting whose law and whose order they meant) still worked even now.

Concerning the Rubbish in Man

During this period, former lieutenant Maus was living in Karlsruhe and studying to be an engineer at the technical college there. He had chosen Karlsruhe as his residence because it was near Strasbourg, where Hilda's father lived.

One summer morning while Maus was working in his laboratory in the city, a man walked up to the fence that enclosed the yard of the small villa where he lived and looked over it. He called to the housemaid, who was pushing a baby buggy back and forth in the yard, that he would like to speak with either the man or the lady of the house.

"What for?"

"It's a private matter."

She gave the tall fellow in his broad-brimmed straw hat a doubtful, appraising glance; he looked like a vagrant. For fear of him, she did not leave the buggy where it was, but pushed it into the house.

Hilda came out, slenderer than she used to be, wearing a red summer dress; she had him pointed out to her. "Where?"

The man was standing at the barred gate, and as she approached he removed his hat.

She asked what he wanted. The stranger, hat in hand, did not answer, but only winked, nodded and looked her in the eye.

She clutched her breast. For God's sake, it was Friedrich, with a disheveled beard, a knotted walking-stick in his hand, sloppy clothes, a red handkerchief hanging out of his jacket pocket—a complete vagabond.

She opened the gate. To the amazement of the maid who had fled to the porch with the buggy, Hilda led the unkempt man inside.

Inside the house, in the living room, Hilda, not at all in command of herself, had him sit in a wicker chair by the window looking out onto the porch. He eased down into it and sighed with comfort, smiling and admitting that he had walked a good deal that day. He nodded toward the child, which had sat up in its buggy outside and was tapping against the windowpane.

"Where have you come from, Friedrich? You've been—released?"

She was still thinking about prison somehow, although that had been a long time ago.

He: That was the last time we saw one another, on Potsdamer Platz, you and that nurse."

And he told her that he had walked here with a few friends from Cologne, and that they wanted to go on hiking cross-country.

"Why, Friedrich?" (To think that this was Friedrich!)

"It's summer, Hilda, a fine time to hike."

Hilda: "And—what do you do? Do you have a profession? Don't you teach anymore?"

"In a school, you mean? No. I've given that up. That didn't work anymore."

She was horrified. Then it was true, he had come down in the world.

Hilda: "And your mother, Friedrich, what does she say to this?"

He laughed good-naturedly. "She was just as worried as you are.

She asked me the same questions you are at first. But now she's content with me."

"She moved to Cologne?"

"Yes. But now—she has gone on another journey herself, my good mother."

Hilda laid her head on the table and wept.

That's why he was like this. There was no one to care for him. No one was watching out for him.

She stood up. "Friedrich, Maus isn't here, he'll be coming in an hour. You're our guest of course. We have enough room. I'll show you where you can put your things."

But he went on sitting there peacefully, his straw hat on his knees; he shook his head and thanked her. He had friends here and was only staying for a few days, perhaps a week.

She wanted to know his address.

He laughed softly and shook his head. He would come back tomorrow when Maus was home.

At first, when Hilda had recognized him at the fence, she had felt the need to throw her arms around his neck, it was Friedrich after all. But then he had looked so changed, had such a strange way about him and was so very silent. So that when he was gone, she stood there at the gate depressed and uneasy. She watched him walk away. Something had been taken from her. She had lived these last years so at peace with her vision of Friedrich, the thought of him had been precious to her, her guardian spirit. And now?

But what had happened to him then? What had caused this, just the death of his mother? Perhaps he was ill again, was that it?

Becker's appearance alarmed Maus even more than it had Hilda, although she had prepared him for it. One thing was certain to Maus at once: it must be the result of the old psychological problems. As they sat with him again now on the porch, Becker avoided all questions having to do with the kind of life he was leading. Nor did he reveal where he was living, saying only that it was somewhere outside of town. They doubted whether he even had a roof over his head.

He took the occasion to ask about the Maus family and how things were going for them, because that was really why he had come this way.

Although he found this rather curious, there was nothing for Maus to do but to tell about himself and Hilda and their child. And then he had to say more about how he had resigned from service with the

517

government troops, since this interested Becker. He hadn't liked it anymore, his heart was no longer in it, and so now he was planning to be an engineer. (Why was he telling him all this? Apart from everything else, to his horror he discovered he had nothing in common with the man.)

Friedrich had high praise for Maus and smiled gently at Hilda. He replied that everything had really been so difficult right after the war, dreadfully difficult, tensions and conflicts everywhere you turned, and how all that had melted away now and things were back to going their old way.

Maus interrupted, "But how about yourself, Becker. Why won't you tell us about yourself? You've certainly not gone back to your old ways. Won't you give us some clue about yourself? Don't you consider us your friends? Are we no longer worthy of being let in on things?"

Becker, at ease and sure of himself: "But why not? Just ask."

Maus exchanged a glance with Hilda. "Friedrich, you were a teacher."

Becker: "I already told Hilda that I'm no longer one. It didn't work out. I couldn't handle it, and gave it up."

Maus shook his head. "I don't understand. It was your profession."

Becker: "Before the war. And then after my prison term I really gave it an honest try. I wanted to be around schools as long as that was an option for me. But it didn't work out, believe me. And besides, there was no point in it. You're wondering why. There's no point in trying to heat with a stove when you know that the coal you pour in at the top is going to fall out at the bottom. You wouldn't go on doing such useless work over the long haul either. If you sow, you also want to reap. I could not see how to educate children—not in opposition to parents, in opposition to the state, in opposition to the world about them."

Maus: "But why should that be? Do you have to be opposed to parents and the state?"

Friedrich: "Yes."

Hilda asked: "Why, Friedrich?"

He sighed. "That's a broad topic, Hilda. Pity the man who has been condemned to teach in these days. What do people really want, what do the parents, the nation, the state want? Growth, prosperity, peaceful conditions, just as before the war, and we are supposed to prepare their children, our students, for those things, which means we are supposed to lie to them and keep them ignorant. I don't care who tries to do that, he won't be able to carry it off. The war cannot be ignored. It's still there. Peace treaties mean nothing. We can rebuild as much as we like, we're paying the bill without having first asked the innkeeper for it. And even good intentions are of no use. Whether we like it or not, we must get down to the causes of the war and draw some conclusions. For just a casual glance will show you that the old causes are still at work. A few people tried to do something, Spartacus for example, although they only scratched the surface of things with their struggle against capitalism, which is not the only thing to blame. But other people don't even scratch the surface."

Maus clapped his hands together. "What is all this about the war after all these years. You've recuperated completely, and we're all glad to have the war behind us, isn't that right, Hilda?"

But an old vision had passed before Hilda's eyes: Becker lying badly wounded in the military hospital, and he had called out, before he ever started back home, "Don't let them fool you, resist their so-called facts, I swear by all that's holy"—Becker during his long crisis there on the chaise longue, his mother, dead now, beside him, and always battling with the question of guilt and responsibility, until he could find no answers and reached for the rope. And she had had to go to him, rescue him, and a demon had tried to hold her back.

Becker: "The war is a nightmare, Maus. But it has not disappeared, nor is it any less real because you don't think about it. What is the nature of war?

"I was reading recently in Isaiah: 'The wicked are like the troubled sea, when it cannot rest, whose waters cast up mire and dirt.' That sea, Maus, that is in us all. It cannot rest. Wars reveal how things are with us. Why are there wars? The sea is always trying to cast up its rubbish. It wants to cleanse itself. A futile task. It thinks it can do that. But it can't."

Maus set his face as if he were enjoying the discussion. "So, as nearly as I can see, you're not banking on either the middle class or the communists, and of course not on the nationalists."

Hilda: "And why can't the sea cleanse itself, Friedrich, when that is what lies deepest inside us? There must be a way to cleanse it."

He looked across to her with his great, wise eyes. "There is, Hilda, of course. But who really talks seriously about it? Who are the people who are arguing with one another? Maus said it: the middle class, the communists and the nationalists. What are they thinking about? About the dirt and the rubbish? The communists are cheerful souls and hope to get around us by making a few changes. The middle class wants to be left in peace. And the nationalists are not about to let their war be torn from their clenched teeth. They have even thought it all through carefully and have come to terms with all the dirt and rubbish that has been cast up out of them. They have observed the wickedness, cruelty, malice and brutality in mankind that Isaiah was talking about, and they glory in it. Yes, they present this rubbish to us as the essence of mankind, as his nature. It's just been misinterpreted till now. It's nothing bad. That's how they've brought the age into basic harmony with their thesis. They are conscious pagans."

Maus: "They were saying that back in Döberitz, admitting it openly."

Becker: "You see, they boast of it, they are proud of their discovery. Heroic and heathen is what they want to be, and they preach it with pride and without guilt. But as you must know, there is no such thing as true paganism anymore. After Christianity, the only possibility is a renegade paganism. They're simply antichrists."

Hilda placed her arm on the table, resting her head in her hand. She gave an involuntary groan. The nightmare was there. She asked, "And the future?"

Becker: "We have fallen into the hands of the powers of darkness. What these pagans are preaching has strength and cunning. It's sly. They have gathered the evil and unholy knowledge of our age about them. They have Satan's muscles of iron and his malice. There's no holding them back. For this is their age."

Hilda wrung her hands. "And you can just say it as easily as that, Friedrich? The future is going to belong to these pagans? Then I wish I had never given birth to a child."

Becker bent over to pat her hand and look into her eyes. "Enjoy the blessing of the child, Hilda. It will not fall into these pagans' hands, because it is your child."

And he had stood up heavily, and bent down over the table, stroking his beard.

"But I must go now. I only wanted to look in on you."

Hilda cast a glance at Maus. At that Maus threw his arm around Becker's shoulder and drew him off to one side.

"Can I help you in any way, Becker, do anything for you? Won't you stay here with us at least for another hour and eat with us?"

Becker answered calmly, turning his hat in his hands, "If Hilda could give me some bread and fruit to take along, I'd welcome that."

Out in the yard, as Hilda slipped him the package tied up in string, he waggled a finger at her. "Is there only bread in there?"

And then she found herself sitting in bewilderment out on the porch after he had gone. She held the child on her lap and tried to smile as Maus returned from seeing Becker to the gate.

*   *   *

Maus sat down beside her, looking very earnest.

"Really Hilda, in his presence you get the feeling we're headed into another war. Everything comes back again."

"What do you think of what he says, Hans?"

Maus: "It's horrible to admit it, but much of it is true."

She looked at the child in her arms.

"Her name is Hilda, after me, and Johanna, after you, and we almost named her Fredericka in memory of the war and of Friedrich. I'm very glad we didn't do that."

It had grown cool out on the porch. Hilda gave the child to the maid. They went into the living room and sat down. Neither of them took the spot at the window where he had sat.

Hilda: "I've spoken to you before this about my impression that Friedrich has something mysterious about him, something wild and dissolute, and all that has grown stronger than before. Back then, in the military hospital, if you remember, he didn't seem like that. It had not emerged from him. He was always cheerful and free and confident. But now something is driving him and will not leave him in peace. He is without house or home. He accepts nothing. Why must he throw it all away?"

Maus (perhaps because of you, Hilda?): "Has he snapped, somehow, Hilda?"

Hilda shook her head energetically.

"No, he hasn't snapped, you shouldn't think that of him. It's how he is. It's inside him, and it's how I know he is. But what a picture of misery. And he's hungry and doesn't take care of himself. And then he rages against these pagans who glorify the awful things that people have inside them. And all the while he belongs with them somehow. Yes, Hans, somehow he's bound up with them."

She shook herself. "And now he's all wound up in religion. But what kind of a religion is that? A thing without joy, without happiness or blessing. Something—that's almost like a curse."

The Vultures on Wotan's Shoulders

Meanwhile, Satan walked next to Friedrich down the sunny suburban street and spoke to him.

"Did you have your eyes open, Friedrich? Wouldn't it be better if you put an end to it all? They have a child. How happy they are sitting there together. How wonderful Hilda looks, not like Mona Lisa anymore, she's slender and grave now, a new person. And Maus, how fine and earnest and at peace. He has grown. And here you are, wandering around in rags, freezing, hungry, and you can't hide it any longer. To the next bridge, Friedrich, and then take the plunge."

Becker agreed. "The creature you see here dragging along in rags truly does not deserve to live and to share in the goods of this world. He should drown and hang a millstone around his neck besides, as punishment for having failed so miserably."

Satan: "That should be your motto. You know human nature. Man's vices are irradicable. The prophet Isaiah, whom you just quoted, is right. Human nature is a troubled sea, whose waves cast up nothing but rubbish and dirt."

Becker: "Let's go to the bridge I crossed on the way here. Beyond it, on that slope over there, my two friends are lying and expecting me."

"Those lazy fellows. They're fond of you because there's nothing to them."

Becker: "You're right."

Satan: "You're only reinforcing their weakness. Be done with them. Get rid of this rubbish as well. Pour the sewage out."

"And afterward?"

"Death."

Becker leaned against the bridge railing and looked into the water.

He said, "Death. You said, death. My friend, I recognize you now. You were waiting there for me at Hilda's, to take your revenge because you failed with me once before back then. You're thinking: this time he won't escape me. I can see it clearly."

Satan: "What can you see clearly?"

Becker: "Just what I said."

Satan: "Then go on over and join your fellow tramps and give them something to stuff their guts."

Becker made a slight wave of his hand. "Get out of here, you. You're getting on my nerves."

When Friedrich made his last visit three days later (Hilda waited for him with a heavy heart—if only he had never come at all), he brought Hilda a freshly picked bouquet of wildflowers, and for Maus he had a sealed letter that he asked him to read later, and for the child he had a cheap necklace with a cross. A frightened Hilda stuffed the necklace into her apron pocket at once.

This time—they sat out on the porch—he refused even to drink the glass of buttermilk she offered him. She had already prepared a package for him. He said they had to continue their wanderings, toward the east. They wanted to go on through Bavaria into Austria.

"What do you want in Austria?" Hilda asked.

He laughed, and now she could see why he most likely wouldn't eat with them: he was missing both upper and lower teeth in the front. He could chew only with difficulty. His heavy beard hid the defect.

He answered, "It's only a matter of direction. We'll move toward the east, and perhaps that's where we'll land. Perhaps not. Something can always happen along the way."

Maus risked a cautious remark. "I would guess that in many places where a man's a stranger the police show an interest in him."

"That's happened to us often enough. It happens even within the borders of the Reich. And then you spend a while in jail."

Hilda: "Have you been in jail, Friedrich, since prison I mean?"

He, earnestly: "You stick out, you have no job. As far as the police are concerned you're a tramp. And then there are brawls, and there are drunks."

Hilda pointed at his mouth. "I'm sorry, but is that how you lost your teeth?" (What a torment to imagine Friedrich in this condition.)

"Only a few of them. The others fell out on their own. Teeth appear to be hard, solid organs, but they're incredibly sensitive, like a baby. In any case, the loss of two of my teeth resulted in a piece of good luck for me. The man who was drunk and knocked them out became my good friend afterward. He was sorry, and from then on it was my job to keep him from drinking. He is the director."

Maus: "The director. Who's that?"

"You remember the sad affair, I'm sure, about my last school director in Berlin who couldn't keep himself under control. It's him."

Maus's eyes grew large. "I thought the man was beaten to death at the time."

"Yes. It's the immortal director. I walked beside him on his way to the grave. Then I met this drunkard, who can't control himself either. It's him."

They all fell silent.

Becker: "I have another immortal with me as well, young Heinz. That was the senior student who was involved in the affair and whom I found with your help inside police headquarters. While I was still serving my sentence he was killed fighting government troops in central Germany."

Maus: "And he's with you now?"

Becker: "I picked him up on this side of Cologne, a brave lad, a very sensible fellow. But he doesn't know what to do with his energy. He belongs to those new pagans who fought on the Baltic front. He was a part of the Ehrhardt troops. Now I have taken him under my wing.

But he's feeling the old urge again, wants to join the Foreign Legion."

Maus: "With the French?"

Becker: "In the desert, in Africa. It's the restlessness in him, and his bad conscience. He is one of the ones who wanted to ride roughshod over the bourgeois world with fire and sword, in order to—yes, in order to do what? That's what he has finally had to ask himself. And afterward he was just as bad off as he was before."

Hilda listened attentively. "Friedrich, you say you're traveling together, you and this Heinz and the director. And what's the purpose? What do you all want, what drives you on?"

"We're wandering. And we don't want to die of starvation, and you can protect yourself best when there are two or three of you. And as you go, you talk about a lot of things and get used to one another."

Hilda: "And that's all?"

Friedrich: "Yes. And some things become easier for them to understand then, things they did not like so well at first."

Hilda: "But you could stop most anywhere, couldn't you, and earn your bread in peace. Why don't you just stop somewhere? Are you disgusted with other people, don't you like anyone? Friedrich, I believe you don't love your fellowman."

He was undisturbed by her anger.

"That's what my mother said too. She threw that up to me a lot. It must look that way, I suppose. But it's because of love, Hilda, that I prefer to wander about freely. What else should I do, what else is there for me? I was tossed out of the human order of things at one point. It would take another totally new decision on my part for me to find a foothold here again. And making that decision is what I cannot do. It doesn't even entice me. If you had been through what I've been through, it wouldn't entice you either. As I said, we, my friends and I, think about all of this and talk about it every day. That's what keeps us together. The two of them have repudiated Europe and its cities. But they don't know how to gain more clarity about things, and where to find a new basic outline. And I help them, and we all teach each other. They are already far enough along in accepting my ideas that they don't look to the politicians and the parties for help or want to join up with them."

Hilda took a deep breath. "I know, Friedrich, but to look to God."

Becker: "Yes. For a long time they couldn't see it. They thought I had some panacea, and instead all I have is the word, and an old, used word at that. Gradually, as we have wandered and lived together, they have grasped the meaning of it. Perhaps there's some love in that, too,

Hilda. They cannot think about things anymore now without that word."

Hilda was being drawn in now, against her will.

Maus: "Not to look to others, not to look to politics and not to one's self, but only to the world to come—that's unhealthy. That is not what you should say to them. That's short-circuiting the connection between man and God."

Friedrich: "It doesn't have to be a short circuit, Maus. It only is for those for whom the syllable God remains an empty one. But it can be filled, be filled up with everything that we call truth and life, and then with even more truth and life than our own senses and thoughts can comprehend, in fact with everything for which our souls long— beauty, goodness, love. And when you have squeezed everything into that one syllable and have bound yourself to it, then there'll be no short circuit. For that one word contains all the fullness, all that is most true, and most alive. God is not the world to come, but reality, whole and fulfilled."

Becker's face literally shone. Maus and Hilda, as they sat there next to him—so proud and happy, but savage, too, a jungle of hair on his head, and that disheveled beard, his boots all muddy—both thought, how can you help this man?

Hilda gave Maus a signal, and he left the room on some pretense or other. Meanwhile, she went to work on Friedrich. She pressed her way inside him, trying to convince him to leave this life behind him.

But the attempt grew more and more curious. She was almost seduced herself. For now that he was alone with her, he became a totally free man. He enjoyed being with her, she had to tell him all over again about herself, about Maus, about the child. He listened attentively and as interested as if he were a member of the family who had suddenly reappeared. He gave her kindly, brotherly, even fatherly advice, so that she was ashamed of having spoken to him about any lack of love for his fellowman. How glad he was that she was living happily with Maus. The things he said during this tête-à-tête and the way he acted moved her deeply. She understood now suddenly what it was that drove him on and why he behaved the way he did. And at the end she felt grateful, as if he had given her a gift. All she wanted now was that he should not leave. Or at least that he would come this way more frequently. She was worried about him.

He seemed to be cheered by this, but then all at once he changed and started whispering to himself, frightening her. His expression had turned dark.

She did not know that he was rebuking Satan, who had joined in her pleas.

Meanwhile Maus had put the music for *Tristan and Isolde* on the piano, remembering a conversation from so long ago, one he and Friedrich had had as their train pulled sadly away from the military hospital in Alsace. As Hilda escorted their guest into the room, Maus took him by the arm and showed him the music. Becker still owed him that, to play it for him. Becker sat down slowly on the piano bench.

His eyes read over the notes, he placed his fingers on the keys, and began, as if compelled, to play the overture. He would stop at times, but then, after a pause, he would start in again, finally the music began to flow and he played as far as the middle section and beyond, ending finally with his face all bright as he turned to his audience and said, "What a world it is, Maus, what a world it was before the war. Do you hear this music? How wonderful, how splendid it is. After all these long years I sense that now just as I did then, perhaps even more so. Yes, that is the beauty of this earth, the joy of unconquerable love that blossoms between two human beings."

Hilda had been sitting on the low stool that stood next to the piano. "You see, Friedrich."

He smiled down at her (you're trying to entice me) and then turned back to the music again. He played the motif of love's yearning and whispered, "You say, 'You see?' Who is it that says, 'You see?' That is unconquerable love. We say 'unconquerable,' but it must be conquered ultimately. For it is a fire and burns hot. Shall the world go up in flames? Shall that be who is set up as our lord, Cupid, our grand master?"

He stood up and sat down again at some distance from the piano, at Maus's desk. He looked as if he had retreated from the music. From there he said, "What's going on with these two, with Tristan and Isolde? Their love is unbounded, and the sum of their yearning is to erase the word 'and' between them. They want nothing but each other, Tristan wants only Isolde, Isolde only Tristan. And that is why there should be no more Tristan and no more Isolde, but only the single 'you.' They want nothing less than that. But what is that? The divine teacher says that man and wife shall be one flesh. He does not say they shall be 'one.' But the final and highest bliss for Tristan is the cessation of all personality, the great and last extinction, unconsciousness, the supreme desire."

526

Maus looked over to Hilda. "Don't you find that wonderful, Hilda, the most beautiful of dreams?"

Hilda: "And what do you think, Friedrich?"

Friedrich: "Not even death can accomplish that, not even death can conquer that little word 'and.' The ancient legend of Tristan tells simply and straightforwardly about the fate of two people who love each other with a love that ought not to be. Because Isolde was already married, and Tristan, the man she loved, was tied to King Mark by the bonds of friendship. But their love broke through that barrier, and the result was death."

Suddenly Maus thought: he is speaking about himself. I am King Mark, and he is Tristan, Hilda is Isolde. Maus looked over at Hilda, she was crouched there, holding her hand to her eyes. The bearded Becker looked straight ahead. Maus had the feeling: the two of them are thinking the same thing I am, I stand between them just as King Mark did. Why is Friedrich bringing up all these old things?

Becker betrayed no sign of excitement. He went on speaking as before. "And what did Richard Wagner make of this? He took this old, lovely, sad material and poured the poison of a drug over it. For to him it is no longer a question of love. He really needs that love potion to account for what happens here between Tristan and Isolde. Indeed, the two of them are poisoned. They begin to fantasize and to go off into ecstasies. They swim upon waves of lewd, moaning, languishing music. They demand that an end be made to their addiction—because they are addicted, they suffer from it, all the while wallowing ever deeper in it, and finally there is only one possibility, one goal, one supreme moment, as with every addiction, which is the complete devastation and dissolution and the end of the person—death itself, which, so we believe, marks the total abrogation of the personality.

"By the way, this is nothing new for Richard Wagner. In the *Ring des Nibelungen* as well, without a love potion, true, there's another couple gone wild, Siegfried and Brünnhilde. They sing: 'Let us perish laughing, let us die, giving way. Valhalla, shining world, farewell oh splendid glory of the gods, end in bliss.' That is what Siegfried and Brünnhilde sing. And what is the point of it all, where does it lead? They celebrate love in death, because you kill two birds with one stone that way: you have your ecstasy, without which they cannot live—this time it's not from alcohol—and you have the end of personality, which they cannot deal with, which they cannot stand to live with any longer. They flee from the strict demands of their personalities, which cannot be silenced; and they liquidate them instead, or believe they have liquidated them, with a theatrical crash and boom. They throw at God's feet the gift that they don't know what to do with. But you can't fool God. You can't escape him. Because the nothing that they desire does not exist."

After a pause, while the other two sat there silent, without so much as moving, he added, "The work is dreadfully representative of its time. Love-death, alcohol-death, opium-death, war-death and all the other deaths to which men want to flee."

It did Maus good to hear this. He was freed, released from the evil spell, there was no talk about King Mark in this. Maus replied, "You've certainly lost the enthusiasm for Tristan that you once had."

Hilda buried her head in her hands. I've understood you. You want to show me what love can lead to. Perhaps you would very much have liked to let yourself be pulled down the mad path of a Tristan. I myself was all too close to doing it and wanted to abandon myself, but now I have Maus and my child and everything is fine. But you, how fortunate for me that we went our separate ways. You're not fooling me. You accuse Tristan, but it's still there inside you, this same thing or something like it. I can see that you haven't tamed it.

Hilda had to leave the room in order to free herself from the sight of Becker and calm herself.

When she returned, Friedrich was about to say good-bye. He felt compelled to make a few remarks about Maus's handsome study, and then he moved toward the door.

Maus and Hilda were deeply touched. They felt that this was an hour they would long remember. Hilda held onto him at the door.

"Don't forget us."

Becker stroked his beard. She gazed in sorrow at his tattered suit. He said, while he walked arm in arm between them through the yard, "How could I forget you two—you, Hilda, who stood by me in those difficult days and who has meant so much to me, and you, Hans, who lay beside me in the hospital all those long months and then rode home with me and who shared so much of my life with me? I won't forget. I'm happy I've seen that you're both doing so well."

He promised to stop in whenever he was in the area. But they both felt that they would never see him again.

He left a very distracted Hilda behind him. She wept for him a great deal, and grew closer to Hans than ever.

The breath of something mysterious had touched them both. Neither of them had been "young" before Becker's visit. But afterward, they were both very cautious and earnest.

528

According to legend, great vultures sit upon the shoulders of the pagan god Wotan; they fly up into the air whenever Wotan rises up to do some momentous deed. Neither Hilda nor Maus heard the chair fall that Wotan knocked over as he stood up, nor the heavy fall of his footstep, nor his chariot rolling above the clouds—but they did hear the croaking of the vultures flying before him. Then they saw how the sun grew dark and then bright again as its light was caught up in their immense wings.

Christ the King

And so Becker, a tall, bearded and increasingly frail man, made his way through the provinces of Germany for several years.

He had periods when he burned like a flame and others when he crept into hiding. He always found new friends, and people tried to help him. They would find him a position as a private tutor, an escort, a traveling companion, but he could not be depended on. After a while he would be seized by unrest. A visible strain would come over him, he would become nervous and need to be alone. In the little room where he chose to live, they would often find him weeping or pacing silently back and forth for hours on end, or brooding and reading the Bible. Whoever his landlord happened to be would notice that he had not even lain down to rest during the night. After a few months the condition would abate, he would become approachable and friendly again, would go out among people. He had fought it off, as he put it. But then he would "hit the road."

Sometimes people would give him new clothes. He accepted them, but only in order to give them to others soon afterward. He would not allow anyone to take away the "right to poverty" that he often emphasized. There was great happiness to be found in poverty, and everyone would be much happier if only they were willing to be poor.

"What would happen if we all thought as you do?" people asked him again and again.

His answer was: "And what has happened to you? Mankind cannot bear prosperity." And he cited the Bible verse: "It is sown in weakness, it is raised in power."

The director and Heinz had left him long ago. They both went off during one of his gloomy spells, as he lay in a shelter for homeless men—the former succumbed to drink, and Heinz, who had fought with Ehrhardt in the Baltic, went to Algeria to enlist in the Foreign Legion. When Becker came to himself again, he lamented: "Why did

I not go with them, with the director to drink and numb myself, the love-death, the opium-death, the alcohol-death, or with Heinz into the desert?" But then the shades of the war dead came to him, all those others, and they wrung their hands, and he knew what he owed them.

For, this much he knew: just as we have been constantly sinking into the earth—plants and animals and men—for millions of years now, building the new earth that rises up, so too our souls sink into the billowing realm of death, where the others await us and ask us what we have brought with us and what we have done to rescue them.

For earth has a place in the order of justice. And the claim of justice never ends. Nor does the punishment of those who violate it ever cease.

How I must weep when I recall those countless poor men, those boys, who died without having fulfilled their lives, unaware. How can I appear before them empty-handed.

Once Satan, with whom he grappled in his months of eclipse, suggested to him that he would be better off going to a monastery and seeking peace there.

Friedrich answered, "You don't convince me. You know what's happening. You know the host of the poor whom you hunt down and dupe, never giving them a moment's rest. You are an angel and have fallen away from God, and so you know how things stand with humankind: that although we live we are dead as well, and do not know what to do with our own reason. A new flood will engulf the world. We are damned, and a new Noah must be born. I wander about to help, to prepare the way for him, for that strong and pious man. What would I do in a monastery?"

Satan: "And what are you doing outside it? What is hidden away inside mankind? What have you talked yourself into? There is evil in man's body. I should know. You drive me out. Let your flood come. It will be the salvation of all of you."

Friedrich: "The flood will come. That is the sign that there is justice. But there is grace as well. Let me see you, you poor wretched spook. How battered you are by justice, and because you have withdrawn yourself from grace. How fine that I am not you, but a human being and can submit myself to grace."

He attacked the false "realism" of his age.

"A man is sitting upon a powerful horse, he puffs himself up and beams down to those below him: look at me, how heavy and mighty I am. Listen to my saddle and harness, how it cracks, and to the hooves of my horse. That is life.

"But when his saddle cracks and the hooves clatter and he beams down from his horse and waves to us to admire and follow him, we see that he's riding a shadow horse, galloping through the fog of a moor.

"For is that truth for which he goes to war? They are nothing but phantoms and fantasies."

He called them idealists, all those who had constructed some fragmentary image of men for themselves.

"I remember a book written long ago by a Frenchman," he once told a circle of students in southern Germany, "which talks of how young people cannot get to the top fast enough. And then there are wives who suddenly get the notion to become nuns or abesses, even though they already live within the sphere of their duties as housewives and mothers—and then there are men and women who thirst to be great martyrs, even though they cannot deal with their own daily drudgery." And then he told of his own experiences in Berlin and how he had wanted to find reality, nothing but reality, and how that had thrust him away from ideas that are only illusions, and how quite unexpectedly he had found enlightenment in holy scripture. It had been a cleansing thunderstorm. But even then he had not grasped reality all at once. That had only come to him totally during the crisis at police headquarters, where he had sat there trapped inside together with the people whose ideas and theories he had fought. He had dismissed their ideas, but now he saw the reality of these fighters and saw that it didn't matter about their ideas, that they made do in one way or another with their theories and dogmas. You could have supplied them with others just as well; but now because of those theories a great injustice was being done them and they were being eradicated— without anyone seeing them, these fighters, these human beings, for what they were. But they were right. Their opponents only wanted to turn loose their own wickedness on them.

At other times he spoke about the disarray within man, from which man tried to flee by attempting to improve his state or his society, even though in doing so he never could escape the sphere of his own iniquity.

"As far as what is within us goes, many people present man as if that inner world does not even exist or is only tangential. And there are others for whom that seems too silly, and who maintain that the inner world of man is only a suppression of the beast that cannot be allowed to vent its fury in the outside world. Healing consists then of letting the beast free, what they call a return to nature. But all these are fantasies, spinning in circles.

"We are not nature in the same way that animals, plants and stones are. We have another nature than that nature. We do not develop out of our weakness and lack of resistance. Like Laocoön and his snakes, we are constantly wrapped up in nature and in danger of truly relapsing into it. But there is still an immortal soul that makes us what we are and that fights against this. An immortal soul has been wedded to an animal in mysterious and terrible nuptials. We do not comprehend, and it will always be beyond our powers of understanding, why this bridegroom has chosen this bride, why this marriage."

People asked: "According to that, then, the best thing would be to free oneself from this animal, to mortify oneself in some medieval fashion and to pray."

Becker: "I assume that this was not said ironically. omeone kills himself, then he is indeed free of the animal. But all the rest is quite another matter. The little word 'and' between body and soul cannot be gotten rid of in our world. But praying and mortification do in any case get us further than walking about armed with rifles. Only he who knows God and his justice knows reality, and can think and act realistically. Only he can muster real courage without placing exaggerated value on poverty, sickness and imprisonment."

The Ballet of Electors on the Siegesallee

There was calm in Germany in those days.

The people had betrayed the hosts of the dead, and thought no more of them, as was only fitting.

Friedrich Ebert and his henchman Gustav Noske were not to enjoy their victory. Revenge was dealt out. The heaviest punishment, however, was yet to fall (later) on the German people (and on the people of other nations).

Since Ebert had spared the officers and junkers, he was forced to endure all manner of things at their hands. They reproached him from the start for having been chosen president of the Reich by a constituent assembly rather than by general elections. They forced him to compete with them in matters of chauvinism, in which he invested a great deal of effort. By 1920, the gentlemen were trying to toss off the cart the man they themselves had set up there. But Herr Kapp did not pull it off. During this putsch it became apparent that there was still a living core to the revolution. Ebert was forced to flee (still not from a nation calling him to account, but from the junkers and officers, his wards, who were dealing with him just as he had expected they would), first to Dresden, then to Stuttgart. Monstrous as it may seem, he was permitted to return; only Noske fell by the wayside.

Friedrich Ebert lived for several years as president of this unfortunate excuse of a state that he had helped to create. His successor, of course, was a general. The country, with a poison in its bones that the revolution had not been able to purge, recovered slowly from the war, while getting ready for a new one.

In order to hold onto the lessons learned in the war, a League of Nations was created as well, into which the ailing countries were slowly to grow. But several of them did not belong to it at all, others were excluded, and the rest quarreled openly and in secret.

As soon as it became clear that the men of the old warrior caste had returned to Germany's helm, everything along the Siegesallee was set in motion. And now the margraves, electors and kings did not limit themselves to the Siegesallee, but extended their ballet out across the graves of the revolutionaries.

They waltzed in the dark across the zoo and into the city. They went out to the graves of Karl and Rosa and filled the air in Friedrichsfelde with their shouts of joy.

They hurried off on their marble legs, askew and misshapen though they were, to Bremen and to the Ruhr, where General Maerker had laid out so many lovely spots for them.

As a walking host of spirits, they raced to Wesel and Bielefeld, where they found all sorts of things to laugh about.

And so they rattled, waddled and dashed through Zeitz, Merseburg, Halle, Leipzig and Munich like a carnival procession.

The old gentlemen had not had such a rousingly merry good time for ages. Each time, they needed weeks after returning from these joyous trips to recover from their excesses. Squirrels brought them rubbing compounds made of beetles that they had snatched away from some ravens. But then afterward the electors got into a fight with the ravens who tried to peck back the gravy that had been stolen from them.

Moreover, the old gentlemen who had to stand there in wind and rain grew more and more critical in their remarks about the weather in Berlin. According to reports, the monuments that stood in Rome or Paris had things much better. They actually considered extending their nocturnal excursions as far as Florence and then simply staying there.

That would have been a surprise for the residents of Florence: one day, one morning, there would stand suddenly the entire Siegesallee from Berlin, and no one would know where they had come from and what it all meant. Only that they were Germans, that you could see. Did they want to found the Holy Roman Empire again perhaps? But you couldn't ask them, since they were made of stone, and besides— they didn't understand Italian.

Before the old gentlemen could proceed to carry out their decision, however, they learned that people in Berlin wanted to degrade them and transfer them to a side street. And that offended them so much that they did not go for a single walk after that; they even stayed put at night, merely making comments about the decadence of the times.

As is well known, marble is a material that loses its elasticity when it is not used, and then, even with moaning and groaning, it can't be made to bend. And that is what happened to the margraves, electors and kings.

And when after a while they had been grumbling up there on their pedestals, sharing curses with one another across the pavement and carrying on conversations—they could no longer scramble up and down. It was the disease of marble in its old age.

And so they let things be. Even their conversations bored them. And finally they were marble, and nothing else.

The Second Snare: Storming the Churches

Until the end of the twenties, Friedrich Becker—a tall, bearded, bent man, a remarkable figure out of step with the times, a living recollection of the last war—still went his way among the provinces of Germany.

In Westphalia he incited poor people to revolt on several occasions, and was arrested. At his trial he denied being in the pay of any political party, and attacked his judges, all so well-fed, as bailiffs of injustice. Where had they got the notion of accusing him of making cause with the Reds? It was not his fault that justice had no place among the well-to-do.

No sooner was he released, when one Sunday he lay in ambush for pious people in front of a church as they climbed out of their carriages and cars, and barred their entry. And when the preacher himself wanted to pass to enter the church with his robes, clerical bands and prayerbook, he cursed him and demanded, amidst the cheers of the people gathered about—evidently his accomplices—that the churches be closed, that these parsons were only defiling the word of God.

Several times he forced his way into churches in small towns, dis-

534

turbing worship services and interrupting the preacher. He instructed the congregations to go home, that they would do better to look after things there and to see how their neighbors were doing. The preacher should be ashamed of chewing around on the word of God Sunday after Sunday, even though he knew better. They were the most corrupt capitalists in the world, because they exploited the most sacred thing man had. They gorged themselves and pandered to the depravity of their congregations.

Although he mostly hung about in villages, he began to call attention to himself. Reporters viewed him as a curiosity and wanted to interview him, but they were turned away. But to other people he would on any occasion proclaim what he thought of Christianity here in Germany and what he held to be true devotion and piety. The very religion that was meant to do battle with comfort and human weakness had been degraded to an item of creature comforts, to a luxury. It was because the need had grown so great, because no one knew any longer the true God who had fallen into the hands of the rich and their venal priests, that the Savior had descended to earth and set matters to rights, and had taken his terrible sacrificial death upon himself. So that now everyone could see: this is what God did for men, and this is how they treated his own son. But he wants to free them all the same. He loves them and calls to them. He wants to be their king, and they are to follow his banner. These were the glad tidings.

In court he would always defend himself in the same way:

"Do not expect from me, since I am not a priest nor a member of a church, to preach the gospel in such a way that these scoundrels can keep a tighter hold on what they have stolen and continue to practice their injustice. He did not go to war and die by the millions for that."

He was spoken of as the Red Parson, and the Reds did not attack him publicly, although they mocked him and were afraid of him because he took some of their people away from them.

As had Luther before him, he posted messages on church doors, warning the congregation not to attend church and commanding them to starve out their pastors, so that the clergy too could learn what poverty was and then take their stand on the side of the common people.

He would often wander in the company of an old man in a long white robe whom no one saw. The man urged him not to be afraid, and instructed him in heavenly things.

It was old Johannes Tauler.

Becker, weak, undernourished and exposed to the ravages of the weather, learned from him:

Every man has been assigned to a higher, invisible creature, and that creature a still higher and more splendid one. Men sometimes call them angels, and they are correct in so far as these higher creatures do lead finally to God and they come from God and can be considered his messengers. They are the stairway to the invisible life.

"Am I approaching that invisible life?" asked Becker. "Is that death?"

Tauler answered, "Yes. You are approaching it. You call it death. Many things are already losing their form for you, Friedrich. You are already no longer able to differentiate many things."

"And who is the angel who leads me?"

"Antoniel is his name. He will stand by you when the time has come for you to leave this earthly world. Fear not when he steps up to you."

Becker was amazed. "Cannot I come to God on my own? Is not Jesus the way and the gate?"

Johannes Tauler: "God's works are vast and unending. You know that he has created more than the visible world. Only a fraction of that has been revealed to you."

While the clouds gathered darkly above Europe and general unrest grew, Becker's call sounded forth: "Christ the King, Christ the King over all the world. Take heart, rise up, do not fear death. There is no death but the death of the flesh."

The result was that many people joined with him, seeing in him a serious expounder of ancient teachings. He knew the people who walked with him, and knew that what they thought was not what he meant. But he did not want to reject them. Contact with them strengthened him in his terrible, but profound conviction that God's tribunal was about to be held, and that the corruption of these days would be washed away in a flood.

Without any encouragement from Becker, this movement (it could be called that by now) gained ground. His friends went far beyond anything that he had said and declared both the state and the social order invalid. Becker was himself carried along with all this. For public insurrection and similar acts he was sentenced to prison for weeks, later on for months at a time. That he had once been a teacher in an academy and an officer would at times increase his sentence, at times decrease it.

But then, given his freedom once more, he attended a nationalist convention, and a mighty laugh of mockery arose when the speaker pointed him out so that everyone noticed his presence. At their unanimous request he had to speak to them. For he was, after all, a former front line soldier.

But once he began to take them to task for their pride in their own strivings, for they strove in the wrong arena, that is for the nation, and a nation could give back no more than what they put into it, the storm broke. People screamed: "Tell that to the Entente!" "Stupid idiot, go get a job with a circus."

And in unison they screamed, "shut him up," until, with ostensible regrets, the chairman asked Becker to leave the podium. Waves of laughter accompanied him down the steps, and as he slowly left the hall, his face to the ground, a mock military cordon was built to greet him.

He grew wilder and wilder. He could feel himself that he was moving down a dangerous path, but he did not want to slow down. He was no longer afraid of "politics." He spoke of burning down the churches, these new Bastilles. He went the socialist dictum that religion is the opium of the masses one better by asserting that traditional Christianity in this country was no religion at all, only an attack on religion, its goal being to open the door to a new paganism. It should be cast aside. There were in fact instances of arson in churches, and these were credited to him. He was put back in prison again.

And released once more, he burrowed into himself. Despair cast him down. He was shaken by fanaticism. How could one check the oncoming doom? Where should he attack, how was he to endure life?

"Yet once again, God, send us thy son once again. Thou hast given us too heavy a burden. Do not leave us alone. Once again, God.

"O word of God, become flesh once again, speak to us, walk among us, and do let us not turn to stone. Jesus, our very breath, our life, our light, come thou once again.

"All saints and martyrs have suffered in vain. All life weeps in hopeless despair.

"Yet once again."

The Third Snare: The Wager

And then near the close of the twenties, Friedrich Becker came to Hamburg, sat down in a shabby bar and ate what they set before him. And the Devil sat down with him to keep him company.

"Taste good?" he asked Friedrich.

"Thanks, not bad," he answered over his plate.

Satan asked, "Why aren't you drinking anything, it's a bar you know? If you just say the word to the barkeep, he'll not begrudge you one little glass."

"I don't drink."

The Devil fell silent then, only to begin once again after a bit.

"I know that you've had problems with drinkers, with the director and so on. Tell me, Friedrich, sitting here in this filthy bar, eating what someone puts on a tin plate for you, you must think you're somebody really special, must be working with a vengeance to eradicate your own ego. You're gambling that the last shall be first, and that he who humbles himself shall be exalted."

"What are you aiming at, you scoundrel?"

But the Devil had been following Friedrich for months now, and he knew what was going on inside him and why he was staring so blankly straight ahead and why his emaciated face twitched the way it did. It was written on his brow and in his eyes: a wasted life. Friedrich had wound up in a dead end and was standing in exactly the same spot as before the war, when he had been struggling with himself, trying to find truth and a fair wind that would speed his ship onward. In those days it had only been Hilda's tears and sorrow that had saved him from ruin. But neither Hilda nor anything else was in sight, and that was what Satan was banking on.

And just then a fat bargeman with a red face entered the bar, a leather jacket over his shoulders—it was summer—cursing the owners and captains who didn't want to hire him.

Satan said, "Take a look at him."

Friedrich answered, "What's so special about him?"

And Satan gave him a little nudge of the elbow.

"Ah, Friedrich, how would it be to be like him. What's so special? Nothing, just that, nothing. He's a garbage heap, a bit of mortar, a clump of earth, one of those you work so hard for and who won't listen to you. One of those whom only a new flood will help. Take a good look at it up close, use your magnifying glass. You've wandered the countryside enough and have fought your way to a standstill. They laughed at you. They don't need you. How often have they thrown you in prison now because you won't leave them in peace, and besides that you're just a tramp, and there are lots of those, and the best place for them is the workhouse. Look the fellow over, take a good look at how he's sitting there at the table pouring himself a fresh glass of beer from his bottle, lifting the glass, licking his lips and swallowing it with such gusto, he's halfway to heaven by now, needs nothing else to get there.

"What do you want to do with that, Friedrich? What's involved in

538

that except gluttony and greed and lechery? Don't fool yourself. You want to be a realist, right. That's an animal. Don't start talking to him about his soul. He's never heard of it. A soul is a luxury he has no use for. Look at him, how he's turned around to catch the barkeep's eye again; his bottle's empty, he wants to order another. What is his life, Friedrich, but eating, drinking, women and sleep, and then going through the whole routine over again, and then once more? And all the rest of you are of the same caliber, you included, dear Friedrich, my dear Becker, or as in the old days, Doctor Friedrich Becker, first lieutenant, teacher at an academy. Why delude yourselves? You're made of matter, that's all, and that matter can't become anything more than what it has in it, and you can turn it and twist it and hammer and chisel it as much as you like."

Becker said coldly, "I'm listening."

Satan: "And that's just how they manage their politics and build their governments. So let them, if they don't want to do anything else. And their murders and wars, it's all of a piece. You get on their nerves, haven't you noticed by this time?"

Becker replied calmly, "That's not how they are."

Satan laughed in his face, making Friedrich flinch. "Friedrich, I'm serious, what's to become of you? You can't sink any lower. And all of this for a couple of crank ideas that came to you in your so-called moment of enlightenment. Any psychiatrist could tell you what that's about. Give it up, Friedrich. You've put yourself through enough. Now's the time to get back to the banquet of life while the lights are still burning."

Becker, calmly: "That's not how people are."

Satan: "I'm sure you know best."

But he knew already what Friedrich was really thinking. And Satan edged closer. "How would it be, my friend, if you would take this whole matter really seriously for once? Here we stand, one viewpoint against the other. It would please me no end if you could prove to me I'm wrong."

"You think I'll find nothing human in them?"

Satan laughed aloud. "Human, why, by the ton, nothing but humanness!"

And that made Friedrich slam his fist on the table so that the barkeep looked up in amazement from washing his glasses. "It's agreed, then. How do you want me to go about it?"

Satan: "Go sit next to him."

So Friedrich sat down at the table with the noisy bargeman and started up a conversation with him. Satan sat on the other side of the table, and after a while he whispered, "Well, what's he like."

Friedrich: "A poor wretched fellow, coarse and crude. What did you suppose he was like?"

Satan: "Just what we need, then, a simple man, one of those of whom it can be said: he was a man, take him for all in all. Give him a try, why don't you?"

Friedrich: "I told you already. What do you want me to do?"

"Take his cap and put it on your head and take a pull from his glass."

Which Becker did. The bargeman enjoyed the joke. He grew much more cheerful right away. Satan snapped his fingers, stood up and gave Friedrich a slap on the back.

"Now observe him from close up, and try your luck. I can go now. I'll come back later."

And at once Becker sensed what had happened to him. The devil had slipped the other fellow's soul into his own breast, and something like a mangy dog was jumping around inside him, and he would have to live with it. The bargeman seemed to feel that a load had been taken from him. He cursed less, he laughed and acted silly and harmless. He amused the people around him. He proved to be such a jolly character that even the barkeep enjoyed the fun and stood him his drinks.

Becker ran after him when he left, slamming the door behind him. He wanted to set all this back in order right away. He was so perplexed and worried by this terrible existence within his own breast. But in the small, winding streets he lost the man. And when he checked in the bar later, looking for the Devil, he wasn't to be found either.

And so Friedrich martialed his forces, pulled himself together and swore that now that he'd made his bed he would lie in it. He would show Satan what he was made of. The scoundrel would lose his teeth from having bit into him. And after all, why not? The Savior had come two thousand years before and had taken the sins of all mankind upon him. He ought to be able to take the imposition of just a single soul, and show the Evil One what he could do if he only wanted to.

Settling Accounts

And what did Friedrich do now?

He drew this strange, wicked soul to him and tried to thrust his way into its beating heart, into its heart of hearts. He tried to discover what it was. He tried to strike fire from its stone. He did indeed work

540

hard at it. But he had not prepared himself for such cynical evil. The fellow proved to be so vile and pigheaded that Friedrich soon began to tremble.

He put up with the torments that the rascal within his breast inflicted on him. But now there was no place of solitude, no hour in which he found rest and in which he could call upon himself. He had taken it upon himself to appease an angry soul, but that soul, instead of letting itself be appeased, turned the tables on him and attacked. He obliged it, for his tactic was to offer no resistance, hoping sooner or later to entice from it the pure gold that it bore within. But the fellow didn't yield up the gold. On the contrary, he forced Friedrich to hand over his own.

Friedrich became quarrelsome. He felt driven to go down to the docks and take up with whores, and the drinking never stopped. And one night, as Friedrich lay in a flophouse, he caught himself (though it was not him, not really him) brooding over the fact that he had no money, and laying plans for stealing his neighbor's boots, and in the end he did steal them, too.

And the evil soul, who mocked him and found all his trials very funny, cunningly led him into a church one Sunday, and made Friedrich, to his own disgust and horror, open his mouth wide and erupt in obscene words and blasphemies. He only barely got away safely afterward.

And then one morning it happened that as Friedrich was sitting on a park bench, the Devil sat down next to him and whispered, "He's drowned."

"Who?"

"Your fellow. No one will contest your right to him now. You can now do with him whatever your heart desires. Take off with it to the far ends of the earth if you like. That's pretty fine, don't you think?"

And then with a grin Satan murmured cozily, "You're stuck with him now, Friedrich, my mighty hero."

Friedrich's shoulders sagged while Satan watched him with interest.

"Or are you ready to admit you've lost the bet? You've bit off more than you can chew with him, right? Yes, talking doesn't help much with him. He's not easily reached with good advice. But then who is, for that matter? All wise men have come to that conclusion before this."

And he rubbed his chin and blew on his hand.

"I put on a similar show once before, years ago, about ten or eleven to be precise. Though there was a different motive behind it all for the two personages involved. In that one, I set up a tête-à-tête between two lovely souls who had not been able to find one another in life, he was named Hannes and she was Rosa. They sought each other for different reasons. She was sitting in a prison in Breslau, he had been dead for a while and was not at all in agreement with that. They went at it pretty wildly in her cell in Breslau for a while. They held regular orgies, and went off on grand pleasure trips. She, Rosa, loved him passionately. But on one matter they could not agree. She was really funny about it," he broke out in loud laughter, "she didn't want him to eat her alive."

Jovially, Satan clapped his drooping friend on the shoulder.

"Hello there, old friend, don't take it so hard. Take it easy. I'm not trying to take your bargeman away from you."

Friedrich: "I can do without your sympathy."

The devil: "Do you want to keep him?"

"Forever. So that you can see, once and for all, who it is you're dealing with."

"As the gentleman wishes," the devil saluted. "I like my Spaniards proud. I hope you continue to enjoy yourself."

And he disappeared into the crowd of strollers.

After that, it was clear that the life of Friedrich Becker—who was dealing with the Devil and had fallen into his hands once before— would come to a terrible end.

He wrestled, breast to breast, with this alien soul, which now let its entire rage loose on him. He was ground down by it. It set its teeth on his nipple and clasped him tight, as once Hannes had clasped Rosa. Its behavior in his breast was frenzied. Sometimes he had the impression (and not a false one) that it did not live there alone, but had brought in similar alien spirits to keep it company, and that they had turned his inner self into a Brocken where they celebrated their ghastly Walpurgis Night.

Friedrich was severely wounded during a robbery to which his companion had incited him; he was pulled off to safety by the others involved, and lay in a dilapidated garage that served as a tool shed. An old woman, the mother of one of the thieves, brought him soup and water.

Friedrich lay there, half conscious.

And he had a vague sense that he had lost his way.

He realized that the shot had come to him as a boon. For he had already decided to entrust himself entirely to this alien soul and to throw himself in the water, down to where the body of the bargeman was rotting.

542

In the shed, on rags and straw, he lay in delirium. The little poodle of the woman who brought him food would slip in at night to sleep with him.

And on the third night, Friedrich raised himself up on his hands and called out to Tauler, his teacher:

"Tauler, Johannes Tauler, my teacher, I'm nearing my end. Take this alien soul from me so that I may speak to you alone."

Tauler whispered: "Finally you have found your way to me."

Friedrich: "Tauler, my teacher, look at what torment I'm in. See what they have burdened me with. Free me. Stand by me against the Evil One and prevent him from speaking his lies, from clinging to them, from saying that he has won and that there is nothing in man but an animal and wickedness and baseness."

Tauler whispered: "In the name of the most holy God, Friedrich, what are you demanding of me?"

"Stand by me, my teacher, the spirit of lies is already celebrating his victory."

Tauler: "You got yourself involved with the Devil. What have you done with yourself? Who are you? Do you not know that not even God succeeded in convicting Satan of his crimes, and that he had to cast him down into the abyss?"

"I could not bear his chatter. I could not look on while the flood rose and the Evil One opened his mouth and said with no one to contradict him: All your labors for mankind have been in vain, I alone am ruler of this world. Tell me yourself, Tauler, did I not have to forbid Satan such effrontery—even if it placed me in danger of being torn to pieces? Have I not done what was demanded of me?"

Tauler veiled his face with a white cloth.

"Oh, Friedrich, and what about you yourself? My child, are you not a human being? Who are you that you should involve yourself in such a struggle? Are you not yourself one of those whom you must struggle against? Have you never yet noticed that you, too, stand on the other side? Satan has recognized you for what you are better than you yourself have. He knows the primal guilt that all men bear in them, because he himself has planted it in you. That is why he was able to get hold of you in your pride and egg you on, and you fell into his trap."

"I did not want to despair, my teacher. I wanted to tear myself to pieces, be dragged through the mire, because I saw all the sordidness. At least I wanted to do my part in suffering for the guilty."

"Friedrich, that is not your part to play. What have you presumed for yourself? Where are the gentleness, the humility, the patience, those great virtues? You had them once, and then your own vehemence swallowed you up. Friedrich, the masks are being lowered. Ah, I am filled with dread. It is as if knots were being tied in my breast."

"Must I die, Tauler?"

The long white robes of the old man fluttered as if blown by the wind. His curly hair wafted. He murmured as he bent down to Friedrich and laid his delicate, aged hand on his brow, "You have lost, my child. Ah, you have lost. Lost. May the unfathomable mercy of God receive you."

And then dread passed over his face, and he vanished.

And then, there sat Satan, gigantic, towering above the roof of the shed, his hide shiny like a horse's, and he bent his long horse's muzzle down to him. The hair of his mane flew into Becker's mouth.

Satan's nostrils dilated with pleasure; he snorted and mimicked the wise old man:

"You have lost, my child. Ah, you have lost. Lost."

He whinnied his laughter. "It's true, you admit it yourself, I take it. And now I can relieve you of your tormentor too, the one you've had a go at, the subject of all your research. He was not a monster, don't curse him, he was simply no better than all the rest." Satan tapped a front hoof on Friedrich's breast. "Come on, little rascal, you've done your job well. And extend him your thanks, Herr Experimenter, Herr Teacher, Herr Professor, Doctor Friedrich Becker, because he has so richly added to your knowledge."

The alien soul hissed like a tea kettle as it passed out of Friedrich's mouth and settled down next to him on the rags as a thick-headed moth.

Satan: "Be off, little rascal, get to work. Here's an extra kick."

And the moth fluttered about in the trash and tried to hide. Satan inflated his cheeks and puffed and snorted after him. The insect bounced off the wall like a ball, fell to the floor, fluttered up, and finally found a chink in the roof to fly off through.

Satan used his tail to swat away the swarm of flies buzzing about him. He sat down and propped up his front legs.

"There he goes and he'll not be back. And now I'll wait until you're ready, Friedrich. Because we'll chase each of you individually. My people need something to keep them busy."

And suddenly, as he looked down on poor, parched and bloodless Friedrich, lying there on his rags, he emitted clear, high tones that turned into a soundless laugh.

"The wise old man has told you everything already. All this fidgeting about won't help you humans at all, strike what poses you will.

You've had it in you from primeval days on, got it from me, and I'll not set you free. You were created in the image of God, but in my image as well. And you can't talk your way out of that with all your big words. Look at yourself, here at the end now. Where did your whole grand conversion get you? All your compassion and all that rolling of your eyes? It was childishness, the ostrich sticking its head in the sand. And that is why I set my sights on you, my son, so that you might learn that there is no joking with me. Now, you see, they've left you in the lurch. What is man without me? Nothing. Zero point zero. Flat on your face. You lie flat on your face. You've lost, and now you'll pay, now you'll pay."

But Friedrich felt relieved. He took a deep breath. The evil shade had left him.

A weariness flowed through his limbs. He smiled, he could smile again.

His thoughts dissolved and fused with the things about him.

Things lost their contours.

All things lost their names.

And a yearning rose up in his breast, a yearning for something celestial, distant, serene, beyond all names and thoughts and matter. His soul whispered tender words to it.

Antoniel had come, soundlessly as a cloud. Satan's hooves clattered. He had stood up, and now he pricked his ears.

Friedrich asked, melting with happiness, "Are you my friend Antoniel?"

No answer.

"Are you Antoniel? Why don't you speak?"

No answer.

"Why are you clad in black? Why do you hide your face, why you as well?"

The angel wept. His hot tears fell on Friedrich's brow.

"What have I done wrong, Antoniel? Have mercy on me."

"It is not for me to have mercy. It is not for me to do that. You could not hear. You could not fall to your knees and pray: Lord, thou who hast created this world, I thank thee, I praise thee, I extol thee, I am thy creature, I am blessed through thee. Thy will be done, on earth as it is in heaven."

Friedrich screamed. He prostrated himself.

And through the mind of this dying man, dreamlike memories thronged—of his kind mother as she bent down over him and fussed with his pillows—and Hilda walking past the foot of his bed in her nurse's uniform, turning at the door to smile at him. Mona Lisa, she came back and gave him her lips to kiss—Heinz letting him calm him down—the director pulling the belt tight on his blue silk robe and nodding to him, his poor brother—and the Havel, the wide, flowing Havel, he is rowing, Krug is there as well, and young girls in white summer dresses, it is a Sunday, how wonderful.

Friedrich groaned. Oh beautiful earth, God's earth, I must leave you now. Have I not loved you enough, have I not praised God enough in you, where did I go wrong?

And he cast himself down and wrung his hands behind Antoniel, whose broad cloak had opened, giving off a delicate white light; and Friedrich, wailing as he sensed hell itself crushing him with an infernal, iron-shod kick, has already left earthly air, has slipped out of his earthly shell, cast aside the steaming ballast of lust and torment, of meadows, forests and rivers and mountains.

And the sweat of death breaks out on the brow of this poor soul, the sweat of exertion, of escape, of bursting the chains, of leaving the prison—and it floats.

See, how it rises and no longer knows who it was, his soul in the dungeon of a body.

He begs Antoniel: "Don't leave me, Antoniel, don't desert me, Antoniel. Don't hand me over to the Evil One, Antoniel."

Antoniel answers:

"It is not for me to do.

"Fear the Lord. Fear the Lord.

"Friedrich, let it fall. Yield.

"There is no place. There is no time. I shall show you the way."

Then the horse of hell let its ponderous weight fall upon him, trying to squash him on the ground—when two fiery figures emerged from the darkness, two fiery lions approaching him from a whirlwind. And the horse of hell gave a cry of battle, leapt to one side, lowered its head, foaming at the mouth, and charged them.

They were smaller than Satan, and he struck their heads with his hooves. He sprayed them with his slaver. Their roars were mixed with his whinnyings and snortings.

The lions leaped into the air and bit at his belly. They sprang up onto his back and fastened their teeth into the nape of his neck. He threw himself over on top of them, and they had to release him. He tried to trample them to death. But they snapped at his fetlocks.

With a scream of pain, he tore himself away and swept up into the air, his blood dribbling down onto the earth. Wherever it fell, fire

broke out, and murderous thoughts arose. He stormed away, surrounded and concealed by his screaming assistants.

"Come, Friedrich. I am holding you. I shall not let you go. You
cannot make it alone. Fear the Lord. Cry to him with every breath.

"Do you hear them singing from the heavenly Jerusalem?

"The holy city, it lies afar, no man can take it by force.

"The holy city beyond the mountains, beyond the snowy peaks. It
lies there, showered in flower petals. All the blood of the martyrs and
saints rains down upon it. The city lies afar, the hovel of God.

"And he shall wipe away all tears, and there shall be no more death,
neither sorrow, nor crying, neither shall there be any more pain."

And when the old woman came the next morning with her lively
dog, Friedrich was lying there on his face and did not move. And
when she turned him over, bloody foam and slime flowed from his
mouth and down his chin. She pressed his glassy eyes shut. He had let
life's mask fall.

Afterward they had one damnable time with the body. Because they
didn't want any police there in the shed—and what should they do
with it?

They waited till the day had passed, and that evening they loaded
their dead pal onto a vegetable cart under some crates and drove him
down to the docks. They stuffed him in a coal sack and put him into a
little motorboat, and in the dark they made a little tour of the harbor,
during which they eased the sack down into the water, with no one the
wiser.